The Orion Book of Murder brings together the three phases of murder: the lawbreakers, famous police detectives and the private eyes. With stories from leading writers such as Ruth Rendell, Sue Grafton, James Ellroy, Agatha Christie, Colin Dexter and Lynda La Plante, this is a unique collection of the world's greatest crime stories, expertly introduced and put in their historical context by anthologist and crime-fiction specialist Peter Haining.

Peter Haining is an internationally known anthologist and writer on crime fiction whose books have been published in over a dozen languages. He was a 1992 Edgar nominee by the Mystery Writers of America for his Centenary study of Agatha Christie's work on stage, film, radio, and TV, *Murder in Four Acts*, and was recently featured in BBC TV's 'Bookmark' Programme. Peter Haining is married with three grown-up children and lives in rural Suffolk.

Also edited by Peter Haining

The Television Detectives' Omnibus
The Television Late Night Horror Omnibus
The Television Crimebusters' Omnibus
The Frankenstein Omnibus
Murder At The Races
Murder On The Railways

THE ORION BOOK OF
MURDER

BOOK ONE
CRIME

BOOK TWO
DETECTION

BOOK THREE
PUNISHMENT

edited by
PETER HAINING

ORION

An Orion paperback
First published in Great Britain by Orion in 1996
This paperback edition published in 1997 by Orion Books Ltd,
Orion House, 5 Upper St Martin's Lane, London WC2H 9EA

A CIP catalogue record for this book
is available from the British Library.

ISBN: 0 75280 915 6

Typeset by Deltatype Ltd, Birkenhead, Merseyside
Printed and bound in Great Britain by
Clays Ltd, St Ives plc.

For JONATHAN WARING
Whose only crime is to work
in the book business

Contents

Contents

Contents

MURDER

BOOK ONE

CRIME
Criminals and Killers

Introduction

NICHOLAS RHEA

'I'm all for crime,' says the man unwittingly about to become the first victim in Agatha Christie's classic *And Then There Were None* (1939) about a group of ill-fated guests summoned to a private island just off the coast of Devon. 'May I propose a toast? Here is to crime!'

We all agree with those sentiments, if we are honest. For what reader has not occasionally felt a sudden affinity, even sympathy, with the killer, especially if the victim is evil, vicious or just someone we don't like very much? And isn't even the most law-abiding citizen occasionally unable to resist a twinge of envy when a criminal suddenly gets away with his villainy? It's the contrary nature of mankind at work – or what distinguishes us from the computer.

Of course, it's also true that we expect the law, in the shape of the police, a private detective or an investigator, to catch up with the wrongdoer in the end – or else our belief in the law and order which holds society together would be totally undermined. But there is no denying that the vicarious thrill of being privy to a crime is one of the main reasons why the genre has been so popular with readers ever since Edgar Allan Poe invented the story of 'ratiocination' (as he called it) in 'The Murders in the Rue Morgue' (1841). In it he created what is arguably one of the world's most popular kinds of literary entertainment: the story which combines the irresistible ingredients of crime, detection and punishment.

In this first of three selections will be found a group of

landmark short stories by some of the twentieth century's most distinguished names in the genre. Their subjects range from serial killers to kidnappers, and from gangsters to juvenile delinquents, as well as stories of assassination, sadism and strangulation, not forgetting crimes of passion, fraud and blackmail; plus – closest to home of all – the *malice domestique*. In each and every one the focus is very much on the criminal and his world – it will be the turn of the police and the investigators in the next two selections.

Criminals – the best of them – are often as memorable in their way as the custodians of the law, and in the pages which follow you will find some of the most unforgettable. Each story, I rather feel, emphasises that last line in *The Maltese Falcon* spoken by Sam Spade as he reluctantly turns a killer over to the police: 'If they hang you,' he says wryly, 'I'll always remember you.'

Man With a Hobby

ROBERT BLOCH

OFFENCE FILE

CRIME: Serial killer

PLACE: Cleveland, USA

YEAR: 1957

BRIEFING: Serial killers are undoubtedly the most feared murderers in modern crime. Amongst the best known are, surely, Jack the Ripper, who slaughtered prostitutes in the back-streets of Victorian London, and the incredibly violent 'Axe-man of New Orleans', who cut his victims to pieces in their homes during the years 1911 to 1919. Both generated sensational newspaper reports, caused widespread fear among the general public, and their identities remain a mystery to this day. Such men – if indeed they were men! – have been described as 'the impresarios of the crime world', for while most murderers endeavour to remain anonymous, these multiple killers went to extraordinary lengths to create special effects at the scenes of their crimes. Today's serial killers, such as Jeffrey Dahmer and Fred West, may not have been as prone to exhibitionism, but the horror of what they did has also been felt worldwide.

AUTHOR: Robert Bloch (1917–94) has written a number of short stories and novels about multiple killers, three of which featured real people: Jack the Ripper, Lizzie Borden and the insidious Herman W. Mudgett of his native Chicago. In 1959, while still a struggling writer for the weird pulp magazines, Bloch wrote one of the landmark crime novels of this century, *Psycho*, about the gentle-looking killer Norman Bates in his Gothic-style Hollywood motel. When the story was filmed the following year by Alfred Hitchcock with Anthony Perkins it became one of the highest-grossing black and white motion pictures ever produced. Indeed, its unforgettable portrait of a psychopathic killer did not so much start a trend as launch one, for there have since been two sequels (both starring Perkins, who has called the role of Bates 'the Hamlet of horror parts') and a continuing series of similar movies including *Texas Chainsaw Massacre, Nightmare on Elm Street, Silence of the Lambs* and *Seven*. Robert Bloch also returned to the theme of deranged killers and psychopathology in several of his later bestselling books – although he always disclaimed any specialist knowledge – including *The Scarf* (1947), a first-person narrative about a strangler; *The Kidnapper* (1954), a book much disliked by critics for its 'cold, clinical and unsparing honesty'; *The Couch* (1962), the account of a mass murderer; and *Night of the Ripper* (1984), a *tour de force* in which he proposed an ingenious solution to the century-old mystery. 'Man With a Hobby' also features a psychopath, known only as 'The Cleveland Torso Slayer', and was first published – appropriately – in *Alfred Hitchcock's Mystery Magazine* of March 1957 ... just two years before the story of another killer was to make both men household names.

***

It must have been around ten o'clock when I got out of the hotel. The night was warm and I needed a drink.

There was no sense trying the hotel cocktail lounge, because the place was a madhouse. The bowling convention had taken that over, too.

Walking down Euclid Avenue, I got the impression that Cleveland was full of bowlers. And most of them seemed to be looking for a drink. Every tavern I passed was jammed with shirt-sleeved men, all wearing their badges. Not that they needed extra identification – nearly all of them carried their own bowling balls in the standard round bag. And most of them carried loads, too.

Funny, the way bowlers like to drink. Scratch a bowler and you generally draw alcohol instead of blood. Even old Washington Irvine knew that, when he wrote about Rip Van Winkle and the dwarfs.

Well, there were no dwarfs in this crowd – just man-sized drinkers. And any sound of thunder from the distant mountain peaks would have been drowned out by the shouting and the laughter.

I wanted no part of it. So I turned off Euclid and kept wandering along, looking for a quiet spot. My own bowling bag was getting heavy. Actually, I'd meant to take it right over to the depot and check it in a locker until train time, but I needed that drink first.

Finally I found a place. It was dim, it was dingy, but it was also deserted. The bartender was all alone down at the far end of the bar, listening to the tail end of a double-header on the radio.

I sat down close to the door, and put the bag on the stool next to me. Then I signalled him for a beer. 'Bring me a bottle,' I said. 'Then I won't have to interrupt you.'

I was only trying to be polite, but I could have spared myself the trouble. Before he had a chance to get back to following the game, another customer came in.

'Double Scotch, never mind the wash.'

I looked up.

The bowlers had taken over the city, all right. This one was a heavily built man of about fifty, with wrinkles

7

extending well up towards the top of his bald head. He wore a coat, but carried the inevitable bowling bag – black, bulging, and very similar to mine. As I stared at him, he set it down very carefully on the adjoining bar stool and reached for his drink.

He threw back his head and gulped. I could see the pasty white skin ripple along his neck. Then he held out the empty glass. 'Do it again,' he told the bartender. 'And turn down the radio, will you, Mac?' He pulled out a handful of bills.

For a moment the bartender's expression hovered midway between a scowl and a smile. Then he caught sight of the bills fluttering down on the bar, and the smile won out. He shrugged and turned away, fiddling with the volume control, reducing the announcer's voice to a distant drone. I knew what he was thinking. *If it was beer I'd tell him to go take a jump, but this guy's buying Scotch.*

The second Scotch went down almost as fast as the volume of the radio.

'Fill 'er up,' said the heavy-set man.

The bartender came back, poured again, took his money, rang it up; then he drifted away to the other end of the bar. Crouching over the radio, he strained to catch the voice of the announcer.

I watched the third Scotch disappear. The stranger's neck was red now. Six ounces of Scotch in two minutes will do wonders for the complexion. It will loosen the tongue, too.

'Damn ball game,' the stranger muttered. 'I can't understand how anyone can listen to that crud.' He wiped his forehead and blinked at me. 'Sometimes a guy gets the idea there's nothing in the world but baseball fans. Bunch of crazy fools yelling their heads off over nothing, all summer long. Then comes fall and it's the football games. Same thing, only worse. And right after that's finished, it's basketball. Honest to God, what do they see in it?'

'Everybody needs some kind of a hobby,' I said.

'Yeah. But what kind of a hobby do you call that? I mean, who can get excited over a gang of apes fighting to grab some kind of a ball?' He scowled. 'Don't kid me that they really care who wins or loses. Most guys go to a ball game for a different reason. You ever been out to see a game, Mac?'

'Once in a while.'

'Then you know what I'm talking about. You've heard 'em out there. Heard 'em yelling. That's why they really go – to holler their heads off. And what are they yelling most of the time? I'll tell you. *Kill the umpire!* Yeah, that's what they're screaming about. *Kill the umpire!*'

I finished the last of my beer quickly and started to slide off the stool. He reached out and rapped on the bar. 'Here have another, Mac,' he said. 'On me.'

I shook my head. 'Sorry, got to catch a train out of here at midnight,' I told him.

He glanced at the clock. 'Plenty of time.' I opened my mouth to protest, but the bartender was already opening a bottle and pouring another Scotch. And the stranger was talking to me again.

'Football is worse,' he said. 'A guy can get hurt playing football. Some of 'em get hurt bad. That's what the crowd like to see. And boy, when they start yelling for blood, it's enough to turn your stomach.'

'I don't know,' I said. 'After all, it's a pretty harmless way of releasing pent-up aggression.'

Maybe he understood me and maybe he didn't, but he nodded. 'It releases something, like you say, but I ain't so sure it's harmless. Take boxing and wrestling, now. Call that a sport? Call that a hobby? People want to see somebody get clobbered. Only they won't admit it.'

His face was quite red now. He was starting to sweat.

'And what about hunting and fishing? When you come right down to it, it's the same thing. Only there you do the killing yourself. You take a gun and shoot some dumb animal. Or you cut up a live worm and stick it on a hook and that hook cuts into a fish's mouth, and you sort of get a thrill out of it, don't you? When the hook goes in and it cuts and tears—'

'Now wait a minute,' I said. 'What makes you think that people are all such sadists?'

He blinked at me for a moment. 'Never mind the two-dollar words,' he told me. 'You know it's true. Everybody gets the urge, sooner or later. Stuff like ball games and boxing don't really satisfy it, either. So we gotta have a war, every so often. Then there's an excuse to do real killing. Millions.'

Nietzsche thought *he* was a gloomy philosopher. He should have known about Double-Scotches.

'What's your solution?' I tried hard to keep the sarcasm out of my voice. 'Do you think there'd be less harm done if they repealed the laws against murder?'

'Maybe.' The baldheaded man studied his empty glass. 'Depends on who got killed. Suppose you just knocked off tramps and bums. Or a floozie, maybe. You know, somebody without a family or relatives or anything. Somebody who wouldn't be missed. You could get away with it easier, too.'

I leaned forward, staring at him.

'Could you?' I asked.

He didn't look at me. He gazed down at his bowling bag for a moment before replying.

'Don't get me wrong, Mac,' he said, forcing a grin. 'I ain't no murderer. But I was just thinking about a guy who used to do it. Right here in this town, too. This was maybe twenty years ago.'

'You knew him?'

'No, of course not. Nobody knew him, that's the

whole point. That's how he always got away with it. But everybody knew about him. All you had to do was read the papers. They called him the Cleveland Torso Slayer. He did thirteen murders in four years, out in Kingsbury Run and around Jackass Hill. Cops went nuts trying to find the guy. Figured he came into town on weekends, maybe. Then he'd pick up some bum and lure him down into a gully or the dumps near the tracks. Promise to give him a bottle, or something. Did the same thing with women. And then he used his knife. He wasn't playing games, trying to fool himself. He went for the real thing. With real thrills and a real trophy at the end. You see, he liked to cut 'em up. He liked to cut off their—'

I stood up and reached for my bag. The stranger laughed.

'Don't be scared, Mac,' he said. 'This guy must of blown town back in nineteen thirty-eight or so. Maybe when the war come along in Europe he joined up over there. Went into some commando outfit and kept on doing the same thing – only then he was a hero instead of a murderer, see? Anyway, he did it honest. He wasn't trying to pretend. He wasn't one of those chicken-liver types who—'

'Easy, now,' I said. 'Don't go getting yourself excited. It's your theory, not mine.'

He lowered his voice. 'Theory? Maybe so, Mac. But I run into something tonight that'll really rock you. What do you suppose I been tossing down all these drinks for?'

'I thought all bowlers drank,' I told him. 'But come to think of it, if you actually feel that way about sports, then why are you a bowler?'

The baldheaded man leaned close to me. 'Who said I was a bowler?' he murmured.

I opened my mouth, but before I could answer him there was another noise. We both heard it at the same time – the sound of a siren, down the street.

The bartender looked up. 'Heading this way, sounds like, doesn't it? Do you think—'

But the baldheaded man was already on his feet and moving towards the door.

I hurried after him. 'Here, don't forget your bag.'

He didn't look at me. 'Thanks,' he muttered. 'Thanks, Mac.'

And then he was gone. He didn't stay on the street, but slipped down a narrow alley between two adjoining buildings. In a moment he had disappeared. I stood in the doorway as the siren's wail choked the street. A squad car pulled up in front of the tavern, its motor racing. A uniformed sergeant had been running along the sidewalk, accompanying it, and he came puffing up. He glanced at the sidewalk, glanced at the tavern, glanced at me.

'See anything of a big, baldheaded guy carrying a bowling bag?' he panted.

I had to tell him the truth. 'Why, yes. Somebody went out of here only a minute ago—'

'Which way?'

I gestured between the buildings and he shouted orders at the men in the squad car. It rolled off, but the sergeant stayed behind.

'Tell me about it,' he said, pushing me back into the tavern.

'All right, but what's this all about?'

'Murder. Over at the bowling convention, in the hotel. About an hour ago. The bellboy saw him coming out of her room, figured maybe he was a grab artist because he used the stairs instead of the elevator.'

'Grab artist?'

'Prowler – you know, they hang around conventions, sneak into rooms and pick up stuff. Anyway, he got a good look at the guy and notified the house dick. The house dick checked the room number and laughed it off. He knew there was some old bat up there who'd been turning a few fast tricks off the convention gang. So he thought the guy who came out was probably just a customer. Then a little while later, one of the maids happened to notice that the door to the room was part-way open, so she took a look inside. Found this dame right on the bed. She'd been carved, but good.'

I took a deep breath. 'The man who was just in here,' I said. 'He kept talking about the Cleveland torso slayings. But I thought he was just drunk, or ribbing me. Do you think he . . .'

The sergeant grunted. 'That your bowling bag?' he asked, pointing at the bar stool.

I nodded.

'Open it up,' he commanded.

I opened it. It took a long time because my hands were trembling.

He stared down at the bowling ball and sighed.

'All right. He took his with him, didn't he?'

I nodded again.

'Then he's our man,' the sergeant told me. 'The bellboy's description checks out with the one a newsie gave us just down the street from here. He saw him coming this way.'

'And that's how you traced him to this tavern?' I asked.

'Yeah. That and one thing more. His bowling bag.'

'Somebody saw it, described it?'

'No, they didn't have to describe it. It left a trail. Notice how I was running along the sidewalk out there? I was following the trail. And take a look at the floor under the stool.'

I looked.

'You see, he wasn't carrying a bowling ball in that bag. Bowling balls don't leak.'

I sat down on the stool and the room began to spin. Then I raised my head. A patrolman came into the tavern. He'd been running, judging from the way he wheezed, but his face wasn't red. It was greenish-white.

'Get him?' snapped the sergeant.

'What's left of him.' The patrolman looked away. 'He must have hopped the fence in back of the block here and ran down across the tracks. He couldn't have seen this freight switching, and it backed up—'

'Dead?'

The patrolman nodded. 'Lieutenant's down there right now. And the meat wagon. But they're gonna have to scrape him off the tracks. Nothing for identification so far, and they'll never get anything off the body.'

The sergeant swore softly under his breath. 'Then we can't know for sure,' he said. 'Maybe he was just a sneak thief after all.'

'One sure way of finding out,' the patrolman said. 'Hanson's coming up with his bag. It was thrown clear of the freight when it hit.'

As we faced the door Patrolman Hanson walked in. He was carrying the bowling bag. The sergeant took it out of Hanson's hands and set it up on the bar.

'Was this what he was carrying?' he asked me.

'Yes,' I said.

Then I turned away. I didn't want to watch the sergeant open the bag. I didn't want to see their faces when they looked inside. But of course, I heard them. I think Hanson got sick.

So I started to get up again, but the sergeant had other ideas. He wouldn't let me go until I gave him an official statement. He wanted a name and address, and he got them, too. Hanson took it all down and made me sign it.

I told him all about the conversation with the stranger, the whole theory of murder as a hobby, the idea of choosing bums and floozies as victims because they weren't likely to be missed.

'Sounds screwy when you talk about it, doesn't it?' I concluded. 'All the while, I thought it was a gag.'

The sergeant glanced at the bowling bag, then looked at me. 'It's no gag,' he said. 'That's probably just how the killer's mind worked. I know all about him – everybody on the force has studied those torso-slaying cases inside and out. The story makes sense. The murderer left town twenty years ago, when things got too hot. Probably he did join up over in Europe, and maybe he stayed on with the occupation forces after the war ended. Then he got the urge to come back to his old home town and start all over again.'

'Why?' I asked.

'Who knows? Maybe it *was* a hobby with him. A sort of a game he played. And he liked to win trophies. But can you imagine the nerve he had, walking into a bowling convention and pulling off a stunt like that? Carrying a bowling bag so he could take the head along for a souvenir?'

I guess he saw the look on my face because he put his hand on my shoulder. 'Sorry,' he said. 'I know how you feel. Had a pretty close shave yourself, just talking to him. Probably the cleverest psychopathic murderer who ever lived. Just consider yourself lucky.'

I nodded and headed for the door. I could still make that midnight train, now. And I agreed with the sergeant about the close shave, the cleverest psychopathic murderer in the world. I agreed that I was lucky, too.

I mean there at the last moment, when that stupid sneak thief ran out of the tavern, and I gave him the bowling bag that leaked.

It was lucky for me that he never noticed I'd switched bags with him.

Accident

AGATHA CHRISTIE

OFFENCE FILE

CRIME: Poisoner

PLACE: Rural England

YEAR: 1934

BRIEFING: Poisoning is one of the oldest forms of murder on record. English criminal history, in particular, is full of cases that have made their principals notorious all over the world. Names like 'Wainewright the Poisoner', Thomas Griffiths Wainewright, who was transported to Australia in 1837 after a lifetime of using strychnine on his victims; the notorious Dr William Palmer who ten years later administered antimony in order to kill at least fourteen people; the lovelorn Madeleine Smith who shocked all Scotland when she poisoned her lover with arsenic in 1857; and Frederick Seddon, who, with his wife, poisoned a lodger in their North London home in 1912. Poison, in its many forms, is also credited with being one of the major elements discovered in cases of *malice domestique*.

AUTHOR: Agatha Christie (1890–1976) was for many years the undisputed 'Queen of Crime' and her work is still hugely popular today. Her fame was earned not only because of the creation of that immortal pair of sleuths, Hercule Poirot and Miss Jane Marple, but because for half a century she was the supreme practitioner of the tale

Must see
Mrs. Valaitis

See me i homework
open brought in

Level _____ test will be on _____

of domestic crime – regardless of whether it took place in an English country house or a typical suburban home. Agatha also had a special knowledge of poisons which she cunningly employed in many of her mysteries, knowledge she had gained during the early years of the First World War while separated from her young army officer husband who was away on duty. In his absence, she had taken up voluntary work as a pharmaceutical dispenser at her local hospital in Torquay and there learned all about drugs, medicines and the power of poisons. In the Second World War – long after she had become famous as a crime novelist – Agatha again served as a volunteer in a London dispensary where she had the opportunity to refresh her knowledge with the latest developments in pharmaceuticals. Once more, in the aftermath of war, she was able to make full use of this new information in her subsequent novels. Indeed, few other crime writers have so cleverly utilised a knowledge of drugs and medicines to underpin their fiction – as she demonstrates in the following mystery about Margaret Merrowdene who, after being accused of poisoning her first husband, has now married again. But what is it, Agatha Christie asks, about this woman and her 'look of an Italian madonna', that arouses such suspicions in people . . .

***

'. . . And I tell you this – it's the same woman – not a doubt of it!'

Captain Haydock looked into the eager, vehement face of his friend and sighed. He wished Evans would not be so positive and so jubilant. In the course of a career spent at sea, the old sea captain had learned to leave things that did not concern him well alone. His friend, Evans, late CID inspector, had a different philosophy of life. 'Acting on information received—' had been his motto in early days, and he had improved upon it to the extent of finding out his own information. Inspector Evans had been a very smart, wide-awake officer, and had justly earned the promotion which had been his. Even now, when he had retired from the force, and had settled down in the country cottage of his dreams, his professional instinct was still alive.

'Don't often forget a face,' he reiterated complacently. 'Mrs Anthony – yes, it's Mrs Anthony right enough. When you said Mrs Merrowdene – I knew her at once.'

Captain Haydock stirred uneasily. The Merrowdenes were his nearest neighbours, barring Evans himself, and this identifying of Mrs Merrowdene with a former heroine of a *cause célèbre* distressed him.

'It's a long time ago,' he said rather weakly.

'Nine years,' said Evans, accurate as ever. 'Nine years and three months. You remember the case?'

'In a vague sort of way.'

'Anthony turned out to be an arsenic eater,' said Evans, 'so they acquitted her.'

'Well, why shouldn't they?'

'No reason in the world. Only verdict they could give on the evidence. Absolutely correct.'

'Then that's all right,' said Haydock. 'And I don't see what we're bothering about.'

'Who's bothering?'

'I thought you were.'

'Not at all.'

'The thing's over and done with,' summed up the captain. 'If Mrs Merrowdene at one time of her life was unfortunate enough to be tried and acquitted for murder—'

'It's not usually considered unfortunate to be acquitted,' put in Evans.

'You know what I mean,' said Captain Haydock

irritably. 'If the poor lady has been through that harrowing experience, it's no business of ours to rake it up, is it?'

Evans did not answer.

'Come now, Evans. The lady was innocent – you've just said so.'

'I didn't say she was innocent. I said she was acquitted.'

'It's the same thing.'

'Not always.'

Captain Haydock, who had commenced to tap his pipe out against the side of his chair, stopped, and sat up with a very alert expression.

'Hallo – allo – allo,' he said. 'The wind's in that quarter, is it? You think she wasn't innocent?'

'I wouldn't say that. I just – don't know. Anthony was in the habit of taking arsenic. His wife got it for him. One day, by mistake, he takes far too much. Was the mistake his or his wife's? Nobody could tell, and the jury very properly gave her the benefit of the doubt. That's all quite right and I'm not finding fault with it. All the same – I'd like to *know*.'

Captain Haydock transferred his attention to his pipe once more.

'Well,' he said comfortably. 'It's none of our business.'

'I'm not so sure . . .'

'But surely—'

'Listen to me a minute. This man, Merrowdene – in his laboratory this evening, fiddling round with tests – you remember—'

'Yes. He mentioned Marsh's test for arsenic. Said *you* would know all about it – it was in *your* line – and chuckled. He wouldn't have said that if he'd thought for one moment—'

Evans interrupted him.

'You mean he wouldn't have said that if he *knew*.

19

They've been married how long – six years you told me? I bet you anything he has no idea his wife is the once notorious Mrs Anthony.'

'And he will certainly not know it from me,' said Captain Haydock stiffly.

Evans paid no attention, but went on: 'You interrupted me just now. After Marsh's test, Merrowdene heated a substance in a test-tube, the metallic residue he dissolved in water and then precipitated it by adding silver nitrate. That was a test for chlorates. A neat unassuming little test. But I chanced to read these words in a book that stood open on the table: "H_2SO_4 decomposes chlorates with evolution of Cl_4O_2. If heated, violent explosions occur, the mixture ought therefore to be kept cool and only very small quantities used."'

Haydock stared at his friend.

'Well, what about it?'

'Just this. In my profession we've got tests too – tests for murder. There's adding up the facts – weighing them, dissecting the residue when you've allowed for prejudice and the general inaccuracy of witnesses. But there's another test of murder – one that is fairly accurate, but rather – dangerous! *A murderer is seldom content with one crime.* Give him time, and a lack of suspicion, and he'll commit another. You catch a man – has he murdered his wife or hasn't he? – perhaps the case isn't very black against him. Look into his past – if you find that he's had several wives – and that they've all died shall we say – rather curiously? – then you *know*! I'm not speaking *legally*, you understand. I'm speaking of *moral* certainty. Once you *know*, you can go ahead looking for evidence.'

'Well?'

'I'm coming to the point. That's all right if there *is* a past to look into. But suppose you catch your murderer at his or her first crime? Then that test will be one from which you get no reaction. But suppose the prisoner is acquitted – starting life under another name. Will or will not the murderer repeat the crime?'

'That's a horrible idea!'

'Do you still say it's none of our business?'

'Yes, I do. You've no reason to think that Mrs Merrowdene is anything but a perfectly innocent woman.'

The ex-inspector was silent for a moment. Then he said slowly: 'I told you that we looked into her past and found nothing. That's not quite true. There was a stepfather. As a girl of eighteen she had a fancy for some young man – and her stepfather exerted his authority to keep them apart. She and her stepfather went for a walk along a rather dangerous part of the cliff. There was an accident – the stepfather went too near the edge – it gave way, and he went over and was killed.'

'You don't think—'

'It was an accident. *Accident!* Anthony's overdose of arsenic was an accident. She'd never have been tried if it hadn't transpired that there was another man – he sheered off, by the way. Looked as though he weren't satisfied even if the jury were. I tell you, Haydock, where that woman is concerned I'm afraid of another – accident!'

The old captain shrugged his shoulders.

'It's been nine years since that affair. Why should there be another "accident", as you call it, now?'

'I didn't say now. I said some day or other. If the necessary motive arose.'

Captain Haydock shrugged his shoulders.

'Well, I don't know how you're going to guard against that.'

'Neither do I,' said Evans ruefully.

'I should leave well alone,' said Captain Haydock. 'No good ever came of butting into other people's affairs.'

But that advice was not palatable to the ex-inspector. He was a man of patience but determination. Taking leave of his friend, he sauntered down to the village, revolving in his mind the possibilities of some kind of successful action.

Turning into the post office to buy some stamps, he ran into the object of his solicitude, George Merrowdene. The ex-chemistry professor was a small dreamy-looking man, gentle and kindly in manner, and usually completely absent-minded. He recognised the other and greeted him amicably, stooping to recover the letters that the impact had caused him to drop on the ground. Evans stooped also and, more rapid in his movements than the other, secured them first, handing them back to their owner with an apology.

He glanced down at them in doing so, and the address on the topmost suddenly awakened all his suspicions anew. It bore the name of a well-known insurance firm.

Instantly his mind was made up. The guileless George Merrowdene hardly realised how it came about that he and the ex-inspector were strolling down the village together, and still less could he have said how it came about that the conversation should come round to the subject of life insurance.

Evans had no difficulty in attaining his object. Merrowdene of his own accord volunteered the information that he had just insured his life for his wife's benefit, and asked Evans's opinion of the company in question.

'I made some rather unwise investments,' he explained. 'As a result my income has diminished. If anything were to happen to me, my wife would be left very badly off. This insurance will put things right.'

'She didn't object to the idea?' inquired Evans casually. 'Some ladies do, you know. Feel it's unlucky – that sort of thing.'

'Oh, Margaret is very practical,' said Merrowdene,

smiling. 'Not at all superstitious. In fact, I believe it was her idea originally. She didn't like my being so worried.'

Evans had got the information he wanted. He left the other shortly afterwards, and his lips were set in a grim line. The late Mr Anthony had insured his life in his wife's favour a few weeks before his death.

Accustomed to rely on his instincts, he was perfectly sure in his own mind. But how to act was another matter. He wanted, not to arrest a criminal red-handed, but to prevent a crime being committed, and that was a very different and a very much more difficult thing.

All day he was very thoughtful. There was a Primrose League Fête that afternoon held in the grounds of the local squire, and he went to it, indulging in the penny dip, guessing the weight of a pig, and shying at coconuts all with the same look of abstracted concentration on his face. He even indulged in half a crown's worth of Zara, the Crystal Gazer, smiling a little to himself as he did so, remembering his own activities against fortune-tellers in his official days.

He did not pay very much heed to her singsong droning voice – till the end of a sentence held his attention.

'. . . And you will very shortly – very shortly indeed – be engaged on a matter of life or death . . . Life or death to one person.'

'Eh – what's that?' he asked abruptly.

'A decision – you have a decision to make. You must be very careful – very, very careful . . . If you were to make a mistake – the smallest mistake—'

'Yes?'

The fortune-teller shivered. Inspector Evans knew it was all nonsense, but he was nevertheless impressed.

'I warn you – *you must not make a mistake*. If you do, I see the result clearly – a death . . .'

Odd, damned odd. A death. Fancy her lighting upon that!

'If I make a mistake a death will result? Is that it?'

'Yes.'

'In that case,' said Evans, rising to his feet and handing over half a crown, 'I mustn't make a mistake, eh?'

He spoke lightly enough, but as he went out of the tent, his jaw set determinedly. Easy to say – not so easy to be sure of doing. He mustn't make a slip. A life, a valuable human life depended on it.

And there was no one to help him. He looked across at the figure of his friend Haydock in the distance. No help there. 'Leave things alone,' was Haydock's motto. And that wouldn't do here.

Haydock was talking to a woman. She moved away from him and came towards Evans and the inspector recognised her. It was Mrs Merrowdene. On an impulse he put himself deliberately in her path.

Mrs Merrowdene was rather a fine-looking woman. She had a broad serene brow, very beautiful brown eyes, and a placid expression. She had the look of an Italian madonna which she heightened by parting her hair in the middle and looping it over her ears. She had a deep rather sleepy voice.

She smiled up at Evans, a contented welcoming smile.

'I thought it was you, Mrs Anthony – I mean Mrs Merrowdene,' he said glibly.

He made the slip deliberately, watching her without seeming to do so. He saw her eyes widen, heard the quick intake of her breath. But her eyes did not falter. She gazed at him steadily and proudly.

'I was looking for my husband,' she said quietly. 'Have you seen him anywhere about?'

'He was over in that direction when I last saw him.'

They went side by side in the direction indicated, chatting quietly and pleasantly. The inspector felt his admiration mounting. What a woman! What self-command. What wonderful poise. A remarkable woman – and a very dangerous one. He felt sure – a very dangerous one.

He still felt very uneasy, though he was satisfied with his initial step. He had let her know that he recognised her. That would put her on her guard. She would not dare attempt anything rash. There was the question of Merrowdene. If he could be warned . . .

They found the little man absently contemplating a china doll which had fallen to his share in the penny dip. His wife suggested going home and he agreed eagerly.

Mrs Merrowdene turned to the inspector: 'Won't you come back with us and have a quiet cup of tea, Mr Evans?'

Was there a faint note of challenge in her voice? He thought there was.

'Thank you, Mrs Merrowdene. I should like to very much.'

They walked there, talking together of pleasant ordinary things. The sun shone, a breeze blew gently, everything around them was pleasant and ordinary.

Their maid was out at the fête, Mrs Merrowdene explained, when they arrived at the charming old-world cottage. She went into her room to remove her hat, returning to set out tea and boil the kettle on a little silver lamp. From a shelf near the fireplace she took three small bowls and saucers.

'We have some very special Chinese tea,' she explained. 'And we always drink it in the Chinese manner – out of bowls, not cups.'

She broke off, peered into a cup and exchanged it for another with an exclamation of annoyance.

'George – it's too bad of you. You've been taking these bowls again.'

'I'm sorry, dear,' said the professor apologetically.

'They're such a convenient size. The ones I ordered haven't come.'

'One of these days you'll poison us all,' said his wife with a half-laugh. 'Mary finds them in the laboratory and brings them back here, and never troubles to wash them out unless they've anything very noticeable in them. Why, you were using one of them for potassium cyanide the other day. Really, George, it's frightfully dangerous.'

Merrowdene looked a little irritated.

'Mary's no business to remove things from the laboratory. She's not to touch anything there.'

'But we often leave our teacups there after tea. How is she to know? Be reasonable, dear.'

The professor went into his laboratory, murmuring to himself, and with a smile Mrs Merrowdene poured boiling water on the tea and blew out the flame of the little silver lamp.

Evans was puzzled. Yet a glimmering of light penetrated to him. For some reason or other, Mrs Merrowdene was showing her hand. Was this to be the 'accident'? Was she speaking of all this so as deliberately to prepare her alibi beforehand? So that when, one day, the 'accident' happened, he would be forced to give evidence in her favour? Stupid of her, if so, because before that—

Suddenly he drew in his breath. She had poured the tea into the three bowls. One she set before him, one before herself, the other she placed on a little table by the fire near the chair her husband usually sat in, and it was as she placed this last one on the table that a little strange smile curved round her lips. It was the smile that did it.

He knew!

A remarkable woman – a dangerous woman. No waiting – no preparation. This afternoon – this very afternoon – with him here as witness. The boldness of it took his breath away.

It was clever – it was damnably clever. He would be able to prove nothing. She counted on his not suspecting – simply because it was 'so soon'. A woman of lightning rapidity of thought and action.

He drew a deep breath and leaned forward.

'Mrs Merrowdene, I'm a man of queer whims. Will you be very kind and indulge me in one of them?'

She looked inquiring but unsuspicious.

He rose, took the bowl from in front of her and crossed to the little table where he substituted it for the other. This other he brought back and placed in front of her.

'I want to see you drink this.'

Her eyes met his. They were steady, unfathomable. The colour slowly drained from her face.

She stretched out her hand, raised the cup. He held his breath. Supposing all along he had made a mistake.

She raised it to her lips – at the last moment, with a shudder, she leant forward and quickly poured it into a pot containing a fern. Then she sat back and gazed at him defiantly.

He drew a long sigh of relief, and sat down again.

'Well?' she said.

Her voice had altered. It was slightly mocking – defiant.

He answered her soberly and quietly: 'You are a very clever woman, Mrs Merrowdene. I think you understand me. There must be no – repetition. You know what I mean?'

'I know what you mean.'

Her voice was even, devoid of expression. He nodded his head, satisfied. She was a clever woman, and she didn't want to be hanged.

'To your long life and to that of your husband,' he said significantly, and raised his tea to his lips.

Then his face changed. It contorted horribly . . . he

tried to rise – to cry out . . . His body stiffened – his face went purple. He fell back sprawling over the chair – his limbs convulsed.

Mrs Merrowdene leaned forward, watching him. A little smile crossed her lips. She spoke to him – very softly and gently . . .

'You made a mistake, Mr Evans. You thought I wanted to kill George . . . How stupid of you – how very stupid.'

She sat there a minute longer looking at the dead man, the third man who had threatened to cross her path and separate her from the man she loved.

Her smile broadened. She looked more than ever like a madonna. Then she raised her voice and called: 'George, George! . . . Oh, do come here! I'm afraid there's been the most dreadful accident . . . Poor Mr Evans . . .'

Evidence in Camera

MARGERY ALLINGHAM

OFFENCE FILE

CRIME: Strangler

PLACE: Essex

YEAR: 1949

BRIEFING: Strangling is another ancient form of murder and was amongst the commonest types of killing to be found in criminal records until the last century, when the gun and other deadly weapons took over. In Britain, one of the most notorious cases of strangling was that of Amelia Dyer, known as the 'Baby Farmer', who choked to death at least seven children who were left in her care before her arrest and execution at Newgate Prison in 1896. In America, the infamous 'Boston Strangler', Albert DeSalvo, killed a total of thirteen women between June 1962 and January 1964, and was sentenced to life imprisonment in 1967. Six years later he was found dead in his cell at Walpole State Prison, Massachusetts, stabbed through the heart.

AUTHOR: Margery Allingham (1904–66) grew up on a remote part of the coast of Essex – an area renowned for smuggling and piracy where many an excise officer or recalcitrant criminal was silenced by strangling. Indeed, her first book, *Blackkerchief Dick: A Tale of Mersea*, written while she was in her teens and published in 1923, was about smugglers on the Essex salt marshes and included one very graphic description of the murder of a customs man by a rope around his neck. After studying literature and dramatic art, Margery divided her time between London and a home at Tolleshunt d'Arcy on the Essex coast where she produced a series of crime and mystery novels that were full of drama and excitement and quite evidently inspired by the world she knew so intimately. In 1929 she also added another important detective to the crime genre, the astute Albert Campion, who made his debut in *The Crime at Black Dudley*. He subsequently appeared in over twenty-five volumes, not to mention being adapted for the cinema and, later, a TV series starring Peter Davison. Some of her best short stories are, however, about criminals and murderers in which she offers vivid characterisation and a rare insight into human psychology. 'Evidence in Camera' is set in St Piers, a small estuary town undoubtedly modelled on her own Tolleshunt d'Arcy, and concerns the hunt for a homicidal maniac who has already strangled five women. Although there is no record of such a killing in the area, it was in this same vicinity, just a few years ago, that Jeremy Bamber was tried for the wholesale murder of his family and jailed for life . . .

***

There are people who might consider Chippy Wager unethical and others who go a great deal further. At the time I am telling you about he was on the *Cormorant*, which is not that paper's real name, but why make enemies if you don't have to? He was, and is, of course, a photographer; one of those boys who shoot through a cop's legs and jump on the boot of the limousine so that you can see the Society bride in tears as she takes her first cold look at the man she's got. They pay those lads plenty, but Chippy had uses for money, mainly liquid, and he made another income on the side by taking photographs privately of practically everything from the Mayor and Corporation to the local beauty queen.

We went down to St Piers for the fifth murder. I was on the old *Post* at the time, and when I say 'we' went, I mean among others. The Southern Railway put on one excursion train for the Press and another for the police when the body of Mrs Lily Clark was found.

The story was simple and, if you like that sort of thing, good. Briefly, someone was killing off middle-aged women redheads in seaside towns. There had been a summer of it. In May Mrs Wild was killed in Whichborne, in June Mrs Garrard at Turnhill Bay, and by July the murderer had got round to Southwharf and had attended to a Mrs Jelf. In August he chose a fashionable resort just outside the polo ground at Prinny's Plage, and in September there was this latest affair at St Piers.

In all five instances the details were astonishingly similar. Each victim was respectable, homely in appearance, in the habit of letting rooms to visitors, and either naturally or artificially auburn haired. Each woman was found strangled in a secluded place in the open air, with her untouched handbag beside her. Each woman lost some trifling ornament, such as a cheap ear-ring, a gold clasp from a chain bracelet, a locket containing edelweiss, and once, in Mrs Hollis's case, a small silver button with a regimental crest upon it.

Not once was any trace of the murderer seen either before or after the crime, and by the time the St Piers news came through, the Press were on the verge of being bored. There was still plenty to write about, but nothing new. The *Cormorant* and its sisters, who had worked themselves up to screaming hysterics in July, were showing signs of exhaustion, and even the heavies, like ourselves and the *World*, were falling back on such items as the slayer's preference for the new moon.

From my own purely personal point of view the thing

was becoming a nightmare, and the principal reason for that was Chippy Wager. I had first met him when I travelled down to Whichborne in May. On that occasion there were seventeen of us in a carriage which might have held ten without active inconvenience, and although he was the last to arrive he was in a corner seat with only myself atop of him before the journey was halfway over. I do not know how he did this. My impression is that there was a jolt in a tunnel and that when we came out into the light there he was, slung with cameras, sitting just underneath me.

Chippy is a thin rag of a man with a surprisingly large square head in which, somewhere low down in front, has been inserted the bright predatory face of an evil child. Whenever I think of him, I receive a mental picture of white lashes on red lids and a row of widely spaced uneven teeth bared in a 'Have you got anything I want?' smile.

His is hardly one of the dressy professions but I have seen his *confrères* blench when confronted by some of his ensembles. Peterson, my opposite number on the *World*, insists that the man finds his clothes lying about in hotel bedrooms. When I first saw him he was certainly wearing jodhpurs, carefully tailored for a larger leg, a green cardigan buttoning on the wrong side, and a new cheap sports coat adorned by a single gigantic beer-stain. Every pocket, one frankly marsupial, bulged strangely rather than dangerously and he carried as much gear as a paratrooper.

I remember my conversation with him on that occasion. I had pulled back my sleeve to glance at the time and he prodded me in the back.

'That's a good watch,' he said. 'Ever had it photographed?'

I said that, strange as it might seem to him, such a notion had never entered my head.

'It's wise,' he assured me seriously. 'In case you ever had it pinched, see? Gives the busies something to go on. I'll do it for you when we get in. Won't cost you more than half a bar. You're married, of course. Got any kids?'

I told him no, and he seemed hurt.

'Kids make good pictures,' he explained. 'Kids and dogs. Got a dog?'

Again I had to disappoint him.

'Pity,' he said. 'What a pal, eh? What a pal. You might pick up one down here. There's a chap only five miles out who breeds Irish wolfhounds. I'll put you on to him and we'll take a spool. Surprise the wife, eh?'

After that the man became an incubus, haunting me as I drank furtively in corners or hunted our murderer with one eye behind me, so to speak, lest I myself should be waylaid. I could, I suppose, have got rid of him with brutality and the fishy eye, but I could not bring myself to do it. He was so fearful, so unmitigatedly awful that he fascinated me; and then, of course, he was so infuriatingly useful. There was a rumour that he was lucky, but that explanation did him less than justice. He was indefatigable, and his curious contacts and side jobs sometimes provided him with most useful breaks, as, for instance, when he nipped down to Whichborne station to oblige a man who wanted a shot of his greyhound and got instead a very fine one of the Yard's Chief Inspector Tizer getting off the train at a time when no one was sure if the local police had appealed to the Yard and, if so, who was going to be sent.

By the time the murderer had got round to St Piers, Chippy was most anxious that the homicidal nut should be apprehended and the case finished. His reason was personal and typical. I happened to know about it because he had confided it to me one night in a hostelry at Prinny's Plage. I can see him now, pointing to the brewers' almanac which hung on the varnished match-boarding of the bar wall.

'Look, chum,' he said, his forefinger tracing out the dates, 'next new moon is September sixteen, isn't it? Don't think I'm complaining about that. It'll still be summer then and the seaside suits me. But what about the month after? New moon, October fourteen. I don't want anything awkward to happen then, do I?'

I made a point of never giving him encouragement and I said nothing, knowing perfectly well I should not silence him.

'October fourteen.' He was indignant. 'The Distillers Livery Company Conference begins on the fourteenth. Fancy missing that. What a tragedy, eh? What a tragedy!'

That was in August. We were all expecting the September murder, though naturally there was no way of telling where it was going to crop up. When the news broke, it was very nearly an anticlimax. As Petersen said, there would have been almost more news value in the story if it hadn't occurred. No one was pleased. The livelier dailies had planted men at most of the larger southern watering-places, but no one had thought of St Piers, cheap and respectable, out on the mudflats of the estuary. We had a local correspondent there, as we had in every town in the country. The last thing he had sent us, according to the book, was an account of a stork which had been seen flying inland one evening in June the previous year. According to his story, the phenomenon had caused wild excitement in the town. It appeared to be that sort of place.

I managed to avoid Chippy going down, but I saw his back disappearing into the Railway Tavern as I picked up a taxi at the station. I was glad of the respite, for the newsflash which had come in was so familiar in its wording – 'Body of well-matured woman found strangled. Lonely woodland. Auburn haired. Chief

Inspector Tizer hurrying to scene' – that I felt a wave of pure nausea at the prospect of having to deal with him as well.

St Piers was much as I had feared. At first it is only the light and the faint smell of iodine which warns the newcomer that the coast is at hand, but towards the front, where the architecture veers towards Victorian Moorish, a faded ocean licks a dun-coloured strand and the shops sell coloured buckets and sticks of sweet rock and crested china to take home.

I found our local correspondent, a tobacconist called Cuffley, in his shop on the parade. He was waiting for me on the step, every hair in his moustache electrified with excitement. He had leapt to the job, had been on the spot soon after the body had been discovered, and had even written a short piece which began, as I remember, 'Mad Killer Visits St Piers At Last. A baleful sun rose early this morning over the municipally maintained woodland behind the Kursaal and must have shone down unheeding for quite a space on the ghastly blue contorted lips of a respected local resident . . .'

However, he had got the victim's name and address for me and had written it down in block caps, on the back of one of his trade cards: MRS LILY CLARK, KNOLE, SEAVIEW AVENUE. It was the same sort of name and the same sort of address as all the others in the long weary business, and when he told me with delight that he had recognised a relation of the dead woman among his customers, and had gone to the length of having her waiting for me in the little room behind the shop, I knew before I saw her exactly the kind of gal I was going to find. The sameness of all five cases was slightly unnerving. I recognised at once both her horror and the dreadful secret enjoyment she was finding in it. I had seen it often that summer.

Her story, too, was a fifth variation of a tale I had heard four times already. Like her predecessors, Mrs

Clark had been a widow. She had not exactly dyed her hair but she had touched it up. She had not taken in lodgers in the ordinary way, being much too refined. But, yes, on occasions she had obliged. The idea of her going for a walk with a man she did not know! Well, if the situation had not been so tragic the relation would have had to laugh, she would, really.

I asked the question I had grown used to asking. 'Was she a nice woman? Did you like her?' I was prepared for the girl's hesitation and the faint uneasiness, the anxiety to speak well of the dead. I remembered comments on the other women. 'She had a temper.' 'You would not call her exactly generous.' 'She liked her own way.' 'She could be very nice when she wanted to.'

This time Mr Cuffley's customer, in speaking of Mrs Clark, said something which seemed to me to sum up them all.

'Oh, she was all for herself,' she said grimly and shut her mouth like a vice.

At Sub-Divisional Police Headquarters there was no information of a startling character. Mrs Clark had met her death at some time before midnight and in the process she had not been robbed. Fifteen pounds in treasury notes had been found in the mock-crocodile handbag which still hung from her arm. The sergeant in charge spoke of the negligence of the criminal in this respect with an amazement which bordered upon indignation. The only blessed thing she had lost, he said regretfully, was a silver tassel which had hung from the old-fashioned silver brooch she wore in her lapel, and, of course, her life.

As in all the earlier crimes, there was absolutely no suspect. There were no visitors staying at Knole, Seaview Avenue, and so far no one had come forward to report having seen the woman out with a stranger. I sent my story off and took a bus to the Kursaal. Half the town appeared to have the same idea, and I joined a stream of consciously casual strollers advancing purposefully up a threadbare path between ragged ill-used trees. The body had been found in a dusty glade where cartons and little scraps of paper grew instead of anemones. The spot needed no signpost. The police had got their screens up and I could see Inspector Tizer's hunched shoulders appearing above one of them.

The sightseers stood around at a police-prescribed distance, and here again nothing was new. In the last few months reams had been written about the avid, open-mouthed defectives who had come to stare at the last couch of each of the victims, and here as far as I could see they all were once more. I felt certain I had seen the dreary man with the fascinated blue eyes and the watchchain full of darts' medals at every road accident, case of illness in the street, or mere surface reconstruction at which I had had the misfortune to be present. The adolescent girl with the weeping baby brother was familiar, too, and as for the plump, middle-aged man with the broad smile, I was sure I had seen him, or someone like him, grinning at the scene of every catastrophe in my experience.

I had a word with Tizer, who was not pleased to see me and had nothing to tell me. He is never sanguine and by this time his gloom was painful. I came away feeling as nearly as sorry for him as I was for myself.

The Press was there in force and I walked down the hill with Petersen. We came on Chippy at the turning where the path divides. He was busy, as usual, and he appeared to be taking a photograph of a holiday trio, two plump blondes in tight slacks and brassières, with a flushed lout wriggling between them. There could be only one explanation of the performance and I was gratified if surprised to see he had the grace not to notice me.

'Grafters and buskers on fairgrounds call it mug-

faking, I believe,' observed Petersen as we turned into the
White Lion. 'What does he charge them? Half a dollar?
It's an interesting comment on the price of whisky.' He
has an acid little voice.

For the rest of the week the case dragged on. We had
our hopes raised by several false alarms. Tizer thought he
had a lead and went scampering to St Leonards with a
trail of us behind him, but the chase led nowhere. From
our point of view it was all very dull. The weather turned
cold, and three of the best hotels ran out of Scotch. I saw
Chippy now and again but he did not worry me. He was
picking up plenty of work, I gathered, and, if his glazed
eyes in the evening were any guide, appeared to find it
profitable.

He had a new friend, I was interested to see. So far I
have not mentioned Chippy's friends. It is one of his
major disadvantages that he always seems to discover a
local drinking companion who matches, if not exceeds,
the man himself in pure unpresentableness. On this
occasion he had chummed up with the fat man I had seen
grinning at the scene of the crime, or if it was not he it
was someone very like him. I had nothing against the
man save that if I had seen but the soles of his feet
through a grating or the top of his hat from a bus I
should have known unerringly that he was a fellow for
whom I should never have the slightest possible use. He
had crumbs in the creases of his blue serge waistcoat, his
voice was hoarse and coarse and negligible, and the
broad vacant grin never left his face.

Chippy went about with him most of the time, and I
was grateful for my release. I was agitating the office for
my recall on the Saturday and should have left, I think,
by Sunday had not I made a sudden startling discovery.
Chippy was trying to avoid me, and not only me but
every other newspaper man in the town.

At first I could not bring myself to believe it, but

having ceased to hide from him I suddenly found I saw very little of him, and then that Sunday morning we met face to face on the steps of the Grand. In the normal way it would have been I who had become wooden faced and evasive and he who pursued me to insist on the morning snifter, but today he slunk from me, and for the first time in my life I thought I saw him discomposed. I even stood looking after him as he shuffled off, his harness clumping round his shanks; but it was not until I was drinking with Petersen and one or two others some fifteen minutes later that the truth occurred to me.

Someone had asked if Chippy had gone since he had not seen him lately, while somebody else observed that he too had noticed a singular freshness in the atmosphere.

Petersen defended him at once with all that charity of his which is far more lethal than straight attack, and I stood quite still looking at the big calendar over the bar.

Of course. I could not think why I had not realised it before. For Chippy, time was growing pretty short.

I was so anxious that Petersen, whom I love like a brother and who knows me nearly as well, should not cotton on to my idea that I wasted several valuable minutes in which I hope was misleading casualness before I drifted off. From that moment I hunted Chippy as he had never hunted me, and it was not too easy an undertaking, since, as I have said, the place was stiff with pressmen and I was more than anxious not to raise any general hue and cry.

I hunted carefully and systematically, and for the best part of the day I was fighting a conviction that he had vanished into air. But just before six, when I was growing desperate, I suddenly saw him, still festooned with cameras, stepping ashore from a so-called pleasure steamer which had been chugging a party round the bay for the best part of three hours. The other people looked to me like the same crowd who had tramped up to the wood behind the Kursaal the day after the body was found. The adolescent girl with the baby brother was certainly there, and so was Chippy's buddy of the moment, the fat man with the smile.

From that moment I do not think I lost sight of him or them either. Shadowing them was comparatively simple. The whole party moved, it seemed by instinct, to the nearest hostelry, and from there in due course they moved to the next. So it went on throughout the whole evening, when the lights first came out yellow in the autumn haze, and too, when they shone white against the quickening dark.

I do not know when Chippy first became aware that I was behind him. I think it was on the second trip up the Marine Boulevard, where the bars are so thick that no serious drinking time is lost in transit. I met his eyes once and he hesitated but did not nod. He had a dreadful group round him. The man with the smile was still there, and so was a little seedy man with a cap and a watchchain, and two plump blondes in slacks. I recognised them all and none of them, if I make myself clear.

I could feel Chippy trying to shake me off, and after a while I realised that he was going somewhere in particular, heading somewhere definitely if obliquely, like a wasp to its nest. His red eyes wandered to the clock more and more often, I noticed, and his moves from pub to pub seemed quicker and more frequent.

Then I lost him. The party must have split. At any rate I found myself following one of the blondes and a sailor who I felt was new to me, unless, of course, it was not the same blonde but another just like her. I was in the older and dirtier part of the town, and closing time, I felt with dismay, could not possibly be far off. For some time I searched in a positive panic, diving into every lighted doorway and pushing every swinging door. As far as I remember, I neglected even to drink, and it may be it was that which saved me.

At any rate I came finally to a big, ugly, old-fashioned drinking-house on a corner. It was as large and drab and inviting as a barn, and in the four-ale bar, into which I first put my head, there was no one at all but a little blue-eyed seedy man wearing a flat cap and a watchchain weighted with medals.

He was sitting on a bench close to the counter, drinking a pint with the quiet absorption of one who has been doing just that for the last two hours. I glanced at him sharply but there was no way of telling if he had been the same seedy little man with medals who had been with Chippy's party. It was not that I am unobservant, but such men exist not in hundreds but in thousands in every town in or off the coast, and there was nothing distinctive about this one. Also he was alone.

I turned away and would have passed on down the street, when I noticed that there was a second frontage to the building. I put my head in the first door I came to and saw Chippy's back. He was leaning on the bar, which was small and temporarily unattended, the landlord having moved farther along it to the adjoining room. At first I thought he was alone, but on coming into the room I saw his smiling friend reclining on a narrow bench which ran along the inner wall.

He was still beaming, but the vacancy of his broad face intensified, if one can say such a thing, and I knew he must have ceased to hear anything Chippy was telling him long ago. Chippy was talking. He always talks when he is drunk, not wanderingly or thickly but with a low intensity some people find unnerving. He was in full flight now. Soft incisive words, illustrated by the sharp gestures of one hand, flowed from him in a steady forceful stream. I had to go very close up behind him to hear what he was saying.

'Trapped,' he whispered to his friend's oblivion. 'Trapped for life by a woman with a sniff and a soul so mean – so *mean* – so MEAN . . .' He turned and looked at me. 'Hullo,' he said.

I remember I had some idea that in that condition of his I could fool him that I'd been there all the time or was not there at all, I forget which. Anyway, I certainly stood looking at him in surprise without speaking. The thing that surprised me was that he had his old Rolleiflex, the thing he used for close inside work, hanging round his neck with the sight-screens, or whatever they call them, up ready for action.

He returned my stare with friendliness at first, but I saw caution creep across his eyes, tomcat fashion, and presently he made an effort.

'Goodbye,' he said.

The barman saved me answering him by bustling back, wiping the wood and thrusting a tankard at me all in one motion. He rattled the money I gave him in the till and waddled off again, after nodding to Chippy in a secret important way I entirely misunderstood.

'She was mean, was she?' I ventured, mumbling into my beer.

'As hell,' Chippy agreed, and his red eyes wandered up to look over my shoulder towards the door. 'Come in, son,' he said softly.

A pallid youth was hesitating in the doorway and he came forward at once, a long cardboard roll held out before him like a weapon. He was white with excitement, I thought, and I did not suppose it was at the sight of us.

'Dad said you were to have these and he'd see you tomorrow.'

I could see by the way Chippy took the parcel that it was important, but he was so casual, or so drunk, that he almost dropped it, and did scatter some of the coins that he gave the boy. He carried them in handfuls in his jacket pocket, apparently.

As soon as the kid had gone, Chippy tore the paper off the roll and I could see it consisted of four or five huge blown-up photographic prints, but he did not open them out, contenting himself with little squints at each corner, and I could see nothing.

The smiling man on the bench moved but did not rise. His eyes were tightly shut but he continued to grin. Chippy looked at him for some time before he suddenly turned to me.

'He's canned,' he said. 'Canned as a toot. I've been carting him round the whole week to have someone safe to talk to, and now look at him. Never mind. Listen to me. Got imagination?'

'Yes,' I assured him flatly.

'You'll need it,' he said. 'Listen. He was young, a simple ordinary friendly kid like you or I were, and he came to the seaside on his holiday. Years ago, I'm talking about. Only one week's holiday in the year.' He paused for the horror to sink in. 'One week and she caught him. God, think of it!'

I looked at the smiling man on the bench and I must have been a little whistled myself for I saw no incongruity in the tale.

'He was *ordinary*!' shouted Chippy suddenly. 'So ordinary that he might be you or me.'

I did not care for that and I spoke sharply.

'His wife caught him, you say?'

'No.' He lowered his voice to the intense stage again. 'Her mother. The landlady. She worked it. Twisted him.' He made a peculiar bending movement with his two hands. 'You know, said things. Made suggestions. Forced it. He had to marry the girl. Then he had hell. Couldn't afford it. Got nagged night and day, day and night. Got him down.'

He leaned towards me and I was aware of every one of his squat uneven teeth.

'He grew old,' he said. 'He lost his job. Got another, buying old gold. Used to go round buying old gold for a little firm in the Ditch who kept him skint. It went on for years and years. Years and years. A long time. Then it happened. He began to see her.'

'Who?' I demanded. 'His wife?'

'No, no.' Chippy was irritated. 'She'd left him, taken all he had, sold the furniture and scarpered with another poor mug. That was years ago. No, he began to see the mother.'

'Good God,' I said, 'and she was red-haired, I suppose?'

'And mean,' he told me solemnly. 'Mean as hell.'

I was trembling so much I had to put my beer down.

'Look here, Chippy,' I began, 'why wasn't he spotted? Why didn't *she* spot him?'

He took me by the coat collar.

'Imagination,' he whispered at me. 'Use it. Think. He married the girl thirty years ago, but this year he began to see the mother as she used to be.'

Our heads were very close together over the bar and his soft urgent voice poured the story at me.

'He's been travelling round the coast for years buying old gold. Everybody knows him and nobody notices him. Millions of women recognise him when he taps at their doors and very often they sell him little things. But he was ill last winter, had pleurisy, had to go into hospital. Since he's been out he's been different. The past has come back to him. He's been remembering the tragedy of his life.' He wiped his mouth and started again.

'In May he saw her. At first she looked like a woman he knew called Wild, but as they were talking her face changed and he recognised her. He knew just what to do. He told her he'd had a bargain he didn't feel like passing on to his firm. Said he'd got a ring cheap and if she'd meet him he'd show it to her and maybe sell it to her for the same money he paid for it. She went, because she'd known him for two or three years coming round to the door, and she didn't tell anybody because she thought she was doing something shady, see?'

'And when he got her alone he killed her?' I whispered.

'Yes.' Chippy's voice held an echoed satisfaction. 'Paid her out at last. He went off happy as an old king and felt freed and content and satisfied until June, when he went to Turnhill Bay and knocked all unsuspecting at a door in a back street and – *saw her again.*'

I wiped my forehead and stood back from him.

'And at Southwharf, and at Prinny's Plage?' I began huskily.

'That's right. And now St Piers,' said Chippy. 'Whenever there's a new moon.'

It was at this precise moment that the smiling drunk on the bench opened his eyes and sat straight up abruptly, as drunks do, and then with a spurt set out at a shambling trot for the door. He hit the opening with a couple of inches to spare and was sucked up by the night. I yelled at Chippy and started after him, pausing on the threshold to glance back.

Chippy leant there against the bar, looking at me with fishlike unintelligence. I could see he was hopeless and the job was mine. I plunged out and saw the smiling man about fifty yards down the street. He was conspicuous because he kept to the middle of the road and was advancing at a perfectly extraordinary trot which had a skip or a gallop in it every two or three yards, as if he were jet-propelled. I was not in sprinting form myself, but I should certainly have caught him and broken my heart if I had not tripped over a grating thirty feet from the pub door.

It was as I was getting up that I looked over my

shoulder and saw Chief Inspector Tizer and the local Super, together with a couple of satellites, slipping quietly into the bar I had left. It was just enough to make me stone-cold sober and realise I might have got the story wrong. I slid into the pub behind the police.

Chippy was standing at the bar with Tizer on one side of him and the local man on the other. The five enlarged prints were spread out on the wood, and everyone was so engrossed in them that I came quietly up behind and saw everything over Chippy's own head.

They were five three-quarter-length portraits of the same man. Each one had been taken out of doors in a gaping crowd, and on each print a mid-section was heavily circled with process-white. In each case, within the circle, was a watchchain hung with darts' medals and other small decorations which might easily have been overlooked had not attention thus been called to them. In the first portrait the watchchain carried two medals and a cheap silver ear-ring. In the second, a gold clasp from a chain bracelet had been added. In the third, a small locket. In the fourth, a silver button. And in the fifth there hung beside the rest an ugly little tassel from an old-fashioned brooch.

Tizer, who is one of those men who look as if they have been designed by someone who was used to doing bison, put a fist as big as a ham on Chippy's little shoulder.

'You're trying to tell me you only noticed this yesterday and you had the outstanding luck to find the earlier photographs in your file?' His tone was pretty ugly, I thought, but Chippy shrugged himself free. Like myself, he was sober enough now.

'I am lucky,' he said coldly, 'and observant.' He glanced at the barman, who was fidgeting in the archway where the counter ran through into the other room. 'Ready, George?'

'Yes, he's still there, Mr Wager. I've slipped round and shut the doors on him. He's sitting very quiet, just drinking his beer.'

He lifted the flap and the police moved forward in a body. Chippy turned to me.

'Poor little blob,' he said. 'He's quite happy now, you see, till the next new moon.'

'When you will be otherwise engaged, I seem to remember,' I said acidly.

He glanced at me with a sudden smile and adjusted his camera.

'That's right,' he said. 'There's sympathy in this business, but no sentiment. Wait just a minute while I get the arrest.'

Round Trip

W. R. BURNETT

OFFENCE FILE

CRIME: Gangster

PLACE: Chicago, USA

YEAR: 1929

BRIEFING: The 'twenties in America saw the rapid emergence of an entirely new form of criminal: the gangster. These ruthless villains, who ruled by the machine-gun, took a stranglehold on vice, gambling and bootlegging in the biggest cities of the USA. The most notorious was undoubtedly Al Capone, nicknamed 'Scarface', who graduated from petty crime to controlling all the rackets in Chicago, with most of the local police and politicians on his payroll. His ruthless disposal of enemies and rebel gangsters was legendary. In Britain, the only real rivals to Capone were the Kray twins, Reginald and Ronald, whose 'firm' ran the London underworld in the 'sixties with a similar mixture of threats, violence and murder.

AUTHOR: William Riley Burnett (1899–1982), an unpublished Idaho novelist and playwright before he moved to Chicago in the late 'twenties and there found his true *métier*, is the man credited with immortalising the gangster in fiction. His novel, *Little Caesar*, published in 1929, is today regarded as the book which typifies the whole genre. A remarkable chronicle of the rise and fall of a tough Chicago gangster, Cesare Bandello, known as Rico, it was the first naturalistic crime novel as well as being the first piece of fiction about the power of the criminal underworld. Based on Burnett's acute observation of Chicago's gangsters and racketeers, it was an instant publishing sensation – selling half a million copies – and made the author a household name. *Little Caesar* similarly revolutionised the movies when it was adapted for the screen in 1930, establishing Edward G. Robinson as a major Hollywood star. It set the benchmark against which all the subsequent gangster pictures have been judged, right up to and including *The Godfather* (1972) and its sequels. Burnett's later novels and screenplays set further standards in the crime genre, especially *Scarface* (1932), with Paul Muni playing a gangster modelled on Al Capone; *High Sierra* (1941), starring Humphrey Bogart as a former convict whose past crimes catch up with him; and *The Asphalt Jungle* (1950), which was initially a movie featuring Sterling Hayden, and ten years later the inspiration for a ground-breaking TV series starring Jack Warden. 'Round Trip' is one of W. R. Burnett's few short stories and has a special significance in that it, too, is about a gangster in the days of Al Capone and was first published in *Harper's Magazine* in 1929 . . . the self-same year that *Little Caesar* astonished readers of crime fiction everywhere.

* * *

It was about ten o'clock when the lookout let George in. The big play was usually between twelve and three, and now there were only a few people in the place. In one corner of the main room four men were playing bridge, and one of the centre wheels was running.

'Hell, Mr Barber,' the lookout said. 'Little early tonight, ain't you?'

'Yeah,' said George. 'Boss in?'

'Yeah,' said the lookout, 'and he wants to see you. He was grinning all over his face. But he didn't say nothing to me.'

'Somebody kicked in,' said George.

'Yeah,' said the lookout, 'that's about it.'

Levin, one of the croupiers, came over to George.

'Mr Barber,' he said. 'The Spade just left. He and the Old Man had a session.'

George grinned and struck at one of his spats with his cane.

'The Spade was in, was he? Well, no wonder the Old Man was in a good humour.'

'How do you do it, Mr Barber?' asked the croupier.

'Yeah, we been wondering,' put in the lookout.

'Well,' said George, 'I just talk nice to 'em and they get ashamed of themselves and pay up.'

The croupier and the lookout laughed.

'Well,' said the croupier, 'it's a gift, that's all.'

Somebody knocked at the entrance door, and the lookout went to see who it was. The croupier grinned at George and walked back to his chair. George knocked at Weinberg's door, then pushed it open. As soon as he saw George, Weinberg began to grin and nod his head.

'The Spade was in,' he said.

George sat down and lighted a cigar.

'Yeah, so I hear.'

'He settled the whole business, George,' said Weinberg. 'You could've knocked my eyes off with a ball bat.'

'Well,' said George, 'I thought maybe he'd be in.'

'Did, eh? Listen, George, how did you ever pry The Spade loose from three grand?'

'It's a business secret,' said George and laughed.

Weinberg sat tapping his desk with a pencil and staring

at George. He never could dope him out. Pretty soon he said: 'George, better watch The Spade. He's gonna try to make it tough for you.'

'He'll try.'

'I told him he could play his IOUs again, but he said he'd never come in this place as long as you was around. So I told him goodbye.'

'Well,' said George, 'he can play some then, because I'm leaving you.'

Weinberg just sat there tapping with his pencil.

'I'm fed up,' said George. 'I'm going to take me a vacation. I'm sick of Chi. Same old dumps, same old mob.'

'How long you figure to be away?' asked Weinberg.

'About a month. I'm going over east. I got some friends in Toledo.'

'Well,' said Weinberg, 'you'll have a job when you get back.'

He got up, opened a little safe in the wall behind him, and took out a big, unsealed envelope.

'Here's a present for you, George,' he said. 'I'm giving you a cut on The Spade's money besides your regular divvy. I know a right guy when I see one.'

'OK,' said George, putting the envelope in his pocket without looking at it.

'Matter of fact,' said Weinberg, 'I never expected to see no more of The Spade's money. He ain't paying nobody. He's blacklisted.'

George sat puffing at his cigar. Weinberg poured out a couple of drinks from the decanter on his desk. They drank.

'Don't get sore now,' said Weinberg, 'when I ask you this question, but listen, George, you ain't going to Toledo to hide out, are you?'

George got red in the face.

'Say . . .' he said, and started to rise.

'All right! All right!' said Weinberg hurriedly. 'I didn't think so, George, I didn't think so. I just wondered.'

'Tell you what I'll do,' said George. 'Get your hat and I'll take you down to The Spade's restaurant for some lunch.'

Weinberg laughed but he didn't feel like laughing.

'Never mind, George,' he said. 'I just wondered.'

'All right,' said George. 'But any time you get an idea in your head I'm afraid of a guy like The Spade, get it right out again, because you're all wrong.'

'Sure,' said Weinberg.

After another drink they shook hands, and George went out into the main room. There was another table of bridge going now, and a faro game had opened up.

The lookout opened the door for George.

'I won't be seeing you for a while,' said George.

'That so?' said the lookout. 'Well, watch your step wherever you're going.'

George got into Toledo late at night. He felt tired and bored, and he didn't feel any better when the taxi-driver, who had taken him from the depot to the hotel, presented his bill.

'Brother,' said George, 'you don't need no gun.'

'What's that!' exclaimed the taxi-driver, scowling.

'You heard me,' said George. 'You don't need no gun.'

'Well,' said the taxi-driver, 'that's our regular rate, Mister. Maybe you better take a street car.'

Then he climbed into his cab and drove off. George stood there staring at the cab till it turned a corner.

'Damn' hick!' he said. 'Talking to me like that!'

The doorman took his bags.

'You sure got some smart boys in this town,' said George.

The doorman merely put his head on one side and grinned.

There were three men ahead of George at the desk, and he had to wait. The clerk ignored him.

'Say,' said George, finally, 'give me one of them cards. I can be filling it out.'

The clerk stared at him and then handed him a card. George screwed up his mouth and wrote very carefully: Mr Geo. P. Barber, Chicago, Ill.

The clerk glanced at the card and said: 'You'll have to give us an address, Mr Barber, please.'

'Allard Hotel,' said George. 'Listen, I'm tired, and I can't be standing around in this lobby all night.'

'Yes, sir,' said the clerk. 'About how long will you be here?'

'I don't know,' said George. 'It all depends.'

As soon as George was settled in his room he unpacked his bag and undressed slowly. He still felt tired and bored.

'Some town,' he said. 'Why, the way them birds act you'd think this *was* a town.'

He turned out the lights, lighted a cigarette, and sat down at a window in his pyjamas. It was about twelve o'clock and the streets were nearly empty.

'Good Lord,' he said. 'Why, in Chi it's busier than this five miles north.'

He flung the cigarette out the window and climbed into bed. He lay thinking about The Spade and Weinberg. Finally he fell asleep.

He woke early the next morning, which was unusual for him, and discovered that he had a headache and a sore throat.

'Hell!' he said.

He pulled on his clothes hurriedly and went across the street to a little Italian restaurant with a green façade and an aquarium in the window. The place was empty. He sat down at a table in the front and stared out into the street. A waiter came over and handed him a menu. The waiter was tall and stooped, with a dark, sad face. He studied George for a moment, then addressed him in Italian. George turned and stared at the waiter. He did not like to be reminded that he had been born Giovanni Pasquale Barbieri.

'Talk American! Talk American!' he said.

'Yes, sir,' said the waiter. 'You a stranger here?'

'Yeah,' said George.

'I seen you come out of the hotel, so I thought you was.'

'Yeah,' said George, with a certain amount of pride, 'I'm from Chicago.'

'Me, too,' said the waiter. 'My brother's got a plumbing shop on Grand Avenue.'

'Yeah?' said George. 'Well, I live 4000 numbers north on Sheridan.'

'That so? Pretty swell out there, ain't it?'

'Not bad,' said George. 'Say what do you do around here for excitement?'

The waiter smiled sadly and shrugged.

'That's what I thought,' said George.

'If I ever get me some money I'm going back to Chicago,' said the waiter.

George ate his breakfast hurriedly and gave the waiter a big tip. The waiter smiled sadly.

'Thank you. We don't get no tip around here like that.'

'Small town, small money,' said George.

The waiter helped him on with his overcoat, then George returned to the hotel. He didn't know what to do with himself, so he went to bed. When he woke up his headache was worse and he could hardly swallow.

'By God, if I ain't got me a nice cold,' he said.

He dressed in his best blue-serge suit and took a taxi down to Chiggi's. Chiggi was in the beer racket and was making good. He had a new place now with mirrors all around the wall and white tablecloths. The bouncer took him back to Chiggi's office. Chiggi got up and shook hands.

'Hello, George,' he said. 'How's tricks?'

'I ain't starving.'

'In bad over in Chi?'

'Me? I should say not.'

Chiggi just grinned and said nothing.

'Listen,' said George, 'does a guy have to be in bad to leave Chi?'

'Well,' said Chiggi, 'the only guys I ever knew that left were in bad.'

'Here's one that ain't.'

'That's your story, anyway,' said Chiggi, grinning.

The bouncer came and called Chiggi, and George put his feet up on Chiggi's desk and sat looking at the wall. From time to time he felt his throat. Once or twice he sneezed.

'It's a damn' good thing I didn't come over on a sleeper; I'd've had pneumonia,' he thought.

Chiggi came back and they organised a poker game. George played listlessly and dropped two hundred dollars. Then he went out into the dance hall, got himself a girl, and danced a couple of times. The music wasn't bad, the floor was good, and the girl was a cute kid and willing, but George wasn't having a good time.

'Say,' he thought, 'what the devil's wrong with me?'

About two o'clock he left Chiggi's, got a taxi, and went back to the hotel. It was raining. He sat hunched in one corner of the taxi with his coat collar turned up.

He went to bed as soon as he could get his clothes off, but he didn't sleep well and kept tossing around.

At eleven o'clock the next morning he came down into the lobby. He went over to the mail clerk to ask if he had any mail; not that he was expecting any, but just to give the impression that he was the kind of man that got mail, important mail. The girl handed him a sealed envelope with his name on it. Surprised, he tore it open and read:

> . . . as your stay is marked on our cards as indefinite, and as you are not listed among our reservations, we must ask that your room be vacated by six tonight. There are several conventions in town this week and it is absolutely necessary that we take care of our reservations.
>
> W. W. Hurlburt, Asst. Mgr.

'Well, tie that!' said George.

The girl at the mail desk stared at him.

'Say, sister,' he said, 'where's the assistant manager's office?'

She pointed. He went over and knocked at the door, and then went in. A big, bald-headed man looked up.

'Well?'

'Listen,' said George, 'are you the assistant manager?'

'I am,' said the big man.

George tossed him the letter.

'Sorry,' said the big man, 'but what can we do, Mr Barber?'

'I'll tell you what you can do,' said George. 'You can tear that letter up and forget about it.'

'Sorry.'

'You think I'm going to leave, I suppose?'

'Well,' said the big man, 'I guess you'll have to.'

'Oh, that's it,' said George, smiling. 'Well, try to put me out.'

The big man stared at him.

'Yeah,' said George. 'Try to put me out. I'd like to see somebody come up and put me out. I'll learn them something.'

'Well, Mr Barber,' said the big man, 'as a matter of fact, it is a little unusual for us to do anything like this. That is, it's not customary. But we were instructed to do so. That's all I can tell you.'

George stared at him for a moment. 'You mean the bulls?'

'Sorry,' said the big man. 'That's all I can tell you.'

George laughed.

'Well,' he said, 'I'm staying, so don't try to rent that room.'

He went out, banging the door, ate his dinner at the Italian restaurant across the street, talked with the waiter for a quarter of an hour and gave him another big tip; then he took a taxi out to Chiggi's. But Chiggi had been called to Detroit on business. George had a couple of cocktails and sat talking with Curly, the bouncer, about Chicago Red, who had once been Chiggi's partner, and Rico, the gang leader, who had been killed by the police in the alley back of Chiggi's old place. At four o'clock George got a taxi and went back to the hotel. All the way to the hotel he sat trying to figure out why he had come to Toledo. This was sure a hell of a vacation!

The key clerk gave him his key without a word, and George smiled.

'Bluffed 'em out,' he said.

But when he opened his door he saw a man sitting by the window reading a magazine. His hand went involuntarily toward his armpit. The man stood up; he was big and had a tough, Irish face.

'My name's Geygan,' said the man, turning back his coat. 'I want to see you a minute. Your name's Barber, ain't it?'

'Yeah,' said George. 'What's the song, flatfoot?'

Geygan stared at him. 'You talking to me, kid?'

'There ain't nobody else in the room that I see,' said George.

'Smart boy,' said Geygan. 'Come over till I fan you.'

'You'll fan nobody,' said George. 'What's the game?'

Geygan came over to George, whirled him around, and patted his pockets; then he lifted George's arms and felt his ribs; then he slapped his trouser legs. George was stupefied.

Geygan laughed. 'I thought you Chicago birds packed rods,' he said.

'What would I do with a rod in this tank town!' said George.

'All right,' said Geygan. 'Now listen careful to what I say. Tonight you leave town. Get that? You birds can't light here. That's all. We've had some of you birds over here and we don't like you, see? Beat it and no questions asked. You stick around here and we'll put you away.'

George grinned. 'Putting it on big, hunh?'

'Yeah. You better not be in the city limits at twelve tonight or . . .'

'Listen,' said George, interrupting, 'you hick bulls can't bluff me that easy. Just try and do something, that's all. Just try and do something. You ain't got a thing on me.'

'All right,' said Geygan.

Geygan went out. George took off his overcoat and sat down in the chair by the window.

'Can you beat that!' he thought. 'It's a damn' good thing I got my rods in the trunk. Why, that mug actually fanned me. Yeah. Say, what kind of a town is this, anyway? No wonder Chicago Red hit for home!'

He got up and unlocked his trunk. There was a false bottom in it where he kept his guns and his liquor. That was safe. Well, they didn't have a thing on him. Let them try and put him out. All the same, he began to feel uneasy. But, hell, he couldn't let these small-town cops scare him.

He was taking off his shoes when somebody knocked at the door.

'I wonder what the game is,' he thought.

Then he went over and opened the door. Geygan and two other plainclothesmen stepped in.

'There he is, chief. You talk to him. He won't listen to me.'

'Say,' said the chief, a big grey-haired man, 'they tell me you've decided to prolong your visit.'

'Yeah,' said George, 'indefinitely.'

'Well,' said the chief, 'if you want to stay here, why, I guess we can accommodate you. Fan him, Buck.'

'Say,' said George, 'I been fanned so much I got calluses.'

'That's too bad,' said the chief. 'Go ahead, Buck.'

Buck whirled George around and gave him the same kind of search Geygan had given him, with this difference: he found a gun in his hip pocket, a small nickel-plated .32. George stared at the gun and began to sweat.

'Geygan,' said the chief, 'you didn't do a very good job.'

'I guess not,' said Geygan.

'You never found that cap pistol on me,' said George, staring hard at Buck.

'Will you listen to that, Buck!' said the chief. 'He thinks you're a magician.'

'Why, you planted that gun on me,' said George. 'That's a hell of a way to do.'

'Well,' said the chief, 'when your case comes up, you can tell it all to the judge.'

'My case!' cried George.

'Why, sure,' said the chief. 'We send 'em up for carrying rods here.'

George stood looking at the floor. By God, they had him. Wasn't that a break. Well, it was up to Chiggi now.

'Listen,' said the chief, 'we ain't looking for no trouble and we're right guys, Barber. I'll make you a little proposition. You pack up and take the next train back to Chicago and we'll forget about the .32.'

'He don't want to go back to Chicago,' said Geygan. 'He told me.'

George walked over to the window and stood there looking down at the street.

'OK,' he said, 'I'll go.'

'All right,' said the chief. 'Buck, you stick with the Chicago boy and see that he gets on the right train.'

'All right, chief,' said Buck.

Geygan and the chief went out. Buck sat down and began to read a newspaper.

Weinberg was sitting at his desk, smoking a big cigar, when George opened the door. Seeing George, he nearly dropped his cigar.

'Hello, boss,' said George.

'By God, I thought you was a ghost,' said Weinberg. 'What's wrong with your voice?'

'I caught a cold over in Toledo.'

'You been to Toledo and back already! Did you go by airplane?'

George grinned.

'No, but I made a quick trip. What a hick town. You ought to go there once, and look it over.'

'Chicago suits me,' said Weinberg.

George sat down, and Weinberg poured him a drink. George didn't say anything, but just sat there sipping his drink.

Pretty soon Weinberg said: 'George, I was hoping you'd stay in Toledo for a while. Rocco was in the other night and he told me that The Spade was telling everybody that your number was up.'

George grinned.

'Ain't that funny!'

Weinberg didn't think it was funny, but he laughed and poured himself another drink.

'Yeah,' said George, 'that's the best one I've heard this year.'

Morning Visit

JAMES HADLEY CHASE

OFFENCE FILE

CRIME: Sadist

PLACE: Cuba

YEAR: C. 1940

BRIEFING: Peter Kurten, the 'Monster of Dusseldorf', who carried out a series of sadistic sexual killings of young women in Germany in the late 'twenties and early 'thirties, was as infamous for a time as Jack the Ripper – for whom he expressed a profound admiration. He caused a wave of fear until he was caught, tried for nine murders, and guillotined in Cologne in 1931. America's most infamous sadistic killer was Albert Fish, who added cannibalism to his sadomasochism and was electrocuted at Sing Sing Prison in 1936; while in the annals of British crime, Neville George Heath, the suave RAF officer with abnormal sexual lusts who killed two young women and was hanged in 1946, enjoys the same dubious distinction on this side of the Atlantic.

AUTHOR: James Hadley Chase (1906–85), a London-born former children's encyclopaedia salesman and book wholesaler, was inspired by the works of W. R. Burnett and several other hardboiled American crime writers to attempt a similar kind of novel. The result was *No Orchids For Miss Blandish* (1939), the story of a beautiful heiress kidnapped by a mob of American gangsters who sadistically abuse, beat and sexually assault her. It became a million seller and is still claimed today to be one of the bestselling mysteries ever published. The phenomenal success of this book and the author's choice of subsequent titles with a similar mixture of sex and violence, turned Chase into the acknowledged king of thriller writers in Britain and Europe – a position he maintained for much of his writing life. It was an astonishing achievement for a man who was writing about American localities he had never visited and authentically describing a criminal milieu and its villains about which he had no personal knowledge. In fact, Chase used maps, travel guides and dictionaries of American slang for his eighty novels, which were virtually all set in the USA. He carried his readers along with fast-paced action, complex plots and unforgettable characters, ranging from unscrupulous private eyes to ex-CIA agents and insurance fraud investigators: all of whom constantly tangled with beautiful and voraciously sexual females. However, his sadistic treatment of women in a number of stories got Chase into trouble with some critics and, on occasions, even the authorities. In fact, attempts were made to ban several of his books – although these self-same titles were soon to be made into Hollywood movies. The following uncompromising story of sadism and torture is believed to have been one of the main reasons why a collection of Chase's short stories, entitled *Get A Load Of This*, which was scheduled to be published in 1941, failed to appear on the bookstalls. Indeed, 'Morning Visit' was not published in the UK until forty years later and is here making its first anthology appearance.

* * *

The Lieutenant stopped and held up his hand. Over to his right he had seen the farm, half hidden by a clump of coconut palms.

The four negro soldiers shuffled to a standstill, grounding their rifles and leaning on them.

Overhead the sun beat down on the little group. The Lieutenant, the sweat oozing out of his fat hide, wriggled his body inside his uniform which stuck to him uncomfortably. He was acutely aware of the great patches of damp that stained his white uniform; and he cursed the heat, the President and, above all, the ABC terrorists.

Contemptuously he regarded the four negroes, who stood staring with vacant eyes on the ground, like emasculated cattle. 'This is the place,' he said, thrusting forward his bullet head. 'Two of you to the right; two to the left. No noise. No shooting – use your bayonets if there's trouble.'

He drew his sword. The steel blade flashed in the sunlight.

The soldiers opened out and advanced towards the farm at a trot. They held their heads down, and their rifles hung loosely in their hands. As they shambled over the uneven ground they looked like bloodhounds picking up a scent.

The Lieutenant moved forward at a slower pace. He walked gingerly, as if he were treading on eggshells. Inside his once beautiful uniform, his fat body cringed at the thought of a bullet smashing into him. He took the precaution of keeping the coconut palms between him and the farm. When he could no longer shelter himself behind the slender trunks he broke into a run. The heat waves coiled round him like a rope as he lumbered over the rough ground.

The four soldiers had already reached the farm, and they stood in an uneven circle, waiting for the Lieutenant to come up. They were more animated now. They knew that very soon they would be back in the barracks out of the heat of the afternoon sun.

The farm was a squat dwelling, with a palm-thatched roof and whitewashed walls. As the Lieutenant approached cautiously, the door of the place opened and a tall, poorly dressed Cuban stepped into the sunshine.

The soldiers jerked up their rifles, threatening him with the glittering bayonets. The Cuban stood very still, his hands folded under his armpits, and his face wooden.

The Lieutenant said, 'Lopez?'

The Cuban's eyes flickered round at the soldiers, seeing only the ring of steel before him. He looked at the Lieutenant. 'Yes,' he said, a dry rustle in his voice.

The Lieutenant swung his sword. 'You may have heard of me,' he said, a wolfish smile pulling at his mouth. 'Ricardo de Crespedes.'

Lopez shuffled his feet in the sand. His eyes flinched, but his face remained wooden. 'You do me much honour, señor,' he said.

The Lieutenant said, 'We'll go inside,' and he stepped past Lopez, holding his sword at the alert. He walked into the dwelling.

Lopez followed him with two of the soldiers. The other two stood just outside the door.

The room was very poor, shabby, and dirty. De Crespedes moved to the rough table standing in the middle of the room and rested his haunches on it. He unbuttoned the flap on his revolver-holster and eased the revolver so that he could draw it easily. He said to one of the soldiers, 'Search the place.'

Lopez moved uneasily. 'Excellency, there is no one here – only my wife.'

The negro went into the other room. De Crespedes said, 'See if he's armed.'

The other soldier ran his big hands over Lopez, shook his head, and stepped back. De Crespedes hesitated, then reluctantly put up his sword. There was a long, uneasy pause.

The negro came back from the other room pushing a Cuban woman before him.

De Crespedes looked at her and his small eyes gleamed. The woman ran to Lopez and clung to him, her face blank with fear. She wore a white blouse and skirt; her feet were bare. De Crespedes thought she was extraordinarily nice. He touched his waxed moustache and smiled. The movement was not lost on Lopez, who tightened his hold on his wife.

De Crespedes said: 'You're hiding guns here. Where are they?'

Lopez shook his head. 'I have no guns, Excellency. I am a poor farmer – I do not trade in guns.'

De Crespedes looked at the woman. He thought her breasts were superb. The sight of her drew his mind away from his duty and this faintly irritated him, because he was quite a good soldier. He said a little impatiently: 'It will be better for you to say so now than later.'

The woman began to weep. Lopez touched her shoulder gently. 'Quiet,' he said, 'it's Ricardo de Crespedes.'

The Lieutenant drew himself to his full height and bowed. 'He is right,' he said, rolling his bloodshot eyes a little. The woman could feel his rising lust for her.

Lopez said desperately: 'Excellency, there has been some mistake—'

De Crespedes lost patience. He told the soldiers to search the place for guns. As the negroes began hunting he pulled the woman away from Lopez. 'Come here,' he said, 'I want to look at you.'

Lopez opened his mouth, but no sound came to him, his eyes half closed and his hands clenched. He knew he could do nothing.

The woman stood close to de Crespedes, her hands clasped over her breasts. Her fear stirred his blood.

'Do you understand why I'm here?' he said, putting his hand on her bare arm. 'Traitors are arming the people against the President. Guns have been hidden here. We know that. Where are they?'

She stood quivering like a nervous horse, not daring to draw away from him. She said, 'Excellency, my man is a good man. He knows nothing about guns.'

'No?' De Crespedes pulled her closer to him. 'You know nothing about these terrorists? Nothing about plots to overthrow Machado?'

Lopez stepped forward, pushing his wife roughly away, so that de Crespedes' hold was broken. 'We know nothing, Excellency.'

De Crespedes shoved himself away from the table. His face hardened. 'Seize this man,' he barked.

One of the soldiers twisted Lopez's arms behind him and held him.

The woman ran her fingers through her thick hair. Her eyes grew very wide. 'Oh no . . . no . . .' she said.

De Crespedes himself supervised the search, but they found nothing. He went out into the sunlight again and shouted to the remaining soldiers to look round the outside of the farm. Then he came back. He stood in the doorway, looking at Lopez. 'Where are the guns?' he said. 'Quick – where are they?'

Lopez shook his head. 'We know nothing about guns, Excellency.'

De Crespedes turned to the soldier. 'Hold him very tightly.' Then he began to walk towards the woman. She turned to run into the other room, but the other soldier was standing against the door. He was smiling, and his teeth looked like piano keys. As she hesitated, de Crespedes caught up with her and his hand fell on the back of her blouse. He ripped it from her. She crouched against the wall, hiding her breasts with her hands, weeping softly.

De Crespedes looked over his shoulder at Lopez.
'When you are dead,' he said, 'I will have your woman –
she is good.'

Lopez controlled himself with a great effort. He was
completely powerless in the grip of the soldier.

De Crespedes said to the soldiers who came in at this
moment, 'Cut off his fingers until he's ready to talk.'

The woman screamed. She fell on her knees in front of
de Crespedes, wringing her hands. 'We know nothing,
Excellency,' she said wildly. 'Don't touch my man.'

De Crespedes looked down at her with a smile. Then
he put his dusty boot on her bare breasts and shoved her
away. She fell on her side and lay there, her head hidden
under her arms.

The soldiers forced Lopez to sit at the table, and they
spread his hands flat on the rough wood. Then, using his
bayonet like a hatchet, one of the negroes lopped off a
finger.

De Crespedes sat looking at the blood that ran across
the table and dripped on to the floor. He stood up with a
little grimace of disgust.

A thin wailing sound came from Lopez, although he
didn't open his lips. The two soldiers who held him
shifted as they strained to keep his hands in position.

'Until he talks,' de Crespedes said, unhooking his
jacket and removing his sword-belt.

The negro raised his bayonet and brought it down with
a swish. There was a little clicking sound as it went
through bone, and he had difficulty in getting the blade
out of the hard wood.

De Crespedes threw his jacket and sword-belt on the
bench and walked over to the woman. With a grunt, he
bent over her. Taking her under her arms, he dragged her
into the other room. He threw her on the bed. Then he
went back and kicked the door shut. He noticed that it

was very hot in the room, although the shutters kept out the sun.

The woman lay on her side, her knees drawn up to her chin. She kept her eyes shut, and her lips moved as she prayed. De Crespedes lowered his bulk on to the bed. He took her knees in his hands and turned her on her back. Then he forced her knees down and ripped the rest of her clothes from her. He did not hurry, and once, when she resisted, pushing at him with her small hands, he thumped her on her chest with his fist, like he was driving in a nail with a hammer.

Then, because he knew this rigid body could give him no pleasure, and because he had much experience, he set about breaking her down. His two hands settled on her arms and his fingers dug into her soft muscles. Her eyes opened and she screamed. He leant on her, crushing her with his bulk, and dug further with his fat, thick fingers. It was not long before the violence of the pain turned the woman into a weeping, gibbering thing of clay on the bed. And when he took her, she lay placid, her tears falling on his shoulder.

Later on, one of the soldiers had to go out and get a bucket of water to throw over Lopez, and although they did many things to him, they could not get him to speak, so they lost patience with him and they killed him.

When de Crespedes came out of the room he found his soldiers standing uneasily waiting for him. He looked down at Lopez and stirred him with his boot. He wiped his face with the back of his hand and yawned. 'Did he talk?' he asked indifferently. He was thinking of the long tramp back to the barracks. When they shook their heads, he shrugged and put on his jacket. He was feeling devilishly tired. Listlessly he tightened the sword-belt round his thick middle and put on his cap. Then he went back and looked at Lopez again. 'It is possible he knew nothing about guns,' he said half aloud, 'they've made a lot of mistakes before.' He shrugged and turned to the door.

The soldiers picked up their rifles and moved after him. Outside, he paused. 'The woman,' he said irritably, 'I was forgetting the woman.' He looked at one of the soldiers. 'Attend to her. Use your bayonet.'

While they waited in the blinding heat, he thought regretfully how much better it would have been if she had loved him. There was little satisfaction to be had from a weeping woman. Still, he felt better for it. Women were necessary to him.

When the soldier came out, they gave him time to clean his bayonet and then they all tramped across the uneven ground towards the barracks.

Murder Comes Easy

EVAN HUNTER

OFFENCE FILE

CRIME: Juvenile delinquency

PLACE: New York

YEAR: 1953

BRIEFING: Young criminals are common to all nations, but very few have become as infamous as Nathan Leopold and Richard Loeb, two teenage youths from prominent Chicago families who, in 1924, killed the fourteen-year-old son of a millionaire businessman and then tried to demand $10,000 in ransom money. Because of their ages, both escaped the death penalty and went to prison for life. In Britain, the case of Derek Bentley and Christopher Craig, two teenagers who were involved in the murder of a policeman in 1952, became the subject of a highly controversial case – with Bentley, nineteen, being hanged though he had played no direct part in the violence, and Craig, sixteen, who had actually fired the gun, 'detained at Her Majesty's pleasure' because he was under age.

AUTHOR: Evan Hunter (b. 1926), famous as a mainstream novelist and creator (as Ed McBain) of the hugely popular 87th Precinct police mysteries, was also one of the pioneer writers of stories about juvenile delinquents in the early 'fifties, which became known as 'JDs' or 'Juvies' and constituted a crime genre of their own. Hunter effectively launched this new trend with his novel *The Blackboard*

Jungle in 1954, which exposed for the first time in fiction the violence and racial tension in a secondary school in a slum district of New York. Filmed the following year, it became notorious for the riots it provoked among young audiences in America and Britain, and also as the first movie to utilise the new music sensation, rock 'n' roll. Drawn from Evan Hunter's own recent experiences teaching in two New York high schools, *The Blackboard Jungle* also made readers uncomfortably aware of a world of teenage crime close to their own doors, where young delinquents killed without a second thought, teenage girls casually took up prostitution, and drugs were quickly becoming an overwhelming problem for the police and local authorities. Hunter developed this same theme further in a series of short stories written between 1953 and 1955 for magazines such as *Real, Manhunt* and *Adventure* which caused him to be acclaimed by Ellery Queen as 'one of the earliest mystery writers to be irresistibly attracted to the violence and crime prevalent among teenagers and to use the material creatively'. His stories, Queen added, came from behind the newspaper headlines – 'tragic, frightening episodes of life in the modern jungle'. Here is such a tale, 'Murder Comes Easy', written for *Real* magazine of March 1953, and amongst the earliest of Hunter's 'Juvies' to explore the world of violence, drugs and brutal young hoodlums. In Manny Cole he offers a chillingly authentic portrait of a young delinquent who will stop at nothing – even murder – in the service of a local mob leader . . .

* * *

The whole thing was almost too easy. I had the lock open in about ten seconds, and all I used was a nail file. I stepped inside out of the cold, closed the door gently behind me, stood quietly with my back to it. I didn't hurry. I eased the .45 out of my coat pocket and checked the clip. Then I shoved the clip home. It made a small click in the darkness of the foyer.

The house branched out from the foyer, one half leading to the kitchen area, the other to the living room and the bedrooms. I knew the house by heart because Mr Williams had gone over the floor plan with me a hundred times.

'This is a big one, Manny,' he'd said. 'A real big one. You do this one right, and you're in. What I mean, *in*.'

I felt good about that. He'd picked me for the gig, and I knew it was an important one. He could have picked one of the punks, but he wanted it done right, and so he came to Manny Cole. And this would be the one. After this one, I'd be in the upper crust, one of the wheels. It had to be done right.

The living room was dark, just the way Mr Williams had said it would be. I released the .45's safety with my thumb and stepped on to the thick pile rug that led off the foyer. From the back of the house, trickling under the narrow crack of a bedroom door, amber light spilled on to the rug in a thin, warm wash. I moved through the living room slowly, past the spinet against one wall, past the big picture window with the drawn drapes. I walked straight to the radio-phono combination, fumbled with its dials for a few seconds, and then turned it on full blast.

A jump tune blared into the room, shattering the silence of the house. I tuned the station in more clearly, listening to the high screech of a trumpet beating out a bop chorus. The door to the bedroom popped open, and Gallagher came out.

He was in his undershirt and shorts, blue-striped shorts that hugged his fat middle. He waddled forward with a surprised look on his face, and his stubby fingers reached for a light switch. There was a small click, and then the living room was filled with light. He looked worse with the light on him.

There was lipstick on his face, and I knew why, but that didn't concern me at the moment. Only Gallagher concerned me. His blue eyes were opened wide, embedded deep in the fleshy folds of his face. His mouth flapped open when he saw the .45 in my fist, and I thought he'd spit out his teeth. Then his face paled, and he began to shake, and the fat shivered all over him.

'Who . . . who are you?' he asked.

I chuckled a little. 'Mr Williams sent me,' I said.

'Williams!' The word came like an explosion, and his face turned a shade paler. He knew what was coming.

'Mr Williams doesn't like the way you've been doing things,' I said.

Gallagher wet his lips. 'What doesn't he like?'

'Lots of things,' I told him. 'The fur heist the other night, for example. He doesn't like people who do things like that.'

'Those furs were mine,' Gallagher shouted over the blast of the trumpet. 'Bart knew that.'

I shook my head. 'Mr Williams says they were his.'

The music stopped and an announcer began talking. His voice sounded strange in the quiet room.

'So . . . so . . . what are you going to do?'

'I'm going to kill you, Gallagher.'

'For God's sake, kid, you can't . . .'

'As soon as the music starts again,' I told him. 'If you've got a religion, pray.'

'Look, kid, for the love of—'

'Gallagher, this is a job, like picking up garbage or shining shoes. Just like that. I'm deaf as far as you're concerned. Understand? I can't hear anything. I'm deaf.'

The music started then, and panic whipped across Gallagher's face. He saw my eyes tighten, and he turned to run towards the bedroom, and that's when I cut loose. I fired low, with the barrel tilted so that the slug would rip upward.

The first one caught him just above the kidneys, spun him around, and slammed him into the wall. He didn't seem to know whether he should reach for the blood, or whether he should cover the rest of him. And while he was deciding, I pumped two more slugs into him. They tore into his face, nearly ripping his head off.

He fell to the floor, and the fat wiggled for a second before it was still.

I looked down at him just long enough to see the red puddle forming under his head. Then I turned away.

'Come on out,' I said.

There was a soft whimper in the bedroom, but no movement.

'Come on, come on.'

I heard bare feet padding on the rug, and then she was standing in the doorway. She'd thrown a robe around her, and she'd done it pretty quickly because she was still fastening the belt at the waist. The robe belonged to Gallagher, apparently, and it didn't help much to cover her. The initials RG were over the pocket, but the pocket was nowhere near where it should have been. It hung far to the right of her rounded shoulders.

She had hair like a bed of charcoal, and it hung over one eye. Her lips had a fresh-kissed look, the way they can look only when the lipstick has been bruised into the flesh. Her eyes might have been smouldering a few minutes ago, but they were scared now. Her lips opened a little, and her eyes dropped quickly to the .45, and then over to Gallagher. She took a deep breath, and then stepped back a pace.

She didn't say anything. She just looked at me with that frightened-animal look in her eyes, wide and brown, and she kept backing away, moving towards the bed. She almost tripped on a pile of silk stockings and underwear on the floor. She looked down quickly, caught her balance, and then started to pull the robe closed over her breasts.

She hesitated for a moment, swallowed hard, and then caught her hand in mid-motion.

'A fat slob like Gallagher,' I said. I shook my head. 'I can't get over it.'

She was staring at me. 'You're . . . you're just a kid,' she said.

'Shut up!'

'Look, I . . . I don't know Gallagher from a hole in the wall. I was just here, you understand? I got a call, that's all, and I came. It's a job, like you told Gallagher. A . . . a business.'

'Sure,' I said. I grinned and took a step closer to her. 'You scared, baby?'

'N – n – no.'

'You should be. You should be damned scared.'

'Kid, please. I'll do whatever you say. Anything. Anything at all, kid. Only . . .'

'Only what?'

'Only . . . Anything you say.'

'You want to get out of this alive?' I asked. 'Is that it?'

She smiled and took a step closer to me, confident of herself now, confident of her body and what it would get her.

The smile was still on her face when I fired. I made it clean and quick. A fast one that caught her right over the bridge of her nose. She was dead before she hit the rug. Quickly, silently, I left the apartment.

Betty didn't understand. Nothing I said mattered. She sat with the open paper in front of her and a coffee cup in her right hand. The steam from the coffee rose up and swirled around her nose. She didn't understand, and she didn't like it. Her mouth told me that.

'You look lousy when you've got a puss on,' I told her.

'Then I'm going to look lousy for a long time,' she said. She was blonde, almost nineteen, with her hair cropped close to the oval of her face. She had green eyes that were blazing at me now, and tiny white teeth that were exposed when she pulled back her lips in a snarl. Her folks had split up when she was seventeen, and she'd taken a job downtown, and she rented her own pad. She was my girl, you know, and she was a real pretty piece, except when she was angry like now.

'Look, baby—' I said.

'Don't "baby" me, Manny. Just don't.'

'Well, what the hell *do* you want?' I was beginning to get a little sore, too. I mean, what the hell! Enough is enough.

'You know what I want,' she snapped.

'I don't know, and I'm not going to guess.'

Her face got soft, the way I liked to see it, and her voice softened to match it.

'When's it going to end, Manny?'

'I don't know what you're talking about.'

The anger flared in her again. 'You know damn well what I'm talking about!'

'All right, I know, and it's never going to end. All right?'

'Who are you going to kill next?'

'Nobody,' I said. 'I'm not going to ever kill anybody. I ain't killed anybody so far. Just you remember that.'

She slapped the newspaper with the back of her hand. 'This Gallagher, and the girl—'

'I don't know anything about this Gallagher. And I don't know anything about his damned whore.'

Betty looked at me across the table, and she shook her head slowly. 'You're a fool, Manny. You really are a fool.'

I got up, shoving my chair back so hard that it fell over. 'I don't have to take this kind of crap. I'll be damned if I have to take it.'

'Where are you going?' she asked.

'None of your damn business!'

'To your friends? To your big Mr Williams?'

'Oh, can it and sell it,' I told her. I slammed the door

behind me and walked down to the '48 Chevvy parked at the curb. I yanked open the door, nearly ripping off the loose handle, and climbed in behind the wheel. What the hell could you do with a woman like Betty? She didn't understand that I'd be driving a Caddy in a few years, that we'd have the best, everything. She didn't understand that I was sick of Brokesville, that I wanted to be up there where I could wallow in the stuff. Or maybe she thought it was an easy pull, like walking up to some guy and saying, 'Man, I want the big time, you know? Lay it on me.'

Sure, just like that.

Damn it, you had to fight for everything you got in this world. There was always another guy waiting to step on you if you let him. I wasn't going to let him. Mr Williams liked me. He'd given me the Gallagher kill when there were a dozen punks slavering at the lips for it. You could bet on that, all right.

So she rode me for it. She didn't understand this was all for both of us – that Manny Cole would be a big man soon, almost like Mr Williams.

I turned on the ignition, started the bus, and pulled away from the curb. She'd see. When the loot began pouring in, she'd change her tune pretty damn quick. As soon as the loot began pouring in.

Turk was riding high when I found him. He looked at me glassy-eyed for a few seconds, and then he said, 'Hey, Cole. How's it, man?'

I remembered when Turk had been a top boy in the organisation. I remembered how I'd gotten close to him first, just to get near Mr Williams. He wasn't so top now.

'What's the word, Turk?' I asked.

'I hear you ventilated Gallagher nice,' he said. 'Real nice.'

I looked around over my shoulder. 'Hey, man,' I said, 'get off that. Cool it fast.'

'Sure, Cole, sure.' The dreamy look came back into his eyes again. He'd been mainlining it for a long time now. I felt sorry for the big slob. He'd been a good man long ago. Before he hit the skids and before he met heroin. Now he was getting slop details, rustling chicks for the big boys when they wanted them, stuff like that. He had a double-tread of puncture marks on his arms and was starting the second tread on his legs. This was the guy I'd looked up to a few years back.

'Where is everybody?' I asked.

'Huh? What was that, Cole?' The glassy eyes opened, sunken deep in the once-full face.

'The boys. Where?'

'Oh, yeah. Down at Julie's, I think. Yeah, Julie's got a game going.'

'Thanks, Turk.'

'Not at all,' he said politely. He coughed then and added, 'You got a fin, Cole? I can get a couple caps for a fin, and I ain't been fixed since the Ice Age.'

I dug into my wallet, opened it. I didn't let Turk see that all I had was a fin and a deuce. I pulled out the fin and laid it on him. 'Here, man,' I said. 'Blow your skull.'

'Well, thanks, Cole. Thanks a million. Hey, thanks.'

I left him staring down at the fin, and hopped into the Chevvy, heading for Julie's dump. Julie was close to the top, and he'd started out the way I had. Mr Williams liked him, too, but since I'd come around, Julie wasn't getting many of the big jobs any more. I figured Julie for maybe another year or two, and then goodbye. You had to stay on your toes all the time, and Julie had dropped his guard when he'd let me squeeze my way in. So, Julie was on the way out.

I parked the car between Second and Third and walked down to Julie's. He still wasn't living big, but he hadn't played it right. He was from nowhere, Julie, and I wondered how he'd ever got so close to the top in the first place. I rapped on the door, saw Cappy's eye appear in a crack the width of a dime.

'Oh, Cole,' he said.

The door swung wide, and I stepped into the room. 'Hello, Cappy. How's it going?'

'*Comme ci comme ça*,' he said, pulling his face into a grimace.

'Where's the game?' I asked.

'In the bedroom. You playing?'

'Oh, I don't know,' I said casually. 'Any action?'

Cappy shrugged his narrow shoulders. 'I ain't playing,' he said. He slumped down into a chair near the door, and I headed for the bedroom. When I walked in, the guys at the table, both sitting and standing, looked up.

'Hey, Cole! Look, guys! It's the big kid himself.'

'How goes it, man? Give us all the cool jive, mister.'

'Hear you punched some holes last night!'

'Nice work, Cole.'

That's the way the talk was drifting until Julie cut in.

'We playing cards or greeting punks?' he asked.

The boys all shut up, as if Julie had clamped a big hand over all their mouths. I looked at him across the table. He was holding his cards out in a tight fan, and his black brows were pulled together over beady brown eyes. He had a thin, curving nose and a cigar pointed up from his lips, tilting so that it almost touched his nose. He didn't look at me. He kept staring at his hand while the boys waited for me to say something.

'What was that, Julie?' I asked.

'You heard me, Cole. You're disrupting the game.'

'Seems you're the only one I'm disrupting, Julie.'

He looked up then, his brows lifted. Slowly and carefully, he put his card fan down on the table. 'Yeah,' he said, 'maybe it's only me you're disrupting.'

'Well, you know what you can do about it, Julie.'

'And what's that, Cole?'

'You can shove it up your—'

He backed away from the table so fast that I didn't know he'd moved for a second. He walked around the players quickly and rammed a big hand at me, wrapping it in the lapels of my jacket.

He brought his other hand back across his chest and then sideways, catching me across the face with his knuckles. My head bounced back, and then his forward slap caught me on the other cheek.

That was all I needed.

I brought my balled fist forward in a short, chopping jab to Julie's gut. He was surprised, all right. He was so surprised that he dropped my jacket and was reaching under his armpit when my other fist looped up and exploded on the point of his jaw. His lips flew open and the cigar flopped out of his mouth. He still had his hand on the bunny-in-the-hutch, so I picked up my knee fast and rammed it into his groin. He folded over like a jack-knife, and I brought my fist down on the back of his neck hard, hard enough to crack a couple of vertebrae. He pitched forward like a drunken sailor, kissed the floor with his face, and then sprawled out without a care in the world. Julie was out.

I kicked him in the ribs to make sure, wanting to break a few, but figuring maybe Mr Williams wouldn't like the way I'd roughed him up.

'Get this crud out of here,' I said. 'How can you play with that stink in here?'

The boys laughed it up, and then one of them dragged him out of the bedroom. I sat down at the card table and played a few hands, just to let them know I could sit in Julie's chair any day. When I lost the deuce, I left.

The word came from Mr Williams two days later. It came down through Turk, and for a minute I thought Turk was just hopped and talking through the top of his skull. I figured that Turk would never dream that up, though, no matter how wigged he was, so I went up to see Mr Williams fast.

He was sitting behind a big desk. He had blond hair, and blond eyebrows, and pale blue eyes that pinned you to the wall.

'Hello, Manny,' he said. 'Pull up a chair.'

I sat down, and my eyes ran over the hand-tailoreds he was wearing, and over the glistening pinky-ring, the manicured nails. He was the top. King of the hill. I watched him light a cigarette with a thin, rolled-gold lighter.

'A little trouble, Manny,' he said.

'Anything I can do to help, Mr Williams?'

'Well, it's a little trouble concerning you,' he said. He blew out a stream of smoke, pinned me with his eyes again.

'Oh,' I said lamely. 'You mean Julie. I—'

'To hell with Julie,' Mr Williams said. 'He had it coming to him. I'm glad you worked him over.'

'Well, thanks. I—'

'Your girlfriend,' Mr Williams said.

'My . . . girl?'

'She was here, Manny. Just a little while ago.'

'Betty? Here?'

'She made a lot of threats, Manny. She said she was going to the police. She said she was sick and tired of your taking orders from a big crook.' He paused. 'Do you think I'm a big crook, Manny?'

'No. No, Mr Williams. You have to excuse Betty. She's just a kid. Sometimes, she . . .'

'No, Manny,' he said coldly. 'She doesn't "sometimes" any more. Things have gone much too far, I'm afraid.'

'Wh – what do you mean by that, Mr Williams?'

'I mean she talks too much. She said she'd give us a week, Manny. After that, she'd go to the police and tell them all about Gallagher and the girl. And a few others.'

'She . . . she said that?'

'I don't like it. I don't like it at all. Not that she can touch us, Manny. She'd have a hard time proving anything. But I had big plans for you. You're young, a boy, one of the best boys I've got. I hadn't counted on a hysterical woman, though.'

'I . . . I'm sorry, Mr Williams. I'll talk to her. I'll . . .'

'Talk!' he said. 'Nonsense! Do you think you can talk her out of this?' He was mildly disturbed now. He got up and began pacing the room, back and forth in front of the desk. 'Once a woman acquires a loose tongue, she never gets rid of it. She needs more than talk.'

'But . . .'

'If you want to go places in this organisation, you'll know what to do, I won't have to tell you. You'll know.'

'I . . . I don't understand.'

'You've got a week, Manny. After that, your girl begins screaming, and we'll be shaking the police out of our hair for a month after that. Disturbances like that annoy me.'

'A week,' I repeated dumbly.

'It's too bad you're attached to her, Manny. It's really too bad. A woman like that can be a millstone around a man's neck. Unless something is done about it.'

I nodded and got up. When I reached the door, Mr Williams smiled and said, 'You could be a big man in this organisation, Manny. A really big man. Think it over.'

And I thought it over. I thought it over for four days, then I tried talking to Betty. It didn't get me very far.

'I don't want to listen,' she said. 'You either quit your Mr Williams, or I go to the police. That's it, Manny. I've had enough.'

'You ain't had nothing,' I said. 'Baby, we'll be in the chips. I'm moving up. Mr Williams—'

'I'll scream!' she shouted. 'If you mention his name once more, I'll scream.'

'Baby—'

'Shut up! Shut up, Manny!' She started crying then, and

I've never known what to do with a chick that bawls, so I left her alone and walked the streets for a while.

I found Turk, and I bought a few joints from him. Marijuana was candy to Turk. It never gave him a jolt, but he was willing to sell it so he could get his paws on the needlestuff. I lit up one of the joints, sucking it in with loose lips, mixing it with air for a bigger charge. The street got longer and the buildings seemed to tilt a little, but outside of that, I didn't feel a thing.

I lit the other joint and smoked it down to a roach, and then I stuck a toothpick in that and got the last harsh, powerful drags out of it. I flew down the street, then, and I forgot all about Betty and her goddamn loose mouth. I was on a big cloud, and the city was just a toy city down below me, and I felt good. Hell, I felt terrific.

It didn't last. You pick up, and the charge is great, but it wears off and you got the same old problem again. Unless you're Turk, and then your big problem is getting the stuff that makes you forget.

On the sixth day, I knew what I had to do.

She went to a movie that night, and I walked the streets thinking it all over in my mind. Around eleven o'clock, I took a post in an alley near her pad. I knew the way she came home. She always came home the same way. The army .45 was in my pocket. It felt heavy, and my palm sweated against the walnut stock.

I heard her heels, and I knew it was her when she was still a block away. She crossed the street under the lamp-post and the light danced in her hair, threw little sparkles across the street. She walked like a queen, Betty, with her shoulders back, and her fine, high breasts firm under her coat. Her heels tapped on the pavement and she came closer and I took the automatic out of my pocket.

When she reached the alley, I said, 'Betty,' soft, in a whisper.

She recognised my voice, and she turned, her eyebrows lifting, her mouth parted slightly. I fired twice, only twice.

The gun bucked in my hand and I saw the holes go right through her forehead, and she fell back without screaming, without making a sound. I didn't look back. I cut down the alley and over towards Eighth Avenue. I dropped the gun down a sewer, then, and I walked around for the rest of the night. It was a long, long night.

The party was a big one. I stayed close to Mr Williams all night, and he called me his boy, and all the punks came around and looked up to me and I could see they were thinking, 'That Cole is a tough cat, and a big man.'

I was wearing a tailormade suit. I'd laid down two hundred skins for it. My pinky-badge was white and clear even if I'd got it at a hock shop. It was a big party, all right, and all the big wheels were there, and Manny Cole was one of them. They were afraid of me, and they respected me. Even Julie. Julie maybe respected me more than all the rest.

The usual punks were there, too, eager, falling all over Mr Williams, waiting for the big kill, the one that would put them up there on top of the heap. Mr Williams introduced me to a young squirt named Davis, Georgie Davis or something. He said the kid was worth watching, that he'd done nicely on a few gigs so far. I watched the kid, and a few times I caught him watching me back, and there was a hungry, glittering look in his eyes.

I didn't get home until five in the morning. The dawn was creeping over the edge of the night in a grey, lazy way.

I stood in the kitchen in the quiet apartment. I had the money to move out of there now, but I hadn't made the break yet. I pulled back the curtain, and I looked down over the rooftops, the way I used to long ago when Betty would come up to see me, when we were both a little younger – when Betty was alive.

It got chilly in the apartment. The chill reached through

my skin and settled in my bones. I tossed the curtain aside and walked over to the phone, flipping open the pad. I'd written the number down when it was an important number to know, when I'd been a punk like Georgie Davis and when this number belonged to a guy on the top.

'Hello?' The voice was tired, not a big shot's voice.

'Hello, Turk,' I said. 'This is Manny Cole.'

'Oh, hello, Mr Cole, how are you? What can I do for you?'

I smiled a little. 'Turk, bring a girl over. I feel lonely, Turk.'

'A girl?' Turk said. 'Why sure, Mr Cole. Any particular kind?'

Mister Cole again. The smile got bigger on my face. 'Use your own judgment, Turk. You know what I like.'

'Sure, Mr Cole. Right away.'

'Incidentally, Turk . . .' I heard the click on the other end of the line, and I knew he'd hung up. I really didn't have anything more to tell him, but I had felt like talking a little more. Slowly, I put the phone back into the waiting cradle.

The apartment was quiet, very quiet. I walked into the bedroom and stood before the dresser, looking down at the framed picture of Betty. I looked at it for a long time.

Then I went to the phone and sat down near it, wondering who I could call, wondering who I could talk to. I lit a cigarette, studied the burning end.

I knew who I wanted to talk to.

I put her out of my mind. I thought of other things. I thought of Georgie Davis, the young punk who'd eyed me at the party. And I thought of all the other punks who'd stare at me with the bright gleam in their eyes and the hungry look on their faces. The young punks eager for a kill, eager for a lot of things.

I thought about them for a long time.

When the doorbell rang, I knew it was the girl.

I knew it couldn't have been anyone else, but it took me a

long time to open that door. And when I did open it, I had one hand on the slippery .45 in my pocket, and I was sweating. I wasn't scared, but I was sweating.

I was sweating because I knew I'd have to open a lot of doors in the days and nights to come –

And one of them would not open on a smiling girl.

The Flaw in the System

JIM THOMPSON

OFFENCE FILE

CRIME: Conman

PLACE: Unnamed American city

YEAR: Early 'sixties

BRIEFING: The confidence trickster has been a notorious if colourful figure in criminal history for several centuries. Few more so than Victorian England's Charles Peace, a scourge of the police for twenty years, and a master of disguise with a glib tongue, nimble fingers and a habit of always being one step ahead of the law. He committed two murders which finally led to his capture and hanging in 1879. He was followed by 'Mad Fred' Deeming who conned hundreds of victims in Australia and South Africa, returned to his native England and, after committing six murders in the course of his frauds, was executed in 1892. In the US, Raymond Fernandez and Martha Beck earned the epithet of 'The Lonely Hearts Killers' plus the reputation of being 'America's most hated killers' for conning lonely middle-aged women out of their money and murdering at least twenty. The couple were executed at Sing Sing Prison in 1951.

AUTHOR: Jim Thompson (1906–77) was an author of paperback originals and an occasional Hollywood scriptwriter who remained unheralded during his lifetime, but has now received posthumous acclaim for his work – in particular his darkly accurate pictures of smalltime con artists, congenital liars and occasional killers. At the forefront of his brilliant but meagre output – mostly written in 1953 and 1954, with a handful more in the early 'sixties – is *The Grifters* (1963), about three con artists making their picaresque progress across western USA. In 1990, the book was adapted for the screen by Donald Westlake, directed by Stephen Frears and superbly acted by Anjelica Huston, John Cusack and Annette Bening to earn the accolade of cult movie. This success further enhanced Thompson's reputation as well as demonstrating to a worldwide audience that here was a master of the American *noir* thriller. Among the other Jim Thompson titles which have been brought to the screen are *The Killer Inside Me* (1952), filmed in 1975 with Stacy Keach; *A Hell of a Woman* (1954), made in 1979 with Marie Trintignant; and *The Kill Off* (1954), a 1989 feature with Loretta Gross that several critics have claimed shows Thompson's nihilism at its most objective. Summing up his contribution to crime fiction, critic Nigel Algar wrote recently, 'Jim Thompson did not so much transcend the genre of mystery fiction as shatter its conventions.' The conman in 'The Flaw in the System' is unlike any other to be found in the pages of crime fiction: an artist who practises his deceptions in a way that is as simple as it is puzzling – but which, in turn, makes him all the more dangerous to his victims . . .

***

I watched him as he came up the mezzanine steps to the Credit Department, studying his worn suit, his frayed necktie, his scuffed shoes. Knowing, even as I waved him to a new-account booth – with the very first question I asked him – that he was strictly on the sour side. And feeling a kind of surly happiness in the knowledge.

For an instalment house – a dollar-down-the-rest-of-your-life outfit – we didn't catch many sour ones. They knew they couldn't beat us – how can you fast-talk a machine? – so they left us alone. But here was this guy, an N.G. from the word go, with a hundred and seventy-five bucks in sales slips! I wondered what the hell was wrong with our clerks, why they hadn't sent him up for an OK in the beginning instead of wasting their time on him.

I looked up from the slips, sharply, all set to read him off. I looked into his eyes – the warmest, friendliest eyes I had ever seen, in the kindliest face I had ever seen. And all I could think of was that somehow, in some way acceptable to the home office, I had to let him have the stuff. I spoke to him, asked a question, in a tone that was almost pleading and apologetic. He shook his head.

'No,' he said pleasantly. 'I cannot make a fifty per cent down payment. The fact of the matter is, I cannot make any down payment at all.'

'Well,' I said regretfully, 'I'm awfully sorry, sir, but I don't think—'

I broke off, unable to tell him, however politely, that the deal was no soap. I had a feeling that if the friendly warmth in those eyes died out, something very necessary to me would die with it.

So I filled out a sales contract – just writing down the answers he gave me without comment or further discussion. When I was through, I made a few telephone calls and then I took the contract in to Dan Murrow's office. Dan was our credit manager.

He scanned the contract swiftly, mumbling to himself: 'One seventy five with no d.p. Unemployed. N.G. from credit bureau. N.G. from two other accounts. No property. Hotel-resident – no permanent address. No –

get outta here!' Dan yelled suddenly. 'What are you bothering me with this for?'

'I'm sorry,' I said. 'Handle it for me, will you, Dan?'

'What the hell's there to handle?' he snarled. 'What's wrong with you?' But he snatched up the contract and headed outside. I stayed where I was, listening.

I heard Dan say, 'Now, look, mister. I don't know what you're trying to pull, see, but—' And then his voice changed. Suddenly it became the same way mine had been, soft and humble and apologetic. Begging for the good will of a man who was not only a total stranger, but an out-and-out deadbeat to boot.

Well . . .

The guy left. Dan came back into his office, gave me a thousand-watt glare, and jerked his thumb towards the door. He didn't say anything. It didn't look like a good time for me to say anything, so I went back to my desk and made out a duplicate on the contract.

All our records were made in duplicate, the dupes going to the home-office store and to Mr Dorrance, the head credit manager. Mr Dorrance trusted no one. He left nothing to chance. As long as you did exactly as you were instructed to do, you were all right. If you didn't – well, however sharp and tough you were, Dorrance was a lot sharper and a lot tougher. He had his eyes on you all the time, and he made sure you knew it.

It was a good system. You might get sore at the whole blasted world, or you might get to where you just didn't give a damn, or you might even quit. But the system rocked right along, permitting no errors, working perfectly.

At least, it always had worked perfectly until now.

Dan Murrow didn't speak to me the rest of the afternoon. But by quitting time he had straightened out a little, and we went to a place for a few beers. He was still kind of on the belligerent side. Sheepishly belligerent. He knew the account was sour – that it just couldn't be anything else – but he tried to pretend it wasn't.

'A hundred and seventy-five bucks,' he said. 'With our mark-up, that's around ninety dollars profit. What kind of credit manager would I be if I chased away that kind of dough?'

'Yeah,' I said. 'I guess that's right.'

'So maybe he's a toughie,' Murrow went on. 'We got a legal department, ain't we? We've got collectors – boys that know how to make the tough ones soft. Sooner or later we'll catch that cookie on a job, and when we do . . .'

His voice trailed away. He looked at me, his eyes strangely bewildered.

Obviously we weren't going to catch the guy on a job. We weren't going to catch him with any attachable assets. This would be the way he made his living – by gypping stores and hocking or selling the merchandise. And there wasn't a thing we could do about it.

It wasn't fraud, because there'd been no misrepresentation. He was a deadbeat, but legally speaking he wasn't a crook.

His first payment fell due on the following Saturday. Naturally he didn't meet it, so Murrow put a collector on to him. The collector reported back that the guy had skipped town. Whether he was lying or not, I don't know. Murrow had an idea he was, but he couldn't see that it mattered much.

'*If* we collect,' he said, '*if* – which we can't – it wouldn't help us any with Dorrance. We broke the rules, see? Like drawing to an inside straight, only ten times worse. Maybe a miracle might happen and we'd fill the straight. But it's still all wrong. We could pay this account ourselves, but Dorrance wouldn't like it one jot better.'

We sweated out the weekend, wondering what Dorrance would do and knowing that whatever it was, it wouldn't be nice. Late Monday afternoon Murrow came to the door of his office and motioned for me to come inside. He looked a little pale. His hand shook as he closed the door behind me.

'Dorrance,' I said.

'Yeah. His secretary, I mean.' Murrow grinned sickishly, trying to make his voice sound satirical. 'Mr Dorrance wants a full report on that very peculiar account,' he recited. 'A detailed report, setting forth any reasons we have – *if* we have any – for opening such an account.'

'Yeah?' I said. 'Well . . .'

'We got to think of something, Joe.' He leaned across the desk, desperately. 'Some way we got to get ourselves off the hook. It means our jobs if we don't. It might mean even more than that. Yeah,' he nodded, as I looked at him startled. 'We had no good reason to OK that guy, so could be we had a bad one. But then again maybe we were in cahoots with him, splitting the take.'

'Well . . .' I spread my hands helplessly.

'Let's start at the beginning,' Murrow said. 'Why did you do what you did, anyway? Why didn't you just turn this character down yourself instead of passing him on to me?'

'I – well, I just didn't want to,' I said. 'It wasn't as if he was compelling me, or hypnotising me, or anything like that. And it wasn't because I felt sorry for him. It was just – well, it doesn't make any sense – it sounds crazy now. But – but—'

'I know,' Murrow murmured. And then he brought himself up sharp. 'Go on and spill it! Maybe we can come up with something.'

'Well,' I hesitated. 'It was like I had to do it to prove something. That I was a person – a human being, not just part of a system. That there wasn't any system big enough to keep me from making a mistake, just like there wasn't any big enough to keep me from doing the right thing. So – well, I guess that's why I did it. Because it was the only way, it seemed, that this guy would go on liking me. And I was afraid that if he ever stopped liking me, I – I just wouldn't be any more. I'd have moved off into a world I could never come back from.'

Murrow looked at me silently. After a moment he let out a scornful grunt – rather, he tried to. 'Brother!' he snorted. 'Are you a big help!'

'How about you?' I said. 'Why didn't you give him a turndown?'

'Never mind about me!' he snapped. 'Because I'm stupid, that's why. Because I got so many dumb clucks working for me, I'm getting dumb myself . . . Well, you got anything else to say?'

I shook my head. 'Nothing that would make any sense.'

'Let's have it,' Murrow said wearily. 'You haven't *been* making any sense, so why should you begin now?'

'I was just wondering,' I said. 'I mean, I wasn't wondering exactly, but— He stuck two other stores in town besides ours. He could have made a clean sweep, yet he only took two. But those two are the same kind of outfits we are.'

'So?' Murrow frowned. 'So he plays the instalment houses. What about it?'

'Not just the instalment houses. A certain *type* of instalment house,' I said. 'The hard-boiled kind. The iron-clad system houses. Places where every contingency is provided for by the system, where the human element is ruled out . . . The system says no sales to the unemployed. No sales to transients. It says that if a risk looks very bad, we must insist on a down payment that practically covers the wholesale cost of the merchandise.

It allows for *no* exceptions under *any* circumstances. It doesn't allow us to think or feel – to do anything but apply our own special yardstick and throw out anyone who doesn't measure up to each and every one of the rules. Why, one of the saints themselves could walk in here and if he didn't—'

'Chop it off,' Murrow said. 'Get to the point.'

'I've already got to it,' I said. 'This guy knows exactly how we operate – yet he chooses us. He deliberately makes things tough on himself. Why did he do it? If he was just after the merchandise. If, I mean, he was doing it just for himself instead of – uh—'

'Yeah?' Murrow said grimly. 'Yeah?'

'Nothing.' I turned towards the door. 'I guess I'd better be getting back to work.'

I had just sat down at my desk when Murrow came out. He asked me for a description of the guy, adding roughly that at least I could help him that much.

'Well . . .' I tried to remember. 'He seemed awfully friendly. Really friendly and kind, you know. The way he smiled at me, it was like he'd known me for a long time – as if he knew me better than I knew myself.'

'Nuts!' Murrow yelled. 'Do you or don't you remember what he looked like?'

'What about you?' I said. 'You talked to him longer than I did.'

Murrow wheeled around, stamped into his office and slammed the door shut behind him.

Naturally he didn't send any report to Dorrance – how could he? There was nothing to report. And there was nothing we could do but wait until Dorrance called again . . . demanding an explanation for the unexplainable.

But Dorrance didn't call.

A week passed.

Two weeks.

And there wasn't a single peep from the home store.

I suggested to Murrow hopefully that maybe there had been a slip-up, that the matter had got buried somewhere and was now in the process of being forgotten. But Murrow said there wasn't a chance – not with our system.

'That's what they want us to think – that we got away with something. We think that, see, so maybe we'll try something else.' And when we do . . .'

'But we aren't going to! We haven't tried anything yet, have we? We made this one mistake – kind of a mistake – but from now on—'

'I'll tell you what,' Murrow said. 'If you've borrowed anything against your petty cash, you'd better pay it back. Check the collectors – make sure they don't hold dough over from one day to the next. Keep your accounts posted right up to the minute. Have everything in perfect order, understand? Because if it isn't – if there's anything wrong at all – we'll be in the soup. A hell of a lot deeper than we are right now.'

I did what he told me to.

Four days later Dorrance showed up.

It was on a Saturday, a few minutes before closing time. He lingered near the entrance until the last of our customers had left; then he came up the stairs, a big man with a flabby face and eyes that were like two chunks of ice.

He answered our nervous greetings with the merest of nods. He cleared off a desk – waving me away when I started to help him – and started laying out the contents of two heavy briefcases.

'All right,' he said, spreading out his records – picking one contract, *the* contract from among them and placing it deliberately to one side. 'You know why I'm here. If I want to know anything I'll ask you. If I want you to do anything I'll tell you. Got that? Good. Now open the safe, unlock the cash drawer, and bring your account files over here.'

It was almost midnight when he finished checking us. Almost five hours – with Murrow and me hanging around red-faced and embarrassed. Feeling unaccountably guilty and looking a hell of a lot guiltier. Hardly speaking unless we were spoken to or moving unless we were ordered to.

Five solid hours of waiting and watching – while Dorrance did his damnedest to spot something crooked.

Then, at last, he was through. He leaned back in his chair, massaged his eyes briefly with a thumb and forefinger and gave us another of those infinitesimal nods.

'That does it,' he said. 'You boys are OK.'

Something inside of me snapped. Before I could stop myself I blurted out an angry, 'Thanks. I'll bet that disappoints you, doesn't it?'

'Now, now,' Murrow said quickly. 'Mr Dorrance is just doing his job.'

'Then it's one hell of a job!' I said. 'He comes in here late at night and—'

'Yes,' said Dorrance quietly. 'Yes, it's one hell of a job, son. I'll be glad to see the day when it isn't necessary – which unfortunately, it seems to be at present. This is the tenth store I've hit in the past three weeks. Four of them didn't check.'

'Well,' I said. 'I didn't mean to say that – that—'

'It gave me quite a start,' Dorrance went on. 'Of course there's always bound to be a little gypping – one-shot, off-and-on stuff. But these birds had been doing it regularly. They'd invented a system for beating our system . . . I wonder –' He hesitated, then his eyes strayed to that laid-aside contract. 'I've been wondering why I didn't foresee that it would happen. We've discouraged individuality, anything in the way of original thinking.

All decisions were made at the top and passed down. Honesty, loyalty – we didn't feel that we had to worry about those things. The system would take care of them. The way the system worked – supposedly – a man simply *had* to be loyal and honest.

'Well, obviously, we were all wet; we found those four stores I mentioned, and God knows how many others there are like them. And about all I can say is we were asking for it. If you won't let a man think for you, he'll think against you. If you don't have any feeling for *him*, you can't expect him to have any for *you*.'

He paused, picking up that lone contract and glanced at us questioningly. Murrow and I didn't say anything. Dorrance shrugged.

'Now let's face it,' he said. 'This man has stuck store after store in our chain. He's hit us for thousands of dollars. How he got away with it, we don't know. None of our men have been able to explain. But there *is* an explanation – several of 'em, in fact ... Perhaps he worked for an outfit like ours at one time. He knew you people had been pushed to the top of the arc in one direction and that you were all set to swing the other way – out of resentment, frustration, anger. The desire to do something for once that *didn't* make any sense. All he had to do was catch you at the right time, and you'd let him walk off with the store.

'Or it could be that he's simply a damned clever conman operating in a new field. A good conman would know that the easiest people to take are those who've never been taken – people who supposedly know all the angles, who are so sure that no one would even try to beat them and they're a cinch for the first man who does.' Dorrance paused, then went on.

'He's a very dangerous man. He did us a good turn, indirectly, by starting this investigation, but that doesn't change the situation. He's a menace – as dangerous as they come – and if we ever spot him again he's got to be treated as one. Just grab him, understand? Latch on to him, and we'll figure out a legal charge later. Why, a man like that – he could wreck us if he took a notion to! He could wreck our entire economy!'

Murrow glanced uneasily at the contract, wondering, as I did, what Dorrance intended to do about it. And about us. Then Murrow said nervously that he didn't imagine the guy would be back. 'Do you, Mr Dorrance?'

'Why not?' Dorrance snapped. 'Why don't you think he'll be back?'

'Well –' Murrow looked at me uncomfortably. 'I'm not sure, of course. It was just an idea. But—'

'Dan means it wouldn't be smart for him to come back,' I said. 'He'd know that we'd be on the lookout for him.'

'Oh,' said Dorrance. After a long moment he pushed himself up from his chair and reached for his coat. 'That wraps it up, I guess. Now let's get out of here. You boys have to work tomorrow, and I have to travel. As for that contract, throw it in your p-and-ls. Can't collect on it, so it might as well go into profit-and-loss.'

Murrow and I didn't move; we just weren't up to moving yet. And we couldn't think of anything to say either. But there was an unspoken question in the air. Dorrance answered it snappishly, as he packed his briefcases.

'What's the matter with you?' he said, not looking at us. 'You can't put two and two together? Do I have to draw you a diagram? That fellow hit the home store hard too – hit us the hardest of all. I personally OKed him for four hundred dollars . . .'

He sounded sore, but he didn't look it. Somehow he looked kind of happy.

Blurred View

JOHN D. MACDONALD

OFFENCE FILE

CRIME: Blackmailer

PLACE: San Francisco

YEAR: 1964

BRIEFING: People in all walks of life, from libidinous Cabinet Ministers to adulterous housewives, have been the object of blackmail – some of whom have made headlines, with a great many more who have not. One of England's most infamous blackmailers was Dr Neill Cream, who practised as a physician in Chicago and London as a cover for his nefarious activities which fed his obsession for sex, crime and murder. As he was about to die on the gallows in November 1892, Cream is said to have begun the sentence, 'I am Jack the . . .' just before the rope snapped tight. In America in 1923, the unsolved murder of a pretty young model, Dot King, who was well known to have a number of rich admirers in New York, has long been ascribed to her being involved in a complex blackmail plot.

AUTHOR: John D. MacDonald (1916–87), another crime writer whose early work was published in paperback, has been described by fellow mystery author Richard Condon as 'the great American storyteller'. Although perhaps best known as the creator of the Fort Lauderdale detective-thief Travis McGee, who makes his living recovering stolen property and outwitting crooked businessmen, the topics of blackmail and corruption have been recurring themes in his work. One of his earliest non-McGee novels, *The Only Girl in the Game* (1960), is a tale of blackmail featuring an innocent young woman trapped into working for a criminal syndicate operating a Las Vegas casino; and corruption is the main theme in *Condominium* (1977), concerning a corporate swindle. MacDonald brought an MBA degree from the Harvard School of Business Administration and a formidable intelligence to the writing of his crime stories and always kept himself up to date on the latest financial scams in case he needed the information for any of his plots. His very first novel, *The Brass Cupcake*, published in 1950, was an instant success, selling one and a half million copies, ensuring that his name was ever-present in book stores and that, in time, he was to be the most renowned original paperback crime novelist of his generation. MacDonald's insight into human psychology – in particular what turns an honest man into a criminal or makes a gentle man a murderer – also earned him numerous awards from crime writers' associations on both sides of the Atlantic. His regular output of two new titles per year has been much missed by his fans since his death. 'Blurred View', originally published in *This Week* magazine in 1964, is MacDonald at his most ingenious as he recounts what seems like a classic case of blackmail – *until* the surprise ending is reached . . .

* * *

The funeral was a wretched affair. I suppose it was done as tastefully as one would expect. But great gaudy swarms of Gloria's friends from the television industry came up from the Los Angeles area. They were dressed sedately, but still managed to seem like flocks of bright birds, men and women alike, their eyes bright and sharp and questing.

They had been at the inquest too, turning out in numbers which astonished the officials. I had not been surprised. If I learned any one thing from my marriage, it was that those people are incurably gregarious. They had absolutely no appreciation of privacy and decorum. Their ceaseless talk is like the chatter of birds, and largely incomprehensible to the outsider.

After the funeral I settled a few final details before going away. The lawyer had me sign the necessary things. Gloria had managed to squirrel away more than I expected, and she had invested it very shrewdly indeed. My own affairs were in a temporary lull. Bernard, at the gallery, made the usual apology about not being able to move more of my work, and offered his condolences, for the tenth time. I closed the Bay house and flew to the Islands.

Helen's greeting was sweet and humble and adoring. She is a small, plain woman, quite wealthy, a few years older than I. She was most restful after the contentious flamboyance of Gloria. Her figure is rather good. During the weeks we had together she made several shy hints about marriage, but the unexpected size of Gloria's estate gave me the courage to think of Helen as a patron rather than a potential wife.

We returned to Los Angeles by ship, in adjoining state-rooms, and parted warmly in that city. She was to return to New York to visit her children and settle some business matters concerning her late husband's estate, then fly back out to San Francisco to be near me.

I moved back into the Bay house and listed it with a good broker. It is a splendid house, set high over the rocks, but a little too expensive to maintain, and a little too conspicuous for the bachelor life I contemplated. Also, there was a silence about it when I was alone there which made me feel uneasy, and made it difficult for me to work in the big studio which Gloria and I had designed together.

After I had been there alone for five days, a seedy little man arrived in the afternoon. He drove up in a battered little car and came to the door carrying a big manila envelope in his hand.

He was trying to say he had something to show me. He was humble, and nervous, and had a little recurring smile like a sudden grimace. He smelled sweaty. Something about him alarmed me. Reluctantly I led him back through the house to the studio.

He said, 'Mr Fletcher, I just want to work something out. That's all. I don't want you should get the wrong idea about anything. It's just one of those things. And we can work something out. The thing is, to talk it over.'

I'd had my share of bad dreams about this kind of situation. My voice sounded peculiar to me as I said, 'I don't know what you're talking about.'

He had put the envelope on a work table. He said, 'What I do, I'm assistant manager, Thrifty Quick. My brother-in-law, he's a doctor, got a home right over there across the way. You can't see it today, it's too misty. The thing is, I was laid up in April. Dropped a case on my foot, and I stayed over there with my sister. I guess I'm what they call a shutter bug. I'm a real nut on photography. It keeps me broke, I'm telling you.'

'Mr Walsik, I haven't the faintest . . .'

'What I was fooling with, long-lens stuff on thirty-five millimetre. I was using a Nikon body and a bunch of adaptors, a tripod of course, and I figured it out it came to f22, sixteen hundred millimetres, and I was using Tri-X. I don't suppose the technical stuff means anything to you, Mr Fletcher.'

'You don't mean anything to me, Mr Walsik.'

'Figuring back, it had to be April tenth. A clear

morning and no wind. Wind is bad when you use that much lens. You can't get sharpness. The thing is, I was just experimenting, so I had to find some sharp-edged object at a distance to focus on, so I picked the edge of that terrace out there. I took some shots at different exposures, and after a while I thought I could see somebody moving around on the terrace. I took some more shots. I made notes on exposure times and so on. You know, you have to keep track or you forget.'

I sat down upon my work stool. This was the monstrous cliché of all murders, I had thought it a device of scenario writers, the accidental little man, the incongruous flaw. With an effort I brought my attention back to what he was saying.

'. . . in the paper that she was all alone here, Mr Fletcher, and you proved you were somewhere else. Now I got to apologise for the quality of this print. It's sixteen by twenty, which is pretty big to push thirty-five millimetre, and there was some haze, and that fast film is grainy, but here you take a look.'

I took the big black-and-white print and studied it. I was at the railing, leaning, arms still extended. He had caught her in free fall toward the rocks, some six feet below my outstretched hands, her fair hair and nylon peignoir rippled upward by the wind of passage. It brought it all back, scooping her up from the drugged and drowsy bed, walking with her slack warm weight, seeing her eyes open and hearing her murmurous question in the instant before I dropped her over the wall. The print was too blurred for me to be recognisable, or Gloria. But it was enough. The unique pattern of the wall was clear. It could no longer be 'jumped or fell'. And with that picture, they could go back and pry at the rest of it until the whole thing fell apart.

When he took the picture out of my hands I looked up at him. He stepped backward very quickly and said in a shaking voice, 'I got the negative in a safe place, with a letter explaining it.'

'What do you want?' I asked him.

'Like I said, I just want to work something out, Mr Fletcher. The way I figure if I try to push too hard what I'll do is spoil everything. What I want is for life to be a little easier. So I could get a little bit better apartment in a handier neighbourhood. And there's some lenses and camera equipment I want to buy. I won't be a terrible burden, you understand. But I don't want to sell you the negatives. I want like a permanent-type thing, the way people get an annuity. I've got some bills I want to pay off, so the first bite, believe me, is bigger than the ones I'll want later on. I was figuring it out. If you can get a thousand for me now, then in three or four months I'll come back like for five hundred. I don't see why we can't work it out this way. I want you to be comfortable with it, so you won't try to upset anything.'

He was actually pleading with me. And obviously frightened. And I found myself reappraising marriage to Helen. She could more readily afford Mr Walsik. I had no choice, of course. I had to agree.

He told me where to meet him, and when, and I promised to bring along the thousand dollars in tens and twenties. After he had left I had two stiff drinks and began to feel better. In ridding myself of Gloria I had saddled myself with Walsik, but he seemed a good deal easier to manage.

I found him two nights later exactly where he said he would be, in one of the rear booths of a tiresome little neighbourhood bar. I handed him the envelope and he tucked it away. As I got up to leave, two burly chaps grabbed me, snapped steel on my wrist, and bustled me out to an official sedan.

They tell me that I held out for fourteen hours before I

finally began to give them those answers as deadly to me as the cyanide will be in the gas chamber.

After it was over, they let me sleep. The next afternoon they brought Walsik to see me. He was not seedy. He was not humble. His voice was not the same. He had that odd febrile, animal glitter so typical of Gloria's friends in the industry.

'While you were on the grass-skirt circuit, Frank baby,' he said, 'we borrowed your pad. We brought the long lenses. We rigged the safety net. A big crew of willing volunteers, baby, all the kids who loved Gloria. We guessed that's how you did it. We took maybe fifty stills of Buddy dropping Nina over the wall. How did you like my performance, sweetie? You bought it good. After you bought it, we brought the law into it, to watch you give me money. Sit right there, Frank baby. Sit there and bug yourself with how stupid you were.'

I heard him leave, walking briskly down the corridor, humming a tune. Somebody said something to him. He laughed. A door clanged shut. And I began to go over it all, again and again and again . . .

The Sweetest Man in the World

DONALD E. WESTLAKE

OFFENCE FILE

CRIME: Fraud

PLACE: New York

YEAR: 1967

BRIEFING: Three men dominate the history of fraud in the twentieth century: Ivar Kreuger, the Swedish financier known as 'The Match King', who tried to gain a worldwide monopoly of match production using long-term dollar loans, and whose assets, after his suicide, were discovered to be largely fictitious; Horatio Bottomley, the English financier, journalist and politician whose Victory Bond scheme proved to be just one of many frauds that brought down his career; and the American tycoon Bernie Cornfield, whose IOS group based in Switzerland was also shown to be an international swindle. Organised crime groups such as the Mafia and Murder Incorporated have also been masters of the big fraud – with business conglomerates and banking institutions as their prime targets – while clever individuals have similarly worked swindles on ordinary men and women, with phoney business schemes, worthless investments and fake insurance policies as the tools of their trade.

AUTHOR: Donald E. Westlake (b. 1933), a former US Air Force pilot and onetime actor, has become the writer most associated with tales of organised crime. Indeed, in story after story, he has demonstrated his particular belief that crime is actually not very different from any other type of business enterprise – and the intelligent criminal is just one more example of 'Organisation Man'. In Westlake's early novels like *Killing Time* (1961), about the running of a corrupt upstate New York town, he dealt with organised crime from the inside with great objectivity; but over the years elements of humour and the absurd have crept into his work in the shape of bungled robberies and inept confidence tricks. In 1962, by way of contrast, he adopted the pen name Richard Stark and started a series of novels about Parker, a cold-blooded professional thief, who was later transferred to the screen in *Point Blank* featuring Lee Marvin (1967). Not content with this, Westlake invented a second major character, Mitch Tobin, a guilt-ridden former New York cop turned private eye, whose adventures appear under the name Tucker Coe. More recently still, he has begun writing a number of capers about a group of inept thieves led by criminal *manqué* John Archibald Dortmunder. For this remarkable display of virtuosity, Donald Westlake has won numerous awards, including three Edgars and a Grand Master Award from the Mystery Writers of America, as well as an Oscar nomination for his screenplay of Jim Thompson's *The Grifters*. In 'The Sweetest Man in the World', written in 1967, he mixes his deadpan humour and fascination with organised crime in the tale of a clever fraud . . . and its even cleverer denouement.

* * *

I adjusted my hair in the hall mirror before opening the door. My hair was grey, and piled neatly on top of my head. I smoothed my skirt, took a deep breath, and opened the door.

The man in the hallway was thirtyish, well dressed, quietly handsome, and carrying a briefcase. He was also somewhat taken aback to see me. He glanced again at the apartment number on the door, looked back at me, and said, 'Excuse me, I'm looking for Miss Diane Wilson.'

'Yes, of course,' I said. 'Do come in.'

He gazed past me uncertainly, hesitating on the doorstep, saying, 'Is she in?'

'I'm Diane Wilson,' I said.

He blinked. '*You're* Diane Wilson?'

'Yes, I am.'

'The Diane Wilson who worked for Mr Edward Cunningham?'

'Yes, indeed.' I made a sad face. 'Such a tragic thing,' I said. 'He was the sweetest man in the world, Mr Cunningham was.'

He cleared his throat, and I could see him struggling to regain his composure. 'I see,' he said. 'Well, uh – well, Miss Wilson, my name is Fraser, Kenneth Fraser. I represent Transcontinental Insurance Association.'

'Oh, no,' I said. 'I have all the insurance I need, thank you.'

'No, no,' he said. 'I beg your pardon, I'm not here to *sell* insurance. I'm an investigator for the company.'

'Oh, they all say that,' I said, 'and then when they get inside they *do* want to sell something. I remember one young man from an encyclopaedia company – he swore up and down he was just taking a survey, and he no sooner—'

'Miss Wilson,' Fraser said determinedly, 'I am *definitely* not a salesman. I am not here to discuss your insurance with you; I am here to discuss Mr Cunningham's insurance.'

'Oh, I wouldn't know anything about that,' I said. 'I simply handled the paperwork in Mr Cunningham's real estate office. His private business affairs he took care of himself.'

'Miss Wilson, I—' He stopped, and looked up and down the hallway. 'Do we have to speak out here?' he asked.

'Well, I don't know that there's anything for us to talk about,' I said. I admit I was enjoying this.

'Miss Wilson, there *is* something for us to talk about.' He put down the briefcase and took out his wallet. 'Here,' he said. 'Here's my identification.'

I looked at the laminated card. It was very official and very complex and included Fraser's photograph, looking open-mouthed and stupid.

Fraser said, 'I will *not* try to sell you insurance, nor will I ask you any details about Mr Cunningham's handling of his private business affairs. That's a promise. Now, *may* I come in?'

It seemed time to stop playing games with him; after all, I didn't want him getting mad at me. He might go poking around too far, just out of spite. So I stepped back and said, 'Very well then, young man, you may come in. But I'll hold you to that promise.'

We went into the living-room, and I motioned at the sofa, saying, 'Do sit down.'

'Thank you.' But he didn't seem to like the sofa when he sat on it, possibly because of the clear plastic cover it had over it.

'My nieces come by from time to time,' I said. 'That's why I have those plastic covers on all the furniture. You know how children can be.'

'Of course.' He said. He looked around, and I think the entire living-room depressed him, not just the plastic cover on the sofa.

Well, it was understandable. The living-room was a natural consequence of Miss Diane Wilson's personality, with its plastic slipcovers, the doilies on all the tiny tables, the little plants in ceramic frogs, the windows with venetian blinds *and* curtains *and* drapes, the general air of overcrowded neatness. Something like the house Mrs Muskrat has in all those children's stories.

I pretended not to notice his discomfort. I sat down on the chair that matched the sofa, adjusted my apron and skirt over my knees, and said, 'Very well, Mr Fraser. I'm ready to listen.'

He opened his briefcase on his lap, looked at me over it, and said, 'This may come as something of a shock to you, Miss Wilson. I don't know if you were aware of the extent of Mr Cunningham's policy holdings with us.'

'I already told you, Mr Fraser, that I—'

'Yes, of course,' he said hastily. 'I wasn't asking, I was getting ready to tell you myself. Mr Cunningham had three policies with us of various types, all of which automatically became due when he died.'

'Bless his memory,' I said.

'Yes. Naturally. At any rate, the total on these three policies comes to one hundred twenty-five thousand dollars.'

'Gracious!'

'With double indemnity for accidental death, of course,' he went on, 'the total payable is two hundred fifty thousand dollars. That is, one quarter of a million dollars.'

'Dear me!' I said. 'I would never have guessed.'

Fraser looked carefully at me. 'And you are the sole beneficiary,' he said.

I smiled blankly at him, as though waiting for him to go on, then permitted my expression to show that the import of his words was gradually coming home to me. Slowly I sank back into the chair. My hand went to my throat, to the bit of lace around the collar of my dress.

'Me?' I whispered. 'Oh, Mr Fraser, you must be joking!'

'Not a bit,' he said. 'Mr Cunningham changed his beneficiary just one month ago, switching from his wife to you.'

'I can't believe it,' I whispered.

'Nevertheless, it is true. And since Mr Cunningham did die an accidental death, burning up in his real estate office, and since such a large amount of money was involved, the routine is to send an investigator around, just to be sure everything's all right.'

'Oh,' I said. I was allowing myself to recover. I said, 'That's why you were so surprised when you saw me.'

He smiled sheepishly. 'Frankly,' he said, 'yes.'

'You had expected to find some sexy young thing, didn't you? Someone Mr Cunningham had been having an – a relationship with.'

'The thought had crossed my mind,' he said, and made a boyish smile. 'I do apologise,' he said.

'Accepted,' I said, and smiled back at him.

It was beautiful. He had come here with a strong preconception, and a belief based on that preconception that something was wrong. Knock the preconception away and he would be left with an embarrassed feeling of having made a fool of himself. From now on he would want nothing more than to be rid of this case, since it would serve only to remind him of his wrong guess and the foolish way he'd acted when I'd first opened the door.

As I had supposed he would, he began at once to speed things up, taking a pad and pen from his briefcase and saying, 'Mr Cunningham never told you he'd made you his beneficiary?'

'Oh, dear me, no. I only worked for the man three months.'

'Yes, I know,' he said. 'It did seem odd to us.'

'Oh, his poor wife,' I said. 'She may have neglected him but—'

'Neglected?'

'Well.' I allowed myself this time to show a pretty confusion. 'I shouldn't say anything against the woman,' I went on. 'I've never so much as laid eyes on her. But I do know that not once in the three months I worked there did she ever come in to see Mr Cunningham, or even call him on the phone. Also, from some things he said—'

'What things, Miss Wilson?'

'I'd rather not say, Mr Fraser. I don't know the woman, and Mr Cunningham is dead. I don't believe we should sit here and talk about them behind their backs.'

'Still, Miss Wilson, he did leave his insurance money to you.'

'He was always the sweetest man,' I said. 'Just the sweetest man in the world. But why would—' I spread my hands to show bewilderment.

Fraser said, 'Do you suppose he had a fight with his wife? Such a bad one that he decided to change his beneficiary, looked around for somebody else, saw you, and that was that.'

'He was always very good to me,' I said. 'In the short time I knew him I always found Mr Cunningham a perfect gentleman and the most considerate of men.'

'I'm sure you did,' he said. He looked at the notes he'd been taking, and muttered to himself. 'Well, that might explain it. It's nutty, but—' He shrugged.

Yes, of course he shrugged. Kick away the preconception, leave him drifting and bewildered for just a second, and then quickly suggest another hypothesis to him. He clutched at it like a drowning man. Mr Cunningham had had a big fight with Mrs Cunningham. Mr Cunningham had changed his beneficiary out of hate or revenge, and had chosen Miss Diane Wilson, the dear middle-aged lady he'd recently hired as his secretary. As Mr Fraser had so succinctly phrased it, it was nutty, but—

I said, 'Well, I really don't know what to say. To tell the truth, Mr Fraser, I'm overcome.'

'That's understandable,' he said. 'A quarter of a million dollars doesn't come along every day.'

'It isn't the amount,' I said. 'It's how it came to me. I have never been rich, Mr Fraser, and because I never married I have always had to support myself. But I am a good secretary, a willing worker, and I have always handled my finances, if I say so myself, with wisdom and economy. A quarter of a million dollars is, as you say, a great deal of money, but I do not *need* a great deal of money. I would much rather have that sweet man Mr Cunningham alive again than have all the money in the world.'

'Of course.' He nodded, and I could see he believed every word I had said.

I went further. 'And particularly,' I said, 'to be given money that should certainly have gone to his wife. I just wouldn't have believed Mr Cunningham capable of such a hateful or vindictive action.'

'He probably would have changed it back later on,' Fraser said. 'After he had cooled down. He only made the change three weeks before – before he passed on.'

'Bless his soul,' I said.

'There's one final matter, Miss Wilson,' he said, 'and then I'll leave you alone.'

'Anything at all, Mr Fraser,' I said.

'About Mr Roche,' he said. 'Mr Cunningham's former partner. He seems to have moved from his old address, and we can't find him. Would you have his current address?'

'Oh, no,' I said. 'Mr Roche left the concern before I was hired. In fact, Mr Cunningham hired me because, after Mr Roche left, it was necessary to have a secretary in order to be sure there was always someone in the office.'

'I see,' he said. 'Well –' He put the pad and pen back into the briefcase and started to his feet, just as the doorbell rang.

'Excuse me,' I said. I went out to the hallway and opened the door.

She came boiling in like a hurricane, pushing past me and shouting. 'Where is she? Where is the hussy?'

I followed her into the living-room, where Fraser was standing and gaping at her in some astonishment as she continued to shout and to demand to know where *she* was.

I said, 'Madam, please. This happens to be my home.'

'Oh, does it?' She stood in front of me, hands on hips. 'Well then, you can tell me where I'll find the Wilson woman.'

'Who?'

'Diane Wilson, the little tramp. I want to—'

I said, 'I am Diane Wilson.'

She stood there, open mouthed, gaping at me.

Fraser came over then, smiling a bit, saying, 'Excuse me, Miss Wilson, I think I know what's happened.' He turned to the new visitor and said, 'You're Mrs Cunningham, aren't you?'

Still open mouthed, she managed to nod her head.

Fraser identified himself and said, 'I made the same mistake you did – I came here expecting to find some vamp. But as you can see—' And he gestured at me.

'Oh, I *am* sorry,' Mrs Cunningham said to me. She was a striking woman in her late thirties. 'I called the insurance company, and when they told me Ed had changed all his policies over to you, I naturally thought – well – you know.'

'Oh, dear,' I said. 'I certainly hope you don't think—'

'Oh, not at all,' Mrs Cunningham said, and smiled a bit, and patted my hand. 'I wouldn't think that of *you*,' she said.

Fraser said, 'Mrs Cunningham, didn't your husband tell you he was changing the beneficiary?'

'He certainly didn't,' she said with sudden anger. 'And neither did that company of yours. They should have told me the minute Ed made that change.'

Fraser developed an icy chill. 'Madam,' he said, 'a client has the right to make anyone he chooses his beneficiary, and the company is under no obligation to inform anyone that—'

'Oh, that's all right,' I said. 'I don't need the money. I'm perfectly willing to share it with Mrs Cunningham.'

Fraser snapped around to me, saying, 'Miss Wilson, you aren't under any obligation at all to this woman. The money is legally and rightfully yours.' As planned, he was now one hundred per cent on my side.

Now it was time to make him think more kindly of Mrs Cunningham. I said, 'But this poor woman has been treated shabbily, Mr Fraser. Absolutely shabbily. She was married to Mr Cunningham for – how many years?'

'Twelve,' she said, 'twelve years,' and abruptly sat down on the sofa and began to sob.

'There, there,' I said, patting her shoulder.

'What am I going to *do*?' she wailed. 'I have no money, nothing. He left me nothing but debts! I can't even afford a decent burial for him!'

'We'll work it out,' I assured her. 'Don't you worry, we'll work it out.' I looked at Fraser and said, 'How long will it take to get the money?'

He said, 'Well, we didn't discuss whether you want it in instalments or in a lump sum. Monthly payments are usually—'

'Oh, a lump sum,' I said. 'There's so much to do right away, and then my older brother is a banker in California. *He'll* know what to do.'

'If you're sure—' He was looking at Mrs Cunningham, and didn't yet entirely trust her.

I said, 'Oh, I'm sure this poor woman won't try to cheat me, Mr Fraser.'

Mrs Cunningham cried, 'Oh, God!' and wailed into her handkerchief.

'Besides,' I said, 'I'll phone my brother and have him fly east at once. He can handle everything for me.'

'I suppose,' he said, 'if we expedite things, we could have your money for you in a few days.'

'I'll have my brother call you,' I said.

'Fine,' he said. He hesitated, holding his briefcase. 'Mrs Cunningham, are you coming along? Is there anywhere I can drop you?'

'Let the woman rest here awhile,' I said. 'I'll make her some tea.'

'Very well.'

He left reluctantly. I walked him to the front door, where he said to me, quietly, 'Miss Wilson, do me a favour.'

'Of course, Mr Fraser.'

'Promise me you won't sign anything until your brother gets here to advise you.'

'I promise,' I said, sighing.

'Well,' he said, 'one more item and I'm done.'

'Mr Roche, you mean?'

'Right. I'll talk to him, if I can find him. Not that it's necessary.' He smiled and said goodbye and walked away down the hall.

I closed the door, feeling glad he didn't think it necessary to talk to Roche. He would have found it somewhat difficult to talk to Roche, since Roche was in the process of being buried under the name of Edward Cunningham, his charred remains in the burned-out real estate office having been identified under that name by Mrs Edward Cunningham.

Would Roche have actually pushed that charge of embezzlement he'd been shouting about? Well, the question was academic now, though three months ago it had seemed real enough to cause me to strangle the life out of him, real enough to cause me to set up this hasty and desperate – but, I think, rather ingenious – plan for getting myself out of the whole mess entirely. The only question had been whether or not our deep-freeze would preserve the body sufficiently over the three months of preparation, but the fire had settled that problem, too.

I went back into the living-room. She got up from the sofa and said, 'What's all this jazz about a brother in California?'

'Change of plans,' I said. 'I was too much the innocent, and you were too much the wronged woman. Without a brother, Fraser might have insisted on hanging around, helping me with the finances himself. And the *other* Miss Wilson is due back from Greece in two weeks.'

'That's all well and good,' she said. 'But where is this brother going to come from? She doesn't have one, you know – the real Miss Wilson, I mean.'

'I know.' That had been one of the major reasons I'd hired Miss Wilson in the first place – aside from our general similarity of build – the fact that she *had* no relatives, making it absolutely safe to take over her apartment during my impersonation.

My wife said, 'Well? What are you going to do for a brother?'

I took off the grey wig and scratched my head, feeling great relief. 'I'll be the brother,' I said. 'A startling resemblance between us.'

She shook her head, grinning at me. 'You are a one, Ed,' she said. 'You sure are a one.'

'That's me,' I said. 'The sweetest man in the world.'

Prediction

CHESTER HIMES

OFFENCE FILE

CRIME: Assassin

PLACE: New York

YEAR: 1969

BRIEFING: Assassins, mostly politically motivated, have been a stark and terrible fact of life for centuries: though in more recent times certain killings stand out more graphically than others. Abraham Lincoln, for example, the sixteenth President of the United States, was shot down by the actor John Wilkes Booth at Fords Theatre in Washington, DC in April, 1865. The thirty-fifth President, John F. Kennedy, was also hit by rifle fire, aimed at him (allegedly) by Marxist sympathiser Lee Harvey Oswald as he drove through Dallas, Texas in November 1963. Among other famous people who have been the target of assassins can be listed Archduke Franz Ferdinand of Austria (June, 1914), whose murder led to the outbreak of the First World War; Leon Trotsky (August, 1940), killed with an ice pick almost certainly on the orders of Stalin; and, most recent of all, the Israeli Prime Minister, Yitzhak Rabin (November, 1995).

AUTHOR: Chester Himes (1909–84) has been described as the first writer to use the crime story for political reasons. He was a dedicated Black Protest novelist who brought a new quality to the American detective story with his series of books about two Harlem policemen, Coffin Ed Johnson and Grave Digger Jones. Despite being born into a middle-class Missouri family, Himes fell into criminal ways and it was as he neared the end of a seven-year prison sentence in Ohio State Penitentiary that he decided to try writing crime fiction in the style of his hero, Dashiell Hammett, and 'tell it like it is'. His first mystery novel, *A Rage in Harlem*, was published in France in 1959 and became an immediate bestseller. Himes's subsequent exploits of the two black detectives won him a wide circle of admirers who believe him to be the man who launched the sociological crime novel with his 'violent and amusing microcosm of black criminal activities in New York'. For his part, Himes insisted on referring to these books ironically as 'Harlem domestic detective stories'. Violence in American society was, though, the most enduring theme in his work and Himes invariably wrote about this as a detached observer making no distinction between good and evil – although he was not above introducing elements of the grotesque and the absurd. For some years, Himes planned to end the Coffin Ed and Grave Digger series with both of them getting killed while trying to prevent a black revolution. Although he finally gave up the idea, he did confess that in his opinion, 'The only way the American Negro will ever be able to participate in the American way of life is by a series of acts of violence – it's tragic, but it's true.' In 'Prediction', Chester Himes has turned his vision into a short story to relate what is surely the most uncompromising account of an assassin that has ever been written . . .

***

The police parade was headed north up the main street of the big city. Of the thirty thousand policemen employed by the big city, six thousand were in the parade. It had been billed as a parade of unity to demonstrate the capacity of law enforcement and reassure the 'communities' during this time of suspicion and animosity between the races. No black policemen were parading, for the simple reason that none had been asked to parade and none had requested the right to parade.

At no time had the races been so utterly divided despite the billing of unity given to the parade. Judging from the appearances of both the paraders and the viewers lining the street, the word 'unity' seemed more applicable than the diffident allusion to the 'races', for only the white race was on view and it seemed perfectly unified. In fact the crowd of all-white faces seemed to deny that a black race existed.

The police commissioner and the chiefs of the various police departments under him led the parade. They were white. The captains of the precinct stations followed, and the lieutenants in charge of the precinct detective bureaus and the uniformed patrolmen followed them. They were all white. As were all of the plainclothes detectives and uniformed patrolmen who made up the bulk of the parade following. All white. As were the spectators behind the police cordons lining the main street of the big city. As were all the people employed on that street of the big city. As were all the people employed on that street in department stores and office buildings who crowded to doors and windows to watch the police parade pass.

There was only one black man along the entire length of the street at the time, and he wasn't in sight. He was standing in a small, unlighted chamber to the left of the entrance to the big city's big Catholic cathedral on the main street. As a rule this chamber held the poor box of the big cathedral from which the daily donations were collected by a preoccupied priest in the service of the cathedral at six p.m. each day. But now it was shortly past three o'clock and there were almost three hours before collection. The only light in the dark room came through two slots where the donations were made, one in the stone front wall opening on to the street and the other through the wooden door opening into the vestibule. The door was locked and the black man had the chamber to himself.

Chutes ran down from the slots into a closed coin box standing on legs. He had removed the chutes which restricted his movements and he now sat straddling the coin box. The slot in the stone front wall gave him a clear view of the empty street, flanked by crowds of white civilians, up which the policemen's parade would march. Beside him on the floor was a cold bottle of lemonade collecting beads of sweat in the hot humid air. In his arms he held a heavy-calibre blued-steel automatic rifle of a foreign make.

The muzzle of the barrel rested on the inner edge of the slot in the stone wall and was invisible from without. He sat patiently, as though he had all the time in the world, waiting for the parade to come into sight. He had all of the remainder of his life. Subjectively, he had waited four hundred years for this moment and he was not in a hurry. The parade would come, he knew, and he would be waiting for it.

He knew his black people would suffer severely for this moment of his triumph. He was not an ignorant man. Although he mopped the floors and polished the pews of this white cathedral, he was not without intelligence. He knew the whites would kill him too. It was almost as though he were already dead. It required a mental effort to keep from making the sign of the cross, but he knew the God of this cathedral was white and would have no tolerance for him. And there was no black God near by, if in fact there was one anywhere in the US. Now at the end of his life he would have to rely upon himself. He would have to assume the authority which controlled his life. He would have to direct his will which directed his brain which directed his finger to pull the trigger; he would have to do it alone, without comfort or encouragement, consoled only by the hope that it would make life safer for the blacks in the future. He would have to believe that the children of the blacks who would suffer now would benefit later. He would have to hope that the whites would have a second thought if it was their own blood being wasted. This decision he would have to take alone. He would have to control his thoughts to formulate what he wanted to think. There was no one to shape them for him. That is the way it should have been all along. To take the decisions, to think for himself, to die without application. And if his death was in vain and the whites would never accept the blacks as equal human beings, there would be nothing to live for anyway.

Through the slot in the stone front wall of the cathedral he saw the first row of the long police parade come into view. He could faintly hear the martial music of the band which was still out of sight. In the front row a tall, sallow-skinned man with grey hair, wearing a grey civilian suit, white shirt and black tie, walked in the centre of four red-faced, gold-braided chief inspectors. The black man did not know enough about the police organisation to identify the police departments from the uniforms of their chiefs but he recognised the man in the civilian suit as the police commissioner from pictures he had seen in the newspapers. The commissioner wore highly polished spectacles with black frames which glinted in the rays of the afternoon sun, but the frosty blue eyes of the chief inspectors, squinting in the sun, were without aids.

The black man's muscles tightened, a tremor ran

through his body. This was it. He lifted his rifle. But they had to march slightly farther before he could get them into his sights. He had waited this long, he could wait a few seconds longer.

The first burst, passing from left to right, made a row of entries in the faces of the five officers in the lead. The first officers were of the same height and holes appeared in their upper cheekbones just beneath the eyes and in the bridges of their noses. Snot mixed with blood exploded from their nostrils and their caps flew off behind, suddenly filled with fragments of their skulls and pasty grey brain matter streaked with capillaries like gobs of putty finely laced with red ink. The commissioner, who was slightly shorter, was hit in both temples and both eyes, and the bullets made star-shaped entries in both the lenses of his spectacles and the corneas of his eyeballs and a gelatinous substance heavily mixed with blood spurted from the rims of his eye sockets. He wore no hat to catch his brains and fragments of skull, and they exploded through the sunny atmosphere and splattered the spectators with goo, tufts of grey hair and splinters of bone. One skull fragment, larger than the others, struck a tall, well-dressed man on the cheek, cutting the skin and splashing brains against his face like a custard pie in a Mack Sennett comedy. The two chiefs on the far side, being a shade taller than the others, caught the bullets in their teeth. These latter suffered worse, if such a thing was possible. Bloodstained teeth flew through the air like exotic insects, a shattered denture was expelled forward from a shattered jaw like the puking of plastic food. Jawbones came unhinged and dangled from shattered mouths. But the ultimate damage was that the heads were cut off just above the bottom jaws, which swung grotesquely from headless bodies spouting blood like gory fountains.

What made the scene so eerie was that the gunshots

could not be heard over the blasting of the band and the soundproof stone walls of the cathedral. Suddenly the heads of five men were shattered into bits without a sound and by no agent that was immediately visible. It was like the act of the devil; it was uncanny. No one knew which way to run from the unseen danger but everyone ran in every direction. Men, women and children dashed about, panic-stricken, screaming, their blue eyes popping or squinting, their mouths open or their teeth gritting, their faces paper white or lobster red.

The brave policemen in the lines behind their slaughtered commissioner and chiefs drew their pistols and rapped out orders. Captains and lieutenants were bellowing to the plainclothes detectives and uniformed patrolmen in the ranks at the rear to come forward and do their duty. And row after row of the captains and lieutenants were shot down with their service revolvers in their hands. After the first burst the black man had lowered his sights and was now shooting the captains in the abdomens, riddling hearts and lungs, livers and kidneys, bursting potbellies like paper sacks of water.

In a matter of seconds the streets were strewn with the carnage, nasty grey blobs of brains, hairy fragments of skull looking like sections of broken coconuts, bone splinters from jaws and facial bones, bloody, gristly bits of ears and noses, flying red and white teeth, a section of tongue; and slick and slimy with large purpling splashes and gouts of blood, squashy bits of exploded viscera, stuffed intestines bursting with half-chewed ham and cabbage and rice and gravy, were lying in the gutters like unfinished sausages before knotting. And scattered about in this bloody carnage were what remained of the bodies of policemen, still clad in blood-clotted blue uniforms.

Spectators were killed purely by accident, by being caught in the line of fire, by bullets that had already passed through the intended victims. It was revealing that most of these were clean, comely matrons snugly fitting into their smooth white skins and little girl children with long blonde braids. Whether from reflex or design, most mature men and little boys had ducked for cover, flattening themselves to the pavement or rolling into doorways and underneath parked cars.

The black man behind the gun had not been seen nor had his hiding place been discovered. The front doors of the cathedral were closed and the stained glass windows high up in the front wall were sealed. The slot in the wall for donations to charity was barely visible from the street and then only if the gaze sought it out deliberately. And it was shaded by the architecture of the clerestory so that the dulled blued-steel gun barrel didn't glint in the sun. As a consequence the brave policemen with their service revolvers in their hands were running helter-skelter with nothing to shoot at while being mown down by the black killer. The white spectators were fortunate that there were no blacks among them, despite the accidental casualties, for had these irate, nervous cops spied a black face in their midst there was no calculating the number of whites who would have been killed by them accidentally. But all were decided, police and spectators alike, that the sniper was a black man, for no one else would slaughter whites so wantonly, slaughter them like a sadist stomping on an ant train. And in view of the history of all the assassinations and mass murders in the US, it was extraordinarily enlightening that all the thousands of whites caught in a deadly gunfire from an unseen assassin, white police and white civilians alike, would automatically agree that he must be black. Had they always experienced such foreboding? Was it a pathological portent? Was it inherited? Was it constant, like original sin? Was it a presentiment of the times? Who knows? The whites had always been as secretive of their fears and failings as had the blacks.

But it was the most gratifying episode of the black man's life. He experienced spiritual ecstasy to see the brains flying from those white men's heads, to see the fat arrogant bodies of the whites shattered and broken apart, cast into death. Hate served his pleasure; he thought fleetingly and pleasurably of all the humiliations and hurts imposed on him and all blacks by whites; in less than a second the complete outrage of slavery flashed across his mind and he could see the whites with a strange, pure clarity eating the flesh of the blacks and he knew at last that they were the only real cannibals who had ever existed. Cordite fumes stung his eyes, seared his lungs, choking him.

When he saw the riot tank rushing up the wide main street from police headquarters to kill him, he felt only indifference. He was so far ahead they could never get even now, he thought. He drew in the barrel of his gun to keep his position from being revealed and waited for his death, choking and almost blinded. He was ready to die. By then he had killed seventy-three whites – forty-seven policemen and twenty-six men, women and children civilians – and had wounded an additional seventy-five, and although he was never to know this figure, he was satisfied. He felt like a gambler who has broken the bank. He knew they would kill him quickly, but that was satisfactory too.

But, astoundingly, there remained a few moments of macabre comedy before his death arrived. The riot tank didn't know where to look for him. Its telescoped eye at the muzzle of the 20 mm cannon stared right and left, looking over the heads and among the white spectators, over the living white policemen hopping about the dead, up and down the rich main street with its impressive stores, and in its frustration at not seeing a black face to shoot at it rained explosive 20 mm shells on the black plaster of Paris mannequins displaying a line of beach-ware in a department store window.

The concussion was devastating. Splintered plate glass filled the air like a sandstorm. Faces were split open and lacerated by flying glass splinters. One woman's head was cut completely off by a piece of flying glass as large as a guillotine. Varicoloured wigs flew from white heads like frightened long-haired birds taking flight. And many others, men, women and children, were stripped stark naked by the force of the concussion.

On seeing bits of the black mannequins sailing past, a rookie cop loosed a fusillade from his .38 calibre police special. With a reflex that appeared shockingly human, on hearing itself shot upon from the rear, the tank whirled about and blasted two 20 mm shells into the already panic-stricken policemen, instantly blowing twenty-nine of them to bits and wounding another one hundred and seventeen with flying shrapnel.

By then the screaming had grown so loud that suddenly motion ceased, as though a valve in the heart had stopped, and with the cessation of motion the screaming petered out to silence like the falling of a pall. Springing out of this motionless silence, a teenage youth ran across the blood-wet street and pointed with his slender arm and delicate hand at the coin slot in the front of the cathedral. All heads pivoted in that direction as though on a common neck, and the tank turned to stare at the stone wall with its blind eye also. But no sign of life was visible against the blank stone wall and the heavy wooden doors studded with brass. The tank stared a moment as if in deep thought, then 20 mm cannon shells began to rain upon the stone, and people fled from the flying rock. It did not take long for the cannon to reduce the stone face of the cathedral to a pile of rubbish. But it took all of the following day to unearth the twisted rifle and a few scraps of bloody black flesh to prove the black killer had existed.

In the wake of this bloody massacre the stock market crashed. The dollar fell on the world market. The very structure of capitalism began to crumble. Confidence in the capitalistic system had an almost fatal shock. All over the world millions of capitalists sought means to invest their wealth in the Communist East.

Good night.

Going Through The Motions

LAWRENCE BLOCK

OFFENCE FILE

CRIME: Kidnapper

PLACE: Maine, USA

YEAR: 1981

BRIEFING: Kidnapping is another crime to be found in great numbers in the annals of law breaking. The Lindbergh case in March 1932 in which the twenty-month-old baby son of the famous aviator, Charles A. Lindbergh, was snatched from his luxurious home in New Jersey and a $50,000 ransom note left in his place is familiar all over the world. The infant was subsequently found dead in a shallow grave not far from the Lindbergh home, and although an illegal German immigrant, Bruno Hauptman, was arrested and later sent to the electric chair at Trenton State Prison, doubt has always remained whether he was in fact the actual kidnapper. There is, however, no doubt as to the guilt of Edward Hickman, known as 'The Fox', who used kidnapping and murder to raise money in Los Angeles in 1928 and was subsequently hanged; nor in the case of Donald Neilson, known as the 'Black Panther' because of the black hood he wore over his head, who kidnapped and murdered several victims in Yorkshire and was sentenced to life imprisonment in 1976.

AUTHOR: Lawrence Block (b. 1938), a former editor

in a New York literary agency who wrote paperback originals for some years, is now recognised as one of the most versatile writers in the crime story genre and has recently started to receive the honours his talent so richly deserves, including two Edgars and the 1994 Grand Master Award from the Mystery Writers of America. Apart from the work bearing his own name, Block has written several mysteries under the pseudonyms of Chip Harrison and Paul Kavanagh. He created a trio of memorable series characters: the reluctant spy Evan Tanner whose unique ability to go without sleep makes him a round-the-clock toiler in the world of espionage; Matt Scudder, the humane ex-New York cop who, as a part-time private eye, gets all the dirtiest cases; and the inimitable burglar, Bernie Rhodenbarr. All Block's stories are notable for the oddball figures who cross the paths of his central characters. The author himself travels a lot to find locations for his books and subscribes to what he describes as 'a lot of arcane publications' which provide him with many of the unusual ideas that make his plots so unique. Of his protagonists, Block says, 'They're usually windows through whom one sees the world rather than characters who are involved with what's happening – that's true of Hammett's detective and Chandler's and all of the archetypal characters.' The following story is an excellent example of the author's ideas put into words, and when first published in *Ellery Queen's Mystery Magazine* in August 1981 it was introduced with this single, loaded sentence: 'As quietly tense and moving a story as you've ever read about one of the most heartbreaking of crimes . . .'

* * *

On the way home I picked up a sack of burgers and French fries at the fast-food place near the Interstate off-ramp. I popped a beer, but before I got it poured or the meal eaten I checked my phone-answering machine. There was a message from Anson Pollard asking me to call him right away. His voice didn't sound right, and there was something familiar in what was wrong with it.

I ate a hamburger and drank half a beer, then made the call. He said, 'Thank God, Lou. Can you come over here?'

'What's the matter?'

'Come over and I'll tell you.'

I went back to the kitchen table, unwrapped a second hamburger, then wrapped it up again. I bagged the food and put it in the fridge, poured the rest of the beer down the sink.

The streetlights came on while I was driving across town to his place. No question, the days were getting longer. Not much left of spring. I switched on my headlights and thought how fast the years were starting to go, and how Anson's voice hadn't sounded right.

I parked at the head of his big circular driveway. My engine went on coughing for ten or twenty seconds after I cut the ignition. It'll do that, and the kid at the garage can't seem to figure out what to do about it. I'd had to buy my own car after the last election, and this had been as good as I could afford. Of course it didn't settle into that coughing routine until I'd owned it a month, and now it wouldn't quit.

Anson had the door open before I got to it. 'Lou,' he said, and gripped me by the shoulders.

He was only a year older than me, which made him forty-two, but he was showing all those years and more. He was balding and carried too much weight, but that wasn't what did it. His whole face was drawn and desperate, and I put that together with his tone of voice and knew what I'd been reminded of over the phone. He'd sounded the same way three years ago when Paula died.

'What's the matter, Anse?'

He shook his head. 'Come inside,' he said. I followed him to the room where he kept the liquor. Without asking, he poured us each a full measure of straight bourbon. I didn't much want a drink but I took it and held on to it while he drank his all the way down. He shuddered, then took a deep breath and let it out slowly.

'Beth's been kidnapped,' he said.

'When?'

'This afternoon. She left school at the usual time. She never got home. This was in the mailbox when I got home. It didn't go through the mails. They just stuck it in the box.'

I removed a sheet of paper from the envelope he handed me, unfolded it. Words cut from a newspaper, pasted in place with rubber cement. I brought the paper close to my face and sniffed at it.

He asked me what I was doing. 'Sometimes you can tell by the smell when the thing was prepared. The solvent evaporates, so if you can still smell it it's recent.'

'Does it matter when they prepared the note?'

'Probably not. Force of habit, I guess.' I'd been sheriff for three terms before Wallace Hines rode into office on the Governor's coat-tails. Old habits die hard.

'I just can't understand it,' he was saying. 'She knew not to get in a stranger's car. I don't know how many times I told her.'

'I used to talk about that at school assemblies, Anse. "Don't go with strangers. Don't accept food or candy from people you don't know. Cross at corners. Don't ever play with an old icebox." Lord, all the things you have to tell them.'

'I can't understand it.'

'How old is Bethie?' I'd almost said *was*, caught myself in time. That would have crushed him. The idea that she might already be dead was one neither of us would voice. It hung in the room like a silent third party to the conversation.

'She's nine. Ten in August. Lou, she's all I've got in the world, all that's left to me of Paula. Lou, I've got to get her back.'

I looked at the note again. 'Says a quarter of a million dollars,' I said.

'I know.'

'Have you got it?'

'I can raise it. I'll go talk to Jim McVeigh at the bank tomorrow. He doesn't have to know what I need it for. I've borrowed large sums in cash before on a signature loan, for a real estate deal or something like that. He won't ask too many questions.'

'Says old bills, out of sequence. Nothing larger than a twenty. He'll fill an order like that and think it's for real estate?'

He poured himself another drink. I still hadn't touched mine. 'Maybe he'll figure it out,' he said. 'He still won't ask questions. And he won't carry tales, either.'

'Well, you're a good customer down there. And a major stockholder, aren't you?'

'I have some shares, yes.'

I looked at the note, then at him. 'Says no police and no FBI,' I said. 'What do you think about that?'

'That's what I was going to ask you.'

'Well, you might want to call Wally Hines. They tell me he's the sheriff.'

'You don't think much of Hines.'

'Not a whole lot,' I admitted, 'but I'm prejudiced on the subject. He doesn't run the department the way I did. Well, I didn't do things the way my predecessor did, either. Old Bill Hurley. He probably didn't think much of me, old Hurley.'

'Should I call Hines?'

'I wouldn't. It says here they'll kill her if you do. I don't know that they're watching the house, but it wouldn't be hard for them to know if the Sheriff's Office came in on the operation.' I shrugged. 'I don't know what Hines could do, to tell you the truth. You want to pay the ransom?'

'Of course I do.'

'Hines could maybe set up a stakeout, catch the kidnapper when he picks up the ransom. But they generally don't release the victim until after they get away clean with the ransom.' If ever, I thought. 'Now as far as the FBI is concerned, they know their job. They can look at the note and figure out what newspaper the words came from, where the paper was purchased, the envelope, all of that. They'll dust for fingerprints and find mine and yours, but I don't guess the kidnapper's were on here in the first place. What you might want to do, you might want to call the Bureau as soon as you get Bethie back. They've got the machinery and the knowhow to nail those boys afterward.'

'But you wouldn't call them until then?'

'I wouldn't,' I said. 'Not that I'm going to tell you what to do or not to do, but I wouldn't do it myself. Not if it were my little girl.'

We talked about some things. He poured another drink and I finally got around to sipping at the one he'd poured for me when I first walked in. We'd been in that same room three years ago, drinking the same brand of whiskey. He'd managed to hold himself together through Paula's funeral, and after everybody else cleared out and Bethie was asleep, he and I settled in with a couple of bottles. Tonight I would take it easy on the booze, but that night three years ago I'd matched him drink for drink.

Out of the blue he said, 'She could have been, you know.' I missed the connection. 'Could have been your little girl,' he explained. 'Bethie could have. If you'd have married Paula.'

'If your grandmother had wheels she'd be a tea cart.'

'But she'd still be your grandmother! Isn't that what we used to say? You could have married Paula.'

'She had too much sense for that.' Though the cards might have played that way, if Anson Pollard hadn't come along. Now Paula was three years dead, dead of anaphylactic shock from a bee sting, if you can believe it. And the woman I'd married, and a far cry from Paula she was, had left me and gone to California. I heard someone say that the Lord took the United States by the State of Maine and lifted, so that everything loose wound up in Southern California. Well, she was and she did, and now Anse and I were a couple of solitary birds growing long in the tooth. Take away thirty pounds and a few million dollars and a nine-year-old girl with freckles and you'd be hard pressed to tell us apart.

Take away a nine-year-old girl with freckles. Somebody had done just that.

'You'll see me through this,' he said. 'Won't you, Lou?'

'If it's what you want.'

'I wish to hell you were still the sheriff. The voters of this county never had any sense.'

'Maybe it's better that I'm not. This way I'm just a private citizen, nobody for the kidnappers to get excited about.'

'I want you to work for me after this is over.'

'Well, now.'

'We can work out the details later. By God, I should have hired you the minute the election results came in. I figured we knew each other too well, we'd been through too much together. But you can do better working for me than you're doing now, and I can use you, I know I can. We'll talk about it later.'

'We'll see.'

'Lou, we'll get her back, won't we?'

'Sure we will, Anse. Of course we will.'

Well, you have to go through the motions. There was no phone call that night. If the victim's alive they generally make a call and let you hear their voice. On tape, maybe, but reading that day's newspaper so you can place the recording in time. Any proof they can give you that the person's alive makes it that much more certain you'll pay the ransom.

Of course nothing's hard and fast. Kidnapping's an amateur crime and every fool who tries it has to make up his own rules. So it didn't necessarily prove anything that there was no call.

I hung around, waiting it out with him. He hit the bourbon pretty hard but he was always a man who could take on a heavy load without showing it much. Somewhere along the way I went into the kitchen and made a pot of coffee.

A little past midnight I said, 'I don't guess there's going to be a call tonight, Anse. I'm going to head for home.'

He wanted me to stay over. He had reasons – in case there was a call in the middle of the night, in case something called for action. I told him he had my number and he could call me at any hour. But we both knew his real reason – he didn't want to be alone there. I thought about staying with him and decided I didn't want to. The hours were just taking too long to go by, and I didn't figure I'd get a good night's sleep under his roof.

I drove right on home. I kept it under the speed limit because I didn't want one of Wally Hines's eager beavers coming up behind me with the siren wailing. They'll do that now. We hardly ever gave out tickets to local people when I was running the show, just a warning and a soft one at that. We saved the tickets for the leadfoot tourists. Well, another man's apt to have his own way of doing things.

In my own house I popped a beer and ate my leftover hamburger. It was cold with the grease congealed on it, but I was hungry enough to get it down. I could have had something out of Anse's refrigerator but I hadn't been hungry while I was there.

I sat in a chair and put on Johnny Carson but didn't even try to pay attention. I thought how little Bethie was dead and buried somewhere and nobody would likely ever find her. Because that was the way it read, even if it wasn't what Anse and I dared to say to each other. I sat there and thought how Paula was dead of a bee sting and my wife was on the other side of the continent and now Bethie. Thoughts swirled around in my head like water going down a bathtub drain.

I was up a long while. The television was still on when they were playing the Star Spangled Banner, and I might as well have been watching programmes in Japanese for all the sense they made to me.

Somewhere down the line I went to bed.

I was eating a sweet roll and drinking a cup of coffee when he called. There'd been a phone call just moments earlier from the kidnapper, he told me, his voice hoarse with the strain of it all.

'He whispered. I was half asleep, I could barely make out what he was saying. I was afraid to ask him to repeat anything. I was just afraid, Lou.'

'You get everything?'

'I think so. I have to buy a special suitcase, I have to pack it a certain way and chuck it in a certain spot at a certain time.' He mentioned some of the specifics. I was only half listening. Then he said, 'I asked them to let me talk to Bethie.'

'And?'

'It was as if he didn't even hear me. He just went on telling me things, and I asked him again, and he hung up.'

She was dead and in the ground, I thought.

I said, 'He probably made the call from a pay phone. Most likely they're keeping her at a farmhouse somewhere and he wouldn't want to chance a trace on the call. He wouldn't have her along to let her talk, he wouldn't want to take the chance. And he'd speed up the conversation to keep it from being traced at all.'

'I thought of that, Lou. I just wished I could have heard her voice.'

He'd never hear her voice again, I thought. My mind filled with an image of a child's broken body on a patch of ground, and a big man a few yards from her, holding a shovel, digging. I blinked my eyes, trying to chase the image, but it just went and hovered there on the edge of thought.

'You'll hear it soon enough,' I said. 'You'll have her back soon.'

'Can you come over, Lou?'

'Hell, I'm on my way.'

I poured what was left of my coffee down the sink. I took the sweet roll with me, ate it on the way to the car. The sun was up but there was no warmth in it yet.

In the picture I'd had, with the child's corpse and the man digging, a light rain had been falling. But there'd been no rain yesterday and it didn't look likely today. A man's mind'll do tricky things, fill in details on its own. A scene like that, gloomy and all, it seems like there ought to be rain. So the mind just sketches it in.

On the way to the bank he said, 'Lou, I want to hire you.'

'Well, I don't know,' I said. 'I guess we can talk about

it after Bethie's back and all this is over, but I'm not even sure I want to stay around town, Anse. I've been talking with some people down in Florida and there might be something for me down there.'

'I can do better for you than some strangers down in Florida,' he said gruffly. 'But I'm not talking about that, I'm talking about now. I want to hire you to help me get Bethie back.'

I shook my head. 'You can't pay me for that, Anson.'

'Why the hell not?'

'Because I won't take the money. Did you even think I would?'

'No. I guess I just wish you would. I'm going to have to lean on you some, Lou. It seems a lot to ask as a favour.'

'It's not such a much,' I said. 'All I'll be doing is standing alongside you and backing you up.' Going through the motions with you, I thought.

I waited in the car while he went into the bank. I might have played the radio but he'd taken the car keys with him. Force of habit, I guess. I just sat and waited.

He didn't have the money when he came out. 'Jim has to make a call or two to get that much cash together,' he explained. 'It'll be ready by two this afternoon.'

'Did he want to know what it was for?'

'I told him I had a chance to purchase an Impressionist painting from a collector who'd had financial reverses. The painting's provenance was clear but the sale had to be a secret and the payment had to be in cash for tax purposes.'

'That's a better story than a real estate deal.'

He managed a smile. 'It seemed more imaginative. He didn't question it. We'd better buy that suitcase.'

We parked in front of a luggage and leather goods store on Grandview Avenue. I remembered they'd had a holdup there while I was sheriff. The proprietor had been shot in the shoulder but had recovered well enough. I went in with him and Anson bought a plaid canvas suitcase. The whisperer had described the bag very precisely.

'He's a fussy son of a gun,' I said. 'Maybe he's got an outfit he wants it to match.'

Anse paid cash for the bag. On the drive back to his house I said, 'What you were saying yesterday, Anse, that Bethie could have been mine. She's the spit and image of you. You'd hardly guess she was Paula's child.'

'She has her mother's softness, though.'

A child's crumpled body, a man turning shovels of earth, a light rain falling. I kept putting the rain into that picture. A mind's a damn stubborn thing.

'Maybe she does,' I said. 'But one look at her and you know she's her father's daughter.'

His hands tightened on the steering-wheel. I pictured Paula in my mind, and then Bethie. Then my own wife, for some reason, but it was a little harder to bring her image into focus.

Until it was time to go to the bank we sat around waiting for the phone to ring. The whisperer had told Anse there wouldn't be any more calls, but what guarantee was that?

He mostly talked about Paula, maybe to keep from talking about Bethie. It bothered me some, the turn the conversation was taking, but I don't think I let it show.

When the phone finally did ring it was McVeigh at the bank, saying the money was ready. Anse took the new plaid suitcase and got in his car, and I followed him down there in my own car. He parked in the bank's lot. I found a spot on the street. It was a little close to a fireplug, but I was behind the wheel with the motor running and didn't figure I had much to worry about from Wally's boys in blue.

He was in the bank a long time. I kept looking at my watch and every few hours another minute would pass. Then he came out of the bank's front door and the suitcase looked heavier than when he'd gone in there. He came straight to my car and went around to the back. I'd left the trunk unlocked and he tossed the suitcase inside and slammed the lid shut.

He got in beside me and I drove. 'I feel like a bank robber,' he said. 'I come out with the money and you've got the motor running.'

My car picked that moment to backfire. 'Some get-away car,' I said.

I kept an eye on the rearview mirror. I'd suggested taking my car just in case anybody was watching him. McVeigh might have acted on suspicions, I'd told him, and might say something to law-enforcement people without saying anything to us. It wouldn't do to be tailed to the overpass where the exchange was supposed to take place. If the kidnappers spotted a tail they might panic and kill Bethie.

Of course I didn't believe for a moment she was still alive. But you play these things by the book. What else can you do?

No one was following us. I cut the engine when we got to the designated place. It was an overpass, and a good spot for a drop. A person could be waiting below, hidden from view, and he could pick up the suitcase and get out of there on foot and nobody up above could do anything about it.

The engine coughed and sputtered and finally cut out. Anse told me I ought to get it fixed. I didn't bother saying that nobody seemed to be able to fix it. 'Just sit here,' I told him. 'I'll take care of it.'

I got out of the car, went around to the trunk. He was watching as I carried the plaid suitcase and sent it sailing over the rail. I heard the car door open, and then he was standing beside me, trying to see where it had landed. I pointed to the spot but he couldn't see it, and I'm not sure there was anything to see.

'I can't look down from heights,' he said.

'Nothing to look at anyway.'

We got back in the car. I dropped him off at the bank, and on the way there he asked if the kidnappers would keep their end of the bargain. 'They said she'd be delivered to the house within the next four hours,' he said. 'But would they take the chance of delivering her to the house?'

'Probably not,' I told him. 'Easiest thing would be to drive her into the middle of one town or another and just let her out of the car. Somebody'll find her and call you right off. Bethie knows her phone number, doesn't she?'

'Of course she does.'

'Best thing is for you to be at home and wait for a call.'

'You'll come over, Lou, won't you?'

I said I would. He went to get his car from the lot and I drove to my house to check the mail. It didn't take me too long to get to his place, and we sat around waiting for a call I knew would never come.

Because it was pretty clear somebody local had taken her. An out-of-towner wouldn't have known what a perfect spot that overpass was for dropping a suitcase of ransom money. An out-of-towner wouldn't have sent Anse to a specific luggage shop to buy a specific suitcase. An out-of-towner probably wouldn't have known how to identify Bethie Pollard in the first place.

And a local person wouldn't dare leave her alive, because she was old enough and bright enough to tell people who had taken her. It stood to reason that she'd been killed right away, as soon as she'd been snatched, and that her corpse had been covered with fresh earth before the ransom note had been delivered to Anson's mailbox.

After I don't know how long he said, 'I don't like it, Lou. We should have heard something by now.'

'Could be they're playing it cagey.'

'What do you mean?'

'Could be they're watching that dropped suitcase, waiting to make sure it's not staked out.'

He started. 'Staked out?'

'Well, say you'd gone and alerted the Bureau. What they might have done is staked out the area of the drop and just watched and waited to see who picked up the suitcase. Now a kidnapper might decide to play it just as cagey his own self. Maybe they'll wait twenty-four hours before they make their move.'

'God.'

'Or maybe they picked it up before it so much as bounced, say, but they want to hold on to Bethie long enough to be sure the bills aren't in sequence and there's no electric bug in the suitcase.'

'Or maybe they're not going to release her, Lou.'

'You don't want to think about that, Anse.'

'No,' he said. 'I don't want to think about it.'

He started in on the bourbon then, and I was relieved to see him do it. I figured he needed it. To tell the truth, I had a thirst for it myself right about then. Plain flat sitting and waiting is the hardest thing I know about, especially when you're waiting for something that's not going to happen.

I was about ready to make an excuse and go on home when the doorbell rang. 'Maybe that's her now,' he said. 'Maybe they waited until dark.' But there was a hollow tone in his voice, as if to say he didn't believe it himself.

'I'll get it,' I told him. 'You stay where you are.'

There were two men at the door. They were almost my height, dressed alike in business suits and holding guns, nasty little black things. First thought I had was they were robbers, and what crossed my mind was how bad Anse's luck had turned.

Then one of them said, 'FBI,' and showed me an ID I didn't have time to read. 'Let's go inside,' he said, and we did.

Anse had a glass in his hand. His face didn't look a whole lot different from before. If he was surprised he didn't show it.

One of them said, 'Mr Pollard? We kept the drop site under careful observation for three full hours. In that time no one approached the suitcase. The only persons who showed up were two boys approximately ten years old, and they never went near the suitcase.'

'Ten years old,' Anse said.

'After three hours Agent Boudreau and I went down and examined the suitcase. The only contents were dummy packages like this one.' He showed a banded stack of bills, then riffled it to reveal that only the top and bottom bills were currency. The rest of the stack consisted of newspaper cut the size of bills.

'I guess your stakeout wasn't such a much,' I said. 'Anse, why didn't you tell me you decided to call the Bureau after all?'

'Jim McVeigh called them,' he said. 'They were there when I went to get the money. I didn't know anything about it until then.'

'Well, either we beat 'em to the drop site or they don't know much about staking a place out. You get people who aren't local and it's easy for them to make a mistake, I guess. The kidnappers just went and switched suitcases on you. You saw a suitcase still lying in the weeds and you figured nobody'd come by yet, but it looks like you were wrong.' I took a breath and let it out slow. 'Maybe they saw you there after they told Anse not to go to the cops. Maybe that's why Bethie's not home yet.'

'That's not why,' one of them said. Boudreau, I guess

his name was. 'We were there to see you fling that case over the railing. I had it under observation through high-powered field glasses from the moment it landed and I didn't take my eyes off it until we went and had a look at it.'

Must have been tiring, I thought, staring through binoculars for three full hours.

'Nobody touched the suitcase,' the other one said. 'There was a rip in the side from when it landed. It was the same suitcase.'

'That proves a lot, a rip in the side of a suitcase.'

'There was a switch,' Boudreau said. 'You made it. You had a second suitcase in the trunk of your car, underneath the blankets and junk you carry around. Mr Pollard here put the suitcase full of money in your trunk. Then you got the other case out of the trunk and threw it over the railing.'

'Her father taught her not to go with strangers,' the other one said. I never did get his name. 'But you weren't a stranger, were you? You were a friend of the family. The sheriff, the man who lectured on safety procedures. She got in your car without a second thought, didn't she?'

'Anse,' I said, 'tell them they're crazy, will you?'

He didn't say anything.

Boudreau said, 'We found the money, Mr Pollard. That's what took so long. We wanted to find it before confronting him. He'd taken up some floorboards and stashed the money under them, still in the suitcase it was packed in. We didn't turn up any evidence of your daughter's presence. He may never have taken her anywhere near his house.'

'This is all crazy,' I said, but it was as if they didn't hear me.

'We think he killed her immediately on picking her up,' Boudreau went on. 'He'd have to do that. She knew him, after all. His only chance to get away with it lay in murdering her.'

My mind filled with that picture again. Bethie's crumpled body lying on the ground in that patch of woods the other side of Little Cross Creek. And a big man turning the damp earth with a shovel. I could feel a soreness in my shoulders from the digging.

I should have dug that hole the day before. Having to do it with Bethie lying there, that was a misery. Better by far to have it dug ahead of time and just drop her in and shovel over her, but you can't plan everything right.

Not that I ever had much chance of getting away with it, now that I looked at it straight on. I'd had this picture of myself down in the Florida sun with more money than God's rich uncle, but I don't guess I ever really thought it would happen that way. I suppose all I wanted was to take a few things away from Anson Pollard.

I sort of tuned out for a while there. Then one of them – I'm not even sure which one – was reading me my rights. I just stood there, not looking at anybody, least of all at Anse. And not listening too close to what they were saying.

Then they were asking me where the body was, and talking about checking the stores to find out when I'd bought the duplicate suitcase, and asking other questions that would build the case against me. I sort of pulled myself together and said that somebody was evidently trying real hard to frame me and I couldn't understand why, but in the meantime I wasn't going to answer any questions without a lawyer being present.

Not that I expected it would do me much good. But you have to make an effort, you have to play the hand out. What else can you do? You go through the motions, that's all.

The Corder Figure

PETER LOVESEY

OFFENCE FILE

CRIME: Crime of passion

PLACE: Surrey and France

YEAR: 1985

BRIEFING: Real life crimes of passion were the subject of chapbooks and broadsheets which sold in vast quantities long before the development of the crime novel, and surviving examples of these publications which describe the terrible acts of lovers driven to murder, each illustrated with lurid, woodblock illustrations, are now keenly collected. Examples that are particularly sought after include the early nineteenth-century case of the Suffolk squire William Corder who killed his lover, Maria Marten, in 1827, and buried her corpse in a Red Barn which gave rise to the enduring epithet by which the crime is remembered. Another example is the story of Henry Landru, France's infamous 'Bluebeard', whose philanderings led him to dispose of ten women before he was caught and guillotined in 1922. An equally famous case which has been featured in both films and on television is that of Ruth Ellis, the London nightclub manager who shot dead her lover outside a pub in 1955 and became the last woman in Britain to be hanged.

AUTHOR: Peter Lovesey (b. 1936), previously an RAF education officer and lecturer in London, has been described as the most popular and consistent writer of 'historical' crime fiction – novels and short stories which draw on notorious real life cases. Indeed, when his first novel, *Wobble To Death*, was published in 1970 it was hailed as something completely new in the genre with its depiction of everyday life in Victorian times and the exploits of two members of Scotland Yard's newly formed CID, Sergeant Cribb and Constable Thackery. Lovesey's subsequent novels about the pair – which have also inspired two TV series starring Alan Dobie and William Simons – highlighted the limited resources available to police investigators at the time and showed them to be hindered as much by their superiors as the criminals they pursued. Peter Lovesey has denied that the Cribb stories are pastiches, but rather 'Victorian police procedural novels'. Lovesey, in fact, researches his history with painstaking care and his text is invariably peppered with fascinating details of unusual people and authentic events. He has won both the Gold and Silver Dagger Awards presented by the Crime Writers' Association, and in a recent article about him the *Mail on Sunday* recommended his seventeenth novel, *Bertie and the Crime of Passion* (1994), as the perfect introduction to his work for new readers. 'The Corder Figure' is one of Lovesey's best short stories utilising a historical background – in this case the aforementioned William Corder. In it he cleverly combines undertones of the 170-year-old *crime passionel* with a very contemporary example of illicit passions.

***

Mrs D'Abernon frowned at the ornamental figure on the shelf above her. She leaned towards it to read the name inscribed in copperplate on the base.

'Who was William Corder?'

'A notorious murderer.'

'How horrid!' She sheered away as if the figure were alive and about to make a grab at her throat. She was in the back room of Francis Buttery's secondhand bookshop, where cheap sherry was dispensed to regular buyers of the more expensive books. As a collector of first editions of romantic novels of the 'twenties and 'thirties, she was always welcome. 'Fancy anyone wanting to make a porcelain effigy of a murderer!'

'White earthenware,' Buttery told her as if that were the only point worth taking up. 'Staffordshire. I took it over with the shop after the previous owner passed on. He specialised in criminology.' He picked it up, a glazed standing figure about ten inches in height.

'The workmanship looks crude to me,' ventured Mrs D'Abernon, determined not to like it. 'I mean, it doesn't compare with a Dresden shepherdess, does it? Look at the way the face is painted – those daubs of colour on the cheeks. You can see why they needed to write the name on the base. I ask you, Mr Buttery, it could be anyone from the Prince of Wales to a peasant, now couldn't it?'

'Staffordshire portrait figures are not valued as good likenesses,' Buttery said in its defence, pitching his voice at a level audible to browsers in the main part of the shop. He believed that a bookshop should be a haven of culture, and when he wasn't broadcasting it himself he played Bach on the stereo. 'The proportions are wrong and the finishing is too stylised to admit much individuality. They are primitive pieces, but they have a certain naive charm, I must insist.'

'Insist as much as you like, darling,' said Mrs D'Abernon, indomitable in her aesthetic judgments. 'You won't convince me that it is anything but grotesque.' She smiled fleetingly. 'Well, I might give you vulgar if you press me, as I'm sure you'd like to.'

Buttery sighed and offered more sherry. These

sprightly married women in their thirties and forties who liked to throw in the occasional suggestive remark were a type he recognised, but hadn't learned how to handle. He was thirty-four, a bachelor, serious-minded, good-looking, gaunt, dark, with a few silver signs of maturity at the temples. He was knowledgeable about women – indeed, he had two shelf-lengths devoted to the subject, high up and close to the back room, where he could keep an eye on anyone who inspected them – but he had somehow failed to achieve what the manuals described as an intimate relationship. He was not discouraged, however – for him, the future always beckoned invitingly. 'The point about Staffordshire figures,' he persisted with Mrs D'Abernon, 'is that they give us an insight into the amusements of our Victorian ancestors.'

'Amusements such as murder?' said Mrs D'Abernon with a peal of laughter. She was still a pretty woman, with blonde hair in loose curls that bobbed when she moved her head.

'Yes, indeed!' Buttery assured her. 'The blood-curdling story of a man like Corder was pure theatre, the stuff of melodrama. The arrest, the trial, and even the execution. Murderers were hanged in public, and thousands came to watch – not just the rabble, but literary people like Dickens and Thackeray.'

'How macabre!'

Buttery gave the shrug of a man who understands human behaviour. 'That was the custom. Anyway, the Staffordshire potters made a tidy profit out of it. I suppose respectable Victorian gentlemen felt rather high-hat and manly with a line of convicted murderers on the mantelpiece. Of course, there were other subjects, like royalty and the theatre. Sport, as well. You collected whatever took your fancy.'

'And what did Mr William Corder do to earn his place on the mantelpiece?'

'He was a scoundrel in every way. No woman was safe with him, by all accounts,' said Buttery, trying not to sound envious. 'It happened in 1827, way out in the country in some remote village in Suffolk. He was twenty-one when he got a young lady by the name of Maria Marten into trouble.'

Mrs D'Abernon clicked her tongue as she took a sidelong glance at the figure.

'The child didn't survive,' Buttery went on, 'but Corder was persuaded to marry Maria. It was a clandestine arrangement. Maria dressed in the clothes of a man and crossed the fields with Corder to a barn with a red roof, where her luggage was stored and a gig was supposed to be waiting to take them to Ipswich. She was not seen alive again. Corder reappeared two days after and bluffed it out for months that Maria was living in Ipswich. Then he left the district and wrote to say that they were on the Isle of Wight.'

'And was he believed?' asked Mrs D'Abernon.

'By everyone except one tenacious woman,' said Buttery. 'That was the feature of the case that made it exceptional. Mrs Marten, Maria's mother, had two vivid dreams that her daughter had been murdered and buried in the Red Barn.'

'Ah! The intrusion of the supernatural,' said Mrs D'Abernon in some excitement. 'And did they find the poor girl there?'

'No one believed Mrs Marten at first, not even her husband, but, yes, eventually they found Maria buried under the floor. It was known as the Red Barn Murder and the whole nation was gripped by the story. Corder was arrested and duly went to the gallows.' He paused for effect, then added, 'I happen to have two good studies of the case in fine condition, if you are interested.'

Mrs D'Abernon gave him a pained look. 'Thank you,

but I don't care for that sort of reading. Tell me, what is it worth?'

'The figure of Corder? I've no idea.'

'It's an antique, isn't it? You ought to get it valued.'

'It's probably worth a few pounds, but I don't know that I'd care to sell it,' said Buttery, piqued that she had dismissed the books so offhandedly.

'You might, if you knew how much you could get for it,' Mrs D'Abernon remarked with a penetrating look. 'I'll make some inquiries. I have a very dear friend in the trade.'

He would have said, 'Don't trouble,' but he knew there was no stopping her. She was a forceful personality.

And the next afternoon, she was back. 'You're going to be grateful to me, Mr Buttery,' she confidently informed him as he poured the sherry. 'I asked my friend and it appears that Staffordshire figures are collectors' items.'

'I knew that,' Buttery mildly pointed out.

'But you didn't know that the murderers are among the most sought after, did you? Heaven knows why, but people try to collect them all, regardless of their horrid crimes. Some of them are relatively easy to obtain if you have a hundred pounds or so to spare, but I'm pleased to inform you that your William Corder is extremely rare. Very few copies are known to exist.'

'Are you sure of this, Mrs D'Abernon?'

'Mr Buttery, my friend is in the antique trade. She showed me books and catalogues. There are two great collections of Staffordshire figures in this country, one at the Victoria and Albert Museum and the other owned by the National Trust, at Stapleford Park. Neither of them has a Corder.'

Buttery felt his face getting warm. 'So my figure could be valuable.' He pitched his voice lower. 'Did your friend put a price on it?'

'She said you ought to get it valued by one of the big

auctioneers in London and she would be surprised if their estimate was lower than a thousand pounds.'

'Good gracious!'

Mrs D'Abernon beamed. 'I thought that would take your breath away.'

'A thousand!' said Buttery. 'I had no idea.'

'These days, a thousand doesn't go far, but it's better than nothing, isn't it?' she said as if Buttery were one of her neighbours on Kingston Hill with acres of grounds and a heated swimming pool. 'You might get more, of course. If you put it up for auction, and you had the V and A bidding against the National Trust . . .'

'Good Lord!' said Buttery. 'I'm most obliged to you for this information, Mrs D'Abernon.'

'Don't feel under any obligation whatsoever, Mr Buttery,' she said, flashing a benevolent smile. 'After all the hospitality you've shown me in my visits to the shop, I wouldn't even suggest a lunch at the Italian restaurant to celebrate our discovery.'

'I say, that *is* an idea!' Buttery enthused, then, lowering his voice again, 'That is, if your husband wouldn't object.'

Mrs D'Abernon leaned towards Buttery and said confidentially, 'I wouldn't tell him, darling.'

Buttery squirmed in his chair, made uneasy by her closeness. 'Suppose someone saw us? I'm pretty well known in the High Street.'

'You're probably right,' said Mrs D'Abernon, going into reverse. 'I must have had too much sherry to be talking like this. Let's forget it.'

'On the contrary, I shall make a point of remembering it,' Buttery assured her, sensing just in time that the coveted opportunity of a liaison was in danger of slipping by. 'If I find myself richer by a thousand pounds, I'll find some way of thanking you, Mrs D'Abernon, believe me.'

On Wednesday, he asked his part-time assistant, James, to manage the shop for the day. He got up earlier than usual, packed the Corder figure in a shoebox lined with tissue, and caught one of the commuter trains to London. In his corduroy jacket and bowtie he felt mercifully remote from the dark-suited businessmen ranged opposite him, most of them doggedly studying the City news. He pictured Mrs D'Abernon's husband reading the same paper in the back of a chauffeur-driven limousine, his mind stuffed with stock-market prices, uninterested in the dull, domestic routine he imagined his wife was following. Long might he remain uninterested!

The expert almost cooed with delight when Buttery unwrapped his figure. It was the first William Corder he had ever seen and a particularly well-preserved piece. He explained to Buttery that Staffordshire figures were cast in simple plaster moulds, some of which were good for up to two hundred figures, while others deteriorated after as few as twenty castings. He doubted whether there were more than three or four Corders remaining in existence, and the only ones he knew about were in America.

Buttery's mouth was dry with excitement. 'What sort of price would you put on it?' he asked.

'I could sell it today for eight hundred,' the expert told him. 'I think in an auction it might fetch considerably more.'

'A thousand?'

'If it went in one of our sales of English pottery, I would suggest that figure as a reserve, sir.'

'So it might go for more?'

'That is my estimation.'

'When is the next sale?'

The expert explained the timetable for cataloguing and pre-sale publicity. Buttery wasn't happy at the prospect of waiting several months for a sale, and he inquired whether there was any way of expediting the procedure. With some reluctance, the expert made a phone call and arranged for the Corder figure to be added as a late item to the sale scheduled the following month, five weeks ahead.

Two days later, Mrs D'Abernon called at the shop and listened to Buttery's account of his day in London. She had sprayed herself lavishly with a distinctive floral perfume that subdued even the smell of the books. She appeared more alluring each time he saw her. Was it his imagination that she dressed to please him?

'I'm so thrilled for you,' she said.

'And I'm profoundly grateful to you, Mrs D'Abernon,' said Buttery, ready to make the suggestion he had been rehearsing ever since he got back from London. 'In fact, I was wondering if you would care to join me for lunch next Wednesday as a mark of my thanks.'

Mrs D'Abernon raised her finely plucked eyebrows. 'I thought we had dismissed the possibility.'

'I thought we might meet in Epsom, where neither of us is so well known.'

She gave him a glimpse of the beautiful teeth. 'How intriguing!'

'You'll come?'

She put down her sherry glass. 'But I think it would be assuming too much at this stage, don't you?'

Buttery reddened. 'How, exactly?'

'One shouldn't take anything for granted, Mr Buttery. Let's wait until after the sale. When did you say it is?'

'On May fifteenth, a Friday.'

'The fifteenth? Oh, what a pity! I shall be leaving for France the following day. I go to France every spring, before everyone else is on holiday. It's so much quieter.'

'How long will you be away?' Buttery asked, unable to conceal his disappointment.

'About a month. My husband is a duffer as a cook. He can survive for four weeks on rubbery eggs and burnt bacon, but that's his limit.'

Buttery's eyes widened. The future that had beckoned ever since he had started to shave was now practically tugging him by the sleeve. 'You go to France without your husband?'

'Yes, we always have separate holidays. He's a golfer, and you know what they're like. He takes his three weeks in July and plays every day. He doesn't care for travel at all. In fact, I sometimes wonder what we *do* have in common. Do you like foreign travel, Mr Buttery?'

'Immensely,' said Buttery huskily, 'but I've never had much opportunity – until this year.'

She traced the rim of the sherry glass with one beautifully manicured finger. 'Your thousand pounds?'

'Well, yes.' He hesitated, taking a glance through the shop to check that no one could overhear. 'I was thinking of a trip to France myself, but I don't know the country at all. I'm not sure where to head for.'

'It depends what you have in mind,' said Mrs D'Abernon, taking a sip of the sherry and giving Buttery a speculative look. 'Personally, I adore historical places, so I shall start with a few days in Orléans and then make my way slowly along the Loire Valley.'

'You can recommend that?'

'Absolutely.'

'Then perhaps I'll do the same. I say,' he added, as if the idea had just entered his head, 'wouldn't it be fun to meet somewhere in France and have that celebration meal?'

She registered surprise like a star of the silent screen. 'Yes, but you won't be going at the same time as I – will you?'

Buttery allowed the ghost of a smile to materialise fleetingly on his lips. 'It could be arranged.'

'But what about the shop?'

'Young James is perfectly capable of looking after things for me.' He topped up her glass, sensing that it was up to the man to take the initiative in matters as delicate as this. 'Let's make a rendezvous on the steps of Orléans Cathedral at noon on May eighteenth.'

'My word, Mr Buttery! – Why May eighteenth?'

'So that we can drink a toast to William Corder. It's the anniversary of the Red Barn Murder. I've been reading up the case.'

Mrs D'Abernon laughed. 'You and your murderer!' There was a worrying pause while she considered her response. 'All right, May eighteenth it is – provided, of course, that the figure is sold.'

'I'll be there whatever the outcome of the sale,' Buttery rashly promised her.

Encouragingly, she leaned forward and kissed him lightly on the lips. 'So shall I.'

When she had gone, he went to his Physiology and Anatomy shelf and selected a number of helpful volumes to study in the back room. He didn't want his inexperience to show on May eighteenth.

The weeks leading up to the auction seemed insufferably long to Buttery, particularly as Mrs D'Abernon appeared in the shop only on two occasions, when by sheer bad luck he happened to be entertaining other lady customers in the back room. He wished there had been time to explain that it was all in the nature of public relations, but on each occasion Mrs D'Abernon curtly declined his invitation to join the sherry party, excusing herself by saying she had so many things to arrange before she went to France. For days, he agonised over whether to call at her house – a big detached place overlooking the golf course – and eventually decided against it. Apologies and explanations on the doorstep didn't accord with the cosmopolitan image he intended to present in Orléans.

So he made his own travel arrangements, such as they were: the purchase of an advance ticket for the cross-Channel ferry, some traveller's cheques, and a map of the French railway system. Over there, he would travel by train. He gathered that Mrs D'Abernon rented a car for her sightseeing, and that would have to do for both of them after Orléans because he had never learned to drive. He didn't book accommodation in advance, preferring to keep his arrangements flexible.

He also invested in some new clothes for the first time in years: several striped shirts and cravats, a navy blazer, and two pairs of white, well-cut trousers. He bought a modern suitcase and packed it ready for departure on the morning after the auction.

On May fifteenth, he attended the auction. He had already been sent a catalogue, and the Corder figure was one of the final lots on the list, but he was there from the beginning, studying the form, spotting the six or seven dealers who between them seemed to account for three quarters of the bids. They made him apprehensive after what he had once read about rings that conspired to keep the prices low, and he was even more disturbed to find that a number of items had to be withdrawn after failing to reach their reserve prices.

As the auction proceeded, Buttery felt increasingly nervous. This wasn't just the Corder figure that was under the hammer – it was his rendezvous with Mrs D'Abernon, his initiation into fleshly pleasures. He had waited all his adult life for the opportunity and it couldn't be managed on a low budget. She was a rich, sophisticated woman, who would expect to be treated to the best food and wines available.

'And so we come to Lot 287, a very fine Staffordshire figure of the murderer, William Corder . . .'

A pulse throbbed in Buttery's head and he thought for a moment he would have to leave the sale-room. He took deeper breaths and closed his eyes.

The bidding got under way, moving rapidly from 500 pounds to 750. Buttery opened his eyes and saw that two of the dealers were making bids on the nod at an encouraging rate.

'Eight hundred,' said the auctioneer.

There was a pause. The bidding had lost its momentum.

'At eight hundred pounds,' said the auctioneer. 'Any more?'

Buttery leaned forward anxiously. One of the dealers indicated that he had finished. This could be disastrous. Eight hundred pounds was below the reserve. Perhaps they had overvalued the figure.

'Eight fifty on my left,' said the auctioneer, and Buttery sat back and breathed more evenly. Another dealer had entered the bidding. Could he be buying for the V & A?

It moved on, but more slowly, as if both dealers baulked at a four-figure bid. Then it came.

'A thousand pounds.'

Buttery had a vision of Mrs D'Abernon naked as a nymph, sipping champagne in a hotel bedroom.

The bidding continued to 1,250 pounds.

The auctioneer looked around the room. 'At 1,250 pounds. Any more?' He raised the gavel and brought it down. 'Hudson and Black.'

And that was it. After the auctioneer's commission had been deducted, Buttery's cheque amounted to 1,125 pounds.

Three days later, in his blazer and white trousers, he waited at the rendezvous. Mrs D'Abernon arrived twenty minutes late, radiant in a primrose-yellow dress and wide-brimmed straw hat, and pressed her lips to Buttery's, there on the cathedral steps. He handed her the box containing an orchid that he had bought in Orléans that morning. It was clearly a good investment.

'So romantic! And two little safety-pins!' she squeaked in her excitement. 'Darling, how thoughtful. Why don't you help me pin it on?'

'I reserved a table at the Hotel de Ville,' he told her as he fumbled with the safety-pin.

'How extravagant!'

'It's my way of saying thank you. The Corder figure sold for over a thousand pounds.'

'Wonderful!'

They had a long lunch on the hotel terrace. He ordered champagne and the food was superb. 'You couldn't have pleased me more,' said Mrs D'Abernon. 'To be treated like this is an almost unknown pleasure for me, Mr Buttery.'

He smiled.

'I mean it,' she insisted. 'I don't mean to complain about my life. I am not unloved. But this is another thing. This is romance.'

'With undertones of wickedness,' commented Buttery.

She frowned. 'What do you mean?'

'We're here by courtesy of William Corder.'

Her smile returned. 'Your murderer. I was meaning to ask you: why did he kill poor Maria?'

'Oh, I think he felt he was trapped into marriage,' Buttery explained. 'He was a philanderer by nature. Not a nice man at all.'

'I admire restraint in a man,' said Mrs D'Abernon.

'But of course,' Buttery responded, with what he judged to be the ironic smile of a man who knows what really pleases a woman.

It was after three when, light-headed and laughing,

they stepped through the hotel foyer and into the sunny street.

'Let's look at some shops,' Mrs D'Abernon suggested.

One of the first they came to was a jeweller's. 'Aren't they geniuses at displaying things?' she said. 'I mean, there's so little to see in a way, but everything looks exquisite. That gold chain, for instance. So elegant to look at, but you can be sure if I tried it on, it wouldn't look half so lovely.'

'I'm sure it would,' said Buttery.

'No, you're mistaken.'

'Let's go in and see, then. Try it on and I'll give you my opinion.'

They went in, and after some rapid mental arithmetic Buttery parted with three thousand francs to convince her that he really had meant what he said.

'You shouldn't have done it, you wicked man!' she told him, pressing the chain possessively against her throat. 'It was only a meal you promised me. I can't think why you did it.'

Buttery decided to leave her in suspense. Meanwhile, he suggested a walk by the river. They made their way slowly down the rue Royale to the quai Cypierre. In a quiet position with a view of the river, they found a *salon de thé*, and sipped lemon tea until the shadows lengthened.

'It's been a blissful day,' said Mrs D'Abernon.

'It hasn't finished yet,' said Buttery.

'It has for me, darling.'

He smiled. 'You're joking. I'm taking you out to dinner tonight.'

'I couldn't possibly manage dinner after the lunch we had.'

'Call it supper, then. We'll eat late, like the French.'

She shook her head. 'I'm going to get an early night.'

He produced his knowing smile. 'That's not a bad idea. I'll get the bill.'

Outside, he suggested taking a taxi and asked where she was staying.

She answered vaguely, 'Somewhere in the centre of town. Put me off at the cathedral and I can walk it from there. How about you? Where have you put up?'

'Nowhere yet,' he told her as he waved down a cab. 'My luggage is at the railway station.'

'Hadn't you better get booked in somewhere?'

He gave a quick, nervous laugh. She wasn't making this easy for him. 'I was hoping it wouldn't be necessary.' The moment he had spoken, he sensed that his opportunity had gone. He should have sounded more masculine and assertive. A woman like Mrs D'Abernon didn't want a feeble appeal to her generosity. She wanted a man who knew what he wanted and took the initiative.

The taxi had drawn up and the door was open. Mrs D'Abernon climbed in. She looked surprised when Buttery didn't take the seat beside her.

He announced, 'I'm taking you to lunch again tomorrow.'

'That would be very agreeable, but—'

'I'll be on the cathedral steps at noon. Sweet dreams.' He closed the door and strode away, feeling that he had retrieved his pride and cleared the way for a better show the next day. After all, he had waited all his life, so one more night in solitary was not of much account.

So it was a more assertive Buttery who arrived five minutes late for the rendezvous next day, found her already waiting, and kissed her firmly on the mouth. 'We're going to a slightly more exotic place today,' he told her, taking a decisive grip on her arm.

It was an Algerian restaurant on the fringe of the red-light district. Halfway through their meal, a belly dancer came through a bead curtain and gyrated to taped music. Buttery clapped to the rhythm. At the end, he tossed the girl a five-franc piece and ordered another bottle of wine.

Towards three p.m. Mrs D'Abernon began to look restless.

'Had enough?' asked Buttery.

'Yes. It was wonderfully exciting and I enjoyed every minute of it, but I have to be going. I really must get back to my hotel and wash my hair. It must be reeking of cigar smoke and I made an appointment for a massage and manicure at five.'

'I'll give you a massage,' Buttery informed her with a no-nonsense statement of intention that pleased him as he said it. It more than made up for the previous day's ineptness.

'That won't be necessary, thank you,' responded Mrs D'Abernon, matching him in firmness. 'She's a qualified masseuse and beautician. I shall probably have a facial as well.'

He gaped at her. 'How long will that take?'

'I'm in no hurry. That's the joy of a holiday, isn't it?'

Buttery might have said that it was not the joy he had in mind, but he was too disconcerted to answer.

'We could meet again tomorrow for lunch, if you like,' offered Mrs D'Abernon.

He said, letting his resentment show, 'Do you really want to?'

She smiled benignly. 'Darling, I can think of nothing I would rather do.'

That, Buttery increasingly understood, was his problem. Mrs D'Abernon liked being treated to lunch, but there was nothing she would rather do. Each day that week she made some excuse to leave him as soon as possible afterwards: a hair appointment, a toothache, uncomfortable shoes. She declined all invitations to dinner and all suggestions of nightclubbing or theatre-going.

Buttery considered his position. He was going through his traveller's cheques at an alarming rate. He was staying at a modest hotel near the station, but he would have to pay the bill some time, and it was mounting up because he spent each evening drinking alone in the bar. The lunches were costing him more than he had budgeted and there was nearly always a taxi fare to settle.

In the circumstances, most men planning what Buttery had come to France to achieve would have got discouraged, cut their losses, and given up, but Buttery was unlike most other men. He still nursed the hope that his luck would change. He spent many lonely hours trying to work out a more successful strategy. Finally, desperation and his dwindling funds drove him to formulate an all-or-nothing plan.

It was a Friday, and they had lunch at the best fish restaurant in Orléans, lobster scooped wriggling from a tank in the centre of the dining-room and cooked to perfection, accompanied by a vintage champagne. Then lemon sorbet and black coffee. Before Mrs D'Abernon had a chance to make her latest unconvincing excuse, Buttery said, 'I'd better get you back to your hotel.'

She blinked in surprise.

'I'm moving on tomorrow,' Buttery explained. 'Must get my travel arrangements sorted out before the end of the afternoon.' He beckoned to the waiter.

'Where do you plan to visit next?' asked Mrs D'Abernon.

'Haven't really decided,' he said as he settled the bill. 'Nothing to keep me in Orléans.'

'I was thinking of driving to Tours,' Mrs D'Abernon quickly mentioned. 'The food is said to be outstanding there. I could offer you a lift in my car if you wish.'

'The food isn't so important to me,' said Buttery.

'It's also very convenient for the chateaux of the Loire.'

'I'll think it over,' he told her as they left the restaurant. He hailed a taxi and one drew up immediately. He opened the door and she got in. 'Hotel Charlemagne,' he told the driver as he closed the door on Mrs D'Abernon. He noticed her head turn at the name of the hotel. It hadn't been difficult to trace. There weren't many that offered a massage and beauty service.

She wound down the window. 'But how will I know—?' Her words were lost as the taxi pulled away.

Buttery gave a satisfied smile as he watched it go.

He went to the florist's and came out with a large bouquet of red roses. Then he returned to his hotel and took a shower.

About seven, he phoned the Hotel Charlemagne and asked to speak to Mrs D'Abernon.

Her voice came through. 'Yes?'

In a passable imitation of a Frenchman, Buttery said, 'You are English? There is some mistake. Which room is this, please?'

'Six fifty-seven.'

He replaced the phone, went downstairs to the bar, and ordered his first vodka and tonic.

Two hours later, carrying the roses, he crossed the foyer of the Charlemagne and took the lift to the sixth floor. The corridor was deserted. He found 657 and knocked, pressing the bouquet against the spy-hole.

There was a delay, during which he could hear sounds inside. The door opened a fraction. Buttery pushed it firmly and went in.

Mrs D'Abernon gave a squeak of alarm. She was dressed in one of the white bathrobes that the best hotels provide for their guests. She had her hair wrapped in a towel and her face was liberally coated in a white cream.

'These are for you,' said Buttery in a slightly slurred, yet, he confidently believed, sexy voice.

She took the roses and looked at them as if a summons had been served on her. 'Mr Buttery! I was getting ready for bed.'

'Good,' said Buttery, closing the door. He crossed to the fridge and took out a half bottle of champagne. 'Let's have a nightcap.'

'No! I think you'd better leave my room at once.'

Buttery moved closer to her, smiling. 'I don't object to a little cream on your face. It's all right with me.' He snatched the towel from her head. The colour of her hair surprised him. It was brown, and grey in places, like his own. She must have been wearing a blonde wig all the times he had taken her to lunch.

Mrs D'Abernon reacted badly. She flung the roses back at him and said, 'Get out of here!'

He was not discouraged. 'You don't mean that, my dear,' he told her. 'You really want me to stay.'

She shook her head emphatically.

Buttery went on. 'We've had good times together, you and I. Expensive lunches.'

'I enjoyed the lunches,' conceded Mrs D'Abernon in a more conciliatory vein. 'Didn't I always express my appreciation?'

'You said you felt romantic.'

'I did, and I meant it!'

'Well, then.' He reached to embrace her, but she backed away. 'What's the matter with you? Or is something the matter with me?'

'No. Don't think me unappreciative, but that's enough for me, to have an escort during the day. I like to spend my evenings alone.'

'Come on, I've treated you well. I've spent a small fortune on you.'

'I'm not to be bought,' said Mrs D'Abernon, edging away from the bed.

'It's not like that at all,' Buttery insisted. 'I fancy you, and I reckon you fancy me.'

She gave an exasperated sigh. 'For pity's sake, Mr Buttery, I'm a married woman. I'm used to being fancied, as you put it. I'm sick of it, if you want to know. All evening he ignores me, then he gets into bed and thinks he can switch me on like the electric blanket. Coupling, that's all it is, and I want a break from it. I don't want more of it. I just crave a little innocent romance, someone to pay me some attention over lunch.' Then Mrs D'Abernon made her fatal mistake. She said, 'Don't spoil it now. This isn't in your nature. I picked you out because you're safe. Any woman could tell you're safe to be with.'

Safe to be with? He winced, as if she had struck him, but the effect was worse than that. She had just robbed him of his dream, his virility, his future. He would never have the confidence now to approach a woman again. He was finished before he had ever begun. He hated her for it. He hated her for going through his money, cynically eating and spending her way through the money he had got for his Corder figure.

He grabbed her by the throat.

Three days later, he returned to England. The French papers were full of what they described as the Charlemagne killing. The police wished to interview a man, believed to be English, who had been seen with the victim in several Orléans restaurants. He was described as middle aged, going grey, about 5ft 8ins and wearing a blue blazer and white trousers.

In Buttery's well-informed opinion, that description was worse than useless. He was 5ft 9ins in his socks, there was no grey hair that anyone would notice, and thirty-four was a long way from being middle aged. Only the blazer and trousers were correct, and he had dumped them in the Loire after buying jeans and a T-shirt. He felt amused at the problems now faced by all the middle-aged Englishmen in blue blazers staying at the Charlemagne.

He experienced a profound sense of relief at setting foot on British soil again at Dover, but it was short lived. The immigration officer asked him to step into an office and answer some questions. A CID officer was waiting there.

'Just routine, sir. Would you mind telling me where you stayed in France?'

'Various places,' answered Buttery. 'I was moving along the Loire Valley. Angers, Tours, Poitiers.'

'Orléans?'

'No. I was told it's a disappointment historically. So much bombing in the war.'

'You heard about the murder there, I expect?'

'Vaguely. I can't read much in French.'

'An Englishwoman was strangled in her hotel bed-room,' the CID man explained. 'She happens to come from the same town as you.'

Buttery made an appropriate show of interest. 'Really? What was her name?'

'Mildred D'Abernon. You didn't meet her at any stage on your travels?'

He shook his head. 'D'Abernon. I've never heard of her.'

'You're quite sure?'

'Positive.'

'In that case, I won't detain you any longer, Mr Buttery. Thank you for your co-operation.'

In the train home, he tried to assess the case from the point of view of the police. In France, there was little, if anything, to connect him with the murder. He had travelled separately from Mrs D'Abernon and stayed in a different hotel. They had met for lunch, but never more than once in the same restaurant and it was obvious that the descriptions provided by waiters and others could have applied to hundreds, if not thousands, of Englishmen. He had paid every bill in cash, so there was no question of his being traced through the traveller's cheques. The roses he had bought came from an old woman so short-sighted that she had tried to give the change to another customer. He had been careful to leave no fingerprints in the hotel room. The unremarkable fact that he came from the same Surrey suburb as Mrs D'Abernon and had been in France at the same time was hardly evidence of guilt.

All he had to do was stay cool and give nothing else away.

So he was irritated, but not unduly alarmed, when he was met off the train by a local policeman in plain clothes and escorted to a car.

'Just checking details, sir,' the officer explained. 'We'll give you a lift back to your place and save you the price of a taxi. You live over your bookshop, don't you?'

'Well, yes.'

'You answered some questions at Dover about the murder in Orléans. I believe you said you didn't know Mrs D'Abernon.'

'That's true.'

'Never met the lady?'

Buttery sensed a trap.

'I certainly didn't know her by name. Plenty of people come into the shop.'

'That clears it up, then, sir. We found a number of books in her house that her husband understands had been bought from you. Do you keep any record of your customers?'

'Only if they pay by cheque,' said Buttery with a silent prayer of thanks that Mrs D'Abernon had always paid in cash.

'You don't mind if I come in, then, just to have a glance at the accounts?'

The car drew up outside the shop and the officer helped Buttery with his cases.

It was after closing-time, but James was still there. Buttery nodded to him and walked on briskly to the back room, followed by the policeman.

'Nice holiday, Mr Buttery?' James called. 'The mail is on your desk. I opened it, as you instructed.'

Buttery closed the door and took the account book off its shelf. 'If I'd had any dealings with the woman, I'm sure I'd remember her name,' he said as he held it out.

The officer didn't take it. He was looking at an open parcel on Buttery's desk. It was about the size of a shoebox. 'Looks as if someone's sent you a present, sir.'

Buttery glanced into the box and saw the Corder figure lying in a bed of tissue paper. He picked it out, baffled. There was a letter with it from Hudson and Black, dealers in *objets d'art*. It said that the client they had represented in the recent auction had left instructions on the day of the sale that the figure of William Corder should be returned as a gift to its seller with the enclosed note.

The policeman picked out a small card from the wrappings, frowned at it, stared at Buttery, and handed it across.

Buttery went white. The message was handwritten. It read: You treated me to romance in a spirit of true generosity. Don't think badly of me for devising this way to show my gratitude. I can well afford it.

It was signed: Mildred D'Abernon.

Below was written: P.S. Here's your murderer.

Gravy Train

JAMES ELLROY

OFFENCE FILE

CRIME: Petty crook

PLACE: Los Angeles

YEAR: 1990

BRIEFING: Most smalltime crooks and petty criminals have dreamed of making it big in the crime underworld, but only a few have achieved this dubious distinction. In America, Dion O'Bannion, an Irish-born hoodlum who had been a paid muscleman and safeblower, rose to become boss of the illicit liquor racket in Chicago in the 'twenties until he was shot down by unknown assassins and earned this enduring epitaph from his rival, Al Capone: 'His head got away from his hat.' Among the Kray twins' gang in London in the 'sixties was 'Mad Frankie' Fraser, another East End petty criminal who survived prison sentences and the demise of the brothers' 'firm' to become something of a television personality recently, expounding on the rackets of his times.

AUTHOR: James Ellroy (b. 1948), a reformed petty criminal from Los Angeles who was recently described by *Armchair Detective* as 'the most fiercely original modern crime writer', prefers to call himself in the argot of the world which he has left but of which he has become the leading chronicler, 'the mad dog of contemporary crime fiction'. He is certainly the most uniquely qualified of modern writers to depict American low life, having been arrested thirty-five times for petty crime when he was young, served various jail sentences for burglary, and conquered both drink and drug addiction before turning to writing, at which he has proved spectacularly successful. His first novel, *Brown's Requiem* (1981), a detective case, is now regarded as a classic of its kind – although he has subsequently abandoned the genre to tell stories that reflect the LA underworld of crime, corruption and obsessive sex about which he knows so much. The brutal sex murder of Ellroy's mother when he was ten formed the basis of *Clandestine* (1982), which gave a clear indication of the direction his fiction was going, and it was with a series of four books known as the 'LA Quartet' – *The Black Dahlia* (1987), *The Big Nowhere* (1988), *LA Confidential* (1990) and *White Jazz* (1992) – that he earned widespread recognition as the leading exponent of what is referred to as American *noir*. Petty crook Stan 'The Man' Klein, the central figure in 'Gravy Train', is one of the characters Ellroy first introduced in the Quartet – pimp, burglar, car thief and scam artist, Stan is always on the lookout to make an easy dollar. In this story – which Ellroy wrote for the winter 1990 issue of *Armchair Detective* – Stan is hired to look after the pampered bull terrier of a recently deceased wealthy man and soon finds himself knee deep in sh**.

***

Out of the Honor Farm and into the work force: managing the maintenance crew at a Toyota dealership in Koreatown. Jap run, a gook clientele, boogies for the shitwork and me, Stan 'The Man' Klein, to crack the whip and keep on-duty loafing at a minimum. My probation officer got me the gig: Liz Trent, skinny and stacked, four useless Masters degrees, a bum marriage to a guy on methadone maintenance and the hots for yours truly. She knew I got off easy: three convictions resulting from the scams I worked with Phil Turkel – a phone sales racket that involved the deployment of hardcore loops synced to rock songs and Naugahyde Bibles embossed with glow-in-the-dark pictures of the Rev. Martin Luther King, Jr – a hot item with the shvartzes. We ran a drug recovery crashpad as a front, subhorned teenyboppers into prostitution, coerced male patients into phone sales duty and kept them motivated with Benzedrine-laced espresso – all of which peaked at twenty-four grand jury bills busted down to three indictments apiece. Phil had no prior record, was strung out on cocaine and got diverted to a drug rehab; I had two GTA convictions and no chemical rationalisations – bingo on a year County time, Wayside Honor Rancho, where my reputation as a lacklustre heavyweight contender got me a dorm boss job. My attorney, Miller Waxman, assured me a sentence reduction was in the works; he was wrong – counting 'good time' and 'work time' I did the whole nine and a half months. My consolation prize: Lizzie Trent, Waxman's ex-wife, for my PO – guaranteed to cut me a long leash, get me soft legitimate work and give me head before my probationary term was a month old. I took two out of three: Lizzie had sharp teeth and an overbite, so I didn't trust her on the trifecta. I was at my desk, watching my slaves wash cars, when the phone rang.

I picked up. 'Yellow Empire Imports, Klein speaking.'

'Miller Waxman here.'

'Wax, how's it hangin'?'

'A hard yard – and you still owe me money on my fee. Seriously, I need it. I lent Liz some heavy coin to get her teeth capped.'

The trifecta loomed. 'Are you dunning me?'

'No, I'm a Greek bearing gifts at ten per cent interest.'

'Such as?'

'Such as this: a grand a week cash and three hots and a cot at a Beverly Hills mansion, all legit. I take a tensky off the top to cover your bill. The clock's ticking, so yes or no?'

I said, 'Legit?'

'If I'm lyin', I'm flyin'. My office in an hour?'

'I'll be there.'

Wax worked out of a storefront on Beverly and Alvarado – close to his clientele – dope dealers and wetbacks hot to bring the family up from Calexico. I double parked, put a 'Clergyman on Call' sign on my windshield and walked in.

Miller was in his office, slipping envelopes to a couple of Immigration Service goons – big guys with that hinky look indigenous to bagmen worldwide. They walked out thumbing C-notes; Wax said, 'Do you like dogs?'

I took a chair uninvited. 'Well enough. Why?'

'Why? Because Phil feels bad about lounging around up at the Betty Ford Clinic while you went inside. He wants to play catch up, and he asked me if I had ideas. A plum fell into my lap and I thought of you.'

Weird Phil: facial scars and a line of shit that could make the Pope go Protestant. 'How's Phil doing these days?'

'Not bad. Do you like dogs?'

'Like I said before, well enough. Why?'

Wax pointed to his clients' wall of fame – scads of framed mugshots. Included: Leroy Washington, the 'Crack King' of Watts; Chester Hardell, a TV preacher indicted for unnatural acts against cats; the murderous Sanchez family – scores of inbred cousins foisted on LA as a result of Waxie's green card machinations. In a prominent spot: Richie 'The Sicko' Sicora and Chick Ottens, the 7-Eleven Slayers, still at large. Picaresque: Sicora and Ottens heisted a convenience store in Pacoima and hid the salesgirl behind an upended Slurpee machine to facilitate their escape. The machine disgorged its contents: ice, sugar and carcinogenic food colouring; the girl, a diabetic, passed out, sucked in the goo, went into sugar shock and kicked. Sicora and Ottens jumped bail for parts unknown – and Wax got a commendation letter from the ACLU, citing his tenacity in defending the LA underclass.

I said, 'You've been pointing for five minutes. Want to narrow it down?'

Wax brushed dandruff off his lapels. 'I was illustrating a point, the point being that my largest client is not on that wall because he was never arrested.'

I feigned shock. 'No shit, Dick Tracy?'

'No shit, Sherlock. I'm referring, of course, to Sol Bendish, entrepreneur, bail bondsman supreme, heir to the late great Mickey Cohen's vice kingdom. Sol passed on recently, and I'm handling his estate.'

I sighed. 'And the punch line?'

Wax tossed me a keyring. 'He left a twenty-five-million-dollar estate to his dog. It's legally inviolate and so well safeguarded that I can't contest it or scam it. You're the dog's new keeper.'

My list of duties ran seven pages. I drove to Beverly Hills wishing I'd been born canine.

'Basko' lived in a mansion north of Sunset; Basko wore cashmere sweaters and a custom-designed flea collar that emitted minute amounts of nuclear radiation guaranteed not to harm dogs – a physicist spent three years developing the product. Basko ate prime steak, Beluga caviar, Häagen-Dazs ice cream and Fritos soaked in ketchup. Rats were brought in to sate his blood lust; rodent mayhem every Tuesday morning, a hundred of them let loose in the back yard for Basko to hunt down and destroy. Basko suffered from insomnia and required a unique sedative: a slice of Velveeta cheese melted in a cup of hundred-year-old brandy.

I almost shit when I saw the pad; going in the door my knees went weak. Stan Klein enters the white-trash comfort zone to which he had so long aspired.

Deep pile purple rugs everywhere.

A three-storey amphitheatre to accommodate a gigantic satellite dish that brought in four hundred TV channels.

Big screen TVs in every room and a comprehensive library of porn flicks.

A huge kitchen featuring two walk-in refrigerators: one for Basko, one for me. Wax must have stocked mine – it was packed with the high-sodium, high-cholesterol stuff I thrive on. Rooms and rooms full of the swag of my dreams – I felt like Fulgencio Batista back from exile.

Then I met the dog.

I found him in the pool, floating on a cushion. He was munching a cat carcass, his rear paws in the water. I did not yet know that it was the pivotal moment of my life.

I observed the beast from a distance.

He was a white bull terrier – muscular, compact, deep in the chest, bow-legged. His short-haired coat gleamed in the sunlight; he was so heavily muscled that flea-nipping required a great effort. His head was perfect good-natured misanthropy: a sloping wedge of a snout, close-set beady eyes, sharp teeth and a furrowed brow that gave him the look of a teenaged kid scheming trouble. His left ear was brindled – I sighed as the realisation hit me, an epiphany – like the time I figured out Annie 'Wild Thing' Behringer dyed her pubic hair.

Our eyes met.

Basko hit the water, swam and ran to me and rooted at my crotch. Looking back, I recall those moments in slow motion, gooey music on the sound track of my life, like those frenchy films where the lovers never talk, just smoke cigarettes, gaze at each other and bang away.

Over the next week we established a routine.

Up early, roadwork by the Beverly Hills Hotel, Basko's a.m. dump on an Arab sheik's front lawn. Breakfast, Basko's morning nap; he kept his head on my lap while I watched porno films and read sci-fi novels. Lunch: blood-rare fillets, then a float in the pool on adjoining cushions. Another walk; an eyeball on the foxy redhead who strolled her Lab at the same time each day – I figured I'd bide my time and propose a double date: us, Basko and the bitch. Evenings went to introspection: I screened films of my old fights, Stan 'The Man' Klein, feather-fisted, cannon fodder for hungry schmucks looking to pad their records. There I was: six-pointed star on my trunks, my back dusted with Clearasil to hide my zits. A film editor buddy spliced me in with some stock footage of the greats; movie magic had me kicking the shit out of Ali, Marciano and Tyson. Wistful might-have-been stuff accompanied by Basko's beady browns darting from the screen to me. Soon I was telling the dog the secrets I always hid from women.

When I shifted into a confessional mode, Basko would scrunch up his brow and cock his head; my cue to shut up was one of his gigantic mouth-stretching yawns. When he started dozing, I carried him upstairs and tucked him in. A little Velveeta and brandy, a little goodnight story – Basko seemed to enjoy accounts of my sexual exploits best. And he always fell asleep just as I began to exaggerate.

I could never sync my sleep to Basko's: his warm presence got me hopped up, thinking of all the good deals I'd blown, thinking that he was only good for another ten years on earth and then I'd be fifty-one with no good buddy to look after and no pot to piss in. Prowling the pad buttressed my sense that this incredible gravy train was tangible and would last – so I prowled with a vengeance.

Sol Bendish dressed antithetical to his Vegas-style crib: tweedy sports jackets, slacks with cuffs, Oxford cloth shirts, wingtips and white bucks. He left three closets stuffed with Ivy League threads just about my size. While my canine charge slept, I transformed myself into his sartorial image. Jewboy Klein became Jewboy Bendish, wealthy contributor to the UJA, the man with the class to love a dog of supreme blunt efficacy. I'd stand before the mirror in Bendish's clothes – and my years as a pimp, burglar, car thief and scam artist would melt away – replaced by a thrilling and fatuous notion: finding *the* woman to complement my new persona . . .

I attacked the next day.

Primping formed my prelude to courtship: I gave Basko a flea dip, brushed his coat and dressed him in his best spiked collar; I put on a spiffy Bendish ensemble: navy blazer, grey flannels, pink shirt and penny loafers. Thus armed, we stood at Sunset and Linden and waited for the Labrador woman to show.

She showed right on time; the canine contingent sniffed each other hello. The woman deadpanned the action; I eyeballed her while Basko tugged at his leash.

She had the freckled look of a rare jungle cat – maybe a leopard/snow tiger hybrid indigenous to some jungleland of love. Her red hair reflected sunlight and glistened gold – a lioness's mane. Her shape was both curvy and svelte; I remembered that some female felines actually stalked for mates. She said, 'Are you a professional dogwalker?'

I checked my new persona for dents. My slacks were a tad too short; the ends of my necktie hung off kilter. I felt myself blushing and heard Basko's paws scrabbling on the sidewalk. 'No, I'm what you might want to call an entrepreneur. Why do you ask?'

'Because I used to see an older man walking this dog. I think he's some sort of organised crime figure.'

Basko and the Lab were into a mating dance – sniffing, licking, nipping. I got the feeling Cat Woman was stalking me – and not for love. I said, 'He's dead. I'm handling his estate.'

One eyebrow twitched and flickered. 'Oh? Are you an attorney?'

'No, I'm working for the man's attorney.'

'Sol Bendish was the man's name, wasn't it?'

My shit detector clicked into high gear – this bimbo was pumping me. 'That's right, Miss?'

'It's Ms Gail Curtiz, that's with a T, I, Z. And it's Mr?'

'Klein with an E, I, N. My dog likes your dog, don't you think?'

'Yes, a disposition of the glands.'

'I empathise. Want to have dinner some time?'

'I think not.'

'I'll try again, then.'

'The answer won't change. Do you do other work for the Bendish estate? Besides walk the man's dog, I mean.'

'I look after the house. Come over some time. Bring your Lab, we'll double.'

'Do you thrive on rejections, Mr Klein?'

Basko was trying to hump the Lab – but no go. 'Yeah, I do.'

'Well, until the next one, then. Good day.'

The brief encounter was Weirdsville, USA – especially Cat Woman's Strangeville take on Sol Bendish. I dropped Basko off at the pad, drove to the Beverly Hills library and had a clerk run my dead benefactor through their information computer. Half an hour later I was reading a lapful of scoop on the man.

An interesting dude emerged.

Bendish ran loan-sharking and union protection rackets inherited from Mickey Cohen; he was a gold star contributor to Israel bonds and the UJA. He threw parties for under-privileged kids and operated his bail bond business at a loss. He lost a bundle on a homicide bond forfeiture: Richie 'Sicko' Sicora and Chick Ottens, the 7-Eleven slayers, Splitsvilled for Far Gonesville, sticking him with a two-million-dollar tab. Strange: the *LA Times* had Bendish waxing philosophical on the bugout, like two mill down the toilet was everyday stuff to him.

On the personal front, Bendish seemed to love broads, and eschew birth control: no less than six paternity suits were filed against him. If the suit-filing mothers were to be believed, Sol had three grown sons and three grown daughters – and the complainants were bought off with chump change settlements – weird for a man so given to charity for appearance's sake. The last clippings I scanned held another anomaly: Miller Waxman said Bendish's estate came to twenty-five mill, while the papers placed it at a cool forty. My scamster's brain kicked into very low overdrive . . .

I went back to my routine with Basko and settled into days of domestic bliss undercut with just the slightest touch of wariness. Wax paid my salary on time; Basko and I slept entwined and woke up simultaneously, in some kind of cross-species psychic sync. Gail Curtiz continued to give me the brush; I got her address from Information and walked Basko by every night, curious: a woman short of twenty-five living in a Beverly Hills mansion – a rental by all accounts – a sign on the lawn underlining it: 'For Sale. Contact Realtor. Please Do Not Disturb Renting Tenant.' One night the bimbo spotted me snooping; the next night I spotted her strolling by the

Bendish/Klein residence. On impulse, I checked my horoscope in the paper: a bust, no mention of romance or intrigue coming my way.

Another week passed, business as usual, two late-night sightings of Gail Curtiz sniffing my turf. I reciprocated: late-night prowls by her place, looking for window lights to clarify my take on the woman. Basko accompanied me; the missions brought to mind my youth: heady nights as a burglar/panty raider. I was peeping with abandon, crouched with Basko behind a eucalyptus tree, when the shit hit the fan – a crap-o, non-Beverly Hills car pulled up.

Three shifty-looking shvartzes got out, burglar's tools gleamed in the moonlight. The unholy trio tiptoed up to Gail Curtiz's driveway.

I pulled a non-existent gun and stepped out from hiding; I yelled, 'Police Officer! Freeze!' and expected them to run. They froze instead; I got the shakes; Basko yanked at his leash and broke away from me. Then pandemonium.

Basko attacked; the schmucks ran for their car; one of them whipped out a cylindrical object and held it out to the hot pursuing hound. A streetlamp illuminated the offering: a bucket of Kentucky Colonel ribs.

Basko hit the bucket and started snouting; I yelled 'No!' and chased. The boogies grabbed my beloved comrade and tossed him in the back seat of their car. The car took off – just as I made a last leap and hit the pavement memorising plate numbers, a partial read: P-L-blank-0016. BASKO BASKO BASKO NO NO—

The next hour went by in delirium. I called Liz Trent, had her shake down an ex-cop boyfriend for a DMV run-through on the plate and got a total of fourteen possible combinations. None of the cars were reported stolen; eleven were registered to Caucasians, three to southside blacks. I got a list of addresses, drove to Hollywood and bought a .45 automatic off a fruit hustler known to deal good iron – then hit darktown with a vengeance.

My first two addresses were losers: staid sedans that couldn't have been the kidnap car. Adrenalin scorched my blood vessels; I kept seeing Basko maimed, Basko's beady browns gazing at me. I pulled up to the last address seeing double: silhouettes in the pistol range of my mind. My trigger finger itched to dispense .45 calibre justice.

I saw the address, then smelled it: a wood-framed shack in the shadow of a freeway embankment, a big rear yard, the whole package reeking of dog. I parked and sneaked back to the driveway gun first.

Snarls, growls, howls, barks, yips – floodlights on the yard and two pitbulls circling each other in a ring enclosed by fence pickets. Spectators yipping, yelling, howling, growling and laying down bets – and off to the side of the action my beloved Basko being primed for battle.

Two burly shvartzes were fitting black leather gloves fitted with razor blades to his paws; Basko was wearing a muzzle embroidered with swastikas. I padded back and got ready to kill; Basko sniffed the air and leaped at his closest defiler. A hot second for the gutting: Basko lashed out with his paws and disembowelled him clean. The other punk screamed; I ran up and bashed his face in with the butt of my roscoe. Basko applied the *coup de grâce*: left-right paw shots that severed his throat down to the windpipe. Punk number two managed a death gurgle; the spectators by the ring heard the hubbub and ran over. I grabbed Basko and hauled ass.

We made it to my sled and peeled rubber; out of nowhere a car broadsided us, fender to fender. I saw a white face behind the wheel, downshifted, brodied, fishtailed and hit the freeway doing eighty. The attack car was gone – back to the nowhere it came from. I whipped off Basko's muzzle and paw weapons and threw them out the window; Basko licked my face all the way to Beverly Hills.

More destruction greeted us; the Bendish/Klein/Basko pad had been ransacked, the downstairs thoroughly trashed: shelves overturned, sections of the satellite dish ripped loose, velvet flocked Elvis paintings torn from the walls. I grabbed Basko again; we hotfooted it to Gail Curtiz's crib.

Lights were burning inside; the Lab was lounging on the lawn chomping on a nylabone. She noticed Basko and started demurely wagging her tail; I sensed romance in the air and unhooked my sidekick's leash. Basko ran to the Lab; the scene dissolved into horizontal nuzzling. I gave the lovebirds some privacy, sneaked around to the rear of the house and started peeping.

Va Va Va Voom through a back window. Gail Curtiz, nude, was writhing with another woman on a tigerskin rug. The gorgeous brunette seemed reluctant: her face spelled shame and you could tell the perversity was getting to her. My beady eyes almost popped out of my skull; in the distance I could hear Basko and the Lab rutting like cougars. The brunette faked an orgasm and made her hips buckle – I could tell she was faking from twenty feet away. The window was cracked at the bottom; I put an ear to the sill and listened.

Gail got up and lit a cigarette; the brunette said, 'Could you turn off the lights, please?' – a dead giveaway – you could tell she wanted to blot out the dyke's nudity. Basko and the Lab, looking sated, trotted up and fell asleep at my feet. The room inside went black; I listened extra hard.

Smutty endearments from Gail; two cigarette tips glowing. The brunette, quietly persistent: 'But I don't understand why you spend your life savings renting such an extravagant house. You *never* spell things out for me, even though we're . . . And just who is this rich man who died?'

Gail, laughing. 'My daddy, sweetie. Blood test validated. Momma was a car hop who died of a broken heart. Daddy stiffed her on the paternity suit, among many other stiffs, but he promised to take care of me – three million on my twenty-fifth birthday or his death, whichever came first. Now, dear, would you care to hear the absurdist punch line? Daddy left the bulk of his fortune to his dog, to be overseen by a sharpie lawyer and this creep who looks after the dog. *But* – there has to be some money hidden somewhere. Daddy's estate was valued at twenty-five million, while the newspapers placed it as much higher. Oh, shit, isn't it all absurd?'

A pause, then the brunette. 'You know what you said when we got back a little while ago? Remember, you had this feeling the house had been searched?'

Gail: 'Yes. What are you getting at?'

'Well, maybe it *was* just your imagination, or maybe one of the other paternity suit kids has got the same idea, maybe that explains it.'

'Linda, honey, I can't think of that just now. Right now I've got you on my mind.'

Small talk was over – eclipsed by Gail's ardour, Linda's phoney moans, I hitched Basko to his leash, drove us to a motel safe house and slept the sleep of the righteously pissed.

In the morning I did some brainwork. My conclusions: Gail Curtiz wanted to sink my gravy train and relegate Basko to a real dog's life. Paternity suit intrigue was at the root of the Bendish house trashing and the 'searching' of Gail's place. The car that tried to broadside me was driven by a white man – a strange anomaly. Linda, in my

eyes a non-dyke, seemed to be stringing the lust-blinded
Gail along – could she also be a paternity suit kid out for
Basko's swag? Sleazy Miller Waxman was Sol Bendish's
lawyer and a scam artist bent from the crib – how did he
fit in? Were the shvoogies who tried to break into Gail's
crib the ones who later searched it – and trashed my
place? Were they in the employ of one of the paternity
kids? *What was going on?*

I rented a suite at the Bel-Air Hotel and ensconced
Basko there, leaving a grand deposit and detailed instructions on his care and feeding. Next I hit the Beverly Hills
Library and reread Sol Bendish's clippings. I glommed
the names of his paternity suit complainants, called Liz
Trent and had her give me DMV addresses. Two of Sol's
playmates were dead; one was address unknown, two –
Marguerita Montgomery and Jane Hawkshaw – were
alive and living in Los Angeles. The Montgomery woman
was out as a lead: a clipping I'd scanned two weeks ago
quoted her on the occasion of Sol Bendish's death – she
mentioned that the son he fathered had died in Vietnam. I
already knew that Gail Curtiz's mother had died – and
since none of the complainants bore the name Curtiz, I
knew Gail was using it as an alias. That left Jane
Hawkshaw: last known address 8902 Saticoy Street in
Van Nuys.

I knocked on her door an hour later. An old woman
holding a stack of *Watchtowers* opened up. She had the
look of religious crackpots everywhere: bad skin, spaced-
out eyes. She might have been hot stuff once – around the
time man discovered the wheel. I said, 'I'm Brother Klein.
I've been dispatched by the Church to ease your conscience in the Sol Bendish matter.'

The old girl pointed me inside and started babbling
repentance. My eyes hit a framed photograph above the

fireplace – two familiar faces smiling out. I walked over and squinted.

Ultra-paydirt: Richie 'Sicko' Sicora and another familiar-looking dude. I'd seen pics of Sicora before – but in this photo he looked like someone *else* familiar. The resemblance seemed very vague – but niggling. The other man was easy – he'd tried to broadside me in darktown last night.

The old girl said, 'My son Richard is a fugitive. He doesn't look like that now. He had his face changed when he went on the run. Sol was going to leave Richie money when he turned twenty-five, but Richie and Chuck got in trouble and Sol gave it out in bail money instead. I've got no complaint against Sol and I repent my unmarried fornication.'

I superimposed the other man's bone structure against photos I'd seen of Chick Ottens and got a close match. I tried, tried, tried, to place Sicora's pre-surgery resemblance, but failed. Sicora pre-plastic, Ottens already sliced – a wicked brew that validated non-dyke Linda's theory straight down the line . . .

I gave the old woman a buck, grabbed a *Watchtower* and boogied southside. The radio blared hype on the Watts homicides: the monster dog and his human accomplice. Fortunately for Basko and myself, eyewitnesses' accounts were dismissed and the deaths were attributed to dope intrigue. I cruised the bad boogaloo streets until I spotted the car that tried to ram me – parked behind a cinderblock dump circled by barbed wire.

I pulled up and jacked a shell into my piece. I heard yips emanating from the back yard, tiptoed around and scoped out the scene.

Pitbull City: scores of them in pens. A picnic table and Chick Ottens noshing bar-b-q'd chicken with his snazzy new face. I came up behind him; the dogs noticed me and sent out a cacophony of barks. Ottens stood up and wheeled around going for his waistband. I shot off his kneecaps – canine howls covered my gun blasts. Ottens flew backwards and hit the dirt screaming; I poured bar-b-q sauce on his kneeholes and dragged him over to the cage of the baddest-looking pit hound of the bunch. The dog snapped at the blood and soul sauce; his teeth tore the pen. I spoke slowly, like I had all the time in the world. 'I know you and Sicora got plastic jobs, I know Sol Bendish was Sicora's daddy and bailed you and Sicko out on the 7-Eleven job. You had your goons break into Gail Curtiz's place and the Bendish pad and all this shit relates to you trying to mess with my dog and screw me out of my gravy train. Now I'm beginning to think Wax Waxman set me up. I think you and Sicora have some plan going to get at Bendish's money, and Wax ties in. You got word that Curtiz was snouting around, so you checked out her crib. I'm a dupe, right? Wax's patsy? Wrap this up for me or I feed your kneecaps to Godzilla.'

Pit Godzilla snarled an incisor out of the mesh and nipped Ottens where it counts. Ottens screeched; going blue, he got out, 'Wax wanted . . . you . . . to . . . look after . . . dog . . . while him and . . . Phil . . . scammed a way to . . . discredit paternity . . . claims . . . I . . . I . . .'

Phil.

My old partner – I didn't know a thing about his life before our partnership.

Phil Turkel was Sicko Sicora, his weird facial scars derived from the plastic surgery that hid his real identity from the world.

'Freeze suckah.'

I looked up. Three big shines were standing a few yards away, holding Uzis. I opened Godzilla's cage; Godzilla burst out and went for Chick's face. Ottens screamed; I tossed the bucket of chicken at the gunmen; shots sprayed the dirt. I ate crabgrass and rolled, rolled, rolled, tripping cage levers, ducking, ducking, ducking.

Pitbulls ran helter skelter, then zeroed in: three soul brothers dripping with soul sauce.

The feast wasn't pretty. I grabbed an Uzi and got out quicksville.

Dusk.

I leadfooted it to Wax's office, the radio tuned to a classical station – I was hopped up on blood, but found some soothing Mozart to calm me down, and highballed it to Beverly and Alvarado.

Waxman's office was stone silent; I picked the back door lock, walked in and made straight for the safe behind his playmate calendar – the place where I knew he kept his dope and bribery stash. Left-right-left: an hour of diddling the tumblers and the door creaked open. Four hours of studying memo slips, ledgers and little black book notations and I trusted myself on a reconstruction.

Labyrinthine, but workable: private eye reports on Gail Curtiz and Linda Claire Woodruff – the two paternity suit kids Wax considered most likely to contest the Bendish estate. Lists of stooges supplied by Wax contacts in the LAPD: criminal types to be used to file phoney claims against the estate, whatever money gleaned to be kicked back to Wax himself. Address book names circled: snuff artists I knew from jail, including the fearsome Angel 'Fritz' Trejo. A note from Phil Turkel to Waxman: 'Throw Stan a bone – he can babysit the dog until we get the money.' A diagram of the Betty Ford Clinic, followed by an ominous epiphany: Wax was going to have Phil and the real paternity kids clipped. Pages and pages of notes in legalese – levers to get at the extra fifteen million Sol Bendish had stuffed in Swiss bank accounts.

I turned off the lights and raged in the dark; I thought of escaping to a nice deserted island with Basko and some nice girl who wouldn't judge me for loving a bull terrier more than her. The phone rang – and I nearly jumped out of my hide.

I picked up and faked Wax's voice. 'Waxman here.'

'Ees Angel Fritz. You know your man Phil?'

'Yeah.'

'Ees history. You pay balance now?'

'My office in two hours, homeboy.'

'Ees bonaroo, homes.'

I hung up and called Waxman's pad; Miller answered on the second ring. 'Yes.'

'Wax, it's Klein.'

'Oh.' His voice spelled it out plain: he'd heard about the southside holocaust.

'Yeah, "Oh." Listen, shit-bird, here's the drift. Turkel's dead, and I took out Angel Trejo. I'm at your office and I've been doing some reading. Be here in one hour with a cash settlement.'

Waxman's teeth chattered; I hung up and did some typing: Stan Klein's account of the whole Bendish/Waxman/Turkel/Ottens/Trejo scam – a massive criminal conspiracy to bilk the dog I loved. I included everything but mention of myself and left a nice blank space for Wax to sign his name. Then I waited.

Fifty minutes later – a knock. I opened the door and let Wax in. His right hand was twitching and there was a bulge under his jacket. He said, 'Hello, Klein,' and twitched harder; I heard a truck rumble by and shot him point blank in the face.

Wax keeled over dead, his right eyeball stuck to his law school diploma. I frisked him, relieved him of his piece and twenty large in cash. I found some papers in his desk, studied his signature and forged his name to his confession. I left him on the floor, walked outside and pulled over to the pay phone across the street.

A taco wagon pulled to the curb; I dropped my quarter, dialed 911 and called in a gunshot tip –

anonymous citizen, a quick hangup. Angel Fritz Trejo rang Wax's doorbell, waited, then let himself in. Seconds dragged; lights went on; two black & whites pulled up and four cops ran inside brandishing hardware. Multiple shots – and four cops walked out unharmed.

So in the end I made twenty grand and got the dog. The LA County Grand Jury bought the deposition, attributed my various dead to Ottens/Turkel/Trejo/Waxman *et al* – all dead themselves, thus unindictable. A superior court judge invalidated Basko's twenty-five mill and divided the swag between Gail Curtiz and Linda Claire Woodruff. Gail got the Bendish mansion – rumour has it that she's turning it into a crash-pad for radical lesbian feminists down on their luck. Linda Claire is going out with a famous rock star – androgynous, but more male than female. She admitted, elliptically, that she tried to 'hustle' Gail Curtiz – validating her dyke submissiveness as good old American fortune hunting. Lizzie Trent got her teeth fixed, kicked me off probation and into her bed. I got a job selling cars in Glendale – and Basko comes to work with me every day. His steak and caviar diet has been replaced by Gravy Train – and he looks even groovier and healthier. Lizzie digs Basko and lets him sleep with us. We're talking about combining my twenty grand with her life savings and buying a house, which bodes marriage: my first, her fourth. Lizzie's a blast: she's smart, tender, funny and gives great skull. I love her almost as much as I love Basko.

A Flash of White

ANDREW VACHSS

OFFENCE FILE

CRIME: Stalker

PLACE: New York

YEAR: 1994

BRIEFING: The stalker has become the nightmare criminal of the 'nineties, especially where Royalty are concerned – both Princess Anne and the Princess of Wales have been followed – and for people in showbusiness. The phenomenon is now referred to as 'Erotomania' to define what amounts to a bizarre and erotic fascination with celebrities that can lead to threats and even suggestions of murder. To take one example, 'Moon Maniac' DeWitt Cook stalked young female child stars in Los Angeles from 1939–40, sexually assaulted a number of society women, and was finally arrested and imprisoned for life following the murder of a student in 1940. To date, the most infamous stalker is Mark Chapman, the fan of the Beatles, who followed John Lennon around New York for three days in December 1980 before finally shooting him five times at point blank range with a .38 revolver.

AUTHOR: Andrew Vachss (b. 1953), a crime novelist and lawyer, has been called 'one of the most terrifying writers around', while US reviewer Nicholas Pileggi was even more emphatic recently when he said that, 'Vachss writes about a criminal world where even wiseguys fear to tread.' He has, in fact, come to the genre with excellent qualifications, having previously been a social worker in the 'hell's kitchens' of New York, a field investigator for Save the Children in Biafra during the country's savage civil war, and the director of a maximum security prison for young offenders. It was as a result of these experiences – and in particular the atrocities against children that he uncovered while conducting an investigation into sexually transmitted diseases for the US Public Health Service in Ohio and West Virginia – that Vachss started writing to give vent to his sense of moral outrage and produced stories that are notable for their terse and uncompromising prose. His debut novel, *Flood* (1985), about a rapist and murderer, brought him to immediate attention, and subsequent works including *Hard Candy* (1990) and *Down in the Zero* (1995) have made him a cult favourite. Vachss has also created a special legal practice that has earned him international recognition as one of the very few lawyers who will represent only children and youths victimised by abuse, neglect, molestation or incest. Not surprisingly, he believes urgent changes in the law are required and was recently quoted as saying, 'Monsters are made, not born.' In 'A Flash of White' he brilliantly describes how one such monster has turned into a terrifying stalker. It is not a story for those of a nervous disposition.

***

The bitch in 24-G is a whore. A real slut. She parades around in front of her bedroom window in her underwear, trying on different outfits. Sometimes she looks right out the window. She knows I'm here.

The highrise has a lot of windows. They all have

different coverings: curtains, drapes, Levelor blinds. The bitch in 24-G has curtains, but she never draws them.

I have a diagram of the building that I made myself. I go in and out all the time. I make deliveries for a florist. They got me that job when they let me out.

I really don't need the job. I have the money my mother left me. But the bitch from the Probation Department, she said I have to have employment.

The bitch in 19-E just came home. She's a pig. When she gets home, she throws off all her clothes, right on the floor. When she comes back into the front room, she has a towel wrapped around her. She doesn't even pick up her clothes until she has a drink. I'm sure it's liquor, because she takes so long to put it together.

I wouldn't drink liquor.

There's a blonde in 16-F that I really hate. She's the biggest bitch of them all. She walks like there's a poker stuck up her ass. I'd like to stick a poker up her ass. A red-hot poker.

A thought like that, I'm supposed to snap the rubber band. The one I have to wear around my wrist. I have to remind myself that those are bad thoughts.

They taught me that inside. Before they let me go.

I never would have gone inside at all except for that bitch. I got caught lots of times. My mother always got me a lawyer. Nothing ever happened. They sent me to counselling twice. The important thing was, I never hurt anybody. I just looked at them, mostly. When I went inside one of their houses, they were never home. I only took panties. That's where bitches keep their secrets, in their panties. If you hold them, you know their secrets. They belong to you.

The last time they caught me was when the bitch got

me sent away. The District Attorney. Not the real District Attorney, not the head man. A woman. While I was locked up, she got a search warrant for my room. My lawyer said she was able to get it in the middle of the night because I had my ninja outfit on when they caught me. And the piano-wire garrotte.

They almost gave my mother a heart attack, charging in there like that. They found my stuff. My stalker's journal, my magazines, even the straight razor. The bitch DA told the judge I was dangerous. A ticking bomb, she said. They wouldn't let me out on bail.

That's when the bitch tricked me. She had me brought to this room to talk to me. My lawyer was there. He said I didn't have to answer any questions. The bitch said she knew there was a reason why I went prowling. That's what she called it, prowling. It sounded good when she said it. Strong. Not like I was a freak or anything.

She had a theory, she said. About why I did it. If she was right, maybe I wasn't a criminal after all. Maybe I was a sick person. Maybe I needed help.

I started to say something, but my lawyer stopped me. We were just there to listen, he said. Just listen.

The bitch started talking about my mother. I saw what she was doing, so I explained the truth to her. It was all just normal discipline. Children need discipline. She never really hurt me. I love my mother.

My lawyer was shaking his head. Not to stop me, like he was sad or something.

The judge sentenced me to this place. For treatment, he said. I didn't know what it was going to be like.

But I bet the bitch knew.

I had to talk. All the time. Every day. Talk about what was inside my head, what I was feeling. They showed me pictures. Lots of pictures. Different kinds. Movies too.

Videotapes. They would ask me, does this make me excited? Was I aroused?

After a few months, they put this cuff on me. Right around my . . . thing. They could tell when I got aroused. From the pictures. They had stories too. On tape. You sit in a chair and close your eyes and put on the earphones and the stories come.

I had to wear the cuff while I heard the stories.

They did something else to me too. Shock. They had this tape of a woman being tied up. And whipped. I watched it. They made me watch it. And when the cuff filled up, I got a shock.

After a while, I didn't get shocked any more. I didn't get hard when I saw women get hurt.

They made me masturbate. Alone in my room. Over and over again. First I had to masturbate every time I thought about a woman getting hurt. I was the one who got hurt. My . . . thing was all red and raw. I had to have medicine for it. But they made me keep doing it.

After a while, I didn't have those thoughts any more.

Then they made me masturbate to sex images. Sex with women. Romantic sex, they called it. They had movies of that too. Kissing, holding. Slow moving.

I had to see therapists too. They made me talk about my mother. About the closet. About being tied up. About the time she caught me playing with my . . . thing. And what she made me do. With her panties.

I have to wear a rubber band on my wrist. If I ever get a thought about hurting women, I snap it. It reminds me of the place, and the shocks.

My mother was killed while I was inside. She was mugged. Somebody followed her up in the elevator and pushed in the door right behind her. She got hit over the head with something hard and she died. Whoever killed her took money from her pocketbook and other stuff from the apartment.

I went to the funeral. The therapists said I shouldn't feel guilty because I hadn't been home. It wasn't my fault. I asked if the killer had sex with her after he hit her.

I live in the apartment now.

The woman in 16-F just came in. I could just barely see her in the living-room. She walked into the bedroom. She never raises the blinds in any room except the living-room. Even there, she only keeps them open a little bit. I can never see much. In the bedroom, the window is open. Just a slit. I saw a flash of white. Maybe her panties, just coming off. I cranked up the zoom on the telescope, aiming right at the slit. Nothing. I waited. Another flash of white. I couldn't tell what it was.

The lousy bitch. A tease is worse than anything.

I was only home about an hour when the buzzer rang. I knew who it was. My lousy bitch of a probation officer.

I have to let her in. My lawyer explained it to me. It's part of my probation. Like the treatment centre was. If I don't do what they say, they can violate me. That's what my lawyer said: they can violate me.

If they do that, the judge could send me to prison. A real prison. For a long time.

I let her in. She sat down on the couch across from me. She crossed her legs. I could hear the nylon. I didn't look – I know how the bitch watches me.

She asked me about the job. I told her I like flowers. They always smell good. I like bringing them to people.

She asked me about counselling. I told her I still go. Twice a week. And once to the group, too.

She asked me about if it bothered me to have a woman probation officer. I told her no – I like women now.

When I said that, she said she wanted to see my

bedroom. I was scared. But she walked in there by herself. When she saw the telescope, she got angry. I was afraid she was going to do something to me for a minute. I told her it was for astronomy. She said she didn't care what it was for, it better not be there the next time she came back.

The bitch. I wonder what's inside her. I'd like to take a look inside her. With the telescope.

After she left, I was very stressed. I was shaking. I tried to be calm. She hadn't found my other stuff. I do a lot of research. I have books. Lock-picking. *Black Dragon Death Grip Techniques. Secrets of the Ninja.*

There's a woman I write to. I never met her, but she sent me pictures. I send her a money order with every letter and she sends me a letter back. She is my slave. She does whatever I tell her to do. She is a bitch too, but a tame bitch. She knows better than to disobey me. I got her name from one of the guys in group therapy. He said it's an outlet, a release thing. So we don't get worked up and maybe hurt somebody for real.

Every time I get a letter from her, I want to hurt some bitch even worse.

I looked out the window. The redhead in 18-H was home. She doesn't go out much. She has a man who comes to visit her. I always know when the man is coming. She gets dressed in sexy clothes. When he comes there, she treats him like a king. Brings him drinks, lights his cigar, sits on his lap. He's an old, fat man. Bitches always go for money.

She was just lying on her couch, watching TV. I saw her hand go between her legs. She knows I'm watching.

I looked into 16-F. A long time. I couldn't tell if the blonde was home. Then I saw it, the flash of white.

They are going to come for me soon. Coming to violate me, the bitches. All of them.

I have my list. I have my list of bitches. Everything about them. Some are from my delivery route. Only the ones where I actually got in the house. But I like the ones in the building across from me the best. I'm in their houses all the time, with my telescope.

I may only get one of them before they come for me. I'll get one. I'll have her. And then I'll always have her. In my mind. No matter where they put me, I can always have her. Again and again.

So I have to make a choice.

24-G is a whore. She deserves whatever happens to her.

19-E is a pig, a dirty slob of a bitch.

18-H lets a fat old man do anything he wants to her.

16-F, she's the worst bitch of all. The way she walks. The way she keeps me from seeing her. Just that flash of white.

That's what decided me. I need to know what that white flash is.

I'm in the corridor now, right outside 16-F. It's late in the afternoon – she won't be home for another hour or so.

This is so easy.

The lock picks really work. I can hear the last tumbler fall. I'm going in now. The bitch isn't home, so there won't be a chain on the door.

I'm going to step inside and wait for her. Teach her a lesson.

The door opens. It's dark in here. But I'll find her secret.

From the back room . . . a flash of white . . .

Teeth.

Remain Nameless

LYNDA LA PLANTE

OFFENCE FILE

CRIME: Professional killer

PLACE: London

YEAR: The present

BRIEFING: The hired killer has been a hit man for all kinds of crime and outlawed organisations, from the Mafia to Palestinian terrorists – not forgetting the occasional unscrupulous individual with the necessary money to pay for his deadly talents. Some of these men have ultimately been caught and brought to justice, but a few have reaped the rewards of their 'art' and disappeared without trace. A well-documented instance is that of the bizarre Robinson Hill case in Houston, Texas in 1971, when the mysterious death of a wealthy doctor's wife led to accusations against her husband and then his death at the hands of a professional gunman before he could be brought to trial. Four years later, an international killer known as Carlos narrowly escaped capture when his hiding place in London was raided by Scotland Yard and a 'hit list' was discovered, full of the names of famous people he was after, including Lord Sainsbury, Yehudi Menuhin and Bernard Delfont. The assassin for hire has also been a popular figure in crime fiction: most memorably Arthur Raven in Graham Greene's *A Gun For Sale* (1936) and the eponymous anti-hero of *The Day of the Jackal* by Frederick Forsyth (1971).

AUTHOR: Lynda La Plante (b. 1946), formerly an actress who worked in cabaret, theatre, films and television before turning to writing, is now one of the most successful creators of crime series for British television. The three Granada series of *Prime Suspect*, starring Helen Mirren as Detective Chief Inspector Jane Tennison – 'the most important female character television has brought us', according to one review – have attracted vast audiences and the same kind of international acclaim that greeted her earlier productions, *Widows*, *Civvies* and *Framed*. Her novels, including *The Legacy*, *Bella Mafia* and *Entwined*, with their strong elements of crime and mystery, have also been bestsellers. Lynda La Plante's great talent is to get inside the heads of her characters – their problems, their fears and their motivations. This is superbly in evidence in 'Remain Nameless', a brutal and yet poignant story about a hired killer and his fate. It is, I think, a salutary and very appropriate tale with which to end a group of stories about crime.

***

He had often wondered what it would be like, dying, perhaps because he had killed so many. He didn't expect it would be so painless. He knew he had been carried and he heard a female voice, hysterically, repeatedly asking: 'Is he dead?' There had also been a man's lower tone and he had detected fear in his voice. 'Control won't like this.'

Now the man was searching through his clothes, swearing as he opened the sticky, blood-soaked wallet. 'Nothing, no driving licence, nothing with the ugly bastard's name on it . . . ah! What's this?'

A small black-and-white photograph of a little boy, dark haired, wearing a hand-knitted pullover and baggy grey shorts, his socks wrinkled at his ankles. He looked as if he was weeping. In childish writing was written the single word 'Me'.

'We still don't know who the hell he is.' She was calmer now and he felt her thin fingers pushing at the pulse in his neck. He opened his mouth, trying to speak, and she started to scream. Blood trickled from his mouth, dripped from his thick, broken nose; he only wanted to tell her his name.

He was travelling now, he could feel the movement of the vehicle, then bliss as the oxygen mask was placed over his face. It was strange, his body felt warm on the outside but cold on the inside.

'What's your name?'

'Can you hear me?'

'Who sent you?'

He felt as if he were flying, unaware they were wheeling him on a stretcher towards the operating room. The sounds, the corridors, the disembodied voices, the strange overhead lights – was he entering heaven? Was this the journey? And the eerie noise he couldn't make out, was it the scissors as they cut away his blood-soaked clothes?

The massive man's body was a map of scars, with two deep purple sockets from bullets. He was at least six feet seven inches tall and weighed around eighteen stone, but he was muscular, had possibly at one time been a boxer – it was obvious that he was a fighter. The new, fresh, gaping wounds, five in all, were centred around his heart.

A nurse leaned over him and he opened his eyes. They were deep blue, fringed with thick black lashes; there was no pain or fear in them. Beautiful, innocent eyes. 'What's your name?' she said softly.

She leaned closer. He tried to speak, his mouth opened and shut like a fish. He growled and gritted his teeth in a final effort to speak, but she was afraid, he frightened her. He had made frightening people his business, his art. He trusted no one, he had no one, and now fear was the last thing he had on his mind. All he wanted was for someone to know his name, the name his real mother had given him, the one he had before they sent him to the home. The one he had before his life turned bad.

There was no softness any more, no peace, no heavenly journey. He died in a scream of impotent agony because he could not say his name, it hurt too much. It was excruciating to remember what little time he'd had in his life that had been happy.

'It looks like he's crying.'

'What?'

'The little boy in the photograph,' she said, about to pass it over. Then her fingers felt the deep indentations left by the pen where the stranger had written the single word 'Me'.

'Funny why he didn't write his name,' she said.

MURDER

BOOK TWO

DETECTION
Police and Detectives

Introduction

'Why are TV police shows so arresting?' the *Sunday Times* asked recently, and then answered the question by stating that as a nation we are obsessed with crime – 'from nostalgia for the country copper in *Heartbeat*, to Morse the solitary hero fighting crime and his own demons'.

The police story has certainly become one of the most popular developments in the crime genre during the past half century. Although novels and short stories about policemen of all ranks have been appearing ever since the 'thirties, it was not until twenty years later, due particularly to *Dixon of Dock Green*, that the custodians of the law became stars on the small screen, too. Dixon, the reassuring, decent, hardworking bobby, was the crucial element in what is now acknowledged to have been the first police series to attract a mass audience, running uninterrupted from 1955 to 1976. It was on the strength of this remarkable achievement that the man on the beat was soon followed by the senior ranks, up to and including Chief Constable. The cops on the box had arrived.

In fiction, there has been a similar huge growth of interest in stories featuring various ranks of policemen, with Detective Inspectors – the men (and, of late, women) closest to the cutting edge of crime fighting – very much to the fore. Recently, too, we have begun to see members of the Force as less heroic, less sure of their capabilities and certainly more flawed as individuals. In a sentence, they have become more like us, their readers and viewers.

This selection represents a cross-section of the best-known crime fighters in blue. Presented in ascending order of rank from PC to Commissioner, the stories offer a fascinating portrait of the battle against crime and criminals as it is carried out at the different levels of the police hierarchy. It is, I believe, the first time this concept has been used in a crime anthology.

In an essay on the British Police Procedural Novel, crime writer Michael Gilbert (who is represented here) wrote, 'When detective story writers started to shy away from the talented amateur, with his odd personal habits, who solved problems by the application of intellect alone, and appeared to possess a formula which enabled him to succeed in detection without really trying, it was inevitable that they should turn to the police story. They knew that murderers, in real life, were caught by policemen. They suspected – and a little research soon proved – that policemen did not catch murderers by taking thought. They caught them by taking statements.'

Welcome, then, to the policeman's manor . . .

A Case of Christmas Spirit

NICHOLAS RHEA

DETECTIVE FILE

OFFICER: Police Constable Nick Rowan

FORCE: Aidensfield, North Yorkshire

TIME: c. 1965

CASES: *Constable on the Hill* (1978), *Constable on the Prowl* (1980), *Along the Lanes* (1986), *Constable by the Stream* (1991), *Constable about the Parish* (1996) etc.

PROFILE: PC Nick Rowan (played by Nick Berry) is television's most famous bobby on the beat since PC George Dixon of Dock Green (Jack Warner) in the BBC TV series which ran for over twenty years. Though Nick is a much younger man, who covers his moorland patch on a Francis Barnet police motorbike (unlike Dixon who patrolled his East End beat on foot), he, too, has caught the imagination of viewers as a solid, friendly and dependable arm of the law. Set just before the arrival of the 'Swinging 'Sixties' revolution in fashions, attitudes and morals, TV episodes of *Heartbeat* have revealed Nick as an idealist who has exchanged the London Met for the rural calm of North Yorkshire – though he soon finds it is not quite the country idyll he expected. He discovers that the life of a village copper is a mixture of social worker, legal adviser, farmer's assistant, even odd-job man – with crime-solving almost an after-thought.

Keeping a constant watch on Nick is the stentorian figure of Sergeant Blaketon (Derek Fowlds), a real stickler for detail, although Nick has an ally in the Aidensfield station in plodding PC Ventress (William Simons). The one thorn in the side of all these officers is the lovable rogue Claude Jeremiah Greengrass (Bill Maynard), forever plotting some deal just on the edge of the law. During the early series of *Heartbeat*, Nick lived with his GP wife, Kate (Niamh Cusack), but following her tragic death from leukaemia, his name has been romantically linked with the village nurse, Maggie Bolton (Kazia Pelka). Together all these ingredients have made Nick and the series one of the most popular on television, with audiences in excess of seventeen million.

CREATOR: Nicholas Rhea is the pen name of Peter Walker (b. 1936) who was himself a policeman for thirty years in the North Yorkshire moorlands where the *Heartbeat* stories are set. Joining the Force as a police cadet when he was sixteen, Peter rose from being a rural beat copper to an inspector before retiring in 1982. Since then he has produced a variety of books under various pseudonyms, including the Constable series, the first-person cases of a young PC, based on his own experiences and written as Nicholas Rhea. When the rights to these sixteen novels were bought by Yorkshire TV, the central character was renamed Nick Rowan, and *Heartbeat* was created, with its mixture of Yorkshire scenery filmed around Goathland (not far from where the author himself still lives) and a soundtrack of 'sixties music. But despite these changes, Peter Walker still insists, 'Being a village copper in those days really was the way you see it in *Heartbeat* – and Nick Berry is exactly the way I saw myself.' In this opening story about the most junior rank of policeman, Nick and Jeremiah Greengrass form an unexpected and unlikely partnership to solve a seasonal

mystery. 'A Case of Christmas Spirit' offers a welcome
return to Aidensfield for the millions of admirers of the
TV series, and was written especially for this collection.

***

The trumpeting of a fractured exhaust pipe heralded
the arrival of Glenys Hutchinson at Aidensfield
Stores. Amid a salvo of bangs and blasts the rusty, mud-
spattered Morris Traveller halted before me. Anyone else
with a faulty exhaust would avoid the village constable –
but not Glenys. Cheerful always, she disarmed me with a
smile.

'I'm in a rush, Constable, and I know what you're
going to say. I just haven't had time to get it fixed . . . I'll
get a replacement from Claude Jeremiah, then I want a
word about the Christmas party, so don't go away . . .'

And with that, Glenys disappeared into the shop. In
her mid-thirties with delightful elfin features, she had
striking white teeth, short dark hair and dark eyes with a
hint of freckles about her nose. Her slender, attractive
body was now broadening as she approached middle age
but she didn't seem to care. She rushed about in old
clothes – she was as poor as the proverbial church mouse
yet always found the time and energy to do things for
others.

The moorland smallholding she ran with her husband
barely produced a living wage, which explained their
poverty and grotty car. It was invariably parked in the
village as she went about her self-imposed tasks. Unfortunately, there was usually something wrong with it. That
was not surprising because it carried everything from
cattle food to live poultry.

Consequently the interior was as mucky as the exterior
but that didn't worry Glenys either. Alec's constant
struggle to earn a living meant he rarely had time for

outings, so it was Glenys who sallied forth with piglets in the back or eggs on the floor. Many trips resulted in rusty bits dropping off or strange noises among the moving parts. Neither had money to lavish on their decaying vehicle, nor had they spare cash to spend on new clothes in spite of striving ceaselessly on their miniature ranch. Few could remember the last time Glenys had her hair done or bought herself a new dress, but in spite of her poverty, she was never gloomy. She went cheerfully about life in the most robust manner.

I was acquainted with Glenys because of that faulty vehicle – either the exhaust was hanging loose, a mudguard was flapping, the number plate was illegible or lightbulbs had blown and I had to tell her to correct the defects. If Sergeant Blaketon noticed them, she'd be in trouble – and so would I! To be fair, she or Alec did obtain secondhand replacements from Claude Jeremiah Greengrass, although I did wonder where Claude found his supplies – some were in very good condition. In spite of it all, I never took the Hutchinsons to court – village bobbies didn't do that sort of thing. A word at the right time was sufficient.

Lately, though, Glenys had become forgetful. She began to leave her car doors unlocked with the key in the ignition. I'd often warned her it was an invitation to thieves; even in the moorland calm of Aidensfield, but she'd say, 'Nobody steals cars in Aidensfield, Constable Nick!'

'There's always a first time,' was my standard retort, whereupon she would merely smile and thank me – then promptly do it again. She existed in a permanent whirl of activity and I wondered if she and Alec ever experienced moments of calm with one another. Although their work on the smallholding was so time consuming, Glenys helped the old folks with shopping, sometimes giving them eggs or vegetables she could ill afford. She lit their fires in winter or cooked their meals, and in addition, always ran the annual Christmas Party in Aidensfield village hall.

In this case, she did persuade others to help with the food or Christmas presents. Claude Jeremiah Greengrass always played Father Christmas and I helped with the decorations and Christmas tree. Lots of people had a job but it was Glenys who made things happen. As Christmas approached, she raced around with her old Morris full of Christmassy things instead of hens or piglets – and that's what she was doing now. This year's party was fast approaching and she seemed more cheerful and lively than usual.

I went to peer into her car and sure enough, she'd left the keys in the ignition! As I sighed in exasperation, Edna Pryer appeared behind me. She was the fifty-year-old purveyor of Aidensfield gossip and had also noticed the noisy arrival of Glenys.

'You should do something about that noise, Constable! And I say it's a pity Glenys Hutchinson hasn't a family to keep her at home! That's what I say. Rushing about like she does . . .'

'She does a lot of good work,' I countered. 'Some old folks rely on her.'

'She ought to spend more time with that husband of hers, then she might produce a family. I'm not surprised she hasn't children, all that gallivanting about.'

'Really?' I had no intention of fuelling Edna's gossip.

'There's no secrets in a place like this – you ought to know! They've had all the tests and they're both all right. Too much rushing about, that's what I say.'

'Those old people and children, they're her family.' I spoke in defence of Glenys. 'If she can't have children herself, it explains all her good work for others.'

'She's as busy as a wasp in a jam jar. It's time she

settled down, Constable,' and Edna stomped away, having imparted her vision of the ideal world.

If Glenys couldn't have a child, it might explain her activities. She loved people; she needed them and gave them lots of her time, and gifts, too – useful things like food.

As Edna left me, Glenys emerged with her arms full of groceries. She placed them in her car, then turned to go back into the shop, saying, 'I'd forget my head if it was loose!' She laughed as she rushed away. 'Mr Stead's out of tea, Miss Browne needs more washing powder and my Alec's run out of toothpaste . . . you won't forget the meeting tomorrow, will you, Nick? About the Christmas Party.'

'No,' I assured her. 'I won't. And you weren't going to leave those keys in the ignition, were you?'

She issued a massive sigh and laughed. 'I'll only be a minute . . . keep an eye on it for me, will you?'

And so I stood guard upon the muddy old Traveller – and noticed its tax disc expired at the end of December. I'd have to remind her to renew it.

The Aidensfield Christmas party was on the Tuesday before Christmas and comprised an afternoon session for children with Father Christmas, games and food. This was followed by an evening interlude for older adults, with presents for pensioners, a supper and old-time dancing. The party ended with more dancing to pop music for the younger element.

Glenys had persuaded old Mrs Habton to wrap the presents and put names on them; they'd be ready for collection on the morning of the party. When I was chatting to Mrs Habton, she told me, 'I did enjoy doing the parcels but I had no idea Mr Greengrass was a pensioner!'

'Neither had I!' I had to admit. 'He's kept that very quiet!'

'The Post Office told me,' grinned Mrs Habton. 'He sneaks in to draw his pension, but if anybody's there, he pretends he's shopping. He's very secretive about his age, you know . . .'

'Really?' I commented, wondering why Claude wished to conceal his advancing years.

But as party day approached, there were more important things than Claude Jeremiah's age to worry about. Glenys told me she'd bought a splendid replacement exhaust from Claude and announced she would collect Mrs Habton's parcels and deliver them to the hall, at the same time collecting the cooked turkeys from the butcher, some bread rolls from the baker, bottles of orange juice and lemonade from the Co-op and the specially baked Christmas cake from Mrs Cooper of Elsinby. There was a box of spirits to collect from the off-licence in Ashfordly, too – bottles of gin, whisky and brandy which were raffle prizes.

But this year, there was a secret and very pleasant job to do. Chairman of the Parish Council, Stanley Preston, had approached committee members to suggest, 'Glenys does all this with no thought of a reward in spite of being so short of money, so how about a surprise presentation to her at the party?'

Everyone had agreed but some had asked, 'What on earth shall we get her?'

'She could do with some new clothes, a nice dress or suit, shoes, something special,' was the general consensus among the ladies. 'She's desperately hard up.'

'What about a gift voucher, then she could get what she wants?' was another idea. 'She might be insulted if we restrict it to clothes.'

It was decided there would be a cash collection to provide an open gift voucher for Glenys. She could treat herself to whatever she wanted, the proviso being that the gift would be for her, and her alone, not to be given to any of the villagers. As the days grew colder and the darkening nights carried a threat of snow on the moors, I got the job of making the collection. I managed to raise £46 10s. 6d., a very useful sum when a weekly wage was around £12. I knew that Alec and Glenys existed on much less – the voucher would be a wonderful present. Somehow, the villagers managed to keep the secret from Glenys.

On the morning before the party, as I was patrolling on my motorbike, a few isolated snowflakes floated from the grey clouds. I was concerned that snow was forecast and hoped it wouldn't hinder the party arrangements.

That morning, Glenys collected the presents so carefully wrapped and labelled by Mrs Habton, along with other party items. Placing everything in her car, she drove into Ashfordly to collect the spirits from the off-licence and decided to do some last-minute shopping of her own. She needed a Christmas card for Alec, and all he wanted as a present was a new pair of corduroys, if she could afford them. Glenys had saved up, and there would be just time to buy the cords before returning to Aidensfield. The snow held off but the sky remained grey and threatening.

In Ashfordly, Glenys collected the spirits and placed the bottles in her car before walking to the stationer's. She hadn't noticed two youths watching her, and by the time she emerged with Alec's card, her car had gone. At first, she didn't believe it. She searched the street, the car park, the side streets . . . but the Traveller wasn't there. It took several minutes to realise it had been stolen, along with all the food, the presents, the drinks and extra items for Aidensfield's Christmas party.

Devastated, Glenys just stood on the pavement and wept.

By chance, I was on my way to Ashfordly police station and saw the unhappy figure sobbing in the street. I parked the motorbike and went to her.

'Glenys?'

'Oh, Nick . . . thank God it's you. It's awful . . . I'm so ashamed . . . it's ruined, everything's ruined.'

"What's ruined? What's happened?"

'You're going to be very angry. You warned me . . .' she sobbed. 'My car's gone, stolen. It was right here. It's got all the party stuff inside as well. It's all gone, every bit of it. All that work, all for nothing . . .'

This was the latest in a long spate of similar car thefts, but I didn't ask if she'd left the keys in the ignition! Her eyes moist with tears, she pleaded, 'What can I do? It's all my fault . . . all those children will be waiting . . .'

I put a comforting arm around her shoulders and said, 'Come on, the police station's just around the corner. We'll circulate details, it can't be far away.'

Sergeant Blaketon confirmed that several cars had been stolen in recent months and not recovered. They'd contained handbags, cameras and things of similar value, but those taken in the last few days had contained either cigarettes or spirits, so popular with thieves at Christmas. Alf Ventress circulated a description of the Traveller and its contents by radio, so within minutes, every patrolling constable was aware of the theft.

'What am I going to do if you don't find it?' she sobbed.

'Make sure she gets home, Constable.' Sergeant Blaketon was firm. 'And do something about that party. Then ask Greengrass what he knows about Mrs Hutchinson's car!'

'Claude wouldn't steal her car, Sergeant!' I protested.

'Ask him all the same!' and Sergeant Blaketon stalked out of the office leaving PC Ventress in charge of the hunt for Glenys's old car.

If you want news to travel quickly in Aidensfield, you make an announcement in the shop or you tell Edna. The village bush-telegraph then outsmarts any other system of news transmission, so within minutes of my return, I made sure everyone knew about the theft. None the less, it was doubtful if we would trace the Traveller or its precious load. Our dilemma was whether to replace the stolen items now or wait in case the vehicle was quickly traced with its load intact. It was now 11 a.m. – the party was scheduled to start at four p.m. for the children, with Father Christmas arriving at six p.m. We could tolerate a short wait. As I walked towards the hall, trying to determine a course of action, Claude Jeremiah Greengrass and Alfred, his scruffy dog, emerged from Claude's old truck outside the pub.

'Ah, Claude, I want a word with you,' I hailed him.

'I know nowt about Glenys's car,' were his first words.

'Not if it contained your Christmas present?' I put to him.

'My present?' he blinked. 'What are you talking about?'

'You're a pensioner, Claude. You're entitled to a present.'

'Pensioner? Me? You must be joking.'

'Your secret's out, Claude. We've a list from the Post Office.'

He paused for a moment, then whispered, 'Look, if this gets out, I'm finished. Who'll give me work if they think I'm too old and past it?'

'So, Claude,' I smiled. 'Let's make a deal – you tell me who's nicking those cars and I might forget you're a pensioner.'

He blinked furiously then whispered, 'I'm no copper's nark, you know, but, well, it's not decent, is it? Pinching presents for kids and pensioners.'

'Very nobly spoken, Claude, so what can you tell me?'

He led me from prying eyes and told me that two Ashfordly youths were preying on cars left unattended during Christmas shopping expeditions. When the owners were out of sight, the lads would drive away the cars and steal any spirits, wines, beers or cigarettes before abandoning the vehicles.

'I'm not saying who it is, mind,' Claude said. 'I mean, I can't be seen grassing to the constabulary – but they drive them stolen cars into that old army camp in Speckledale. It's used as a scrapyard, you know, unofficial, like,' and he blinked repeatedly.

'Thanks, Claude.'

'Is there a reward? Not that I want this making public, mind, but, well, a chap has to live . . .'

'Your secret will be your reward, Claude!' and I left him, realising that I now knew the source of his secondhand spares business. Within minutes I was on my way to collect Sergeant Blaketon, and half an hour later, we drove deep into the moors to locate the deserted camp. There, among dozens of abandoned cars, ancient and modern, was the scruffy old Traveller. We had found a car thieves' dumping ground and Sergeant Blaketon was delighted.

'We'll mount observations on this place,' he assured me. 'I reckon we'll soon catch one of 'em red-handed!'

Glenys's Traveller still had the keys in the ignition but the spirits and Christmas fare had gone. The presents were intact, however, and so, having examined it for fingerprints, I drove it back to Aidensfield.

I was fair to Claude – I removed his parcel so I could slip it to him beyond the gaze of the public and warn him to keep away from the old camp! We were able to obtain some more turkeys and spirits for the party and so, by the time everyone began to arrive, the drama was over.

Claude was wonderful as Father Christmas but the climax was Stanley Preston's presentation to Glenys.

Everyone was delighted that Alec had come too; both he and Glenys were in their best clothes. This was unusual – had the couple discovered our plot? We felt not; we felt sure our surprise was complete. So why *had* Alec come? Perhaps the theft had unsettled Glenys and she needed his support? Was she blaming herself for what had happened? I began to wonder whether Glenys was going to give up her voluntary work. Clearly, she was going to announce something, but before she did so, Stanley Preston mounted the stage. Glenys hurried forward.

'Before you say your thankyous,' I heard her say, 'I'd like to say something.'

'There is a matter I must deal with first, Glenys,' said Stanley firmly but very diplomatically. 'And then you can take the stage. I'll do my thankyou afterwards.'

He called for silence then began to praise Glenys for her selfless work. Standing before the crowd, she grew very embarrassed and then he said, 'On behalf of the people of Aidensfield, Glenys, I would like to present you with this gift token. We wish you the happiest of Christmases . . . but we insist, Glenys, that this gift is personal, for you.'

She was dumbfounded, but Alec eased her on to the stage to collect it and she ascended the steps to loud applause. She saw the large amount on the token and began to weep with happiness, wiping her eyes with her free hand.

'This is so lovely,' she sniffed. 'And I know somebody who can use this . . .'

'No,' Stanley interrupted. 'It's for you, no one else.'

'It'll be for our baby,' she said coyly. 'At last, Alec and I are going to have a child. We can get some baby clothes and a cot . . . You've no idea how happy we are, we wanted you all to be the first to know. But it means I won't be able to organise the party next year . . .'

Her remaining words were lost among the joy which flowed towards Glenys, Alec and their unborn child as the snow gently descended upon Aidensfield that night.

The Second Skin

MICHAEL GILBERT

DETECTIVE FILE

OFFICER: Sergeant Patrick Petrella

FORCE: Metropolitan Police, London

TIME: 1958

CASES: *Blood and Judgement* (1959), *London Manhunt* (1967), *The Body of a Girl* (1972), *Petrella at Q* (1977) etc.

PROFILE: Patrick Petrella is a traditionally hardworking and dedicated member of the Met who began his career at Crown Road police station, Highside in the 'fifties. He has progressed steadily up the ladder, to Detective Inspector, and is currently a Detective Chief Inspector. Well built, slightly earnest in appearance, and generally unflappable, he dresses in dark suits and occasionally wears a hat over his neatly trimmed hair. Petrella is a man respected by his fellow officers and accorded a healthy regard by the city's criminals, and during his career he has tackled virtually every type of crime from blackmail to arson, theft to murder, and even taken on that most hated of all villains – the cop killer. Off duty he enjoys a glass of port and a good book. His first cases appeared as short stories in *Ellery Queen's Mystery Magazine* in 1958, to be followed the next year by a full-length novel, *Blood and Judgement*, in which a female body was discovered near a reservoir by three little boys, setting Petrella off on an exceptionally difficult manhunt. The book was recommended by the American critic Anthony Boucher as one of the best mystery novels of 1959 and Petrella has never looked back, in dozens of short stories and a handful of novels.

CREATOR: Michael Gilbert (b. 1912) has been a practising lawyer as well as a mystery-story writer for over forty years, and the *Encyclopaedia of Mystery and Detection* has called him 'one of the finest of the Post-World War Two generation of detective story writers'. In his early days as a London solicitor in Lincoln's Inn he became legal adviser to Raymond Chandler, who in turn proved an inspiration when he began to write crime fiction. Gilbert's work is highly regarded for its complex plotting and well-rounded characters. 'The Second Skin' is one of Patrick Petrella's early cases when he was still a sergeant at Highside in 1958 – but even then he was showing all the qualities of perseverance, attention to detail and interest in people which have made him such an outstanding detective.

***

The table was the first thing which caught your eye as you came into the room. Its legs were of green-painted angle-iron, bolted to the floor; its top was a solid block of polished teak.

Overhead shone five white fluorescent lights.

On the wide, shadowless, aseptic surface of the table the raincoat looked out of place, like some jolly, seedy old tramp who has strayed into an operating theatre. A coat is such a personal thing, almost a second skin. As it loses its own shape and takes on the outlines of its wearer, as its pockets become a repository of tobacco flakes and sand and fragments of leaves, and its exterior becomes spotted with more unexpected things than rain, so a coat takes on a life of its own.

There was an element of indecency, Petrella thought, in tearing this life from it. The earnest man in rimless glasses and a white laboratory overall had just finished going over the lining with a pocket-sized vacuum cleaner that had a thimble-shaped container. Now he was at work on the exterior. He cut a broad strip of adhesive tape and laid it on the outside of the coat, pressing it down firmly. He then marked the area with a special pencil and pulled the tape off.

There was nothing visible to the naked eye on the under surface of the tape, but the laboratory man seemed satisfied.

'We'll make a few microslides,' he said. 'They'll tell us anything we want to know. There's no need for you to hang around if you don't want to.'

Sergeant Petrella disliked being told, even indirectly, that he was wasting his time. If the truth must be told, he did not care for Scientific Assistant Worsley at all.

'All right,' he said. 'I'll push off and come back in a couple of hours.'

'To do the job completely,' said Worsley, 'will take about six days.' He looked complacently at the neat range of Petri dishes round the table and the test samples he had so far extracted. 'Then perhaps another three days to tabulate the results.'

'All the same,' said Petrella, 'I'll look in this evening and see what you have got for me.'

'As long as you appreciate,' said Worsley, 'that the results I give you will be unchecked.'

'I'll take the chance.'

'That, of course, is for you to decide.' The laboratory man's voice contained a reproof: impetuous people, police officers; unschooled in the discipline of science;

jumpers to conclusions. People on whom careful controlled research was usually wasted. Worsley sighed audibly.

Sergeant Petrella said nothing. He had long ago found out that it was a waste of time antagonising people who were in a position to help you.

He consulted his watch, his notebook, and his stomach. He had a call to make in Wandsworth, another in Acton and a third in South Harrow. Then he would come back to the forensic science laboratory to see what Worsley had got for them. Then he would go back to Highside and report to Superintendent Haxtell.

All this activity – and, indirectly, the coat lying on the laboratory table – stemmed from a discovery made by a milkman at 39 Carhow Mansions. Carhow Mansions is a tall block of flats overlooking the southern edge of Helenwood Common.

Miss Martin, who lived alone at 39, was a woman of about thirty. Neither beautiful nor clever; nor ugly, nor stupid. She was secretary to Dr Hunter who had a house and consulting room in Wimpole Street. She did her work well and was well paid for it.

The flat, which was tucked away on the top storey and was smaller than the others in the block, was known as a 'single' – which means that it had about as little accommodation as one person could actually exist in. A living-room which was also a dining-room. A cubbyhole which served as a bedroom. Another cubbyhole called a kitchen and another called a bathroom. Not that Miss Martin had ever been heard to complain. She had no time to waste on housework and ate most of her meals out. Her interests were Shakespeare and tennis.

Which brings us to the milkman who, finding Friday's milk bottle still unused outside the door of flat 39 on Saturday, mentioned the matter to the caretaker.

The caretaker was not immediately worried. Tenants

often went away without telling him, although Miss Martin was usually punctilious about such matters. Later in the morning his rounds took him up to 39 and he looked at the two milk bottles and found the sight faintly disturbing. Fortunately he had his passkey with him.

Which brought Superintendent Haxtell on to the scene in a fast car. And Chief Superintendent Barstow from District Headquarters. And photographic and fingerprint detachments, and a well-known pathologist, and a crowd on the pavement, and a uniformed policeman to control them; and, eventually, since Carhow Mansions was in his district, Sergeant Petrella.

Junior detective sergeants do not conduct investigations into murders but they are allowed to help, in much the same way as a junior officer helps to run a war. They are allowed to do the work, while their superiors do the thinking. In this case there was a lot of work to do.

'I don't like it,' said Barstow in the explosive rumble which was his normal conversational voice. 'Here's this girl, as ordinary as apples and custard. No one's got a word to say against her. Her life's an open book. Then someone comes in and hits her on the head. Not once – five or six times.'

'Any one of the blows might have caused death,' agreed the pathologist. 'She's been dead more than twenty-four hours. Probably killed on Friday morning. And I think there's no doubt that that was the weapon.'

He indicated a heavy long-handled screwdriver.

'It could have belonged to her,' said Haxtell. 'Funny thing to find in a flat like this though. More like a piece of workshop equipment.'

'All right,' said Barstow. 'Suppose the murderer brought it with him. Ideal for the job. You could force a front door with a thing like that. But it's still' – he boggled over the word and its implications – 'it's still mad.'

And the further they looked, and the wider they spread their net, the madder it seemed.

Certain facts, however, came to light at once. Haxtell talked to Dr Hunter of Wimpole Street within an hour. The doctor explained that Miss Martin had not come to work on Friday because he himself had ordered her to stay in bed. 'I think she'd been overworking her eyes,' said the doctor. 'That gave her a headache, and the headache in turn affected her stomach. It was a form of migraine. What she needed was forty-eight hours on her back, with the blinds down. I told her to take Friday off and come back on Monday only if she felt well enough. She's been with me for nearly ten years now. An excellent secretary, and such a nice girl.'

He spoke with so much warmth that Haxtell, who was a cynic, made a mental note of a possible line of inquiry. But nothing came of it. The doctor, it developed, was very happily married.

'That part of it fits all right,' said Haxtell to Chief Superintendent Barstow. 'She was in bed when the intruder arrived. He hit her as she was coming out of her bedroom.'

'Then you think he was simply a housebreaker?'

'I imagined so. Yes,' said Haxtell. 'The screwdriver looks like the sort of thing a housebreaker would carry. You could force an ordinary mortice lock right off with it. He didn't have to use it in this instance because she used a simple catch lock that a child of six could open. I don't doubt he merely slipped it with a piece of talc.'

'But why did he choose her flat?'

'Because it was an isolated one on the top floor. Or because he knew her habits. Just bad luck that she should have been at home at that time.'

'Bad luck for her,' agreed Barstow, sourly. 'Well, we've got the machine working. We may turn something up.'

Haxtell was an experienced police officer. He knew

that investigating a murder was like dropping a stone into a pool of water. He started two inquiries at once. Everybody within a hundred yards of the flat was asked what they had been doing and whether they had noticed anything. And everyone remotely connected with Miss Martin, by ties of blood, friendship or business, was sought out and questioned.

It is a system which involves an enormous amount of work for a large number of people, and has only one thing in its favour: it is nearly always successful in the end.

To Sergeant Petrella fell the task of questioning all the other tenants in the building. This involved seven visits. In each case at least one person, it appeared, had been home all Friday morning. And no one had heard anything at all, which was disappointing. Had anything unusual happened on Friday morning? The first six people to whom this inquiry was addressed scratched their heads and said they didn't think anything had. The seventh mentioned the gentleman who had left census papers.

Now by then Petrella was both hot and tired. He was, according to which way you looked at it, either very late for his lunch or rather early for his tea. He was on the point of dismissing the gentleman with the census papers when the instinct – which guides all good policemen – drove him to persevere with one further inquiry. Had he not done so, the Martin case would probably have remained unsolved. But as the sergeant probed, a curious little story emerged. The gentleman had not actually left any papers behind him. He had been making preliminary inquiries as to the number of people on the premises so that further arrangements for the census could be made. The census papers themselves would be issued later.

Petrella trudged down three flights of stairs (it is only in a grave emergency that policeman are allowed to use private telephones) and rang up the Municipal Returning Officer from a call box. After that he revisited the first six flats. The occupants unanimously agreed that a 'man from the Council' had called on them that Friday morning. They had not mentioned it because Petrella had asked if anything 'unusual' had happened. There was nothing in the least unusual in men from the Council snooping round. Petrella asked for a description and collected, from his six informants, the following: the man in question was 'young', 'youngish', 'and sort of middle-aged' (the last from a teenaged daughter in 37); he was bareheaded and had tousled hair; he was wearing a hat; he had a shifty look (flat 34), a nice smile (teenaged daughter); couldn't say, didn't really look at him (the remainder); he was about six foot, five foot nine, five foot six, and didn't notice; he had an ordinary sort of voice; he was wearing an old Harrovian tie (old gentleman in ground-floor flat 34); he seemed to walk with rather a stiff sort of leg, almost a limp (four out of six informants).

Petrella hurried back to Crown Road police station where he found Haxtell and Barstow in conference.

'There doesn't seem to be much doubt,' he reported, 'that it was a sneak thief posing as a Council employee. I've checked with the Council and they are certain he couldn't have been genuine. His plan would be to knock once or twice. If he got no answer he'd either slip the lock or force it. He drew blank at the first seven flats – someone answered the door in each of them. When he got to 39, on the top floor, I expect Miss Martin didn't hear him. The migraine must have made her pretty blind and deaf.'

'That's right,' said Barstow. 'And then she came out and caught him at it. So he hit her.'

'The descriptions aren't much good,' said Haxtell, 'but we'll get all the pictures from the CRO of people known to go in for this sort of lark. They may sort someone out for us.'

'Don't forget the most important item,' said Barstow. 'The limp.'

Petrella said, 'It did occur to me to wonder whether we ought to place too much reliance on the limp, sir.'

He received a glare which would have daunted a less self-confident man but he persisted.

'He would have to have somewhere to hide that big screwdriver. It was almost two feet long. The natural place would be a pocket inside his trouser leg. That might account for the appearance of a stiff leg.'

Haxtell avoided Barstow's eye.

'It's an idea,' Haxtell said. 'Now just get along and start checking on this list of Miss Martin's known relations.'

'There was one other thing—' Petrella went on.

'Do you know,' observed Chief Superintendent Barstow unkindly, 'why God gave young policemen two feet but only one head?'

Petrella took the hint and departed.

But the idea kept gnawing at Petrella and later that day, when he was alone with Superintendent Haxtell, he voiced it again.

'Do you remember,' he said, 'about six months ago, I think it was, we had an outbreak of this sort of thing in the Cholderton Road, Park Branch area? A man cleared out three or four blocks of flats, and we never caught him. He was posing as a Pools salesman then.'

'The man who left his coat behind?'

'That's right,' said Petrella. 'With Colonel Wing.'

Colonel Wing was nearly ninety and stone deaf, but still spry. He had fought in one Zulu and countless Afghan wars and the walls of his top-floor living-room in Cholderton Mansions were adorned with a fine selection of assegais, yataghans, and knobkerries. Six months before the Martin case he had had an experience which might have unnerved a less seasoned warrior. He was not an early riser. Pottering out of his bedroom one fine morning at about eleven o'clock he found a man kneeling in front of his sideboard and quietly sorting out the silver. It was difficult to say who had been more taken aback. The intruder had jumped up and run from the room. Colonel Wing had regretfully dismissed the idea of trying to spear him with an assegai from the balcony as he left the front door of the flats, and had rung up the police. They had made one curious discovery.

Hanging in the hall was a strange raincoat.

'Never seen it before in my life,' insisted Colonel Wing. 'D'you mean to say the fellow had the cheek to hang his coat up before starting work? Wonder he didn't help himself to a whisky and soda while he was about it.'

Haxtell said that he had known housebreakers to do just that. He talked to Colonel Wing at length about the habits of criminals; and removed the coat for examination. Since the crime was only an attempted robbery, it was not thought worthwhile wasting too much time on it. A superficial examination produced no results in the way of name tabs or tailor's marks, but the coat was carefully placed in a cellophane bag and stored.

'I'd better have a word with him,' suggested Petrella.

He found Colonel Wing engaged in writing a letter to the *United Services Journal* on the comparative fighting qualities of Zulus and Russians. The Colonel listened to the composite descriptions of the more recent intruder, and said that, so far as he could tell, they sounded like the same man. His intruder had been on the young side of middle age, of medium height, and strongly built.

'There's one thing,' said the Colonel. 'I saw him in a good light, and I may be deaf but I've got excellent eyesight. There's a tiny spot in his left eye. A little red spot, like a fire opal. You couldn't mistake it. If you catch him, I'll identify him for you.'

'The trouble is,' said Petrella, 'that it looks as if he's never been through our hands. Almost the only real lead we've got is that coat he left behind him at your place. We're going over it again – much more thoroughly this time.'

Thus the coat had grown in importance. It had improved its status. It had become an exhibit in a murder case.

'Give it everything,' said Haxtell to the laboratory. And the scientists prepared to oblige.

That evening, after a weary afternoon spent interrogating Miss Martin's father's relatives in Acton and South Harrow, Petrella found himself back on the Embankment. The forensic science laboratory observes civilised hours and Mr Worsley was on the point of removing his long white overall and replacing it with a rather deplorable tweed coat with homemade leather patches on the elbows.

'I've finished my preliminary work on the right-hand pocket,' he said. 'We have isolated arrowroot starch, pipe tobacco, and a quantity of common silver sand.'

'Splendid,' said Petrella. 'Splendid. All I have now got to do is to find a housewife who smokes a pipe and has recently been to the seaside and we shall be home and dry.'

'What use you make of the data we provide must be entirely a matter for you,' said Mr Worsley coldly. He was already late for a meeting of the South Wimbledon Medico-Legal Society to whose members he had promised a paper titled *The Part of the Laboratory in Modern Crime Detection*.

Petrella went back to Highside.

Here he found a note from Superintendent Haxtell which ran: 'A friend of Miss Martin's has suggested that some of these were, or might have been, boyfriends of the deceased. I am seeing the ones marked with a cross. Would you tackle the others?'

There followed a list of names and addresses ranging from Welwyn Garden City to Morden. Petrella looked at his watch. It was half-past seven. With any luck he could knock off a few of the names before midnight.

In the ensuing days the ripples spread, wider and wider, diminishing in size and importance as they became more distant from the centre of the disturbance. Petrella worked his way from near relatives and close friends, who said, 'How terrible! Whoever would have thought of anything like that happening to Marjorie,' and then through more distant connections who said, 'Miss Martin? Yes, I know her. I haven't seen her, for a long time,' all the way out to the circumference where people simply looked bewildered and said, 'Miss Martin? I'm sorry, I don't think I remember anyone of that name.' And on being reminded that they had danced with her at a tennis club dance two years before, they said, 'If you say so, I expect it's right – but I'm dashed if I can remember what she looked like.'

It was in the course of the third day that Petrella called at a nice little house in Herne Hill. The name was Taylor. Mr Taylor was not at home but the door was opened by his wife, a cheerful redhead who banished her two children to the kitchen when she understood what Petrella was after. Her reactions were the standard ones. Apprehension, followed as soon as she understood that what Petrella wanted had nothing to do with her, by a cheerful communicativeness. Miss Martin was, she believed, her husband's cousin. That is to say, not his cousin but his second cousin, or something like that. Her husband's father's married sister's husband's niece. So far as she knew they had only met her once, and that was six months before, at the funeral of Miss Martin's mother who was, of course, sister to her husband's uncle by marriage.

Petrella disentangled this complicated relationship without too much difficulty. He was already a considerable expert on the Martin family tree. But unfortunately Mrs Taylor could tell him nothing more. Her acquaintance with Miss Martin was confined to this single occasion and she had not set eyes on her since. Her husband, who was a commercial traveller for Joblox, the London paint firm, was unlikely to be back until very late. He was on a tour in the Midlands, and his return home depended on the traffic. Petrella said he quite understood. The interview remained in his memory chiefly because it was on his way back from it that he picked up his copy of the laboratory report on the raincoat.

The scientists had done themselves proud. Not one square inch of the coat's surface, interior or exterior, had escaped their microscopic gaze. Petrella cast his eye desperately over the eight closely typed foolscap pages. Stains on the exterior had been isolated, chemically tested, and proved beyond reasonable doubt to be, in two cases, ink, in one case rabbit blood, and in one case varnish. A quantity of sisal-hemp fluff had been recovered from the seam of the left-hand cuff and some marmalade from the right-hand one. A sliver of soft wood, originally identified on the Chatterton Key Card as ordinary *pinus sylvestris*, was now believed to be *Chamaecyparis Lawsoniana*. In the right-hand pocket had been discovered a number of fragments of oyster shell and a stain of oil shown by quantitative analysis to be thick oil of the sort used in marine engineering.

Petrella read the report in the underground between Charing Cross and Highside. When he reached Crown Road he found Haxtell in the CID room. The Superintendent had in front of him the reports of all his visits made so far. There were two hundred and thirty of them. Petrella added the five he had completed that afternoon and was about to retire when he remembered the laboratory report and cautiously added that, too, to the pile. He was conscious of thunder in the air.

'Don't bother,' said Haxtell. 'I've had a copy.' His eyes were red-rimmed from lack of sleep. 'So has the Chief Superintendent. He's just been here. He wants us to take some action on it.'

'Action, sir?'

'He suggests,' said Haxtell in ominously quiet tones, 'that we re-examine all persons interviewed so far' – his hand flickered for a moment over the pile of papers on the table – 'to ascertain whether they have ever been interested in the oyster-fishing industry. He feels that the coincidence of oyster shell and marine oil must have some significance.'

'I see, sir,' said Petrella. 'When do we start?'

Haxtell stopped himself within an ace of saying something which would have been both indiscreet and insubordinate. Then to his eternal credit, he laughed instead.

'We are both,' he said, 'going to get one good night's rest first. We'll start tomorrow morning.'

'I wonder if I could borrow the reports until then,' said Petrella.

'Do what you like with them,' said Haxtell. 'I've got three days' routine work to catch up with.'

Petrella took the reports back with him to Mrs Cat's where that worthy widow had prepared a high tea for him, his first leisured meal in three days. Sustained by a mountainous dish of sausages and eggs and refreshed by his third cup of strong tea, he started on the task of proving the theory that had come to him.

Each paper was skimmed, then put to one side. Every now and then he would stop, extract one, and add it to a much smaller pile beside his plate. At the end of an hour Petrella looked at the results of his work with satisfaction. In the small pile were six papers – six summaries of interviews with friends or relations of the murdered girl. If his theory was right, he had thus at a stroke, reduced the possibles from two hundred and thirty-five to six. And of those six possibles only one was a probable. He knew it in his heart of hearts.

There came back into his mind the visit he had made that afternoon. It was there, in that place and no other, the answer lay. There he had glimpsed, without realising it, the end of the scarlet thread which led to the heart of this untidy, rambling labyrinth. He thought of a nice redheaded girl and two redheaded children, and unexpectedly he found himself shivering.

It was dusk before he got back to Herne Hill. The lights were on in the nice little house, upstairs and downstairs, and a muddy car stood in the gravel driveway leading to the garage. Sounds suggested that the redheaded children were being put to bed by both their parents and were enjoying it.

One hour went by, and then a second. Petrella had found an empty house opposite and he was squatting in the yard, his back propped against a tree. The night was warm and he was quite comfortable, and his head was nodding on his chest when the front door of the house opposite opened, and Mr Taylor appeared.

He stood for a moment, outlined against the light from the hall, saying something to his wife. He was too far off for Petrella to make out the words. Then he came down the path. He ignored his car and made for the front gate for which Petrella was thankful. He had made certain arrangements to cope with the contingency that Mr Taylor might use his car, but it was much easier if he remained on foot.

A short walk took them both pursuer and pursued, to

the door of the King of France public house. Mr Taylor went into the saloon. Petrella himself chose the private bar. Like most private bars it had nothing to recommend it save its privacy, being narrow, bare, and quite empty. But it had the advantage of looking straight across the serving counter into the saloon.

Petrella let his man order first. He was evidently a well-known character. He called the landlord Sam, and the landlord called him Mr Taylor.

Petrella drank his own beer slowly. Ten minutes later the moment for which he had been waiting arrived. Mr Taylor picked up a couple of glasses and strolled across with them to the counter. Petrella also rose casually to his feet. For a moment they faced each other, a bare two paces apart, under the bright bar lights.

Petrella saw in front of him a man of youngish middle age, with a nondescript face, neutral-coloured tousled hair, perhaps five foot nine in height, and wearing some sort of old school tie.

As if aware that he was being looked at, Mr Taylor raised his head; and Petrella observed, in the left eye, a tiny red spot. It was, as Colonel Wing had said, exactly the colour of a fire opal . . .

'We showed his photograph to everyone in the block,' said Haxtell with satisfaction, 'and all of them picked it out straight away, out of a set of six. Also the Colonel.'

'Good enough,' said Chief Superintendent Barstow. 'Any background?'

'We made a cautious inquiry at Joblox. Taylor certainly works for them. But he's what they call an outside commission man. He sells in his spare time and gets a percentage on sales. Last year he made just under a hundred pounds.'

'Which wouldn't keep him in his present style.'

'Definitely not. And of course a job like that would be

very useful cover for a criminal side line. He would be out when and where he liked, and no questions asked by his family.'

Barstow considered the matter slowly. The decision was his.

'Pull him in,' he said. 'Charge him with the job at Colonel Wing's. The rest will sort itself out quickly enough when we search his house. Take a search warrant with you. By the way, I never asked you how you got on to him. Has he some connection with the oyster trade?'

Petrella said cautiously, 'Well no, sir. As a matter of fact, he hadn't. But the report was very useful corroborative evidence.'

'Clever chaps, these scientists,' said Barstow.

'Come clean,' said Haxtell, when the Chief Superintendent had departed. 'It had nothing to do with that coat, did it?'

'Nothing at all,' said Petrella. 'What occurred to me was that it was a very curious murder – presuming it was the same man both times. Take Colonel Wing: he's full of beans, but when all's said and done he's a frail old man, over ninety. He saw the intruder in a clear light and the man simply turned tail and bolted. Then he bumps into Miss Martin, who's a girl, but a muscular young tennis player, and he *kills* her, coldly and deliberately.'

'From which you deduced that Miss Martin knew him, and he was prepared to kill to preserve the secret of his identity. Particularly as he had never been in the hands of the police.'

'There was a bit more to it than that,' said Petrella. 'It had to be someone who knew Miss Martin, *but so casually that he would have no idea where she lived.* Mightn't even remember her name. If he'd had any idea that it was the flat of someone who knew him he wouldn't have touched it with a barge pole. What I was looking for, then, was someone who was distantly connected with Miss Martin, but happened to have renewed his acquaintance with her recently. He had to be a very distant connection, you see – *but they had to know each other by sight*. There were half a dozen who would have filled the bill. I had this one in my mind because I'd interviewed Mrs Taylor only that afternoon. Of course, I'd have tried all the others afterwards. Only it wasn't necessary.'

There was neither pleasure nor satisfaction in his voice. He was seeing nothing but a nice redheaded girl and two nice redheaded children . . .

It was perhaps six months later that Petrella ran across Colonel Wing again. The Taylor case was now only an uncomfortable memory, for Mr Taylor had taken his own life in his cell at Wandsworth and the redheaded girl was now a widow. Petrella was on his way home, and he might not have noticed him, but the Colonel came right across the road to greet him, narrowly missing death at the hands of a motorcyclist of whose approach he had been blissfully unaware.

'Good evening, Sergeant,' the old man said. 'How are you keeping?'

'Very well, thank you, Colonel,' said Petrella. 'And how are you?'

'I'm not getting any younger,' said the Colonel. Petrella suddenly perceived that the old man was covered with embarrassment. He waited patiently for him to speak.

'I wonder,' said the Colonel at last, 'it's an awkward thing to have to ask, but could you get that coat back – you remember –?'

'Get it *back*?' asked Petrella. 'I don't know. I suppose so.'

'If it was mine, I wouldn't bother. But it isn't. I find it's my cousin Tom's. I'd forgotten all about it, until he reminded me.'

Petrella stared at the old man.

'Do you mean to say—'

'Tom stayed the night with me – he does that sometimes, between trips. Just drops in. Of course, when he reminded me, I remembered—'

'Between trips,' repeated Petrella weakly. 'He isn't by any chance an oyster fisherman?'

It was the Colonel's turn to stare.

'Certainly not,' he said. 'He's one of the best-known breeders of budgerigars in the country.'

'Budgerigars?'

'Very well known for them. I believe I'm right in saying he introduced the foreign system of burnishing their feathers with oil. It's funny you should mention oysters though. That's something he's very keen on. Powdered oyster shell in the feed. It improves their high notes.'

Petrella removed his hat in a belated salute to the forensic science laboratory.

'Certainly you shall have your coat back,' he said. 'It'll need a thorough cleaning and a little repairing, but I am delighted to know that at last it is going to be of use to someone.'

Blood Brothers

CHRISTIANNA BRAND

DETECTIVE FILE

OFFICER: Inspector Cockrill

FORCE: Kent County Police

TIME: 1965

CASES: *Heads You Lose* (1941), *The Crooked Wreath* (1946), *London Particular* (1952), *Tour de Force* (1955), *Rabbit Out of a Hat* (1967) etc.

PROFILE: Inspector 'Cockie' Cockrill is a complete contrast to Petrella – an eccentric, omniscient detective rather than a follower of police procedural methods. A shrewd, occasionally sharp-tongued officer based at Heronsford in Kent, he is invariably shabbily dressed, with his hat crammed down over his head and his fingers dark stained from too many hand-rolled cigarettes. Cockrill is actually a few inches shorter than the required height for police officers – but no one should be fooled by this or his appearance because behind the brown eyes and aquiline nose, the Inspector possesses acute powers of observation which have enabled him time and again to unmask the real criminal among the most unlikely assembly of suspects. Generations of readers have been trying to outwit 'Cockie' Cockrill, but most usually come unstuck because of red herrings and false clues which he, of course, sees through. The little detective made his debut in *Heads You Lose* (1941), in which the decapitated head of a spinster lady sparked off a gruesome murder hunt. This was followed by a wartime mystery, *Green For Danger* (1944), which has been praised as one of the great detective novels of all time, and was filmed two years later with Alastair Sim as a rather lankier Inspector than his fans had expected. Accounts of his career have, sadly, been rather intermittent since the 'seventies.

CREATOR: Christianna Brand is the pseudonym of Mary Christianna Lewis (b. 1907), who worked in a variety of occupations, including governess, receptionist, dancer, model and salesgirl, before writing her first mystery novel, *Death in High Heels* (1941), which, she said, was inspired by fear of a fellow worker! Her subsequent crime stories – especially those about Inspector Cockrill – have won her a number of awards from writers' associations on both sides of the Atlantic and there are some critics who consider her best work to be the equal of Agatha Christie's. In the following short story written in 1965, the irascible 'Cockie' sets out to unravel a curious mystery involving the famous Birdswell twins – the 'blood brothers' of the title.

***

'And devoted, I hear,' he says. 'David and Jonathan,' he says. 'In fact you might properly be called,' he says, with that glitter in his eye, 'blood brothers?'

Well, he can sneer but it's true we was pally enough, Fred and me, till Lydia came along. Shared the same digs in the village – Birdswell's our village, if you know it? – Birdswell, in Kent. Everyone in Birdswell knows us – even if they can't easily tell the difference between us – and used to say how wonderful it was, us two so alike, with our strong legs and big shoulders and curly red hair, like a kid's: and what a beautiful understanding we had, what a bond of union. People talk a lot of crap about identical twins.

Lydia couldn't tell the difference between us either – seemingly. Was that my fault? Fair enough, she was Fred's girl first – unless you counted her husband, and to some extent you did have to count him: six foot five, he is, and it isn't only because he's the blacksmith that they call him in the village, Black Will. But she switched to me of her own accord, didn't she? – even if I wasn't too quick to disillusion her, the first time she started with her carryings-on, mistaking me for Fred. '*I* can't help it if she fancies me more than you, now,' I said to Fred.

'You'll regret this, you two-timing, double-crossing bastard,' said Fred: he always did have a filthy temper, Fred.

Well, I did regret it: and not so very long after. Fred and me shares a car between us – a heavy old bashed-up, fourth-hand 'family model', but at least it goes. And one evening, when he'd slouched off, ugly and moody as he was those days, to poach the river down by the Vicarage woods, I picked up Lydia and took her out in it, joy-riding. Not that there was much joy in it. We hadn't been out twenty minutes when, smooching around with Lydia, I suppose, not paying enough attention to the road – well, I didn't see the kid until I'd hit him. Jogging along the grass verge he was, with his little can of blackberries: haring home as fast as his legs would go, a bit scared, I daresay, because the dark was catching up on him. Well – the dark caught him up all right: poor little bastard. I scrambled out and knelt down and turned him over; and got back again, quick. 'He's gone,' I said to Lydia, 'and we'd best be gone too.' She made a lot of fuss, woman-like, but what was the point of it? If he wasn't dead now, he would be mighty soon, there wasn't any doubt of it:

lying there with the can still clutched in his fat little hand and the blackberries spilt, and scattered all around him. I couldn't do nothing; if I could have I daresay I'd have waited, but I couldn't. So what was the use of bringing trouble on myself, when the chances were that I could get clear away with it?

And I did get clear away with it. The road was hard and dry, the cars that followed and stopped must have obscured my tyre marks, if there were any. They found half a footprint in the dried mud, where I'd bent over him; but it was just a cheap, common make of shoe, pretty new so it had no particular marks to it; and a largish size, of course, but nothing out of the ordinary. No one knew I'd been on that road – everything Lydia did with us two was done in deep secret, because of Black Will. Will was doing time at the moment, for beating up a keeper who came on him, poaching (we all spent most of our evenings poaching). But he'd be back some day.

And Fred promised me an alibi, when I told him about it: clutching at his arm, shaking a bit by this time, losing confidence because Lydia was threatening to turn nasty. 'I'll say you was in the woods with me,' he said. And he did, too. They came to our door, 'regulation police enquiries'; but Lydia wouldn't dare to tell, not really, I could see that in the light of day, and they had no other sort of reason to suspect me, especially. And nobody did – it could have been any stranger, speeding along the empty country roads. Fred pretended to be reluctant to alibi me, cagey about saying where we was – because of the poaching. He managed it fine, it sort of threw their interest halfway in a different direction. I thought it was decent of Fred, considering about me and Lydia. But brotherly love is a wonderful thing, isn't it?

Or isn't it? Because it hadn't been all for nothing. No sooner was I clear of that lot than he says to me: 'Well – has she told you?'

'Told me what?' I says. 'Who? Lydia?'

'Lydia,' he says. 'She's having a baby.'

'Well, don't look at me,' I said, and quick. 'I've only been going with the girl a couple of weeks.'

'And her husband hasn't been going with her at all,' said Fred. 'On account of he's been in prison for the past five months.'

'For half killing a man,' I said, thoughtfully; and I looked Fred up and down. Fred and me are no weeds, like I said; but Black Will, he's halfway to a giant.

'And due out at the end of October,' said Fred.

'Well, good luck to the two of you,' says I. 'It's nothing to do with me. I had her for a couple of weeks, and now even that's over. She reckons I ought to have stopped and seen to the kid: she's given me the bird.'

'She'll give you more than the bird,' he says 'and me too when Will comes home. When he knows about the baby, he'll beat the rest out of her; and then God help you and me too.'

'The baby could be Jimmy Green's,' I said. 'Or Bill Bray's. She's been out with them, too.'

'That's her tales,' he said, 'to make you jealous. They're a sight too scared of Will to let Lydia make up to them. And so ought you and I to have been too, if we'd had any sense.' Only where Lydia was concerned, there never seemed to be time to have sense; and six months ago, Fred said, Black Will's return had seemed like an aeon away. 'So what are you going to do?' I said.

'What are *you* going to do?' he said. 'A hit-and-run driver – you can get a long stretch for that. The kid wasn't dead yet, when they found him.'

Good old brotherly love! – Fred worrying about me, when after all I *had* pinched his girl. And him in such trouble himself.

We went out in the car, where no one could hear us: our old landlady's pretty deaf and takes no interest at all in our comings and goings, but Fred wasn't taking no chances . . .

Because it was all Fred's idea: that I will say, and stick to it – it was Fred's idea. Dead men tell no tales, said Fred; nor dead girls, neither. 'If they find she's in the family way – it's like you said, she was spreading it around she'd been going with half the village. Once she was past talking, Will couldn't pin it on us two: not to be certain.'

'Speak for yourself,' I said.

'She'd be past talking about the hit-and-run, too,' he said. 'You say she's sore about that. She won't tell now, because it means admitting she was joyriding with you; but once Black Will gets it out of her that she was – and he will – then she'll tell about the accident too; it'll make her feel easier.'

'So what do you suggest?' I said. '*I'm* not killing the girl, I can tell you that, flat.'

'No,' he said. 'I'll do that. You've done one killing,' he said, not too pleasantly, I thought, 'that'll do for you. All I want from you now is an alibi.'

'What, me alibi you?' I said. 'No one'd believe it for a minute. One twin speaking up for another – the whole village would testify how "close" we are.' (The whole village not knowing anything about us and Lydia.)

But Fred had thought of all that too. If a straight alibi failed, he said, there were other ways of playing it. He had it all worked out – suspiciously well worked out, I ought to have thought; but he gave me no time for thinking. 'It won't come to any alibi, our names probably won't even come into it – as you say, the baby could be fathered on half the male population of Birdswell. But if it does – well, you alibi for me, I alibi for you; they'll know it was one of us, but they'll never know which of us; and if they don't know which of us, they'll have to let both of us go.'

'And Black Will?' I said. 'When we've not only seduced his wife, but murdered her – which one of us will *he* let go?'

'Oh, well,' he said, 'we'd have to clear out anyway, if it got as far as that: start again somewhere else. But the chances are a hundred to one it'll never come to it. After all, no one suspected you of the hit-and-run affair.'

He kept coming back to that: and sort of – nastily. I didn't forget that I'd done him wrong, pinching his girl. But that was his lever, really: while he kept reminding me, he could pretty well force me to go in with him – he was in trouble, but I was in trouble deeper.

So we worked it out: we worked out everything, to the last detail. This was Tuesday, we'd do it Thursday night. I'd see nothing more of the girl; but he'd get her to go driving with him on pretence of talking over the baby business. And he'd lead round to the accident, advising her, maybe, to confess to the police it was me; and drive past where it happened. And get her to get out of the car and show him where the boy was lying . . . And then – well, then there'd be a second hit-and-run killing on that lonely corner. 'You got away with it,' he kept saying. 'Why not another?'

There was a kind of – well, justice, in it, I thought. After all, it was because she was threatening to tell about the hit-and-run that I was letting her be murdered. 'But what about clues?' I said. 'Even I left a footprint.'

He had worked that out too. He and I are the same size, of course, and most of our clothes are the same as one another's. Not for any silly reason of dressing identical, but simply because when he'd go along shopping, I'd go along too, and mostly we'd like the same things; or he'd buy something and it'd be a success, so I'd buy the same, later. We must dress the same on the night, he said, because of the alibi: and we checked our stuff over, shoes, grey flannels, shirts, without jackets – this all happened in September. Our blue poplins were in the wash – we'd worn them clean Sunday, and second-day Monday; so it would have to be the striped wool-and-nylon – a bit warm for this weather, if anyone remarked it, but we'd have to risk that, I said, we daren't ask the old woman to wash out our blue ones special. The last thing we wanted, was to do anything out of the ordinary. That was what the police looked for: the break in routine. That was asking for it.

Our shoes were the same: same size, same make, bought together; a rubber sole with bars across it, but, like I said, new enough not to be worn down, or have any peculiarities. And everything else we'd wear identical: not only for the alibi, but in case of bits caught in the girl's fingernails or what-not – you've only got to read the papers. Not that he meant to get near enough for that. But she might not – well, she might not kick-in at once, if you see what I mean; he might have to get out of the car and do something about it. And in case of scratches, he said, I'd better be prepared to get some scratches on my own hands too – we could say we'd been blackberrying or something.

'Blackberrying,' I said. 'That'd be bloody likely! We both detest blackberries, everybody knows it: or anyway, the old woman knows it, we never touch her blackberry pie.' I knew he'd only said it to remind me of the kid: him and his little can of blackberries, spilt all around him . . .

'Oh, well,' he said, 'say we got scratched pushing through the brambles down by the river. Do your poaching down by the bramble patch.'

But she didn't scratch him. It was all a bit grim, I think: he couldn't be sure she was properly done in and he had to get out of the car and have a look and – well, go back and take a second run at her. But she didn't have the strength left to scratch him. All the same, he looked pretty ghastly when finally we met in the moonlight, in the Vicarage woods. He didn't say anything, just stood there, staring at me with a sort of sick, white heaviness. I couldn't exactly say anything either; it was worse than, talking it over, I'd thought it ever would be. I sort of – looked a question at him; and he gave me a weary kind of nod and glanced away towards the river. It was easier to talk about my angle, so I said, at last: 'Well, I saw the Vicar.'

'But did he see you?' he said. We'd agreed on the Reverend, because he always walked across the church of a Thursday evening: you'd be sure of passing him, if you went at a certain time.

'Yes,' I said. 'He saw me. I gave a sort of grunt for "good evening" and he said "Going poaching?" and gave me a bit of a grin. You'd better remember that.' He nodded again but he said nothing more; and more to ease the silence than anything else, I said: 'Is the car all right? Not marked?'

'What does it matter if it is?' he said. 'It's marked all over, no one could say what's old or what's new: you know that, from bashing the boy.' As for bits of her clothing and – blood and all that, he'd had the idea of spreading a bit of plastic over the front of the car before he – well, did it. He produced the plastic folded in a bit of brown paper and we wrapped the whole lot round a stone and sank it, then and there, in the river. There was blood on the plastic all right. It gave me the shudders.

But next thing he said, I really had something to shudder at. He said: 'Anyway, *your* number's up, mate. She's shopped you.'

'Shopped me?' I said. I stood and stared at him.

'Shopped you,' he said. 'She'd already sent off an anonymous note to the police. About the hit-and-run.'

'How do you know?' I said. I couldn't believe it.

'She told me so,' he said. 'It was on her conscience.'

Her conscience. Lydia's conscience! I started to laugh,

a bit hysterical, I suppose, with the strain of it. He put his hand on my wrist and gave me a little shake. 'Steady lad,' he said. 'Don't lose your head. I'm looking after you.' It wasn't like him to be so demonstrative, but there you are – it's like the poem says, when times are bad, there isn't no friend like a brother. 'It's just a matter of slanting the alibi,' he said.

Well, we'd worked that out, too; like I said. There'd always be a risk that they wouldn't accept a brother's alibi, that we two was together. The other time, about the accident, they'd had no special reason to suspect me, they'd accepted that all right; but this might at any moment turn into a murder enquiry. And a murder enquiry into *us*, now they knew about the hit-and-run. But as he said – we had the alternative.

I hadn't counted on its being Inspector Cockrill. When I realised it was him – come all the way over from Heronsford – I knew they meant business. And to be honest, it struck a bit chill to the heart of me. A little man he is, for a policeman, and near retiring age, he must be – he looks like a grandfather; but his eyes are as bright as a bird's and they seem to look right into you. He came into the old woman's best parlour and he had us brought in there, and he looked us up and down. 'Well, well,' he said, 'the famous Birdswell twins! You certainly are identicals, aren't you?' And he gave us a look of a sort of fiendish glee, or so it seemed to me, and said: 'And devoted, I hear? An almost mystic bond, I hear? David and Jonathan, Damon and Pythias and all the rest of it? In fact,' he said, 'you might properly be called – blood brothers?'

We stood in front of him, silent. He said at last: 'Well, which is which? And no nonsense.'

We told him: *and* no nonsense.

'So you're the one that killed the child?' he said to me. 'And drove on, regardless.'

'I never was near the child,' I said. 'I was in the woods, on Monday evening – poaching.'

'Yours is the name stated in the anonymous letter.'

'I don't know who wrote the letter,' I said. 'But no one can tell us apart, me and my brother.'

'Even your fancy girl?' he said. 'It appears it was she who wrote the letter.'

'I don't know what you mean,' I said, 'by my fancy girl.'

'Well, everybody else does,' he said. 'All the village knows she was playing you off, one against the other. And grinning behind their hands, waiting for her husband's homecoming.'

'But all the village can't tell us two apart,' I said. 'I was out poaching.'

'That's a damn lie,' says Fred, playing it the way we'd agreed upon. 'That was me, poaching.'

'One of you was poaching?' says Inspector Cockrill, very smooth. 'And one of you was with the lady? And even the lady couldn't have said which was which?'

He said it sort of – suggestive. 'I daresay she might,' I said, 'later on in the proceedings. But there couldn't have been any proceedings that night, there wouldn't have been time: because the accident happened.'

'Why should she say so positively that it was you, then?'

'I daresay she thought it was,' I says. 'I daresay he told her so. She'd finished with him: it would be the only way he could get her.'

'I see,' said Inspector Cockrill. 'How very ingenious!' I didn't know whether he meant how ingenious of Fred to have thought of it then, or of me to think of it now.

'Don't you listen to him, sir,' says Fred. 'He's a bloody liar. I wasn't with the girl that night. I tell you – I was poaching.'

'All right, you were poaching,' said Inspector Cockrill. 'Any witnesses?'

'Of course not. You don't go poaching with witnesses. I used to go with him,' says Fred, bitterly gesturing with his head towards me, 'but not since he pinched my girl, the bloody so-and-so.'

'And last night?' says the Inspector softly. 'When the girl was murdered?'

'Last night too, the same,' said Fred. 'I was in the woods, poaching.'

'You call *me* a liar!' I said. 'It was me in the woods. The Vicar saw me going there.'

'It was me the Vicar saw,' said Fred. 'I told him, Good evening, and he laughed and said. "Going poaching?"'

'There!' said Inspector Cockrill to me, like a teacher patiently getting the truth from a difficult child. 'How could he know *that*? Because the Vicar will surely confirm it?'

'He knows it because I told him,' I said. 'I told him I'd been poaching and I hoped the Vicar hadn't really realised where I was going.'

'Very ingenious,' said Inspector Cockrill again. 'Ve-ry ingenious.' It seemed like he couldn't get over it all, sitting there, shaking his head at the wonder of it. But I knew he was playing for time, I knew that we'd foxed him.

And Fred knew too. He suggested, reasonably: 'Why should you be so sure, sir, that the girl was murdered? Why not just a second hit-and-run?'

'A bit of a coincidence?' said Inspector Cockrill, mildly. 'Same thing, in the same place and so very soon after? And when on top of it, we find that the girl was threatening a certain person with exposure, about the *first* hit-and-run . . .' He left it in the air. He said to his sergeant: 'Have you collected their clobber?'

'Yessir,' said the sergeant. 'Two pairs of shoes' – and

he gave the Inspector a sort of nod, as if to say, Yes, they look as if they'll match very nicely – 'and all the week's laundry.'

'Including Monday's?' says Cockrill.

'Including Monday evening's, sir. The old woman washes of a Monday morning. Anything they've worn after that – which includes two shirts to each, sir – is in two laundry baskets, one in each bedroom.'

'Two baskets?' he says, looking more bright eyed than ever. 'That's a bit of luck. Their laundry's kept separate, is it?'

'Yes, it is,' says Fred, though I don't know what call he had to butt in. 'His in his room, mine in mine.'

'And no chance of its getting mixed up?' said Inspector Cockrill. He fixed Fred with that beady eye of his. 'This could be important.'

Fred, of course, was maintaining the mutual-accusation arrangement we'd agreed upon. 'Not a chance, sir,' he said a bit too eagerly.

I wasn't going to be left out. I said: 'Not the slightest.'

'That's right, sir,' says the sergeant. 'The old lady confirms it.'

'Good,' said Cockrill. He gave a few orders and the sergeant went away. People were still buzzing about, up in our bedrooms. 'I'm coming,' called up the Inspector, to someone at the head of the stairs. He turned back to us. 'All right, Cain and Abel,' he said, 'I'll leave you to stew in it. But in a day or two, as the song says, "I'll be seeing you." And when I do, it'll be at short notice. So stick around, won't you?'

'And if we don't?' I said. 'You've got nothing against us, you can't charge us; you've got no call to be giving us orders.'

'Who's giving orders?' he said. 'Just a little advice. But before you ignore the advice – take a good, hard, look at yourselves. You won't need any mirrors. And ask yourselves,' he said, giving us a good, hard, long look on his own account, from the soles of our feet to the tops of our flaming red heads, 'just how far you'd get . . .'

So that was that; and for the next two days, we 'stewed in it': David and Jonathan, Cain and Abel – like he'd said, blood brothers.

On the third day, he sent for us, to Heronsford police station. They shoved Fred into one little room and me in another. He talked to Fred first, and I waited. All very chummy, fags and cups of tea and offers of bread and butter: but it was the waiting . . .

Long after I knew I couldn't stand one more minute of it, he came. I suppose they muttered some formalities, but I don't remember: Fred and I might hate one another, and by this time we did, well and truly, there's no denying it – but it was worse, a thousand times worse, without him there. My head felt as though it were filled with grey cotton-wool, little stuffy, warm clouds of it. He sat down in front of me. He said: 'Well – have you come to your senses? Of course, you killed her?'

'If anyone killed her,' I said, clinging to our patter, 'it must have been him.'

'Your brother?' he said. 'But why should your brother have killed her?'

'Well,' I says, 'if the girl was having a baby—'

'A baby?' he says, surprised; and his eyes got that bright, glittering look in them. He said after a minute of steady thinking: 'But she wasn't.'

'She wasn't?' I said. 'She *wasn't*? But she'd told him—'

Or hadn't she told him? Something, like an icicle of light, ice-cold, piercing, brilliant, thrust itself into the dark places of my cotton-wool mind. I said: 'The bloody, two-timing, double-crossing bastard . . . !'

'*He* didn't seem,' said the Inspector, softly, 'to expect her to have been found pregnant.'

So that was it! So *that* was it! So as to get me to agree

to the killing, to get me to assist with it . . . I ought to have been more fly – why should Fred, of all people, be so much afraid of Black Will as to go in for murder? Will's a dangerous man, but Fred's not exactly a softie . . . The icicle turned in my mind and twisted, probing with its light-rays into the cotton-woolliness. Revenge! Cold, sullen, implacable revenge upon the two of us – because Lydia had come to me: because I had taken her. Death for her: and I to be the accomplice in her undoing – in my own undoing. And for me . . . I knew now who had sent the anonymous note about the hit-and-run accident: so easily to be 'traced' (after she was dead) to Lydia.

But yet – he was as deep in it as I was: deeper, had he but known it. I said, fighting my way up out of the darkness: 'Even if she *had* been pregnant, it wouldn't have been my fault. I'd only been going a couple of weeks with the girl.'

'That's what you say,' he said.

'But all the village—'

'All the village knew there were goings-on; nobody knew just where they went on, or when. You must, all three, have been remarkably careful.'

I tried another tack. 'But if she wasn't pregnant – why should I have killed her?'

'You've just told me yourself that you thought she was,' he said.

'Because he told me – my brother told me. Now, look, Inspector,' I said, trying to think it out as I went along, trying to ram it home to him, 'you say she wasn't having a baby? So why should I have thought she was? *She* wouldn't have told me, if she hadn't been: why should she? It was he who told me: it was my brother. But you say yourself, he knew it wasn't true. So why should he have told me?'

He looked at me, cold as ice. He said: 'That's easy. He wanted you to kill her for him.'

He wanted *me* to kill her! I could have laughed. The thing was getting fantastic, getting out of hand; and yet at the same time I had the feeling that the fantasy was a hard, gripping, grim fantasy, that, once it had its hold on me, would never shake loose. I stammered out: 'Why should he have wanted her killed?'

'Because,' he said, 'she was threatening to tell that it was he who ran the child down, and left it to die.' And he said, cold and bitter: 'I have no wish to trap you. We know that it was your brother who killed the child: we have proof of it. And we know it was you who killed the girl. We have proof of that too: there's her blood on your cuff.'

On my cuff. Where he had put his hand that night: taking my wrist in his grasp, giving me a brotherly little shake 'to steady me'. I remembered how I'd thought, even then, that it wasn't like him to be so demonstrative.

Putting his hand on my wrist – fresh from the blood-smeared plastic. Making such a point, later on, about there being no chance of our soiled shirts getting confused, one with the other's . . .

So there it is. I wonder if we'll be doing our time in the same prison? – sharing the same cell, maybe? – we two blood brothers . . .

Because he'll be doing time all right, as well as me. While I'm doing my time for *his* killing of the girl – he'll be doing his, for my killing of the child.

Well – that's all right with me. He'll be first out, I daresay (is it murder to leave a kid to die, in case, when he gets better, he tells? I suppose not: the actual knocking-down would be accidental, after all). So Fred'll be out, first: and Black Will will be there to meet him when he comes. By the time I get out, I daresay Will will be 'in' for what he done to Fred; may even have got over it all by then – it looks like being a very long time away.

But can you beat it? – working it out so far ahead,

leading up to it so softly, so craftily . . . And all for revenge: revenge on his own twin brother!

After all, what *I* did, was done in self-preservation: there was no venom in it, I wished him no harm. That night after the accident, I mean: when, clutching his arm, begging him to help me – just to be on the safe side, I rubbed his sleeve with the juice of a blackberry.

Duello

HENRY WADE

DETECTIVE FILE

OFFICER: Inspector John Poole

FORCE: CID, Scotland Yard

TIME: 1930

CASES: *Policeman's Lot* (1933), *Bury Him Darkly*
(1936), *Lonely Magdalene* (1940), *Too Soon To Die*
(1953), *Gold Was Our Grave* (1954) etc.

PROFILE: A deceptively ordinary-looking man in
appearance, John Poole is a hidden dynamo of energy
who mixes good manners with tact and exceptional
judgment of character. He has an easy smile and his
steady grey eyes often sparkle when he is on the verge of
uncovering a clue. College educated and entering the
Force at police training school in 1929, he has risen
quickly through the ranks to become the youngest
Inspector in Scotland Yard's CID squad, where he is
often assigned the cases that others are nervous about
handling. By 1953 his career reaches its climax when he
is promoted to the rank of Chief Inspector, and he marks
the landmark in *Too Soon To Die* by solving a particularly tricky murder case that is related to the devious
attempts by a wealthy family to avoid inheritance tax and
financial ruin.

CREATOR: Henry Wade, whose real name was Baronet

Henry Aubrey-Fletcher (1887–1969), was a former Grenadier Guardsman who won the DSO and Croix de Guerre while on active service in the First World War. After leaving the army, he held several honorary positions in Buckinghamshire, including JP and High Sheriff, and devoted the rest of his time to writing crime novels, the majority of which featured Inspector Poole. In so doing he earned himself the accolade of 'one of the really major figures of the Golden Age of the mystery story', from the American critic Charles Shibuk. As a master of the realist police novel, Wade has been compared to Freeman Wills Crofts, but sadly few of his books have remained in print since his death. Apart from the precise young CID man Poole, he also wrote a number of stories about Constable John Bragg, described as 'inquisitive as a mongoose, unshakeable as a bulldog'. Amongst Henry Wade's short stories about Inspector Poole, 'Duello' has a particular interest for me – not only because of the ingenuity that the CID man shows in solving a double killing, but because it is set partly in Enfield where I was born and partly in Broxbourne, Hertfordshire, where I began my working life as an author and anthologist!

***

'Like the good old times, isn't it? All for the love of a lady.'

The speaker was a uniformed police Superintendent, ponderous in build and patriarchal in manner. His companion was a considerably younger man in plain clothes, whose firm mouth and steady grey eyes were becoming only too well known to the underworld – Detective Inspector Poole, of the CID. The two men were standing on a stretch of sodden grass – a clearing in a wood; at their feet lay two other men, both in evening clothes – short coat, black tie, one wearing a white waistcoat, one a black – and both dead. In the right hand of each was clasped a small automatic pistol and each white shirt-front was saturated with a dark smear of blood.

'Lady or money, Superintendent. Hardly politics in these days, I'm afraid. Who found them?'

'Sergeant Robins, here. A farm labourer reported at Broxbourne this morning that there was an empty car with its lights on standing outside Cowheath Wood – this wood. Robins jumped on a bike and came along, found the car, did a bit of exploring into the wood and came across these chaps. Like a sensible fellow he got straight back to his station and telephoned for me – Enfield, my headquarters are. I came along with the doctor, had a look – and went off myself and telephoned to the Yard – and here you are. Dr Vammer just confirmed fact of death, then I sent him away and said we'd have him back later.'

Poole stroked his chin thoughtfully.

'You had some reason for calling in the CID, Superintendent. On the face of it, it's a job you could have tackled yourself.'

Superintendent Cox chuckled.

'Yes, Mr Poole,' he said. 'I had a reason; you'll probably spot it for yourself when you've had a look round.'

Poole nodded.

'If it's not a straightforward case,' he said, 'footprints are going to be important – can you tell me how much the ground's been disturbed?'

'I think so. Robins showed me exactly the line he'd followed, in and out – he didn't come closer than ten paces or so – said he knew a stiff when he saw one. The doctor and I followed in his footsteps – as you and I have just done; of course we came right up but we didn't trample round. I think you'll find their footmarks quite distinct from ours. Now you go ahead.'

For a minute or so Poole continued to gaze down at the bodies of the two duellists – as apparently they were. One was a middle-aged man of fair size – perhaps five feet ten, but not heavily built. The other was younger and smaller, of rather dapper type, but possessed – Poole thought – of an excellent pair of shoulders. He lay on his side, with one arm flung out behind him – the right arm, in the hand of which was clasped the .38 Colt. Glancing at his feet, with a view to identifying footprints, the detective saw that they were small, even for his size, and that the evening shoes had sharply pointed toes. The older man's feet were larger, and the shoes squarer, there should be no difficulty in distinguishing the two footprints, though there was probably no importance in them.

'Square Toes' also lay on his side, his knees slightly drawn up, one ankle turning inwards in a curiously unnatural manner. His hand, also, clasped a .38 Colt; it seemed as if the two men must have fired simultaneously, at very close range, though not so close as to leave powder marking on the linen shirt-fronts. It was an intriguing affair; such a thing as a duel was almost unheard of in these days and in this case it seemed as if the men had been bent upon killing each other, without thought of one surviving.

'Know who they are, sir?'

Superintendent Cox drew some papers from his pocket.

'One comes from Cheshunt – this one – George Horne; here's his card. The other hadn't a card but he had some letters, addressed to Julian de Lange, Cadorna Mansions, Putney. I don't know anything about either of them, though Cheshunt's in my division; enquiries being made now about Horne.'

'Right, sir. I'll telephone to the Yard to look up de

Lange. Odd position this chap Horne's in – that ankle, I mean.'

Poole took hold of the legs of the older man and tried to straighten them, but they were quite immovable. De Lange's legs were nearly straight but they also were quite stiff.

'Doctor say anything about time of death, sir?'

'He put it between twelve and three; Horne's *rigor* was a bit more advanced, but he's an older man – arteries harder.'

With considerable difficulty the detective disengaged the Colt from Horne's hand, drew out the magazine, extracted the round from the chamber, and looked down the barrel.

'The worse of these automatics is that it's so jolly difficult to tell how many rounds have been fired,' he said. 'The good old-fashioned revolver kept its spent cartridge in the cylinder – you only had to count. These things spit them out as they reload and you have to hunt on the ground – you can never be sure if you've found all there are. Are you an expert on guns, sir? Can you tell by the fouling of the barrel how many shots have been fired?'

Superintendent Cox shook his head.

'I can't, and I doubt if anyone else can – within a round. There's not much fouling in this, but I can't guarantee that only one shot's been fired. What's the doubt? They could hardly have missed each other at this range.'

Poole smiled.

'Scotland's Yard's got to justify your calling it in, sir,' he said.

A similar examination was made of de Lange's Colt, with equally indeterminate result.

'I'll just go over these footprints before I look for the shell,' said Poole.

Although the ground was soft enough to take a good impression wherever the earth was exposed, there was so much grass that no clear line of tracks could be distinguished. In the clearing where the bodies lay Poole had the greatest difficulty in picking out any distinct footprints, but nearer the edge of the wood – under the trees – there was no grass, only moss with many bare patches of earth. Here – in a line between the bodies and the deserted car – were several clearly defined footprints which Poole, a shoe from each victim in his hands, had no difficulty in identifying as those of the dead men. 'Pointed Toes' – de Lange – gave particularly clear marks, except where in one or two places those of 'Square Toes' were partially superimposed upon them.

The detective spent a considerable time over these footprints; finally, he called to the Superintendent, who was still standing by the bodies.

'Which of those men would you say was the heavier, sir?'

Mr Cox studied the bodies with a practised eye.

'Horne, I should say; he's inches taller. De Lange has got big shoulders, of course – may have the bigger bones.'

'There's no doubt about it from these tracks; de Lange is distinctly the heavier – his impressions are definitely deeper than Horne's.'

He stood for a while in silence, studying the tracks at his feet.

'It's a funny thing, sir,' he said. 'These men came here with the obvious intention of killing each other – look at the range they fired at, with both pistols loaded – and yet one wasn't afraid of being murdered by the other. These tracks show that de Lange walked in front, and Horne followed behind him – could easily have shot him in the back. Psychology's an odd thing. Well, sir, I suppose we must go to Cheshunt now; I'll just have a hunt round for those shells. The bodies can go off to the doctor; will you ask him to weigh them, sir, and let me know at the Cheshunt station.'

A thorough search of the ground round the bodies produced, as was to be expected, two spent cartridge-cases. Although the grass was fairly long, Poole felt pretty sure that there were no more. He next turned his attention to the car; it was a 12 hp Yorrick saloon, fairly new – its upholstery clean and yielding no clue of any sort. Poole got leave to borrow it and also Sergeant Robins; taking leave of the Superintendent he drove off towards Cheshunt.

Having learnt from the local police that Mr George Horne was a married man with no children, living in a small house called Five Oaks, about half a mile west of the town, Poole decided to call upon the Vicar, with the double object of getting him to break the news to the widow and of learning any local gossip.

Rev. James Partacle was an elderly man with an obviously sympathetic nature. He was genuinely distressed by the news brought by the detective and at once bustled off on his painful errand, murmuring, 'Poor girl; poor young girl.' Mrs Partacle, to whom the Vicar referred Poole for information, was perhaps more worldly than her husband; she was deeply intrigued by the detective's news and was able and willing to throw considerable illumination upon it.

The Hornes, it appeared, had come to Five Oaks soon after their marriage four years previously. For a time they appeared a happy and attached couple, but as time went on it became evident that Quirril Horne, a pretty and excitable woman at least ten years younger than her husband, was finding life on the outskirts of a London suburb extremely dull. For a time this difficulty was met by her husband taking her two or three nights a week to theatres and nightclubs in London, but this life soon began to tell upon a hardworked City man and gradually he became more reluctant to take her, more fretful when he did. There was nothing unusual in the situation – it was a commonplace of postwar life – but none the less a tragedy.

Inevitably as her husband cooled off Mrs Horne began to look for other cavaliers; she had no difficulty in finding them. There had been no actual scandal but there was 'talk'; a London 'gigolo' was mentioned. There were no children to draw the couple together; they were drifting (so Mrs Partacle) to – this.

When the Vicar returned, Poole learnt that Mrs Horne, who had been 'desperately worried' at her husband's absence, was now 'prostrated with grief'. The Vicar trusted that it would not be necessary to intrude upon her sorrow. Poole gave a non-committal reply, thanked Mr and Mrs Partacle for their help, and drove straight to Five Oaks. Leaving Sergeant Robins in the car outside the drive gate, Poole walked towards the house. The drive, some fifty yards long, was of new, well-kept gravel and showed clearly the single track of a car, the tyres being of the same make as those borne by the Yorrick. From the Cheshunt police Poole had discovered that there had been heavy rain on the previous night from about nine to eleven p.m. – probably the car had gone out after eleven and had come in (if it had been out at all that day) before nine.

A red-eyed maid admitted Poole, informed him that Mrs Horne was in the drawing-room and added that she was in a 'terrible state, crying her head off'. The detective was suitably impressed and asked for a few words with his informant in the kitchen. As they passed down the passage the girl jerked her thumb at a door. Poole paused for a moment and heard the sound of deep sobbing within – it was indeed a severe attack that should last half an hour after the breaking of the news by the kindly Vicar.

In the kitchen Poole learnt that the cook, who ordinarily lived in the house, was away till midday, having been given leave to attend her sister's wedding in Devonshire on the previous day. Ethel herself – the house parlourmaid – did not sleep in the house, but with her parents in Cheshunt. She had given Mr Horne his (cold) supper at 7.45 p.m. the previous evening – Mrs Horne was in London and not returning till late – and, after washing up and turning down the beds, had left the house at about ten p.m. There was, therefore (Poole observed), no independent witness of anything that might have occurred in the house after that hour. Ethel certainly did not know that Mr Horne was expecting anyone that evening, though of course he may have come after she left. Mr Horne always dressed for dinner, whether he was alone or not.

Having learnt so much, Poole thought he had kept Mrs Horne, who had probably heard the front doorbell ring, waiting long enough. Ethel was persuaded – against her will – to tap at the drawing-room door and announce him.

Mrs Horne, dressed in a fawn skirt and a striped jumper, was lying on a sofa, an embroidered shawl over her legs. She did not attempt to rise when Poole entered, but greeted him with the shadow of a smile and a gesture towards a chair. Her eyes were red, but her colour was high, and she gave the detective the impression of being hysterical rather than prostrated with grief.

Poole made the usual apology for intrusion, followed by the stock question as to when she had seen her husband last.

Quirril Horne put a lace handkerchief to her mouth and stared at the detective with wide-open eyes; she seemed to be stifling her emotion.

'Yesterday morning – when he went to catch – (sob) – his train. I went up – in the afternoon – to shop – I –

never – saw him again – oh my God.' She turned on her
side, buried her face in her arm, and sobbed wildly.

Poole allowed a minute to pass.

'And when did you see Mr de Lange last?' he asked
quietly.

The sobs ceased abruptly. Slowly Quirril lifted her
head and looked at the detective, her eyes large with
innocent surprise.

'De Lange?' she said. 'Who's he?'

'The man who was found dead beside your husband. I
thought perhaps he was a – an acquaintance of yours.'

Mrs Horne sat bolt upright, her eyes flashing.

'Oh!' she exclaimed. 'How dare you? What are you
suggesting? Oh how monstrous!'

'I have suggested nothing, madam. I only asked . . .'

'Oh, but you did! You think he is my lover – that my
husband killed him – that they fought a duel for me. Oh,
what shall I do? How cruel! How terrible!'

There was no longer any anger in Mrs Horne's eyes,
but there was a sparkle of something else – was it
excitement? . . . Suddenly it dawned upon Poole that Mr
Partacle's 'poor young girl' was intensely enjoying the
scene!

The detective's manner changed at once. He rose to his
feet; when he spoke, his voice was cold and incisive.

'Mrs Horne, it is my duty to warn you of your
position. In the eyes of the law murder has been
committed; if you, being aware of the circumstances,
conceal your knowledge from the police, you are rendering yourself liable to be charged as an accessory either
before or after the fact. It is perfectly easy for the police
to find out whether or not you knew Mr de Lange and
when you were last with him. I strongly advise you to be
absolutely frank with me.'

Poole realised that he was talking like a magazine
detective but he felt sure that that was the only kind of

talk that Mrs Horne would appreciate. Certainly it had
the desired effect; Quirril altered her pose. Dropping her
voice into a low and earnest key she made what she
called her 'confession'. Julian de Lange had been her
lover. Her husband began to suspect their 'guilty passion'
(sic) and last night Julian – with whom she had been
dining and dancing in town – had insisted on coming
down with her and having it out with George. She herself
had retired to her bedroom ('What else could I do,
Inspector? My position was terrible!') and for half an
hour had listened to loud and angry voices from
downstairs. Then the front door had slammed, she heard
the garage doors pulled back and the car being started up
and driven away. She could not imagine what had
happened – had her husband driven away and left her?
Or had he merely driven his rival to the station to catch a
workman's train? ('An anticlimax that you'd have hated,'
thought Poole.)

'I lay awake all night,' Quirril concluded, 'racking my
brains, torturing myself with suspense. Oh, it was
horrible, horrible! And then this morning – Mr Partacle
coming – to hear that they were both dead – that they
had killed each other for me – what my feelings have
been – my remorse – my guilty remorse!'

Tears, sobs, heaving shoulders – all the reactions
familiar to the devotee of the cinema. The woman was
evidently quite incapable of genuine feeling – of appreci-
ating the true horror of her position.

Utterly disgusted, Poole decided to cut the 'scene'; he
would probably have to return to it, but he wanted fresh
air – morally as well as physically. There were one or two
points to be cleared up before he could decide whether
the case was as straightforward as it appeared or whether
the curious doubt that had come into his mind was based
upon solid foundations. Rejoining Sergeant Robins, he
drove the dead man's car back to Cheshunt police

station. The sergeant in charge at once handed him a message from the doctor who was examining the bodies. Both men had died of gunshot wounds inflicted some time between midnight and three a.m. There was nothing to show whether the wounds were self-inflicted or not; the weight of Horne was 12st. 12oz., and of de Lange 11st. 8oz.

Poole felt his interest, deadened as it had been by his disgust at Mrs Horne's behaviour, quicken into active life. Horne was more than a stone heavier than his rival and yet his footprints were appreciably less deep and clear than those of de Lange!

For twenty minutes Poole sat, wrapped in thought; by the end of that time he had worked out a theory that might cover the known facts. Driving the Hornes' Yorrick into the yard at the back of the police station, he went over it again with a magnifying glass, but without discovering anything either to confirm or disprove his theory. A reference to the Register of Firearms records was more enlightening and he drove back to Five Oaks with a grim tightening of his mouth.

Making his way this time to the back door, where he would not have to pass the drawing-room window, the detective gently knocked and was admitted by a flustered Ethel.

'Your master's dressing-room,' he said. 'Can you show it to me without letting Mrs Horne know?'

Ethel goggled but she led the way up a miniature back stairs in silence. The dressing-room was small but well furnished – a good mahogany wardrobe, a bow-fronted chest of drawers, and a boot-cupboard. It was to the latter that Poole turned his attention; opening the door he pulled out seven pairs of shoes and placed them side by side in a row on the floor – two pairs of black, one of brown, golf shoes, tennis shoes, old evening shoes and red slippers; with the exception of the latter they were all evidently built from the same last. Drawing from the small attaché case that he carried the evening shoe that he had removed from the dead man's foot for identifying footprints, he compared it carefully with the shoes in front of him; without a shadow of doubt they were also made from the same last.

'How many pairs has he got altogether?' asked Poole in a low voice. 'There'll be another pair of day shoes perhaps?'

Ethel was looking at the display with a puzzled expression. 'That's a funny thing,' she said. 'I can't call to mind ... oh, well, I suppose I did – I've been that flustered today.'

'What can't you remember?' asked Poole sharply.

'Cleaning them London shoes.'

'Do you mean the ones he was wearing when he came back from London yesterday? Probably they're still downstairs.'

'Not they; he didn't have but two pairs. It's one of them two,' said Ethel, whose grammar was not her strong point.

'You usually clean them; when?'

'Not till latish as a rule – morning I mean. Master, he'd take 'em off of an evening of course and I'd take 'em down to the pantry. But he always put on another pair and another suit come the morning – rested the molly-coddles or something, he said. I usen't as a rule to brush till after I'd cleared breakfast.'

'Had you cleared breakfast when I came this morning?'

'No I hadn't – not to say properly, I mean. One or two things I'd brought into the pantry, but I was that flustered-like, what with Master not being back and her that jumpy and excited ...'

'Then when did you clean the shoes?'

'I didn't. Leastways I s'pose I must 'a done. But I don't know when – I don't recollect doing it.'

Poole seized the two pairs of black shoes.

'Which pair was he wearing yesterday?' he asked.

The question seemed unreasonable, so twin were the two parts, but Ethel knew her job better than her quantities. She looked carefully at the pairs, then touched the ones in Poole's left hand.

'Them. That tag's gone – I noticed it yesterday morning.'

'Look at them carefully – can you tell me whether you cleaned them or not?'

'Well, look at them? They're clean enough, ain't they?' Ethel's voice had a tang of indignation.

'I mean did *you* clean them?'

The girl stared at him, looked at the shoes again, turned them over – and straightened herself abruptly. 'That I didn't – they ain't black under the arches – master was dead on that – look 'ere.' She seized the other pair and, turning both over, displayed the difference to Poole.

The detective rose slowly to his feet.

'The suit?' he said.

Ethel half turned towards the wardrobe, but stopped. 'I'll take my Davy it was still in the pantry when you come just now,' she said.

'Get it,' he returned, and to himself, 'Not likely to be that one.'

While the girl was away he hunted through the suits in the wardrobe but evidently found nothing that interested him. Nor did the suit of conventional London clothes brought by Ethel afford any enlightenment. Returning to the shoes he examined them carefully with a pocket magnifying glass and this time appeared satisfied with what he saw.

'That's enough to go on,' he muttered.

Dismissing Ethel, he quietly descended the front stairs and, after listening for a moment at the drawing-room door, walked straight in. To his surprise, he found Mrs

Horne still lying on the sofa, her legs covered with the embroidered shawl. He had not expected that a woman of her temperament would hold that pose so long. Without apology for his intrusion he came straight to the point.

'Would you mind telling me who looks after your husband's clothes, madam?' he asked.

Quirril stared at him in evident surprise.

'Why, Ethel, of course – the parlourmaid,' she replied after a pause.

'Nobody else?'

'No. Why should they?'

'You don't yourself do so?'

'Certainly not – I make him stockings sometimes, that's all.'

'You don't, for example, ever clean his shoes?'

For the first time Poole thought he saw genuine emotion in the girl's face – the emotion of fear.

She did not answer, but stared at him with hard eyes – a look which he returned. Suddenly, as he watched her, there came to him a possible explanation of her attitude – her physical attitude.

'Will you come with me and help me go through the things in his dressing-room?' he asked.

There was no mistaking the look on her face now.

'Why do you want to do that?' she asked harshly. 'Can't you leave me alone – the very day that my husband dies!'

Poole rose to his feet.

'It's my duty to go through his things – I must do it now,' he said.

She sat upright and seemed about to follow him, but checked herself and sank back on her cushions, putting her hand to her eyes.

'I feel so ill,' she said, weakly. 'I can't do it – do fetch a doctor or someone.'

'I'm going now,' the detective replied, inexorably, moving towards the door. But Quirril did not move and as he closed the door behind him Poole realised that his first stratagem had failed. Going to the kitchen, he gave some instructions to Ethel and slipped out into the garden. Making his way carefully to the drawing-room window he crouched down, with his head just below the sill. There was a minute's pause and the front door banged. Poole slowly raised his head till he could see into the room. Quirril Horne was sitting bolt upright on the sofa, staring at the door – her back was almost to him, so that he could not read the expression on her face, though he guessed it accurately enough. Again a pause and, unexpectedly, the door banged again. Poole saw his prey stiffen. Pause, and again a bang. Pause, bang. Pause, bang. Pause, bang. It was more than any nerves, however sound – and Quirril's surely were not that – could stand. Swinging her feet to the floor, she sprang up and took three quick steps towards the door, then staggered and came to an abrupt stop. For a moment she stood in the centre of the room, then turned and limped slowly back to the sofa. Poole could see her face now – on it was deeply engraved pain and misery. Pity for the first time stirred in his heart, mingling with the triumph that he felt at this complete confirmation of his guess.

Going back into the house, he stopped Ethel's door-banging activities and obtained from her the further information that he required. Then, with a rather heavy heart, he returned to the drawing-room.

'Mrs Horne,' he said. 'I may have to take you into custody on a charge of being concerned in the murder of either your husband or Mr de Lange. I am going to ask you some questions but I must warn you that what you answer may be used as evidence and that you are not obliged to answer if you do not want to.'

As he spoke he saw, to his intense astonishment,

Quirril's expression change from misery to alertness to excitement – almost pleasure. The dramatic value of the situation was outweighing her personal fears!

'Ask your questions,' she exclaimed. 'I will decide whether to answer them when I hear them.'

'Were you dancing with Mr de Lange in London last night?'

'You know I was – I told you. There's no crime in that.'

'Why did you stop?'

Quirril stared at him.

'Why? Because we'd had enough I suppose – no, it was because Julian wanted to come down here and have it out with George – I told you that too.'

'No other reason?'

'No – what do you mean?'

Poole leant forward.

'You didn't stop because you had rubbed the skin off your heels so badly that you couldn't walk three steps across a room?' he asked.

Slowly the colour ebbed out of the girl's face – fear again pushing the 'dramatic' into the background.

'I put it to you,' Poole followed up, 'that you rubbed the skin off your heels when you walked back from Cowheath Wood in your husband's shoes last night. Is that so?'

The girl buried her face in her hands and remained so, motionless, while the detective's calm, inexorable voice continued.

'In the Firearms Register of this district, Mrs Horne, your husband is registered as holding a .38 Colt automatic.'

A pause, but Quirril did not move.

'You are also registered as holding a similar automatic, Mrs Horne. These two weapons bear the numbers of, and in fact are the two that were found in the hands of the dead men this morning. I put it to you that you at least knew . . .'

Quirril flung up her head, her face once more flushed, her eyes sparkling.

'Yes, I knew!' she cried. 'And much more than that! You're a clever man, inspector; you'll find it all out in time. I'll tell you – no, no, don't stop me; I know what I'm doing. I'll tell you now – I may not if you take me to the police station. I told you that Julian wanted to have it out with George – that wasn't true; he didn't – it was the last thing he wanted. I got him down here, pretending George was away from home. You should have seen their faces when they met in this room! George simply blew up and Julian lost his temper too – it was terrific!'

The girl's eyes flashed with enjoyment of the recollection.

'I thought they'd fight, but instead of that they cooled off – they hadn't either of them got the guts. I don't mean they made it up – anything but – but they became coldly hating instead of hotly, as I wanted. George actually offered to drive Julian to the station, because it was raining! While he was gone for the car, I slipped my gun into Julian's hand and told him to shoot George – we could easily arrange it to look like suicide. He wouldn't – wanted to, but funked it – pushed the gun back at me. When George came back into the room I walked up to him and shot him myself through the heart.

'There was no one else in the house and not another house within earshot. I mopped up what little blood had got on to the carpet and filled Julian up with whisky – and a plan. I put on an old pair of George's flannel trousers and the shoes he'd been wearing and my own mac and a cap. I pretended it was because I should be less noticeable as a man than as a woman, but really of course it was to make footprints like George – Julian was too much of a fool to think of them.

'The car was already at the door – it had stopped raining. We drove to Cowheath Wood and Julian carried George to that clearing – I followed. We had put the gun into George's hand at once – after wiping off my fingerprints – and we arranged him (as Julian thought) to look like suicide. Then when Julian straightened up I shot him through the heart in exactly the same way with George's gun, that I'd got out of his desk – and there it was – a duel!

'Of course, I had to kill Julian. I'd have been in his power for ever if I hadn't – he was quite capable of blackmail. I killed George because I couldn't stand him any longer – and because – because – oh, you wouldn't understand that.'

The look in Quirril's eyes as she spoke was certainly a complex one – it would have needed, Poole thought, an alienist to interpret it fully.

'The grass was long in the clearing and down a ride that crossed the wood – I knew it well; we often used to picnic there. I felt sure my footprints wouldn't show on it if I shuffled along and that you would only look at the two tracks – George's and Julian's you would think, leading from the car to the bodies. I don't know what made you suspect me.'

She paused interrogatively, but as Poole remained silent, continued: 'I walked home but, though it was only two miles George's awful shoes rubbed the most ghastly places on my heels. I didn't notice – I was too excited – till the damage was done. I struggled home, burnt the trousers in the hot water furnace, cleaned George's shoes, and went to bed. When I woke up my feet were awful. I didn't dare stay in bed – I knew I should be made to get up and I couldn't let anyone see me walk into a room – so I dressed and lay on the sofa. I don't know how you spotted . . . Good God, Julian!'

Poole, who had been watching the girl's face, saw it

suddenly stiffen into a look of terror, her gaze fixed over his shoulder towards the door. He spun round, caught by the age-old and never-failing trick, and in that moment a revolver crashed.

'That's a type that I don't understand,' said Superintendent Cox, gazing down at the dead woman. Poole had repeated to him Quirril's extraordinary story and still more extraordinary manner.

'Wartime adolescence and postwar demoralisation,' said Poole. 'I've seen them in London – nightclubs full of them – though they don't generally go to such lengths. Lot of good qualities in her too – brains and pluck – up to the eyes in pluck.'

'I wonder there wasn't any blood in the car,' said the matter-of-fact Superintendent.

'She was too sharp for that, sir – wrapped him up in something I expect, and burnt it like the trousers. I looked for it, of course.'

'What put you on to it, Poole – that it wasn't what it looked?'

'Well, I knew you'd seen something, sir, or you wouldn't have called in the Yard. So I didn't take things for granted. Horne's ankle was the first thing – it was bent over. The fall couldn't have done that, and if it was permanent, it would have shown in the footprints, which were straight enough. It simply followed that he couldn't have made them. The bent ankle, too, suggested a cramped position, for a stiffening body in the car. Then there was the *rigor*. The doctor said Horne's was more advanced than de Lange's – suggested age as the cause: but Horne wasn't old or decrepit – a much simpler explanation was that he died earlier than de Lange did. Then again, those footprints – de Lange's, the lighter man's – more deeply marked than Horne's – why? Than Horne's? But Horne hadn't made them – then who had?

They were made with his shoes, without a shadow of doubt. Who had access to his shoes? His wife.

'Then there was Mrs Partacle's account of the Hornes; Mrs Horne's own extraordinary manner and what she called her "confession" – finally, the Firearms Register, showing her as the owner of one of the automatics. I was a damn fool, though, to forget that it showed him as holding a service revolver as well as the Colt; I ought to have searched for it – she'd got it under the cushions on the sofa all the time I suppose.'

There was silence for a moment, as the two men looked down at the still form, the shattered head now veiled by Poole's silk handkerchief.

The younger man was the first to speak.

'Will you tell me, sir, what made you think it wasn't straight?' Superintendent Cox chuckled.

'People don't fight duels nowadays,' he said. 'And besides, why were de Lange's shoes limed with clay but Horne's had only respectable drive gravel on them?'

The Suitcase

FREEMAN WILLS CROFTS

DETECTIVE FILE

OFFICER: Inspector Joseph French

FORCE: CID, Scotland Yard

TIME: 1956

CASES: *Inspector French's Greatest Case* (1924), *The 12.30 from Croydon* (1934), *Death of a Train* (1946), *The Mystery of the Sleeping Car Express* (1956) etc.

PROFILE: Known laconically to his colleagues at the Yard as 'Soapy Joe', Inspector Joseph French gives the impression of being easygoing and difficult to ruffle – which is most probably why the crime historian H. R. F. Keating has referred to him as 'the Mr Plod of fictional sleuths'. His comfortably dressed appearance and twinkling blue eyes match his unaggressive personality, which can, however, lure the unsuspecting law-breaker into drawing the wrong conclusions about his skills of detection. For patience is very much French's middle name and his always thorough investigations have proved him to be an expert manhunter with a unique ability to break seemingly unbreakable alibis. His thirty years of dedicated service have seen him rewarded with promotion to Chief Inspector and, finally, Superintendent. As a man who loves travel, French is always at his most perceptive when investigating crimes on the railways and he has broken a good many cases as a direct result of his knowledge of the rail system.

CREATOR: Freeman Wills Crofts (1879–1957) had actually been a construction engineer on the railways in Northern Ireland for over twenty years before a severe illness confined him to bed and he decided to while away the hours writing a crime novel. The result was *The Cask* (1920), in which the solution was arrived at through the use of timetables, and the book is widely regarded in crime fiction circles as a masterpiece as well as one of the definitive crime novels. Inspector French played the central role in many of Crofts's subsequent mysteries and earned the acclaim from critic Melvyn Barnes of being 'arguably the greatest police detective, whose solid and tireless work enabled countless readers to identify with his triumphs and frustrations'. The case of 'The Suitcase' is a fine example of 'Soapy Joe' at work on a murder case on the railway – solid and methodical as always in the face of what seems like a watertight alibi.

***

Albert Rank shivered in the chill wind which was blowing along the platform of Thorpe station on this late February afternoon. Wearing a thin, soiled waterproof and carrying a small suitcase, he shrank behind a stack of luggage. He wished to avoid notice, for he was on a terrible errand: no less than the murder of his enemy, David Turner.

Rank was porter, boots and general factotum in a small hotel in North London. He was a careful, hardworking man, unmarried, and three months earlier had been good-humoured, cheerful, and contented. Then all at once something seemed to go wrong, and one blow after another fell upon him, till he had reached his present unhappy situation.

It began about money. A friend of his was employed in a training stable, and from him Rank learnt that sure money was to be made out of horses, if only one had the necessary inside knowledge. This knowledge the friend claimed. Rank was persuaded to back the friend's fancy.

At first he had the usual beginner's luck, followed in due course by the usual disastrous losses. His difficulties increased till for the sake of a few pounds he was faced with the loss of his job and everything he held dear.

In his distress he lost his head. A large number of minor smash-and-grab raids had taken place in this North London area, all, it was believed, the work of one gang. Rank determined to try his hand at the game, believing that his work would be put down to the gang. It was of course fantastically foolish, but he felt sure he could get away with it.

The scene of his exploit was to be a small newsagent's shop. He had watched the place and knew that the ancient proprietor disappeared for tea each afternoon, leaving the young girl assistant in charge. On a dark and blustery November afternoon Rank entered, asked for cigarettes, and when the girl opened the cash register for change, he grabbed the little wad of notes it contained.

The affair didn't work out quite as he had hoped. There was a slight delay in releasing the notes from under their clip, and the girl's cries brought the proprietor running. Before Rank could get away the old man had seized him. To free himself Rank hit out. As he ran from the shop he saw his victim falling backwards. He got safely away, but next day he learnt from the papers that the man had struck his head in the fall and was dead.

Rank was overwhelmed. The last thing he had wished was to hurt anyone, and he would have given all he had many times over to bring the man back to life. Then, as the immediate horror dulled, fear for his own safety took its place. He sweated as he pictured the arrival at the hotel of two large men and with a shrinking terror thought of what might follow. But one, two, and three days passed without incident, and gradually he began to breathe more freely.

Then on the third evening the blow fell, though it was not the one he had been dreading. As he left the hotel for a short break a stranger fell in beside him.

'Name of Turner,' said the man. 'David Turner. You're Albert Rank?'

Rank admitted it.

'I saw what happened on Tuesday,' Turner continued. 'I heard the girl scream and I saw you run out. I waited till the police came and I told them.'

Rank's heart missed a beat. Then tremulously he muttered: 'You're mistaken. I was at no shop.'

'Quite,' the other answered. 'You can tell that to the police when the time comes.'

A remnant of Rank's courage was coming back. 'I don't believe you,' he declared. 'If you'd made an accusation the police would have come to question me. They haven't.'

'I'm not all that fool,' Turner replied. 'I told them I recognised your face but couldn't place you. But don't you make any mistake. I can remember who you are at any time, and then it'll be you for the eight o'clock walk.'

Rank glanced at the other's face. There was greed in it and an unholy joy, but of softness or mercy no trace. The man would do what he said. 'What do you want?' Rank asked thickly.

'Ah, that's better.' Turner's manner grew almost friendly. 'Half the swag and a pound a week and I'll forget what I saw. I mean as long as the pound goes on.'

Rank exclaimed at the extortion. He pleaded, he threatened, he declared he couldn't pay, all to no purpose. In the end, as he had known from the beginning, he had to agree.

When Turner left him he was in despair. From now on he would be in Turner's power. Sooner or later there would be further demands. A chance word might give him away: not merely his happiness nor his comfort, but his *life*! Only too clearly he saw that while Turner lived he would know neither safety nor happiness. Gradually the thought of the man's death became an obsession.

He had now learnt a good deal about Turner. He was a passenger guard and worked on the slower trains of the main East Coast route between London and Edinburgh. His way home led him past the hotel, and on different occasions he had noticed Rank.

Rank now wondered if some accident could happen along the line. As he thought over it almost unconsciously a plan formed in his mind. He would travel by one of Turner's trains. He would get him alone in his van. And then –!

It was for this purpose that, with a heavy cosh hidden under his clothes, he was now at Thorpe station awaiting the London train. At 5.30 to the minute it came in. From previous inspection he had learnt that the dining-car was the sixth from the rear and that the five coaches between it and the van were of the side-corridor type, with luggage shelves and lavatories at their ends. He also knew that only one guard was in charge: his enemy, David Turner.

Unostentatiously mingling with the crowd, Rank approached the train. He was the last to get into the coach immediately behind the dining-car. There he placed his suitcase on one of the shelves, got out again, and strolled along the platform to the last coach. He climbed in, quietly entered the lavatory beside the van and bolted the door, having gripped the handles in his handkerchief. A few seconds later the train started.

From Thorpe to Selcaster, the next stop and for which Rank held a third single, was an hour's run. During it he had counted on the corridor being clear, for at this time of year the train was seldom crowded, and the first dinner was not served till after Selcaster.

At zero hour he left the lavatory and passed through the swaying vestibule into the van. When Turner saw him he jumped up.

'Good Lord, Rank! What's the ruddy idea?'

'Just a word with you, Turner.'

'Not here. If you're seen I'll get it in the neck.'

'I'll not be a minute. See, I've got a scheme with money in it, but it would take two to get it. Will you join me?'

This was an opening which Turner could not resist. He hesitated, and Rank drew a paper from his pocket. It bore an imaginary plan. 'House, full of valuables and empty. Not overlooked. See, here's a sketch.'

As Turner grudgingly bent forward to examine the paper, Rank struck. Turner pitched forward and lay motionless.

A wave of sheer terror swept over Rank as he straightened up and put away his cosh. Now he was in real danger. If a passenger were to come into the van, he was as good as hanged. He felt an overwhelming urge to rush from the place.

He fought it down. Failure to stick to his plan would mean certain disaster. He must indeed get as far from the van as possible, but not by headlong flight. That near lavatory would not be far enough, for at Selcaster porters would be grouped where the van stopped, and he might be seen leaving. Therefore he must pass unnoticed along the corridor. He had worked out how this was to be done.

He slipped the sketch into his pocket and drew on a pair of rubber gloves. Then, setting his teeth, he knelt down and began to strip the uniform off the body. He found it harder than he had expected. Indeed, he grew panicky, it took so long. But at last it was done. Quickly he put on the uniform over his own clothes, coat and all. This was why he had shivered in a featherweight waterproof. Owing to Turner's being about his height, but of a sturdier build, the uniform fitted reasonably well. Indeed, it was this fact of their relative sizes that had suggested his plan. With rubber pads in his cheeks and the peak of the uniform cap pulled low over his eyes, he was satisfied no one would recognise him, specially in the dimly lit corridor.

One other precaution remained to be taken. Before leaving the van he made a space in a pile of luggage, dragged the body in, and covered it with suitcases. Discovery of the crime at Selcaster was inevitable, but not, he hoped, till he had left the station.

Having glanced quickly round to make sure he had forgotten nothing, he left the van, and summoning all his strength of will, walked in a leisurely yet businesslike way down the corridor. To his relief he met no one. At last he reached the end of the fifth coach and drew the door to behind him. He was now in the little space containing the luggage shelves, the lavatory, and the vestibule leading to the dining-car. Picking up his suitcase, he went into the lavatory. As he bolted the door some of his anxiety dropped away from him. The worst was now over and so far all had gone well.

The suitcase contained his overcoat and a hat. Having taken these out, he stripped off the guard's uniform and his rubber gloves and, together with the cosh, cap, and waterproof, packed them in the case. His plan required it to be weighted but the weight must not take up much room. He had found the very thing in an old cast-iron door from the front of the patent stove in the hall of his hotel. This door, which had been renewed because its enamel had been burnt off, had been left beside the rubbish bin for the dustmen to take away. Rank had protected himself here too. If its absence were noticed, it would naturally be assumed that the men had taken it.

At last the train began to slacken speed and presently drew in to the platform at Selcaster. Rank stepped out and walked off, neither dawdling nor hurrying. He reached the exit in the middle of a throng of others, handed up his ticket, and left the station. A sigh of relief burst from him. Now he was practically safe. One further precaution and he would be absolutely so.

He knew Selcaster, in fact he had prospected it for the purpose of this very expedition. He turned along the river and soon reached a suburban area and an outlying bridge. Though the wind had fallen, it remained cold and raw and there were few people on the roads. Rank passed on to the bridge, which was deserted. Halfway across he took a cord from his pocket, put it through the handle of the suitcase, and lowered the latter from the parapet. When it reached the water he let go one end of the cord and the suitcase sank without splash or sound. Returning to the centre of the town, he boarded a bus to Wrexborough, a town some fifteen miles along the railway to the south. There he walked about till the next train left for London. He took a single ticket and joined it without incident.

As he sat in his third-class compartment he went over what he had done. Yes, he was safe! He had left absolutely no clue whatever. No detective officer, no matter how skilful and gifted, could possibly trace him. No one knew of his association with Turner, and the girl in the shop had not seen his face. Nothing could connect him with either crime.

In the subsidiary matters apart from the actual murder he had been equally circumspect. The suitcase, cap, and waterproof he had bought in different shops in the East End while wearing a disguise. For his whole-day absence from London he had an adequate explanation. He had gone to his birthplace, Notfield, and had there spent the day visiting hotel after hotel, asking what chances there were of a job. The reason he would give would be that his gambling debts were making life unpleasant in London, and he was considering a fresh start elsewhere. The Notfield hotel proprietors would confirm his statement, and it was unlikely that he had been noticed on the bus from Notfield to Thorpe, an hour's run taken in the late afternoon to enable him to join Turner's train.

At 9.55 the train drew into King's Cross. If challenged, Rank would say he had come direct from Notfield, arriving at St Pancras at 10.10. To support this theory he walked to St Pancras, returning to the hotel after the 10.10 came in. When he had registered the time of his arrival by asking the cook for a bite of supper, he felt that his worries at long last were over.

Rank had pitted himself against society, but unhappily for him, society in this instance was represented by Superintendent French of New Scotland Yard. For French the case began with a telephone message from the Chief Constable of Selcaster, recounting the facts and saying that as Guard Turner was a Londoner, he had decided to hand over to the Yard. 'Our Inspector Cutler,' he concluded, 'is travelling up in the train and should be with you a little after ten.'

At ten French returned to the Yard and in due course Cutler was announced. 'Ah, Inspector, sit down,' French greeted him. 'You've had a spot of trouble in Selcaster?'

Cutler agreed, saying that he had been instructed to make inquiries in the train, which had started as soon as they had got another guard.

French nodded. 'Tell me what you did.'

Cutler had begun by interviewing the dining-car staff. They were positive that no one had passed through the car between Thorpe and Selcaster. Therefore the criminal's activities had been confined to the coaches following. A search of these revealing nothing helpful, Cutler had gone through the compartments, questioning passengers and taking their names. By the time this was done they were approaching King's Cross.

Several passengers had noticed that during the run a guard had walked forward along the corridor, but no one had observed him returning. The man indeed had vanished. It was further established that no traveller had been absent from his compartment for more than two or three minutes.

'A pretty problem,' said French. 'Well, Inspector, you've got your work cut out for you. Meantime we'll look into it from this end.'

French was as good as his word. During the next day or two discreet inquiries brought out a number of facts. The dead guard had lived quietly in lodgings. He had been rather unsocial, had had a doubtful reputation where money was concerned, and on the whole was not popular. But there was nothing to indicate that he had had a serious enemy.

Selcaster reported that a search for the uniform had proved fruitless. It had not been thrown out of the train nor hidden on the railway premises, nor had anyone been seen wearing it.

French had put Inspector Ludlow in charge of the London inquiry and now the two men sat talking it over. 'As Turner was the only guard on the train,' French was saying, 'and as his uniform has vanished, it follows that the man seen walking down the corridor was wearing the uniform, and was therefore the murderer.'

'Clear enough, sir.'

'Something arises out of that, surely? The murderer was somewhere near Turner's height and of slighter build, else he couldn't have got the uniform on over his clothes.'

Ludlow slapped his thigh. 'That's good, sir! It hadn't occurred to me.'

'Another point,' continued French. 'The murderer left the train at Selcaster. We know that because there was no one in the lavatories or corridor and no stranger entered a compartment during the journey.'

'OK, sir.'

'As the uniform was not in the train, the murderer must have taken it with him. A strange guard would certainly have been noticed, therefore he wasn't wearing it, and as he couldn't carry it over his arm, he must have packed it in something. What would he use?'

They agreed that of all receptacles, a suitcase was the most likely. So French reached the first milestone on the road to a completed case.

'A step further,' he went on. 'Imagine yourself guilty of the murder and carrying that uniform about with you. Would you feel happy?'

'I'd feel happier with a can of nitroglycerine,' grinned Ludlow.

'That's it. If it's found, you hang. So you'd get rid of it, at once, there in Selcaster. No waiting till you got to London. Then find the suitcase. Spot of work for the Selcaster men.'

French rang up the Selcaster Chief Constable.

'We've already got that in hand, Mr French,' was the reply. 'We're going into it thoroughly. We've offered a good reward, and that will ensure that we get it if an outsider finds it. We're examining areas closed to the public.'

'If I may suggest it, what about rubbish tips?'

'We're having all loose places dug over.'

'The river?'

'There are few places he could have dropped it in

unseen: a length of wharf, two bridges and so on. We're having them dragged.'

French felt that he himself could have done no more. 'Splendid!' he congratulated. 'If it's there you'll get it.'

The prophecy was soon fulfilled. Dragging operations were successful, and when French reached the Yard two mornings later he found the suitcase waiting for him. Accompanying it was a note saying that the discovery had been kept absolutely secret.

The second milepost!

The inquiry now took a different turn. French entrusted the suitcase, the waterproof and cap, the cosh and the stove door to different officers. The first four drew blanks, but the fifth made progress.

'Find out from the makers of the stove if any similar doors were sent out as replacements during recent weeks,' French directed Ludlow. A list was soon obtained, and Ludlow went round the London purchasers. In due course he visited Rank's hotel, and there the proprietress identified the door from the shape of the bare patch. When Ludlow found that the porter was of about Turner's height but of slighter build, that for some time he had seemed worried, and that he had had leave on the day of the murder, he felt a satisfying thrill. Leaving a man to shadow Rank, he hurried back to the Yard.

'Good work,' said French. 'He's our man right enough, but we must have more proof. He'll put up some alibi for the day of the crime, and we'll get him over that. Bring him in.'

So milepost three came and went.

Since the murders Rank had been living through a veritable nightmare. Added to the gnawing worry of his debts was now the shadow of a ceaseless fear. Every caller at the hotel, every policeman he met, set his heart racing and his hands trembling. Like so many before him, he felt that there was nothing he would not give to call back the past. The thought added to his despair.

When one day he entered the hotel to find two large men waiting for him, a cold weight of dread settled down on him. But they were polite, even friendly. Admitting that they were police officers, they said they thought he might be able to help them in an inquiry they were making. Would he have any objection to coming to see Superintendent French, who was handling the matter?

During the silent drive Rank called up his reserves of courage. He had a perfect alibi. All he had to do was to steel his nerves and stick to his story.

French's beginning made the former difficult. In a serious voice he told him that the inquiry was concerned with the death of David Turner, and that he needn't answer any question unless he liked. Then he went on: 'We understand that you were absent from work on the day of the crime. Would you care to tell us where you were?'

Rank breathed more freely. He was prepared for this, and his answer was true, except in respect of the time between four and eight. He explained that during the day he had visited hotel managers, and in this later period had had supper in a Notfield café. He had then walked about, revisiting the scenes of his youth.

It seemed to go down well. French nodded, then turned to an incomprehensible sideline. 'Looking for a job at Notfield? I follow. If you had got one did you mean to remain on there, without any explanation to your old employer?'

Rank didn't understand it, but he drove himself to reply promptly. 'Certainly not. I'd have gone back and worked my notice.'

French nodded again. 'You mean you didn't intend to stay overnight?'

'No, of course not.'

'Then why,' French said quietly, 'did you take that with you?'

As he spoke he pointed across the room and there, suddenly pushed forward into view, was the suitcase. Rank stared at it, frozen with horror. Beneath its stained cover he seemed to see the shadowy outline of a cosh and a uniform. Slowly he pitched forward in a faint.

Confirmation

JOHN HARVEY

DETECTIVE FILE

OFFICER: Detective Inspector Charles Resnick

FORCE: Nottingham CID

TIME: 1996

CASES: *Lonely Hearts* (1989), *Rough Treatment* (1990), *Wasted Years* (1993), *Cold Light* (1994), *Living Proof* (1995) etc.

PROFILE: Charlie Resnick has been described as the misfit copper with a curious, passive charm. A man with a middle-aged paunch due to unhealthy food, bags under his eyes from too little sleep, he operates in the gritty and down-at-heel areas of Nottingham which are said to have among the highest number of cases of violent crime and murder per head in England: a fair proportion of which fall into Resnick's lap. Several of his cases have involved him crucially with women – a fact which frequently causes him to dwell on the state of his own lovelife. When not at work, Charlie fills in time on his own drinking and listening to jazz. With his Polish roots, quartet of cats named after jazz legends, and general feeling of disillusionment with police politics, Resnick is a multidimensional policeman who throws himself into an investigation as much to escape his loneliness as to solve the crime. In America, he has been greeted by reviewers as 'one of the most fully realised characters in modern crime fiction', while *The Times* recently said that he has now become established as the latest addition to 'that select band of cold but cultured English inspectors like Morse and Dalgliesh'.

CREATOR: John Harvey (b. 1948) started writing and editing while he was at school and later in college. For some years he worked as a teacher, at the same time continuing to write a whole batch of pseudonymous paperback novels. In 1976 he created his first private eye, Londoner Scott Mitchell, in *Amphetamines and Pearls*, and followed this with three more titles which, he says, were heavily influenced by the works of Raymond Chandler. It was in 1989 that he found his own voice with the first Resnick novel, *Lonely Hearts*, and added a new figure to the pantheon of memorable contemporary police detectives. John has also written scripts for television, including Central TV's series, *Hard Cases*, and was closely involved in the making of the BBC TV version of *Resnick*, starring Tom Wilkinson. The story 'Confirmation' is a new case for the lonely DI that John wrote especially for this collection.

***

Terry Cooke went to the pool every morning because it was good for his health. His doctor had told him so. Or, rather, his doctor had said, squinting above a pair of glasses held together with orange Elastoplast, 'Terry, you're going to have to change your lifestyle, that is if you're going to have any life at all. Future tense.'

A quarter past eleven on a sunny January morning, Terry was finally in Dr Max Bone's surgery after forty minutes shared with old copies of the *Guardian* magazine and the usual selection of bad backs, hacking coughs, and unmarried mums-to-be about to drop their firstborn on the worn carpet. The *Guardian*, for Christ's sake, where did Bone think this was, West Bridgford? And there was the doc ignoring his request for a referral to a chiropodist so Terry could get rid of his troublesome bunion on the NHS, and engaging him instead on issues of mortality. Life or death. His. Terry's.

'I'll stop smoking,' Terry said, prepared to be alarmed.

'You should.'

'Cut back on the drink.'

'Yes.'

'For pity's sake, I'm not even fifty.'

'You want to be?'

Terry got up from the chair and walked to the window. In the street outside, two kids in bomber jackets, neither of them above ten years old, and both wearing nearly-new Nike trainers that had come down the chimney with Santa, were dismantling a black and silver mountain bike whose owner had optimistically left it chained to a parking meter.

'Exercise,' the doctor said.

Terry couldn't see himself in one of those poncey jogging suits, sidestepping the dog shit round the edges of Victoria Park.

'Specifically, swimming; that's the thing.'

The only time in the last fifteen years Terry had been swimming, Carrington Lido had still been an open-air pool and not a bunch of cramped chi-chi houses with satellite dishes the size of dinner plates and shiny gold numbers on the doors.

'It's not just the aerobic activity,' Bone said, 'though you need that without question. It's the effect of the water. Calming.' He removed his glasses and pinched the bridge of his nose. 'It's the stress, Terry, it's making too great demands upon the heart.'

His back to the window, Terry could feel it, angry and irregular against his ribs. Cautiously, he returned to the chair and sat down. 'Swimming,' he said, uncertainly. 'That'd really make a difference?'

Bone nodded. 'If not, I know a wonderful masseuse. Shiatsu. Unfortunately not on the National Health.'

Terry thought he would try the swimming first. He shook Bone's hand and, out on the street, clipped the ear of an eight-year-old demanding a pound to look after his car, make sure no one tried to nick the radio, see it didn't get scratched.

'Listen, you, I find one mark on that motor you're for it. This is Terry Cooke you're talking to, right?'

'Yeah, and my Dad's Frank Bruno.'

Terry shrugged; anything was possible. He walked as far as the corner of Carlton Road and sat in the side bar of an empty pub with a half of bitter and a large Bells. Stress, the doc was right. Terry had it in spades.

There was his daughter, Sarah, for instance. Several months back she had followed her mother's inexact path and taken the overnight National Express north to Edinburgh. No note, no reason, though Sarah's gran, Terry's own mum, that is, had acted strangely about the whole thing and Terry was sure she knew more about it than she was letting on. One of these fine days, when she'd suckled enough gin, it'd all come pouring out. Till then, it was the occasional reversed-charge call from Sarah and a postcard of Greyfriar's Bobby with a scrawled message to say that she and her mum were fine. Terry could imagine the pair of them shacked up in some scabby flat, more likely than not a squat. As long as her mother wasn't into sharing needles, it might not work out so bad.

At least it made it easier with Eileen, Terry's live-in girlfriend. Eileen was a stripper of considerable abilities who, since moving in with Terry, had taken herself upmarket and now specialised in delivering personalised birthday messages dressed in her own version of a WPC's uniform.

Terry tried to tell himself he didn't mind Eileen going out and cuffing some spotty car salesman to a chair while she gave him a tongue lashing, but the truth was that he did. After all, the first time he'd ever laid eyes on her himself, it had been the speed with which she'd got down to her spangled g-string that had taken his eye. Slowly, very slowly. Now whenever Eileen went out on a job, part of him was terrified she'd encounter some muscled hard boy who worked out six days a weeks and made love like a power machine on the seventh. Twenty-three, Eileen, and young enough, just about, to be Terry's daughter herself.

Sarah . . . then Eileen . . . and the star over the sodding stable hadn't long faded before Inspector bloody Charlie Resnick had been sniffing round the secondhand shop Terry rented out by Bobbers Mill. Resnick like some scruffy Santa with a ho-ho-ho and turkey gravy on his tie, offering to do a special New Year inventory of suspect goods. It was only good luck that Terry had been there himself that day, and not his gormless nephew Raymond, otherwise it might not have been so easy to steer Resnick away from the several gross of Sega and Nintendo that had escaped the Christmas market. To say nothing of the camcorders.

Stress? Of course he was suffering from stress. A life like this, how could it be anyway else? But fifty was something he did want to see. It wasn't altogether off the cards that he and Eileen might want to start a family.

Terry lowered himself into the water gradually – none of those bravura dives off the pool edge for him – and began the first of thirty slow, laborious lengths. Not so very long from now he'd be back out and across the road, sitting in the market café with a strong tea and a sausage cob.

Resnick got into the station that morning late and less than happy. His own car was in for what might prove to be its last ever service and the Vauxhall he'd borrowed had recently been used for a spot of undercover observation and smelled of hastily bottled urine and too many Benson Kingsize. Halfway along Lower Parliament Street a corporation bus driver had ploughed into the back of a Burger King delivery truck and the consequent brouhaha had blocked the traffic both ways from the Theatre Royal to the Albert Hall and Institute.

'Bit of a lie-in?' Millington asked when Resnick finally pushed his way through the door to the CID room, the smile edging its way, ferret-like, from beneath the sergeant's moustache. 'Deserved.'

'Last night's files on my desk?' Resnick asked, barely breaking stride en route to the partitioned-off section that was his office.

'Likely need a bit of an update by now.'

'Tea, Graham,' Resnick said. 'I don't suppose there's any chance of a cup of tea?' Coffee was his preference, but experience had long since taught him that within the confines of the station the cup that cheers was the safer choice.

'Kev,' Millington called, head inclined towards the far corner of the room.

'Boss?' Telephone in hand, Kevin Naylor peered round from his desk.

'When you've a minute, get kettle on, mash some more tea.'

Naylor sighed, spoke into the receiver, made a mark alongside the list of names and addresses on his desk and got to his feet. He glanced across at Lynn Kellogg as he passed, Lynn sitting impervious at her computer, strolling through the county data base detailing offenders with a penchant for carrying firearms with malicious intent.

That'll be the day, he thought, when anyone dares ask her to make the bloody tea in this team.

Leaning over the shuffle of folders and papers that covered his desk, Resnick scanned through the outline of the previous night's events. Three men had been arrested and held in the cells overnight: two on charges of drunk and disorderly; the third, apparently sober, had driven his fibreglass-bodied invalid tricycle into a Kentucky Fried Chicken franchise and attempted to run over his ex-lover, who was one of the customers.

There had been eleven burglaries reported from the Victorian splendours of the Park estate and seven more, all of them in the same short street, from the less salubrious east side of the Alfreton Road. Carl Vincent was out there now, checking some of these door to door, while Naylor was talking to other aggrieved homeowners on the phone.

All routine: it was the last entry in the night's incident file which claimed most of Resnick's attention. At eleven minutes past three a message had been received giving information of a burglary taking place at a television and electrical goods suppliers in Radford. The officers who had responded, PCs Mark McFarlane and Mary Duffy, had initially reported seeing no obvious signs of forced entry, but in the narrow alley at the rear had run into a gang of four men armed with a sawn-off shotgun, iron bars and a long-handled sledgehammer. A mercy, Resnick thought, that the shotgun had not been brought into play, though he was by no means certain the officers would have agreed. Mark McFarlane was in Queen's with a suspected fractured skull and Mary Duffy was in an intensive care bed in the same hospital, a splintered rib having pierced her lung. Such descriptions as they had been able to give of their assailants were necessarily brief and incomplete – balaclavas and coveralls, boots and gloves – it had been dark in the alley and McFarlane's torch had been smashed early in the struggle.

Resnick snapped open the door from his office. 'Graham . . .'

'On its way. Kev, what you doing with that tea?'

'This pair in hospital,' Resnick said, 'when did we last get a report?'

'Not above half-hour back. No change.'

Resnick nodded. 'Any list yet of what was taken?'

'I've called the owner twice,' Millington said, handing Resnick his favourite Notts County mug. 'Promised it within the hour.'

'Get on to them again, Graham. Sitting on it this long, likely all they're busying themselves with is massaging the totals for the insurance. If they keep stalling, maybe you should get down there yourself.'

Millington nodded, right.

'Sir,' Lynn said, swivelling at her desk. 'I've got a print-out of likely candidates for carrying the shotgun. Local, anyhow.'

'Good. Cross-check with the information officer at Central, might be a body or two worth pulling to get things started. Let me know how it's going when I get back.' Resnick took a couple of swallows at his tea and set it down. 'I'm off out to the hospital, take a look at the wounded, see if anything's jogged their memory.' He hoped the traffic had died down and that Duffy and McFarlane would be up to talking to him when he arrived.

He was hoping in vain. McFarlane had lost consciousness again by the time Resnick got to his side and all that Mary Duffy could tell him through bruised lips was that one of their attackers had seemed taller than the rest, two or three inches over six foot, and another might have been stockier and shorter than the other two.

'Voices?' Resnick asked. 'Accents?'

Quietly, Duffy began to cry. 'I'm sorry, sir. I'm sorry.'
Resnick patted her hand and hoped she wouldn't notice when he glanced at his watch.

Terry Cooke collected his tea and roll from the counter and went to his normal seat by the window. Across Gedling Street, the stalls of the open market were attracting a slow scuffle of elderly shoppers, collars turned up against the keenness of the wind. He watched as a lean, slope-shouldered figure, white haired, turned away from where he had been buying what looked like a couple of pounds of potatoes, a few carrots and onions, and crossed towards the café.

Like Terry, Ronnie Rather was a creature of routine. Monday, Wednesday, Friday, he would push his olive-green shopping trolley sedately from stall to stall, before treating himself to tea and toast and a small cigar that burned like anthracite and had a similar flinty smell. On alternate Fridays, he splashed out on beans as well.

Since Ronnie had been adhering to this particular routine longer than Terry himself, and had made a habit, when it was vacant, of sitting at the window table, Terry could hardly object when – as today – the old man parked up his trolley against the table edge and joined him.

'Ron.'

'Terry.'

There would be no more said until Ronnie had cut his slices of toast into thin strips – soldiers, Terry's mum would have called them, when she had been readying them for the young Terry to dip into his boiled egg – which Ronnie would then sprinkle with salt before chewing methodically. Two or three pieces despatched into the gurgles and groans of Ronnie's antique digestive system and Terry's breakfast companion would lean forward across the table, resting on one elbow, and engage him in conversation.

Which usually meant, as was the way with those old jossers well above the pensionable age, talking about the dim and distant past when a pint of beer was a pint of beer and the sound of a horse-drawn cart approaching along the road outside was enough to send every self-respecting householder running for his dustpan and broom. Or, in Ronnie Rather's case, when there was a dance hall on every corner, each of them keeping a dozen or more musicians in fulltime employment, and when names like Joe Loss and Jack Hylton were enough to quicken the pulse and set up a tremble at the back of the knees.

Trombone, Ronnie had played; first or second chair with every dance band ever to grace Mayfair and the West End or tour the provinces, where, according to Ronnie, so many women would throng round the stage door it often needed the police to clear them away. If he had really done all the things he claimed, played with all those people in all those places, Terry figured Ronnie Rather had to be the wrong side of eighty if he was a day. Which was just about right.

'Here, Terry . . .' Ronnie began, and Terry waited for the night the Prince of Wales came into the Savoy and insisted that everyone else was sent packing so that he and Mrs Simpson could dance alone. Or the time at the Queensbury Club just before the end of the war, when Glen Miller recognised him in the audience and insisted that he step up and sit in with the band.

But no, it was 'Terry, you hear about them two poor bloody coppers, got their heads smashed in?'

Terry nodded; he had heard it on the news driving to the pool. A gang of four masked men, heavily armed, disturbed while carrying out a burglary – well, he reckoned he could fit names to at least two of those hidden faces, possibly three, and it wouldn't surprise him if by the time he got out to the shop there hadn't been a call enquiring, in the most roundabout of terms, if he might be interested in enlarging his stock to the tune of a couple of dozen state-of-the-art wide-screen, digital-sound TVs.

'One of 'em a woman, an' all, that's what sticks in my craw. The bloke, copper, I mean, whatever's comin' to him, fair deal. But not the woman – only a kid, too.' Ronnie Rather shook his head in disgust and a piece of undigested toast reappeared at one corner of his mouth. 'Call me old-fashioned, if you like. Don't hold with hitting women, never have.'

'No, no,' Terry said. 'I agree with you there. Ninety-nine per cent.' And he did. 'Listen, Ronnie,' he said, checking what remained of his tea was too cold to drink, 'like to stick around and chat, but you know how it is, got to run. Business. See you soon, yes?'

Ronnie nodded and watched as Terry scooted out through the door and hurried off to where his car was parked on a meter outside the leisure centre doors. Ulcer, Ronnie thought watching him, that's what he's going to get if he doesn't watch out. An ulcer at least.

Millington and his merry team had stuck the proverbial pin in Lynn Kellogg's list of likely candidates and, backed up by a crew of eager uniforms, each and every one of them anxious to avenge their fellow officers, had gone knocking on doors and feeling collars on the Bestwood and Broxtowe estates and in those all-day pubs and twenty-four-hour snooker halls where villains of like minds were wont to congregate. Great sport, but to little longterm avail.

'Anything, Graham?' Resnick asked.

It was late enough in the afternoon for any pretence at daylight to have given up the ghost, and the sergeant's moustache was drooping raggedly towards his upper lip. 'Bugger all!'

It would have taken Petula Clark herself to have walked into the CID room and given out with 'The Other Man's Grass (Is Always Greener)' – a perennial favourite of Millington's – to bring the smile back to his eyes.

'I thought Ced Petchey . . .'

'Ced Petchey coughed to a break-in out at the University Science Park which netted a couple of outmoded Toshibas and three cartons of double-sided three-and-a-half-inch floppy disks.'

'Ah. I thought we'd already charged the Haselmere youth with that one?'

'Precisely.'

It was that time of the day when Resnick's energy was at its lowest and his need for a quick caffeine injection at its most pronounced. 'Look at it this way, Graham. What we've done today, clear out the dead wood. Tomorrow, we'll strike lucky.'

'We bloody better.'

Resnick thought there was no harm in giving luck a helping hand. He left his car on the lower floor below the Victoria Centre and took the lift up to the covered market. Doris Duke was winding sprigs of greenery into a bouquet in which pink and white carnations featured prominently.

'Three of these for your mates out at the hospital this morning, Mr Resnick. By the sound of it, fortunate they wasn't wreaths.'

Resnick slid a ten-pound note along the surface where she worked. 'If you've a customer for that already, Doris, you could make me up another.'

'Fifteen, Mr Resnick. Got to be worth that, at least.'

'Prices going up, Doris? I didn't see a sign.'

Doris pushed the bouquet away and sat straighter on her stool, hooking the heels of her shoes over the lower rungs. 'Special orders, special price; you know how it goes.' She lifted a pack of ten Embassy from the breast pocket of her pink overall, leaned sideways and slid a lighter from the side pocket of her jeans.

Resnick set five pound coins, each neatly balanced on top of the other, down on the centre of the ten-pound note.

'Word is it's Coughlan. He was the one carrying.' Doris's voice could only just be heard.

'Whoever that was,' Resnick said, 'didn't do the beating.'

'I'm sorry, Mr Resnick,' Doris said, 'this time of the year they're scarce, good blooms. That's the best I can do for now.'

Resnick nodded. 'Look after yourself, Doris.'

'You too.'

Somehow, when he walked away in the direction of the Italian coffee stall, Resnick forgot to take his bouquet.

'Coughlan,' Millington said sceptically. 'Bit of a change of pace for him, isn't it?'

'Self-improvement, Graham. Most likely comes from listening to his probation officer.'

Resnick and Millington were in the left-side bar of the Partridge, what would have been called the Public in more openly divided times. Their fellow drinkers – and it was not crowded – were either single men staring morosely into pints of mixed, or students wearing slimming black and sporting silver rings.

'You think it's true?' Millington asked. He was trying not to stare at a skinny seventeen-year-old, the largest of whose three noserings was decorated with three emerald stones and from whose left eyebrow a tiny crucifix hung from a loop of chain.

'About Coughlan?' Resnick said.

'They get themselves pierced all over? All over their bodies?'

'I don't know, Graham. No idea.' He knew the superintendent's daughter had come back from her first term at university with a gold stud in the side of her ear and a plaited ring through her navel.

'Blokes, too.' Millington shook his head, eyes close to watering at the prospect of a pierced foreskin.

'Coughlan, Graham.'

'It's good information?'

'More often than not.'

'Go wading in, all we're like to do is warn him off. Come up empty handed.'

Resnick nodded. Coughlan had been involved in maybe a dozen break-ins in the past two years, but each foray to turn over the council house he lived in off Bracknell Crescent had found the neat three-bedroom semi as clean, in Millington's words, as a pair of Julie Andrews's knickers. A shotgun, though; for Coughlan that was a step in a dubious direction. Why go armed to do an empty shop in the wee small hours? Maybe he was trying to get the feel of it, readying himself for bigger things.

'No word who he was working with?'

''Fraid not.'

'What's that cousin of his called? Barker? Breaker?'

'Breakshaw. Norbert Breakshaw.'

'Didn't he go down for five last time?'

'Carrying a weapon with criminal intent.'

'Maybe the shotgun was his.'

'Then what was Coughlan doing carrying it?'

'Norbert likely give it him to hold, leave his hands free for belting McCrory and the girl. He's a nasty bastard. Certificates to prove it.'

'One thing, Graham, isn't he still inside? Lincoln?'

'I'll check first thing. If he's out and we can put the pair of them together, Breakshaw and Coughlan . . .'

'Confirmation, Graham, that's what we need. Confirmation.'

'Right,' said Millington. 'Sup up and we'll have another before I get home to the missus. Chicken chasseur tonight, unless I'm much mistaken. Say what you like about Marks, you know, can't fault 'em for reliability.'

Resnick's quip about Karl or Groucho remained frozen on his lips.

Terry Cooke had fallen asleep with the *Mail* open on his lap and orchestral versions of Burt Bacharach's hits lilting out of the stereo. When he opened his eyes with a start, Eileen was framed in the living-room mirror and the violins were just cascading into the theme of 'This Guy's In Love With You'. There were times, Terry thought, life could be pretty nearly perfect.

'I was just going,' Eileen said. She was wearing a red dress, tight at the hips, high black heels, and her red hair was pinned high above her head. A camel coat was slung over one arm.

'Without saying goodbye?' Terry smiled.

'You looked so peaceful.'

'So?'

Smiling, she crossed the room and he turned to greet her, Eileen bending to plant a red-lipped kiss on the oval of thinning hair where the scalp showed through.

'What time'll you be back?'

'Late.'

'Why don't you let me meet you?'

She took a step away. 'Terry, let's not start all that again, eh?'

When they had first started living together he had insisted upon picking her up outside whichever hotel or club she had been working, but Eileen had insisted it was bad for business and finally convinced him it was true. No birthday boy for whom she'd just table-danced in a g-string and policewoman's hat would enjoy the sight of her being whisked away by her live-in lover, likely back home to a bowlful of hot cereal and his and hers mugs of Ovaltine. 'It won't do, Terry, it's bad for the image. You've got to see that?'

Terry knew she was right; knew, too, what she wasn't quite saying – picked up by some bloke old enough to be my father.

Most nights now, unless he had to go out on a bit of business himself, Terry stayed home, television turned low so he'd hear the cab pulling up outside, the clatter of Eileen's heels up to the door.

'What is it tonight?' he asked.

'A stag night and two twenty-firsts.'

'OK, see you later. Have fun.'

Eileen hated lying to him, but sometimes he didn't leave her any choice. If Terry knew she'd gone back to working the pubs – not often, and then only when the landlord had organised a lock-in, which meant bigger tips and less chance of the punters getting out of control – he would not be happy. But that was what Eileen missed, working an audience, feeling all their eyes on you and knowing if you played it right you could keep them there, glued. That feeling of control.

For tonight, she'd been brushing up one of her old routines with a banana and half a dozen ping-pong balls; if that didn't put at least a couple of hundred quid in the pot, she didn't know what would.

No chicken chasseur for Resnick to go home to; no wife. A predatory black cat to greet him, hungry, at the front door and three others, more docile, waiting inside. After seeing to them, he fixed himself a sandwich from gorgonzola and smoked ham, forked two pickled cucumbers from a jar and snapped open a bottle of Pilsner Urquel. In the front room, he fished out an old vinyl album, *Eddie Condon's Treasury of Jazz*, bought a hundred years ago, and set it to play. When Billy Butterfield was taking the introduction to 'I've Got a Crush on You', trumpet and piano with the verse to themselves, Resnick recalled seeing Butterfield in person – the 'seventies it would have been – down the M1 at a club in Leicester, a portly old boy wearing stay-pressed flannels and a blue wool blazer. The number was coming to an end, Ralph Sutton filigreeing under the final chords, when the telephone rang. Resnick recognised Ronnie Rather's voice right away.

Ronnie was in the downstairs bar of the Old Vic. 'Get your skates on, Charlie, and you'll just catch the last set.'

The band were into something modal, bluesy; sax and rhythm set up on a low stage deep to the rear of the low-ceilinged room. Maybe half the tables were taken, couples mostly, caught up in quiet conversation. Ronnie Rather was sitting midway between the door and the stand, his white hair resting back against the wall, eyes closed, listening.

Resnick went over to the bar, and when the girl had solved seven across she got to her feet and served him a bottle of Worthington White Shield, which she left him to pour for himself, and a large brandy with a touch of lemonade. Dropping his change back into his suit pocket, he stayed there listening: all of the musicians he recognised, was on nodding terms with; he had seen them playing in everything from pubs like this to the pit band at the theatre: they were of an age. 'Second Nature' was what they were calling themselves now; the last time he had seen them it had been something else. The pianist,

Resnick thought, had likely been with Billy Butterfield when he had seen him in Leicester.

As the number came to an end, a tenor cadenza over bowed bass, Resnick walked back across the room and placed the brandy down alongside Rather's empty glass.

'Cheers, Charlie.'

'Pleasure.'

Ronnie nodded in the direction of the band. 'Heard Mel Thorpe do his Roland Kirk, have you?'

'Not recently.'

Ronnie tasted his brandy and lemonade and smiled. 'Considering he's not black or blind, he does a pretty fair job.'

On flute now, the soloist sang, hummed and grunted as he blew, spurring himself along with intermittent shouts and hollers which raised the temperature of the playing to the point that one or two of the audience began drumming on their tabletops and the barmaid set aside her crossword puzzle in favour of polishing glasses. The applause was sustained and earned.

'I saw him, you know, Charlie. Roland Kirk. St Pancras Town Hall. Nineteen sixty-four.'

Resnick nodded. He had seen Kirk once himself, but later, not more than a year before the end of his life – Birmingham, he thought it had been, but for once he wasn't sure. The musician had already suffered one stroke and played with one side of his body partially paralysed; it had been like watching a tornado trapped in a basket, a lion shorn and bereft in a cage.

'This business with the copper, Charlie. The girl . . .'

'Mary Duffy.'

'If you say so. I don't like it, treating women like that.'

Resnick allowed himself a smile. 'One of nature's gentlemen, that what you're saying, Ronnie?'

'Oh, I've known a few in my time, Charlie. Young women, I mean.'

'I'll bet you have.'

'And never raised a finger, not to any of them. Not one.'

Resnick nodded again, drank some beer. The band were playing a ballad, medium tempo, 'The Talk of the Town'.

'Bumped into Terry Cooke,' Ronnie said, 'café by the market, Victoria Park. Soon as I mentioned it, the break-in and that, he turned all pale and couldn't wait to be on his way.'

'You don't think he was involved?'

'Terry? Not directly, no. Have a heart attack minute anyone said boo to him in the dark.'

'What then?'

'Mates with Coughlan, isn't he?'

'And this was Coughlan's job?'

'Word is, on the street.'

'I didn't know,' Resnick said, 'Cooke and Coughlan were close.'

'Who Cookie was close to,' Ronnie explained, 'was Coughlan's wife.'

'Second or third?'

'Third. Marjorie. Cookie was having it away with her the best part of a year. That was before he cottoned on to this young bit of skirt he's got now. Anyway, while all this was going on, he got himself into a card school with Coughlan. Poker. Dropped a lot of money there on occasion, so I heard. His way of paying for it, I suppose.'

'Coughlan didn't know?'

'Some blokes,' Ronnie said, leaning a shade closer to Resnick as if letting him into a greater confidence, 'get off on the idea their bird's fresh from shagging someone else. Whether Coughlan's one of those, it's difficult to tell. But him and Cookie, still speaking. Doing business.'

'You think Coughlan's going to be looking to his old

pal Terry, then, to help him offload from the other night?'

Ronnie paused to applaud a particularly nice piece of piano. 'Wouldn't you, Charlie? What friends are for.'

Resnick bought another large brandy, nothing for himself. 'Any word Breakshaw might have been involved?'

'Norbert? Not so's I've heard. But it'd make sense. Evil bastard. When he kicked inside his old lady's womb, he'd have been wearing steel-capped Doc Martin's.'

The hand Resnick slipped down into Rather's jacket pocket held three twenty-pound notes. 'Look after yourself, Ronnie.'

Ronnie nodded and leaned back, closing his eyes.

When Terry Cooke arrived, waved through the lock-in on Coughlan's say-so, Eileen was down on all fours on the bar, waving an unzipped banana above her head and asking, should she put it in, if there was anyone there man enough to eat it out.

When Coughlan had phoned, the last thing Terry had wanted to do was be seen drinking with him so soon after the break-in and what had followed, but Coughlan had assured him it was a private party. Mates. No prying eyes. He hadn't said anything about Eileen. Maybe he hadn't known. Maybe he had.

Now Coughlan gripped Terry firmly by the upper arm and led him into a corner, some distance from the core of the chanting crowd.

'You'll not be bothered,' Coughlan said, 'not seeing the show. Nothing you won't have seen before.'

Terry looked into Coughlan's face but, heavy and angular, it gave nothing away. In a wedge of mirror to his right, Terry could see the shimmer of Eileen's nearly nude body as she lowered herself into a squatting position, facing out. The banana was nowhere to be seen.

Confirmation

'What's up, Terry? Nothing the matter?'

Terry shook his head and tried to look away.

'Come over all of a muck sweat.'

'Bit of a cold. Flu, could be.'

'Scotch, that's what you need. Double.'

The crowd, grinning, egging one another on, clapped louder and louder as Eileen arched backwards, taking her weight on the palms of her hands, the first brave volunteer being pushed towards her by his mates.

'Not hungry yourself, Terry?' Coughlan enquired, coming back with two glasses of Bells. 'Had yours earlier, I daresay.'

'What's going on?' Terry asked, feeling his own perspiration along his back and between his legs, smelling it through the cigarette smoke and beer. 'What's all this about?'

'Marjorie sends her love,' Coughlan said. 'Told her I'd be seeing you tonight.'

'For fuck's sake, Coughlan!'

'Exactly.' Coughlan's hand was back on his shoulder, like a vice, and Terry, the glass to his lips, almost let it slip from his hand. 'Bygones be bygones, eh, Terry? So much shafting under the bridge. Besides, things change, move on . . .' There was a loud roar from the jubilant crowd and then cheers. '. . . Musical beds, you might say. Keeps things fresh. Revives the appetite.' Coughlan looked pointedly towards the mirror, turning Terry so that he was forced to do the same. 'Lovely young girl like that, Terry, shouldn't take much persuading to get her round my place of an evening. Once in a while.' His face twisted into a smile. 'Genuine redhead, natural. I like that.'

Terry held his glass in both hands and downed the Scotch.

'I could have let Norbert loose on you, Terry. He'd

have loved that. But no, this way's best. Pals. Pals, yes, Terry?'

Terry said nothing.

'And then there's the stuff from the other night. 'Course I don't expect you to take it all. Dozen sets, say? Sony? VCRs? Stereo? Matt black, neat, you'll like those. I'll have them round your place tomorrow night. One, one-thirty. Norbert, I expect he'd like to make delivery himself.'

Terry Cooke looked at the floor.

'I shouldn't wait around, Terry, to take her home. Someone'll see she gets a lift, you don't have to fret.'

Back on her feet and shimmying along the bar to 'Dancing Queen', Eileen caught sight of Terry for the first time as he pushed through the door, spotted him and almost lost her step.

There was a light burning on the landing, another in the back room, and Eileen stood for a full minute on the step, key poised, running over her excuses in her head. She'd half expected to get back and find her bags on the pavement, clothes flung all over the privet hedge. Thought, when she got inside, that he might be waiting with a knotted towel in his hand, wet, she'd known men do that; at least his fist. But he was sitting, Terry, in the old round-backed chair that was usually his mother's, cup of tea cold in his hand.

'Terry, I . . .'

'You get on,' Terry said. 'Time you've had your shower and that, I'll be up.' He didn't look her in the face.

Twenty minutes later, when he slid into bed beside her, the backs of her legs were still damp from the shower and he shivered lightly as he pressed against her.

'Terry?'

'Yes?'

'Put out the light.'

Resnick and Millington were in the shop when Terry Cooke arrived, not yet ten-thirty and Millington poised to buy a nearly-new book club edition of *Sense and Sensibility* for his wife, while Resnick was thumbing through the shoebox of CDs, looking for something to equal the set of Charlie Parker Dial sessions he'd bought there once before.

Terry's nephew, Raymond, stood in the middle of the room like a rabbit caught in headlights.

'Ray-o,' Terry said, 'get off and see a film.'

'They don't open till gone twelve.'

'Then wait.'

'You know why we're here?' Resnick asked once Raymond had gone.

'Maybe.'

'We've heard one or two whispers,' Millington said, making himself comfortable on a Zanussi washing machine. 'Concerning a certain nasty incident the other night.'

'Not down to me,' Terry said hastily.

'Of course not,' Resnick assured him. 'We'd never believe that it was. But others, maybe known to you . . .'

'You see, we've heard names,' Millington said. 'Confirmation, that's all we need.'

'Though if you give us more . . .'

'Confirmation and more . . .'

Terry felt the muscles tightening along his back; he ought never to have missed his morning swim. 'These names . . .'

'We thought,' Resnick said, 'you might tell us.'

'Remove,' Millington said, 'any suggestion that we put words into your mouth.'

Terry felt the pressure of Coughlan's hand hard on his shoulder, remembered the sick leer on his huge face when he had talked about sharing Eileen. 'Coughlan,' he said. 'Him for certain.'

'And?'

'Breakshaw. Norbert Breakshaw.'

'Thank you, Terry,' Resnick said, letting a Four Seasons anthology fall back into the box; just so many times, he thought, you could enjoy 'Big Girls Don't Cry'.

'Here,' Millington said. 'How much for this?'

'There's something else,' Terry said, 'something else you'll want to know.'

When Norbert Breakshaw parked the van close to the back entrance to Terry Cooke's business premises, he wasn't alone; Francis Farmer and Francis's brother-in-law, Tommy DiReggio, were with him. Norbert had brought them along, partly for the company, partly to help him shift the gear; they had been with Norbert and Coughlan at the original break-in. Francis had hung back once Norbert had started swinging the sledgehammer and things got a little out of hand, but Tommy had enjoyed the chance to let fly with an iron bar, get the boot in hard.

'There's a light on,' Norbert said. 'He's waiting for us.'

Not quite right. What was waiting for them was a team of some twenty officers, two of them, Millington included, having drawn arms just in case.

Burdened down by boxes of expensive electricals, Francis and Tommy had no chance to run; Norbert's retreat back to the van was cut off by a phalanx of men and women eager to try out their newly issued long-handled truncheons.

'Just like the military in the Gulf,' Millington explained in the canteen later. 'Not so often you get a chance to give the hardware a try, battle conditions and all.'

Resnick had taken Vincent and Naylor for back-up, but

left them downstairs, watching over Coughlan's wife as she offered them a choice of Ceylon or Darjeeling. Resnick read Coughlan his rights as the big man dressed, hesitating for longer than was strictly necessary over the striped tie or the plain blue. Either way, the custody sergeant would never let him take it with him into the cells.

'Some bastard fingered me, I suppose,' Coughlan said, walking ahead of Resnick out of the room.

'Your mistake,' Resnick said, 'doing a job with Breakshaw, letting him wade into those officers the way he did.'

'It wasn't Cookie, was it?' Coughlan stood facing Resnick at the foot of the stairs.

'Terry? No,' Resnick said. 'Besides, I thought the two of you were close. Family, almost. Last thing I should have thought he'd want to do, drop you in it. Unless you've given him reason, of course.'

'Whatever time is it?' Eileen asked. The faintest glow from the streetlamp, orange, filtered through the curtain of the room.

Terry picked up the clock and brought it closer to his face. 'Half three.'

'What you doing still awake?'

'Can't sleep.'

She turned towards him, careful not to let the cold air into the bed. 'You're not worried, are you?'

'What about?'

'I don't know. I thought maybe the other night . . .'

'Shush.' Leaning forward, he kissed her lightly on the mouth. 'It's happened. Done.'

'I won't do it again.'

'You said.'

'I pr—'

Again he stopped her, this time with his hand. 'Don't. Don't promise. There isn't any need.'

She moved her mouth so that first one, then two of his fingers were between her lips. Terry reached down and hooked his thumb inside the top of his boxer shorts, easing them lower till he could kick them away to the end of the bed.

'I don't deserve you, you know,' Eileen said, reaching for him, his tongue for that moment where his fingers had been.

'Yes,' he said, when he could speak again. 'Yes, sweetheart, you do.'

This had to be a better way, Terry thought, of relieving stress. No matter what the doctor said.

Auld Lang Syne

IAN RANKIN

DETECTIVE FILE

OFFICER: Detective Inspector John Rebus

FORCE: Edinburgh CID

TIME: 1993

CASES: *Knots & Crosses* (1987), *Wolfman* (1992), *Mortal Causes* (1993), *Let It Bleed* (1995) etc.

PROFILE: Scottish Detective Inspector John Rebus is good at his job but something of a loner – a man who prefers investigating on his own, likes going out on a limb and has a low regard for teamwork. His is a state of mind that has been shaped by the traumatic events of his life. Born in Fife, he was raised mostly by his father, a smalltime stage hypnotist, and joined the army after leaving school. Eight years spent in the Parachute Regiment turned Rebus into a tough, resourceful and resilient man who then sought admission to the SAS. However, so gruelling was the training that Rebus suffered a nervous breakdown during the last section of the course and had to be invalided out of the army. Following a period of convalescence in his native Fife, John decided to try the City of Edinburgh Police where his experiences and attitudes made his progress through the ranks to that of DI slow and not without incident. Along the way he has married and divorced, as well as gaining an assistant, Detective Sergeant Brian Holmes.

Rebus is a man who finds it difficult to make friends and has a habit of just carrying along the people he needs, regardless of whether they are friends or contacts. He has a nice way with puns and attracts female companionship without great difficulty – although he finds making a commitment hard and often retreats alone to his tenement flat on the outskirts of Edinburgh. John Rebus has been aptly described as 'a classic personality detective in the tradition of Holmes right through to Morse'.

CREATOR: Like Inspector Rebus, Ian Rankin (b. 1960) was born in Fife, and after graduating from the University of Edinburgh worked – by his own admission – in a variety of unusual jobs including 'grape-picker, swineherd, taxman, alcohol researcher, hi-fi journalist and punk musician'. The success in Britain of the first novel about his solitary hero, *Knots & Crosses*, has been followed by similar acclaim in America where his books are admired for their atmospheric portrayal of the dark side of Edinburgh life – 'a picture of a Scotland the tourist never sees', to quote critic Janet Hutchings. Ian has been elected a Hawthornden Fellow, won the prestigious Chandler-Fulbright Award which enabled him to study in America for a year, and has received a Silver Dagger from the Crime Writers' Association in London. 'Auld Lang Syne' was written for *Ellery Queen's Mystery Magazine* in January 1993 and finds Rebus reluctantly at work on Hogmanay when most of his fellow Scots, good citizens and those of criminal intentions alike, are out and about – though not necessarily celebrating . . .

***

Places Detective Inspector John Rebus did not want to be at midnight on Hogmanay: number one, the Tron in Edinburgh.

Which was perhaps, Rebus decided, why he found himself at five minutes to midnight pushing his way through the crowds that thronged the area of the Royal Mile outside the Tron Kirk. It was a bitter night, a night filled with the fumes of beer and whisky, of foam licking into the sky as another can was opened, of badly sung songs and arms around necks and stooped, drunken proclamations of undying love, proclamations which would be forgotten by morning.

Rebus had been here before, of course. He had been here at midnight on Hogmanay, ready to root out the eventual troublemakers, to break up fights and crunch across the shattered glass covering the cobblestones. The best and worst of the Scots came out as another New Year approached: the togetherness, the sharpness, the hugging of life, the inability to know when to stop, so that the hug became a smothering stranglehold. These people were drowning in a sea of sentiment and sham. 'Flower of Scotland' was struck up by a lone voice for the thousandth time, and for the thousandth time a few more voices joined in, all falling away at the end of the first chorus.

'Gawn yirsel there, big man.'

Rebus looked around him. The usual contingent of uniformed officers was going through the annual ritual of having hands shaken by a public suddenly keen to make friends. It was the WPCs Rebus felt sorry for, as another slobbering kiss slapped into the cheek of a young female officer. The police of Edinburgh knew their duty: they always offered one sacrificial lamb to appease the multitude. There was actually an orderly queue standing in front of the WPC waiting to kiss her. She smiled and blushed. Rebus shivered and turned away. Four minutes to midnight. His nerves were like struck chords. He hated crowds. Hated drunken crowds more. Hated the fact that another year was coming to an end. He began to push through the crowd with a little more force than was necessary.

People Detective Inspector John Rebus would rather not be with at midnight on Hogmanay: number one, detectives from Glasgow CID.

He smiled and nodded towards one of them. The man was standing just inside a bus shelter, removed from the general scum of the road itself. On top of the shelter, a Mohican in black leather did a tribal dance, a bottle of strong lager gripped in one hand. A police constable shouted for the youth to climb down from the shelter. The punk took no notice. The man in the bus shelter smiled back at John Rebus. He's not waiting for a bus, Rebus thought to himself, he's waiting for a bust.

Things Detective Inspector John Rebus would rather not be doing at midnight on Hogmanay: number one, working.

So he found himself working, and as the crowd swept him up again, he thought of Dante's *Inferno*. Three minutes to midnight. Three minutes away from hell. The Scots, pagan at their core, had always celebrated New Year rather than Christmas. Back when Rebus was a boy, Christmasses were muted. New Year was the time for celebration, for first-footing, black bun, madeira cake, coal wrapped in silver foil, stovies during the night and steak pie the following afternoon. Ritual after ritual. Now he found himself observing another ritual, another set of procedures. A meeting was about to take place. An exchange would be made: a bag filled with money for a parcel full of dope. A consignment of heroin had entered Scotland via a west-coast fishing village. The CID in Glasgow had been tipped off but failed to intercept the package. The trail had gone cold for several days, until an informant came up with the vital information. The dope was in Edinburgh. It was about to be handed on to an east-coast dealer. The dealer was known to Edinburgh CID, but they'd never been able to pin a major possession charge on him. They wanted him badly. So did the west-coast CID.

'It's to be a joint operation,' Rebus's boss had informed him, with no trace of irony on his humourless face. So now here he was, mingling with the crowds, just as another dozen or so undercover officers were doing. The men about to make the exchange did not trust one another. One of them had decided upon the Tron as a public enough place to make the deal. With so many people around, a double cross was less likely to occur. The Tron at midnight on Hogmanay: a place of delirium and riot. No one would notice a discreet switch of cases, money for dope, dope for money. It was perfect.

Rebus, pushing against the crowd again, saw the money-man for the very first time. He recognised him from photographs. Alan Lyons, 'Nal' to his friends. He was twenty-seven years old, drove a Porsche 911, and lived in a detached house on the riverside just outside Haddington. He had been one of Rab Philips's men until Philips's demise. Now he was out on his own. He listed his occupation as 'entrepreneur'. He was sewerage.

Lyons was resting his back against a shop window. He smoked a cigarette and gave the passersby a look that said he was not in the mood for handshakes and conversation. A glance told Rebus that two of the Glasgow crew were keeping a close watch on Lyons, so he did not linger. His interest now was in the missing link, the man with the package. Where was he? A countdown was being chanted all around him. A few people reckoned the New Year was less than ten seconds away; others, checking their watches, said there was a minute left. By Rebus's own watch, they were already into the New Year by a good thirty seconds. Then, without warning, the clock chimes rang and a great cheer went up. People were shaking hands, hugging, kissing. Rebus could do nothing but join in.

'Happy New Year.'

'Happy New Year, pal.'

'Best of luck, eh?'

'Happy New Year.'

'All the best.'

'Happy New Year.'

Rebus shook a Masonic hand, and looked up into a face he recognised. He returned the compliment – 'Happy New Year' – and the man smiled and moved on, hand already outstretched to another well-wisher, another stranger. But this man had been no stranger to Rebus. Where the hell did he know him from? The crowd had rearranged itself, shielding the man from view. Rebus concentrated on the memory of the face. He had known it younger, less jowly, but with darker eyes. He could hear the voice: a thick Fife accent. The hands were like shovels, miner's hands, but this man was no miner.

He had his radio with him, but trapped as he was in the midst of noise, there was no point trying to contact the others on the surveillance. He wanted to tell them something. He wanted to tell them he was going to follow the mystery man. Always supposing, that was, he could find him again in the crowd.

And then he remembered: Jackie Crawford. Dear God, it was Jackie Crawford!

People Rebus did not want to shake hands with as the old year became the new: number one, Jackie 'Trigger' Crawford.

Rebus had put Crawford behind bars four years ago for armed robbery and wounding. The sentence imposed by the judge had been a generous stretch of ten years. Crawford had headed north from court in a well-guarded van. He had not gained the nickname 'Trigger' for his quiet and homely outlook on life. The man was a headcase of the first order, gun-happy and trigger-happy. He'd taken part in a series of bank and building society robberies; short, violent visits to High Streets across the Lowlands. That nobody had been killed owed more to strengthened glass and luck than to Crawford's philanthropy. He'd been sent away for ten, he was out after four. What was going on? Surely, the man could not be out and walking the streets *legally*? He had to have broken out, or at the very least cut loose from some day-release scheme. And wasn't it a coincidence that he should bump into Rebus, that he should be here in the Tron at a time when the police were waiting for some mysterious drug peddler?

Rebus believed in coincidence, but this was stretching things a bit too far. Jackie Crawford was somewhere in this crowd, somewhere shaking hands with people whom, a scant four years before, he might have been terrorising with a sawn-off shotgun. Rebus had to do something, whether Crawford was the 'other man' or not. He began squeezing through the crowd again, this time ignoring proffered hands and greetings. He moved on his toes, craning his head over the heads of the revellers, seeking the square-jawed, wiry-haired head of his prey. He was trying to recall whether there was some tradition in Scotland that ghosts from your past came to haunt you at midnight on Hogmanay. He thought not. Besides, Crawford was no ghost. His hands had been meaty and warm, his thumb pressing speculatively against Rebus's knuckles. The eyes which had glanced momentarily into Rebus's eyes had been clear and blue, but uninterested.

Had Crawford recognised his old adversary? Rebus couldn't be sure. There had been no sign of recognition, no raising of eyebrows or opening of the mouth. Just three mumbled words before moving on to the next hand. Was Crawford drunk? Most probably: few sane and sober individuals visited the Tron on this night of all nights. Good; a drunken Crawford would have been unlikely to recognise him. Yet the voice had been quiet and unslurred, the eyes focused. Crawford had not seemed drunk, had not acted drunk. Sober as a judge, in fact. This, too, worried Rebus.

But then, *everything* worried him this evening. He couldn't afford any slip-ups from the operation's Edinburgh contingent. It would give too much ammo to the Glasgow faction: there was a certain competitive spirit between the two forces. For 'competitive spirit' read 'loathing'. Each would want to claim any arrest as *its* victory; and each would blame any foul-up on the other.

This had been explained to him very clearly by Chief Inspector Lauderdale.

'But surely, sir,' Rebus had replied, 'catching these men is what's most important.'

'Rubbish, John,' Lauderdale had replied. 'What's important is that we don't look like arseholes in front of McLeish and his men.'

Which, of course, Rebus had already known; he just liked winding his superior up a little the better to watch him perform. Superintendent Michael McLeish was an outspoken and devout Catholic, and Rebus's chief did not like Catholics. But Rebus hated bigots, and so he wound up Lauderdale whenever he could and had a name for him behind his back: the Clockwork Orangeman.

The crowd was thinning out as Rebus headed away from the Tron and uphill towards the castle. He was, he knew, moving away from the surveillance and should inform his fellow officers of the fact, but if his hunch was right, he was also following the man behind the whole deal. Suddenly he caught sight of Crawford, who seemed to be moving purposefully out of the crowd, heading on to the pavement and giving a half-turn of his head, knowing he was being followed.

So he had recognised Rebus, and now had seen him hurrying after him. The policeman exhaled noisily and pushed his way through the outer ring of the celebrations. His arms ached, as though he had been swimming against a strong current, but now that he was safely out of the water, he saw that Crawford had vanished. He looked along the row of shops, separated each from the other by narrow, darkened closes. Up those closes were the entrances to flats, courtyards surrounded by university halls of residence, and many steep and worn steps leading from the High Street down to The Mound. Rebus had to choose one of them. If he hesitated, or made the wrong choice, Crawford would make good his escape. He ran to the first alley and, glancing down it, listening for footsteps, decided to move on. At the second close, he chose not to waste any more time and ran in, passing dimly lit doorways festooned with graffiti, dank walls, and frozen cobbles. Until, launching himself down a flight of steps into almost absolute darkness, he stumbled. He flailed for a handrail to stop him from falling, and found his arm grabbed by a powerful hand, saving him.

Crawford was standing against the side of the alley, on a platform between flights of steps. Rebus sucked in air, trying to calm himself. There was a sound in his ears like the aftermath of an explosion.

'Thanks,' he spluttered.

'You were following me.' The voice was effortlessly calm.

'Was I?' It was a lame retort and Crawford knew it. He chuckled.

'Yes, Mr Rebus, you were. You must have gotten a bit of a shock.'

Rebus nodded. 'A bit, yes, after all these years, Jackie.'

'I'm surprised you recognised me. People tell me I've changed.'

'Not that much.' Rebus glanced down at his arm, which was still in Crawford's vicelike grip. The grip relaxed and fell away.

'Sorry.'

Rebus was surprised at the apology, but tried not to let it show. He was busy covertly studying Crawford's body, looking for any bulge big enough to be a package or a gun.

'So what were you doing back there?' he asked, not particularly interested in the answer, but certainly interested in the time it might buy him.

Crawford seemed amused. 'Bringing in the New Year, of course. What else would I be doing?'

It was a fair question, but Rebus chose not to answer it. 'When did you get out?'

'A month back.' Crawford could sense Rebus's suspicion. 'It's legit. Honest to God, Sergeant, as He is my witness. I haven't done a runner or anything.'

'You ran from *me*. And it's Inspector now, by the way.'

Crawford smiled again. 'Congratulations.'

'Why did you run?'

'Was I running?'

'You know you were.'

'The reason I was running was because the last person I wanted to see tonight of all nights was you, Inspector Rebus. You spoilt it for me.'

Rebus frowned. He was *looking* at Trigger Crawford, but felt he was talking to somebody else, someone calmer and less dangerous, someone, well, *ordinary*. He was confused, but still suspicious. 'Spoilt what exactly?'

'My New Year resolution. I came here to make peace with the world.'

It was Rebus's turn to smile, though not kindly. 'Make peace, eh?'

'That's right.'

'No more guns? No more armed robberies?'

Crawford was shaking his head slowly. Then he held open his coat. 'No more shooters, Inspector. That's a promise. You see, I've made my own peace.'

Peace or piece? Rebus couldn't be sure. He was reaching into his own jacket pocket, from which he produced a police radio. Crawford looked on the level. He even sounded on the level, but facts had to be verified. So he called in and asked for a check to be made on John Crawford, nickname 'Trigger'. Crawford smiled shyly at the mention of that name. Rebus held on to the radio, waiting for the computer to do its stuff, waiting for the station to respond.

'It's been a long time since anyone called me Trigger,' Crawford said. 'Quite some time.'

'How come they released you after four?'

'A bit less than four, actually,' corrected Crawford. 'They released me because I was no longer a threat to society. You'll find that hard to believe. In fact, you'll find it *impossible* to believe. That's not my fault, it's yours. You think men like me can never go straight. But we can. You see, something happened to me in prison. I found Jesus Christ.'

Rebus knew the look on his face was a picture, and it caused Crawford to smile again, still shyly. He looked down at the tips of his shoes.

'That's right, Inspector. I became a Christian. It wasn't any kind of blinding light. It took a while. I got bored inside and I started reading books. One day I picked up the Bible and just opened it at random. What I read there seemed to make sense. It was the Good News Bible, written in plain English. I read bits and pieces, just flicked through it. Then I went to one of the Sunday services, mainly because there were a few things I couldn't understand and I wanted to ask the minister about them. And he helped me a bit. That's how it started. It changed my life.'

Rebus could think of nothing to say. He thought of himself as a Christian, too, a sceptical Christian, a little like Crawford himself perhaps. Full of questions that needed answering. No, this couldn't be right. He was *nothing* like Crawford. Nothing at all like him. Crawford was an animal; his kind never changed. Did they? Just because he had never met a 'changed man', did that mean such a thing did not exist? After all, he'd never met the Queen or the Prime Minister either. The radio crackled to life in his hand.

'Rebus here,' he said, and then listened.

It was all true. The details from Crawford's file were being read to him. Model prisoner. Bible class. Recommended for early release. Personal tragedy.

'Personal tragedy?' Rebus looked at Crawford.

'Ach, my son died. He was only in his twenties.'

Rebus, having heard enough, had already switched off the radio. 'I'm sorry,' he said. Crawford just shrugged, shrugged shoulders beneath which were tucked no hidden shotguns, and slipped his hands into his pockets, pockets where no pistols lurked. But Rebus held out a hand towards him.

'Happy New Year,' he said.

Crawford stared at the hand, then brought out his own right hand. The two men shook warmly, their grips firm.

'Happy New Year,' said Crawford. Then he glanced back up the close. 'Look, Inspector, if it's all right with you, I think I'll go back up the Tron. It was daft of me to run away in the first place. There are plenty of hands up there I've not shaken yet.'

Rebus nodded slowly. He understood now. For Crawford, the New Year was something special, a new start in more ways than one. Not everyone was given that chance.

'Aye,' he said. 'On you go.'

Crawford had climbed three steps before he paused. 'Incidentally,' he called, 'what were *you* doing at the Tron?'

'What else would I be doing there on New Year?' replied Rebus. 'I was working.'

'No rest for the wicked, eh?' said Crawford, climbing the slope back up to the High Street.

Rebus watched until Crawford disappeared into the gloom. He knew he should follow him. After all, he *was* still working. He was sure now that Crawford had been speaking the truth, that he had nothing to do with the drug deal. Their meeting had been coincidence, nothing more. But who would have believed it? Trigger Crawford a 'model prisoner'. And they said mankind no longer lived in an age of miracles.

Rebus climbed slowly. There seemed more people than ever on the High Street. He guessed things would be at their busiest around half past midnight, with the streets emptying quickly after that. If the deal was going to go through, it would take place before that time. He recognised one of the Glasgow detectives heading towards him. As he spotted Rebus, the detective half-raised his arms.

'Where have you been? We thought you'd buggered off home.'

'Nothing happening then?'

The detective sighed. 'No, nothing at all. Lyons looks a bit impatient. I don't think he's going to give it much longer himself.'

'I thought your informant was airtight?'

'As a rule. Maybe this will be the exception.' The detective smiled, seemingly used to such disappointments in his life. Rebus had noticed earlier that the young man possessed badly chewed fingernails and even the skin around the nails was torn and raw-looking. A stressed young man. In a few years he would be overweight and then would become heart attack material. Rebus knew that he himself was heart attack material: h.a.m., they called it back at the station. You were lean (meaning fit) or you were ham. Rebus was decidedly the latter.

'So anyway, where were you?'

'I bumped into an old friend. Well, to be precise, an old adversary. Jackie Crawford.'

'Jackie Crawford? You mean Trigger Crawford?' The young detective was rifling through his memory files. 'Oh yes, I heard he was out.'

'Did you? Nobody bothered to tell me.'

'Yes, something about his son dying. Drug overdose. All the fire went out of Crawford after that. Turned into a Bible basher.'

They were walking back towards the crowd. Back towards where Alan Lyons waited for a suitcase full of heroin. Rebus stopped dead in his tracks.

'Drugs? Did you say his son died from drugs?'

The detective nodded. 'The big H. It wasn't too far from my patch. Somewhere in Partick.'

'Did Crawford's son live in Glasgow, then?'

'No, he was just visiting. He stayed here in Edinburgh.' The detective was not as slow as some. He knew what Rebus was thinking. 'Christ, you don't mean . . . ?'

And then they were both running, pushing their way through the crowd, and the detective from Glasgow was shouting into his radio, but there was noise all around him, yelling and cheering and singing, smothering his words. Their progress was becoming slower. It was like moving through water chest-high. Rebus's legs felt useless and sore and there was a line of sweat trickling down his spine. Crawford's son had died from heroin, heroin purchased most probably in Edinburgh, and the man behind most of the heroin deals in Edinburgh was waiting somewhere up ahead. Coincidence? He had never really believed in coincidences, not really. They were convenient excuses for shrugging off the unthinkable.

What had Crawford said? Something about coming here tonight to make peace. Well, there were ways and ways of making peace, weren't there? 'If any mischief should follow, then thou shalt give life for life.' That was from Exodus. A dangerous book, the Bible. It could be made to say anything, its meaning in the mind of the beholder.

What was going through Jackie Crawford's mind? Rebus dreaded to think. There was a commotion up ahead, the crowd forming itself into a tight semicircle around a shopfront. Rebus squeezed his way to the front.

'Police,' he shouted. 'Let me through, please.'

Grudgingly, the mass of bodies parted just enough for him to make progress. Finally he found himself at the front, staring at the slumped body of Alan Lyons. A long smear ran down the shop window to where he lay and his chest was stained dark red. One of the Glasgow officers was trying unsuccessfully to stem the flow of blood, using his own rolled-up coat, now sopping wet. Other officers were keeping back the crowd. Rebus caught snatches of what they were saying.

'Looked like he was going to shake hands.'

'Looked like he was hugging him.'

'Then the knife . . .'

'Pulled out a knife.'

'Stabbed him twice before we could do anything.'

'Couldn't do anything.'

A siren had started near by, inching closer. There were always ambulances on standby near the Tron on Hogmanay. Beside Lyons, still gripped in his left hand, was the bag containing the money for the deal.

'Will he be all right?' Rebus said to nobody in

particular, which was just as well since nobody answered. He was remembering back a month to another dealer, another knife . . . Then he saw Crawford. He was being restrained on the edge of the crowd by two more plainclothes men. One held his arms behind him while the other frisked him for weapons. On the pavement between where Crawford stood and Alan Lyons lay dying or dead there was a fairly ordinary-looking knife, small enough to conceal in a sock or a waistband, but enough for the job required. More than an inch of blade was excess. The other detective was beside Rebus.

'Aw, Christ,' he said. But Rebus was staring at Crawford and Crawford was staring back, and in that moment they understood one another well enough. 'I don't suppose,' the detective was saying, 'we'll be seeing the party with the merchandise. Always supposing he was going to turn up in any event.'

'I'm not so sure about that,' answered Rebus, turning his gaze from Crawford. 'Ask yourself this: how did Crawford know Lyons would be in the High Street tonight?' The detective did not answer. Behind them, the crowd was pressing closer for a look at the body and then making noises of revulsion before opening another can of lager or half-bottle of vodka. The ambulance was still a good fifty yards away. Rebus nodded towards Crawford.

'He knows where the stuff is but he's probably dumped it somewhere. Somewhere nobody can ever touch it. It was just bait, that's all. Just bait.'

And as bait it had worked. Hook, line, and bloody sinker. Lyons had swallowed it, while Rebus, equally fooled, had swallowed something else. He felt it sticking in his throat like something cancerous, something no amount of coughing would dislodge. He glanced towards the prone body again and smiled involuntarily. A headline had come to mind, one that would never be used.

LYONS FED TO THE CHRISTIAN.

Someone was being noisily sick somewhere behind him. A bottle shattered against a wall. The loudest voices in the crowd were growing irritable and hard edged. In fifteen minutes or so, they would cease to be revellers and would be transformed into troublemakers. A woman shrieked from one of the many darkened closes. The look on Jackie Crawford's face was one of calm and righteous triumph. He offered no resistance to the officers. He had known they were watching Lyons, had known he might kill Lyons but he would never get away. And still he had driven home the knife. What else was he to do with his freedom?

The night was young and so was the year. Rebus held out his hand towards the detective.

'Happy New Year,' he said. 'And many more of them.'

The young man stared at him blankly. 'Don't think you're blaming us for this,' he said. 'This was your fault. You let Crawford go. It's Edinburgh's balls-up, not ours.'

Rebus shrugged and let his arm fall to his side. Then he started to walk along the pavement, moving further and further from the scene. The ambulance moved past him. Someone slapped him on the back and offered a hand. From a distance, the young detective was watching him retreat.

'Away to hell,' said Rebus quietly, not sure for whom the message was intended.

Sweating It Out With Dover

JOYCE PORTER

DETECTIVE FILE

OFFICER: Detective Chief Inspector Wilfred Dover

FORCE: Murder Squad, Scotland Yard

TIME: 1980

CASES: *Dover One* (1964), *Dover and the Unkindest Cut of All* (1967), *Dover Strikes Again* (1973), *It's Murder With Dover* (1973) etc.

PROFILE: The fattest, laziest and most inefficient member of Scotland Yard's famed Murder Squad, Dover is certainly one of the oddest creations in crime fiction, comparable only perhaps with Rex Stout's huge, gourmet private eye, Nero Wolfe – indeed Ellery Queen once referred to Dover as 'the most unlikeable sleuth in the history of crime fiction'. The Chief Inspector is vulgar, harsh to the point of offensiveness to his junior officers, and forever thinking of his next meal – which, ideally, he will scrounge off some unsuspecting person. Only when a sumptuous meal is in the offing will Dover switch his manner to one of gross flattery. There is actually little information available as to how this appalling man has achieved such a high ranking at the Yard beyond the suggestion that as no one wanted him in their department he was constantly being moved up the promotion ladder! Dover is a constant moaner – many of his complaints being about his ill-fitting false teeth or stomach upsets caused by overeating – and when he does solve a case it is either from a sudden burst of shrewdness or the hard work of his much put-upon assistant, Sergeant MacGregor. Whichever is the case, Dover will always look after Number One and take any credit going.

CREATOR: Joyce Porter (b. 1924) is the absolute antithesis of her creation, a gentle lady who served in the Women's Royal Air Force for many years before producing a brand of crime fiction which is always highlighted by its comedy and exaggeration. Her creations include the inept secret agent Eddie Brown; the grotesque amateur detective the Honourable Constance Ethel Morrison-Burke; and the obese Chief Inspector Dover, who has featured in more than a dozen novels and short stories since his first acclaimed appearance in *Dover One* (1964). Of her gross fatman she has written, 'The fact that his career as a detective has endured, and even flourished in a mild way, is almost entirely due to the fact that most criminals, incredible as it may seem, are even more inept and stupid.' In 'Sweating It Out With Dover', written in 1980, the combination of a sweltering summer day and a brutal murder make the grunting, snarling, belching Chief Inspector, if anything, even more impossible to bear.

***

Every English summer, no matter how awful the weather is in general, is blessed with one gloriously hot, really sweltering day – and in drought years we sometimes have two. The savage murder of young Elvin Garlick took place on one of these exceptional days when the sky was blue and the sun blazed down. So, too, did Detective Chief Inspector Wilfred Dover's 'investigation'.

Indeed, his conduct of the case and the highly unseasonable weather were not unconnected.

It was getting on for midday when Detective Chief Inspector Dover, chaperoned as always by MacGregor, his young and handsome sergeant, arrived at Skinners Farm. The temperature was already pushing up into the eighties and most people would have been delighted at getting out into the country on such a marvellous day. Chief Inspector Dover, however, wasn't most people and, in spite of appearances, Skinners Farm was only twenty-five miles from Charing Cross and so not really country anyhow.

Charitable people might have thought it was the heat which had addled Dover's brains but, in reality, he was just as slow-witted on even the most temperate day. On this occasion he didn't seem able to get it into his head that Skinners Farm wasn't actually a farm, but an over-restored Georgian house standing in its own grounds and separated from the hurly-burly of the outside world by a couple of fields full of gently ruminating black and white cows.

'I suppose they call it a farm, sir,' said MacGregor, surreptitiously dabbing at the back of his neck with a slightly starched white handkerchief, 'because it was once the farmhouse.'

'Bloody fools,' said Dover, the sweat standing out in beads on his forehead. As a concession to the weather, he had left off his overcoat – but the greasy bowler hat, the blue serge suit, and the down-at-heel boots were the same as ever. ''Strewth,' panted Dover, 'but it's hot!'

'Perhaps we could have the window down a bit, sir,' said MacGregor, who'd been wondering for some time if the peculiar smell in the police car was Dover or merely something agricultural they were spraying on the fields.

'I hope they've shifted that blooming body,' said Dover

querulously as he plucked at his shirt. 'It'll be ponging to high heaven else.'

MacGregor glanced at his watch. 'They may not have moved it yet, sir,' he warned. 'It's only about an hour and a half since they found him, and since I understand he's lying in some sort of copse and reasonably sheltered from the sun—'

'You won't get me going to see it,' declared Dover flatly. 'I'll bet it's all crawling with flies. Here' – he roused himself as the car turned into a driveway – 'are we there?'

The married couple who lived at Skinners Farm were, understandably, in a state of some distress and they greeted the arrival of the two high-powered detectives from Scotland Yard as though it was a heaven-sent solution to all the horrors of that terrible morning. Anxiously hospitable, they conducted a profusely sweating Dover through the house and out on to the comparatively cool and shady veranda.

Here they installed him on a cane chaise longue, plied him with cigarettes, and asked him what he would like in the way of a long, cool drink. Dover, having graciously accepted pretty little Mrs Hewson's suggestion of an iced lager, hoisted his boots up on to the footrest and flopped back. 'Strewth, this was the life! And it was going to take more than a bloody murder case to dislodge him from it.

When, a few minutes later, Mr Hewson came out with the drinks, Dover was more or less obliged to open his eyes. Having half a pint of ice-cold liquid sloshing around in his stomach had quite a bracing effect on him, however, and for a few minutes he was actually sitting up and taking some interest in his surroundings. The veranda, he discovered, overlooked a large and well-kept garden which fell gently away from the house. In the distance was what appeared to be a clump of trees where several figures in dark blue could dimly be seen moving about.

Dover had no wish to strain his eyesight by peering through the heat haze, so he treated himself to a good look at his host instead. Mr Hewson, he ascertained without much interest, was a man of about fifty, but very fit and youthful looking. He was wearing a pair of powder-blue shorts and matching T-shirt, but his manner was far from being carefree and relaxed. As he explained with an uneasy laugh, he wasn't accustomed to stumbling over dead bodies in the middle of a Saturday morning.

Dover relieved his own inner tensions with a good belch and wiped the back of his hand across his mouth. 'You found him, did you?'

'No, not exactly,' said Mr Hewson. 'Tansy, here' – he indicated his wife who was happily engaged in refilling Dover's glass – 'actually found him, but naturally I went down to have a look before I phoned the police. I hoped,' concluded Mr Hewson with a bleak little smile, 'that she'd got it wrong.'

'Still hanging around, are they?' asked Dover through a yawn which gave everybody a fine view of his dentures.

'The local police? Yes. The Inspector's using the phone in the sitting-room and the rest of them are still down there in the old orchard.' Mr Hewson pointed toward the clump of trees which Dover had already more or less noticed. 'They're searching through the undergrowth. Er – do you want me to tell them you're here?'

The last thing Dover wanted was a mob of local flatfoots swarming all over him in that heat. He leered encouragingly at pretty little Mrs Hewson. 'So what happened, missus?' he asked and rattled his now empty glass.

Pretty little Mrs Hewson grew tearful. She'd told her story four times already and really didn't want to go through it all again.

Dover had little sympathy for a woman who seemed incapable of recognising an empty glass when she saw one. 'Oh, get on with it!' he advised impatiently.

Mrs Hewson gulped, dried her eyes on a wisp of a handkerchief, clutched her husband's hand, and complied. 'It's all my fault, actually. If I hadn't decided to grub up the old orchard and turn it into a vegetable garden, none of this would ever have happened. Freddie wasn't a bit keen on the idea – were you, darling? He said he'd do it himself some time but – well, I know how busy he is, so I got hold of this young man from the village to come and do it.'

'What young man?' demanded Dover, sportingly moving his empty glass even nearer so as to give Mrs Hewson every chance.

'The young man who's been murdered. Elvin Garlick. He works for a firm of landscape gardeners so, of course, he's able to borrow their equipment.'

'You mean he was doing the job for you in his own time?' MacGregor, sipping straight lemonade because he didn't drink when he was on duty, was taking notes. Well, somebody in that partnership had to behave responsibly, didn't they?

'Oh, yes!' said Mrs Hewson with some pride. 'And for cash. That way you get it cheaper because nobody has to pay income tax or VAT or anything. The only trouble was,' she added with a disconsolate little moue, 'he could only come on weekends and that meant I couldn't keep it a secret from Freddie. I'd wanted to present him with a *fait accompli*, you see.'

'Ugh,' grunted Dover, just to show he was still awake.

'Well, Elvin arrived about half-past eight this morning.' Mrs Hewson raised her pretty little chin defensively. 'He told me to call him Elvin. He said everybody always did, especially when he was obliging them. Well, I told him exactly what I wanted doing and left him to get on with it.'

'And where were you all this time, sir?' MacGregor turned to Mr Hewson.

'I was still getting up. Saturday's my day off, too, you know.' Freddie Hewson felt that further explanation was required. 'I'm a stockbroker so, of course, I'm in the City all week.'

'So you didn't see Mr Garlick?'

'No. I knew somebody'd come to the house, of course, and then later you could hear his rotivator or whatever churning away down there in the orchard. That's when this naughty little girl here' – Mr Hewson squeezed his wife's hand affectionately – 'finally had to tell me what she was up to.'

'He was ever so surprised!' simpered little Mrs Hewson happily.

'And then what, sir?'

'Well, then nothing, Sergeant. Tansy and I had breakfast out here on the veranda. Garlick was all right then because we could hear him – couldn't we, darling? After breakfast I went round to the back of the house to work on my car. I'm rebuilding a 1934 Alvis and there were a few things I wanted to get done before it got too hot.'

'And you, Mrs Hewson?'

'I was in the kitchen, getting as much as I could ready for dinner tonight. Well, you don't want to spend a glorious day like this slaving over a hot stove, do you?'

'The kitchen's on the far side of the house, too, Sergeant,' explained Mr Hewson, 'so neither of us could see anything going on in the old orchard. And, as I told the other policeman, we didn't hear anything, either. We were both pretty absorbed in what we were doing and, of course, Garlick was a good way off and he wasn't using his machinery the whole time. Well, at about eleven, I suppose it would be, Tansy brought me out a cup of coffee to the garage. She said she was going to take some down to Garlick, too. I would have gone myself, of course, but I'd just started stripping down the clutch and it was all a bit fraught and I really didn't want to leave it.'

'Oh, I didn't mind, lovie!' cooed Mrs Hewson. 'Like I said, I was glad to get out of that kitchen for a few minutes and stretch my legs.'

MacGregor nodded. 'So you walked down to the old orchard with the coffee, Mrs Hewson?'

'That's right. Well, when I got there, I couldn't see or hear Elvin anywhere, so I shouted his name. I wasn't keen to go tramping about down there because it's waist-high in weeds and nettles and things.' Mrs Hewson stretched out her shapely bare legs for the general delectation and to emphasise the point she was making.

MacGregor did, indeed, begin to sweat a bit more freely, but it was many moons since any part of the female anatomy had sent the blood racing through Dover's veins. He merely pushed his bowler hat a bit farther back on his head and inquired if anybody'd got a cigarette to spare.

The murder investigation ground to a halt as the Hewsons obligingly rushed off in all directions to fetch cigarettes, matches, and ashtrays. They finally redeemed themselves by refilling Dover's glass, and it was only when they'd got Dover happily swilling and sucking away that Mrs Hewson was able to finish her story.

The end proved something of an anticlimax. Having received no answer to her shouts, Mrs Hewson had gingerly ventured farther into the old orchard and found Garlick just lying there, face down, with his own pitchfork sticking out of his back. Pretty little Mrs Hewson wasn't sure whether she'd screamed, but she was certain she hadn't touched the body.

'I didn't have to,' she explained unhappily. 'I just knew

he was dead. I dropped everything and came running back up here to tell Freddie.'

Mr Hewson took up the tale. 'I went tearing down to the old orchard,' he said, 'and there he was. I couldn't see any sign of breathing – Garlick was stripped to the waist, by the way – and with that pitchfork pinning him to the ground . . . well, I knew it couldn't be an accident or anything. I left everything just as it was and came back up here and phoned the police.'

'And we had a patrol car here in less than five minutes.' A man who had been waiting just inside the sitting-room for a suitably dramatic moment stepped forward. There was an unmistakable drop of the jaw when he got his first clear look at Dover, but he recovered well and introduced himself. 'Detective Inspector Threlfall, sir. I arrived at eleven twenty-six in response to an urgent summons from the patrol car and I have been in charge of the preliminary investigation since my arrival.'

Detective Inspector Threlfall paused in case the seventeen and a quarter stone of solid flesh stretched out on the chaise longue wished to make some response. It didn't. With the mercury climbing that high in the thermometers, Dover had no energy to spare for social niceties.

Inspector Threlfall cleared his throat and tried again. 'You'll want to see the body, sir.'

That stung Dover into life. 'I bloody shan't!' he growled, the mere thought of venturing out into that hot bright world outside making him feel quite sick.

'The doctor thought that Garlick had been knocked unconscious with a blow across the back of the head, sir.' Inspector Threlfall would never have believed that Dover didn't care a fig either way. 'Then he was run through with the pitchfork while he was still out. Crude, but effective.'

MacGregor took pity on the Inspector. 'Are there any signs as to which way the murderer came, sir?'

Inspector Threlfall shook his head. 'Not so far, Sergeant. Mind you, Buff had been churning things up for a couple of hours before he bought it, so it's a tricky job trying to sort things out. Mind you, the murderer could have come from almost any direction. Crept down this way past the house or come across those fields or' – Inspector Threlfall waved his arms about in the appropriate directions – 'got into the orchard from the other side. You can't see it from here, but there's a road running along there, not fifty yards from where Buff was killed.'

Dover's chair creaked pathetically as he tried to find a more comfortable position.

'Buff?' queried MacGregor with a frown.

Inspector Threlfall shrugged. 'That was his nickname. I've known him since he was old enough to appear before a juvenile court, you know, and he's been a regular customer ever since. We're going to miss him. He'd had a go at pretty well everything – pinching old ladies' pension books, drunk and disorderly, breaking and entering, nicking cars, shoplifting—'

'Good heavens!' gasped Mrs Hewson faintly.

Inspector Threlfall glanced at her with just a touch of contempt. 'That's how he got his job with Wythenshaw's, madam. His probation officer swung it for him. Well, they'd tried everything else. Seems they thought a spell of honest toil might sort him out. I don't know what old Wythenshaw's going to say when he finds out Buff's been "borrowing" all that expensive gear.'

'But he told me his boss was only too willing to lend him the stuff,' protested Mrs Hewson, carefully avoiding her husband's eye.

'Well, he would, wouldn't he, madam?' asked Inspector Threlfall easily. 'Always had a very smooth tongue, young Buff, especially where the ladies were concerned.' He turned back to MacGregor. 'That's where I'd start looking, if I was you, Sergeant. Buff's got more girls into trouble than you and I've had hot dinners. There must be hundreds of fathers and husbands and boyfriends thirsting for his blood – and that's not counting any members of the fair sex who might have had it in for him.'

'It hardly sounds like a woman's crime,' said MacGregor doubtfully. He was dying to get down to the old orchard and see things for himself.

'I don't see why not. You don't need much strength to knock somebody out with a chunk of wood or something, and that pitchfork had prongs as sharp as a razor. It would go through him like a hot knife through butter.'

'Oh, dear!' moaned Mrs Hewson, clamping both hands across her mouth and going as white as a sheet.

Her husband leapt across, and wrapping his arms protectively round her, helped her to her feet. He smiled apologetically at the three stolidly staring policemen. 'She's a bit upset, I'm afraid. I'll get her to have a little lie-down. You don't want us any more just now, do you? I think we've told you all we know.'

Nobody seemed much concerned one way or the other, though Dover did bestir himself to remark that, if Mr Hewson was thinking of making his wife some tea, he – Dover – wouldn't say no to a cup.

'These cold drinks are all right,' said Dover confidingly to an astonished Inspector Threlfall, 'but there's nothing to touch a good hot cup of tea, especially in this bloody weather. It brings you out in a good muck sweat.'

'Oh – quite,' said Inspector Threlfall. 'Er – I was wondering what your plans were, sir.'

'Plans?' Dover squinted suspiciously.

'I thought you might like to pop down to the village, sir, and have a word with the lad's mother. He lived with her and she might just know something. I've got some chaps out making general inquiries around the neighbourhood, but I thought I'd best leave Mrs Garlick for you.'

There was an awkward pause. Not that Dover was hesitating. Wild horses weren't going to shift him off that veranda until the temperature outside dropped by at least twenty degrees, but there was the problem of conveying this message to Inspector What's-his-name without too much loss of face. 'How many people knew he was going to be working here this morning?' asked Dover in an attempt to give himself time to think.

Inspector Threlfall rubbed his chin. 'Not many, I should think. Not if he was borrowing the gear without permission. Besides, it's not the sort of thing you'd expect young Buff to be doing in his spare time. Normally, if he wanted extra money, he'd just nick it.'

MacGregor wiped the perspiration off his upper lip. The veranda was only comparatively cool. 'Maybe he's turned over a new leaf?'

'More likely casing the joint,' said Inspector Threlfall. 'The Hewsons must have been mad to let him come within a mile of this place.'

MacGregor fanned himself gently with his notebook. 'It was more Mrs Hewson, wasn't it? I don't think her husband knew anything about it until Garlick turned up this morning.'

'Seems he wanted that old orchard left just as it was,' said Inspector Threlfall. 'Claims it's a nature reserve or something. I reckon he'll pin her ears back for her when all this is over.'

Most untypically at this stage in the proceedings, Dover was wide awake and listening intently. It wasn't, however, the lethargic conversation about the Hewsons' private life that was claiming his anxious attention, but the more interesting rumbles that were coming from his stomach.

MacGregor laughed a cool, sophisticated, man-of-the-world laugh. 'Hewson'll just have to teach her who's boss, otherwise he won't be able to call his soul his own.'

'Hark who's talking!' jeered Dover, for whom it was never too hot and sticky to be unpleasant. He left his guts to take care of themselves for a moment. 'You could write all you know about married life on a threepenny bit, laddie, and still have room for the Lord's Prayer. Any moron can see that she's got him by the short and curly. What do you expect when a man goes and marries a flighty young thing half his age?'

'I don't think he's quite as—'

'Near as damn it!' snarled Dover, who didn't care to be contradicted, especially when he wasn't feeling too frisky in the first place. 'There's no fool like an old fool.'

'Speaking of marriage,' said Inspector Threlfall – but nobody was listening to him.

Dover had tuned in to those ominous visceral splutterings again and MacGregor was frantically trying to work out if Dover had spotted something he'd missed.

'Do you think it might be a case of jealousy, sir?' MacGregor asked, eyeing Dover doubtfully.

Dover blinked. 'Eh?'

MacGregor grew even more worried. 'The elderly husband, sir, and the attractive young wife? Plus the sexy young man from the village? Do you think there could have been anything between Mrs Hewson and Garlick?' MacGregor appealed to Inspector Threlfall. 'You did say Garlick was attractive to women, didn't you, sir?'

'Like a honeypot to flies,' agreed Inspector Threlfall.

'Or, maybe' – MacGregor was more interested in his own brilliant deductions – 'it was *Mrs* Hewson! She takes the coffee down to the old orchard, say, and Garlick makes improper advances towards her. She repulses him. He persists. She picks up the nearest fallen branch or what-have-you and—'

'Bunkum!' said Dover, coming out in a hot flush at the mere thought of such an expenditure of energy in that heat. 'She'd not have the strength. She's only knee-high to a grasshopper.'

'Garlick wasn't all that big a chap, sir,' said Inspector Threlfall as he remembered that these two Scotland Yard experts hadn't yet even seen the body. 'A woman might have done it. But what I wanted to mention, sir, was about the Hewsons.'

'Well, why don't you spit it out, then? I haven't got all bloody day to sit around waiting for you to come to the point.'

The training that Inspector Threlfall had received at the police school all those years ago stood him in good stead now. Otherwise Skinners Farm might have witnessed another and even bloodier murder. 'They're not actually husband and wife, sir. Not legally, that is.'

Dover shrugged his ample shoulders and folded his hands over his ample paunch. 'So what? It's no skin off my nose.' He closed his eyes against the glare coming in from the garden, only to snap them open again as the desire to score off a brother police officer proved stronger than the longing for a quiet forty winks. 'She wears a wedding ring,' he pointed out, much to MacGregor's amazement because one didn't really expect Dover to notice such things. 'And she calls herself "Mrs".'

'That's as maybe, sir,' said Inspector Threlfall, nobly swallowing the rejoinder he would have liked to have made. 'But they are definitely not married – well, not to each other. Hewson's already got a wife. Or as far as anybody knows, he has.'

'And what the hell's that supposed to mean?'

'It's just that I happened to be involved when she did a bunk, sir. The first Mrs Hewson, that is. I was on duty when Hewson came in to report that she was missing. It must be six years ago, now. He wanted us to find her.'

'But you didn't?'

'There's nothing we can do about a runaway wife, sir.

You know that. I carried out a routine investigation but there was nothing suspicious about her disappearance. All I could do was suggest to Mr Hewson that he try the Salvation Army, not that it was her sort of thing, really.'

Working on the principle that 'talk, talk on the veranda' was a damned sight better than 'walk, walk across that dirty great garden', Dover demanded more details about the first Mrs Hewson and her mysterious disappearance. Inspector Threlfall was obliged to search his memory. As far as he was concerned, the whole incident had been totally unremarkable. It was true that the first Mrs Hewson had cleared out without a word and nobody had heard from her since, but this could be attributed to pure spite.

'Spite?' queried Dover, almost as though he was interested.

'It makes it difficult for Hewson to divorce her, sir. As things stand now, he's got to wait all of seven years and then apply to the courts for permission to presume that she's dead. Meantime, his hands are tied. You can't serve divorce papers on a woman you can't find. Hewson, himself, reckoned that she'd stay out of sight until the seven years was nearly up and then put in an appearance again, just to be bloody-minded. The marriage was pretty well on the rocks when she left home but she seems to have made up her mind not to let him go without a struggle.'

'You're sure there were no signs of foul play?'

'Quite sure, sir. She'd taken all her clothes and jewellery and her passport. There were a couple of suitcases missing and she'd cleared out their joint banking account. Her car turned up a few weeks later. It had been abandoned in the long-stay car park at Gatwick airport but there were no clues in it as to where she'd gone.'

Dover ran a stubby finger round inside his shirt collar.

'Strewth, it was hot! He hoped What's-his-name wasn't going to be all bloody day with that cup of tea. 'Was there another man?'

'Hewson thought there might be, sir, but he didn't know. She was on her own here quite a bit while he was off working in the City.'

'What about her friends?' Dover might not have been the world's most brilliant detective but, in his long years in the police, even he'd managed to pick up a few bits of technique. 'Did she mention to any of them she was thinking of running away?'

Inspector Threlfall shook his head. 'As far as I can remember, sir, she didn't have any friends. At least, not round here.'

'Relations?' Dover had begun thrashing about in his chair like a stranded porpoise.

Inspector Threlfall watched these antics nervously. Was Fatty having some kind of heatstroke or was he merely trying to hoist himself to his feet? 'Only a sister in Ireland, sir, and they hadn't spoken for years.'

With a final wheeze Dover managed to stand up. Too hot to move, it may have been, but, when Nature calls, even the least fastidious of us is obliged to go. Especially if we have bladders as weak as Dover's. 'Bloody foreign muck!' he grumbled. 'It goes straight through you. I don't know why people can't give you proper English beer.' He turned to MacGregor who was trying to pretend that none of this had anything to do with him. 'Where is it, laddie?'

Long association with Dover had taught MacGregor to give a high priority on every possible occasion to locating where 'it' was. 'I believe there's a small cloakroom at the foot of the stairs, sir.'

Dover departed at an urgent trot, leaving a thoughtful silence behind him on the veranda.

Inspector Threlfall loosened his tie. 'He's a bit of a lad, eh?' he said at last.

MacGregor responded with a thin humourless smile and changed the subject. 'Have you any ideas about who killed Garlick, sir?'

'Some,' said Inspector Threlfall, seeing no particular reason to be helpful. Left alone he reckoned he could have solved this case in a couple of hours flat.

'One of his fellow yobboes, sir?'

'Could be.'

'Friday is usually payday,' observed MacGregor carefully. 'Garlick was a bit of a drinker, I think you said?'

'He liked his pint.'

MacGregor closed his notebook to show that this was an off-the-record conversation. 'You often get drunken rows blowing up on a Friday night. Maybe this one didn't get settled until Saturday morning. I mean, who else – except his mates – would have known he'd be working out here this morning? Apart from Mrs Hewson, that is. He'd have hardly spread the news around, would he? And it would only be a local chap who'd know there was easy access to that old orchard from the road.'

Inspector Threlfall contented himself with raising his eyebrows in an enigmatic sort of way. If that was how the clever dicks from the Yard saw it, good luck to 'em! Inspector Threlfall wasn't going to stick his neck out just to show them where they'd gone wrong.

It seemed a very long time before Dover came waddling back. MacGregor tried to get him to continue on down to the scene of the crime while he was still on his feet, but Dover brushed his sergeant's efforts to one side and flopped back into his chair.

'I've just been out round the back,' he announced.

MacGregor's heart sank. Oh, it was all so mortifying!

'But, sir,' he wailed, 'I told you exactly where the cloakroom was!'

Dover flapped an impatient hand. 'Not that, you fool!' he growled. 'I went there first. It was after when I went round the back of the house to have a look. Bloody good thing I did, too. Do you know what? You can't see the kitchen from the garage and you can't see the garage from the kitchen.'

'Sir?'

'That means he did it, laddie!' explained Dover helpfully. He nodded cheerfully at Inspector Threlfall. 'All we need now is a bulldozer and a warrant.'

'I beg your pardon, sir?'

Dover's good humour began to evaporate. If there was one thing that really got to him, it was stupidity, especially on a blooming hot day like this. 'You got cloth ears or something?' he asked Inspector Threlfall savagely. 'I've solved your murder for you. 'Strewth, some people want it with bloody jam on!'

Inspector Threlfall very sensibly clung on to the one bit of this he could understand. 'You've solved the case, sir?'

'It came to me out there,' said Dover, not without a touch of pride. 'I wasn't just twiddling my thumbs, you know. Then I went round the back and Bob's your uncle. It all fits. All you've got to do is dig up the evidence and charge him with murder.'

'But charge – er – who, sir?'

'Well, What's-his-name, you bloody fool!' roared Dover. 'Who else, for God's sake? Look, this morning he waits until his wife – or whatever she is – is safely shut up in the kitchen. Right? Then he nips out of the garage, round the *other* side of the house – get it? – and down across the bloody garden.'

The gesticulations which accompanied this vivid account were a little uncertain as Dover had not actually seen the terrain he was describing. 'He sneaks into this orchard place, finds young Who's-your-father, picks up the nearest blunt instrument, and knocks him out. OK? After that, all he has to do is finish the job off with the pitchfork. Easy as shelling peas.'

Rightly deducing that nothing useful was going to emerge from Inspector Threlfall's feebly gaping mouth, MacGregor himself tried to introduce a note of sanity into the proceedings.

'Are you saying that Mr Hewson murdered Garlick, sir? But why should he? He didn't even know Garlick. In fact' – MacGregor riffled officiously through his note-book – 'he claims that he'd never even seen Garlick until after he was dead. That's a very definite statement, sir, and easy enough to check.'

Dover scowled. Trust MacGregor to start nit-picking! 'He didn't have to know Garlick,' he said sullenly. 'He'd have croaked anybody.'

'You mean Mr Hewson is some sort of homicidal maniac, sir?'

Dover's scowl blackened. If it hadn't been for the excessively hot weather and MacGregor being such a big strapping chap, Dover might have been sorely tempted to go across and belt him one. Insolent young pup! 'Hewson,' he snarled through gritted dentures, 'would have killed *anybody* who started digging that old orchard up.'

The penny dropped and MacGregor could have kicked himself. 'You mean—'

'I mean that's where he buried his first blooming wife!' snapped Dover, making sure that MacGregor didn't steal his thunder this time. 'She didn't run away. He killed her and then buried her with all her clothes and jewellery and stuff out there in that orchard.'

Inspector Threlfall recovered his powers of speech. 'But I investigated the first Mrs Hewson's disappearance, sir, and there were no suspicious circumstances.'

''Strewth,' sneered Dover happily, 'you wouldn't know a suspicious circumstance if it jumped up and bit you! Hewson was just too clever for you, that's all.'

'Well, it's true the marriage wasn't a very happy one,' said Inspector Threlfall, meekly accepting the slur on his professional competence, 'but we took that as a motive for her leaving him.' He glanced across at MacGregor for support. 'I suppose we could have Hewson in again and ask him a few questions.'

Dover reacted to this suggestion with unusual passion. 'Not yet, you bloody don't!' he spluttered indignantly. 'I'm still waiting for that cup of tea he promised me!' This must have sounded a bit thin even to Dover's ears. 'Besides,' he added in an attempt to place his policy of inaction beyond all question, 'I've been invited to lunch.

'Look, why don't you two just push off and get that orchard dug up? It'll probably take you two or three hours. Soon as you find the wife's dead body, you can come and tell me. But not before two o'clock at the earliest, mind! Then we can confront What's-his-name with the facts and get a confession out of him. There's nothing to worry about. He's not the stuff heroes are made of. He'll soon co-operate if we shove him around a bit. And now' – the Dover eyelids drooped slowly over the Dover eyes – 'why don't you just bug off and leave me to have a quiet think?'

Clutching at Straws

RUTH RENDELL

DETECTIVE FILE

OFFICER: Chief Inspector Reginald Wexford

FORCE: Kingsmarkham Police, Sussex

TIME: 1979

CASES: *From Doon with Death* (1964), *Some Lie and Some Die* (1973), *Death Notes* (1981), *Kissing The Gunner's Daughter* (1992) etc.

PROFILE: Comfortably married with two grown-up daughters, Chief Inspector Reg Wexford is in late middle age and while undoubtedly dedicated to his job maintains strong interests outside the Force. He is an intensely domesticated man and close to his wife, Dora, who often provides a respite and ready ear when he wants to escape from the ugliness of a murder enquiry. Described as rather wrinkled and ungainly in appearance, and bulky despite regular bouts of dieting, he has small eyes and curiously shaped, three-cornered ears. A highly moral officer who clings to strong and decent values, Wexford is noted for his tolerance and interest in people, their faults and weaknesses and what makes them commit murder. The Chief Inspector is also never lost for a quotation to offer at any appropriate moment – all drawn from the books which provide another of his off-duty diversions. Apart from the support of his family, Wexford derives a great deal from his strait-laced but determined assistant, Detective Inspector Michael Burden, who is some twenty years his junior.

CREATOR: Ruth Rendell (b. 1930), who has made these two sensitive and complex policemen popular with a huge worldwide audience over the past thirty years, was a local newspaper journalist in West Essex before turning to crime writing and becoming a bestselling author with almost her first book. By Ruth's own admission, Wexford is based on her father: an intellectual and highly moral man who similarly delighted in quoting from literature with all the erudition of a university don! Apart from the series of Kingsmarkham novels, she has also published a number of other books under the pen name of Barbara Vine which have been highly praised for their brilliant psychological insight. A number have been adapted for television in tandem with stories about CI Wexford, who has been continually played since 1990 by George Baker. 'Clutching At Straws' (1979) finds Wexford once again having to use all his powers of tolerance and insight into human nature to cope with the nasty insinuations of local gossip as he endeavours to get to the bottom of what initially seems like the perfectly natural death of a very old lady.

***

They looked shocked and affronted and somehow ashamed. Above all, they looked old. Chief Inspector Wexford thought that in the nature of things a woman of seventy ought to be an orphan, ought to have been an orphan for twenty years. This one had been an orphan for scarcely twenty days. Her husband, sitting opposite her, pulling his wispy moustache, slowly and mechanically shaking his head, seemed older than she, perhaps not so many years the junior of his late mother-in-law.

He wore a brown cardigan with a small neat darn at one elbow and sheepskin slippers, and when he spoke he snuffled. His wife kept saying she couldn't believe her ears, she couldn't believe it, why were people so wicked? Wexford didn't answer that. He couldn't, though he had often wondered himself.

'My mother died of a stroke,' Mrs Betts said tremulously. 'It was on the death certificate, Dr Moss put it on the death certificate.'

Betts snuffled and wheezed. He reminded Wexford of an aged rabbit, a rabbit with myxomatosis perhaps. It was partly the effect of the brown woolly cardigan and the furry slippers, and partly the moustache and the unshaven bristly chin. 'She was ninety-two,' Betts said in his thick catarrhal voice. '*Ninety-two*. I reckon you lot must have got bats in the belfry.'

'I mean,' said Mrs Betts, 'are you saying Dr Moss was telling an untruth? A doctor?'

'Why don't you ask him? We're only ordinary people, the wife and me, we're not educated. Doctor said a cerebral haemorrhage' – Betts stumbled a little over the words – 'and in plain language that's a stroke. That's what he said. Are you saying me or the wife gave Mother a stroke? Are you saying that?'

'I'm making no allegations, Mr Betts.' Wexford felt uncomfortable, wished himself anywhere but in this newly decorated, paint-smartened house. 'I am merely making inquiries which information received obliges me to do.'

'Gossip,' said Mrs Betts bitterly. 'This street's a hotbed of gossip. Pity they've got nothing better to do. Oh, I know what they're saying. Half of them turn up their noses and look the other way when I pass them. All except Elsie Parrish, and that goes without saying.'

'She's been a brick,' said her husband. 'A real brick is Elsie.' He stared at Wexford with a kind of timid outrage. 'Haven't you folk got nothing better to do than listen to a bunch of old hens? What about the real crime? What about the muggings and the break-ins?'

Wexford sighed. But he went on doggedly questioning, remembering what the nurse had said, what Dr Moss had said, keeping in the forefront of his mind that motive which was so much more than merely wanting an aged parent out of the way. If he hadn't been a policeman with a profound respect for the law and for human life, he might have felt that these two, or one of them, had been provoked beyond bearing to do murder.

One of them? Or both? Or neither? Ivy Wrangton had either died an unnatural death or else there had been a series of coincidences and unexplained contingencies which were nothing short of incredible.

It was the nurse who had started it, coming to him three days before. Sergeant Martin brought her to him because what she alleged was so serious. Chief Inspector Wexford knew her by sight, had seen her making her calls, and had sometimes wondered how district nurses could endure their jobs, the unremitting daily toil, the poor pay, the unsavoury tasks. Perhaps she felt the same about his. She was a fair pretty woman, about thirty-five, overweight, with big red hands, who always looked tired. She looked tired now, though she hadn't long been back from two weeks' holiday. She was in her summer uniform, blue and white print dress, white apron, dark cardigan, small round hat, and the stout shoes that served for summer and winter alike. Nurse Radcliffe, Judith Radcliffe.

'Mr Wexford?' she said, 'Chief Inspector Wexford? Yes. I believe I used to look in on your daughter after she'd had a baby. I was doing my midwifery then. I can't remember her name but the baby's was Benjamin.'

Wexford smiled and told her his daughter's name and wondered, looking at the bland faded blue eyes and the stolid set of the neck and shoulders, just how intelligent this woman was, how perceptive and how truthful. He pulled up one of the little yellow chairs for her. His office was cheerful and sunny-looking even when the sun wasn't shining, not much like a police station.

'Please sit down, Nurse Radcliffe,' he said. 'Sergeant Martin's given me some idea what you've come about.'

'I feel rather awful. You may think I'm making a mountain out of a molehill.'

'I shouldn't worry about that. If I do I'll tell you so and we'll forget it. No one else will know of it, it'll be between us and these four walls.'

At that she gave a short laugh. 'Oh, dear, I'm afraid it's gone *much* further than that already. I've three patients in Castle Road and each one of them mentioned it to me. That's what Castle Road gossip is at the moment, poor old Mrs Wrangton's death. And I just thought – well, you can't have that much smoke without fire, can you?'

Mountains and molehills, Wexford thought, smoke and fire. This promised to be a real volcano. He said firmly, 'I think you'd better tell me all about it.'

She was rather pathetic. 'It's best you hear it from someone *professional*.' She planted her feet rather wide apart in front of her and leant forward, her hands on her knees. 'Mrs Wrangton was a very old woman. She was ninety-two. But allowing for her age, she was as fit as a fiddle, thin, strong, her heart as sound as a bell. The day she died was the day I went away on holiday, but I was in there the day before to give her her bath – I did that once a week, she couldn't get in and out of the bath on her own – and I remember thinking she was fitter than I'd seen her for months. You could have knocked me down with a feather when I came back from holiday and heard she'd had a stroke the next day.'

'When did you come back, Nurse Radcliffe?'

'Last Friday, Friday the sixteenth. Well, it's Thursday

now and I was back on my district on Monday and the first thing I heard was that Mrs Wrangton was dead and suggestions she'd been – well, helped on her way.' She paused, worked something out on her fingers. 'I went away June second, that was the day she died, and the funeral was June seventh.'

'Funeral?'

'Well, cremation,' said Nurse Radcliffe, glancing up as Wexford faintly sighed. 'Dr Moss attended Mrs Wrangton. She was really Dr Crocker's patient, but he was on holiday too like me. Look, Mr Wexford, I don't know the details of what happened that day, June second, not first-hand, only what the Castle Road ladies say. D'you want to hear that?'

'You haven't yet told me what she died of.'

'A stroke – according to Dr Moss.'

'I'm not at all sure,' said Wexford dryly, 'how one sets about giving someone a stroke. Would you give them a bad fright or push an empty hypodermic into them or get them into a rage or what?'

'I really don't know.' Nurse Radcliffe looked a little put out and as if she would like to say, had she dared, that to find this out was Wexford's job, not hers. She veered away from the actual death. 'Mrs Wrangton and her daughter – that's Mrs Betts, Mrs Doreen Betts – they hated each other, they were like cat and dog. And I don't think Mr Betts had spoken to Mrs Wrangton for a year or more. Considering the house was Mrs Wrangton's and every stick of furniture in it belonged to her, I used to think they were very ungrateful. I never liked the way Mrs Betts spoke about her mother, let alone the way she spoke *to* her, but I couldn't say a word. Mr Betts is retired now but he only had a very ordinary sort of job in the Post Office and they lived rent-free in Mrs Wrangton's home. It's a nice house, you know, late Victorian, and they built to last in those days. I used to think it badly needed doing up and it was a pity Mr Betts couldn't get down to a bit of painting, when Mrs Wrangton said to me she was having decorators in, having the whole house done up inside and out—'

Wexford cut short the flow of what seemed like irrelevancies. 'Why were the Bettses and Mrs Wrangton on such bad terms?'

The look he got implied that seldom had Nurse Radcliffe come across such depths of naivety. 'It's a sad fact, Mr Wexford, that people can outstay their welcome in this world. To put it bluntly, Mr and Mrs Betts couldn't wait for something to happen to Mrs Wrangton.' Her voice lingered over the euphemism. 'They hadn't been married all that long, you know,' she said surprisingly. 'Only five or six years. Mrs Betts was just a spinster before that, living at home with mother. Mr Betts was a widower that she met at the Over Sixties Club. Mrs Wrangton used to say she could have done better for herself – seems funny to say that about a woman of her age, doesn't it? – and that Mr Betts was only after the house and her money.'

'You mean she said it to you?'

'Well, not just to me, to anybody,' said Nurse Radcliffe, unconsciously blackening the dead woman to whom she showed such conscious bias. 'She really felt it, I think she bitterly resented having him in the house.'

Wexford moved a little impatiently in his chair. 'If we were to investigate every death just because the victim happened to be on bad terms with his or her relations—'

'Oh, no, no, it's not just that, not at all. Mrs Betts sent for Dr Moss on May twenty-third, just four days after Dr Crocker went away. Why did she? There wasn't anything wrong with Mrs Wrangton. I was getting her dressed after her bath and I was amazed to see Dr Moss. Mrs Wrangton said, I don't know what you're doing here, I never asked my daughter to send for you. Just because I overslept a bit this morning, she said. She was so proud of her good health, poor dear, never had an illness in her long life but the once and that was more an allergy than an illness.

'I can tell you why he was sent for, Mr Wexford. So that *when Mrs Wrangton died* he'd be within his rights signing the death certificate. He wasn't her doctor, you see, but it'd be all right if he'd attended her within the past two weeks, that's the law. They're all saying Mrs Betts waited for Dr Crocker to go away, she knew he'd never have accepted her mother's death like that. He'd have asked for a post mortem and then the fat would have been in the fire.'

Nurse Radcliffe didn't specify how, and Wexford thought better of interrupting her again. 'The last time I saw Mrs Wrangton,' she went on, 'was on June first. I had a word with the painter as I was going out. There were two of them but this was a young boy, about twenty. I asked him when they expected to finish, and he said, sooner than they thought, next week, because Mrs Betts had told them just to finish the kitchen and the outside and then to leave it. I thought it was funny at the time, Mrs Wrangton hadn't said a word to me about it. In fact, what she'd said was, wouldn't it be nice when the bathroom walls were all tiled and I wouldn't have to worry about splashing when I bathed her.

'Mr Wexford, it's possible Mrs Betts stopped that work because she knew her mother was going to die the next day. She personally didn't want the whole house redecorated and she didn't want to have to pay for it out of the money her mother left her.'

'Was there much money?' Wexford asked.

'I'd guess a few thousands in the bank, maybe three or four, and there was the house, wasn't there? I know she'd made a will, I witnessed it. I and Dr Crocker. In the presence,' said Nurse Radcliffe sententiously, 'of the legatee and of each other, which is the law. But naturally I didn't see what its *provisions* were. Mrs Wrangton did tell me the house was to go to Mrs Betts and there was a little something for her friend Elsie Parrish. Beyond that, I couldn't tell you. Mind you, Mrs Parrish won't have it that there could have been foul play. I met her in Castle Road and she said, wasn't it wicked the things people were saying?'

'Who is Elsie Parrish?'

'A very nice old friend of Mrs Wrangton's. Nearly eighty but as spry as a cricket. And that brings me to the worst thing. June second, that Friday afternoon, Mr and Mrs Betts went off to a whist drive. Mrs Parrish knew they were going. Mrs Betts had promised to knock on her door before they went so that she could come round and sit with Mrs Wrangton. She sometimes did that. It wasn't right to leave her alone, not at her age. Well, Mrs Parrish waited in and Mrs Betts never came, so naturally she thought the Bettses had changed their minds and hadn't gone out. But they had. They deliberately didn't call to fetch Mrs Parrish. They left Mrs Wrangton all alone but for that young painter, and they'd never done such a thing before, not once.'

Wexford digested all this in silence, not liking it but not really seeing it as a possible murder case. Nurse Radcliffe seemed to have dried up. She slackened back in the chair with a sigh.

'You mentioned an allergy?'

'Oh, my goodness, that was about fifty years ago! Only some kind of hayfever, I think. There's asthma in the family. Mrs Betts's brother had asthma all his life, and Mrs Betts gets urticaria – nettle rash, that is. They're all connected, you know.'

He nodded. He had the impression she had a bomb-shell yet to explode, or that the volcano was about to erupt. 'If they weren't there,' he said, 'how could either of them possibly have hastened Mrs Wrangton's end?'

'They'd been back two hours before she died. When they came back she was in a coma, and they waited *one hour and twenty minutes* before they phoned Dr Moss.'

'Would you have signed that death certificate, Len?' said Wexford to Dr Crocker. They were in the bungalow that housed two consulting rooms and a waiting room. Dr Crocker's evening surgery was over, the last patient packed off with reassurance and a prescription. Crocker gave Wexford rather a defiant look.

'Of course I would. Why not? Mrs Wrangton was ninety-two. It's ridiculous of Radcliffe to say she didn't expect her to die. You expect everyone of ninety-two to die and pretty soon. I hope nobody's casting any aspersions on my extremely able partner.'

'I'm not,' said Wexford. 'There's nothing I'd like more than for this to turn out a lot of hot air. But I do have to ask you, don't I? I do have to ask Jim Moss.'

Dr Crocker looked a little mollified. He and the Chief Inspector were lifelong friends, they had been at school together, had lived most of their lives in Kingsmarkham where Crocker had his practice, and Wexford was head of the CID. But for a medical practitioner, no amount of friendship will excuse hints that he or one of his fellows have been negligent. And he prickled up again when Wexford said, 'How could he *know* it was a stroke without a post mortem?'

'God give me patience! He saw her before she was dead, didn't he? He got there about half an hour before she died. There are unmistakable signs of stroke, Reg. An experienced medical man couldn't fail to recognise them. The patient is unconscious, the face flushed, the pulse slow, the breathing stertorous with a puffing of the cheeks during expiration. The only possible confusion is with narcotic poisoning, but in narcotic poisoning the pupils of the eyes are widely dilated whereas in apoplexy or stroke they're contracted. Does that satisfy you?'

'Well, OK, it was a stroke, but aren't I right in thinking a stroke can be the consequence of something else – of an operation, for instance, or in the case of a young woman, of childbirth, or in an old person even of bedsores?'

'Old Ivy Wrangton didn't have bedsores and she hadn't had a baby for seventy years. She had a stroke because she was ninety-two and her arteries were worn out. The days of our age,' quoted the doctor solemnly, 'are threescore years and ten, and though men be so strong that they come to fourscore years, yet is their strength then but labour and sorrow. She'd reached fourscore years and twelve and she was worn out.'

Dr Crocker had been pacing up and down, getting heated, but now came to sit on the edge of his desk, a favourite perch of his. 'A damn good thing she was cremated,' he said. 'That puts out of court all the ghastliness of exhumation and cutting her up. She was a remarkable old woman, you know, Reg. Tough as old boots. She told me once about having her first baby. She was eighteen, out scrubbing the doorstep when she had a labour pain. Indoors she went, called her mother to fetch the midwife, and lay down on her bed. The baby was born after two more pains, and the daughter came even easier.'

'Yes, I heard there's been another child.' Wexford saw the absurdity of referring to someone who must necessarily be in his seventies as a child. 'Mrs Betts has a brother?' he corrected himself.

'*Had*. He died last winter. He was an old man, Reg, and he'd been bronchial all his life. Seventy-four is old till you start comparing it with Mrs Wrangton's age. She was so proud of her good health, boasted about never being ill. I used to drop in every three months or so as a matter of routine, and when I'd ask her how she was she'd say, I'm fine, Doctor, I'm in the pink.'

'But I understand she'd had some illness connected with an allergy?' Wexford was clutching at straws. 'Nurse Radcliffe told me about it. I've been wondering if anything to do with that could have contributed to — ?'

'Of course not,' the doctor cut in. 'How could it? That was when she was middle-aged and the so-called illness was an asthmatic attack with some swelling of the eyes and a bit of gastric trouble. I fancy she used to exaggerate it the way healthy people do when they're talking about the one little bit of illness they've ever had . . . Oh, here's Jim, I thought I'd heard his last patient leave.'

Dr Moss, small, dark, and trim, came in from the corridor between the consulting rooms. He gave Wexford the very wide smile that showed thirty-two large white teeth which the Chief Inspector had never been able precisely to define as false, as crowns, or simply as his own. The teeth were rather too big for Dr Moss's face which was small and smooth and lightly tanned. His small black eyes didn't smile at all.

'Enter the villainous medico,' he said, 'who is notoriously in cahoots with greedy legatees and paranoid Post Office clerks. What evidence can I show you? The number of my Swiss bank account? Or shall I produce the hammer, a crafty tap from which ensured an immediate subarachnoid haemorrhage?'

It is very difficult to counter this kind of facetiousness. Wexford knew he would only get more fatuous pleasantries, heavy irony, outrageous confessions, if he attempted to rebut any of it or if he were to assure Moss that this wasn't what he had meant at all. He smiled stiffly, tapping his foot against the leg of Crocker's desk, while Dr Moss elaborated on his fantasy of himself as corrupt, a kind of latterday William Palmer, poison-bottle-happy and ever ready with his hypodermic to gratify the impatient next-of-kin.

At length, unable to bear any more of it, Wexford cut across the seemingly interminable harangue and said to Crocker, 'You witnessed her will, I understand?'

'I and that busybody Radcliffe, that's right. If you want to know what's in it, the house and three thousand pounds go to Doreen Betts, and the residue to another patient of mine, a Mrs Parrish. Residue would have been about fifteen hundred at that time, Mrs Wrangton told me, but considering her money was in a building society and she managed to save out of her pension and her annuity, I imagine it'll be a good deal more by now.'

Wexford nodded. By now Dr Moss had dried up, having run out, presumably, of subject matter and witticisms. His teeth radiated his face like lamps, and when his mouth was closed he looked rather ill-tempered and sinister. Wexford decided to try the direct and simple approach. He apologised.

'I'd no intention of suggesting you'd been negligent, Dr Moss. But put yourself in my position—'

'Impossible!'

'Very well. Let me put it this way. Try to understand that in my position I had no choice but to make inquiries.'

'Mrs Betts might try an action for slander. She can count on my support. The Bettses had neither the opportunity nor the motive to do violence to Mrs Wrangton, but a bunch of tongue-clacking old witches are allowed to take their characters away just the same.'

'Motive,' said Wexford gently, 'I'm afraid they did have, the straightforward one of getting rid of Mrs Wrangton who had become an encumbrance to them, and of inheriting her house.'

'Nonsense.' Momentarily the teeth showed in a white blaze. 'They were going to get rid of her in any case. They would have had the house to themselves in any case. Mrs Wrangton was going into a nursing home.' He paused, enjoying the effect of what he had said. 'For the rest of her days,' he added with a touch of drama.

Dr Crocker shifted off the edge of the desk. 'I never knew that.'

'No? Well, it was you told her about a new nursing home opening in Stowerton, or so she said. She told me all about it that day Mrs Betts called me when you'd gone away. Some time at the end of May, it was. She was having the house decorated for her daughter and son-in-law prior to her leaving.'

'Did she tell you that too?' asked Wexford.

'No, but it was obvious. I can tell you exactly what happened during that visit if it makes you happy. That interfering harpy, Radcliffe, had just been bathing her, and when she'd dressed her she left. Thank God. I'd never met Mrs Wrangton before. There was nothing wrong with her, bar extreme old age and her blood pressure up a bit, and I was rather narked that Mrs Betts had called me out. Mrs Wrangton said her daughter got nervous when she slept late in the mornings as she'd done that day and the day before. Wasn't to be wondered at, she said, considering she'd been sitting up in bed watching the World Cup on television till all hours. Only Mrs Betts and her husband didn't know that and I wasn't to tell them. Well, we had a conspiratorial laugh over that, I liked her, she was a game old dear, and then she started talking about the nursing home – what's it called? Springfield? Sunnyside?'

'Summerland,' said Dr Crocker.

'Cost you a lot, that will, I said, and she said she'd got a good bit coming in which would die with her anyway. I assumed she meant an annuity. We talked for about five minutes and I got the impression she'd been tossing around this nursing home idea for months. I asked her what her daughter thought and she said . . .'

'Yes?' prompted Wexford.

'Oh my God, people like you make one see sinister nuances in the most innocent remarks. It's just that she said, "You'd reckon Doreen'd be only too glad to see the back of me, wouldn't you?" I mean, it rather implied she wouldn't be glad. I don't know what she was inferring and I didn't ask. But you can rest assured Mrs Betts had no motive for killing her mother. Leaving sentiment apart, it was all the same to her whether her mother were alive or dead. The Bettses would still have got the house and after her death Mrs Wrangton's capital. The next time I saw her she was unconscious, she was dying. She did die, at seven-thirty, on June second.'

Both Wexford's parents had died before he was forty. His wife's mother had been dead twenty years, her father fifteen. None of these people had been beyond their seventies, so therefore Wexford had no personal experience of the geriatric problem. It seemed to him that for a woman like Mrs Wrangton, to end one's days in a nursing home with companionship and good nursing and in pleasant surroundings was not so bad a fate. And an obvious blessing to the daughter and son-in-law whose affection for a parent might be renewed when they only encountered her for an hour or so a week.

No, Doreen Betts and her husband had no motive for helping Mrs Wrangton out of this world, for by retiring to Summerland she wouldn't even make inroads into that three or four thousand pounds of capital. Her pension and her annuity would cover the fees. Wexford wondered what those fees would be, and remembered vaguely from a few years back hearing a figure of £20 a week mentioned in a similar connection. Somebody's old aunt, some friend of his wife's. You'd have to allow for inflation, of course, but surely it would cost no more than

£30 a week now. With the retirement pension at £18 and the annuity worth, say, another £20, Mrs Wrangton could amply have afforded Summerland.

But she had died first – of natural causes. It no longer mattered that she and Harry Betts hadn't been on speaking terms, that no one had fetched Elsie Parrish, that Dr Moss had been called out to visit a healthy woman, that Mrs Betts had given orders to stop the painting. There was no motive. Eventually the tongues would cease to wag, Mrs Wrangton's will would be proved, and the Bettses settle down to enjoy the rest of their lives in their newly decorated home.

Wexford put it out of his head, apart from wondering whether he should visit Castle Road and drop a word of warning to the gossips. Immediately he saw how impossible this would be. The slander would be denied, and besides, he hardly saw his function as extending so far. No, let it die a natural death – as Mrs Wrangton had.

On Monday morning he was having breakfast, his wife reading a letter just arrived from her sister in Wales.

'Frances says Bill's mother has got to go into a nursing home at last.' Bill was Wexford's brother-in-law. 'It's either that or Fran having her, which really isn't on.'

Wexford from behind his newspaper, made noises indicative of sympathy with and support for Frances. He was reading a verbatim report of the trial of some bank robbers.

'Ninety pounds a week,' said Dora.

'What did you say?'

'I was talking to myself, dear. You read your paper.'

'Did you say ninety pounds a week?'

'That's right. For the nursing home. I shouldn't think Bill and Fran could stand that for long. It's getting on for five thousand a year.'

'But . . .' Wexford almost stammered, 'I thought a couple of years ago you said it was twenty a week for what's-her-name, Rosemary's aunt, wherever they put her?'

'Darling,' said Dora gently, 'first of all, that wasn't a couple of years ago, it was at least *twelve* years ago. And secondly, haven't you ever heard of the rising cost of living?'

An hour later he was in the matron's office of Summerland, having made no attempt to disguise who he was, but presenting himself as there to inquire about a prospective home for an aged relative of his wife's. Aunt Lillian. Such a woman had actually existed, perhaps still did exist in the remote Westmorland village from which the Wexfords had last heard of her in a letter dated 1959.

The matron was an Irishwoman, Mrs Corrigan. She seemed about the same age as Nurse Radcliffe. At her knee stood a boy of perhaps six, and at her feet, playing with a toy tractor, was another of three. Outside the window three little girls were trying to coax a black cat from its refuge under a car. You might have thought this was a children's home but for the presence of half a dozen old women sitting on the lawn in a half circle, dozing, muttering to themselves, or just staring. The grounds were full of flowers, mauve and white lilac everywhere, roses coming out. From behind a hedge came the sound of a lawnmower, plied perhaps by the philoprogenitive Mr Corrigan.

'Our fees are ninety-*five* pounds a week, Mr Wexford,' said the matron. 'And with the extra for laundry and dry-cleaning, sure and you might say five thousand a year for a good round figure.'

'I see.'

'The ladies only have to share a room with one other lady. We bathe them once a week and change their clothes once a week. And if you could please see to it your aunt only had synthetic fabrics, if you know what I mean, for the lot's popped in the washing machine all together. We like the fee a month in advance and paid on a banker's order, if you please.'

'I'm afraid I don't please,' said Wexford. 'Your charges are more than I expected. I shall have to make other arrangements.'

'Then there's no more to be said,' said Mrs Corrigan with a smile nearly equalling the candlepower of Dr Moss's.

'Just out of curiosity, Mrs Corrigan, how do your – er, guests meet your fees? Five thousand a year is more than most incomes would be equal to.'

'Sure and aren't they widows, Mr Wexford, and didn't their husbands leave them their houses? Mostly the ladies sell their houses, and with prices the way they are today that's enough to keep them in Summerland for four years or five.'

Mrs Wrangton had intended to sell her house, and she was having it redecorated inside and out in order to get a better price. She had intended to sell the roof over the Bettses' head – no wonder she had implied to Dr Moss that Doreen Betts would be sorry to see the back of her. What a woman? What malevolence at ninety-two! And who could have said she wouldn't have been within her moral as well as her legal rights to sell? It was her house. Doreen Wrangton might long ago have found a home of her own, ought perhaps to have done so, and as Doreen Betts she might have expected her husband to provide one for her. It is universally admitted to be wrong to anticipate stepping into dead men's shoes. And yet what a monstrous revenge to have on an uncongenial son-in-law, a not always cooperative daughter. There was a subtlety about it that evoked Wexford's admiration nearly as much as its cruelty aroused his disgust. It was a motive all right, and a strong one.

So at last he had found himself in Castle Road, in the

Bettses' living-room, confronting an elderly orphan and her husband. The room was papered in a silvery oyster colour, the woodwork ivory. He was sure that that door had never previously sported a shade lighter than chocolate brown, just as the hall walls had, until their recent coat of magnolia, been gloomily clothed in dark Lincrusta.

When the two of them had protested bitterly about the gossip and the apparent inability of the police to get their priorities right, Doreen Betts agreed without too much mutiny to answer Wexford's questions. To the first one she reacted passionately.

'Mother would never have done it. I know she wouldn't, it was all bluff with her. Even Mother wouldn't have been that cruel.'

Her husband pulled his moustache, slowly shuffling his slippered feet back and forth. His angry excitement had resulted in a drop of water appearing on the end of his nose. It hung there, trembling.

Doreen Betts said, 'I knew she didn't mean to go ahead with it when I said, "Can I tell the builders to leave the upstairs?" And she said, "I daresay." That's what she said, "I daresay," she said, "I'm not bothered either way." Of course she wouldn't have gone ahead with it. You don't even get a room to yourself in that place. Ninety-five pounds a week! They'll put you in a bed at eight o'clock, Mother, I said, so don't think they'll let you sit up till all hours watching TV.'

'Quite right,' said Harry Betts ambiguously.

'Why, if we'd known Mother meant to do a thing like that, we could have lived in Harry's flat when we got married. He had a nice little flat over the freezer centre in the High Street. It wasn't just one room like Mother went about saying, it was a proper flat, wasn't it, Harry? What would we have done if Mother had done a thing like that? We'd have had nowhere.' Her husband's head-shaking, the trembling droplet, the fidgety feet, seemed suddenly to unnerve her. She said to him, distress in her voice, 'I'm going to have a little talk to the officer on my own, dear.'

Wexford followed her into the room where Mrs Wrangton had slept for the last years of her life. It was on the ground floor at the back, presumably originally designated as a dining-room, with a pair of windows looking out on to a narrow concrete terrace and a very long, very narrow garden. No redecorations had been carried out here. The walls were papered in a pattern of faded nasturtiums, the woodwork grained to look like walnut. Mrs Wrangton's double bed was still there, the mattress uncovered, a pile of folded blankets on top of it. There was a television set in this room as well as in the front room, and it had been placed so that the occupant of the bed could watch it.

'Mother came to sleep down here a few years back,' said Mrs Betts. 'There's a toilet just down the passage. She couldn't manage the stairs any more except when nurse helped her.' She sat on the edge of the mattress, nervously fingering a cage-like object of metal bars. 'I'll have to see about her walking frame going back, I'll have to get on to the welfare people.' Her hands resting on it, she said dolefully, 'Mother hated Harry. She always said he wasn't good enough for me. She did everything she could to stop me marrying him.' Mrs Betts's voice took on a rebellious girlish note. 'I think it's awful having to ask your mother's consent to marry when you're sixty-five, don't you?'

At any rate, he thought, she had gone ahead without receiving it. He looked wonderingly at this grey wisp of a woman. Seventy years old, who talked as if she were a fairy princess.

'You see, she talked for years of changing her will and leaving the house to my brother. It was after he died that

the nursing-home business started. She quarrelled out-
right with Harry. Elsie Parrish was in here and Mother
accused Harry in front of her of only marrying me to get
this place. Harry never spoke a word to Mother again,
and quite right too. I said to Mother, "You're a wicked
woman, you promised me years ago I'd have this house
and now you're going back on your word. Cheats never
prosper," I said.'

The daughter had inherited the mother's tongue.
Wexford could imagine the altercations, overheard by
visitors, by neighbours, which had contributed to the
gossip. He turned to look at the framed photograph on a
mahogany tallboy. A wedding picture, *circa* 1903. The
bride was seated, lilies in her lap under a bolster of a
bosom hung with lace and pearls. The bridegroom stood
behind her, frock coat, black handlebar moustache. Ivy
Wrangton must have been seventeen, Wexford calculated, her face plain, puffy, young, her figure modishly
pouter pigeon-like, her hair in that most unflattering of
fashions, the cottage loaf. She had been rather plump
then, but thin, according to Nurse Radcliffe, in old age.

Wexford said quietly, apparently idly, 'Mrs Betts, why
did you send for Dr Moss on May twenty-third? Your
mother wasn't ill. She hadn't complained of feeling ill.'

She held the walking frame, pushing it backwards and
forwards. 'Why shouldn't I? Dr Crocker was away. Elsie
came in at nine and Mother was still asleep, and Elsie
said it wasn't right the amount she slept. We couldn't
wake her, though we shook her, we were so worried. I
wasn't to know she'd get up as fit as a flea ten minutes
after I'd phoned for him, was I?'

'Tell me about the day your mother died, Mrs Betts,
Friday, June second,' he said, and it occurred to him that
no one had yet told him anything much about that day.

'Well . . .' Her mouth trembled and she said quickly,

'You don't think Harry did anything to Mother, do you? He wouldn't, I swear he wouldn't.'

'Tell me about that Friday.'

She made an effort to control herself, clenching her hands on the metal bar. 'We wanted to go to a whist drive. Elsie came round in the morning and I said, if we went out would she sit with Mother, and she said, OK, of course she would if I'd just give her a knock before we left.' Mrs Betts sighed and her voice steadied. 'Elsie lives two doors down. She and Mother had been pals for years and she always came to sit with her when we went out. Though it's a lie' – her old eyes flashed like young ones – 'to say we were always out. Once in a blue moon we went out.'

Wexford's eyes went from the pudding-faced girl in the photograph, her mouth smug and proud even then, to the long strip of turfed-over garden – why did he feel Betts had done that turfing, had uprooted flowers? – and back to the nervous little woman on the mattress edge.

'I gave Mother her lunch and she was sitting in the front room, doing a bit of knitting. I popped down to Elsie's and rang her bell but she can't have heard it, she didn't come to the door. I rang and rang and I thought, well, she's gone out, she's forgotten and that's that. But Harry said, Why not go out just the same? The painter was there, he was only a bit of a boy, twenty, twenty-two, but he and Mother got on a treat, a sight better than she and I ever did, I can tell you. So the upshot was, we went off and left her here with the painter – what was he called? Ray? Rafe? No, Roy, that was it, Roy – with Roy doing the hall walls. She was OK, fit as a flea. It was a nice day, so I left all the windows open because that paint did smell. I'll never forget the way she spoke to me before I left. That was the last thing she ever said to me. "Doreen," she said, "you ought to be lucky at cards. You haven't been very lucky in love." And she laughed and I'll swear Roy was laughing too.'

You're building an edifice of motives for yourself, Mrs Betts, reflected Wexford. 'Go on,' was all he said.

She moved directly into hearsay evidence, but Wexford didn't stop her. 'Roy closed the door to keep the smell out, but he popped in a few times to see if Mother was all right. They had a bit of a chat, he said, and he offered to make her a cup of tea but she didn't want any. Then about half-past three Mother said she'd got a headache – that was the onset of the stroke but she didn't know that, she put it down to the paint – and would he fetch her a couple of her phenacetins from the bathroom. So he did and he got her a glass of water and she said she'd try and have a sleep in her chair. Anyway, the next thing he knew she was out in the hall walking with her walking frame, going to have a lay-down on her bed, she said.

'Well, Harry and me came in at five-thirty and Roy was just packing up. He said Mother was asleep in her bed, and I just put my head round the door to check. She'd drawn the curtains.' Mrs Betts paused, then burst out, 'To tell you the honest truth, I didn't look too closely, I thought, well thank God for half an hour's peace to have a cup of tea in before she starts picking on Harry. It was just about a quarter to seven, ten to seven, before I went in again. I could tell there was something going on, the way she was breathing, sort of puffing out her cheeks, and red in the face. There was blood on her lips.' She looked fearfully at Wexford, looked him in the eye for the first time. 'I wiped that clean before I called the doctor, I didn't want him seeing that.

'He came straight away. I thought maybe he'd call an ambulance but he didn't. He said she'd had a stroke and when people had strokes they shouldn't be moved. We stayed with her – well, doctor and I stayed with her – but she passed away just before half-past.'

Wexford nodded. Something about what she had said was wrong. He felt it. It wasn't that she had told a lie, though she might well have done so, but something else, something that rang incongruously in that otherwise commonplace narrative, some esoteric term in place of a household word . . . He was checking back, almost there, when a footstep sounded in the hall, the door opened, and a face appeared round it.

'There you are Doreen!' said the face, which was very pretty considering its age. 'I was just on my way to – oh, I beg your pardon, I'm intruding.'

'That's all right,' said Mrs Betts. 'You can come in, Elsie.' She looked blankly at Wexford, her eyes once more old and tired. 'This is Mrs Parrish.'

Elsie Parrish, Wexford decided, looked exactly as an old lady should. She had a powdery, violet-cashew, creamy smell, which might equally well have been associated with a very clean baby. Her legs were neat and shapely in grey stockings, her hands in white gloves with tiny darns at the fingertips, her coat silky navy blue over blue flowery pleats, and her face withered rose leaves with rouge on. The bouffant mass of silver hair was so profuse that from a distance it might have been taken for a white silk turban. She and Wexford walked down the street together towards the shops, Elsie Parrish swinging a pink nylon string bag.

'It's wicked the way they gossip. You can't understand how people can be so evil minded. You'll notice how none of them is able to say how Doreen gave Ivy a stroke when she wasn't even there.' Mrs Parrish gave a dry satirical laugh. 'Perhaps they think she bribed that poor young man, the painter, to give Ivy a fright. I remember my mother saying that fright could give you a stroke – an apoplexy, she called it – or too much excitement or drinking too much or overeating even.'

To his surprise, because this isn't what old ladies of elegant appearance usually do or perhaps should do, she opened her handbag, took out a packet of cigarettes, and put one between her lips. He shook his head when the packet was offered to him, watched her light the cigarette with a match from a matchbook with a black shiny cover. She puffed delicately. He didn't think he had ever before seen someone smoke a cigarette while wearing white gloves.

He said, 'Why didn't you go round and sit with Mrs Wrangton, that afternoon, Mrs Parrish?'

'The day she died, you mean?'

'Yes.' Wexford had the impression she didn't want to answer, she didn't want to suggest anything against Doreen Betts. She spoke with care.

'It's quite true I'm getting rather deaf.' He hadn't noticed it. She had heard everything he said, in the open noisy street, and he hadn't raised his voice. 'I don't always hear the bell. Doreen must have rung and I didn't hear. That's the only explanation.'

Was it?

'I thought she and Harry had changed their minds about going out.' Elsie Parrish put the cigarette to her lips between thumb and forefinger. 'I'd give a lot,' she said, 'to be able to go back in time. I wouldn't hesitate this time, I'd go round and check on Ivy whether Doreen had asked me or not.'

'Probably your presence would have made no difference,' he said, and then, 'Mrs Betts had told the builders not to do any work upstairs—'

She interrupted him. 'Maybe it didn't need it. I've never been upstairs in Ivy's house, so I couldn't say. Besides, when she'd sold it the new people might have had their own decorating ideas, mightn't they?'

They were standing still now on the street corner, he about to go in one direction, she in the other. She dropped the cigarette end, stamped it out over-thoroughly with a high heel. From her handbag she took a small lacy handkerchief and dabbed her nostrils with it. The impression was that the tears, though near, would be restrained. 'She left me two thousand pounds. Dear Ivy, she was so kind and generous. I knew I was to have something, but I didn't dream as much as that.' Elsie Parrish smiled, a watery, girlish, rueful smile, but still he was totally unprepared for what she said next. 'I'm going to buy a car.'

His eyebrows went up.

'I've kept my licence going. I haven't driven since my husband died and that's twenty-two years ago. I had to sell our car and I've always longed and longed for another.' She really looked as if she had, a yearning expression crumpling the roses still further. 'I'm going to have my own dear little car!' She was on the verge of executing a dance on the pavement. 'And dear Ivy made that possible!' Anxiously: 'You don't think I'm too old to drive?'

Wexford did, but he only said that this kind of judgment wasn't really within his province. She nodded, smiled again, then whisked off surprisingly fast into the corner supermarket. Wexford moved more slowly and thoughtfully away, his eyes down. It was because he was looking down that he saw the matchbook, and then he remembered fancying he had seen her drop something when she got out that handkerchief.

She wasn't in the shop. She must have left by the other exit into the High Street and now she was nowhere to be seen. Deciding that matchbooks were in the category of objects which no one much minds losing, Wexford dropped it into his pocket and forgot it.

'You want Roy?'

'That's right,' said Wexford.

The foreman, storekeeper, proprietor, whatever he was, didn't ask why. 'You'll find him,' he said, 'doing the Snowcem on them flats up the Sewingbury Road.'

Wexford drove up there. Roy was a gigantic youth, broad shouldered, heavily muscled, with an aureole of thick curly fair hair. He came down the ladder and said he'd just been about to knock off for his tea break, anyway. There was a truckers' café conveniently near. Roy lit a cigarette and put his elbows on the table.

'I never knew a thing about it till I turned up there the next day.'

'But surely when Mrs Betts came in the afternoon before, she asked you how her mother had been?'

'Sure she did. And I said the truth, that the old lady had got a headache and asked for something for it and I'd given it her, and then she'd felt tired and gone in for a lay-down. But there was no sign she was *dying*. My God, that'd never have crossed my mind.'

A headache, Wexford reflected, was often one of the premonitory signs of cerebral haemorrhage. Roy seemed to read his thoughts, for he said quickly, 'She'd had a good many headaches while I was in the place working. Them non-drip plastic-based paints have got a bit of a smell to them, used to turn *me* up at first. I mean, you don't want to get thinking there was anything out of the way in her having an aspirin and laying down, guv. That had happened two or three times while I was there. And she'd shovel them aspirins down, swallow four as soon as look at you.'

Wexford said, 'Tell me about that afternoon. Did anyone come into the house between the time Mr and Mrs Betts went out and the time they got back?'

Roy shook his head. 'Definitely not, and I'd have known. I was working on the hall, see? The front door was wide open on account of the smell. Nobody could have come in there without me seeing, could they? The other old girl – Mrs Betts, that is – she locked the back door before she went out and I hadn't no call to unlock it. What else d'you want to know, guv?'

'Exactly what happened, what you and Mrs Wrangton talked about, the lot.'

Roy swigged his tea, then lit a fresh cigarette from the stub of the last. 'I got on OK with her, you know. I reckon she reminded me of my gran. It's a funny thing, but everyone got on OK with her bar her own daughter and the old man. Funny old git, isn't he? Gave me the creeps. Well, to what you're asking, I don't know that we talked much. I was painting, you see, and the door to the front room was shut. I looked in a couple of times. She was sitting there knitting, watching cricket on the TV. I do remember she said I was making a nice job of the house and it was a pity she wouldn't be there to enjoy it. Well, I thought she meant she'd be dead, you know the way they talk, and I said, "Now come on, Mrs Wrangton, you mustn't talk like that." That made her laugh. She said, "I don't mean that, you naughty boy, I mean I'm going into a nursing home and I've got to sell the place, didn't you know?" No, I said, I didn't, but I reckoned it'd fetch a packet, big old house like that, twenty thousand at least, I said, and she said she hoped so.'

Wexford nodded. So Mrs Wrangton had intended to go ahead with her plans, and Doreen Betts's denial had either been purposeful lying to demolish her motive or a post mortem whitewashing of her mother's character. For it had certainly been black hearted enough, he thought, quite an act it had been, that of deliberately turning your own daughter and her husband out of their home.

He looked back to Roy. 'You offered to make her some tea?'

'Yeah, well, the daughter, Mrs Betts, said to make

myself and her a cup of tea if she wanted, but she didn't want. She asked me to turn off the TV and then she said she'd got a headache and would I go up to the bathroom cupboard and get her aspirins? Well, I'd seen Mrs Betts do it often enough, though I'd never actually—'

'You're sure she said aspirins?' Quite suddenly Wexford knew what it was that had seemed incongruous to him in Mrs Betts's description of her mother's last afternoon of life. Doreen Betts had specified phenacetin instead of the common household remedy. 'You're sure she used that word?' he said.

Roy pursed his mouth. 'Well, now you mention it, I'm not sure. I reckon what she said was, my tablets or the tablets for my head, something like that. You just do say aspirins, don't you, like naturally? I mean, that's what everybody takes. Anyway, I brought them down, the bottle, and gave them to her with a glass of water, and she says she's going to have a bit of shut-eye in her chair. But the next thing I knew she was coming out, leaning on that walking frame the welfare people give her. "I took four, Roy," she says, "but my head's that bad, I reckon it's worse, and I'm ever so giddy."

'Well, I didn't think much of that, they're all giddy at that age, aren't they? I remember my gran. She says she's got ringing in her ears, so I said, "I'll help you into your room, shall I?" And I sort of give her my arm and helped her in and she lay down on the bed with all her things on and shut her eyes. The light was glaring, so I pulled the curtains over and then I went back to my painting. I never heard another thing till Mrs Betts and the old boy come in at half-past five . . .'

Wexford closed *Practical Forensic Medicine* by Francis E. Camps and J. M. Cameron and made his way back to Castle Road. He had decided to discuss the matter no further with Mrs Betts. The presence of her husband, shuffling about almost silently in his furry slippers, his feet like the paws of an old hibernating animal, rather unnerved him. She made no demur at his proposal to remove from the bathroom cabinet the prescription bottle of painkilling tablets labelled: Mrs I. Wrangton, Phenacetin.

Evening surgery had only just begun. Wexford went home for his dinner, having sent two items away for fingerprint analysis. By eight-thirty he was back in the surgery building and again Dr Crocker had finished first. He groaned when he saw Wexford.

'What is it now, Reg?'

'Why did you prescribe phenacetin for Mrs Wrangton?'

'Because I thought it suitable for her, of course. She was allergic to aspirin.'

Wexford looked despairingly at his friend. 'Now he tells me. I'd rather gathered that. I mean, today I caught on, but you might have told me.'

'For God's sake! You *knew*. You said to me, "Nurse Radcliffe told me all about it." Those were your words. You said—'

'I thought it was asthma.'

Crocker sat on the edge of his desk. 'Look, Reg, we've both been barking up the wrong trees. There was asthma in Mrs Wrangton's family. Mrs Betts has nettle rash, her brother was a chronic asthmatic. People with asthma or a family history of asthma are sometimes allergic to acetylsalicylic acid or aspirin. In fact, about ten per cent of such people are thought to have the allergy. One of the reactions of the hypersensitive person to aspirin is an asthmatic attack. That's what Mrs Wrangton had when she was in her forties, that and haematemesis. Which means,' he added kindly for the layman, 'bringing up blood from an internal haemorrhage.'

'OK, I'm not bone ignorant,' Wexford snapped, 'and

I've been reading up hypersensitivity to acetylsalicylic acid—'

'Mrs Wrangton couldn't have had aspirin poisoning,' said the doctor quickly. 'There were never any aspirins in the house. Mrs Betts was strict about that.'

They were interrupted by the arrival of smiling Dr Moss. Wexford wheeled round on him.

'What would you expect to be the result of – let me see – one point two grams of acetylsalicylic acid on a woman of ninety-two who was hypersensitive to the drug?'

Moss looked at him warily. 'I take it this is academic?' Wexford didn't answer. 'Well, it would depend on the degree of hypersensitivity. Nausea, maybe, diarrhoea, dizziness, tinnitis – that's ringing in the ears – breathing difficulties, gastric haemorrhages, oedema of gastric mucosa, possible rupture of the oesophagus. In a person of that age, consequent upon such a shock and localised haemorrhages, I suppose a brain haemorrhage—' He stopped, realising what he had said.

'Thanks very much,' said Wexford. 'I think you've more or less described what happened to Mrs Wrangton on June second after she'd taken four three-hundred-milligram tablets of aspirin.'

Dr Moss was looking stunned. He looked as if he would never smile again.

Wexford passed on an envelope to Dr Crocker.

'Those are aspirins?'

Crocker looked at them, touched one to his tongue. 'I suppose so, but—'

'I've sent the rest away to be analysed. To be certain. There were fifty-six in the bottle.'

'Reg, it's unthinkable there could have been a mistake on the part of the pharmacist, but just supposing by a one-in-a-million chance there was, she couldn't have taken forty-four tablets of aspirin. Not even over the months she couldn't.'

'You're being a bit slow,' said Wexford. 'You prescribed one hundred phenacetin, and one hundred phenacetin were put into that bottle at Fraser's, the chemist's. Between the time the prescription was made up and the day before, or a few days before, or a week before she died, she took forty tablets of phenacetin, leaving sixty in the bottle. But on June second she took four tablets of aspirin. Or, to put it bluntly, some time before June second someone removed those sixty tablets of phenacetin and substituted sixty tablets of aspirin.'

Dr Moss found his voice. 'That would be murder.'

'Well . . .' Wexford spoke hesitantly. 'The hypersensitivity might not have resulted in a stroke. The intent may only have been to cause illness of a more or less severe kind. Ulceration of the stomach, say. That would have meant hospitalisation for Mrs Wrangton. On the Welfare State. No exorbitant nursing-home fees to be paid there, no swallowing up of capital or selling of property. Later on, if she survived, she would probably have been transferred, again for free, to a geriatric ward in the same hospital. It's well known that no private nursing home will take the chronically sick.'

'You think Mrs Betts—?' Dr Moss began.

'No, I don't. For two good reasons, Mrs Betts is the one person who wouldn't have done it this way. If she had wanted to kill her mother or to make her seriously ill, why go to all the trouble of changing over sixty tablets in a bottle, when she had only to give Mrs Wrangton the aspirins in her hand? And if she had changed them, wouldn't she, immediately her mother was dead, have changed them back again?'

'Then who was it?'

'I shall know tomorrow,' said Wexford . . .

Dr Crocker came to him at his office in the police station.

'Sorry I'm late. I just lost a patient.'

Wexford made sympathetic noises. Having walked round the room, eyed the two available chairs, the doctor settled for the edge of Wexford's desk.

'Yesterday,' Wexford began, 'I had a talk with Mrs Elsie Parrish.' He checked the doctor's exclamation and sudden start forward. 'Wait a minute, Len. She dropped a matchbook before we parted. It was one of those with a glossy surface that very easily takes prints. I had the prints on it and those on the phenacetin bottle compared. There were Mrs Betts's prints on the bottle, and a set that were presumably Mrs Wrangton's, and a man's that were presumably the painter's. And there was also a very clear set identical to those on the matchbook.

'It was Elsie Parrish who changed those tablets, Len. She did it because she knew that Mrs Wrangton fully intended to retire to Summerland and that the first money to go, perhaps before the house was sold, would be the few thousands of capital that she and Doreen Betts were to share. Elsie Parrish had waited for years for that money, she wanted to buy a car. A few more years and if she herself survived it would be too late for driving cars. Besides, by then her legacy would have been swallowed up in nursing-home fees.'

'A nice old creature like that?' Dr Crocker said. 'That's no proof, her prints on the bottle. She'll have fetched that bottle often enough for old Ivy.'

'No. She told me she had never been upstairs in Ivy Wrangton's house.'

'Oh, God.'

'I don't suppose she saw it as murder. It wouldn't seem like murder, or manslaughter, or grievous bodily harm, changing tablets in a bottle.' Wexford sat down, wrinkled up his face. He said crossly, dispiritedly, 'I don't know what to do, Len. We've no way of proving Mrs Wrangton died of aspirin poisoning. We can't exhume her, we can't analyse "two handfuls of white dust shut in an urn of brass". And even if we could, would we be so inhumane as to have a woman of – how old is Elsie Parrish?'

'Seventy-eight.'

'Seventy-eight up in court on a murder charge. On the other hand, should she be allowed to profit from her crime? Should she be permitted to terrorise pedestrians in a smart little Ford Fiesta?'

'She won't,' said Crocker.

Something in his voice brought Wexford to his feet. 'Why? What d'you mean?'

The doctor slid lightly off the edge of the desk. 'I told you I'd lost a patient. Elsie Parrish died last night. A neighbour found her and called me.'

'Maybe that's for the best. What did she die of?'

'A stroke,' said Dr Crocker, and went.

The Burglar

COLIN DEXTER

DETECTIVE FILE

OFFICER: Chief Inspector E. Morse

FORCE: Oxford CID

TIME: 1995

CASES: *Last Bus to Woodstock* (1975), *The Dead of Jericho* (1981), *The Wench is Dead* (1989), *The Daughters of Cain* (1994) etc.

PROFILE: Chief Inspector Morse, the melancholy, pessimistic and sometimes gruff policeman, has been described as one of the most cerebral sleuths in contemporary crime fiction. An introverted but highly intelligent man, he has honed his exceptional talents during a long career with the Thames Valley Force at Oxford and won the respect, if not always the affection, of his fellow officers. Morse is also a vulnerable man beneath the surface, a fact which has much to do with a tortured romance that occurred during his college days, and he now prefers, when off duty, to lose himself in the music of Wagner, good books, crossword puzzles or pints of real ale. Middle aged and a confirmed bachelor, he can be relied upon to devote himself wholeheartedly to solving a case and often drives himself and his long-suffering aide, Sergeant Lewis, to the edge of distraction. In the press, Morse is regularly referred to as the nation's favourite detective – largely due to the extraordinary success of the several ITV series of his adventures starring John Thaw and Kevin Whately which attracted audiences in excess of eighteen million viewers!

CREATOR: Colin Dexter (b. 1930), despite the overwhelming success of Morse, remains the same unassuming and courteous man he has always been and still lives in Oxford where for many years he was a university administrator. A passionate crossword puzzle enthusiast, it was this love of unravelling clues that prompted Dexter to create Morse during a family holiday in Wales in 1972. He recalls, 'It was raining and I'd just read a crime novel that I thought was lousy so I sat down to write a better one – and that was the beginning of *Last Bus to Woodstock*, a story about a detective called Morse.' (The name, he says, sprang from his National Service days where he discovered he was very good at transmitting high speed Morse code!) At the most recent calculation, the Morse novels have been translated into seventeen languages and the TV series seen by a total of 750 million viewers worldwide. 'The Burglar', written for *You* magazine in 1994, is another of Morse's wonderfully puzzling little cases, ostensibly just about a break-in. But you may be sure there is more to it than that . . .

***

As he drove into Chaucer Crescent, Sergeant Lewis turned to speak to his passenger.

'Not often you show much interest in things like this, sir.'

Morse shrugged. 'I used to live near him, that's all.'

'Did you know him very well?'

'I've never known anyone very well, Lewis. But he

showed me his collection of cigarette cards once – very fine.'

'Probably not got it any longer.'

'Probably not,' admitted Morse.

'Valuable?'

'Oh yes! No cigarette cards around these days, are there?'

Lewis unfastened the safety belt. 'I wouldn't know. I've never smoked, myself.'

'Well, just don't be too critical of those who do,' said Morse briskly, as he stubbed out his cigarette. 'Anyway, it's good for all of us to do a bit of fourth-grade clerical work occasionally – you know, licking stamps, that sort of thing.'

'I've never actually seen you licking stamps . . .'

'Lewis! I shall go crackers if you use that weasel word "actually" much more.'

Sergeant Lewis took a deep breath. Made no reply. Got out of the car.

Number fourteen was an unremarkable semi-detached property, and the house itself presented a somewhat unkempt appearance – except for the windows, which had recently been replaced. And it was through one of these replacement windows that Mrs Agnes Price, living immediately opposite at number eleven, had observed a man peering into the front ground-floor living-room . . .

'I suppose we'd better go and have a word with the old girl,' said Morse.

What a stressful morning it had become for Mrs Price! She knew that more often than not burglaries took place in the broad light of day rather than by torchlight in the small hours of the morning. But was the man she'd seen a burglar – or at least a potential burglar? There was no way of knowing really, was there?

It was her responsibility, though, to keep an eye on things, because Mr Robertson had left his keys with her –

as he'd left them for each of the past seven years when he'd gone off on his mid-August holidays to Morocco. And it was clear what she ought to do, because the police booklet was quite specific: 'If you see anything at all suspicious, don't hesitate to ring us and ask to speak to your local crime prevention officer.'

She had hesitated though; hesitated too long. But at least her biggest worry was over: the worry that she might be causing the police a lot of needless trouble – and making herself look a fool into the bargain – if it was all a false alarm.

But it hadn't been a false alarm.

The goldfish suddenly gave a flick of its tail and propelled itself upon another of its interminable orbits inside its bowl; and somewhere inside Mrs Price too there was a flick of self-importance as she saw the two men get out of the police car and open her front gate.

After all, this was the second visit from the police that morning.

Pity she'd left things a bit before ringing, thought Lewis, but he made no mention of the fact as he and Morse were seated in Mrs Price's front room (Lewis beside the goldfish bowl) where the elderly widow repeated the evidence she'd given three quarters of an hour earlier.

The first thing she'd noticed was that he was standing there – the man – on the grass in front of Mr Robertson's front window, and sort of peering inside, with his right hand up to his eye – just like the Americans used to salute in the old wartime films. (Morse smiled: nicely put!) Then he'd tried the side gate: locked, though. So he'd come back to the front of the house; and after that – well, she thought he'd gone away. But he hadn't – because he was back again about ten minutes later when he'd gone up to the front door and waited there a while and . . . and sort of listened.

A lot of burglaries took place when properties were empty, didn't they? And she – well, she just hadn't known what to do. She'd considered going over herself but . . . but he might still have been there!

Lewis nodded. 'Much better to ring us – like you did, Mrs Price. That's what we're here for, isn't it, sir?'

But Morse made no reply, apparently unaware that he had been invited to corroborate his sergeant's assertion.

So Mrs Price continued . . . She'd rung the police and the young PC Watson had arrived within ten minutes. They'd gone over to number fourteen together, where she'd let them both in. She'd picked up the letters from the doormat and put them on the hall stand – but she hadn't touched anything else.

Things seemed fairly normal . . . downstairs. 'Except for the french window, of course.' Again Lewis nodded encouragingly. 'But . . . but upstairs, in poor Mr Robertson's bedroom – Oh dear!'

'Would you recognise him again – the burglar?'

She shook her head. 'He'd got his back to me most of the time.'

'Was he white or coloured?'

'White.'

'Fair hair? Dark hair?'

'Darkish.'

'Was it long – or short?'

'Shortish.'

'What was he wearing?'

'I can't really . . .'

'Was he just wearing a shirt? I mean, it's a lovely warm day.'

'Yes I think he was just in his shirtsleeves.'

'Can you remember what colour?'

'Blue – bluish, I think.'

'How old would you say?'

'Young – youngish.'

The 'h' suffix was figuring frequently in Lewis's notebook.

'Was he carrying anything suspicious? You know what I mean . . . like . . .'

But Lewis seemed unable to provide any specific exemplification.

'I think he was carrying something yes. But . . .'

'That's fine. Don't worry!' said Lewis, closing his notebook and getting to his feet. As Mrs Price handed him the keys, he asked one final question. 'How long have you had the goldfish, by the way?'

'Christ! You do ask some stupid questions,' said Morse, as he and Lewis walked over to number fourteen. ' "Was he just wearing a shirt?" ' you said. If he was, he'd have been arrested for indecent exposure, wouldn't he?'

'Mrs Price knew exactly . . .' But Lewis abandoned any further explanation. 'What would you have asked?'

'Me? For a start I'd've asked whether this was normally kept shut,' said Morse, pushing open the decrepit wooden gate. 'Interesting things, gates. See this?' He pointed to the notice lopsidedly nailed across the top bar. 'No Free Newspapers.'

'So we may assume, Lewis, that our suspicious visitor was probably not the paperboy – unless he couldn't read, of course.'

Lewis shook his head. 'Even if he couldn't read, he'd still stick the paper through the letterbox, wouldn't he?'

'So?'

'So what's he doing looking through the window, sir?'

'Ah! Now that's a good question,' said Morse as he pressed the doorbell button – with no audible consequence – before inserting the key into the Yale lock.

A dozen or so envelopes, brown and white, together with a few cards and leaflets, stood neatly stacked where Mrs Price had left them; and Morse quickly fingered through the pile, a slight frown forming on his forehead as he did so. But there was no one to observe such temporary puzzlement, since Lewis had already walked through to the dining-room at the rear of the house where earlier Mrs Price and PC Watson had quickly spotted the one – so far – incontrovertible piece of evidence of the burglar's intrusion; and pretty certainly his means of ingress.

From the french window, which overlooked the semi-wilderness of the back garden, a small pane of glass had been carefully removed. The aperture thus created, though measuring only some few square inches, had clearly been sufficient for the burglar to insert a hand, to reach down, and to turn the dark brown key which now stood in the lock; and which – presumably? – Robertson must have left there.

'Your old friend ought to be shot!' ventured Lewis.

Morse grunted agreement.

'The fingerprint boys'll be pleased, though, sir.'

'Waste o' time, Lewis! We're dealing with a professional here.'

'They're not all that bright, some of 'em.'

'Lewis! You're missing the whole point.'

'Which is?'

'The glass. Where's the glass? Not in here, is it?'

Lewis looked down at the threadbare green carpet. Not a sliver of glass was to be seen. Nor, it appeared, on the concreted area immediately outside.

'No,' continued Morse. 'Somebody as organised as that isn't going to leave his signature. And I wouldn't mind betting that he probably locked up after himself too.'

He was reaching out towards the french window when Lewis laid a hand on his arm.

'Please don't touch anything, sir!'

'Stop treating me like a child!' snapped Morse.

Considerably irked, Lewis followed his superior officer up the stairs, the passageway made even narrower by piles of books stacked at each side of every step. On the small landing, where the door of the front bedroom stood wide open, the two men came face to face straight away with a scene of chaos on a considerable scale.

Bill Robertson, a tall, stooping, seventy-five-year-old bachelor, returned from his annual holiday in Morocco a week late.

At nine a.m. the Heathrow Customs had been ready for him. And on the coach journey back to Oxford, he'd sought to come to terms with the news that the property had been ransacked, and that the police were anxious to be with him when he first set foot in number fourteen again.

'Doesn't seem too much wrong,' he began tentatively, as together with Morse and Lewis he stood first in the hallway, then in the front room; then in the dining-room – where Lewis pointed to the french window, now liberally besprinkled with dusting powder.

It was Robertson who broke the ensuing silence. 'I'm so sorry – really should have had it fixed before I went, shouldn't I?'

'You mean to say . . . ?' began Lewis slowly.

Robertson nodded. 'I was trying to get a bit of gardening done, and the handle of the rake, well, sort of just went straight through the window.'

'And you left the key in the lock,' added Morse quietly.

Robertson nodded like a guilty schoolboy.

'You know,' said Lewis, 'you might just as well have left a notice on the gate telling everybody that the back door was wide open.'

'You're right. But . . . but I'm still a bit surprised that everything's been left so tidy.'

Lewis walked to the foot of the stairs, wondering what

his own immaculately methodical wife would have made of this man's idea of tidiness.

'Just wait a little while, if you will, sir!'

'I'm in for a shock – is that what you're telling me?'

'I'm afraid so,' said Lewis quietly.

In the bedroom all the drawers from the two large mahogany chests had been removed and lay, on their sides or upside down, alongside the single bed, forming (as it were) the basis of a pyramid, whose superstructure comprised (variously) piles of such things as bedlinen, shirts, pyjamas, cardigans; phrase books, maps, paperbacks, diaries; the great motley heap littered at its apex with pens and pencils, bottle-openers, tubes of ointment, and small-denominational coinage, as if the contents of the various canisters and jars scattered around the room had been sprinkled over the entire accumulation.

Robertson stood silent.

And Lewis stood silent.

And Morse himself, after seeing his way past the wreckage, stood silent too, as he looked out over the quiet crescent, where a postman was working his way along the opposite side of the street – a youngish, darkish man wearing a light-bluish short-sleeved shirt; for the morning was just as gloriously warm as it had been at the same time a week previously.

And Morse smiled sadly, if contentedly, to himself, for all the clues now fitted into place: the light-blue shirt; the malfunction of the front-door bell; the card he'd read in the stack of mail inviting the householder to collect a recorded-delivery package; the missing pane in the french window; and, above all, the fecklessness of his former neighbour.

'Take your time, sir!' prompted the gentle Lewis. 'No need to say anything for a while. Just have a quiet look around and try and tell us what's missing.'

Meanwhile, Morse had turned his back on the bedroom window – the replacement bedroom window. Apart from a first perfunctory greeting, he'd said nothing, and still said nothing, although he now saw the whole thing so clearly. Perhaps, given a minute or so longer, he would himself have revealed the extraordinary truth concerning the burglary of number fourteen Chaucer Crescent. But he had no need, for quietly, sadly, Robertson did it for him, as he picked up a Moroccan phrase book from the top of the pyramid.

'You know, gentlemen, it's very difficult for me to tell you what's missing here – if anything – because this room looks to me exactly the same as when I went away!'

Where The Snow Lay Dinted

REGINALD HILL

DETECTIVE FILE

OFFICER: Chief Superintendent Andrew Dalziel

FORCE: Yorkshire CID

TIME: 1993

CASES: *A Clubbable Woman* (1970), *An April Shroud*
(1975), *Deadheads* (1983), *Child's Play* (1987), *Under
World* (1989) etc.

PROFILE: Fat, coarse Chief Superintendent Andy Dalziel (pronounced 'Dee-ell') is inseparable from his thin,
intellectual right-hand man, Detective Inspector Peter
Pascoe, which has caused some admirers of their exploits
to refer to them as the 'Laurel and Hardy of detection'.
The label is made doubly apt by the opening sentence
spoken by Dalziel to Pascoe in *Under World* where he
exclaims, 'Another fine mess you've got me into!'
Described as having a broad slab of a face, Dalziel is
blunt and vulgar, a lifetime policeman now in late middle
age who brings an earthy common sense to every case he
tackles. Pascoe, on the other hand, is a former sociology
graduate who has advanced quickly in the force by way
of sergeant to inspector, although along the way has lost
quite a few of his liberal attitudes and illusions. Despite
their obvious differences, the pair complement each other
quite well and through triumph and adversity have come
to respect one another. Dalziel does, though, like to try

and score points off his younger aide, and the pair have a habit of finding themselves in situations which demand a sense of humour. Black comedy, in fact, is an essential ingredient in many of their cases, and critic Joanne Hayne has observed that their stories 'combine something of the bawdiness of Joyce Porter's Inspector Dover books'.

CREATOR: Reginald Hill (b. 1936) is a North Countryman who was previously a schoolteacher in Essex and an English lecturer in Yorkshire before making his mark as an innovative voice in crime fiction, where his success enabled him to devote himself fulltime to writing. He initially wrote a number of books under different pen names and in different genres, before achieving international recognition with the Dalziel and Pascoe series and winning the Gold Dagger Award for best crime novel of the year from the Crime Writers' Association, and also their Cartier Diamond Dagger for his outstanding contribution to the genre. Hill has also been described by H. R. F. Keating as 'one of the most consistently interesting crime writers of his generation', although he himself likes to keep a low profile and lives quietly in Cumbria with, he says, 'my cats and my conscience'. The books about the brash head of Yorkshire CID and his high-flier assistant, with their layers of plot, character, humour and drama, have inspired two television series: the first rather ill-advisedly featuring the comedians Hale and Pace, but subsequently with great success starring Warren Clarke as Dalziel and Colin Buchanan as Pascoe. 'Where The Snow Lay Dinted' is making its first anthology appearance here, and in it a very hungover Chief Superintendent finds himself unexpectedly caught up in a most baffling case of disappearance.

* * *

Dalziel awoke.

He knew nothing, remembered nothing, and felt neither the desire nor the will to activate cognition.

He lay unmoving and might have so continued for an indefinite period had not a physical sensation finally forced itself upon his embryonic consciousness.

His bollocks were cold.

Time to make contact with the waking world. Nothing rash, minimum risk. He opened his left eye just sufficiently to admit light in the smallest measure known to man, which is a single Scotch in an English pub.

Jesus wept!

Light poured in, white and blinding as if someone had indeed poured a glass of whisky on to his eyeball. He squeezed the eyelid shut and lay still till the dancing white patina had faded from his retina.

Sight no good, so try the other senses . . .

Touch . . . cold, he'd already established that . . .

Sound . . . voices, gently murmuring . . .

Smell . . . antiseptic . . .

Taste . . . *blood*!

Oh God, I'm being operated on and the anaesthetic hasn't took!

'Nobody move!' he bellowed, sitting bolt upright and opening both eyes wide.

In a huge dressing-table mirror he saw a naked fat man with a split lip sitting up in a four-poster bed. On a bedside table stood a half-empty bottle of whisky and a half-full bottle of TCP. Through a tall open window drifted a chilling draught, a blinding white light, and a murmur of voices.

He rolled off the bed on to the floor, landing on a spoor of damp clothes which ran from the doorway to the bedside. After a while he pushed himself to his knees. When his head didn't fall off, he rose fully upright, took three uncertain steps towards the window and, catching hold of the pelmet to maintain verticality, he looked out. And knew at last where, and when, and why he was.

He was in the Hirtledale Arms Hotel on the Yorkshire Moors, it was Boxing Day morning, and it had snowed hard during the night.

It was a scene to touch even the done-over heart of a hungover cop. The sky was delft blue and the still-low rays of the morning sun were gilding the horizoned hills, lending the curves and hollows the sensuous quality of female limbs in repose. Where the foothills gave way to pastureland, the varicosed lines formed by drystone walls were all that marked one field from another. Small trees and bushes sagged beneath the weight of their temporary blossom, while beech and oak and elm stood upright as judges in their wigs of white. About a mile away, the small village of Hirtledale had all but vanished under the sealing snow, but nearer still the fairytale turrets of Hirtledale Castle floated like something imagined by Walt Disney over the icing-sugared battlements.

Dalziel let his gaze drift down to the square of perfect lawn which was the pride and joy of Giles Hartley-Pulman, the hotel's owner. At its centre stood a bronze statue of little St Agnes clutching a lamb, saved from dereliction in Rome (according to the hotel brochure) by a nineteenth-century Lord Hirtledale, and planted here when the hotel building had still been the castle's dower house.

The perfect lawn was now of course a blanket of perfect white, and this seemed to be the focus of attention of the several guests standing on the terrace immediately below Dalziel's window and whose soft conversation he had mistaken for the blasé chit-chat of heartless surgeons.

So what was so interesting? wondered Dalziel.

He returned his attention to the lawn and as his eyes adjusted to the dazzling light, he saw that its surface was not perfect after all.

From the feet of the statue ran a set of small animal hoofprints. The trail swung in a wide circle round the lawn, though always staying well clear of its edges, before returning to the base of the statue.

'Bugger me,' said Andy Dalziel.

His exclamation drew the attention of the watchers below to his presence. They looked up at him with expressions ranging from the amused to the amazed. Among them, he spotted Peter and Ellie Pascoe, who maintained the neutral faces of people who'd seen it all before. If so, they were seeing it all again, for it suddenly occurred to Dalziel that he was stark naked.

Time for retreat. Any road, miracles shouldn't be taken on an empty stomach.

He belched gently, gave a little wave, and called, 'See you at breakfast, I'm fair clemmed.'

As he showered and shaved, memory struggled back into his mind like the sea up a long shallow beach.

At low tide level, things were pretty clear. This time last week, he'd had no plans for Christmas and didn't give a toss. Then Peter Pascoe had let slip that he was planning to spend the break at the Hirtledale Arms, and suddenly Dalziel realised how much he'd been relying on the usual Boxing Day invitation to lunch with the Pascoes.

He must have let it show. Or perhaps Pascoe just felt guilty, because he'd started explaining.

'Not my cup of tea, really, but Ellie's mum, well, you know she's not long widowed and she needs a change of scene, and it takes the pressure off Ellie . . .' Then, with the expansive generosity of one who knew the hotel had long been booked solid, he'd added, 'Look, why not join us? We'd all love to see you there.'

And God, who is a Yorkshireman, had grinned, nipped a guest in the appendix and made sure news of the cancellation reached the hotel five minutes before Dalziel rang.

When he heard the price quoted by Giles Hartley-Pulman (who immediately in Dalziel-speak became Giles Partly-Human), his Scottish/Yorkshire blood curdled. Then he'd asked himself, 'What are you saving for? A cashmere winding sheet and a platinum coffin?' and booked. His reward had been the discovery that one of the things the inclusive price included was wine and liqueurs with Christmas dinner. Somewhere between the turkey and the truffles he had a vague recollection of calculating that profligacy had turned into profit. And he thought he recalled starting on the liqueurs in alphabetical order, but now they sat like an oil slick on the tide of memory, turning it sluggish and opaque well short of high water. What he needed was some mental menstruum and he knew just the formula. First take a precise inch of the Macallan in a tooth glass and toss it straight down to avoid contact with your cut lip. Then add half a pound of streaky bacon, a black pudding, several eggs and a potato scone, and chew gently.

He descended to the dining-room to complete the cure.

As he entered, a voice cried. 'Andy, good morning. Now the Great Detective is among us, the riddle of the perambulating statue will be solved in a trice. Or would you rather we all assembled in the library later?'

This was Freddie Gilmour, a young man who was something in the City and had been Christmassing at Hirtledale for many years with half a dozen like-mindless friends. They had adopted Dalziel in a way which Peter Pascoe found offensively patronising. But Dalziel's huge frame was lead lined, and this imperviousness, plus his prodigious feats of consumerism, had brought these devout free-marketeers to a wondering respect.

'Nay, Fred,' he said. 'I only solve real mysteries. Like if

you put your hand in your pocket and found some of your own money there.'

Followed by a gust of laughter, he crossed the room and joined the Pascoes.

'Morning,' he said.

He couldn't have behaved too badly last night because both Ellie and her mother gave him a welcoming smile, though the former began to fade as little Rosie Pascoe piped up eagerly, 'Uncle Andy, did you see? The statue went for a walk last night and took her little lamb with her.'

'I don't think so, dear,' said her mother who, though having nothing against flights of imagination, was a natural enemy of anything smacking of superstitious credulity. 'I'm sure there's some other explanation.'

'No, they went for a walk, you can see the footprints in the snow, isn't that right, Uncle Andy? Because anything can happen at Christmas.'

Dalziel looked from mother to daughter. The same dark, serious, unblinking gaze, the same expression of expectant certitude.

Pascoe was observing him with a faint grin which said, 'Get out of this one!'

'Aye. Owt can. That doesn't say it will, but.'

Good try, but not good enough.

'But this *has* happened, hasn't it?' insisted the girl. 'You can see the prints.'

'That's right,' agreed the Fat Man. 'What I can't see is anyone to serve me breakfast.'

'I get the impression there's some sort of crisis in the kitchen,' said Pascoe.

'If there's not, there soon will be,' said Dalziel, glad of an excuse to escape Ellie's threatening glare.

He rose, went to the kitchen door, pushed it open and bellowed, '*Shop!*'

Giles Hartley-Pulman, deep in confabulation with his

chef and three young waitresses, jumped six inches in the air. His lean ascetic face was creased with concern, but oddly when he identified the source of the sound, it relaxed ever so slightly.

There had been a moment last night when he would gladly have given half his kingdom for the privilege of never seeing Dalziel again. This had been when he bravely but foolishly attempted to slow if not stem the Fat Man's consumption of claret. To the applause of the other guests, Dalziel had flourished the menu, stabbing with a huge finger at the words 'Wine and Liqueurs, ad lib', and saying, 'Here in Yorkshire we've got a word for a man who's not good as his word! We'll try another bottle of the 'eighty-three.'

A good hotelier knows when to withdraw. He also knows how to get even if the chance offers, and now Hartley-Pulman advanced saying, 'Superintendent Dalziel, thank heaven. There's been a burglary. I was about to phone the police but of course with you on the spot, it seems a shame to drag someone out in these conditions . . . and I should hate for the Press to get involved, asking impertinent questions about my guests . . .'

Meaning, I'd rather not have uniformed plods all over the place, but if I do, I'll make sure the world knows you were pissed the far side of oblivion last night!

Dalziel considered. Hirtledale was on the northernmost fringe of his mid-Yorkshire patch, so he certainly had jurisdiction, if he cared to assert it. On the other hand, he didn't care for Partly-Human imagining he could threaten him.

Postponing decision, he said, 'What's been stolen?'

'Well,' said Hartley-Pulman, savouring the moment. 'It's mainly . . . your breakfast.'

And in the dining-room conversation ceased as a great cry of pain and loss exploded out of the kitchen.

Five minutes later, Peter Pascoe was summoned to join his boss. It didn't take long to put him in the picture.

'Partly-Human's making a list,' Dalziel concluded. 'You talk to the staff, lad. Use your boyish charm.'

'Yes, sir,' said Pascoe, looking unhappily at the chef who was breaking a bowlful of eggs into a pan. He didn't want to be involved in this, but if he was ... 'Sir, shouldn't we seal the kitchen in case Forensic . . .'

'Stuff Forensic,' said Dalziel. 'There's nowt left but eggs and I need to keep me strength up.'

Sighing, Pascoe went in search of the waitresses.

Fifteen minutes later he returned to find Dalziel wiping the pattern off a plate with a slice of bread.

'You've got that aren't-I-clever look,' said the Fat Man.

'We've got a name,' said Pascoe. 'Remember little Billy Bream?'

'In the frame for the Millhouse break-in, but CPS got their knickers in a twist. Still, it gave him a scare and he dropped out of sight.'

'Hirtledale was where he dropped to. His old gran lives there. And Milly Staines, the waitress with the squint, she reckons she saw him hanging around here last night.'

'Grand. Owt else?'

'Maybe. Patty Strang, the pretty blonde, says she glanced out of her window just as the snow was starting and saw someone down the drive. No description except it was too big for little Billy and moving very slowly.'

'Even Billy 'ud move slow carrying this lot,' said Dalziel, producing a list.

Pascoe whistled. As well as twelve pounds of sausage, fifteen pounds of bacon, forty kidneys, thirty kippers, twenty-five black puddings and a kilo of salt, a dozen bottles of champagne had gone.

'One thing's certain, he must have left some tracks.'

'Let's take a look,' said Dalziel.

Close to the building the snow was already churned up, but a few yards down the drive they spotted two lines of footprints, one approaching, one moving away.

'How's your tracking, Pocahontas?' said Dalziel. 'Get your wellies and let's see where these lead us.'

Before they left Pascoe had a quick word with Ellie, who rolled her eyes in not altogether mock rage and said, 'Trouble follows the fat bastard but I don't see that's any reason why you should.'

'We're just going to look at the tracks in the snow,' protested Pascoe.

'Yeah? With a bit of luck he might catch pneumonia. If he does, my sympathy's with the bacilli!'

Freddie and the Free-marketeers must have been ear-wigging on this exchange for, as Pascoe joined Dalziel outside the kitchen, they appeared in the doorway and struck up a rousing chorus of 'Good King Wenceslas'.

'Twits,' muttered Pascoe. 'Wouldn't surprise me if they had something to do with this.'

'Wouldn't displease you, you mean,' said Dalziel, acknowledging the carollers with a friendly two-fingered wave. 'Where's your festive spirit, lad?' And joining in their song at the line 'Mark my footsteps good, my page', he strode off up the drive.

As Pascoe floundered behind, already feeling the cold strike through his soles, the carol's words fell with heavy irony on his tingling ears. 'Heat was in the very sod That the saint had printed'. No chance! You needed a saint for that and all he'd got was the very sod!

Where the drive joined the road, the prints turned towards the village and were joined by another outward set.

'Accomplice,' guessed Dalziel. 'Stayed here to keep watch.'

'Or someone who'd set out before the snow started laying,' Pascoe contradicted sourly.

But as they walked on and he began to warm up, the enchanted silence of the snow began to work its magic on his mood. This was what Christmas was all about: not the gluttonous consumerism of the telly ads but a brief interval in which all the filth and flaws of human existence were cloaked in a mantle of purest white.

They were approaching the gothic archway marking the entrance to the castle estate. They heard the sound of a hunting horn and a merry chatter of distant voices.

'Must be the Boxing Day meet,' said Dalziel. 'I could just sup a stirrup cup. Come on!'

He hurried forward, clearly with every intention of turning in to the castle grounds and inserting himself among the huntsmen. But his haste was almost his undoing for as he reached the gate, there was a drumming of hoofs mingled with shouts and laughter, and next moment a posse of red-coated riders erupted in front of them and galloped across the road into a wood. Pascoe, still in his master's steps, was protected from the worst of the spume of slush thrown up behind them, but Dalziel took the full brunt.

'Fuck me,' he said coming to a halt. 'Rigid!'

He looked, thought Pascoe, like a snowman on a Christmas card, lacking only the carrot nose and old pipe to complete the picture. It was a thought he kept to himself.

Another horseman came through the archway, moving at a more decorous pace. This was a much older man, grey hair showing beneath his black cap. He came to a halt in front of Dalziel and examined him for a moment. What might have been a glint of amusement touched his bright blue eyes but didn't extend to his narrow patrician face as he said courteously, 'Sorry about that. Impetuous youth. I'll speak to them.'

'Aye, but will the buggers listen?' said Dalziel brushing the snow away.

'Eventually, once they've ridden off all their festive excesses. No excuse, of course, but if we recall our own younger days and the tricks we got up to, perhaps we can forgive.'

This appeal seemed to strike a chord in Dalziel who said, 'Aye, well, I'll not die of a bit of snow. Daresay some on 'em enjoyed themselves so much last night, they didn't even get to bed.'

'They were certainly still carousing when I went up,' said the horseman. 'I'd better get after them before they find a frozen pond to ride across. Again my apologies. And Merry Christmas to you both.'

He touched his riding crop to his cap and cantered on.

'Know who that was?' said Dalziel. 'Lord Hirtledale himself.'

'Well, roll on the revolution,' said Pascoe. 'Never thought you were a forelock-tugger, sir.'

'Long time since I had one of those,' said Dalziel equably. 'Thought you'd have been all for his lordship. Doesn't he chair that Bosnian relief gang your missus collects for? Cost me a fiver last time she rattled her can!'

'I don't see how that entitles him to prance around the countryside, slaughtering foxes.'

'Nay, lad, you'd best put that one to the Pope next time you write. Too deep for me. I just hunt villains. Tally ho!'

They had no difficulty in refinding the trail beyond the hoofprints, but when they reached the cobbles of the village High Street, it vanished completely.

'What now?' asked Pascoe.

Dalziel didn't answer straight away but thrust his great head forward and moved it slowly this way and that, like an old bear checking out the scents of the forest on waking from hibernation.

Then showing his teeth in a hungry smile, he said, 'I reckon I'll follow my nose up here. You sniff around further along.'

He vanished down the side of a tiny grey cottage, leaving Pascoe to continue up the street, still scanning the trodden snow in search of the vanished spoor. But the combination of cobbled surface and the fact that people had clearly been out and about in the village made it an impossible task. Only on the doorsteps of some of the cottages fronting the street did the snow lay even enough to take a good print, and all you got here were the perfect circles left by milk bottles.

He turned to cross the street to see if he had any better luck on the other side. And halted abruptly as a puzzling thought came into his mind.

Surely even out here in the country where some trace of old-fashioned standards of service still remained, there was unlikely to be a milk delivery on Boxing Day?

Behind him a door opened. Something hard and cylindrical rammed into his spine making him squeak with pain. And a harsh Yorkshire voice grated, 'Stand still, mister, and state thy business. Now!'

Dalziel meanwhile was pushing open a kitchen door, his nostrils flaring wide.

He found himself looking into the surprised eyes of a slightly built young man sitting at a scarred oak table, topping up a pint pot with Veuve Clicquot. In front of him was a huge plate piled high with the delicious freight of the full English breakfast.

'Morning, Billy,' said the Fat Man genially. 'Cansta spare a sausage?'

Ten minutes later he emerged, chewing pensively. Looking down the street he spotted Peter Pascoe sitting on the wall running round the churchyard, cradling a large plastic carrier bag.

'You look knackered,' said Dalziel as he approached. 'Should take more exercise.'

'Fails my heart I know not how,' said Pascoe. 'What are you eating?'

'Kidney. Billy Bream's back there stuffing his face and washing it all down with bubbly.'

'So why's he not here in handcuffs?' asked Pascoe without much passion.

'He says he found it all on his gran's doorstep this morning when he got back from the hotel.'

'And what had he been doing at the hotel that kept him all night?'

'You recall yon bonny waitress, Patty Strang? That's what he says he was doing at the hotel that kept him all night.'

'And you believe him?'

'Well, she looks a healthy young animal,' said Dalziel. 'Still, I admit that normally I'd have had him in for questioning so quick he'd have got indigestion. But when I opened my mouth to give him the caution, I found myself putting another sausage in. Peter, I think maybe I took a knock on the head last night and it's left me concussed. I've started imagining some very strange things. Tell me to get a grip on myself, then pop back in there and arrest Billy Bream, and I'll give you a big wet kiss.'

Pascoe smiled wanly and said, 'Sorry, sir, not even for such an inducement. You see, I've been having a strange encounter of my own too. With Miss Drusilla Earnshaw of this parish, age eighty-three, vegetarian and devout Methodist, who poked her walking stick in my back and didn't take it away till she'd seen my warrant and my library card. Then she told me a very strange story indeed.'

'I don't think I want to hear it,' said Dalziel.

'I don't imagine you do,' said Pascoe. 'Seems she was woken by a noise outside her cottage not long after midnight. She got up, took hold of her stick and flung open her front door. A man was crouching on the step.'

'Description?' said Dalziel desperately.

'Her eyes are bad. Big, broad and brutish, is the best she can do. But her hearing's fine. To her question, "Who are you?" he replied, "Never fret yourself, luv. It's only Good King Wenceslas." Upon which, she hit him in the mouth with her stick and slammed the door. When she opened it again this morning, she found these on her step.'

He opened the carrier to reveal a bottle of Veuve Clicquot, five sausages and a kipper. Dalziel looked at them, shivered, and touched his wounded lip as the tide of memory finally broke clear of the slick of liqueurs and ran clear and high, and oh, so very cold.

He let his gaze rise to meet Pascoe's. And spoke.

'Well, here it is at last, lad. Your big moment. Ring the Chief Constable, alert the Home Office, call out the SAS, and get yourself put in charge of a nationwide hunt for a well-built man with a cut lip and a bedroom floor covered with damp clothes who might be staying at the Hirtledale Arms Hotel. Could be the making of you.'

'No thanks,' said Pascoe standing upright with sudden decision. 'I'm made already, I reckon. But here's what I do suggest. You go back to the hotel, get in your car, and head for town. I'll say you've been called away on an urgent case. But first I'll go round the village and collect as much of the stuff as I can find. I'll tell Partly-Human that we lost the trail but are ninety per cent sure it was some local lads, having a bit of a joke . . .'

Dalziel was shaking his head.

'Nay, lad. Good try but it won't work. Local lads means yobs and poachers to the likes of Partly-Human.

Vermin. He really would want to call in the SAS to flush 'em out.'

'So what *do* you suggest?' demanded Pascoe, exasperated.

'Well, first off, I'm not going to take advantage of your loyalty to get me off the hook. But I'm touched, lad. Deeply touched.'

His voice broke and he gave a choking cough.

'Please,' said Pascoe. 'No need . . .'

'Nay, I'm right. Bit of kidney got stuck, that's all. No, there are times when a man's got to face up to consequences. What is it I'm always telling you?'

Pascoe thought. None of the things that Dalziel was always telling him, such as he should eat more red meat, or that a university degree was what any convict could get between jerking off and sewing mailbags, seemed to apply.

'Can't think, sir,' he said. 'What is it you're always telling me?'

'Speak the truth and the truth will set you free!'

Pascoe couldn't believe his ears.

'You've never told me that in your life!' he cried. 'Besides, in this instance, it's rubbish. The truth will lock you up. You've got too many enemies, starting with Partly-Human . . .'

'Peter, you always think the worst of people,' remonstrated Dalziel. 'There's good in everyone, especially this time of year. Remember the carol.'

Seeking the tune, he began to intone, ' "Wherefore Christian men be sure, Wealth or rank possessing . . ." '

'You won't have any rank,' insisted Pascoe. 'And precious little wealth. Andy, it's your career . . .'

But Dalziel was away down the street, the words now bursting out in a thunderous baritone.

' "Ye who now do bless the poor Shall yourselves find blessing!" '

Fifteen minutes after his return, he emerged from Hart-ley-Pulman's office looking solemn. Pascoe, waiting anxiously, cried, 'What did he say? What did you tell him?'

'I told him the truth,' said the Fat Man. 'And it's OK, lad. Like the decent chap he is, he listened, he under-stood, he forgave and now he's starting to forget. And I'm off down to the kitchen. All this confessing don't half make you hungry! And it's a shame to waste yon stuff you rescued from the old lady.'

He walked away smiling. He loved Pascoe dearly, but it did his heart good to see those intelligent sensitive features gobsmacked from time to time. Not that he hadn't been touched by the lad's willingness to cover up for him. But why tell lies when the truth was good enough? And in his dealing with Partly-Human he'd spoken nowt but gospel truth.

Of course what most folk forget is, there are four versions of the Gospel.

He'd said, man to man, 'I followed them tracks as far as the castle where I came across Lord Hirtledale and some of his young guests. High spirited lads, but no harm in them. His Lordship and I spoke briefly – man with a mind like that doesn't need things spelt out – and he apologised sincerely for any inconvenience his young friends may have caused. He said . . . but I reckon a chap like you doesn't need things spelt out either. Suffice to say, if you can see your way to keeping this business under your bonnet, you'd be highly obligating someone not a million miles away. No names, no pack drill. In fact the only name you need bother with is mine, 'cos that's the one that'll be on the cheque covering your losses. And I'll tell you, I'll be proud to sign it. What do you say? Draw a line under this lot? It won't be forgotten, I promise.'

Partly-Human was looking at him as if the Michelin guide had just awarded him three stars.

'Well, naturally, in those circumstances, I'm only too happy to oblige. And I must say I'm pleasurably surprised by your part in this, Superintendent.'

'Andy,' said Dalziel. 'Well, it 'ud be a sad world if them as are born to rule it couldn't sow a few wild oats. Tell you what, I bet his lordship 'ud be really chuffed if half the damages went to his Bosnian relief fund, eh, Giles?'

And Partly-Human to his credit hardly blanched as he said, 'I think that's a lovely idea, Andy.'

Driving home the next day, Dalziel grinned at the memory. All right, it had cost him, but he'd really enjoyed his break.

Best of all, though, had been the delight on Rosie's face, not to mention the dismay on her mother's, as they'd all stood on the terrace together before they left and examined the mysterious footprints still visible on the lawn.

'You see, the statue did walk, mum,' insisted the little girl. 'Because it's Christmas. Isn't that right, Uncle Andy?'

'That's right,' said Dalziel winking broadly at Ellie. 'Everyone gets what they want at Christmas. That's what it's all about.'

Everyone who had an Uncle Andy anyway. It was funny, all these clever buggers like Pascoe, and not one of them had thought to speculate why the kitchen thief should have included a kilo of salt in his swag. But the salt had been the first and principal object of the raid. The Wenceslas idea had been an afterthought.

He'd trotted round the still snow-free lawn, marking out the trail of footsteps and hoofprints in salt. On the rest of the frost-hard surface, the big flakes had soon started to settle but for a while those that hit the salt melted away. And when the white coverlet was complete, the spoor of prints remained to baffle the adults and delight the little girl.

Andrew Dalziel threw back his head and laughed long and loud, and God, who is a Yorkshireman, looked fondly down on him and laughed too.

Rosie Pascoe, drowsy by her gran's side in the back of her dad's car, was also looking back on Christmas with much pleasure. Of course, any time spent in the close company of adults was bound to have its baffling elements. Like did her mum and dad *really* like Uncle Andy or not? *She* liked him, because he was funny, and kind, and never worried about being rude. Also, because he was a bit sad sometimes.

She recalled Christmas night when she couldn't get to sleep because of all the day's excitements. Finally she'd got up and looked out of the window. There on the lawn, she'd seen him, Uncle Andy, lumbering around like an old dancing bear with the snowflakes whirling like moths round his great grey head. He'd been pouring something on to the grass, she didn't know what. But she didn't doubt next morning that it had something to do with the statue's supposed footprints.

Now, why Uncle Andy should want people to think the statue had walked, she didn't know. It was silly really. Statues couldn't walk, everyone knew that. But it was what he wanted, and that was enough for her to give him her total uncritical support.

Everyone gets what they want at Christmas . . . even Uncle Andy . . .

She fell asleep with her head on her grandmother's lap.

The Little Copplestone Mystery

NGAIO MARSH

DETECTIVE FILE

OFFICER: Chief Superintendent Roderick Alleyn

FORCE: Scotland Yard

TIME: 1973

CASES: *A Man Lay Dead* (1934), *Died in the Wool* (1945), *Singing in the Shrouds* (1958), *Killer Dolphin* (1966), *Black As He's Painted* (1973) etc.

PROFILE: When Eton-educated Roderick Alleyn (pronounced 'Allen') joined the police in the 'thirties he was undoubtedly a genuine original – the first aristocrat to enter the force. Tall and handsome, he has expressive hands and a deep, soothing voice. He is, in fact, very much a gentleman, elegant in dress, beautifully mannered and able to move freely in what are referred to as 'the best circles'. He is, though, a man of iron resolve, never afraid to take physical action where necessary, and possesses a particular style of detection that can as easily comfort frightened women as alert criminals that he is not a man to be trifled with. In a career which has spanned over forty years he has risen from Inspector to Chief Superintendent, all the time aided by Inspector Fox, a dour little man he delights in referring to as 'Br'er Fox'. He is married to Agatha Troy, a celebrated portrait painter, who frequently offers useful suggestions to her husband when he is involved on a difficult case. Even with the passage of time and all the changes in society, the Chief Superintendent has remained a man who stands by the same ideals of the police force as they were when he first joined.

CREATOR: Ngaio Marsh (1899–1982) named Roderick Alleyn after the Elizabethan actor who founded Dulwich College in London, to which she had paid a visit just the day before she began work on her first novel. Born in New Zealand, she devoted much of her early life to the theatre, first as an actress, then as playwright, director and producer – a dedication which was ultimately rewarded in 1966 when she was made a Dame of the British Empire in recognition of her services to the profession. Ngaio's contribution to the crime genre in the form of the Alleyn mysteries is also highly regarded by critics, especially Howard Haycraft, who wrote that she had 'helped to bring the English detective story to full flower'. Sadly, she produced only a handful of short stories about her formidable Scotland Yard detective, and 'The Little Copplestone Mystery' was the very last of these, written in 1973. It offers a splendid picture of the urbane officer who remains to this day a phenomenon in the history of Scotland Yard's fictional detectives.

***

When the telephone rang, Troy came in, sun dazzled, from the cottage garden to answer it, hoping it would be a call from London.

'Oh,' said a strange voice uncertainly. 'May I speak to Superintendent Alleyn, if you please?'

'I'm sorry. He's away.'

'Oh, dear!' said the voice, crestfallen. 'Er – would that be – am I speaking to Mrs Alleyn?'

'Yes.'

'Oh. Yes. Well, it's Timothy Bates here, Mrs Alleyn. You don't know me,' the voice confessed wistfully, 'but I had the pleasure several years ago of meeting your husband. In New Zealand. And he did say that if I ever came home I was to get in touch, and when I heard quite by accident that you were here – well, I *was* excited. But, alas, no good after all.'

'I *am* sorry,' Troy said. 'He'll be back, I hope, on Sunday night. Perhaps—'

'Will he! Come, *that's* something! Because here I am at the Star and Garter, you see, and so – ' The voice trailed away again.

'Yes, indeed. He'll be delighted,' Troy said, hoping that he would.

'I'm a bookman,' the voice confided. 'Old books, you know. He used to come into my shop. It was always such a pleasure.'

'But of course!' Troy exclaimed. 'I remember perfectly now. He's often talked about it.'

'*Has* he? Has he, really! Well, you see, Mrs Alleyn, I'm here on business. Not to *sell* anything, please don't think that, but on a voyage of discovery; almost, one might say, of detection, and I think it might amuse him. He has such an eye for the curious. Not,' the voice hurriedly amended, 'in the trade sense. I mean curious in the sense of mysterious and unusual. But I mustn't bore you.'

Troy assured him that he was not boring her and indeed it was true. The voice was so much coloured by odd little overtones that she found herself quite drawn to its owner.

'I know where you are,' he was saying. 'Your house was pointed out to me.'

After that there was nothing to do but ask him to visit. He seemed to cheer up prodigiously. 'May I? May I, really? Now?'

'Why not?' Troy said. 'You'll be here in five minutes.'

She heard a little crow of delight before he hung up the receiver.

He turned out to be exactly like his voice – a short, middle-aged, bespectacled man, rather untidily dressed. As he came up the path she saw that with both arms he clutched to his stomach an enormous Bible. He was thrown into a fever over the difficulty of removing his cap.

'How ridiculous!' he exclaimed. 'Forgive me! One moment.'

He laid his burden tenderly on a garden seat. 'There!' he cried. 'Now! How do you do?'

Troy took him indoors and gave him a drink. He chose sherry and sat in the window seat with his Bible beside him. 'You'll wonder,' he said, 'why I've appeared with this unusual piece of baggage. I *do* trust it arouses your curiosity.'

He went into a long excitable explanation. It appeared that the Bible was an old and rare one he had picked up in a job lot of books in New Zealand. All this time he kept it under his square little hands as if it might open of its own accord and spoil his story.

'Because,' he said, 'the *really* exciting thing to me is *not* its undoubted authenticity but – ' He made a conspiratorial face at Troy and suddenly opened the Bible. 'Look!' he invited.

He displayed the flyleaf. Troy saw that it was almost filled with entries in a minute, faded copperplate handwriting.

'The top,' Mr Bates cried. 'Top left-hand. Look at *that*.'

Troy read: ' "Crabtree Farm at Little Copplestone in the County of Kent." Why, it comes from our village!'

'Ah, ha! So it does. Now, the entries, my dear Mrs Alleyn. The entries.'

They were the recorded births and deaths of a family

named Wagstaff, beginning in 1705 and ending in 1870 with the birth of William James Wagstaff. Here they broke off but were followed by three further entries, close together.

> Stewart Shakespeare Hadet. Died: Tuesday, 5th April, 1779. 2nd Samuel 1:10.
> Naomi Balbus Hadet. Died: Saturday, 13th August, 1779. Jeremiah 50:24.
> Peter Rook Hadet. Died: Monday, 12th September, 1779. Ezekiel 7:6.

Troy looked up to find Mr Bates's gaze fixed on her. 'And what,' Mr Bates asked, 'my dear Mrs Alleyn, do you make of *that*?'

'Well,' she said cautiously, 'I know about Crabtree Farm. There's the farm itself, owned by Mr De'ath, and there's Crabtree House, belonging to Miss Hart, and – yes, I fancy I've heard they both belonged originally to a family named Wagstaff.'

'You are perfectly right. Now! What about the Hadets? What about *them*?'

'I've never heard of a family named Hadet in Little Copplestone. But—'

'Of course you haven't. For the very good reason that there never have been any Hadets in Little Copplestone.'

'Perhaps in New Zealand, then?'

'The dates, my dear Mrs Alleyn, the dates! New Zealand was not colonised in 1779. Look closer. Do you see the sequence of double dots – ditto marks – under the address? Meaning, of course, "also of Crabtree Farm at Little Copplestone in the County of Kent".'

'I suppose so.'

'Of course you do. And how right you are. Now! You have noticed that throughout there are biblical references. For the Wagstaffs they are the usual pious offerings. You need not trouble yourself with them. But consult the text awarded to the three Hadets. Just look *them* up! I've put markers.'

He threw himself back with an air of triumph and sipped his sherry. Troy turned over the heavy bulk of pages to the first marker. 'Second of Samuel, one, ten,' Mr Bates prompted, closing his eyes.

The verse had been faintly underlined.

' "So I stood upon him," ' Troy read, ' "and slew him." '

'That's Stewart Shakespeare Hadet's valedictory,' said Mr Bates. 'Next!'

The next was at the fiftieth chapter of Jeremiah, verse twenty-four: ' "I have laid a snare for thee and thou are taken." '

Troy looked at Mr Bates. His eyes were still closed and he was smiling faintly.

'That was Naomi Balbus Hadet,' he said. 'Now for Peter Rook Hadet. Ezekiel, seven, six.'

The pages flopped back to the last marker.

' "An end is come, the end is come: it watcheth for thee; behold it is come." '

Troy shut the Bible.

'How very unpleasant,' she said.

'And how very intriguing, don't you think?' And when she didn't answer, 'Quite up your husband's street, it seemed to me.'

'I'm afraid,' Troy said, 'that even Rory's investigations don't go back to 1779.'

'What a pity!' Mr Bates cried gaily.

'Do I gather that you conclude from all this that there was dirty work among the Hadets in 1779?'

'I don't know, but I'm going to find out. *Dying* to. Thank you, I should enjoy another glass. Delicious!'

He had settled down so cosily and seemed to be enjoying himself so much that Troy was constrained to ask him to stay to lunch.

'Miss Hart's coming,' she said. 'She's the one who bought Crabtree House from the Wagstaffs. If there's any gossip to be picked up in Copplestone, Miss Hart's the one for it. She's coming about a painting she wants me to donate to the Harvest Festival raffle.'

Mr Bates was greatly excited. 'Who knows!' he cried. 'A Wagstaff in the hand may be worth two Hadets in the bush. I am your slave forever, my dear Mrs Alleyn!'

Miss Hart was a lady of perhaps sixty-seven years. On meeting Mr Bates she seemed to imply that some explanation should be advanced for Troy receiving a gentleman caller in her husband's absence. When the Bible was produced, she immediately accepted it in this light, glanced with professional expertise at the inscription and fastened on the Wagstaffs.

'No doubt,' said Miss Hart, 'it was their family Bible and much good it did them. A most eccentric lot they were. Very unsound. Very unsound, indeed. Especially Old Jimmy.'

'Who,' Mr Bates asked greedily, 'was Old Jimmy?'

Miss Hart jabbed her forefinger at the last of the Wagstaff entries. 'William James Wagstaff. Born 1870. And died, although it doesn't say so, in April, 1921. Nobody was left to complete the entry, of course. Unless you count the niece, which I don't. Baggage, if ever I saw one.'

'The niece?'

'Fanny Wagstaff. Orphan. Old Jimmy brought her up. Dragged would be the better word. Drunken old reprobate he was and he came to a drunkard's end. They said he beat her *and* I daresay she needed it.' Miss Hart lowered her voice to a whisper and confided in Troy. 'Not a *nice* girl. You know what I mean.'

Troy, feeling it was expected of her, nodded portentously.

'A drunken end, did you say?' prompted Mr Bates.

'Certainly. On a Saturday night after Market. Fell through the top-landing stair rail in his nightshirt and split his skull on the flagstoned hall.'

'And your father bought it, then, after Old Jimmy died?' Troy ventured.

'Bought the house and garden. Richard De'ath took the farm. He'd been after it for years – wanted it to round off his own place. He and Old Jimmy were at daggers-drawn over *that* business. And, of course, Richard being an atheist, over the Seven Seals.'

'I beg your pardon?' Mr Bates asked.

'Blasphemous!' Miss Hart shouted. 'That's what it was, rank blasphemy. It was a sect that Wagstaff founded. If the Rector had known his business he'd have had him excommunicated for it.'

Miss Hart was prevented from elaborating this theory by the appearance at the window of an enormous woman, stuffily encased in black, with a face like a full moon.

'Anybody at home?' the newcomer playfully chanted. 'Telegram for a lucky girl! Come and get it!'

It was Mrs Simpson, the village postmistress. Miss Hart said, 'Well, *really*!' and gave an acid laugh.

'Sorry, I'm sure,' said Mrs Simpson, staring at the Bible which lay under her nose on the window seat. 'I didn't realise there was company. Thought I'd pop it in as I was passing.'

Troy read the telegram while Mrs Simpson, panting, sank heavily on the window ledge and eyed Mr Bates, who had drawn back in confusion. 'I'm no good in the heat,' she told him. 'Slays me.'

'Thank you so much, Mrs Simpson,' Troy said. 'No answer.'

'Righty-ho. Cheerie-bye,' said Mrs Simpson and with

another stare at Mr Bates and the Bible, and a derisive grin at Miss Hart, she waddled away.

'It's from Rory,' Troy said. 'He'll be home on Sunday evening.'

'As that woman will no doubt inform the village,' Miss Hart pronounced. 'A busybody of the first water and ought to be taught her place. Did you ever!'

She fulminated throughout luncheon and it was with difficulty that Troy and Mr Bates persuaded her to finish her story of the last of the Wagstaffs. It appeared that Old Jimmy had died intestate, his niece succeeding. She had at once announced her intention of selling everything and had left the district to pursue, Miss Hart suggested, a life of freedom, no doubt in London or even in Paris. Miss Hart wouldn't, and didn't want to know. On the subject of the Hadets, however, she was uninformed and showed no inclination to look up the marked Bible references attached to them.

After luncheon Troy showed Miss Hart three of her paintings, any one of which would have commanded a high price at an exhibition of contemporary art, and Miss Hart chose the one that in her own phrase, really did look like something. She insisted that Troy and Mr Bates accompany her to the parish hall where Mr Bates would meet the Rector, an authority on village folklore. Troy in person must hand over her painting to be raffled.

Troy would have declined this honour if Mr Bates had not retired behind Miss Hart and made a series of beseeching gestures and grimaces. They set out therefore in Miss Hart's car which was crammed with vegetables for the Harvest Festival decorations.

'And if the woman Simpson thinks she's going to hog the lectern with *her* pumpkins,' said Miss Hart, 'she's in for a shock. Hah!'

St Cuthbert's was an ancient parish church round whose

flanks the tiny village nestled. Its tower, an immensely high one, was said to be unique. Near by was the parish hall where Miss Hart pulled up with a masterful jerk.

Troy and Mr Bates helped her unload some of her lesser marrows to be offered for sale within. They were observed by a truculent-looking man in tweeds who grinned at Miss Hart. 'Burnt offerings,' he jeered, 'for the tribal gods, I perceive.' It was Mr Richard De'ath, the atheist. Miss Hart cut him dead and led the way into the hall.

Here they found the Rector, with a crimson-faced elderly man and a clutch of ladies engaged in preparing for the morrow's sale.

The Rector was a thin gentle person, obviously frightened of Miss Hart and timidly delighted by Troy. On being shown the Bible he became excited and dived at once into the story of Old Jimmy Wagstaff.

'Intemperate, I'm afraid, in everything,' sighed the Rector. 'Indeed, it would not be too much to say that he both preached and drank hellfire. He *did* preach, on Saturday nights at the crossroads outside the Star and Garter. Drunken, blasphemous nonsense it was and although he used to talk about his followers, the only one he could claim was his niece, Fanny, who was probably too much under his thumb to refuse him.'

'Edward Pilbrow,' Miss Hart announced, jerking her head at the elderly man who had come quite close to them. 'Drowned him with his bell. They had a fight over it. Deaf as a post,' she added, catching sight of Mr Bates's startled expression. 'He's the Verger now. *And* the town crier.'

'What!' Mr Bates exclaimed.

'Oh, yes,' the Rector explained. 'The village is endowed with a town crier.' He went over to Mr Pilbrow, who at once cupped his hand round his ear. The Rector yelled into it.

'When did you start crying, Edward?'

'Twenty-ninth September, 'twenty-one,' Mr Pilbrow roared back.

'I thought so.'

There was something in their manner that made it difficult to remember, Troy thought, that they were talking about events that were almost fifty years back in the past. Even the year 1779 evidently seemed to them to be not so long ago, but, alas, none of them knew of any Hadets.

'By all means,' the Rector invited Mr Bates, 'consult the church records, but I can assure you – no Hadets. Never any Hadets.'

Troy saw an expression of extreme obstinacy settle round Mr Bates's mouth.

The Rector invited him to look at the church and as they both seemed to expect Troy to tag along, she did so. In the lane they once more encountered Mr Richard De'ath, out of whose pocket protruded a paper-wrapped bottle. He touched his cap to Troy and glared at the Rector, who turned pink and said, 'Afternoon, De'ath,' and hurried on.

Mr Bates whispered imploringly to Troy, '*Would* you mind? I *do* so want to have a word – ' and she was obliged to introduce him. It was not a successful encounter. Mr Bates no sooner broached the topic of his Bible, which he still carried, than Mr De'ath burst into an alcoholic diatribe against superstition, and on the mention of Old Jimmy Wagstaff, worked himself up into such a state of reminiscent fury that Mr Bates was glad to hurry away with Troy.

They overtook the Rector in the churchyard, now bathed in the golden opulence of an already westering sun.

'There they all lie,' the Rector said, waving a fatherly hand at the company of headstones. 'All your Wagstaffs, right back to the sixteenth century. But no Hadets, Mr Bates, I assure you.'

They stood looking up at the spire. Pigeons flew in and out of a balcony far above their heads. At their feet was a little flagged area edged by a low coping. Mr Bates stepped forward and the Rector laid a hand on his arm.

'Not there,' he said. 'Do you mind?'

'Don't!' bellowed Mr Pilbrow from the rear. 'Don't you set foot on them bloody stones, mister.'

Mr Bates backed away.

'Edward's not swearing,' the Rector mildly explained. 'He is to be taken, alas, literally. A sad and dreadful story, Mr Bates.'

'Indeed?' Mr Bates asked eagerly.

'Indeed, yes. Some time ago, in the very year we have been discussing – 1921, you know – one of our girls, a very beautiful girl she was, named Ruth Wall, fell from the balcony of the tower and was, of course, killed. She used to go up there to feed the pigeons and it was thought that in leaning over the low balustrade she overbalanced.'

'Ah!' Mr Pilbrow roared with considerable relish, evidently guessing the purport of the Rector's speech. 'Terrible, terrible! And 'er sweetheart after 'er, too. Terrible!'

'Oh, no!' Troy protested.

The Rector made a dabbing gesture to subdue Mr Pilbrow. 'I wish he wouldn't,' he said. 'Yes. It was a few days later. A lad called Simon Castle. They were to be married. People said it must be suicide but – it may have been wrong of me – I couldn't bring myself – in short, he lies beside her over there. If you would care to look.'

For a minute or two they stood before the headstones.

'Ruth Wall. Spinster of this Parish. 1903–21. *I will extend peace to her like a river.*'

'Simon Castle. Bachelor of this Parish. 1900–21. *And God shall wipe away all tears from their eyes.*'

The afternoon having by now worn on, and the others having excused themselves, Mr Bates remained alone in the churchyard, clutching his Bible and staring at the headstones. The light of the hunter's zeal still gleamed in his eyes.

Troy didn't see Mr Bates again until Sunday night service when, on her way up the aisle, she passed him, sitting in the rearmost pew. She was amused to observe that his gigantic Bible was under the seat.

'We plow the fields,' sang the choir, 'and scatter – ' Mrs Simpson roared away on the organ, the smell of assorted greengrocery rising like some humble incense. Everybody in Little Copplestone except Mr Richard De'ath was there for the Harvest Festival. At last the Rector stepped over Miss Hart's biggest pumpkin and ascended the pulpit, Edward Pilbrow switched off all the lights except one and they settled down for the sermon.

'A sower went forth to sow,' announced the Rector. He spoke simply and well but somehow Troy's attention wandered. She found herself wondering where, through the centuries, the succeeding generations of Wagstaffs had sat until Old Jimmy took to his freakish practices, and whether Ruth Wall and Simon Castle, poor things, had shared the same hymnbook and held hands during the sermon; and whether, after all, Stewart Shakespeare Hadet and Peter Rook Hadet had not, in 1779, occupied some dark corner of the church and been unaccountably forgotten.

Here we are, Troy thought drowsily, and there, outside in the churchyard, are all the others going back and back –

She saw a girl, bright in the evening sunlight, reach from a balcony towards a multitude of wings. She was falling – dreadfully – into nothingness. Troy woke with a sickening jerk.

' – on stony ground,' the Rector was saying. Troy listened guiltily to the rest of the sermon.

Mr Bates emerged on the balcony. He laid his Bible on the coping and looked at the moonlit tree tops and the churchyard so dreadfully far below. He heard someone coming up the stairway. Torchlight danced on the door jamb.

'You were quick,' said the visitor.

'I am all eagerness and, I confess, puzzlement.'

'It had to be here, on the spot. If you *really* want to find out – '

'But I do, I do!'

'We haven't much time. You've brought the Bible?'

'You particularly asked—'

'If you'd open it at Ezekiel, chapter twelve. I'll shine my torch.'

Mr Bates opened the Bible.

'The thirteenth verse. There!'

Mr Bates leaned forward. The Bible tipped and moved.

'Look out!' the voice urged.

Mr Bates was scarcely aware of the thrust. He felt the page tear as the book sank under his hands. The last thing he heard was the beating of a multitude of wings.

' – and for evermore,' said the Rector in a changed voice, facing east. The congregation got to its feet. He announced the last hymn. Mrs Simpson made a preliminary rumble and Troy groped in her pocket for the collection plate. Presently they all filed out into the autumnal moonlight.

It was coldish in the churchyard. People stood about in groups. One or two had already moved through the lychgate. Troy heard a voice, which she recognised as that of Mr De'ath. 'I suppose,' it jeered, 'you all know you've been assisting at a fertility rite.'

'Drunk as usual, Dick De'ath,' somebody returned without rancour. There was a general laugh.

They had all begun to move away when, from the shadows at the base of the church tower, there arose a great cry. They stood, transfixed, turned toward the voice.

Out of the shadows came the Rector in his cassock. When Troy saw his face she thought he must be ill and went to him.

'No, no!' he said. 'Not a woman! Edward! Where's Edward Pilbrow?'

Behind him, at the foot of the tower, was a pool of darkness; but Troy, having come closer, could see within it a figure, broken like a puppet on the flagstones. An eddy of night air stole round the church and fluttered a page of the giant Bible that lay pinned beneath the head.

It was nine o'clock when Troy heard the car pull up outside the cottage. She saw her husband coming up the path and ran to meet him, as if they had been parted for months.

He said, 'This is mighty gratifying!' And then, 'Hullo, my love. What's the matter?'

As she tumbled out her story, filled with relief at telling him, a large man with uncommonly bright eyes came up behind them.

'Listen to this, Fox,' Roderick Alleyn said. 'We're in demand, it seems.' He put his arm through Troy's and closed his hand round hers. 'Let's go indoors, shall we? Here's Fox, darling, come for a nice bucolic rest. Can we give him a bed?'

Troy pulled herself together and greeted Inspector Fox. Presently she was able to give them a coherent account of the evening's tragedy. When she finished, Alleyn said, 'Poor little Bates. He was a nice little bloke.' He put his hand on Troy's. 'You need a drink,' he said, 'and so, by the way, do we.'

While he was getting the drinks he asked quite casually, 'You've had a shock and a beastly one at that, but there's something else, isn't there?'

'Yes,' Troy swallowed hard, 'there is. They're all saying it's an accident.'

'Yes?'

'And, Rory, I don't think it is.'

Mr Fox cleared his throat. 'Fancy,' he said.

'Suicide?' Alleyn suggested, bringing her drink to her.

'No. Certainly not.'

'A bit of rough stuff, then?'

'You sound as if you're asking about the sort of weather we've been having.'

'Well darling, you don't expect Fox and me to go into hysterics. Why not an accident?'

'He knew all about the other accidents, he *knew* it was dangerous. And then the oddness of it, Rory. To leave the Harvest Festival service and climb the tower in the dark, carrying that enormous Bible!'

'And he was hell-bent on tracing these Hadets?'

'Yes. He kept saying you'd be interested. He actually brought a copy of entries for you.'

'Have you got it?'

She found it for him. 'The selected texts,' he said, 'are pretty rum, aren't they, Br'er Fox?' and handed it over.

'Very vindictive,' said Mr Fox.

'Mr Bates thought it was in your line,' Troy said.

'The devil he did! What's been done about this?'

'The village policeman was in the church. They sent for the doctor. And – well, you see, Mr Bates had talked a lot about you and they hope you'll be able to tell them something about him – whom they should get in touch with and so on.'

'Have they moved him?'

'They weren't going to until the doctor had seen him.'

Alleyn pulled his wife's ear and looked at Fox. 'Do you fancy a stroll through the village, Foxkin?'

'There's a lovely moon,' Fox said bitterly and got to his feet.

The moon was high in the heaven when they came to the base of the tower and it shone on a group of four men – the Rector, Richard De'ath, Edward Pilbrow, and Sergeant Botting, the village constable. When they saw Alleyn and Fox, they separated and revealed a fifth, who was kneeling by the body of Timothy Bates.

'Kind of you to come,' the Rector said, shaking hands with Alleyn. 'And a great relief to all of us.'

Their manner indicated that Alleyn's arrival would remove a sense of personal responsibility. 'If you'd like to have a look – ?' the doctor said.

The broken body lay huddled on its side. The head rested on the open Bible. The right hand, rigid in cadaveric spasm, clutched a torn page. Alleyn knelt and Fox came closer with the torch. At the top of the page Alleyn saw the word Ezekiel and a little farther down, Chapter Twelve.

Using the tip of his finger Alleyn straightened the page. 'Look,' he said, and pointed to the thirteenth verse. ' "My net also will I spread upon him and he shall be taken in my snare." '

The words had been faintly underlined in mauve.

Alleyn stood up and looked round the circle of faces.

'Well,' the doctor said, 'we'd better see about moving him.'

Alleyn said, 'I don't think he should be moved just yet.'

'Not!' the Rector cried out. 'But surely – to leave him like this – I mean, after this terrible accident – '

'It has yet to be proved,' Alleyn said, 'that it was an accident.'

There was a sharp sound from Richard De'ath.

' – and I fancy,' Alleyn went on, glancing at De'ath, 'that it's going to take quite a lot of proving.'

After that, events, as Fox observed with resignation, took the course that was to be expected. The local Superintendent said that under the circumstances it would be silly not to ask Alleyn to carry on, the Chief Constable agreed, and appropriate instructions came through from Scotland Yard. The rest of the night was spent in routine procedure. The body having been photographed and the Bible set aside for fingerprinting, both were removed and arrangements put in hand for the inquest.

At dawn Alleyn and Fox climbed the tower. The winding stair brought them to an extremely narrow doorway through which they saw the countryside lying vaporous in the faint light. Fox was about to go through to the balcony when Alleyn stopped him and pointed to the door jambs. They were covered with a growth of stonecrop.

About three feet from the floor this had been brushed off over a space of perhaps four inches and fragments of the microscopic plant hung from the scars. From among these, on either side, Alleyn removed morsels of dark-coloured thread. 'And here,' he sighed, 'as sure as fate, we go again. O Lord, O Lord!'

They stepped through to the balcony and there was a sudden whirr and beating of wings as a company of pigeons flew out of the tower. The balcony was narrow and the balustrade indeed very low. 'If there's any looking over,' Alleyn said, 'you, my dear Foxkin, may do it.'

Nevertheless he leaned over the balustrade and presently knelt beside it. 'Look at this. Bates rested the open Bible here – blow me down flat if he didn't! There's a powder of leather where it scraped on the stone and a fragment where it tore. It must have been moved – outward. Now, why, *why?*'

'Shoved it accidentally with his knees, then made a grab and overbalanced?'

'But why put the open Bible there? To read by moonlight? "My net also will I spread upon him and he shall be taken in my snare." Are you going to tell me he underlined it and then dived overboard?'

'I'm not going to tell you anything,' Fox grunted and then: 'That old chap Edward Pilbrow's down below swabbing the stones. He looks like a beetle.'

'Let him look like a rhinoceros if he wants to, but for the love of Mike don't leer over the edge – you give me the willies. Here, let's pick this stuff up before it blows away.'

They salvaged the scraps of leather and put them in an envelope. Since there was nothing more to do, they went down and out through the vestry and so home to breakfast.

'Darling,' Alleyn told his wife, 'you've landed us with a snorter.'

'Then you *do* think – ?'

'There's a certain degree of fishiness. Now, see here, wouldn't *somebody* have noticed little Bates get up and go out? I know he sat all alone on the back bench, but wasn't there *someone?*'

'The Rector?'

'No, I asked him. Too intent on his sermon, it seems.'

'Mrs Simpson? If she looks through her little red curtain she faces the nave.'

'We'd better call on her, Fox. I'll take the opportunity to send a couple of cables to New Zealand. She's fat, jolly, keeps the shop-cum-Post Office, and is supposed to read all the postcards. Just your cup of tea. You're dynamite with postmistresses. Away we go.'

Mrs Simpson sat behind her counter doing a crossword puzzle and refreshing herself with liquorice. She welcomed Alleyn with enthusiasm. He introduced Fox and then he retired to a corner to write out his cables.

'What a catastrophe!' Mrs Simpson said, plunging straight into the tragedy. 'Shocking! As nice a little gentleman as you'd wish to meet, Mr Fox. Typical New Zealander. Pick him a mile away and a friend of Mr Alleyn's, I'm told, and if I've said it once I've said it a hundred times, Mr Fox, they ought to have put something up to prevent it. Wire netting or a bit of ironwork; but, no, they let it go on from year to year and now see what's happened – history repeating itself and giving the village a bad name. Terrible!'

Fox bought a packet of tobacco from Mrs Simpson and paid her a number of compliments on the layout of her shop, modulating from there into an appreciation of the village. He said that one always found such pleasant company in small communities. Mrs Simpson was impressed and offered him a piece of liquorice.

'As for pleasant company,' she chuckled, 'that's as may be, though by and large I suppose I mustn't grumble. I'm a cockney and a stranger here myself, Mr Fox. Only twenty-four years and that doesn't go for anything with this lot.'

'Ah,' Fox said, 'then you wouldn't recollect the former tragedies. Though to be sure,' he added, 'you wouldn't do that in any case, being much too young, if you'll excuse the liberty, Mrs Simpson.'

After this classic opening Alleyn was not surprised to hear Mrs Simpson embark on a retrospective survey of life in Little Copplestone. She was particularly lively on Miss Hart, who, she hinted, had had her eye on Mr Richard De'ath for many a long day.

'As far back as when Old Jimmy Wagstaff died, which

was why she was so set on getting the next-door house; but Mr De'ath never looked at anybody except Ruth Wall, and her head-over-heels in love with young Castle, which together with her falling to her destruction when feeding pigeons led Mr De'ath to forsake religion and take to drink, which he has done something cruel ever since.

'They do say he's got a terrible temper, Mr Fox, and it's well known he give Old Jimmy Wagstaff a thrashing on account of straying cattle, and threatened young Castle, saying if he couldn't have Ruth, nobody else would, but fair's fair and personally I've never seen him anything but nice mannered, drunk or sober. Speak as you find's my motto and always has been, but these old maids, when they take a fancy they get it pitiful hard. You wouldn't know a word of nine letters meaning "pale-faced lure like a sprat in fishy story", would you?'

Fox was speechless, but Alleyn, emerging with his cables, suggested 'whitebait'.

'Correct!' shouted Mrs Simpson. 'Fits like a glove. Although it's not a bit like a sprat and a quarter the size. Cheating, I call it. Still, it fits.' She licked her indelible pencil and triumphantly added it to her crossword.

They managed to lead her back to Timothy Bates. Fox, professing a passionate interest in organ music, was able to extract from her that when the Rector began his sermon she had in fact dimly observed someone move out of the back bench and through the doors. 'He must have walked round the church and in through the vestry and little did I think he was going to his death,' Mrs Simpson said with considerable relish and a sigh like an earthquake.

'You didn't happen to hear him in the vestry?' Fox ventured, but it appeared that the door from the vestry into the organ loft was shut, and Mrs Simpson, having

settled herself to enjoy the sermon with, as she shamelessly admitted, a bag of chocolates, was not in a position
to notice.

Alleyn gave her his two cables: the first to Timothy
Bates's partner in New Zealand and the second to one of
his own colleagues in that country asking for any
available information about relatives of the late William
James Wagstaff of Little Copplestone, Kent, possibly
resident in New Zealand after 1921, and of any persons
of the name of Peter Rook Hadet or Naomi Balbus
Hadet.

Mrs Simpson agitatedly checked over the cables,
professional etiquette and burning curiosity struggling
together in her enormous bosom. She restrained herself,
however, merely observing that an event of this sort set
you thinking, didn't it?

'And no doubt,' Alleyn said as they walked up the lane,
'she'll be telling her customers that the next stop's
bloodhounds and manacles.'

'Quite a tidy armful of lady, isn't she, Mr Alleyn?' Fox
calmly rejoined.

The inquest was at ten-twenty in the smoking-room of
the Star and Garter. With half an hour in hand, Alleyn
and Fox visited the churchyard. Alleyn gave particular
attention to the headstones of Old Jimmy Wagstaff, Ruth
Wall, and Simon Castle. 'No mention of the month or
day,' he said. And after a moment: 'I wonder. We must
ask the Rector.'

'No need to ask the Rector,' said a voice behind them.
It was Miss Hart. She must have come soundlessly across
the soft turf. Her air was truculent. 'Though why,' she
said, 'it should be of interest, I'm sure I don't know. Ruth
Wall died on August thirteenth, 1921. It was a Saturday.'

'You've a remarkable memory,' Alleyn observed.

'Not as good as it sounds. That Saturday afternoon I

came to do the flowers in the church. I found her and I'm not likely ever to forget it. Young Castle went the same way almost a month later. September twelfth. In my opinion there was never a more glaring case of suicide. I believe,' Miss Hart said harshly, 'in facing facts.'

'She was a beautiful girl, wasn't she?'

'I'm no judge of beauty. She set the men by the ears. *He* was a fine-looking young fellow. Fanny Wagstaff did her best to get *him*.'

'Had Ruth Wall,' Alleyn asked, 'other admirers?'

Miss Hart didn't answer and he turned to her. Her face was blotted with an unlovely flush. 'She ruined two men's lives, if you want to know. Castle and Richard De'ath,' said Miss Hart. She turned on her heel and without another word marched away.

'September twelfth,' Alleyn murmured. 'That would be a Monday, Br'er Fox.'

'So it would,' Fox agreed, after a short calculation, 'so it would. Quite a coincidence.'

'Or not, as the case may be. I'm going to take a gamble on this one. Come on.'

They left the churchyard and walked down the lane, overtaking Edward Pilbrow on the way. He was wearing his town crier's coat and hat and carrying his bell by the clapper. He manifested great excitement when he saw them.

'Hey!' he shouted. 'What's this I hear? Murder's the game, is it? What a go! Come on, gents, let's have it. Did 'e fall or was 'e pushed? Hor, hor, hor! Come on.'

'Not until after the inquest,' Alleyn shouted.

'Do we get a look at the body?'

'Shut up,' Mr Fox bellowed suddenly.

'I got to know, haven't I? It'll be the smartest bit of crying I ever done, this will! I reckon I might get on the telly with this. "Town crier tells old-world village death stalks the churchyard." Hor, hor, hor!'

'Let us,' Alleyn whispered, 'leave this horrible old man.'

They quickened their stride and arrived at the pub, to be met with covert glances and dead silence.

The smoking-room was crowded for the inquest. Everybody was there, including Mrs Simpson who sat in the back row with her candies and her crossword puzzle. It went through very quickly. The Rector deposed to finding the body. Richard De'ath, sober and less truculent than usual, was questioned as to his sojourn outside the churchyard and said he'd noticed nothing unusual apart from hearing a disturbance among the pigeons roosting in the balcony. From where he stood, he said, he couldn't see the face of the tower.

An open verdict was recorded.

Alleyn had invited the Rector, Miss Hart, Mrs Simpson, Richard De'ath, and reluctantly, Edward Pilbrow, to join him in the parlour and had arranged with the landlord that nobody else would be admitted. The public bar, as a result, drove a roaring trade.

When they had all been served and the hatch closed, Alleyn walked into the middle of the room and raised his hand. It was the slightest of gestures but it secured their attention.

He said, 'I think you must all realise that we are not satisfied this was an accident. The evidence against accident has been collected piecemeal from the persons in this room and I am going to put it before you. If I go wrong I want you to correct me. I ask you to do this with absolute frankness, even if you are obliged to implicate someone who you would say was the last person in the world to be capable of a crime of violence.'

He waited. Pilbrow, who had come very close, had his ear cupped in his hand. The Rector looked vaguely horrified. Richard De'ath suddenly gulped down his double whisky. Miss Hart coughed over her lemonade and Mrs Simpson avidly popped a peppermint cream in her mouth and took a swig of her port-and-raspberry.

Alleyn nodded to Fox, who laid Mr Bates's Bible, open at the flyleaf, on the table before him.

'The case,' Alleyn said, 'hinges on this book. You have all seen the entries. I remind you of the recorded deaths in 1779 of the three Hadets – Stewart Shakespeare, Naomi Balbus, and Peter Rook. To each of these is attached a biblical text suggesting that they met their death by violence. There have never been any Hadets in this village and the days of the week are wrong for the given dates. They are right, however, for the year 1921 and *they fit the deaths,* all by falling from a height, of William Wagstaff, Ruth Wall, and Simon Castle.

'By analogy the Christian names agree. William suggests Shakespeare. Naomi – Ruth; Balbus – a wall. Simon – Peter; and a Rook is a Castle in chess. And Hadet,' Alleyn said without emphasis, 'is an anagram of Death.'

'Balderdash!' Miss Hart cried out in an unrecognisable voice.

'No it's not,' said Mrs Simpson. 'It's jolly good crossword stuff.'

'Wicked balderdash. Richard!'

De'ath said, 'Be quiet. Let him go on.'

'We believe,' Alleyn said, 'that these three people met their deaths by one hand. Motive is a secondary consideration, but it is present in several instances, predominantly in one. Who had cause to wish the death of these three people? Someone whom old Wagstaff had bullied and to whom he had left his money and who killed him for it. Someone who was infatuated with Simon Castle and bitterly jealous of Ruth Wall. Someone who hoped, as an heiress, to win Castle for herself and who, failing, was determined nobody else should have him. Wagstaff's orphaned niece – Fanny Wagstaff.'

There were cries of relief from all but one of his hearers. He went on. 'Fanny Wagstaff sold everything, disappeared, and was never heard of again in the village. But twenty-four years later she returned, and has remained here ever since.'

A glass crashed to the floor and a chair overturned as the vast bulk of the postmistress rose to confront him.

'Lies! *Lies!*' screamed Mrs Simpson.

'Did you sell everything again, before leaving New Zealand?' he asked as Fox moved forward. 'Including the Bible, Miss Wagstaff?'

'But,' Troy said, 'how could you be so sure?'

'She was the only one who could leave her place in the church unobserved. She was the only one fat enough to rub her hips against the narrow door jambs. She uses an indelible pencil. We presume she arranged to meet Bates on the balcony, giving a cock-and-bull promise to tell him something nobody else knew about the Hadets. She indicated the text with her pencil, gave the Bible a shove, and, as he leant out to grab it, tipped him over the edge.

'In talking about 1921 she forgot herself and described the events as if she had been there. She called Bates a typical New Zealander but gave herself out to be a Londoner. She said whitebait are only a quarter of the size of sprats. New Zealand whitebait are – English whitebait are about the same size.

'And as we've now discovered, she didn't send my cables. Of course she thought poor little Bates was hot on her tracks, especially when she learned that he'd come here to see me. She's got the kind of crossword-puzzle mind that would think up the biblical clues, and would get no end of a kick in writing them in. She's overwhelmingly conceited and vindictive.'

'Still – '

'I know. Not good enough if we'd played the waiting

game. But good enough to try shock tactics. We caught her off her guard and she cracked up.'

'Not,' Mr Fox said, 'a nice type of woman.'

Alleyn strolled to the gate and looked up the lane to the church. The spire shone golden in the evening sun.

'The Rector,' Alleyn said, 'tells me he's going to do something about the balcony.'

'Mrs Simpson, née Wagstaff,' Fox remarked, 'suggested wire netting.'

'And she ought to know,' Alleyn said and turned back to the cottage.

Gideon and the Young Toughs

JOHN CREASEY

DETECTIVE FILE

OFFICER: Commander George Gideon

FORCE: CID, Scotland Yard

TIME: 1970

CASES: *Gideon's Day* (1955), *Gideon's Fire* (1961), *Gideon's Wrath* (1967), *Gideon's Fog* (1974) etc.

PROFILE: Commander George Gideon of the Criminal Investigation Department of Scotland Yard – known to his colleagues of all ranks as 'G. G.' – is a stolid, reassuring senior policeman: professional, thoughtful, hard to anger but absolutely implacable in his devotion to the law. His soft blue eyes and gentle voice belie his tendency to great anger when faced with the two worst crimes in his book – bent policemen and child molesters. Gideon has risen through the ranks at the Yard and drives his men hard, though always fairly. A familiar expression which can put a look of apprehension across the face of everyone in the Yard when it is heard is, 'G. G. is on the warpath!' More than one admirer of this formidable figure has compared his features and convictions to those of the prophet Gideon in the New Testament, from whom, in fact, he got his name! Away from the Met, he has a devoted wife, Kate, and two youngsters who are not beyond giving him the same kind of problems faced by ordinary parents. Gideon's fame is such that tourists have been known to visit Scotland

Yard asking to meet him; while critic Maurice Richardson declared in 1969 that he has 'done more than any other detective in fiction to maintain the reading public's faith in Scotland Yard'. The Gideon stories have been adapted for films – starring Jack Hawkins – and also inspired a TV series with John Gregson in 1965–6.

CREATOR: John Creasey (1908–73), one of the most prolific of all crime writers – he is said to have produced around six hundred books under two dozen different names – created the Commander in 1955 in *Gideon's Day*, which was published under the name of J. J. Marric. The book is a landmark in itself as the first British police procedural novel – an area of crime fiction in which Creasey under various of his pen names proved himself to be a master. Though much of his work is now out of print, his influence has been acknowledged by several of the leading English writers utilising the same style of detection in their mysteries. 'Gideon and the Young Toughs' is a rare short story about the Commander written in 1970 in which 'G. G.' employs all his accumulated procedural skills to discover the *real* reason why a gang of hooligans are causing disturbances in Central London.

***

Possibly places other than Piccadilly could claim to be the hub of the world, but for Gideon, Piccadilly was the true centre of things. It had fascinated him when he had been a child, an adolescent, and – also a long time ago – a rookie policeman. It still fascinated him now that he was Commander Gideon of the CID, the Criminal Investigation Department of the Metropolitan Police Force.

He knew every inch of it.

He knew when any of the vivid electric signs was being changed, or when a new one was going up. He knew when the shops changed hands. He knew what was playing in its theatre and its cinema. He knew the newspaper sellers, the flower sellers – when they were about, these days – and he regarded the statue of Eros rather as he might one of his own children.

In most matters a progressive, he felt a positive hostility to all new architectural and town-planning schemes for Piccadilly Circus; but he had the comfortable feeling that in his lifetime he need worry about nothing more serious than the switch to one-way traffic along Piccadilly itself. *If* that ever came about.

Behind Piccadilly, in Soho, there lurked much crime and vice, as well as fine food, some happiness, and quite a lot of goodness. Piccadilly Circus itself was so brightly lit, so well populated and so well policed, that it was seldom the scene of a crime. A youth or a girl who did not know his or her way about might run into trouble in the side streets, but never in Piccadilly.

Of course, there were days of trouble. Oxford and Cambridge Boat Race night, for instance, or the Welsh or the Irish Twickenham festivals. On such great occasions police were drafted well in advance, and Eros was boarded up. Anyone who managed to climb to the top of the statue and perch some article on the arrow deserved his picture in the newspaper.

These things were as much a part of London as Piccadilly Circus itself.

The outburst of hooliganism which came one hot summer evening did not trouble Gideon. Drunks did sometimes get out of control. High spirits plus hard liquor could create vicious tempers out of cheerfulness.

The second incident, however, was very different.

It happened three nights later.

Police Constable Sturgeon, of the Central London Division, was on duty – alone. He knew that his next big job would be to help keep the traffic moving when the theatres emptied. The plainclothesmen would look after the pickpockets who selected that hour to get busy.

Constable Sturgeon had noticed a group of youths, quite well dressed, rather noisy, coming out of one of the side streets. He glanced round to see if any other constables were near, but saw none. He strolled in the direction of the group, hoping that the sight of his uniform would quiet them. Instead, it seemed to do the opposite – to excite them.

There were six of them. As he approached, they made a cordon across the pavement at the spot where the Circus led into Coventry Street. People behind them and people in front were suddenly hampered. In the bewildering way of all big cities a crowd gathered in a few seconds. No one protested at first; everyone assumed that there had been some kind of accident.

Sturgeon knew that the youths were doing this deliberately.

'Break it up, chaps,' he said in a pleasant voice; he had been warned that a hectoring note was a bad one to start with.

None of the six spoke. Sturgeon only had a split second's warning of what was going to happen. Then they attacked. One made a flying tackle and brought the constable down, and the others swooped.

A woman screamed, and a man shouted, 'Stop that!' in a quivering voice.

Someone called waveringly, '*Police!*'

Sturgeon felt as if a pack of wild dogs had savaged him. As if in the distance he heard the shrill of a police whistle, and then he lost consciousness. But all the assailants were gone by the time the police had rushed in strength to Piccadilly Circus.

'They all got away,' reported Superintendent Lemaitre the next morning. 'Every single perisher. The division had a dozen chaps there inside of five minutes, but it was too late.

A couple of passersby got black eyes trying to stop the swine. And this is the *second* time, George.'

Gideon blocked much of the sunlight coming through the window that overlooked the Embankment. In silhouette he looked huge. His shoulders were hunched and he had one hand deep in his pocket.

'How's Sturgeon?' he demanded.

'Twenty-seven stitches.'

'Can he talk?'

'Not until tomorrow.'

'Have Central check all their chaps, and you check all ours. See if you can get any description of the attackers. Find out if any of them can be identified with those responsible for the outbreak of trouble last week.'

'Right, George,' said Lemaitre.

He knew just how incensed Gideon was about such a thing as this happening on 'his' beat. He was not surprised when Gideon announced, the next day, that he was going to the Charing Cross Hospital, where they had taken PC Sturgeon.

Coming out of the ward was a tall, slim, nice-looking girl. Her eyes were bright, as if shining with tears.

'Are you a friend of Constable Sturgeon?' inquired Gideon.

'I – I'm his fiancée.'

'Oh. I see. I'm Commander Gideon. If you see his parents tell them how sorry I am, won't you? And you can be positive we'll find out who did this and make sure it doesn't happen again.'

'It *mustn't* happen again,' the girl said, and her voice broke. 'It will be weeks before he's able to get about.'

'Mind telling me one thing?' asked Gideon.

'If – if I can.'

'Was he nervous about going to Piccadilly? Did he have any reason to dislike that particular part of his beat?'

'Good heavens, no. I think he loves it.'

Sturgeon himself, barely able to talk, did not say that he 'loved it', but he confirmed that he liked that part of his beat. He did not remember having seen any of his assailants before, and had no idea at all about the possible motive.

'As a matter of fact, sir,' he said huskily, 'I got the idea that they were doing it for sheer enjoyment.'

Gideon arranged for a closer watch to be kept on the Circus and gave instructions for a radio call to be made to the Yard if there seemed to be any gathering of young toughs. There were three or four false alarms in the week. Twice Gideon took Kate, his wife, for a drive as far as Whitehall, and then calmly walked her to Piccadilly.

He chose nightfall. The bright lights, the gay colours, the throngs of people of all nationalities, the chatter of voices, the laughter, the furtiveness, the timidity, the gaping visitors – all these things were part of this place.

On Monday of the next week another police constable saw a group of dark-haired youths who looked as if they might be out for trouble. He signalled a radio car. The car called for help from the Yard. Two policemen approached the group – one from the front, one from behind. Quite suddenly the youths acted exactly as they had with Sturgeon – made a thin cordon across the pavement.

The constable, hand on his truncheon, spoke as if casually.

'Break it up there. Don't let's have any trouble.'

'*Trouble!*' one of the young men spat at him – and they all leapt.

Two plainclothesmen and three more uniformed officers were onto them before the constable was brought down. After a short sharp fight two of the six managed to dash across the road in front of moving traffic and escape. Four were hauled round the corner. A Black Maria was soon on the spot, and they were charged with disturbing the peace.

The next morning Gideon sat in court while the charges

were being heard. A divisional Chief Inspector asked for a remand in custody.

'I really don't see that such a remand is necessary,' said a lawyer appearing for the young toughs. 'These are hard-working lads from good families. They all belong to a social club in Victoria, and have never been in trouble before. They had a little too much to drink and lost their heads, that's all. Each has pleaded guilty, your worship, and I'm sure each will apologise. May I submit that it might well be sufficient to bind them over?'

The four youths looked fresh, bright eyed, even wholesome.

'What – ah – what have you to say to that, Chief Inspector?' inquired the magistrate, a fair man.

'We would like time to obtain more information about the accused, sir.'

'I see. Very well. I shall remand each of the accused for eight days, each on his own recognisances of £25. Can you each find £25?' he asked the accused, as if craftily.

'Yes, sir,' they chorused.

'Silly old fool,' said Lemaitre to Gideon. 'They'll jump their bail – what does he think twenty-five quid means to a chap of eighteen these days?'

'We want to find out all we can about them,' Gideon said. 'And more about the club, too. Oh – and find out if Sturgeon recognises any of them.'

Sturgeon did not.

The youths appeared after their remand, and each was bound over to keep the peace.

'If you ask me they're young savages out to make trouble – they don't need a motive,' Lemaitre said. 'And it might happen again – any time the young louts are looking for kicks. It's a sign of the times, George. That's what it is.'

'It's a sign of nerves when a club like theirs needs a mouthpiece,' Gideon said. 'Have we discovered anything about the place?'

'Seventy or eighty members – mixed sexes – ages seventeen to twenty-one,' reported Lemaitre. 'All the usual club activities.'

'Have a closer eye kept on it,' Gideon ordered.

It was exactly four days later that Lemaitre stormed into Gideon's office, clapped his bony hands together, and twanged, 'Now we're in business, George! A lot of those club members go to Sammy Dench occasionally. Sammy is the smartest fence in London. Now if we could only find out why he uses those kids – put your thinking cap on, George!'

'It's on so tight that it's stuck,' said Gideon. 'Lem, tell Central to act as if it were an anti-vice week. Have uniformed chaps concentrated in Piccadilly Circus, and plainclothesmen in Soho. We've been looking for a motive, and now we have it.'

'What motive?' shrilled Lemaitre.

'They've caused those disturbances as a distraction,' Gideon said. 'They've intended to make us concentrate on Piccadilly – as we have. There'll be another distraction before long, and maybe others. One night, while we're busy coping—'

'Other members of the club will be staging raids in the side streets!' cried Lemaitre.

It happened again three nights later.

This time a knot of seven youths suddenly started fighting and cursing outside the Criterion. Almost at once police whistles shrilled and the police appeared as if from nowhere.

Behind the Circus, in those narrow Soho streets, other youths seemed to erupt from dark doorways. They raided restaurants and theatres, stole the day's receipts, and rushed out – into the arms of waiting police.

'But what made you twig it?' Lemaitre demanded.

'It took me too long really,' said Gideon. 'I was sure no

one would cause trouble in the Circus unless they intended
to risk being caught. They were too slick in getting away to
be just drunks or young savages. I simply went on from
there.'

Before Insulin

J. J. CONNINGTON

DETECTIVE FILE

OFFICER: Chief Constable Sir Clinton Driffield

FORCE: Sussex Police (unspecified)

TIME: 1935

CASES: *Murder in the Maze* (1927), *Mystery at Lynden Sands* (1928), *The Sweepstake Murders* (1931), *Common Sense Is All You Need* (1947).

PROFILE: Sir Clinton Driffield is one of the very few Chief Constables to feature in a series of crime novels and short stories. Still only in his mid-thirties, he has a suntanned face, trim moustache, and a shrewd and penetrating gaze. Driffield's slightly cynical air and tendency to be abrupt when questioning people makes him a forerunner in literary terms of the recent TV series, *The Chief*, in which Martin Shaw appeared as a youthful top policeman, Alan Cade, maverick in style and strongly opinionated. Cade and Driffield are also similar in that they share uneasy relationships with those close to them – in Sir Clinton's case with Squire Wendover, a wealthy landowner and JP with whom he frequently disagrees when they are thrown together as a result of a crime committed in their area. Driffield has risen to the top of his profession because of his remarkable memory and ability to notice important characteristics in even seemingly unimportant people. He enjoys matching his wits with criminals and policemen alike – a trait that has contributed to him being regarded as efficient, though not very likeable. A great feature of all the Chief Constable's cases is the ingenuity of the plotting and his use of scientific and medical information.

CREATOR: J. J. Connington was the pseudonym of Alfred Walter Stewart (1880–1947), a lecturer on physical chemistry and radioactivity, who became the first scientist to recognise the existence of isobaric atoms: hence Sir Clinton's knowledge of science and medicine. Apart from writing a number of major treatises about his scientific experiments, Stewart (as J. J. Connington) wrote a bestselling science fiction novel, *Nordenholt's Millions*, in 1923. This was followed four years later by the first of his cases featuring the Chief Constable, *Murder in the Maze*. Despite the book's popularity, he continued to combine the role of Professor of Chemistry at Queen's University, Belfast with that of crime novelist, earning comparison with another of his distinguished contemporaries in the genre, Freeman Wills Crofts. Stewart was still writing mystery fiction until just a few days prior to his death. 'Before Insulin', published in 1935, not only offers Sir Clinton and Wendover in typical contrary moods as they investigate the impending death of a small boy, but is another example of how skilfully he used his medical knowledge in crime fiction.

* * *

I'd more than the fishing in my mind when I asked you over for the weekend,' Wendover confessed. 'Fact is Clinton, something's turned up and I'd like your advice.' Sir Clinton Driffield, Chief Constable of the county, glanced quizzically at his old friend.

'If you've murdered anyone, Squire, my advice is: keep

it dark and leave the country. If it's merely breach of promise, or anything of that sort, I'm at your disposal.'

'It's not breach of promise,' Wendover assured him with the complacency of a hardened bachelor. 'It's a matter of an estate for which I happen to be sole trustee, worse luck. The other two have died since the will was made. I'll tell you about it.'

Wendover prided himself on his power of lucid exposition. He settled himself in his chair and began.

'You've heard me speak of old John Ashby, the ironmaster? He died fifteen years back, worth £53,000; and he made his son, his daughter-in-law, and myself executors of his will. The son, James Ashby, was to have the life-rent of the estate; and on his death the capital was to be handed over to his offspring when the youngest of them came of age. As it happened, there was only one child, young Robin Ashby. James Ashby and his wife were killed in a railway accident some years ago; so the whole £53,000, less two estate duties, was secured to young Robin if he lived to come of age.'

'And if he didn't?' queried Sir Clinton.

'Then the money went to a lot of charities,' Wendover explained. 'That's just the trouble, as you'll see. Three years ago, young Robin took diabetes, a bad case, poor fellow. We did what we could for him, naturally. All the specialists had a turn, without improvement. Then we sent him over to Neuenahr, to some institute run by a German who specialised in diabetes. No good. I went over to see the poor boy, and he was worn to a shadow, simply skin and bone and hardly able to walk with weakness. Obviously it was a mere matter of time.'

'Hard lines on the youngster,' Sir Clinton commented soberly.

'Very hard,' said Wendover with a gesture of pity. 'Now as it happened, at Neuenahr he scraped acquaintance with a French doctor. I saw him when I was there:

about thirty, black torpedo beard, very brisk and well-got-up, with any amount of belief in himself. He spoke English fluently, which gave him a pull with Robin, out there among foreigners; and he persuaded the boy that he could cure him if he would put himself in his charge. Well, by that time, it seemed that any chance was worth taking, so I agreed. After all, the boy was dying by inches. So off he went to the south of France, where this man – Prevost, his name was – had a nursing home of his own. I saw the place: well-kept affair though small. And he had an English nurse, which was lucky for Robin. Pretty girl she was: chestnut hair, creamy skin, supple figure, neat hands and feet. A lady, too.'

'Oh, any pretty girl can get round you,' interjected Sir Clinton. 'Get on with the tale.'

'Well, it was all no good,' Wendover went on, hastily. 'The poor boy went downhill in spite of all the Frenchman's talk; and, to cut a long story short, he died a fortnight ago, on the very day when he came of age.'

'Oh, so he lived long enough to inherit?'

'By the skin of his teeth,' Wendover agreed. 'That's where the trouble begins. Before that day, of course, he could make no valid will. But now a claimant, a man Sydney Eastcote, turns up with the claim that Robin made a will the morning of the day he died and by this will this Eastcote fellow scoops the whole estate. All I know of it is from a letter this Eastcote man wrote to me giving the facts. I referred him to the lawyer for the estate and told the lawyer – Harringay's his name – to bring the claimant here this afternoon. They're due now. I'd like you to look him over, Clinton. I'm not quite satisfied about this will.'

The Chief Constable pondered for a moment or two.

'Very well,' he agreed. 'But you'd better not introduce me as Sir Clinton Driffield, Chief Constable, etc. I'd better be Mr Clinton, I think. It sounds better for a private confabulation.'

'Very well,' Wendover conceded. 'There's a car on the drive. It must be they, I suppose.'

In a few moments the door opened and the visitors were ushered in. Surprised himself, the Chief Constable was still able to enjoy the astonishment of his friend; for instead of the expected man, a pretty chestnut-haired girl, dressed in mourning, was shown into the room along with the solicitor, and it was plain enough that Wendover recognised her.

'You seem surprised, Mr Wendover,' the girl began, evidently somewhat taken aback by Wendover's expression. Then she smiled as though an explanation occurred to her. 'Of course, it's my name again. People always forget that Sydney's a girl's name as well as a man's. But you remember me, don't you? I met you when you visited poor Robin.'

'Of course I remember you, Nurse,' Wendover declared, recovering from his surprise. 'But I never heard you called anything but "Nurse" and didn't even hear your surname; so naturally I didn't associate you with the letter I got about poor Robin's will.'

'Oh, I see,' answered the girl. 'That accounts for it.'

She looked inquiringly towards the Chief Constable, and Wendover recovered his presence of mind.

'This is a friend of mine, Mr Clinton,' he explained. 'Miss Eastcote. Mr Harringay. Won't you sit down? I must admit your letter took me completely by surprise, Miss Eastcote.'

Wendover was getting over his initial astonishment at the identity of the claimant, and when they had all seated themselves, he took the lead.

'I've seen a copy of Robin's death certificate,' he began slowly. 'He died in the afternoon of September twenty-first, the day he came of age, so he was quite competent to make a will. I suppose he was mentally fit to make one?'

'Dr Prevost will certify that if necessary,' the nurse affirmed quietly.

'I noticed that he didn't die in Dr Prevost's Institute,' Wendover continued. 'At some local hotel, wasn't it?'

'Yes,' Nurse Eastcote confirmed. 'A patient died in the Institute about that time and poor Robin hated the place on that account. It depressed him, and he insisted on moving to the hotel for a time.'

'He must have been at death's door then, poor fellow,' Wendover commented.

'Yes,' the nurse admitted, sadly. 'He was very far through. He had lapses of consciousness, the usual diabetic coma. But while he was awake he was perfectly sound mentally, if that's what you mean.'

Wendover nodded as though this satisfied him completely.

'Tell me about this will,' he asked. 'It's come as something of a surprise to me, not unnaturally.'

Nurse Eastcote hesitated for a moment. Her lip quivered and her eyes filled with tears as she drew from her bag an envelope of thin foreign paper. From this she extracted a sheet of foreign notepaper which she passed across to Wendover.

'I can't grumble if you're surprised at his leaving me this money,' she said, at last. 'I didn't expect anything of the kind myself. But the fact is . . . he fell in love with me, poor boy, while he was under my charge. You see, except for Dr Prevost, I was the only one who could speak English with him, and that meant much to him at that time when he was so lonely. Of course he was much younger than I am; I'm twenty-seven. I suppose I ought to have checked him when I saw how things were. But I hadn't the heart to do it. It was something that gave him just the necessary spur to keep him going, and of course I knew that marriage would never come into it. It did no harm to let him fall in love; and I really did my very best to make him happy, in these last weeks. I was so sorry for him, you know.'

This put the matter in a fresh light for Wendover, and he grew more sympathetic in his manner.

'I can understand,' he said gently. 'You didn't care for him, of course . . .'

'Not in that way. But I was very very sorry for him, and I'd have done anything to make him feel happier. It was so dreadful to see him going out into the dark before he'd really started in life.'

Wendover cleared his throat, evidently conscious that the talk was hardly on the businesslike lines which he had planned. He unfolded the thin sheet of notepaper and glanced over the writing.

'This seems explicit enough. "I leave all that I have to Nurse Sydney Eastcote, residing at Dr Prevost's medical Institute." I recognise the handwriting as Robin's, and the date is in the same writing. Who are the witnesses, by the way?'

'Two of the waiters at the hotel, I believe,' Nurse Eastcote explained.

Wendover turned to the flimsy foreign envelope and examined the address.

'Addressed by himself to you at the institute, I see. And the postmark is twenty-first September. That's quite good confirmatory evidence, if anything of the sort were needed.'

He passed the two papers to Sir Clinton. The Chief Constable seemed to find the light insufficient where he was sitting, for he rose and walked over to a window to examine the documents. This brought him slightly behind Nurse Eastcote. Wendover noted idly that Sir Clinton stood sideways to the light while he inspected the papers in his hand.

'Now just one point,' Wendover continued. 'I'd like to know something about Robin's mental condition towards the end. Did he read to pass the time, newspapers and things like that?'

Nurse Eastcote shook her head.

'No, he read nothing. He was too exhausted, poor boy. I used to sit by him and try to interest him in talk. But if you have any doubt about his mind at that time – I mean whether he was fit to make a will – I'm sure Dr Prevost will give a certificate that he was in full possession of his faculties and knew what he was doing.'

Sir Clinton came forward with the papers in his hand.

'These are very important documents,' he pointed out, addressing the nurse. 'It's not safe for you to be carrying them about in your bag as you've been doing. Leave them with us. Mr Wendover will give you a receipt and take good care of them. And to make sure there's no mistake, I think you'd better write your name in the corner of each of them so as to identify them. Mr Harringay will agree with me that we mustn't leave any loophole for doubt in a case like this.'

The lawyer nodded. He was a taciturn man by nature, and his pride had been slightly ruffled by the way in which he had been ignored in the conference. Nurse Eastcote, with Wendover's fountain pen, wrote her signature on a free space of each paper. Wendover offered his guests tea before they departed, but he turned the talk into general channels and avoided any further reference to business topics.

When the lawyer and the girl had left the house, Wendover turned to Sir Clinton.

'It seems straight enough to me,' he said, 'but I could see from the look you gave me behind her back when you were at the window that you aren't satisfied. What's wrong?'

'If you want my opinion,' the Chief Constable

answered, 'it's a fake from start to finish. Certainly you can't risk handing over a penny on that evidence. If you want it proved up to the hilt, I can do it for you, but it'll cost something for inquiries and expert assistance. That ought to come out of the estate, and it'll be cheaper than an action at law. Besides,' he added with a smile, 'I don't suppose you want to put that girl in gaol. She's probably only a tool in the hands of a cleverer person.'

Wendover was staggered by the Chief Constable's tone of certainty. The girl, of course, had made no pretence that she was in love with Robin Ashby; but her story had been told as though she herself believed it.

'Make your inquiries, certainly,' he consented. 'Still, on the face of it the thing sounds likely enough.'

'I'll give you definite proof in a fortnight or so. Better make a further appointment with that girl in, say, three weeks. But don't drag the lawyer into it this time. It may savour too much of compounding a felony for his taste. I'll need these papers.'

'Here's the concrete evidence,' said the Chief Constable, three weeks later. 'I may as well show it to you before she arrives, and you can amuse yourself with turning it over in the meanwhile.'

He produced the will, the envelope, and two photographs from his pocket book as he spoke and laid them on the table, opening out the will as he put it down.

'Now first of all, notice that the will and envelope are of very thin paper, the foreign correspondence stuff. Second, observe that the envelope is of the exact size to hold that sheet of paper if it's folded in four – I mean folded in half and then doubled over. The sheet's about quarto size, ten inches by eight. Now look here. There's an extra fold in the paper. It's been folded in four and then it's been folded across once more. That struck me as soon as I had it in my hand. Why the extra fold, since it would fit into the envelope without that?'

Wendover inspected the sheet carefully and looked rather perplexed.

'You're quite right,' he said, 'but you can't upset a will on the strength of a fold in it. She may have doubled it up herself, after she got it.'

'Not when it was in the envelope that fitted it,' Sir Clinton pointed out. 'There's no corresponding doubling of the envelope. However, let's go on. Here's a photograph of the envelope, taken with the light falling sideways. You see the postal erasing stamp has made an impression?'

'Yes, I can read it, and the date's twenty-first September right enough.' He paused for a moment and then added in surprise, 'But where's the postage stamp? It hasn't come out in the photo.'

'No, because that's a photo of the impression on the back half of the envelope. The stamp came down hard and not only cancelled the stamp but impressed the second side of the envelope as well. The impression comes out quite clearly when it's illuminated from the side. That's worth thinking over. And, finally, here's another print. It was made, before the envelope was slit to get at the stamp impression. All we did was to put the envelope into a printing-frame with a bit of photographic printing paper behind it and expose it to light for a while. Now you'll notice that the gummed portions of the envelope show up in white, like a sort of St Andrew's Cross. But if you look carefully, you'll see a couple of darker patches on the part of the white strip which corresponds to the flap of the envelope that one sticks down. Just think out what they imply, Squire. There are the facts for you, and it's not too difficult to put an interpretation on them if you think for a minute or two. And I'll add just one further bit of information. The two waiters who acted as witnesses to that will were given tickets for South America, and a certain sum of money each to keep them from feeling homesick . . . But here's your visitor.'

Rather to Wendover's surprise, Sir Clinton took the lead in the conversation as soon as the girl arrived.

'Before we turn to business, Miss Eastcote,' he said, 'I'd like to tell you a little anecdote. It may be of use to you. May I?'

Nurse Eastcote nodded politely and Wendover, looking her over, noticed a ring on her engagement finger which he had not seen on her last visit.

'This is a case which came to my knowledge lately,' Sir Clinton went on, 'and it resembles your own so closely that I'm sure it will suggest something. A young man of twenty, in an almost dying state, was induced to enter a nursing home by the doctor in charge. If he lived to come of age, he could make a will and leave a very large fortune to anyone he chose; but it was the merest gamble whether he would live to come of age.'

Nurse Eastcote's figure stiffened and her eyes widened at this beginning, but she merely nodded as though asking Sir Clinton to continue.

'The boy fell in love with one of the nurses, who happened to be under the influence of the doctor,' Sir Clinton went on. 'If he lived to make a will, there was little doubt that he would leave the fortune to the nurse. A considerable temptation for any girl, I think you'll agree.

'The boy's birthday was very near, only a few days off; but it looked as though he would not live to see it. He was very far gone. He had no interest in the newspapers and he had long lapses of unconsciousness, so that he had no idea of what the actual date was. It was easy enough to tell him, on a given day, that he had come of age, though actually two days were still to run. Misled by the doctor, he imagined that he could make a valid will, being now twenty-one; and he wrote with his own hand a short document leaving everything to the nurse.'

Miss Eastcote cleared her throat with an effort.

'Yes?' she said.

'This fraudulent will,' Sir Clinton continued, 'was witnessed by two waiters of the hotel to which the boy had been removed; and soon after, these waiters were packed off abroad and provided with some cash in addition to their fares. Then it occurred to the doctor that an extra bit of confirmatory evidence might be supplied. The boy had put the will into an envelope which he had addressed to the nurse. While the gum was still wet, the doctor opened the flap and took out the "will", which he then folded smaller in order to get the paper into an ordinary business-size envelope. He then addressed this to the nurse and posted the will to her in it. The original large envelope, addressed by the boy, he retained. But in pulling it open, the doctor had slightly torn the inner side of the flap where the gum lies; and that little defect shows up when one exposes the envelope over a sheet of photographic paper. Here's an example of what I mean.'

He passed over to Nurse Eastcote the print which he had shown Wendover and drew her attention to the spots on the St Andrew's Cross.

'As it chanced, the boy died next morning, a day before he came of age. The doctor concealed the death for a day, which was easy enough in the circumstances. Then, on the afternoon of the crucial date – did I mention that it was September twenty-first? – he closed the empty envelope, stamped it, and put it into the post, thus securing a postmark of the proper date. Unfortunately for this plan, the defacement stamp of the Post Office came down hard enough to impress its image on *both* the sheets of the thin paper envelope, so that by opening up the envelope and photographing it by a sideways illumination the embossing of the stamp showed up – like this.'

He handed the girl the second photograph.

'Now if the "will" had been in that envelope, the "will" itself would have borne that stamp. But it did not; and that proves that the "will" was not in the envelope when it passed through the post. A clever woman like yourself, Miss Eastcote, will see the point at once.'

'And what happened after that?' asked the girl huskily.

'It's difficult to tell you,' Sir Clinton pursued. 'If it had come before me officially – I'm Chief Constable of the county, you know – I should probably have had to prosecute that unfortunate nurse for attempted fraud; and I've not the slightest doubt that we'd have proved the case up to the hilt. It would have meant a year or two in gaol, I expect.

'I forgot to mention that the nurse was secretly engaged to the doctor all this while. And, by the way, that's a very pretty ring you're wearing, Miss Eastcote. That, of course, accounted for the way in which the doctor managed to get her to play her part in the little scheme. I think if I were you, Miss Eastcote, I'd go back to France as soon as possible and tell Dr Prevost that . . . Well, it hasn't come off.'

The Memorial Service

MICHAEL INNES

DETECTIVE FILE

OFFICER: Commissioner Sir John Appleby

FORCE: Metropolitan Police, London

TIME: 1975

CASES: *Death at the President's Lodging* (1936), *The Weight of Evidence* (1943), *The Long Farewell* (1958), *The Bloody Wood* (1966), *Appleby's Other Story* (1974) etc.

PROFILE: Sir John Appleby is undoubtedly the most erudite detective in mystery fiction. He is a well-read officer, patient and good natured, with an empathy towards his job that makes him an ideal role model for anyone following in his footsteps in the Met. Appleby came to the Force with a liberal education, and has risen from Inspector to Detective Inspector and, finally, Commissioner, thanks to his sense of curiosity, his irony, and his dedication to duty. He is noted for his ability to handle sensitive cases involving prominent people in society and government, and this characteristic has undoubtedly impressed his superiors and been instrumental in the steady upward path of his career. Whether looking into cases of fugitives from justice, chicanery in the art world, crime in university life or investigating whimsical village mysteries – four familiar themes in the thirty books and numerous short stories about Appleby –

he can be relied upon to exercise discretion and good judgment and to get his man. Even when hard pressed, Appleby still comes up with an apt literary quotation to fit the moment – and there is no one better at spotting obscure literary allusions in which may lie the solution to a crime.

CREATOR: Michael Innes was the pen name of John Innes Mackintosh Stewart (1906–95) and there is much in the cases of the Commissioner that reflects the author's own life and career. An Oxford scholar and professor of English, Stewart was often referred to as 'the donniest of the donnish school of detective story writing' and he derived enormous pleasure from his dual role of academic and creator of murder and mystery. A lover of detective fiction from his childhood, he produced his first Appleby story, *Death at the President's Lodging*, in 1936 by spending two hours each morning before his day's lectures writing the tale of a murder mystery among the senior dons at a fictional English college. In the next forty years, he progressed his contemplative policeman up the various echelons of the Met, providing him with a happy marriage to a sculptress wife, and ultimately a knighthood for his services to the Force. Even in retirement, Appleby and crime proved inseparable, as 'The Memorial Service', written in 1975, demonstrates. It is a typical example of the man and his method – similar methods of detection, in fact, to those which have been evident throughout these pages, from the enquiries of a humble PC right through to the man at the very top of the police hierarchy.

* * *

In the fashionable church of St Boniface in the Fields (mysteriously so named, since it was in the heart of London) a large and distinguished congregation was assembled to give thanks for the life of the late Christopher Brockbank QC. The two newspaper reporters at the door, discreetly clad in unjournalistic black, had been busy receiving and recording all sorts of weighty names. It was the sort of occasion upon which sundry persons explain themselves as 'representing' sundry other persons even more august than themselves; or sundry institutions, corporations, charities and learned bodies with which the deceased important individual has been associated.

Legal luminaries predominated. An acute observer (and there was at least one such present) might have remarked that a number of these did not settle in their pews, kneel, and bury their noses devoutly in their cupped hands without an exchange of glances in which a hint of whimsical humour fleetingly flickered. *All this for Chris Brockbank!* they appeared to be telling each other. *Just what would he have made of it?*

Sir John Appleby (our acute observer) was representing his successor as Commissioner of Metropolitan Police. For Brockbank long ago, and before he had transformed himself from a leading silk into a vigorous and somewhat eccentric legal reformer, had owned his connections with Scotland Yard, and this fact had to be duly acknowledged today. Appleby possessed only a vague memory of the man, so that a certain artificiality perhaps attended his presence at the service. It hadn't seemed decent, however, to decline a request which was unlikely to occupy him for much more than twenty minutes – nor thirty-five if one counted the time spent in scrambling into uniform and out again.

It would have been hard to tell that it wasn't something quite different – even a wedding – that was about to transact itself. Gravity now and then there had to be, but on the whole a cheerful demeanour is held not improper on such occasions. The good fight has been fought, and nothing is here for tears, nothing to wail or knock the breast. Six weeks had passed, moreover, since Christopher Brockbank's death, and anybody much stunned by grief had thus had a substantial period in which to recover. Whether there had been many such appeared doubtful. Brockbank had been unmarried, and now the front pew reserved for relations was occupied only by two elderly women, habited in old-fashioned and no doubt frequently exhibited mourning, whom somebody had identified for Appleby in a whisper as cousins of the dead man. If anything, they appeared rather to be enjoying their role. It was to be conjectured that they owned some quite obscure, although genteel, situation in society. Nobody had ever heard of any Brockbanks until Christopher QC had come along. In some corner of the globe, Appleby vaguely understood, there was a brother, Adrian Brockbank, who had also distinguished himself – it seemed as a lone yachtsman. But the wandering Adrian had not, it seemed, hoisted himself into a jet for the occasion.

The congregation had got to its feet, and was listening to the singing of a psalm. It was well worth listening to, since the words were striking in themselves and the choir of St Boniface's justly celebrated. The congregation was, of course, in the expectation of playing a somewhat passive part. At such services it is understood that there is to be comparatively little scope for what, in another context, would be called audience participation.

Appleby looked about him. It was impressive that the Lord Chief Justice had turned up, and that he was flanked by two Ministers of the Crown. There were also two or three socially prominent dowagers, who were perhaps recalling passages with Christopher when he had been young as well as gay: these glanced from time to time in benevolent amusement at the two old creatures in the front pew. Among the clergy, and wearing a very plain but very golden pectoral cross, was a bishop who would presently ascend the pulpit and deliver a brief address. In the nave two elderly clubmen (as they ought probably to be called) of subdued raffish appearance were putting their heads together in muttered colloquy. These must liaise with yet another aspect of the dead man's dead life. They were presumably laying a wager with one another on just how many minutes the address would occupy.

The service proceeded with unflawed decorum. An anthem was sung. The bishop, ceremoniously conducted to his elevated perch, began his address. He lost no time in launching upon a character analysis of the late Queen's Counsel; it would have been possible to imagine an hourglass of the diminutive sort used for nicely timing the boiling of eggs as being perched on the pulpit's edge beside him. The analysis, although touching lightly once or twice upon endearing foible, was highly favourable in the main. The dead man, disposed in his private life to charity, humility, gentleness, and the study of English madrigals, had in his professional character been dedicated, stern, courageous, and passionately devoted to upholding, clarifying, reforming his country's laws.

It was now that something slightly untoward occurred. A late arrival entered the church. An elderly man with a finely trimmed grey moustache, he was dressed with the exactest propriety for the occasion; that he was accustomed to such appearances was evident in the mere manner in which he contrived to carry a black silk hat, an umbrella, and a pair of grey kid gloves dextrously in his left hand while receiving from the hovering verger the printed service sheet. Not many of those present thought it becoming to turn their heads to see what was happening. But nobody, in fact, was cheated of a sight of the newcomer for long. He might have been expected (however accustomed to some position of prominence) to slip modestly into a pew near the west door. But this he did not do. He walked with quiet deliberation up the central aisle – very much (Appleby thought) as if he were an integral and expected part of the ritual which he was in fact indecorously troubling. He walked right up to the front pew, and sat down beside Christopher Brockbank's female relatives.

There could be only one explanation. Here was the missing Adrian, brother of the dead man – to whom, indeed, Appleby's recollection sufficed to recognise that he bore a strong family likeness. Perhaps the plane from Singapore or the Bahamas or wherever had been delayed; perhaps fog had caused it to be diverted from Heathrow to a more distant airport; thus rendered unavoidably tardy in his appearance, this much-travelled Brockbank had decided that he must afford a general indication of his presence, and move to the support of the ladies of the family, even at the cost of rendering an effect of considerable disturbance. It must have been – Appleby thought sympathetically – a difficult decision to make.

The address went on. The new arrival listened with close attention to what must now be the tail end of it. And everybody else ought to have been doing the same thing.

But this was not so. The Lord Chief Justice had hastily removed one pair of spectacles, donned another, and directed upon the fraternal appearance in the front pew the kind of gaze which for many years he had been accustomed to bring to bear upon occupants of the dock at the Central Criminal Court. One of the Cabinet Ministers was looking frightened – which is something no Cabinet Minister should ever do. Two of the dowagers were talking to one another in agitated and semi-audible whispers. A third appeared to be on the verge of hysterics. As for the bishop, he was so upset that he let the typescript of his carefully prepared allocution flutter to the floor below, with the result that he was promptly reduced to a peroration in terms of embarrassed improvisation.

But before even this was concluded, the brother – whether, veritable or suppositious – of the late Christopher Brockbank behaved very strangely. He stood up, moved into the aisle, and bowed. He bowed, not towards the altar (which would have been very proper in itself), but at the bishop in his pulpit (and this wasn't proper at all). He then turned, and retreated as he had come. Only, whereas on arriving he had kept his eyes decently directed upon the floor, on departing he bowed to right and left as he walked – much like a monarch withdrawing from an audience chamber through a double file of respectful courtiers. He paused only once, and that was beside the uniformed Appleby, upon whom he directed a keen but momentary glance, before politely handing him his service sheet. Then he resumed his stately progress down the aisle until he reached the church door and vanished.

Somebody would possibly have followed a man so patently deranged, and therefore conceivably a danger to himself or others, had not the Rector of St Boniface's thought it expedient to come to the rescue of the flustered bishop by promptly embarking upon the prayers which, together with a hymn, were to conclude the service. These prayers (which are full of tremendous things) it would have been indecent to disturb. But a hymn is only a hymn, and it was quite plain that numerous members of the congregation were giving utterance not to the somewhat jejune sentiments this one proposed to them, but to various expressions, delivered more or less *sotto voce*, of indignation and stupefaction. The Lord Chief

Justice, moreover, was gesturing. He was gesturing at Appleby in a positively threatening way which Appleby perfectly understood. If Appleby bolted from this untoward and unseemly incident instead of reacting to it in some policemanlike fashion he would pretty well be treated as in contempt of court. This was why he found himself standing on the pavement outside St Boniface's a couple of minutes later.

'Get into this thing,' the Lord Chief Justice said imperiously, and pointed at his Rolls Royce. 'You, too,' he said to the Home Secretary (who was one of the two Ministers who had been giving thanks for the life of the deceased Brockbank). 'We can't let such an outrage pass.'

'An outrage?' Appleby queried, as he resignedly sat down in the car. 'Wasn't it merely that Christopher Brockbank's brother is mildly dotty – nothing more?'

'Adrian merely dotty! Damn it, Appleby, didn't you realise what he was doing? He was *impersonating* Christopher – nothing less. That moustache, those clothes, his entire bearing: they weren't remotely Adrian. They were Christopher *tout court*. Didn't you remark the reaction of those who knew Christopher well? Both those Brockbank brothers were given to brutal and tasteless practical jokes, but this has been the most brutal and tasteless of the lot.'

'They may well have been. In fact, I seem to remember hearing something of the sort about them. But if Adrian has judged it funny to get himself up like Christopher in order to attend Christopher's memorial service that seems to me entirely his own affair. I shall be surprised, Pomfret, if you can tell me he has broken the law.' Appleby smiled at the eminent judge. 'Although, of course, it wouldn't at all do for me not to believe what you say.'

'I don't believe it was Adrian at all. It was Christopher's ghost.' The Home Secretary endeavoured to offer this

in a whimsical manner. It was he who had been looking
patently frightened ten minutes before, and he was
endeavouring to carry this off lightly now. 'Turn up as a
ghost for something like one's own funeral is a joke good
enough to gratify any purgatorial spirit, I'd suppose.
What we've witnessed is the kind of thing those psychic
chaps call a veridical phantasm of the dead.'

'I haven't set eyes on Christopher Brockbank for thirty
years,' Appleby said, 'and his wandering brother Adrian
I've never seen at all. This well-groomed person bowing
himself down the aisle in that crazy fashion was *very* like
Christopher?'

'Very.'

'Thoroughly scandalous,' Lord Pomfret said. 'Not to
be tolerated. Appleby, you must look into it.'

'My dear Chief Justice, I have no standing in such
matters. This uniform is merely ornamental. I'm a retired
man, as you know.'

'Come, come.' The Home Secretary laid a hand on
Appleby's arm in a manner designed as wholly humor-
ous. 'Do as you're told, my boy.'

'Do you know – perhaps I will? The ghost, or
whatever, did a little distinguish me, after all. He stopped
and handed me this.' Appleby was still holding a
superfluous service sheet. 'It was almost as if he was
passing me the ball.'

Much in the way of hard fact about Christopher
Brockbank turned out not easy to come by. He proved to
have been surprisingly wealthy. As the elder of the two
brothers he had inherited a substantial fortune, and to
this he had added a second fortune earned at the Bar.
Uninterested in becoming a judge, he had retired comparatively early, and for the greater part of the year lived in
something like seclusion in the South of France. It was
understood by his acquaintance that this was in the

interest of uninterrupted labour on a work of jurisprudence directed to some system of legal reform. The accident in which he had lost his life had been a large-scale air disaster in the Alpes-Maritimes. He had died intestate, and his affairs were going to take a good deal of clearing up.

It was on the strength of no more than this amount of common knowledge, together with only a modicum of private inquiry, that Appleby eventually called upon a bank manager in the City.

'I understand from an official source,' he began blandly, 'that the late Mr Brockbank kept his private account in this country at your branch.'

'That is certainly true.' The bank manager nodded amiably. He had very clear views, Appleby conjectured, on what information was confidential and what was not. 'He used to spare a few minutes to chat with me upon the occasion of his quite infrequent visits. A delightful man.'

'No doubt. It has occurred to me that, in addition to keeping both a current and a deposit account with you, he may have been in the habit of lodging documents and so forth for safe keeping.'

'Ah.'

'I know that you maintain some sort of strong-room for such purposes, and suppose that your customers can hire strong-boxes of one convenient size or another?'

'Yes, indeed, Sir John. Should you yourself ever have occasion—'

'Thank you. Brockbank did this?'

'Sir John, may I say that, when inquiries of this sort are judged expedient for one reason or another, a request – and it can scarcely be more than a request – is commonly preferred by one of the Law Officers of the Crown?' The manager paused, and found that this produced no more than a composed nod. 'But no doubt there is little point in being sticky in the matter. Let me consult my appropriate file.' He unlocked a drawer, and rummaged. 'Yes,' he said. 'It would appear that Brockbank had such a box.'

'His executors haven't yet got round to inquiring about it?'

'Seemingly not.'

'I'd like you to open it and let me examine the contents.'

'My dear Sir John!' The manager was genuinely scandalised. 'You can scarcely believe—'

'But only in the most superficial way. I have an officer waiting in your outer office who would simply turn over these documents unopened, and apply a very simple test to the envelopes or whatever the outer coverings may prove to be. He will not take, and I shall not take, the slightest interest in what is said.'

For a moment the manager's hand hovered over his telephone. An appeal to higher authority – perhaps to the awful authority of the General Manager himself – was plainly in his mind. Then he took a deep breath.

'Very well,' he said. 'I suppose an adequate discretion will be observed?'

'Oh, most decidedly,' Appleby said.

'So that, for a start, is *that*,' Appleby murmured to the Lord Chief Justice an hour later.

'But surely, my dear Appleby, he would scarcely recognise you at a glance? The years have been passing over us, after all.'

'That is all too true. But the point isn't material. There I was, dressed up for that formal occasion in the uniform of a high-ranking officer of the Metropolitan Police. He felt he could trust me to tumble to the thing.'

'And you are quite sure? *Absolutely* sure? The finger-prints on that service sheet were identical—'

'Beyond a shadow of doubt. Christopher Brockbank

always deposited or withdrew documents from that strong-box in the presence of an official of the bank who was in a position to identify him beyond question. The man who attended Christopher Brockbank's memorial service was Christopher Brockbank himself.'

'And he wanted the fact to be known?'

'He wanted the fact to be known.'

'It makes no sense.'

'What it makes is very good *nonsense*. And there is one kind of nonsense that Brockbank is on record as having a fondness for: the kind of nonsense one calls a practical joke. And I expect he had money on it.'

'Money!' Lord Pomfret was outraged.

'Say a wager with one of his own kidney.'

'We have been most notoriously abused.' Something formidable had come into Pomfret's voice. One could almost imagine that high above his head in the chill London air the scales were trembling in the hand of the blindfolded figure of Justice which crowns the Central Criminal Court.

'I wouldn't deny it for a moment. But I come back to a point I've more or less made before. You can't send a man down, Chief Justice, for attending his own memorial service. It just isn't a crime.'

'But there must be something very like a crime in the hinterland of this impertinent buffoonery.' Lord Pomfret had flushed darkly. 'Steps have been taken to certify as dead a man who isn't dead at all.'

'In a foreign country, and in the context of some hideous and, no doubt, vastly confused air crash. Possibly without any actual knowledge of the thing on Brockbank's own part. Possibly as a consequence of innocent error – error on top of which he has merely piled an audacious joke. And a singularly tasteless joke, perhaps. But not one with gaol at the end of it.'

'We can get him. We can get him for *something*.'

'I don't know what to make of that from a legal point of view.' The retired Commissioner of Police made no bones about glancing at the Lord Chief Justice of England in frank amusement. 'And there will be a good deal of laughter in court, wouldn't you say?'

'You're damn well right.' Not altogether unexpectedly, Lord Pomfret was suddenly laughing himself. 'But what the devil is he going to do now? Just how is he proposing to come alive again?'

'With great respect, m'lud, I suggest your lordship is in some confusion.' Appleby, watching his august interlocutor dive for a whisky decanter and syphon, was laughing too. 'Christopher Brockbank *is* alive. He's in a position, so to speak, in which no further action is necessary.'

'Nor from us either? We leave him to it?'

'Just that I wouldn't say.' Appleby was grave again. 'I confess to being a little uneasy still about the whole affair.'

'The deuce you do!' Now on his feet, the Lord Chief Justice held the decanter poised in air. 'So what? Say when.'

'Only a finger,' Appleby said. 'And I'll continue to look into the thing.'

'With discretion, my dear fellow.' Pomfret was suddenly almost like the bank manager.

'Oh, most decidedly,' Appleby said.

Retired Police Commissioners don't go fossicking in France, and through the courtesy of his successor Appleby received reports in due season. Hard upon the air crash, it transpired, an elderly and distressed English gentleman had appeared upon the scene of the disaster in a chauffeur-driven car. Presenting himself to the *chef de gendarmerie* who was in control of the rescue operations, he had explained that he was Adrian Brockbank, and that he had motored straight from Nice upon hearing of the accident, since he had only too much reason to suppose that his elder brother, Mr Christopher Brockbank QC, had been on board the ill-fated plane. Could he be given any information about this, either way? It was explained to Mr Adrian Brockbank that much confusion inevitably prevailed; that, as often happened on such sad occasions, there was no certainty that an entirely reliable list of passengers' names existed; and that certain necessarily painful and distressing attempts at identification were even then going on. Would Mr Adrian Brockbank care . . . ?

The inquirer steeled himself, and cared. Eventually he had been almost irrationally reluctant to admit the sad truth. A ring on the charred finger of one of the grim exhibits he had, indeed, formally to depose as being his brother's ring. But it seemed so tiny a piece of evidence! Might there not be more? A relevant article of baggage, perhaps, that had in part escaped the heat of the conflagration?

Not – it was explained to Mr Adrian Brockbank – at the moment. But something of the kind might yet turn up. As so often, debris was probably scattered over a very wide area. There was to be a systematic search at first light. With this information, Mr Adrian Brockbank and his chauffeur had departed to a nearby hotel for the night. And in the morning the sombre expectation had been fulfilled. Christopher Brockbank's briefcase had been discovered, along with other detritus, in a field nearly a quarter of a mile away; and it contained a number of recent personal papers and his passport. Whereupon Adrian, formally identifying himself through the production of his own passport and the testimony of his chauffeur, satisfied the requirements of French law by making a deposition before a magistrate. After that again, he made decent arrangements for the disposal of anything that could be called his brother's remains. And then he departed as he had come.

Such had been the highly unsatisfactory death of Christopher Brockbank.

All this, Appleby told himself, didn't remain exactly obscure once you took a straight look at it. Just as it wasn't Adrian who had turned up at the memorial service, so it hadn't been Adrian who had turned up at the grisly aftermath of that aerial holocaust. It had been Christopher on both occasions – and it was impossible to say that throughout the whole affair there had been any positive role played by Adrian at all. This was bizarre – but there was something that was mildly alarming as well. Christopher had *waited*. Equipped with a passport in the name of his brother, equipped no doubt with a duplicate passport in his own name, equipped with the briefcase which he would eventually toss into an appropriate field – equipped with all this, Christopher had waited for a sufficiently substantial disaster within, say, a couple of hours' hard motoring-distance of his French residence. He had certainly had to wait for months – and more probably for years. A thoroughly macabre pertinacity had marked the attaining of his practical joke.

And hadn't the joker overreached himself? Could any place in society remain for a man who, with merely frivolous intent, had deliberately identified an unknown dead body as his own? It seemed not surprising that Christopher hadn't been heard of again since he had walked down that aisle, graciously bowing to a bewildered congregation. Perhaps he had very justifiably lost his nerve.

But even if Adrian didn't come into the story at all, where *was* Adrian? He was almost certainly Christopher's heir, and yet even Christopher's English solicitors appeared to know nothing about him. Perhaps they were

just being more successfully cagey than that bank
manager. Certainly they had, for the moment, nothing to
say – except that Mr Adrian Brockbank spent most of his
time sailing the seven seas.

Appleby was coming to feel, not very rationally, that
time was important. He had told Lord Pomfret that he
was uneasy – which had been injudicious, since he
couldn't quite have explained why. Pomfret, however,
had refrained from catechising him. And now he had the
same feeling still. No Brockbank had died. But two
Brockbanks might be described as lying low. There was
about this the effect of an ominous lull.

And then Christopher Brockbank turned up.

He turned up on Appleby's urban doorstep and was
shown in – looking precisely the man who had put on the
turn in St Boniface's.

'My dear Appleby,' he said, 'I have ventured to call for
the purpose of offering you an apology.' Brockbank's
address was easy and familiar; he might have been
talking to a man he ran into every second week in one
club or another.

'I don't need an apology. But I could do with an
explanation.'

'Ah, that – yes, indeed. But the apology must come
first. For dragging you into the little joke. It started up in
my mind like a creation, you know, just as I was walking
out of that church. There on the service sheet were my
fingerprints, and there were you, who if handed the thing
could be trusted to do as I have no doubt you have done.
A sublimely simple way of vindicating myself as still in
the land of the living.'

'I am delighted you are with us still.' Appleby said this
on a note of distinguishable irony. 'And I accept your
apology at once. And now, may the explanation of the
little joke follow?'

'The explanation is that it has been designed as rather more than a little joke. My idea has been, in fact, to make a real impact upon the complacency of some who are satisfied with the absurd inadequacy of many of our laws. That old fool Pomfret, for example. I have for long been a legal reformer, after all.'

'I see.' Appleby really did see. 'This exploit has been in the interest of highlighting the fact, or contention, that the law is hazardously lax in point of verifying adequately the identity of deceased persons – that sort of thing?'

'Precisely that sort of thing. I shall have established – strikingly because by means of an ingenious prank – that in France and England alike—'

'Quite so, Mr Brockbank. We need not linger on the worth of your intention. But surely you have reflected of late on the extent to which you are likely to be in trouble, under French legal jurisdiction, if not under English? The deception you carried out upon the occasion of that disaster—'

'My dear Appleby, what can you be thinking of? That was my brother Adrian, was it not? This all begins from his proposing to bring off a better joke against *me* than I ever brought off against him. It is on the record, I suppose, that we have both rather gone in for that sort of thing. He was going to confront me with the pleasant position of being legally dead. Well, I capped his joke by, you may say, concurring. I attended – I hope in a suitably devout manner – my own memorial service. So the laugh is going to be on him.'

'Mr Brockbank, I have seldom come across so impudent an imposture!' Appleby suddenly found himself as outraged as the Lord Chief Justice had been. 'Whether your brother has, or has not, been remotely involved in this freakish and indecent affair I do not know. But I *do* know that, six weeks ago in France, you presented yourself as that brother upon an occasion in which such clowning would have been wholly inconceivable' – Appleby paused, and then took a calculated plunge – 'to anybody bearing the character of a gentleman.'

'I withdraw my apology.' Christopher Brockbank had gone extremely pale. 'As for what you allege: prove it. Or get somebody with a legitimate concern in my affairs to prove it. *You* have none.'

'Then I scarcely see why you should be calling on me – except to discover how far I have penetrated to the truth of this nonsense. I am prepared to believe that you had some ghost of serious intention in the way of exposing the weakness of certain legal processes. I accept that notions of what is permissibly funny may differ as between one generation, or one coterie, and another. But your present pack of lies about the conduct of your own brother – lies which I must now suppose you to be intending to make public – is a little too steep for me. Just what are you going to say to your brother when you meet?'

'I don't quite know.' Christopher Brockbank had decided to digest the strong words which had been offered to him. 'But I must certainly decide, since I am on the point of running down to see him now.'

'I beg your pardon?' Appleby stared incredulously at his visitor.

'I said I'm off to see Adrian. I must persuade him I'm not as dead as he has tried to represent me. In a way, he doesn't know that he has not, so to speak, liquidated me quite successfully. Here is more than six weeks gone by since his little turn over my supposed body, and I haven't – so far as he knows – given a chirp. That must be puzzling him, wouldn't you say?'

'Possibly so. Do I understand that your only public appearance has been at that deplorably mistaken memorial service?'

'Yes it has. You may simply take it that it has amused me to lie low.'

'You appear to me to be in love with your own mortality. Now more than ever seems it rich to die: that sort of thing. What if there's a general feeling, Mr Brockbank, that your decease was a welcome event? You might have quite a task in persuading a malicious world that you *are* alive; that you are *you*, in fact, and not some species of Tichborne Claimant.'

'Ah, that's where those fingerprints come in. It's hardly a piece of evidence a conscientious policeman could suppress, eh?'

'No, it is not.' Appleby was becoming impatient of this senseless conversation. 'If your brother Adrian really played that trick at the scene of the disaster – which I do not believe for a moment – he will be gratified to learn that you have taken the consequences of his joke so seriously as pretty well to register your continued existence with the police.'

'But I shan't tell him what I did with that service sheet.' Christopher Brockbank gave a cunning chuckle. 'Not till I'm sure he hasn't got some further joke up his sleeve.' He got to his feet. 'And now I must be off to my brotherly occasion.'

'Far be it from me to detain you. But may I ask, Mr Brockbank, where your brother is to be found?'

'Ah, that will doubtless be becoming public property quite soon. Adrian is a minor celebrity in his way. But, just at the moment, I think I'll keep him to myself.'

The prediction proved accurate. The very next morning's papers carried the news that Adrian Brockbank's yacht had been sighted at anchor off Budleigh Salterton in Devon. It seemed probable that he had arrived unobtrusively in home waters several days earlier.

Appleby endeavoured to absorb this as information of

only moderate interest. Christopher Brockbank had had his joke, and it had involved a breach of the law in France if not in England. He had now gone off to join his nautical brother Adrian, and crow over the manner in which he had taken Adrian's identity upon himself at the inception of the imposture in the Alpes-Maritimes. Something like that must really be what was in Christopher's mind. And it was all very far from being Appleby's business; he ought to be indifferent as to whether those two professional jokers (as they appeared to have been) decided to laugh over the thing together or to quarrel about it. Let them fight it out.

But this line of thought didn't work. Several times in the course of the morning there came back into Appleby's head one particular statement which Christopher had made. It was a statement which just *might* be fraught with a consequence not pretty to think of. At noon Appleby got out his car and drove west.

Budleigh Salterton proved not to run to a harbour. A few unimpressive craft were drawn up on a pebbly beach. Far away on the horizon tankers and freighters ploughed up and down the English Channel; the sea was otherwise empty except for a simple yacht riding at anchor rather far out. Binoculars didn't help to make anything of this. Where one might have been expected to read the vessel's name a tarpaulin or small sail had been spread as if to dry. Appleby appealed to a bystander.

'Do you happen to know,' he asked, 'whose yacht that is?'

'I haven't any idea.' The man addressed, although he appeared to be a resident of the place, was plainly without nautical interests. 'It has been here for some days – except that it went out at dusk yesterday evening, and I happened to see it return at dawn this morning. But I did hear somebody say there was a rumour that the fellow was one of those lone yachtsman types.'

'Do you know where I can hire a rowing-boat?'

'Just down by that groyne, I believe.'

'Thank you very much.'

'May I come on board?' Appleby called out. Adrian Brockbank was very like his brother – even down to the neat grey moustache.

'Not if you're another of those infernal journalists.'

'I'm not. I'm an infernal policeman. A retired one.'

'You can come up, if you like.' And Adrian tossed down a small accommodation ladder. He had appeared only momentarily startled.

'Thank you.' Appleby climbed, and settled himself without ceremony on the gunwale. 'Have you had any other visitors just lately, Mr Brockbank?'

'I see you know my name. Only a journalist, as I say. That was yesterday evening. But I persuaded him to clear out again.'

'What about your brother?'

'I beg your pardon?' Adrian stared.

'Your brother Christopher.'

'Good, God, Mr—'

'Appleby. Sir John Appleby. Yes?'

'My brother Christopher was killed six weeks ago in an air crash. Your question is either ignorant or outrageous.'

'That remains to be proved, sir. And I gather you have been on some extended cruise or other. Just how did you hear this sad news?'

'*Hear* it? Heaven and earth, man! It was actually I who identified Christopher's body. I'd sailed into Nice, and tried to contact him by telephone. They said he was believed to have joined a plane for Paris, and gave some particulars. Then suddenly there was the news of this—'

'So you identified the body, made certain decent

arrangements about it, and then went to sea again. Is that right?'

'It is right. But I'm damned if I know what entitles you—'

'And then, only a few days ago, there was your brother's memorial service at St Boniface's in London. Do you say that you attended it?'

'Certainly I attended it. But as I'd only just berthed here, and had to get hold of the right clothes, I was a bit late for the occasion.'

'I see. Then you came straight back here?'

'Obviously I did. I don't like fuss. I've been lying low.'

'That's something that appears to run in your family. And so, very decidedly, does something else.'

'May I ask what that is?' Adrian was now eyeing Appleby narrowly.

'A rash fondness for ingenious but really quite vulnerable lies. Mr Brockbank, your brother Christopher, having somehow got wind of your arrival here at Budleigh, came down yesterday evening and – I don't doubt – rowed out to see you just as I have done. It was something quite out of the blue. I don't know where you've come from, but you certainly haven't been receiving English news on the way. And here, suddenly, was your brother, chock-full of the craziest and most discreditable of his practical jokes. He'd resolved to attend his own memorial service, partly for the sheer hell of it, and partly to dramatise what he considered some loophole in the law. He'd plotted the thing ingeniously enough, and it had involved his impersonating you at the scene of an air crash. He told you all this in exuberant detail. *You* had been made to appear the joke – this was the best part of *his* joke – and as a result of it he was officially dead until he chose to come alive again.' Appleby paused. 'Mr Brockbank,' he went on quietly, 'you decided that he never *would* so choose.'

'This is the most outrageous—'

'Please don't interrupt. What you said to yourself was this: if Christopher wanted to be dead, let him damned well *be* dead – and let his large fortune pass to his next of kin, yourself. It was all so simple, was it not? Lie One: *you* had sworn to what was in fact the *true* identity of the dead man. Lie Two: *you* had been just in time for the memorial service. Your story would be simple and plausible. The true story, supposing anybody should tumble to it, would be too fantastic for credence. Have I succeeded in stating the matter with some succinctness?'

'You have a kind of professional glibness, Sir John.' Adrian said this perfectly coolly. 'I suppose that for most of your days you've been ingeniously fudging up yarns like this. But it won't wash, you know. It won't wash, at all. You are reckoning that, at every step, it will be possible to collect one or another scrap of circumstantial evidence against me, and that these will just add up. But they won't – not to anything like the total that would persuade a jury of such nonsense. My poor brother met an accidental death in France, and I identified his body, and that's that.'

'On the contrary, your brother was murdered by you on this yacht yesterday evening; doubtless sewn up in canvas with as much in the way of miscellaneous metal objects as you could find on board; and sent over the side – far out at sea – last night.'

'Far out at sea?' It was ironically that Adrian repeated the words. 'Awkward, that. A body is rather a useful exhibit, is it not, when a thin case has to be proved?'

'Mr Brockbank, you entirely mistake the matter. There is absolute proof that your brother Christopher, alive and well, attended his own memorial service. It is a proof which, I know, he proposed to withhold from you for a time – which was perhaps a pity. But the evidence, which I need not particularise, is in my possession.'

'Dear me!' Adrian made a casual gesture which somehow didn't match with a suddenly alert look and a tautened frame. 'And is it in the possession of anybody else?'

'Yes, of several people. Otherwise, I'm bound to say I shouldn't be thus alone with you, Mr Brockbank, in a secluded situation. But it hadn't, I repeat, been evidence in *your* possession. For it wasn't in your brother's mind to mention its existence to you just at present. He was keeping it up *his* sleeve. Rather a muzzy notion, perhaps, but understandable when Brockbank is sparring with Brockbank. It is evidence, incidentally, which was entirely and ingeniously devised by your brother himself.' Appleby paused. 'I may just say that fingerprints come into it. Irrefutable things.'

There was a long silence, and then Adrian Brockbank, who had also been perched on a gunwale, stood up.

'If I may just slip below for a moment,' he said, 'I think I can turn up something which will put a term to this whole absurd affair.'

'As you please.'

It was only after a pause that Appleby had spoken. He might have been staring with interest at some small smudge of smoke on the horizon. For a couple of long minutes he continued immobile, sombrely waiting. For a further minute he continued so – even after the revolver shot had made itself heard. Then he rose with a small sigh and sought the late Adrian Brockbank below.

MURDER

BOOK THREE

PUNISHMENT

Private Eyes and Investigators

Introduction

'Death's at the bottom of everything, Martins,' the tough but sympathetic policeman Calloway warns pulp novelist Rollo Martins when he turns detective in the search for his missing friend, Harry Lime, in Graham Greene's famous murder mystery, *The Third Man* (1950). 'Leave death to the professionals.'

Of course, detectives and avengers outside the ranks of the law have been ignoring such advice and following the example of Martins ever since the days of Sherlock Holmes. For the determination of the inquiry agent and the private eye to be the harbinger of justice and, ultimately, punishment, is of a very special kind and has resulted in a type of story all its own within the crime genre that holds a great attraction for large numbers of readers.

The reason for the popularity of these investigators is not difficult to explain. For they answer a human need to read about extraordinary characters who do the things that the law seemingly cannot – either because of police procedure, legal restrictions or just the inertia of the enforcement agencies concerned.

In the early years of the sleuth in crime fiction, such characters were invariably men like the intellectual Holmes, the playboy Simon Templar or the hardboiled Sam Spade. They, in turn, were followed by new archetypes of their time, like the first black investigator, Virgil Tibbs, the first gay, Pharaoh Love, and the almost superhuman Executioner. More recently still has come a wave of female avengers who are the new stars of the genre. As Marion Shaw wrote in the *Sunday Times* recently, 'In the insatiable market for crime fiction, feminist sleuthing is feeding a very healthy appetite ... Dick Tracy has become a woman.'

Despite the indisputable fact that women have been the most successful crime writers of this century, from Agatha Christie and Dorothy L. Sayers through to current stars such as P. D. James and Ruth Rendell – and there have been a few detective heroines along the way including Miss Marple, Hildegarde Withers and Bertha Cool (little old ladies all) – it has only been since the late 'seventies that the young female detective has become a major figure in the genre. A state of affairs directly attributable to another unarguable fact that for much of the time during the development of the crime genre the necessary qualifications for a sleuth, of bravery, energy, independence and (cruellest of all) intelligence, were just not ascribed by society to women.

Now, though, as we near the millennium, we have a new breed of feminist gumshoes, spearheaded by Sharon McCone, V. I. Warshawski and Kinsey Millhone, who are active, resourceful, cynical, determinedly independent and in every respect a match for their male counterparts. 'They also stalk a modern wasteland,' Marion Shaw has remarked with undisguised admiration, 'and are the avengers of its pitiful detritus.'

In this selection I have brought together the best of the past and the present to demonstrate how the investigators and private eyes of both sexes have become the final arbiters of justice when other means, including the law, have failed. When Sherlock Holmes began his career to fill this need in Victorian London a century ago he was 'the only unofficial consulting detective in the world'. In the following pages you will read just how far his successors have come and with what success in the intervening years.

Somewhere in the City

MARCIA MULLER

INVESTIGATOR FILE

NAME: Sharon McCone, Private Eye

PLACE: San Francisco

TIME: 1989

CASES: *Edwin of the Iron Shoes* (1977), *There's Something in a Sunday* (1989), *Wolf in the Shadows* (1994), *Till the Butchers Cut Him Down* (1995) etc.

DOSSIER: Sharon McCone is crime fiction's first fully realised and realistically portrayed female private detective and represents the most important new development in the genre of this generation. Armed with her Nikkormat camera, .38 hand gun, and behind the wheel of her red MG sports car, she is as readily identifiable as the toughest hardboiled dick of the 'thirties – and as such is the pioneer of her kind. Tough, intuitive and philosophical – in a way not unlike Sam Spade or Lew Archer – she works in San Francisco and is single minded about fighting crime and corruption. Sharon has a very special insight into human nature and is at her best when investigating complex relationships wherein she often discovers the motives and means behind a crime. Single (though often falling in and out of love), practical and independent by nature, she carries out most of her cases on behalf of her co-operative firm, often spotting the vital clues that other investigators – including the law – have missed. Sharon is a true multi-dimensional figure: unorthodox and headstrong, resolute and resilient, scrupulous and sharp, although she can also be compassionate and sensitive. Of her, the *San Francisco Review* said recently with understandable pride, 'She's easily the best of the female detectives.'

CREATOR: Marcia Muller (b. 1953), who lives in northern California, took up writing mystery fiction after obtaining a BA and MA from the University of Michigan and received immediate acclaim for her first Sharon McCone novel, *Edwin of the Iron Shoes*, published in 1977. This ground-breaking work has subsequently caused her to be recognised by crime writer Sue Grafton as 'the founding "mother" of the contemporary female hardboiled private eye' as well as the inspiration for several other 'gumshoe girls'. (Grafton and Sara Paretsky are acknowledged as the two other writers who effected this revolution in crime fiction.) Marcia has subsequently created two more popular series characters – Joanna Stark, a partner in a California art security firm, and Elena Oliverez, a Santa Barbara museum curator and amateur detective – although it is for private eye Sharon that she is best known. In 1993 she was given a Life Achievement Award by the Private Eye Writers of America, becoming the first and to date only woman recipient. 'Somewhere in the City', published in the *Armchair Detective* in 1990, represents an unusually tense case for Sharon as well as being unique among crime short stories by having as its background the terrifying San Francisco earthquake of 1989.

* * *

Somewhere in the City

At 5.04 p.m. on 17 October, 1989, the city of San Francisco was jolted by an earthquake that measured a frightening 7.1 on the Richter Scale. The violent tremors left the Bay Bridge impassable, collapsed a double-decker freeway in nearby Oakland, and toppled or severely damaged countless homes and other buildings. From the Bay Area to the seaside town of Santa Cruz some hundred miles south, sixty-five people were killed and thousands left homeless. And when the aftershocks subsided, San Francisco entered a new era – one in which things would never be quite the same again. As with all cataclysmic events, the question, 'Where were you when?' will forever provoke deeply emotional responses in those of us who lived through it . . .

Where I was when: the headquarters of the Golden Gate Crisis Hotline in the Noe Valley district. I'd been working a case there – off and on, and mostly in the late afternoon and evening hours, for over two weeks – with very few results and with a good deal of frustration.

The hotline occupied one big windowless room behind a rundown coffee house on Twenty-fourth Street. The location, I'd been told, was not so much one of choice as of convenience (meaning the rent was affordable), but had I not known that, I would have considered it a stroke of genius. There was something instantly soothing about entering through the coffee house, where the aromas of various blends permeated the air and steam rose from huge stainless-steel urns. The patrons were unthreatening – mostly shabby and relaxed, reading or conversing with their feet propped up on chairs. The pastries displayed in the glass case were comfort food at its purest – reminders of the days when calories and cholesterol didn't count. And the round face of the proprietor, Lloyd Warner, was welcoming and kind as he waved troubled visitors through to the crisis centre.

On that Tuesday afternoon I arrived at about twenty to five, answering Lloyd's cheerful greeting and trying to ignore the chocolate-covered doughnuts in the case. I had a dinner date at seven-thirty, had been promised some of the best French cuisine on Russian Hill, and was unwilling to spoil my appetite. The doughnuts called out to me, but I turned a deaf ear and hurried out.

The room beyond the coffee house contained an assortment of mismatched furniture: several desks and chairs of all vintages and materials; phones in colours and styles ranging from standard black touchstone to a shocking turquoise Princess; three tattered easy-chairs dating back to the fifties; and a card table covered with literature on health and psychological services. Two people manned the desks nearest the door. I went to the desk with the turquoise phone, plunked my briefcase and bag down on it, and turned to face them.

'He call today?' I asked.

Pete Lowry, a slender man with a bandit's moustache who was director of the centre, took his booted feet off the desk and swivelled to face me. 'Nope. It's been quiet all afternoon.'

'Too quiet.' This came from Ann Potter, a woman with dark frizzled hair who affected the ageing-hippie look in jeans and flamboyant over-blouses. 'And this weather – I don't like it one bit.'

'Ann's having one of her premonitions of gloom and doom,' Pete said. 'Evil portents and omens lurk all around us – although most of them went up front for coffee a while ago.'

Ann's eyes narrowed to a glare. She possessed very little sense of humour, whereas Pete perhaps possessed too much. To forestall the inevitable spat, I interrupted. 'Well, I don't like the weather much myself. It's muggy, and too warm for October. It makes me nervous.'

'Why?' Pete asked.

I shrugged. 'I don't know, but I've felt edgy all day.'

The phone on his desk rang. He reached for the receiver. 'Golden Gate Crisis Hotline, Pete speaking.'

Ann cast one final glare at his back as she crossed to the desk that had been assigned to me. 'It *has* been too quiet,' she said defensively. 'Hardly anyone's called, not even to inquire about how to deal with a friend or a family member. That's not normal even for a Tuesday.'

'Maybe all the crazies are out enjoying the warm weather.'

Ann half-smiled, cocking her head. She wasn't sure if what I'd said was funny or not, and didn't know how to react. After a few seconds her attention was drawn to the file I was removing from my briefcase. 'Is that about our problem caller?'

'Uh-huh.' I sat down and began rereading my notes silently, hoping she'd go away. I'd meant it when I'd said I felt on edge, and was in no mood for conversation.

The file concerned a series of calls that the hotline had received over the past month – all from the same individual, a man with a distinctive raspy voice. Their content had been more or less the same: an initial plaint of being all alone in the world with no one to care if he lived or died; then a gradual escalating from despair to anger, in spite of the trained counsellors' skilful responses; and finally the declaration that he had an assault rifle and was going to kill others and himself. He always ended with some variant on the statement, 'I'm going to take a whole lot of people with me.'

After three of the calls, Pete had decided to notify the police. A trace was placed on the centre's lines, but the results were unsatisfactory; most of the time the caller didn't stay on the phone long enough, and in the instances that the calls could be traced, they turned out to have originated from booths in the Marina district. Finally the trace was taken off, the official conclusion being that the calls were the work of a crank – and possibly one with a grudge against someone connected with the hotline.

The official conclusion did not satisfy Pete, however. By the next morning he was in the office of the hotline's attorney at All Souls Legal Co-operative, where I am chief investigator. And half an hour after that, I was assigned to work the phones at the hotline as often as my other duties permitted, until I'd identified the caller. Following a crash course from Pete in techniques for dealing with callers in crisis – augmented by some reading of my own – they turned me loose on the turquoise phone.

After the first couple of rocky, sweaty-palmed sessions, I'd gotten into it: become able to distinguish the truly disturbed from the fakers or the merely curious; learned to gauge the responses that would work best with a given individual; succeeded at eliciting information that would permit a crisis team to go out and assess the seriousness of the situation in person. In most cases, the team would merely talk the caller into getting counselling. However, if they felt immediate action was warranted, they would contact the SFPD, who had the authority to have the individual held for evaluation at the SF General Hospital for up to seventy-two hours.

During the past two weeks the problem caller had been routed to me several times, and with each conversation I became more concerned about him. While his threats were melodramatic, I sensed genuine disturbance and desperation in his voice; the swift escalation of panic and anger seemed much out of proportion to whatever verbal stimuli I offered. And, as Pete had stressed in my orientation, no matter how theatrical or frequently made, any threat of suicide or violence towards others was to be taken with utmost seriousness by the hotline volunteers.

Unfortunately I was able to glean very little information from the man. Whenever I tried to get him to reveal concrete facts about himself, he became sly and would dodge my questions. Still, I could make several assumptions about him: he was youngish, reasonably well educated, and Caucasian. The traces to the Marina indicated he probably lived in that bayside district – which meant he had to have a good income. He listened to classical music (three times I'd heard it playing in the background) from a transistor radio, by the tinny tonal quality. Once I'd caught the call letters of the FM station – one in the Central Valley town of Fresno. Why Fresno? I'd wondered. Perhaps he was from there? But that wasn't much to go on; there were probably several Fresno transplants in his part of the city.

When I looked up from my folder, Ann had gone back to her desk. Pete was still talking in low, reassuring tones with his caller. Ann's phone rang, and she picked up the receiver. I tensed. Knowing the next call would cycle automatically to my phone.

When it rang some minutes later, I glanced at my watch and jotted down the time while reaching over for the receiver. Four-fifty-eight. 'Golden Gate Crisis Hotline, Sharon speaking.'

The caller hung up – either the wrong number or, more likely, someone who lost his nerve. The phone rang again about twenty seconds later and I answered it in the same manner.

'Sharon. It's me.' The greeting was the same as the previous times, the raspy voice unmistakable.

'Hey, how's it going?'

A long pause, laboured breathing. In the background I could make out the strains of music – Brahms, I thought. 'Not so good. I'm really down today.'

'You want to talk about it?'

'There isn't much to say. Just more of the same. I took

THE ORION BOOK OF MURDER

a walk a while ago, thought it might help. But the people out there flying their kites, I can't take it.'

'Why is that?'

'I used to . . . ah, forget it.'

'No, I'm interested.'

'Well, they're always in couples, you know.'

When he didn't go on, I made an interrogatory sound.

'The whole damn world is in couples. Or families. Even here inside my little cottage I can feel it. There are these apartment buildings on either side, and I can feel them pressing in on me, and I'm here all alone.'

He was speaking rapidly now, his voice rising. But as his agitation increased, he'd unwittingly revealed something about his living situation. I made a note about the little cottage between the two apartment buildings.

'This place where the people were flying kites,' I said, 'do you go there often?'

'Sure – it's only two blocks away.' A sudden note of sullenness now entered his voice – a part of the pattern he'd previously exhibited. 'Why do you want to know about that?'

'Because . . . I'm sorry, I forget your name.'

No response.

'It would be a help if I knew what to call you.'

'Look, bitch, I know what you're trying to do.'

'Oh?'

'Yeah. You want to get a name, an address. Send the cops out. Next thing I'm chained to the wall at SF General. I've been that route before. But I know my rights now; I went down the street to the Legal Switchboard, and they told me . . .'

I was distracted from what he was saying by a tapping sound – the stack trays on the desk next to me bumped against the wall. I looked over there, frowning. What was causing that . . . ?

'. . . gonna take the people next door with me . . .'

I looked back at the desk in front of me. The lamp was jiggling.

'What the hell?' the man on the phone exclaimed.

My swivel chair shifted. A coffee mug tipped and rolled across the desk and into my lap.

Pete said, 'Jesus Christ, we've having an earthquake!'

'. . . The ceiling's coming down!' The man's voice was panicked now.

'Get under the door frame!' I clutched the edge of the desk, ignoring my own advice.

I heard a crash from the other end of the line. The man screamed in pain. 'Help me! Please help—' And then the line went dead.

For a second or so I merely sat there – longtime San Franciscan, frozen by my own disbelief. All around me formerly inanimate objects were in motion. Pete and Ann were scrambling for the archway that led to the door of the coffee house.

'Sharon, get under the desk!' she yelled at me.

And then the electricity cut out, leaving the windowless room in blackness. I dropped the dead receiver, slid off the chair, crawled into the kneehole of the desk. There was a cracking, a violent shifting, as if a giant hand had seized the building and twisted it. Tremors buckled the floor beneath me.

This is a bad one. Maybe the big one that they're always talking about.

The sound of something wrenching apart. Pellets of plaster rained down on the desk above me. Time had telescoped, it seemed as if the quake had been going on for many minutes, when in reality it could not have been more than ten or fifteen seconds.

Make it stop! Please make it stop!

And then, as if whatever powers-that-be had heard my unspoken plea, the shock waves diminished to shivers, and finally ebbed.

Blackness. Silence. Only bits of plaster bouncing off the desks and the floor.

'Ann?' I said. 'Pete?' My voice sounded weak, tentative.

'Sharon?' It was Pete. 'You OK?'

'Yes. You?'

'We're fine.'

Slowly I began to back out of the kneehole. Something blocked it – the chair. I shoved it aside, and emerged. I couldn't see a thing, but I could feel fragments of plaster and other unidentified debris on the floor. Something cut into my palm; I winced.

'God, it's dark.' Ann said. 'I've got some matches in my purse. Can you—'

'. . . Oh, right.'

Pete said, 'Wait, I'll open the door to the coffee house.'

On hands and knees I began feeling my way toward the sound of their voices. I banged into one of the desks, overturned a wastebasket, then finally reached the opposite wall. As I stood there, Ann's cold hand reached out to guide me. Behind her I could hear Pete fumbling at the door.

I leaned against the wall. Ann was close beside me, her breathing erratic. Peter said, 'Goddamned door's jammed.' From behind it came voices of people in the coffee house.

Now that the danger was over – at least until the first of the aftershocks – my body sagged against the wall, giving way to tremors of its own manufacture. My thoughts turned to the lover with whom I'd planned to have dinner: where had he been when the quake hit? And what about my cats, my house? My friends and my co-workers at All Souls? Other friends scattered throughout the Bay Area?

And what about a nameless, faceless man somewhere

in the city who had screamed for help before the phone
went dead?

The door to the coffee house burst open, spilling weak
light into the room. Lloyd Warner and several of his
customers peered anxiously through it. I prodded Ann –
who seemed to have lapsed into lethargy – towards them.

The coffee house was fairly dark, but late-afternoon
light showed beyond the plate-glass windows fronting on
the street. It revealed a floor that was awash in spilled
liquid and littered with broken crockery. Chairs were
tipped over – whether by the quake or the patrons' haste
to get to shelter I couldn't tell. About ten people milled
about, talking noisily.

Ann and Pete joined them, but I moved forward to the
window. Outside, Twenty-fourth Street looked much as
usual, except for the lack of traffic and pedestrians. The
buildings still stood, the sun still shone, the air drifting
through the open door of the coffee house was still warm
and muggy. In this part of the city, at least, life went on.

Lloyd's transistor radio had been playing the whole
time – tuned to the station that was carrying the coverage
of the third game of the Bay Area World Series, due to
start at five-thirty. I moved closer, listening.

The sportscaster was saying, 'Nobody here knows
what's going on. The Giants have wandered over to the
A's dugout. It looks like a softball game where somebody
forgot to bring the ball.'

Then the broadcast shifted abruptly to the station's
studios. A newswoman was relaying telephone reports
from the neighbourhoods. I was relieved to hear that
Bernal Heights, where All Souls is located, and my own
small district near Glen Park were shaken up but for the
most part undamaged. The broadcaster concluded by
warning listeners not to use their phones except in cases
of emergency. Ann snorted and said, 'Do as I say but
not . . .'

Again the broadcast made an abrupt switch – to the station's traffic helicopter. 'From where we are,' the reporter said, 'it looks as if part of the upper deck of the Oakland side of the Bay Bridge has collapsed on to the bottom deck. Cars are pointing every which way, there may be some in the water. And on the approaches—' The transmission broke, then resumed after a number of static-filled seconds. 'It looks as if the Cypress Structure on the Oakland approach to the bridge has also collapsed. Oh my God, there are cars and people—' This time the transmission broke for good.

It was very quiet in the coffee house. We all exchanged looks – fearful, horrified. This was an extremely bad one, if not the catastrophic one they'd been predicting for so long.

Lloyd was the first to speak. He said, 'I'd better see if I can insulate the urns in some way, keep the coffee hot as long as possible. People'll need it tonight.' He went behind the counter, and in a few seconds a couple of the customers followed.

The studio newscast resumed. '. . . fires burning out of control in the Marina district. We're receiving reports of collapsed buildings there, with people trapped inside . . .'

The Marina district. People trapped.

I thought again of the man who had cried out for help over the phone. Of my suspicion, more or less confirmed by today's conversation, that he lived in the Marina.

Behind the counter Lloyd and the customers were wrapping the urns in dish towels. Here – and in other parts of the city, I was sure – people were already overcoming their shock, gearing up to assist in the relief effort. There was nothing I could do in my present surroundings, but . . .

I hurried to the back room and groped until I found my purse on the floor beside the desk. As I picked it up, an aftershock hit – nothing like the original trembler, but strong enough to make me grab the chair for support. When it stopped, I went shakily out to my car.

Twenty-fourth Street was slowly coming to life. People bunched on the sidewalks, talking and gesturing. A man emerged from one of the shops, walked to the centre of the street, and surveyed the façade of his building. In the parking lot of nearby Bell Market, employees and customers gathered by the grocery carts. A man in a butcher's apron looked around, shrugged, and headed for a corner tavern. I got into my MG and took a city map from the side pocket.

The Marina area consists mainly of early twentieth-century stucco homes and apartment buildings built on fill on the shore of the bay – which meant the quake damage there would naturally be bad. The district extends roughly from the Fisherman's Wharf area to the Presidio – not large, but large enough, considering I had a few clues as to where within its boundaries my man lived. I spread out the map against the steering-wheel and examined it.

The man had said he'd taken a walk that afternoon, to a place two blocks from his home where people were flying kites. That would be the Marina Green near the yacht harbour, famous for the elaborate and often fantastical kites flown there in fine weather. Two blocks placed the man's home somewhere on the far side of North Point Street.

I had one more clue: in his anger at me he'd let it slip that the Legal Switchboard was 'down the street'. The switchboard, a federally funded assistance group, was headquartered in one of the piers at Fort Mason, at the east end of the Marina. While several streets in that vicinity ended at Fort Mason, I saw that only two – Beach and North Point – were within two blocks of the Green as well.

Of course, I reminded myself, 'down the street' and 'two blocks' could have been generalisations or exaggerations. But it was somewhere to start. I set the map aside and turned the key in the ignition.

The trip across the city was hampered by near-gridlock traffic on some streets. All the stoplights were out; there were no police to direct the panicked motorists. Citizens helped out; I saw men in three-piece suits, women in heels and business attire, even a ragged man who looked to be straight out of one of the homeless shelters, all playing traffic cop. Sirens keened, emergency vehicles snaked from lane to lane. The car radio kept reporting further destruction; there was another aftershock, and then another, but I scarcely felt them because I was in motion.

As I inched along a major crosstown arterial, I asked myself why I was doing this foolhardy thing. The man was nothing to me, really – merely a voice on the phone, always self-pitying, and often antagonistic and potentially violent. I ought to be checking on my house and the folks at All Souls; if I wanted to help people, my efforts would have been better spent in my own neighbourhood or Bernal Heights. But instead I was travelling to the most congested and dangerous part of the city in search of a man I'd never laid eyes on.

As I asked the question, I knew the answer. Over the past two weeks the man had told me about his deepest problems. I'd come to know him in spite of his self-protective secretiveness. And he'd become more to me than just the subject of an investigation; I'd begun to care whether he lived or died. Now we had shared a peculiarly intimate moment – that of being together, if only in voice, when the catastrophe that San Franciscans feared the most had struck. He had called for help; I had heard his terror and pain. A connection had been established that could not be broken.

After twenty minutes and little progress, I cut west and took a less-travelled residential street through Japantown and over the crest of Pacific Heights. From the top of the hill I could see and smell the smoke over the Marina; as I crossed the traffic-snarled intersection with Lombard, I could see the flames. I drove another block, then decided to leave the MG and continue on foot.

All around I could see signs of destruction now: a house was twisted at a tortuous angle, its front porch collapsed and crushing a car parked at the curb; on Beach Street an apartment building's upper storey had slid into the street, clogging it with rubble; three bottom floors of another building were flattened, leaving only the top intact.

I stopped at a corner, breathing hard, nearly choking on the thickening smoke. The smell of gas from broken lines was vaguely nauseating – frightening, too, because of the potential for explosions. To my left the street was cordoned off; fire-department hoses played on the blaze – weakly, because of damaged water mains. People congregated everywhere, staring about with horror-struck eyes; they huddled together, clinging to one another, many were crying. Firefighters and police were telling bystanders to go home before dark fell. 'You should be looking after your property,' I heard one say. 'You can count on going seventy-two hours without water or power.'

'Longer than that,' someone said.

'It's not safe here,' the policeman added. 'Please go home.'

Between sobs, a woman said, 'What if you've got no home to go to any more?'

The cop had no answer for her.

Emotions were flying out of control among the onlookers. It would have been easy to feed into it – to weep, even panic. Instead, I turned my back to the flaming buildings, began walking the other way, towards

Fort Mason. If the man's home was beyond the barricades, there was nothing I could do for him. But if it lay in the other direction, where there was a lighter concentration of rescue workers, then my assistance might save his life.

I forced myself to walk slower, to study the buildings on either side of the street. I had one last clue that could lead me to the man: he'd said he lived in a little cottage between two apartment buildings. The homes in this district were mostly of substantial size; there couldn't be too many cottages situated in just that way.

Across the street a house slumped over to one side, its roof canted at a forty-five-degree angle; windows from an apartment house had popped out of their frames, and its iron fire escapes were tangled and twisted like a cat's cradle of yarn. Another home was unrecognisable, merely a heap of rubble. And over there, two four-storey apartment buildings leaned together, forming an arch over a much smaller structure . . .

I rushed across the street, pushed through a knot of bystanders. The smaller building was a tumble-down mass of white stucco with a smashed red-tile roof and partially flattened iron fence. It had been a Mediterranean-style cottage with grillework over high windows; now the grilles were bent and pushed outwards, the collapsed windows resembled swollen-shut eyes.

The woman standing next to me was cradling a terrified cat under her loose cardigan sweater. I asked her, 'Did the man who lives in the cottage get out OK?'

She frowned, tightened her grip on the cat as it burrowed deeper. 'I don't know who lives there. It's always kind of deserted-looking.'

A man in front of her said, 'I've seen lights, but never anybody coming or going.'

I moved closer. The cottage was deep in the shadows of the leaning buildings, eerily silent. From above came a groaning sound, and then a piece of wood sheared off the apartment house to the right, crashing on to what remained of the cottage's roof. I looked up, wondering how long before one or the other of the buildings toppled. Wondering if the man was still alive inside the compacted mass of stucco . . .

A man in jeans and a sweatshirt came up and stood beside me. His face was smudged and abraded; his clothing was smeared with dirt and what looked to be blood; he held his left elbow gingerly in the palm of his hand. 'You were asking about Dan?' he said.

So that was the anonymous caller's name. 'Yes. Did he get out OK?'

'I don't think he was home. At least, I saw him over at the Green around quarter to five.'

'He was home. I was talking with him on the phone when the quake hit.'

'Oh, Jesus.' The man's face paled under the smudges. 'My name's Mel; I live . . . lived next door. Are you a friend of Dan's?'

'Yes,' I said, realising it was true.

'That's a surprise.' He stared worriedly up at the place where the two buildings leaned together.

'Why?'

'I thought Dan didn't have any friends left. He's pushed us away ever since the accident.'

'Accident?'

'You must be a new friend, or else you'd know. Dan's woman was killed on the freeway last spring. A truck crushed her car.'

The word 'crushed' seemed to hang in the air between us. I said, 'I've got to try to get him out of there,' and stepped over the flattened portion of the fence.

Mel said, 'I'll go with you.'

I looked sceptically at his injured arm.

'It's nothing, really,' he told me. 'I was helping an old lady out of my building, and a beam grazed me.'

'Well—' I broke off as a hail of debris came from the building to the left.

Without further conversation, Mel and I crossed the small front yard, skirting fallen bricks, broken glass, and jagged chunks of wallboard. Dusk was coming on fast now; here in the shadows of the leaning buildings it was darker than on the street. I moved toward where the cottage's front door should have been, but couldn't locate it. The windows, with their protruding grillework, were impassable.

I said, 'Is there another entrance?'

'In the back, off a little service porch.'

I glanced to either side. The narrow passages between the cottage and the adjacent buildings were jammed with debris. I could possibly scale the mound at the right, but I was leery of setting up vibrations that might cause more debris to come tumbling down.

Mel said, 'You'd better give it up. The way the cottage looks, I doubt he survived.'

But I wasn't willing to give it up – not yet. There must be a way to at least locate Dan, see if he was alive. But how?

And then I remembered something else from our phone conversations . . .

I said, 'I'm going back there.'

'Let me.'

'No, stay here. That mound will support my weight, but not yours.' I moved toward the side of the cottage before Mel could remind me of the risk I was taking.

The mound was over five feet high. I began to climb cautiously, testing every hand and foothold. Twice jagged chunks of stucco cut my fingers; a piece of wood left a line of splinters on the back of my hand. When I neared the top, I heard the roar of a helicopter, its rotors flapping overhead. I froze, afraid that the air currents would precipitate more debris, then scrambled down the other side of the mound into a weed-choked back yard.

As I straightened, automatically brushing dirt from my jeans, my foot slipped on the soft, spongy ground, then sank into a puddle. Probably a water main was broken nearby. The helicopter still hovered overhead; I couldn't hear a thing above its racket. Nor could I see much: it was even darker back here. I stood still until my eyes adjusted.

The cottage was not so badly damaged at its rear. The steps to the porch had collapsed, and the rear wall leaned inward, but I could make out a door frame opening into blackness inside. I glanced up in irritation at the helicopter, saw it was going away. Waited, and then listened . . .

And heard what I had been hoping to. The music was now Beethoven – his third symphony, the 'Eroica'. Its strains were muted, tinny. Music played by an out-of-area FM station, coming from a transistor radio. A transistor whose batteries were functioning long after the electricity had cut out. Whose batteries might have outlived its owner.

I moved quickly to the porch, grasped the iron rail beside the collapsed steps, and pulled myself up. I still could see nothing inside the cottage. The strains of the 'Eroica' continued to pour forth, close by now.

Reflexively I reached into my purse for the small flashlight I usually kept there, then remembered it was at home on the kitchen counter—a reminder for me to replace its weak batteries. I swore softly, then started through the doorway, calling out to Dan.

No answer.

'Dan!'

This time I heard a groan.

I rushed forward into the blackness, following the sound of the music. After a few feet I came up against something solid, banging my shins. I lowered a hand, felt around. It was a wooden beam, wedged crosswise.

'Dan!'

Another groan. From the floor – perhaps under the beam. I squatted and made a wide sweep with my hands. They encountered a wool-clad arm; I slid my fingers down it until I touched the wrist, felt for the pulse. It was strong, although slightly irregular.

'Dan,' I said, leaning closer, 'it's Sharon, from the hotline. We've got to get you out of here.'

'Unh. Sharon?' His voice was groggy, confused. He'd probably been drifting in and out of consciousness since the beam fell on him.

'Can you move?' I asked.

'. . . Something on my legs.'

'Do they feel broken?'

'No, just pinned.'

'I can't see much, but I'm going to try to move this beam off you. When I do, roll out from under.'

'. . . OK.'

From the position at which the beam was wedged, I could tell it would have to be raised. Balancing on the balls of my feet, I got a good grip on it and shoved upwards with all my strength. It moved about six inches and then slipped from my grasp. Dan grunted.

'Are you all right?'

'Yeah. Try it again.'

I stood, grasped it, and pulled this time. It yielded a little more, and I heard Dan slide across the floor. 'I'm clear,' he said – and just in time because I once more lost my grip. The beam crashed down, setting up a vibration that made plaster fall from the ceiling.

'We've got to get out of here fast,' I said. 'Give me your hand.'

He slipped it into mine – long fingered, work rough-ened. Quickly we went through the door, crossed the porch, jumped to the ground. The radio continued to play forlornly behind us. I glanced briefly at Dan, couldn't make out much more than a tall, slender build and a thatch of pale hair. His face was turned from me, toward the cottage.

'Jesus,' he said in an awed voice.

I tugged urgently at his hand. 'There's no telling how long those apartment buildings are going to stand.'

He turned, looked up at them, said, 'Jesus' again. I urged him toward the mound of debris.

This time I opted for speed rather than caution – a mistake, because as we neared the top, a cracking noise came from high above. I gave Dan a push, slid after him. A dark, jagged object hurtled down, missing us only by inches. More plasterboard – deadly at that velocity.

For a moment I sat straddle-legged on the ground sucking in my breath, releasing it tremulously, gasping for more air. Then hands pulled me to my feet and dragged me across the yard toward the sidewalk – Mel and Dan.

Night had fallen by now. A fire had broken out in the house across the street. Its red-orange flickering showed me the man I'd just rescued: ordinary-looking, with regular features that were now marred by dirt and a long cut on the forehead, from which blood had trickled and dried. His pale eyes were studying me; suddenly he looked abashed and shoved both hands into his jeans pockets.

After a moment he asked, 'How did you find me?'

'I put together some of the things you'd said on the phone. Doesn't matter now.'

'Why did you even bother?'

'Because I care.'

He looked at the ground.

I added, 'There never was any assault rifle, was there?'

He shook his head.

'You made it up, so someone would pay attention.'

'. . . Yeah.'

I felt anger welling up – irrational, considering the present circumstances, but none the less justified. 'You didn't have to frighten the people at the hotline. All you had to do was ask them for help. Or ask friends like Mel. He cares. People do, you know.'

'Nobody does.'

'Enough of that! All you have to do is look around to see how much people care about each other. Look at your friend here.' I gestured at Mel, who was standing a couple of feet away, staring at us. 'He hurt his arm rescuing an old lady from his apartment building. Look at those people over by the burning house – they're doing everything they can to help the firefighters. All over the city people are doing things for one another. Goddamn it, I'd never laid eyes on you, but I risked my life anyway!'

Dan was silent for a long moment. Finally he looked up at me. 'I know you did. What can I do in return?'

'For me? Nothing. Just pass it on to someone else.'

Dan stared across the street at the flaming building, looked back into the shadows where his cottage lay in ruins. Then he nodded and squared his shoulders. To Mel he said, 'Let's go over there, see if there's anything we can do.'

He put his arm around my shoulders and hugged me briefly, then he and Mel set off at a trot.

The city is recovering now, as it did in 1906, and as it doubtless will when the next big quake hits. Resiliency is what disaster teaches us, I guess – along with the preciousness of life, no matter how disappointing or burdensome it may often seem.

Dan's recovering, too: he's only called the hotline twice, once for a referral to a therapist, and once to ask for my home number so he could invite me to dinner. I turned the invitation down because neither of us needs dwell on the trauma of October the seventeenth, and I was fairly sure I heard a measure of relief in his voice when I did so.

I'll never forget Dan, though – or where I was when. And the strains of Beethoven's Third Symphony will forever remind me of the day after which things would never be quite the same again.

A Classic Forgery

ROY VICKERS

INVESTIGATOR FILE

NAME: Fidelity Dove, Avenger

PLACE: London and Swallowsbath

TIME: 1924

CASES: 'The Great Kabul Diamond' (1923), 'The St Jocasta Tapestries' (1924), *The Exploits of Fidelity Dove* (1935) etc.

DOSSIER: The petite, angelic-looking Fidelity Dove was the first female crook-turned-righter-of-wrongs. She was preceded only by the incorrigibly criminal Madame Koluchy, the mastermind in *The Brotherhood of the Seven Kings* (1899), the sinister Madame Sara in *The Sorceress of the Strand* (1903) – both novels by the Victorian authoress, Lillie Meade – and *Lady Méchante* (1909), a confidence trickster who convinced the gullible of Boston that she was in contact with Martians and set up a fake cult in Gelett Burgess's novel. Unlike these female villains, Fidelity has changed from master burglar to avenger of all those who have been cheated or robbed by unscrupulous businessmen and brutal criminals – usually enriching herself in the process. A woman of fragile beauty, with mesmerising violet eyes and a strict moral code, Fidelity has at her beck and call several talented admirers including a scientist, Appleby, and a lawyer, Sir Frank Wrawton. Often her exploits bring her into contact with Detective Inspector

Rason of Scotland Yard, who once referred to her as 'the coolest crook in London', although he now admires her ability to outwit even the cleverest criminals. Fidelity moves easily through fashionable society – invariably dressed in grey to complement her eyes and to reinforce her almost puritanical attitude to life. She is unorthodox in her methods and well deserves the accolade that was given to her by Ellery Queen in 1947, that she 'raised the gentle art of craft and cracksmanship to a new peak'.

CREATOR: Originally published as 'by David Durham', the stories of Fidelity Dove were actually written by Roy Vickers (1889–1965), a former court reporter, magazine editor and prolific writer of sensational, topical and crime fiction novels between the two world wars. He used the Durham pseudonym for a number of his early crime stories and it was not until almost a decade after the launching of the series about the ethereal girl avenger, that his real name appeared on a collected edition of the stories. As well as his pioneer Fidelity Dove exploits, Vickers also created a memorable aged criminal mastermind, Jabez Winterbourne, in *The Gold Game* and *Hide Those Diamonds*, plus thirty-eight highly regarded cases about a fictional branch of Scotland Yard known as the Department of Dead Ends, whose sole purpose was to take on cases that other police detectives had failed to solve. Leading this group of painstaking crime-busters was the selfsame Inspector Rason who had learned his craft in the shadow of Fidelity Dove! Both the policeman and the angelic avenger feature in 'A Classic Forgery' in which a devious property speculator thinks he has got the better of Fidelity. Only *thinks*, that is . . .

***

Fidelity Dove is the only thief in history – if thief we must call her – who can claim to have stolen a landscape. Incidentally, she provided our jurists with an illuminating essay on the jurisprudence of forgery.

The particular landscape she stole was that of Swallowsbath. If you have been there in recent years to admire the richly wooded slopes, the verdant meadows, the quaint old-world cottages, and, above all, the fairy glen where the river comes tumbling down a miniature mountain – know that you would have admired a quarry and a saw-mill if Fidelity hadn't stolen the whole countryside – woods, hills, river, village and meadows.

Fidelity's country seat was – and still is – at Swallowsbath. She has a house and some seven acres. The house is a reproduction of an old Tudor farmhouse. When Fidelity first owned it, it was a genuine Tudor farmhouse but—

It happened like this:

Fidelity had been feeling rather tired and had run down to Swallowsbath for a week's holiday, taking only her aged aunt with her. In the four-mile drive from the station the aunt slept and Fidelity gazed out upon her beloved woods and fields. Her car swung up to the genuine Tudor door of 'The Farm House', and Fidelity helped her aunt tenderly out. As she did so, she saw from the faces of her servants that something was amiss. From their incoherent explanations she gathered that the trouble concerned Swallowsbath.

Fidelity rested, bathed and changed into a grey linen frock with a sunbonnet to match. Then she strolled into the village, which consists, as you know, of some dozen-odd cottages and two very nice hotels, built by architects who knew their job and loved Swallowsbath.

She encountered Mrs Jorman in tears.

'Oh, haven't you heard, missie? It's this Mr Stranack. There's the woods and the fairy glen and the 'otels and the 'ole village. He's bought the 'ole place from his poor lordship and we've all got to be out in three months and the 'otels is to be shut—'

'My poor friend, your troubles oppress you so that they seem to you greater than they are.' Fidelity's wonderful violet eyes were lustrous with sympathy. 'He cannot turn you out of your homes.'

'That's what his lordship's agent said, but he can, all the same,' said Mrs Jorman. 'He's employed every man that owns a house on his quarry over at Inchfield and 'e's found cottages of his own for them which he's built a-purpose, so we've all got to go. I wonder you 'aven't 'eard, miss, because, if George's got it right, 'e's goin' to run 'is own railway through your grounds.'

'I fear George, too, is overweighted with sorrow,' said Fidelity. 'I was not his lordship's tenant. The house and the grounds are my own, and I promise you that no railway shall run through them, Mrs Jorman.'

'Well, that's a comfort, I'm sure,' said Mrs Jorman, brightening somewhat. 'I says to George, I says, "You wait till Miss Dove" – oh lawks, miss, 'ere 'e 'is. No, I don't mean George, missie, I mean – I—'

A yellow sports car with a yellow-liveried chauffeur passed them. Mrs Jorman abjectly curtsied. Fidelity Dove studied the occupant from under the frills of her sunbonnet. The car passed on and half a mile further turned into the drive of Fidelity's own house.

'Mrs Jorman, he has gone to call upon me. Goodbye. I will not fail you – and Swallowsbath.'

Mr Stranack's car was slowly emerging from the gates of the Farm House when Fidelity reached them. Mr Stranack leant over the edge of the tonneau. His hard eyes raked Fidelity's slender grey form.

'Say, d'you know where Miss Dove is?'

'Yes, sir,' said Fidelity, dropping a curtsy.

'Well, where is she? Speak up, I can't hear.'

'I am here, sir,' said Fidelity more meekly than ever.

'Eh, what? You Miss Dove? Beg pardon, I'm sure.' Mr Stranack jerked at his hat and lurched out of the car. 'I've come here in the hope of seeing you, Miss Dove. I'm the new owner of Swallowsbath, as I daresay you've heard by now, and I thought maybe you and I could have a chat with something hanging at the end of it for you.'

'Something for me!' echoed Fidelity wonderingly. 'That is very generous of you, Mr Stranack. Will you come into my poor house?'

Mr Stranack came in. He knew so little of panellings and carvings and apostle spoons and primrose Wedgwood that he was able to go on taking it for granted that Fidelity was a dead farmer's daughter and as simple as her sunbonnet.

'I'm a man of few words, Miss Dove,' he explained. 'I've got the whole country hereabouts with the exception of your land and house. I've got it into my head I'd like to have this too. There, I'm not bluffing you. I've let slip I want it. And now I expect you'll ask me a fancy price.'

Fidelity always thought in lightning flashes. During the dialogue in the drive she had decided upon Mr Stranack's fate. Her face took on an expression almost ethereal in its innocence.

'Fancy price!' she repeated. 'That means more than a thing is worth, does it not? Oh, I could never do such a thing! Do you really think that I would ask more money because you have so frankly revealed to me that your heart is set upon buying my property?'

Mr Stranack looked surprised, then wary, then – after a searching glance – extremely pleased.

'Well – it's very fair of you to take that attitude, I'm sure,' he mumbled. 'Well now, suppose we strike a medium. What do you say to five thousand pounds down for the title deeds?'

Lord Carronmere had sold it to Fidelity for just that sum

– because he knew that she understood Swallowsbath. She could have resold it for double had she wished.

Fidelity's sunbonnet had fallen back. Her pale-gold hair framed her face as though she were a haloed saint. Her voice was liltingly sweet.

'Five thousand pounds! But that is surely too much. I will not take advantage of your generosity, Mr Stranack. You are deliberately offering a higher price because I am a woman. If you really wish to buy my property, the price is three thousand.'

Mr Stranack looked almost frightened. She could see him pinching himself to make sure he was awake. Then he pulled himself together.

'Miss Dove, you're the first lady I've met, or man either, come to that, who hasn't tried to take advantage of me. It's a deal. Well, what about the title deeds? May I send my solicitor round here this evening?'

'Oh, please, no!' begged Fidelity. 'I am so frightened of solicitors – and this is a personal matter between you and me, Mr Stranack. Tomorrow evening, if you will call again, I will hand you the title deeds. Then you can let your solicitor do what is necessary and you yourself can bring the remaining papers to me to sign.'

Mr Stranack agreed. He would have agreed to anything. Fidelity knew that it would be quite unnecessary to caution him to say nothing of the deal until it was over. She spoke instead of the Swallowsbath Young Girls' Guild, in which she was so deeply interested. Their meeting-room, it appeared, required a piano. Mr Stranack, to his own surprise, took out his chequebook and fountain pen and presented the Swallowsbath Young Girls' Guild with fifty pounds for a piano. He made the cheque payable to Fidelity and told himself that he had never seen such eyes.

When he had gone, Fidelity called London, and in half an hour was speaking to Appleby, the scientist, perhaps the most remarkable member of that remarkable band which had given life and honour into her keeping.

'Appleby, my friend, can you perform the marvel of throwing a light through parchment so that it becomes transparent as tissue paper? . . . Then you must come and do it. And bring three of our friends, who are to carry with them those unbeautiful crowbars and blowlamps used by burglars. You will arrive, with all secrecy, at midnight tomorrow.'

At half-past nine on the following evening, Mr Stranack left the Farm House with the title deeds in his pocket of the residence and the seven acres. He was to have them conveyanced and in three days return for Fidelity's signature. Fidelity had been gently averse from undue haste.

At midnight, while Swallowsbath slept, Appleby and three of the gang arrived. Appleby brought with him a framework like a drawing-board and a high-power, portable electric lamp. Varley, Maines and Garfield wielded the unbeautiful implements of the burgling profession.

Fidelity welcomed them and opened to them the secret places of her heart.

On the following day Fidelity, once more alone in the house with her utterly insignificant relative, again called London. This time she rang Scotland Yard.

'Good morning, Mr Rason. Fidelity Dove speaking. I want you to help me.'

There was an astounded silence. Then, 'I've helped you about enough, Miss Dove, I should think,' said Rason, who was great hearted enough to be able to make a joke at his own expense.

'Oh, but this time it is something special!' pleaded Fidelity. 'I'm at my house at Swallowsbath. Last night the house was entered by burglars and my safe was broken. I have not said anything to the local police because I have no real confidence in them. There are only two, and their training—'

'I will come, Miss Dove,' said Rason. He said it with a certain ominousness. Fidelity sighed, and closed her eyes as though in prayer.

Rason arrived in the middle of the afternoon. Fidelity met him at the station and drove him over. Fidelity looked lovely as an angel's dream and Rason, in spite of himself, could not help being conscious of the fact. They spoke of the climate, the country, the crops, and in due course they arrived at the Farm House.

'You will have tea before we begin?' asked Fidelity.

'No, thanks,' said Rason, and Fidelity sighed again.

Fidelity took him to the study, showed him a crudely broken safe, bootprints on the cushions and the regulation paraphernalia of a cumbersome burglary. Rason took in the details in a few minutes. He nodded and grinned.

'Just a little bit overdone, Miss Dove, if I may say so!' he said in the height of good temper. 'Ten years ago those bootmarks on the bow-window seat might have passed muster. But they always brush away that kind of thing nowadays.'

They were alone in the room together.

'Don't be insulted by that, Mr Rason,' begged Fidelity, and her voice was tender as the call of birds in a silvery dusk.

'I'm not insulted,' said Rason, smiling still. 'I take it as a compliment to me that you didn't trouble to do it really well. You knew I'd guess it was a fake robbery, however you did it. The nights and nights I've lain awake thinking of your methods, Miss Dove, have taught me something. You know just how the Department compels me to work, and lay your plans accordingly. You know that the Regulations compel me to treat this as a burglary. That's where you have the pull over us. We're never fighting you brain for brain. We're tied down by the laws of evidence and the rules of the Department. I used to think each time I'd got you. I've learnt something since then – including a proverb about a pitcher going to the well.'

'And when the pitcher is broken, Mr Rason?' The perfect voice lingered on the words.

Rason faltered. There was an odd catch in his own as he replied: 'I don't think of that, Miss Dove. It's my duty to break it.'

'Some tea,' suggested Fidelity again, 'and a taste of honey from my hives.'

'Formalities first,' said Rason. 'I shall get into trouble if I don't go through the whole programme.' He spoke wearily. 'Can you give me a list of the articles you've missed from the safe?'

'Two gold candlesticks, the title deeds of this house and its grounds, an altar cloth worked three hundred years ago in Malines, worth even in worldly value a very great deal, my first copy of the *Pilgrim's Progress* and two miniatures of my grandfather.'

Rason noted the items, a sardonic smile on his face. Then he accepted Fidelity's invitation to tea. Again they talked of climate, cattle and countryside. He returned to London by the last train.

'We shall let you know as soon as we have discovered anything,' said Rason formally as he took his departure.

'I feel sure you are already following an important clue,' murmured Fidelity, and her pale-gold lashes swept her cheek.

Three days later Mr Stranack drove up to the Farm House with a deed of conveyance in his pocket. Fidelity was indisposed. He came again next day. Fidelity was out. He telephoned, and Fidelity answered him mildly.

'I am so sorry!' she crooned. 'But I am afraid I cannot receive you tonight as the vicar is dining with me, and Mr Clarges, the agent. Will you send the documents to me and call for them tomorrow morning? . . . Oh, yes, I quite understand that. I will ask my guests to witness my signature.'

Fidelity had barely replaced the receiver before the vicar arrived. Over dinner the conversation inevitably turned to the imminent destruction of Swallowsbath.

'They say,' said the vicar gloomily, 'that he cannot carry out this nefarious scheme unless he can obtain possession of your property, Miss Dove. I gather that it is required for the purposes of a – er – light railway.'

'He asked me to sell him my home,' said Fidelity. 'And of course, I gave him the only answer one could give. It hurt me to disappoint him – he seemed so downcast – and yet his manner to me is most pleasant.'

'The whole thing is an almost inconceivable catastrophe,' said the agent. 'The woods and the fairy glen!' Words failed him.

'Let us not dread misfortune before it comes,' pleaded Fidelity. 'If it should comfort you, my friends, I will not hesitate to say that deep within me is a feeling that this scourge shall pass and our beautiful countryside be preserved.'

The vicar and the agent, who knew nothing of Fidelity save that she was young and beautiful and loved Swallowsbath as they did, looked appropriately comforted, but wondered what Stranack wanted the light railway for.

At ten o'clock on the following morning Mr Stranack was ushered into the study of the Farm House. Spread out on the Queen Anne escritoire was the conveyance of Fidelity's property to himself.

'Good morning, Miss Dove. You have completed that little matter? Very – ah – very kind of you. Just let me run my eyes over it, will you?'

Mr Stranack ran his eye over the document. It was an expert eye. Fidelity Dove's signature, witnessed by the vicar and the agent, gave a property worth ten thousand in the open market and fifty thousand to him, into his possession for a paltry three thousand. A bit of luck, that, stumbling on such astounding ignorance!

'Ah! That's all correct, I think. It only remains for me to ask you for your receipt for three thousand pounds. I have the money here in notes.'

'I have already written the receipt,' said Fidelity, and handed it to him. He examined the receipt, too, found it satisfactory, and then took out his wallet.

'One, two, three, four of five hundred each – that's two thousand – and one for a thousand. Grand total, three thousand. It's a lot of money, Miss Dove, but there – you might have made me pay another five hundred if you hadn't been a perfect lady.'

'Ah, I have no claims to rank,' said Fidelity with beautiful modesty. 'I attempt only to set an example which I pray may be followed by others.'

'So do I,' said Mr Stranack. 'So do I. Ah, there's just one thing. I daresay you noticed in this little piece of paper here' – Mr Stranack tapped the conveyance – 'that you have given me immediate possession, and – er – have included your furniture and effects in the sale. Now, when would it suit you to move? I'll not press you for a week or two, but I'm going to put my men in the grounds in fourteen days from now.'

'My preparations are made,' returned Fidelity. 'I shall leave tomorrow.'

By the end of the week Mr Stranack had removed the furniture. By the end of the month the house had been destroyed with dynamite and preparations were in full swing for running a light railway through the estate.

About a month after Fidelity had left Swallowsbath with Mr Stranack's notes for three thousand pounds in her deep, grey bag, she was sitting in the inner office of Sir Frank Wrawton, her solicitor, weeping bitterly. She had been weeping bitterly for two or three minutes. Sir Frank was just about to suggest sal volatile when Fidelity became coherent.

'The Farm House!' gasped Fidelity. 'My beautiful house at Swallowsbath!'

'Yes?' asked Sir Frank, trying to see whether Fidelity's eyes were wet; for, more than once lately, his fair client had given him furiously to think. 'Yes? Your house – ?'

'It is destroyed – razed to the ground – men are cutting up my beautiful terraces!'

Sir Frank registered incredulity, then consternation. He pressed for more particulars, but it was no use.

Fidelity could not – or would not – go beyond the bare fact she had stated. Each time she was overcome with emotion. Sir Frank had to conduct her to her car and promise to make immediate investigations.

To say that Sir Frank Wrawton was Fidelity's solicitor is to say that he was a highly competent man.

By lunchtime he was in possession of the fact that Fidelity had sold her property absolutely to Mr Stranack. He had had a conversation with the latter's solicitor, had apologised profusely for his interference and wondered exactly why Fidelity had omitted to mention the trifling fact that she had sold the Farm House, with furniture, effects, and seven acres, all complete. He rang up Fidelity with a view to telling her so.

'But it is untrue!' gasped Fidelity. 'I would not sell that property. I *love* it, if indeed it be not impious to love a property.'

Sir Frank made a noise that might have meant anything.

'Oh, light breaks upon me!' exclaimed Fidelity. 'Do you remember I told you about that burglary? My title deeds were amongst the things stolen. Do you think it possible that that can be the explanation?'

Sir Frank did not think it possible.

'The man who has bought the place is practically a

millionaire,' he explained. 'He has a very large backing. It wouldn't pay him to buy a property without making the fullest investigations as to the authority of the vendor. However, I'll look into the matter. It's certainly a point to take up.'

Sir Frank did not have to look very far in the first instance. Mr Stranack's solicitor, severely puzzled by the turn of events, showed Sir Frank the conveyance of the title deeds and Fidelity's receipt for three thousand pounds.

'Three thousand pounds!' exclaimed Sir Frank. 'She gave five thousand for it, and it was worth ten any day. It's preposterous—'

'That is hardly my affair, Sir Frank,' said the other solicitor. 'The deal was conducted by Mr Stranack personally. I was merely instructed to draw up the conveyance. The – er – morality of the deal is outside my province. You and I both know that the legality is unimpeachable. The money, I understand, was paid in notes. Doubtless my client will have the numbers and I'll ask him for them. Miss Dove must have passed them and that should simplify matters.'

It did not simplify matters. It complicated them. The notes, as far as could be ascertained from Fidelity's bank, had never been passed. The numbers were circulated throughout the clearing houses. Nothing happened.

'Well, in effect it amounts to this,' said Sir Frank to Mr Stranack's solicitor. 'My client denies any knowledge of the deal. In other words, she declares that the signatures to these documents are forgeries. Will you allow her access to them? May I bring her here?'

Fidelity was timidly willing to be brought. When she arrived, a poem in grey and silver, Mr Stranack was discovered to be present also.

'Oh, Mr Stranack!' she cried at sight of him. 'They told me it is *you* who have destroyed my house. Tell me that it is not true. I will never believe it of you.'

'Never believe— What the— You sold the house and grounds to me. What have you got to complain of?' raved Mr Stranack.

Fidelity turned to Sir Frank and clung to his arm.

'He bewilders me,' she faltered. 'He declares that I sold him my property. Can it be that he really believes it?'

Sir Frank stroked his chin. Mr Stranack's legal adviser induced Mr Stranack to resume his chair.

'Look here,' began Mr Stranack when he could speak. 'I came to your house twice. I can prove that.'

'You came on my invitation,' said Fidelity, 'because you were interested in the Swallowsbath Young Girls' Guild. You kindly gave me a cheque on the first occasion – for a piano – and then you came to see—'

'Yes, and I've got that cheque in my pocket with your endorsement on the back of it,' broke out Stranack. 'And I've compared it with your signature on the document. You can't repudiate that.'

Fidelity was shown her signature on the document. She glanced from the conveyance to the receipt. Again she turned to Sir Frank.

'Oh, what can I do?' she sobbed. 'I cannot say that that is not my signature. It seems the same in every particular. Yet I did not sign it. I have never seen those documents before.'

'Very well, then, Miss Dove, you declare them to be forgeries?' asked Sir Frank.

'I fear it must be so,' said Fidelity, and gave a quivering sigh. 'Please take me away.'

Events after that moved quickly. First there were the handwriting experts who photographed the signatures, made lantern slides of them, and examined them on the screen. There were five handwriting experts altogether, and they were unanimous in their verdict. The signature of Fidelity Dove on the deed of conveyance and upon the receipt had been traced. Further, as is common in cases of forgery by tracing, the signature had in each case been traced backwards, the tracer beginning with the 'e' of Dove.

There was a further conclave, in which Fidelity's bank manager figured. He examined Mr Stranack's cheque for fifty pounds which had been endorsed by Fidelity, and gave it as his opinion that the tracing had been made on the endorsement. He supported this theory by pointing to a tiny flourish on the 'y' due, doubtless, to a slip of the pen. This flourish had been faithfully copied on the two documents. In the meantime the vicar of Swallowsbath and the agent had been interviewed and immediately denied ever having witnessed Miss Dove's signature to anything. Weight was given to their denial by the fact that the signatures on the documents in no way resembled the signatures with which they provided the investigator.

Further, in a manner unknown to Mr Stranack and his solicitor, and only guessed at by Sir Frank Wrawton, the newspapers got hold of the full facts and made a sensation of it. The newspapers, of course, were very careful in the matter of libel, but – the facts were the facts. Mr Stranack's open letter to the Press stating that he had paid Miss Dove three thousand pounds in notes for a property admittedly worth more than three times that amount, did not improve matters for him. Mr Stranack did not attempt to explain why, on the evidence of the bank, Miss Dove had never passed the notes he stated he had paid her.

'Where are the missing notes?' demanded the *Evening Record*, growing bolder than the rest. 'Mr Stranack has favoured the Press with their numbers, together with the request for our assistance in finding them. Mr Stranack may have all the assistance he requires from ourselves if he will allow a *Record* man to search his London house.'

Mr Stranack, breathing actions for libel, allowed a *Record* man to search his London house. The *Record* man, acting, it must be admitted, on the strength of an anonymous telephone message, found the notes for three thousand, bearing the published numbers, behind the skirting-board in Mr Stranack's dining-room.

When this was added to evidence provided by Scotland Yard that a burglary had been committed at Miss Dove's house from which, amongst other things, her title deeds had been stolen, the case was now complete against Mr Stranack of having caused to be stolen the title deeds of the said property, of ordering an innocent solicitor to make a deed of conveyance in respect thereof, and of forging the signature of Miss Dove and two witnesses. No one would believe that he was interested in Swallowsbath Young Girls' Guild, and the trifling cheque was taken as a trick for obtaining Fidelity's signature.

After the discovery of the notes, Sir Frank Wrawton received a guarded intimation that while Mr Stranack refused to admit Miss Dove's statement, he was in the circumstances prepared to discuss the question of compensating her, for the injury she believed herself to have suffered at his hands.

Fidelity was late for the conference which was to be held at Sir Frank Wrawton's office. When she came in, Sir Frank, Stranack's solicitor and Detective Inspector Rason simultaneously arose. Mr Stranack himself remained seated.

Mr Stranack's solicitor opened the proceedings.

'Madam, my client is of the opinion that the rumour that you intended to take criminal proceedings against him—'

'Pah!' came in an explosion from Mr Stranack. 'You can drop that punk. I've been done brown by a crook and *she's* the one criminal proceedings ought to be taken against.'

The others protested, but Mr Stranack roared on.

'Think I don't know a plant when it's built round me? Who robbed that safe? You yourself, you – Miss Dove – ask the detective. Who traced the signature on the receipt and the deed? You yourself – from the endorsement of my cheque for fifty pounds that you wheedled me into giving you for some tomfool guild. Who planted the notes in my house? One of your burglar pals. Ask the detective again.'

'The place to ask the detective questions of that nature, Mr Stranack,' put in Sir Frank, 'is the witness box in the prosecution of Miss Dove for conspiracy.'

'Mush! Think I don't know that? Think she'd be here if she didn't know she'd got me? That I'm dead certain to be convicted of forgery and arson and a few other trifles if I go into court? As for that detective – I don't mean him no harm, he was the one to put me wise – but it's all punk about a prosecution. I've simply got to listen here and find out how much I've got to pay to get out of it.'

Fidelity looked with the eyes of a pitying, forgiving saint at the man who had evicted the tenantry of Swallowsbath and proposed to scar the countryside for the purpose of gain. Then she touched her eyelids with a wisp of lace and spoke brokenly: 'Sir Frank, you could have protected me from insult. Why did you allow me to come here? But oh! how I grieve for this unhappy man.'

'Play-acting!' shouted Stranack. Then, more hastily, as Fidelity moved towards the door: 'What are you going to do, Miss Dove?'

'I can do nothing. The police are here.' She gave a little bow to Rason. 'I know nothing of the law – but surely, Sir Frank, it is now impossible for me to arrest the hand of Justice?'

'I think Sir Frank will bear me out,' put in Mr Stranack's solicitor, 'when I say that the whole case turns upon your view of the matter, Miss Dove. If you are prepared to accept my client's assurance that he knows nothing of all this – that some preposterous chain of accidents has enmeshed him—'

'Ah, but Mr Warne,' returned Fidelity earnestly, 'does he believe that in his heart?'

Sir Frank caught Rason's eye. Both men looked away with shaking shoulders.

'Well, then, I say this,' sneered Stranack. 'The whole thing is my fault. I was careless. I bought the title deeds from burglars who assured me that your signature was appended. I ought to have taken steps to verify your willingness to deal, but I did not. I gave orders for the demolition of your property. I am sincerely sorry and I beg you to allow me to compensate you.'

Mr Stranack spoke with a virulent irony which clearly proclaimed that he did not believe a word of what he was saying.

'That alters the case, does it not, Sir Frank?' asked Fidelity. 'I would not like to be the means of any fellow creature going to prison. We must not turn our backs upon those who come to us in true penitence.'

'My client offers ten thousand pounds,' said the solicitor.

'That is, roughly, the market value of the property,' said Sir Frank, who had recovered his outward composure. 'It is no offer of moral compensation.'

'Moral compensation,' said Fidelity with a soft upward look which Rason appeared to have seen before. 'I had not thought of that. What moral compensation can there be for the destruction of a thing of beauty? Ah, you cannot pay for that with mere money, Mr Stranack. You can only replace a thing of beauty with another thing of beauty. Can you do this, think you?'

'Oh, yes, I can do it. I'll give you the whole of my title deeds for Swallowsbath – timber rights and the houses and hotels and everything, if you like!' said Mr Stranack, emphasising his own ponderous irony with tremendously hollow laughter.

'That would seem to me true repentance,' said Fidelity with an exalted smile. 'I accept your offer—'

'*What*? D'you think I was serious?' bellowed Mr Stranack, precipitating himself out of his chair.

'You were *joking* on such a subject?' said Fidelity. There was a hushed reproof in every word.

'*Of course* I was joking – if you call it a joke! Do you really think I would be such an imbecile—'

'You were joking,' sighed Fidelity. 'Your heart is hardened and you seek but to deceive me with talk of repentance. You have destroyed my power to help you. Detective Inspector Rason, do your duty.'

'I was joking again,' said Mr Stranack in weak falsetto. 'I meant you to have – the whole – of – Swallowsbath.'

'I do not understand your humour, Mr Stranack,' said Fidelity. 'But it is not for me to deride the mentality of a fellow creature. If you mean what you say, Sir Frank Wrawton will arrange the – er – conveyancing, as I think it is called.'

'Oh, yes, that's what it's called,' moaned Mr Stranack. Fidelity shook her head over him and left the room.

Mr Stranack unbuttoned his waistcoat. The others looked alarmed. but Mr Stranack, when he spoke, spoke mildly – one might almost say reverently.

'I take off my hat to that woman,' he said. 'A thing of beauty – which no mere money can square. In *mere money* I paid thirty-five thousand for Swallowsbath. In *mere money* those two hotels, of which she'll have complete possession, yield a net profit of eight thousand three hundred per annum. The rent roll—'

Mr Stranack's voice trailed off into nothingness.

The Adventure of the Abergavenny Murder

SIR ARTHUR CONAN DOYLE

INVESTIGATOR FILE

NAME: Sherlock Holmes, Consulting Detective

PLACE: London and Wales

TIME: *circa* 1910

CASES: *A Study in Scarlet* (1887), *The Adventures of Sherlock Holmes* (1892), *The Hound of the Baskervilles* (1902), *The Case Book of Sherlock Holmes* (1927) etc.

DOSSIER: The tall, lean, hook-nosed Sherlock Holmes with his deerstalker and Inverness cape was the world's first consulting detective – a man so famous that readers all over the world believe he actually exists and have made his home at 221B Baker Street in London a place of pilgrimage. Admired for his intellect, powers of deduction and scientific knowledge, Holmes is a first-class athlete, enthusiastic violin player, and noted also for his moods and his not infrequent use of cocaine. A restless and excitable man, he owes much of his stability to his friend and companion, Dr John H. Watson, a practising GP of great loyalty and common sense. Although often teased by Holmes and left amazed at his deductions, the good doctor is not above questioning his methods. According to the canon of stories, Holmes was born in

1854, solved his first case while still a student at Oxford, and then set himself up as a consulting detective in Baker Street in 1881. Here for almost a quarter of a century – interrupted only by a hiatus of three years as a result of certain events at the Reichenbach Falls – he used his scientific equipment, library of reference works and commonplace books, in conjunction with his exceptional powers of reason to reassure potential clients before setting out on his cases. Ultimately, Holmes retired to Sussex to raise bees, and there, with a single brief foray just before the First World War, he has remained, his fame ensured by the constant reprinting of his exploits plus many film and television adaptations of the stories so faithfully recorded by Dr Watson.

CREATOR: Sir Arthur Conan Doyle (1859–1930) changed detective story history with the creation of Sherlock Holmes, who was partly based on his Edinburgh tutor, Dr Joseph Bell, and a fair mixture of his own convictions and interests. His medical knowledge, love of unravelling mysteries and his brilliant idea of creating a central figure to run through all his stories, helped to establish a benchmark for all those who followed in the genre. Conan Doyle was a supreme storyteller and few other writers have so evocatively captured the language and times of Victorian London, with its gaslit streets and hansom cabs. He has also been credited with creating arguably the first hardboiled detective – the tough, wisecracking, resourceful Birdy Edwards, the American undercover Pinkerton operative who is involved in Holmes's case of *The Valley of Fear*, published in 1915, almost a decade before the official 'birth' of the genre in America. (Curiously, Dashiell Hammett, one of the founding fathers of the hardboiled genre was, of course, a Pinkerton operative before he became a writer.) Mystery also surrounds this next item – the outline for a Sherlock

The Adventure of the Abergavenny Murder

Holmes story which Conan Doyle never completed. The text was found in manuscript after the author's death by his biographer, Hesketh Pearson, and it is assumed that he either mislaid it or decided against using the plot. The title has been ascribed to it from a remark by Dr Watson and it is here appearing in print for the first time in almost half a century.

***

A girl calls on Sherlock Holmes in great distress. A murder has been committed in her village – her uncle has been found shot in his bedroom, apparently through the open window. Her lover has been arrested. He is suspected on several grounds:

(1) he has had a violent quarrel with the old man, who has threatened to alter his will, which is in the girl's favour, if she ever speaks to her lover again.

(2) a revolver has been found in his house, with his initials scratched on the butt, and one chamber discharged. The bullet found in the dead man's body fits this revolver.

(3) he possesses a light ladder, the only one in the village, and there are the marks of the foot of such a ladder on the soil below the bedroom window, while similar soil (fresh) has been found on the feet of the ladder.

Notwithstanding these damning proofs, however, the girl persists in believing her lover to be perfectly innocent, while she suspects another man, who has also been making love to her, though she has no evidence whatever against him, except that she feels by instinct that he is a villain who would stick at nothing.

Sherlock and Watson go down to the village and inspect the spot, together with the detective in charge of the case. The marks of the ladder attract Holmes's special attention. He ponders – looks about him – inquires if there is any place where anything bulky could be concealed. There is – a disused well, which has not been searched because apparently nothing is missing. Sherlock, however, insists on the well being explored. A village boy consents to be lowered into it, with a candle. Before he goes down Holmes whispers something in his ear – he appears surprised. The boy is lowered and, on his signal, pulled up again. He brings to the surface a *pair of stilts*!

'Good Lord!' cries the detective. 'Who on earth could have expected this?'

'I did,' replies Holmes.

'But why?'

'Because the marks on the garden soil were made by two perpendicular poles – the feet of a ladder, which is on the slope, would have made depressions slanting towards the wall.'

(N.B. The soil was a strip beside a gravel path on which the stilts left no impression.)

This discovery lessened the weight of the evidence of the ladder, though the other evidence remained.

The next step was to trace the user of the stilts, if possible. But he had been too wary, and after two days nothing had been discovered. At the inquest the young man was found guilty of murder. But Holmes is convinced of his innocence. In these circumstances, and as a last hope, he resolves on a sensational stratagem.

He goes up to London, and returning on the evening of the day when the old man is buried, he and Watson and the detective go to the cottage of the man whom the girl suspects, taking with him a man whom Holmes has brought from London, who has a disguise which makes him the living image of the murdered man, wizened body, grey shrivelled face, skull-cap, and all. They have also with them, the pair of stilts. On reaching the cottage, the disguised man mounts the stilts and stalks up the path towards the man's open bedroom window, at the same time crying out his name in a ghastly sepulchral voice. The man, who is already half mad with guilty terrors, rushes to the window and beholds in the moonlight the terrific spectacle of his victim stalking towards him. He reels back with a scream as the apparition, advancing to the window, calls in the same unearthly voice, 'As you came for me, I have come for you!' When the party rush upstairs into his room he darts to them, clinging to them, gasping, and pointing to the window, where the dead man's face is glaring in, shrieks out, 'Save me! My God! He has come for me as I came for him.'

Collapsing after his dramatic scene, he makes a full confession. He has marked the revolver, and concealed it where it was found – he has also smeared the ladder-foot with soil from the old man's garden. His object was to put his rival out of the way, in the hope of gaining possession of the girl and her money.

Raffles and the Dangerous Game

BARRY PEROWNE

INVESTIGATOR FILE

NAME: A. J. Raffles, Gentleman Cracksman

PLACE: London

TIME: *circa* 1910

CASES: *The Amateur Cracksman* (1899), *A Thief in the Night* (1905), *Raffles in Pursuit* (1934), *Raffles Revisited* (1974) etc.

DOSSIER: The handsome and debonair A. J. Raffles has been described as the first and greatest of the crime anti-heroes. Introduced initially as the most accomplished cracksman in Victorian England who lives a totally hedonistic existence and survives solely by his remarkable skill as a robber, he had by the time of the Edwardian era become more socially aware, committing crimes to right injustice and with little thought for personal profit. A figure of great charm and wit, Raffles first turned to crime as a penniless and desperate young man, and soon discovered that burglary gave him a tremendous thrill. By day a social butterfly and outstanding cricketer, the cracksman uses his personality to gain entrance to the world of high society and there plans the many audacious thefts and robberies which he carries out with great coolness and without attracting the slightest suspicion. His façade as a pillar of society is reinforced by living in The Albany, one of the most exclusive addresses in

London, where he maintains a luxurious lifestyle aided by Bunny Manders, a former schoolfriend he rescued from penury and who is privy to his secret life. Following the death of Raffles's creator in 1921, he was revived by another writer, now a reformed character and more of a two-fisted adventurer. His lifestyle and manners are still the same, however, as is his relish for danger.

CREATOR: Ernest William Hornung (1866–1921) was the brother-in-law of Sir Arthur Conan Doyle, and in the wake of the success of the Sherlock Holmes stories, dreamed up Raffles as the antithesis of the great detective. So popular did the cracksman become, that after Hornung's premature death his executors gave permission for the British mystery novelist Philip Atkey (b. 1908), writing as Barry Perowne, to continue his exploits in *The Thriller* and subsequently in *Ellery Queen's Mystery Magazine*. The Raffles legend has, of course, also been enhanced by a number of very successful stage plays, films and TV adaptations, where he has been played by John Barrymore, Ronald Colman and David Niven amongst others. Perowne is regarded by critics as one of the few writers to have continued the adventures of a famous literary figure as successfully as the original author. 'Raffles and the Dangerous Game' was published in 1979 and finds him in Edwardian London facing an encounter with one of his most sinister adversaries, the Tarantula . . .

* * *

All of a sudden, in the fog that blanketed London one midwinter evening, the tall figure of a policeman loomed up at a street corner and, waving a red lantern, brought a hansom jingling to a standstill.

'Sorry, gentlemen,' he told the passengers, who happened to be A. J. Raffles and myself, Bunny Manders, 'this street is closed.'

I had spent the past couple of hours watching Raffles win his match in a tennis tournament in progress at Lord's Cricket Ground, where the building which houses the court for the gentlemanly game of 'real' tennis, or *jeu-de-paume*, is for a spectator about the chilliest place in town.

So, being anxious to thaw myself out with a rum toddy or two at my flat, where Raffles would drop me off on the way to his own bachelor chambers in The Albany, I protested to the bobbie.

'But look here,' I said to him, 'this is Mount Street. I live in this street.'

'Well, sir,' he replied, 'there's been a gas explosion in a house along there on the left.'

'You describe, more or less,' I said, startled, 'the area where *I* live! Raffles, if you'll excuse me—'

Leaving him to pay off the cabbie, I sprang out of the hansom and, breaking into a run along Mount Street, saw above the roof of some house ahead a dull red glow pulsing in the fog. The glow faded out as I arrived upon the scene, but the gabled roof from which clouds of smoke and steam were now billowing up was that of the very house in which I had my domicile.

I stopped dead, incredulous. The windows of the flat on the top floor, the fourth, and of my own flat on the third floor, were shattered, and a brass-helmeted, thigh-booted fireman was in the act of clambering from a ladder into my living-room.

'Mr Manders!' a voice called to me.

I looked round. Firemen's lanterns and the lamps of three Fire Brigade vehicles, one of them of the new horseless type, pallidly mitigated the fog, and I saw that the man who had called to me was Hobday, the hall porter of the house. He was talking to three of the residents.

'Who would have thought it?' said Hobday, as I went over to him. 'A gas explosion in *Mount* Street, sir! In the top flat, it was – Major Torrington's, just above yours, Mr Manders. The Major was out at the time – still is.'

'Luckily for him,' said Charles Chastayne, who occupied the other flat on my floor. A typical man-about-town, who played cards in the best clubs and probably, I suspected, derived his income from it, he was in evening dress, his cape and silk hat blotched with some sort of white stuff. 'I'd only just come in, Manders,' he told me, 'when the big bang shook the whole house.'

'Anyone hurt?' asked Raffles, who had joined us.

'No, sir,' said Hobday. 'I had my hands full getting Lady Davencourt an' her marmosets out of her first-floor flat, into a cab an' off to her sister's. But, my word, I was worried about Miss Van Heysst here, who's unfamiliar with the premises as yet. It was lucky a few lights stayed on for a minute or two, or she mightn't 'ave found her way out, plunged in the dark, an' come over panicky, bein' foreign.'

'I do not at all panic in the least, Mr Hobday – *though foreign*,' said Miss Marika Van Heysst, whose accent was as charming as her person and who had moved recently into the flat below mine. 'Only, see now how it is with us! We have run out safely, yes, but the firemen say we cannot go back in. We say, for how long? They only shake their heads. So we are become refugees in the fog, and your London fog is so *cooold*!'

She drew more closely about her a cloak like Red Riding Hood's, but Miss Van Heysst's cloak, its hood framing her enchanting young face and flaxen hair, was as blue as her forlorn, appealing eyes.

'You make a sensible point, Miss Van Heysst,' agreed the man who occupied the other flat on her floor. A handsome naval officer with a staff job at the Admiralty, he was in uniform, his cap and greatcoat marred here and there with white smears. 'Since we're not allowed back in the house,' he said, 'there's no point in our standing here in the cold. Miss Van Heysst, may I suggest that I seek a cab for you and escort you to a hotel I know of?'

'Oh, Commander Rigby, that would be kind, for if I am lost in the fog alone and meet with your Jack the Ripper, then yes, I panic very much – being foreign,' said Miss Van Heysst, with a flash of her lovely eyes at Hobday as she accepted Clifford Rigby's proffered arm and went off with him into the fog.

'You can trust the Navy with a pretty young woman,' said Chastayne, the cardplayer. 'Or can you?' He shrugged cynically. 'No business of mine. I must go and find somewhere to pig it temporarily myself. Good night, Manders.'

Only then, as Chastayne left us, did it dawn on me that the white smears on his evening cape and on Rigby's greatcoat must have been caused by ceiling plaster falling when the explosion shook the house – and a sudden thought threw my mind into a cerebral commotion.

'Raffles,' I blurted, 'I'll just pop up to my flat – see the damage.'

He gripped my arm, restraining me. 'Nonsense, Bunny, you won't be allowed in. You can have my spare room in The Albany. I take it your goods and chattels are insured, so you've nothing to worry about.'

But I knew otherwise – knew it so damnably well that I did not sleep a wink in his spare room and, while still the lamps were dim yellow blurs in the murk of what passed for dawn, I inserted my key into the front-door lock of the now silent house in Mount Street.

In the dark hall I stood listening. All was still. I struck a match. The light quivered on the walls of the water-drenched, chaotic hall. On a coffer stood a candelabrum with three unused candles in it. Their wicks spluttered wetly but finally lit and, my heart thumping, I stole up the stairs.

The sodden carpet was blotched with plaster-white bootprints all the way up to the second floor, where my candles showed the landing littered with chunks, still wet, of lath-and-plaster. The ceiling must have come down at the moment of the explosion, and down with the ceiling must have come a package of mine – a package so private that, under a sawn section of floorboard in a corner of my living-room immediately above this landing, I had kept the package hidden on the laths between the floor-beams. I peered up, holding my candles higher, and their light showed me the exposed floor-beams and, dangling down from a hole between them, a corner of my water-soaked carpet.

My package must have fallen, with the lath-and-plaster, on to this second-floor landing. I searched vainly through the debris lying here, then crept on up to my living-room, which was a shambles, and checked the hole from above. But there was no possible doubt about it. My package was gone.

I slunk out of the house. I had rather have blown out my brains than tell Raffles what I had now to tell him, but I forced myself to walk back to The Albany, where I found him at breakfast in his chambers.

The lights were on, a coal fire burned cheerfully in the grate, and Raffles, immaculate in tweeds, a pearl in his cravat, his keen face tanned, his dark hair crisp, looked up from *The Times* propped against the coffee pot.

'Chafing-dishes on the sideboard, Bunny. Ring for more toast.'

'I don't want any,' I said. I sat down. 'Raffles, I've had a shock. Due to that damned explosion last night, some private papers of mine have – gone astray. They were wrapped in a yellow silk muffler patterned with red *fleurs-de-lys*, the package tied with cord, the knot sealed with red wax.'

'A colourful package, Bunny, and valuable-looking. Some fireman at work in your flat has probably spotted the package and taken charge of it for you. What *are* these papers – or are they so private you'd rather not tell me?'

'I'd rather not tell you,' I said, 'but I must. Raffles, you know that ever since we were at school together I've had a sort of – well, a compulsion to write? If one has that sort of compulsion, one naturally writes about things that have made a strong impression on one's mind. Somehow, writing them down is the only way one can get them *off* one's mind – especially if they're things it would be suicide to talk about to other people. So these private writings of mine are accounts, no names, or details changed or omitted, of some – recent experiences of ours.'

'*Ours?*'

'Raffles,' I muttered, 'that package contains full accounts of six of our – criminal adventures.'

Silence. Only the rustle of the fire in the grate, the quiet ticking of the clock above it. Then I heard Raffles cross to the fireplace. I thought it was to get the poker, and my scalp tingled in anticipation of a terminal impact upon it. But he was only lighting a cigarette with a spill. I sensed him standing there on the hearthrug, his grey eyes looking down at me, studying me with a clinical detachment. At last he spoke, his tone even.

'I now know, Bunny,' he observed, 'why it's said, of people with the strange compulsion to write, that they've been "bitten by the tarantula".'

He asked me then for further details, and I explained that the package, which did not have my name on the outside, must have been found on the second-floor landing.

'Raffles,' I said, 'your cricket's made your name very well known. If whoever's found that package opens it to see whom it belongs to, and sees your name in a criminal context on every page of those manuscripts, the finder may hand them to the police!'

'Who, if they once start inquiries,' Raffles said, 'could be a bit awkward.'

'We must get out of the country – immediately!'

'And, not knowing whether the police have or have not got that package, have to spend the rest of our lives in Callao?'

'Why Callao, Raffles?'

'Because, as the famous rhyme says, Bunny: "Under no condition is extradition allowed from Callao"! No, we've got to try to trace your package. It may be unopened. We'd better not make overt inquiries in person. I'll get Ivor Kern, our invaluable "fence", to put some of his snoops on to this. Take a room at your club, Bunny. A red light glows for us in the fog. If the light should glow redder still, I'll get word to you. Meantime, keep a suitcase packed handy for instant travel.'

All the things in my flat had been ruined by water from firehouses. I had to buy a suitcase and new togs. And towards the end of a week of torturing suspense, I returned to my club after a fitting at my tailor's and was told that Raffles was waiting for me in the Hastings Room.

I hared up the handsome marble staircase and found Raffles, alone except for a whisky and soda, sitting in a saddlebag chair under a dismal great painting, *The Trial of Warren Hastings*.

'Well, Bunny,' Raffles greeted me, 'we've had a communication.'

'From the police?'

'No,' said Raffles. 'From the Tarantula.'

He handed me a large envelope, which had been

opened, and with shaking hands I drew out the contents – about forty pages of my own handwriting, held together with a paper clip.

'One of your six manuscripts,' Raffles said. 'Came in my mail this morning. No message with it. None needed. The sender holds five more of your writings. This one, obviously, is to serve notice on us.'

'Notice?'

'Of the Bite To Come,' Raffles said.

It came three agonising days later. It was another of my manuscripts. Raffles showed it to me in the Hastings Room. Attached to the manuscript was a typewritten message: 'To A. J. Raffles, Esq: There now remain in the hands of the present writer four further manuscripts from the pen of your confederate, the ineffable Manders.

'To hand these manuscripts to Scotland Yard, and so end the career of an individual who, little suspected of being a criminal, frequents high social and sporting circles, would be less to the purpose of the present writer than to exchange the manuscripts in return for services rendered.

'Here, Mr Raffles, is the particular service required of you:

'Sir Roderick Naismith, a pillar of the British Treasury, frequently has with him, when he leaves his office in the evening, a small dispatch case. Invariably is this so on Friday evenings, when no doubt his dispatch case contains matter for study in his Hampstead home over the weekend.

'In winter, however, Sir Roderick does not go directly home, but proceeds in a cab to Lord's Cricket Ground, where, at six-thirty on Friday evenings, he exercises himself at the aristocratic game of "real" tennis.

'To you, Mr Raffles, a familiar of that exclusive haunt of the nobility and squirearchy, the building which houses the "real" tennis court at Lord's, an opportunity to acquire Sir Roderick's dispatch case should readily present itself.

'On Friday evening, therefore, you will obtain that dispatch case. You will then return to your chambers in The Albany, where, it has been ascertained, the window of your chambers at the rear of the building overlooks Vigo Street. You will place in that window of yours, as a signal that the service has been duly rendered, a reading-lamp with a green shade. You will then receive, by second post the following day, instructions regarding arrangements for the exchange of Sir Roderick's dispatch case in return for your confederate's manuscripts.

'Failure on your part to carry out the specified service will result in the delivery of your partner's manuscripts to Scotland Yard.'

'Oh, dear God!' I said.

'Sir Roderick Naismith's match at Lord's on Friday evening,' Raffles said, 'is one in the intermediate stages of the tennis tournament. He'll be playing against a distinguished soldier, a Field Marshal – Kitchener of Khartoum.' Raffles's eyes glittered. 'Bunny, the Tarantula – so to call that unknown person – has made a significant slip in this missive, a slip that may well indicate a curious element in this whole situation. The ball's now in my court – and I intend to play it.'

'How?'

'By doing, more or less, as the Tarantula demands,' Raffles said. 'But, Bunny, I think you'd do well to keep out of this from here on.'

'I got you into the situation,' I said, 'and I damned well intend to see it through with you – come what may.'

He raised his glass to me.

So the following evening, Friday, found us arriving together, in one of those taximeter-cabs currently challenging the supremacy of London's hansoms and 'growlers', at Lord's, the headquarters of world cricket.

The stands and terraces, gaily stippled in summer with the confetti hues of men's blazers and ladies' parasols, loomed now deserted, spectral in the persistent fog. Only from the tennis-court building, in its secluded corner of the famous demesne, did gleams of gaslight faintly mitigate the dank, muffling vapour.

Capped and ulstered, we entered the building. Just inside the entrance stood a glass case. In this was housed the token trophy of the tournament – token only, as it was one of the priceless treasures at Lord's and never left the ground. Warped, time blackened, worm eaten, the long-handled, curved, stringless old racquet in the glass case was a reminder of that long-ago day when a monarch of France had presented to a monarch of England, as they met in conclave among the pennoned pavilions and glittering shields and lances of the armoured chivalry of both nations, on a French meadow, a gift of tennis balls.

Now, from the unseen court to our left, sounded hollow thuds and bangs, and from the changing-room, to our right, emerged a wiry man carrying a huge basket loaded to the brim with tennis balls of a type little changed since that far-off day of the two monarchs.

'Evening, Mole,' said Raffles.

'Good evening, Mr Raffles,' said Mole, the resident professional. 'Come to see the match? Lord Kitchener and Sir Roderick Naismith are in the court now, warming up. I'm just going in to mark for them.'

He went off with his heavy basket, and Raffles strolled over to the door of the changing-room, glanced in casually, then returned to me.

'Just three men in there, Bunny,' he murmured. 'Let's hope they decide presently to watch the match. Meantime, we'll watch it ourselves.'

Gripping my arm, he opened a door to the left, closed it behind us, and in the almost total darkness of the restricted space for spectators steered me to the rearmost of a half-dozen spartan benches. Through the interstices of a protective net I saw the reflector-shaded, wire-caged gaslights which from aloft shed down their brilliance solely on to the court proper, a stylised version of a barnyard of some ancient abbey in the Avignon of Pope Joan, or Cahors of the turreted bridge, or grey-walled Carcassonne of the many candlesnuffer towers.

But whereas medieval monks, banging balls at each other across a net slung between the monastery cow byre and the barn wall, had played this tennis stripped to their hairshirts, the two gentlemen now in the court here – one of the only eight such courts in England, including Henry VIII's at Hampton Court – were in white flannels and sweaters.

'In these troubled times, Bunny,' Raffles murmured, 'when a European monarch's keeping half of the world nervous by his rapid expansion of his High Seas Fleet, it's good to see Kitchener looking fit.'

I nodded, my gaze on the powerful figure, granite jaw, heavy moustache, and challenging steel-blue eyes of the great soldier, with whom the distinguished senior civil servant, gaunt, grey-haired, shrewd-faced Sir Roderick Naismith of the Treasury, markedly contrasted.

From the marker's niche to the left of the court, where a section of penthouse roof simulated the eaves of a cow byre, Mole appeared, carrying his basket of tennis balls, which he emptied into a trough that already contained hundreds. And the match now began, but here in the dark I was trying to discern how many shadowy figures were spaced about on the benches in front of Raffles and myself. There were, as far as I could make out, only about half a dozen spectators – members here, of course – but presently I became aware of three more men quietly entering. Closing the door behind them, they groped their way to the front bench.

Raffles breathed in my ear, 'The three from the changing-room. Sit tight!'

Silent as a ghost, he was gone from my side. I forced myself to keep my eyes on the game. Sir Roderick was serving, sending the ball, struck underhand, sliding along the penthouse roof. The ball, falling at the far end, was emphatically struck back across the centre net by Lord Kitchener. Sir Roderick's return went high, the ball banging hollowly against a piece of wood – shaped like a Gothic arch and simulating a monastery pigeon-cote – on the wall behind Kitchener.

'Fifteen thirty,' chanted Mole, the marker, as the players changed ends. 'Thirty fifteen – chase four.'

The game continued, the players changing ends as service was won or lost. Twanging of racquets, thudding of balls, thumping of plimsolled feet echoed hollowly in the court.

'Better than three,' rang the voice of Mole. 'Deuce!'

Vicariously, I was with Raffles, breaking now into Sir Roderick's locker in the changing-room. Or surprised red-handed at the job? I did not know. Crypt-cold as it was here in the dark, my gloved hands were clammy with sweat. Because I could not keep a pen out of them, Raffles now risked total ruin – and the grim lines of Omar Khayyám rang in my ears: 'The Moving Finger writes, and having writ—'

' 'Vantage,' chanted Mole. 'Game! Game and set to Lord Kitchener!'

The players met in mid-court to mop their faces with towels proffered to them by Mole from his marker's niche between the netted apertures which represented the window-openings of a monastery cow byre. Sir Roderick's pale face looked as cool as ever, but the hero of Khartoum was considerably ruddier as he dried his brow and his heavy great moustache.

'Have at you again, Naismith,' I heard him growl.

'Good-oh, Field Marshal,' said Sir Roderick.

Halfway through the second set, I became aware, with a start, of a shadow at my side. Raffles was back.

Neither of us said a word until the match was over, with victory to Kitchener, and we made our way out from the tennis-court building into the fog shrouding the cricket ground, when I ventured to ask Raffles how he had got on.

'I'll tell you when I've thought it over,' he said. 'Let's see if we can find a cab of some sort. I'm hoping there may be a message for me at The Albany.'

When we reached his chambers and with a match he popped the gas-globe alight, we saw an envelope lying on the doormat. He tore the envelope open, read the message enclosed, thrust it into his ulster pocket.

'From Ivor Kern,' he said. 'Come on, we've a call to make.'

'On Ivor?'

'No, Bunny. On the Tarantula!'

He turned out the gas, hurried me out of the building by the front entrance to Albany Courtyard and Piccadilly, where we were fortunate enough to get a cab, a four-wheeler. Telling the cabbie to drop us at the corner of Church Walk, Kensington, Raffles thrust me into the dark, cold interior of the cab and, as the horse jingled us off westward, gave me a cigarette.

'Now, Bunny,' he said. 'Consider your lost package. On the night of the explosion in the Mount Street house, just three people passed along the second-floor landing in making their hasty exits from the house. Any one of those three could have spotted and snatched up your valuable-looking package – and, oddly enough, when we had our brief conversation with them in the street each of them was wearing a garment which could have concealed the package. Charles Chastayne was in evening-dress – with cape. Miss Van Heysst had thrown on a hooded cloak –

557

as blue as her eyes. Commander Rigby was in uniform, with a deep-pocketed Navy greatcoat.'

A match flared. We dipped our cigarettes to the flame Raffles held in his cupped hands.

'I had Ivor Kern,' he went on, 'set his snoops to find out where those three persons had taken up their respective temporary abodes – and keep an eye on them. Then came the Tarantula's missive – with its significant slip, the reference to the 'the British Treasury'. Any English person would say, simply, 'the Treasury'. So here was a hint that the writer of the Tarantula missive was a foreigner – and one of our three suspects is a foreigner.'

'Miss Van Heysst!'

'Yes, but she couldn't have written the letter, Bunny. Her English is charming, but if she'd written that letter there'd have been more slips, more foreign locutions. No, if it were she who snatched up your package, she must have shown it to someone – the person, a foreigner fluent in English and well informed on English ways and values, who wrote the Tarantula letter. So who – and what – *is* this person with the very sharp bite?'

Our cab was jingling past the muffled gaslamps and flickering fog-flare braziers of Hyde Park Corner.

'And just what,' Raffles said, 'is the youthful, seductive Miss Van Heysst? A new resident, she moves into a flat adjoining that of Commander Clifford Rigby. A gas explosion puts them on the street. At whom, Bunny, was Miss Van Heysst's forlorn plea of fearing to meet Jack the Ripper in the fog subtly directed, and who takes it up with the gallantry to be expected of the Navy and promptly tucks Little Blue Riding Hood under his wing? Commander Rigby. And what, in these times when the clang of shipbuilders' hammers is resounding threateningly to us across the North Sea, is Rigby? He's a naval officer – *with a staff job at the Admiralty.*'

'Oh, dear God!' I said.

'What an adroit little opportunist,' said Raffles, 'is Miss Van Heysst! But, Bunny, though it seemed to me that a curious element was beginning to creep into this matter of your lost manuscripts, it struck me as odd that the Tarantula was anxious to view the documents in a dispatch case of a senior civil servant at the *Treasury*. If the Tarantula is what I was beginning to suspect, it would have been more understandable if the documents he wanted stolen belonged to, say, Field Marshal Lord Kitchener. Why those of a senior civil servant at the *Treasury*? I decided to have a look at Sir Roderick's documents, in the changing-room at Lord's this evening, and find out.'

'And you did?'

'I did,' said Raffles. 'Naturally, I left the documents intact and Sir Roderick's dispatch case and locker relocked. What the Tarantula, as a foreigner, doesn't realise is that a member at Lord's does *not*, however dire his need, rob another member. It's simply not done. But a brief skim through Sir Roderick's documents made all plain to me. He's an impostor.'

'Sir Roderick Naismith an impostor? Raffles, that's incredible!'

'But true, Bunny. He's a senior civil servant, but not at the Treasury. That ostensible occupation of Sir Roderick's is a mask for his real one. He's the head of our Secret Security Service.'

'I never knew we had such a thing!'

'How could you?' said Raffles. 'It's secret.' He peered out into the fog. 'We'll be arriving any minute now,' he said, and he went on, 'I've no doubt now that the Tarantula is a spymaster. He's evidently learned Sir Roderick's real occupation. And what the Tarantula is anxious to find out is whether any of the agents whose activities in this country he directs and controls are under suspicion. And, significantly enough, Bunny, in Sir

Roderick's dispatch case there's a pencilled list of five names, each with some personal particulars noted against them. The list is headed: "For expulsion from England subject to Firm Evidence of Espionage Activity." Among the names is that of Miss Van Heysst of Mount Street. But *not* the name of the Tarantula.'

'You know his name, then?'

'It's in the note I had just now from Ivor Kern,' Raffles said. 'One of his snoops, who'd traced Miss Van Heysst to a respectable hotel, Garland's, near the Haymarket Theatre, was keeping an eye on her. It seems that this afternoon she went, by a circuitous route, to Richmond Park, a place usually deserted on a foggy afternoon. She met a man at the Priory Lane gate, had a brief talk with him. As I'd instructed, any person she met with was to be followed. So Ivor's snoop followed the man. He lives on the first floor of number eight, Church Walk, Kensington. So we're now about to visit him in his spidery lair,' Raffles said, 'and return his Tarantula bite!'

We were, as always, unarmed, and I was taut with apprehension as Raffles paid off our cab at the corner of Church Walk and we walked along that silent side-street. Here and there, dim light from curtained windows faintly blurred the fog.

'Here we are, Bunny,' Raffles said, 'that house with the number barely visible on the front-door fanlight. He's probably in that first floor where faint edges of light show around the window-curtains. No doubt he's waiting impatiently for word from whatever minion he has skulking in Vigo Street, at the back of The Albany, that a green-shaded reading-lamp has appeared at the window of my chambers. H'm! Now, how're we to trap this hairy Tarantula?' Raffles thought for a moment. 'Tell you what, Bunny. We'll get him worried. Got plenty of small change in your pocket?'

'A fair amount, Raffles.'

'Good. Now, I'm going to try that front door. It'll probably be locked, but may not be bolted – in which case the little implement I used on Sir Roderick's locker at Lord's should serve our purpose. If I can get into the house, you keep well back in the fog and toss coins up at that first-floor window. The man's almost certainly armed, so my prudent course will be to steal in on him from behind when his back's turned as he peers out of the window.'

Instantly grasping Raffles' strategy, I whipped off my gloves, took a handful of small change from my pocket as he moved silently up the two steps to the door under the dim fanlight. As I watched his shadowy figure at work on the door, a vertical line of light suddenly appeared there – and vanished instantly as Raffles, entering, soundlessly closed the door.

Drawing back into the fog, I tossed up a coin at the first-floor window. I heard a tinkle against the glass, a second tinkle as the coin dropped down into the railed basement area. No movement of the curtains ensued, so I tossed up another coin – another – and another. Suddenly, the faint lines of light that edged the window-curtains vanished. Drawing back further into the fog, I sensed, my heart thumping, that the curtains had been parted a little and that some evil, spider-like creature, crouching there at the window of the now dark room, was glaring out balefully into the fog.

Listening intently, I heard no sound from within the room, but I saw the light go on again. For a second Raffles showed himself to me between the curtains, then he closed them. I waited, swallowing with a parched throat. It seemed a long wait before the front door of the house silently opened and closed, and Raffles rejoined me.

We picked up a cab in Kensington High Street, and Raffles gave the cabbie an address in Hampstead.

'I'm afraid, Bunny,' he said, 'I had to violate a rule of ours and use a modicum of violence. I banged the Tarantula's head hard against his floor, to stun him while I relit the gaslight he'd turned out. Still, he was beginning to come round as I left. He'll find he's lost your four manuscripts. They were on his desk. Here they are, still loosely wrapped in your yellow silk muffler.

'There was a locked drawer in his desk. The lock presented no problem. So we're richer by about one thousand pounds – spies' wages, I imagine. I also abstracted from the drawer a batch of the Tarantula's papers – which provide, I fancy, all the "firm evidence" Sir Roderick Naismith needs to justify some expulsions from this country. I noticed Sir Roderick's Hampstead address on letters in his document case, at Lord's, so we'll drop these papers he needs through the letterbox, then drive to Piccadilly Circus and see if we can buy a few flowers.'

I was at a loss to divine why he should want flowers at this hour. However, late as it was when we got back from our Hampstead errand and paid off our cab in Piccadilly Circus, we found this hub of London an oasis of activity in the blanketing fog. The theatres and music halls were disgorging their second-house audiences, the gin palaces their inebriates, into the blurred glow from gaslights and the naked flicker of naphtha fog-flares.

Police whistles shrilled above the clip-clop of hoof-beats, harness-jingle of hansoms, fourwheelers, and rumbling omnibuses, and mingled with the honking of occasional taximeter-cabs and the raucous cries of the Piccadilly flower women sitting beside their big baskets at their usual receipt of custom on the steps of the Eros statue.

'Oy, misters, you gents there!' A cheeky-looking wench, much shawled and petticoated, with a feather boa, huge hat bedecked with ostrich plumes, and high-

heeled button boots, brandished a great bunch of chrysanthemums at Raffles and myself. 'Out lyte, you are! Bin
on the spree, you two 'ave! You'd best tyke a few flowers
'ome – beautiful chrysanths, fresh as a dysy – to sweeten
yer little bit o' trouble-an'-strife!'

'On behalf of my friend here,' said Raffles, 'I'll give
you a sovereign for that fine bunch of chrysanthemums,
and if you'd care for an extra half-bar, you can deliver
them for him at your leisure. The place is not far. It's just
off the Haymarket there – a hotel called Garland's. Hand
the flowers in at the desk and say they're for Miss Van
Heysst, as a *bon voyage* gift from A Gentleman of Mount
Street. Are you on?'

'Mister, for an extra 'arf-bar, the w'y tryde's bin
tonight in this bleedin' fog,' said the wench, 'I'd walk as
far as Seven Dials for yer wiv me whole bloody basket!'

So Raffles gave her the extra half-sovereign and,
raising our caps to the wench, we walked across the
misty Circus towards the nearby Albany.

'There are games, Bunny, *and* games,' Raffles
remarked thoughtfully. ' "Real" tennis is an old one, but
espionage is an older one still – and much more
dangerous. As far as women are concerned, only a brave
woman would play it. It's to be hoped that Miss Van
Heysst doesn't continue her activities in the pay of the
Wilhelmstrasse, or – in the troubled state of Europe
today – she may come to a bad end. That would be a
pity, because she's not only an exceptionally attractive
and very young woman, but also a brave one.'

'Yes,' I said.

'So, I think, Bunny,' Raffles said, 'although she was a
fellow resident of yours in Mount Street for only a short
while, it would be nice for her to have a small tribute of
flowers from you, to take with her when Sir Roderick
Naismith has her escorted aboard the Harwich-to-Hook-
of-Holland boat tomorrow. I wish we'd seen more of her.

She's a most interesting person. According to some particulars against her name in Sir Roderick's list, her real surname is Zeller – and she's believed to use aliases other than Van Heysst.'

'Other aliases?' I said.

He nodded.

'One of them, noted against our Little Blue Riding Hood in Sir Roderick's list, is rather striking,' Raffles said. 'Mata Hari.'

The Smashing of Another Racket

LESLIE CHARTERIS

INVESTIGATOR FILE

NAME: Simon Templar, aka the Saint

PLACE: London

TIME: 1933

CASES: *Meet the Tiger* (1928), *The Saint in New York* (1935), *The Saint Sees It Through* (1946), *Trust The Saint* (1962), *Catch The Saint* (1975) etc.

DOSSIER: Simon Templar, who craves excitement and is not above breaking the law to achieve his ends, is known as 'the modernday Robin Hood' and once expressed his philosophy as seeking 'battle, murder and sudden death with plenty of good beer and damsels in distress and a complete callousness about blipping the ungodly over the beezer'. A tall, good-looking and physically very strong man who is well able to take care of himself in a fight, he is accomplished at sports, horse-riding, flying and automobile racing. Invariably well dressed and instantly attractive to women, Templar makes little attempt to disguise his other identity and is famous for leaving his calling card of a little matchstick man with a halo at the scene of a crime, where his actions may be nefarious but his motives are always pure. He dispenses justice in his own style and often brings criminals to book when the law is unable to touch them. Like his predecessor A. J. Raffles, the Saint has kept up with the times, exchanging his beer for a martini, becoming more of an amateur detective pursuing international criminals, and discovering that damsels in distress have been replaced by modern, liberated women.

CREATOR: Leslie Charteris, who has been credited with 'virtually inventing the modern "Gay Desperado" figure', by critic Jack Adrian, was born Leslie Charles Bowyer Yin (1907–93) in Singapore and lived a life almost as cinematic as that of his famous creation – he was a pearl fisher, gold prospector, rubber planter, tin miner, fairground hand and even a policeman before success as a writer turned him into one of the top-selling authors of his times. When he decided to try writing, he took his *nom de plume* from Colonel Francis Charteris, the legendary founder of the infamous Hellfire club; though, by contrast, Yin picked that of the Knights Templar, the warrior knights who protected pilgrims bound for the Holy Land, for his young crime fighter. Not long after the Saint's debut in print in 1928, Simon Templar became a national hero and was soon featured in films and on television, played by actors as different as Louis Hayward, George Saunders, Roger Moore, Ian Ogilvy and, the very latest, Val Kilmer of Batman fame! Amongst the many short stories that Charteris produced about his hero, a group of twenty-five which he wrote especially for *The Empire News* in 1933 are considered to be the very best. Twenty-four of these were later included in collections – with the sole exception of 'The Smashing of Another Racket' from the 5 November issue, which, prior to this reappearance, has only once been reprinted in a magazine in 1960. Why the tale of a fraudulent publisher suffered this fate was never disclosed by the author during his lifetime, and today can only be a matter of conjecture!

The Smashing of Another Racket

Even the strongest men have their weak moments.

Peter Quentin once wrote a book. Many young men do, but usually with more disastrous results. Moreover he did it without saying a word to anyone, which is perhaps even more uncommon; and even the Saint did not hear about it until after the crime had been committed.

'Next time you're thinking of being rude to me,' said Peter Quentin, on that night of revelation, 'please remember that you're talking to a budding novelist whose work has been compared to Dumas, Tolstoy, Conan Doyle, and others.'

Simon Templar choked over his highball.

'Only pansies bud,' he said severely. 'Novelists fester. Of course, it's possible to be both.'

'I mean it,' insisted Peter seriously, 'I was keeping it quiet until I heard the verdict, and I had a letter from the publishers today.'

There was no mistaking his earnestness; and the Saint regarded him with affectionate gloom. His vision of the future filled him with overwhelming pessimism. He had seen the fate of other young men – healthy, upright, young men who had had a book published.

He had seen them tread the downhill path of pink shirts, velvet coats, long hair, quill pens, cocktail parties, and beards, until finally they sank into the awful limbos of Bloomsbury and were no longer visible to the naked eye. The prospect of such a doom for anyone like Peter Quentin, who had been with him in so many bigger and better crimes, cast a shadow of great melancholy across his spirits.

'Didn't Kathleen try to stop you?' he asked.

'Of course not,' said Peter proudly. 'She helped me. I owe—'

'—it all to her,' said the Saint cynically. 'All right. I know the line. But if you ever come out with "My Work" within my hearing, I shall throw you under a bus . . . You'd better let me see this letter. And order me some more Old Curio while I'm reading it – I need strength.'

He took the document with his fingertips, as if it were unclean, and opened it out on the bar. But after his first glance at the letterhead his twinkling blue eyes steadied abruptly, and he read the epistle through with more than ordinary interest.

Dear Sir,

We have now gone into your novel *The Gay Adventurer*, and our readers report that it is very entertaining and ably written, with the verve of Dumas, the dramatic power of Tolstoy, and ingenuity of Conan Doyle.

We shall therefore be delighted to set up same in best small pica type to form a volume of about 320 pp., machine on good antique paper, bind in red cloth with title in gold lettering, and put up in specially designed artistic wrapper, at cost to yourself of only £600 (Six Hundred Pounds) and to publish same at our own expense in the United Kingdom at a net price of 15s. (Fifteen Shillings); and believe it will form a most acceptable and popular volume which should command a wide sale.

We will further agree to send you on date of publication twelve presentation copies, and to send copies for review to all principal magazines and newspapers; and further to pay you a royalty of 25% (twenty-five per cent) on all copies sold of this Work.

The work can be put in hand immediately on receipt of your acceptance of these terms.

Trusting to hear from you at your earliest convenience, We beg to remain, dear Sir, Faithfully yours, for

HERBERT G. PARSTONE & CO

Herbert G. Parstone,
Managing Director.

Simon folded the letter and handed it back with a sigh of relief.

'OK, Peter,' he said cheerfully. 'I bought that one. What's the swindle, and can I come in on it?'

'I don't know of any swindle,' said Peter puzzledly. 'What do you mean?'

The Saint frowned. 'D'you mean to tell me you sent your book to Parstone in all seriousness?'

'Of course I did. I saw an advertisement of his in some literary paper, and I don't know much about publishers—'

'You've never heard of him before?'

'No.'

Simon picked up his glass and strengthened himself with a deep draught.

'Herbert G. Parstone,' he said, 'is England's premier exponent of the publishing racket. Since you don't seem to know it, Peter, let me tell you that no reputable publisher in this or any other country publishes books at the author's expense, except an occasional highly technical work which goes out for posterity rather than profit. I gather that your book is by no means technical. Therefore you don't pay the publisher: he pays you – and if he's any use he stands you expensive lunches as well.'

'But Parstone offers to pay—'

'A twenty-five per cent royalty. I know. Well, if you were something like a bestseller you might get that; but on a first novel no publisher would give you more than ten, and then he'd probably send you a statement showing a sale of two hundred copies, you'd get a cheque from him for thirty-seven pounds ten, and that's the last trace you'd see of your six hundred quid. He's simply trading on the fact that one out of every three people you meet thinks he could write a book if he tried, one out of every three of 'em try it, and one out of every three of those tries to get it published.

'The very fact that a manuscript is sent to him tells him that the author is a potential sucker, because anyone who's going into the writing business seriously takes the trouble to find out a bit about publishers before he starts slinging his stuff around. The rest of his game is just playing on the vanity of mugs. And the mugs – mugs like yourself, Peter – old gents with political theories, hideous women with ghastly poems, schoolgirls with nauseating love stories – rush up to pour their money into his lap for the joy of seeing their repulsive tripe in print. I've known about Herbert for many years, old lad, but I never thought you'd be the sap to fall for him.'

'I don't believe you,' said Peter glumly.

An elderly mouselike man who was drinking at the bar beside him coughed apologetically and edged bashfully nearer.

'Excuse me, sir,' he said diffidently, 'but your friend's telling the truth.'

'How do you know?' asked Peter suspiciously. 'I can usually guess when he's telling the truth – he makes a face as if it hurt him.'

'He isn't pulling your leg this time, sir,' said the man. 'I happen to be a proofreader at Parstone's.'

The surprising thing about coincidences is that they so often happen. The mouselike man was one of those amazing accidents on which the fate of nations may hinge, but there was no logical reason why he should not have been drinking at that bar as probably as at any other hostel in the district. And yet there is no doubt that if Mr Herbert Parstone could have foreseen the accident he would have bought that particular public house for the simple pleasure of closing it down lest any such coincidence should happen; but unhappily for him Mr Herbert Parstone was not a clairvoyant.

This proofreader – the term, by the way, refers to the occupation and not necessarily to the alcoholic content of the man – had been with Parstone for twelve years, and he was ready for a change.

'I was with Parstone when he was just a small jobbing printer,' he said, 'before he took up this publishing game. That's all he is now, really – a printer. But he's going to have to get along without me. In the last three years I've taken one cut after another, till I don't earn enough money to feed myself properly; and I can't stand it any longer. I've got four more months on my contract, but after that I'm going to take another job.'

'Did you read my book?' asked Peter.

The man shook his head.

'Nobody read your book, sir – if you'll excuse my telling you. It was just put on a shelf for three weeks, and after that Parstone sent you his usual letter. That's what happens to everything that's sent in to him. If he gets his money, the book goes straight into the shop, and the proofreader's the first man who has to wade through it. Parstone doesn't care whether it's written in Hindustani.'

'But surely,' protested Peter half-heartedly, 'he couldn't carry on a racket like that in broad daylight and get away with it?'

The reader looked at him with a rather tired smile on his mouselike features.

'It's perfectly legal, sir. Parstone publishes the book. He prints copies and sends them around. It isn't his fault if the reviewers won't review it and the booksellers won't buy it. He carries out his legal undertaking. But it's a dirty business.'

After a considerably longer conversation, in the course of which a good deal more Scotch was consumed, Peter Quentin was convinced. He was so crestfallen on the way home that Simon took pity on him.

'Let me read this opus,' he said, 'if you've got a spare copy. Maybe it isn't so lousy, and if there's anything in it we'll send it along to some other place.'

He had the book next day; and after ploughing through the first dozen pages his worst fears were realised. Peter Quentin was not destined to take his place in the genealogy of literature with Dumas, Tolstoy, and Conan Doyle. The art of writing was not in him. His spelling had a grand simplicity that would have delighted the more progressive orthographists, his grammatical constructions followed in the footsteps of Gertrude Stein, and his punctuation marks seemed to have more connection with intervals for thought and opening beer-bottles than with the requirements of syntax. Moreover, like most first novels, it was embarrassingly personal.

It was this fact which made Simon follow it to the bitter end, for the hero of the story was one 'Ivan Grail, the Robbin Hood of modern crime,' who could without difficulty be identified with the Saint himself, his 'beutiful wife,' and 'Frank Morris his acomplis whos hard-biten features consealed a very clever brain and witt.' Simon Templar swallowed all the flattering evidence of hero-worship that adorned the untidy pages, and actually blushed. But after he had reached the conclusion – inscribed 'FINNIS' in triumphant capitals – he did some heavy thinking.

Later on he saw Peter again.

'What was it that bit your features so hard?' he asked. 'Did you try to kiss an alligator?'

Peter turned pink. 'I had to describe them somehow,' he said defensively.

'You're too modest,' said the Saint, after inspecting him again. 'They were not merely bitten – they were thoroughly chewed.'

'Well, what about the book?' said Peter hopefully. 'Was it any good?'

'It was lousy,' Simon informed him, with the privileged candour of friendship. 'It would have made Dumas turn in his grave. All the same, it may be more readable after I've revised it for you. And perhaps we will let Comrade Parstone publish it after all.'

Peter blinked. 'But I thought—'

'I have an idea,' said the Saint. 'Parstone has published dud books too long. It's time he had a good one. Will you get your manuscript back from him, Peter – tell him you want to make a few corrections, and that you'll send him his money and let him print it. For anyone who so successfully conceals a very clever brain and wit,' he added cruelly, 'there are much more profitable ways of employing them than writing books, as you ought to know.'

For two weeks after that the Saint sat at his typewriter for seven hours a day, hammering out page after page of neat manuscript at astonishing speed. He did not merely revise Peter Quentin's story – he rewrote it from cover to cover, and the result would certainly not have been recognised by its original creator.

The book was sent in again from his own address, and consequently Peter did not see the proofs. Simon Templar read them himself; and his ribs were aching long before he had finished.

The Gay Adventurer, by Peter Quentin, was formally pushed out upon a callous world about two months later. *The Times* did not notice it, the library buyers did not refill their fountain pens to sign the order forms, lynx-eyed scouts of Hollywood did not rush in with open contracts; but nevertheless it was possible for a man with vast patience and dogged determination to procure a copy, by which achievement Mr Parstone had fulfilled the letter of his contract.

Simon Templar did not need to exercise patience and determination to obtain his copy, because the author's presentation dozen came to his apartment; and it happened that Peter Quentin came there on the same morning.

Peter noticed the open parcel of books, and fell on them at once, whinnying like an eager stallion. But he had scarcely glanced over the first page when he turned to the Saint with wrathful eyes.

'This isn't my book at all,' he shouted indignantly.

'We'll call it a collaboration if you like,' said the Saint generously. 'But I thought you might as well have the credit. My name is famous already – '

Peter had been turning the pages frantically.

'But this – this is awful!' he expostulated. 'It's – it's – '

'Of course it is,' agreed the Saint. 'And that's why you must never tell anyone that I had anything to do with it. When the case comes to court, I shall expect you to perjure yourself blue in the face on that subject.'

After the revelations that have been made in the early stages of this story, no one will imagine that on the same morning Mr Herbert Parstone was pacing feverishly up and down his office, quivering with anxiety and parental pride, stopping every now and then to peer at the latest circulation figures rushed in by scurrying office boys and bawling frantic orders to an excited staff of secretaries, salesmen, shippers, clerks, exporters, and truck drivers.

As a matter of fact, even the most important and reputable publishers do not behave like that. They are usually too busy concentrating on mastering that loose shoulder and smooth follow-through which carries the ball well over that nasty bunker on the way to the fourteenth.

Mr Herbert Parstone was not playing golf, because he had a bad cold; and he was in his office when the Saint called. The name on the card that was sent in to him was unfamiliar, but Mr Parstone never refused to see anyone who was kind enough to walk into his parlour.

He was a short ginger-haired man with the kind of stomach without which no morning coat and gold watch-chain can be seen to their best advantage; and the redness of his prominent nose was not entirely due to his temporary affliction.

'Mr Teblar?' he said, with great but obstructed geniality. 'Please sit dowd. I dode thig I've had the pleasure of beetig you before, have I?'

'I don't think so,' said the Saint pleasantly. 'But any real pleasure is worth waiting for.' He took the precious volume which he was carrying from under his arm, and held it up. 'Did you publish this?'

Mr Parstone looked at it. 'Yes,' he said, 'that is one of our publicashuds. A bost excelledd ad ibportad book, if I bay perbid byself to say so. A book, I bight say, which answers problebs which are dear to every wud of us today.'

'It will certainly have some problems to answer,' said the Saint; 'and I expect they'll be dear enough. Do you know the name of the principal character in this book? Do you know who this biography is alleged to be about?'

'Biography?' stammered Mr Parstone, blinking at the cover. 'The book is a dovel. A work of fickshud. It is clearly explaid—'

'The book is supposed to be a biography,' said the Saint. 'And do you know the name of the principal character?'

Mr Parstone's brow creased with thought.

'Pridcipal character?' he repeated. 'Led be see, led be see. I ought to dough, oughtud I?' He blew his nose several times, sniffed, sighed, and spread out his hand uncertainly. 'Iddn it abazing?' he said. 'The dabe was od the tip of by tug, but dow I cadd rebember id.'

'The name is Simon Templar,' said the Saint grimly; and Mr Parstone sat up.

'What?' he ejaculated.

Simon opened the book and showed him the name in plain print. Then he took it away to a chair and lighted a cigarette.

'Rather rude of you, wasn't it?' he murmured.

'Well, by dear Bister Teblar,' said Parstone winningly. 'I trust you are dot thinkig that any uncomblibendary referedds was intended. Far frob id. These rebarkable coidcidedces will happud. Ad yet it is dot every yug bad of your age who fides his dabe preserved for posterity id such a work as that. The hero of that book, as I rebember him, was a fellow of outstaddig charb—'

'He was a low criminal,' said the Saint virtuously. 'Your memory is failing you, Herbert. Let me read you some of the best passages.'

He turned to a page he had marked.

'Listen to this, Herbert,' he said, ' "Simon Templar was never particular about how he made money, so long as he made it. The drug traffic was only one of his many sources of income, and his conscience was never touched by the thought of the hundreds of lives he ruined by his insatiable avarice. Once, in a nightclub, he pointed out to me a fine and beautiful girl on whose lovely face the ravages of dope were already beginning to make their mark. 'I've had two thousand pounds from her since I started her on the stuff,' he said gloatingly, 'and I'll have five thousand more before it kills her.' I could multiply instances of that kind by the score, and refrain only from fear of nauseating my readers. Sufficient, at least, has already been said to show what an unspeakable ruffian was this man who called himself the Saint." '

However hard it might have been for Mr Parstone to place the name of Simon Templar, he was by no means ignorant of the Saint. His watery eyes popped halfway out of their sockets, and his jaw hardened at the same time.

'So you're the Saint?' he said.

'Of course,' murmured Simon.

'Id your very own words, a low cribidal—'

Simon shook his head.

'Oh, no, Herbert,' he said. 'By no means as low as that. My reputation may be bad, but it's only rumour. You may whisper it to your friends, but the law doesn't allow you to put it in writing. That's libel. And you couldn't even get Chief Inspector Teal to testify that my record would justify anything like the language this book of yours has used about me.

'My sins were always fairly idealistic, and devoted to the squashing of beetles like yourself – not to trading in drugs and grinding the faces of the poor. But you haven't heard anything like the whole of it. Listen to some more.'

He turned to another selected passage.

' "The Saint",' he read, ' "always seemed to derive a peculiar malicious pleasure from robbing and swindling those who could least afford to lose. To my dying day, I shall be haunted by the memory of the fiendish glee which distorted his face when he told me that he had stolen five pounds from a woman with seven children, who had scraped and saved for months to get the money together. He accepted the money from her as a fee for trying to trace the grave of her father, who had been reported 'missing' in 1943. Of course he never made any attempt to carry out his share of the bargain. He played this cruel trick on several occasions, and always with the same sadistic pleasure, which I believe meant far more to him than the actual cash which he derived from it." '

'Is that id the book too?' asked Parstone hoarsely.

'Naturally,' said the Saint. 'That's what I'm reading it from. And there are lots more interesting things. Look here. "The bogus companies floated by Templar, in which thousands upon thousands of widows and orphans were deprived—" '

'Wait!' interrupted Parstone tremblingly. 'This is terrible – a terrible coidcideds. The book will be withdrawd at wuds. Hardly eddywud will have had tibe to read it. Ad if eddy sball cobbensation I cad give—'

Simon closed his book with a smile and laid it on Mr Parstone's desk.

'Shall we say fifty thousand pounds?' he suggested affably.

Mr Parstone's face reddened to the verge of an apoplectic stroke, and he brought up his handkerchief with shaking hands.

'How buch?' he whispered.

'Fifty thousand pounds,' repeated the Saint. 'After all, that's a very small amount of damages to ask for a libel like this. If the case has to go to court, I think it will be admitted that never in the whole history of modern law has such a colossal libel been put on paper. If there is any crime under the sun of which I'm not accused in that book, I'll sit down right now and eat it. And there are three hundred and twenty pages of it – eighty thousand words of continuous and unbridled insult. For a thing like that, Herbert, I think fifty thousand pounds is pretty cheap.'

'You could'n get it,' said Parstone harshly. 'It's the author's liability—'

'I know the clause,' answered the Saint coolly, 'and you may be interested to know that it has no legal value whatsever. In a successful libel action, the author, printer, and publisher are joint tortfeasors, and none of them can indemnify the other. Ask your solicitor. As a matter of fact,' he added prophetically, 'I don't expect I shall be able to recover anything from the author, anyway. Authors are usually broke. But you are both the printer and publisher, and I'm sure I can collect from you.'

Mr Parstone stared at him with blanched lips.

'But fifty thousad pouds is ibpossible,' he whined. 'It would ruid be!'

'That's what I mean to do, dear old bird,' said the Saint gently. 'You've gone on swindling a lot of harmless idiots for too long already, and now I want you to see what it feels like when it happens to you.'

He stood up, and collected his hat.

'I'll leave you the book,' he said, 'in case you want to entertain yourself some more. But I've got another copy; and if I don't receive your cheque by the first post on Friday morning it will go straight to my solicitors. And you can't kid yourself about what that will mean.'

For a long time after he had gone Mr Herbert Parstone sat quivering in his chair. And then he reached out for the book and began to skim through its pages. And with every page his livid face went greyer. There was no doubt about it. Simon Templar had spoken the truth. The book was the most monumental libel that could ever have found its way into print. Parstone's brain reeled before the accumulation of calumnies which it unfolded.

His furious ringing of the bell brought his secretary running.

'Fide me that proofreader!' he howled. 'Fide be the dab fool who passed this book!' He flung the volume on to the floor at her feet. 'Sed hib to be at wuds! I'll show hib. I'll bake hib suffer. By God, I'll—'

The other things that Mr Parstone said he would do cannot be recorded in such a respectable publication as this.

His secretary picked up the book and looked at the title.

'Mr Timmins left yesterday – he was the man you fired four months ago,' she said; but even then Mr Parstone was no wiser.

They Can Only Hang You Once

DASHIELL HAMMETT

INVESTIGATOR FILE

NAME: Sam Spade, Private Eye

PLACE: San Francisco

TIME: 1943

CASES: *The Maltese Falcon* (1929), *A Man Called Spade* (1932), *The Adventures of Sam Spade* (1944) etc.

DOSSIER: Samuel Spade was among the earliest of the new breed of private eyes who appeared in America in the late 'twenties – and he remains to this day one of the most famous of all detectives in crime fiction. A curious-looking man with a long, bony jaw and v-shaped mouth, nostrils and eyebrows which give him the appearance of 'a rather pleasant blond Satan', Sam is tough, cynical and idealistic. His yellow-green eyes see things plain – all things, including himself – and there is an ambiguity about his attitude towards the law which makes him such an intriguing and fascinating character. He has an intimate knowledge of 'his burg' and is familiar with the city's lawmen and gangsters, all of whom treat him with a kind of respect. Sam keeps his lips tight when he smiles, but never loses his ability to laugh at threatening gangsters, trigger-happy policemen, corrupt politicians and, especially, beautiful, seductive women. He is unusual in that he refuses to carry a gun, can be unpredictable and is occasionally wild, but he is not above bending the rules to bring a hood to justice. In a sentence, Sam Spade is the ultimate hardboiled dick.

CREATOR: Dashiell Hammett (1894–1961) was a former Pinkerton detective who grew tired of the profession in the mid-twenties and turned to fictionalising his experiences for the rapidly growing number of crime and mystery pulp magazines. Spade made his debut in *The Maltese Falcon*, a five-part serial in *Black Mask* magazine in 1929 which, when published as a book the following year, became a classic as well as later inspiring a landmark movie with Humphrey Bogart (1941). The story also represented a major new development in the crime genre, breaking away from the published mannerisms and cheerful violence of the English crime tale to create the first truly native American detective story. Of Sam Spade as a character, Dashiell Hammett confessed that he had no particular prototype: 'He is idealised in the sense that he is what most of the private detectives I have worked with would *like* to have been.' Precisely what he meant by that is superbly demonstrated in 'They Can Only Hang You Once'.

* * *

Samuel Spade said, 'My name is Ronald Ames. I want to see Mr Binnett – Mr Timothy Binnett.'

'Mr Binnett is resting now, sir,' the butler replied hesitantly.

'Will you find out when I can see him? It's important.' Spade cleared his throat. 'I'm – uh – just back from Australia, and it's about some of his properties there.'

The butler turned on his heel while saying. 'I'll see, sir,' and was going up the front stairs before he had finished speaking.

Spade made and lit a cigarette.

The butler came downstairs again. 'I'm sorry, he can't be disturbed now, but Mr Wallace Binnett – Mr Timothy's nephew – will see you.'

Spade said, 'Thanks,' and followed the butler upstairs.

Wallace Binnett was a slender, handsome, dark man of about Spade's age – thirty-eight – who rose smiling from a brocaded chair, said, 'How do you do, Mr Ames?' waved his hand at another chair, and sat down again. 'You're from Australia?'

'Got in this morning.'

'You're a business associate of Uncle Tim's?'

Spade smiled and shook his head. 'Hardly that, but I've some information I think he ought to have – quick.'

Wallace Binnett looked thoughtfully at the floor, then up at Spade. 'I'll do my best to persuade him to see you, Mr Ames, but, frankly, I don't know.'

Spade seemed mildly surprised. 'Why?'

Binnett shrugged. 'He's peculiar sometimes. Understand, his mind seems perfectly all right, but he has the testiness and eccentricity of an old man in ill health, and – well – at times he can be difficult.'

Spade asked slowly, 'He's already refused to see me?'

'Yes.'

Spade rose from his chair. His blond Satan's face was expressionless.

Binnett raised a hand quickly. 'Wait, wait,' he said. 'I'll do what I can to make him change his mind. Perhaps if – ' His dark eyes suddenly became wary. 'You're not simply trying to sell him something, are you?'

'No.'

The wary gleam went out of Binnett's eyes. 'Well, then, I think I can—'

A young woman came in crying angrily, 'Wally, that old fool has—' She broke off with a hand to her breast when she saw Spade.

Spade and Binnett had risen together. Binnett said suavely, 'Joyce, this is Mr Ames. My sister-in-law, Joyce Court.'

Spade bowed.

Joyce Court uttered a short, embarrassed laugh and said, 'Please excuse my whirlwind entrance.' She was a tall, blue-eyed, dark woman of twenty-four or twenty-five with good shoulders and a strong, slim body. Her features made up in warmth what they lacked in regularity. She wore wide-legged blue satin pyjamas.

Binnett smiled goodnaturedly at her and asked, 'Now, what's all the excitement?'

Anger darkened her eyes again and she started to speak. Then she looked at Spade and said, 'But we shouldn't bore Mr Ames with our stupid domestic affairs. If – ' She hesitated.

Spade bowed again. 'Sure,' he said, 'certainly.'

'I won't be a minute,' Binnett promised, and left the room with her.

Spade went to the open doorway through which they had vanished, and, standing just inside, listened. Their footsteps became inaudible. Nothing else could be heard. Spade was standing there – his yellow-grey eyes dreamy – when he heard the scream. It was a woman's scream, high and shrill with terror. Spade was through the doorway when he heard the shot. It was a pistol shot, magnified, reverberated by walls and ceilings.

Twenty feet from the doorway Spade found a staircase, and went up it three steps at a time. He turned to the left. Halfway down the hallway a woman lay on her back on the floor.

Wallace Binnett knelt beside her, fondling one of her hands desperately, crying in a low, beseeching voice, 'Darling, Molly, darling!'

Joyce Court stood behind him and wrung her hands while tears streaked her cheeks.

The woman on the floor resembled Joyce Court, but was older, and her face had a hardness the younger one's had not.

'She's dead, she's been killed,' Wallace Binnett said incredulously, raising his white face towards Spade. When Binnett moved his head Spade could see the round hole in the woman's tan dress over her heart and the dark stain which was rapidly spreading below it.

Spade touched Joyce Court's arm. 'Police, emergency hospital – phone,' he said. As she ran towards the stairs he addressed Wallace Binnett: 'Who did—'

A voice groaned feebly behind Spade.

He turned swiftly. Through an open doorway he could see an old man in white pyjamas lying sprawled across a rumpled bed. His head, a shoulder, an arm dangled over the edge of the bed. His other hand held his throat tightly. He groaned again and his eyelids twitched, but did not open.

Spade lifted the old man's head and shoulders and put them up on the pillows. The old man groaned again and took his hand from his throat. His throat was red with half a dozen bruises. He was a gaunt man with a seamed face that probably exaggerated his age.

A glass of water was on a table beside the bed. Spade put water on the old man's face, and, when the old man's eyes twitched again, leaned down and growled softly, 'Who did it?'

The twitching eyelids went up far enough to show a narrow strip of bloodshot grey eyes. The old man spoke painfully, putting a hand to his throat again: 'A man – he – ' He coughed.

Spade made an impatient grimace. His lips almost touched the old man's ear. 'Where'd he go?' His voice was urgent.

A gaunt hand moved weakly to indicate the rear of the house and fell back on the bed.

The butler and two frightened female servants had joined Wallace Binnett beside the dead woman in the hallway.

'Who did it?' Spade asked them.

They stared at him blankly.

'Somebody look after the old man,' he growled, and went down the hallway.

At the end of the hallway was a rear staircase. He descended two flights and went through a pantry into the kitchen. He saw nobody. The kitchen door was shut but, when he tried it, not locked. He crossed a narrow back yard to a gate that was shut, not locked. He opened the gate. There was nobody in the narrow alley behind it.

He sighed, shut the gate, and returned to the house.

Spade sat comfortably slack in a deep leather chair in a room that ran across the front second storey of Wallace Binnett's house. There were shelves of books and the lights were on. The window showed outer darkness weakly diluted by a distant street lamp. Facing Spade, Detective Sergeant Polhaus – a big, carelessly shaven, florid man in dark clothes that needed pressing – was sprawled in another leather chair; Lieutenant Dundy – smaller, compactly built, square faced – stood with legs apart, head thrust a little forward, in the centre of the room.

Spade was saying, '. . . and the doctor would only let me talk to the old man a couple of minutes. We can try it again when he's rested a little, but it doesn't look like he knows much. He was catching a nap and he woke up with somebody's hand on his throat dragging him around the bed. The best he got was a one-eyed look at the fellow choking him. A big fellow, he says, with a soft hat pulled down over his eyes, dark, needing a shave. Sounds like Tom.' Spade nodded at Polhaus.

The detective sergeant chuckled, but Dundy said, 'Go on,' curtly.

Spade grinned and went on, 'He's pretty far gone when he hears Mrs Binnett scream at the door. The hands go away from his throat and he hears the shot, and just before passing out he gets a flash of the big fellow heading for the rear of the house and Mrs Binnett tumbling down on the hall floor. He says he never saw the big fellow before.'

'What size gun was it?' Dundy asked.

'Thirty-eight. Well, nobody in the house is much more help. Wallace and his sister-in-law, Joyce, were in her room, so they say, and didn't see anything but the dead woman when they ran out, though they think they heard something that could've been somebody running down-stairs – the back stairs.

'The butler – his name's Jarboe – was in here when he heard the scream and shot, so he says. Irene Kelly, the maid, was down on the ground floor, so she says. The cook, Margaret Finn, was in her room – third floor back – and didn't even hear anything, so she says. She's deaf as a post, so everybody else says. The back door and gate were unlocked, but are supposed to be kept locked, so everybody says. Nobody says they were in or around the kitchen or yard at the time.' Spade spread his hands in a gesture of finality. 'That's the crop.'

Dundy shook his head. 'Not exactly,' he said. 'How come you were here?'

Spade's face brightened. 'Maybe my client killed her,' he said. 'He's Wallace's cousin. Ira Binnett. Know him?'

Dundy shook his head. His blue eyes were hard and suspicious.

'He's a San Francisco lawyer,' Spade said, 'respectable and all that. A couple of days ago he came to me with a story about his Uncle Timothy, a miserly old skinflint, lousy with money and pretty well broken up by hard living. He was the black sheep of the family. None of them had heard of him for years. But six or eight months ago he showed up in pretty bad shape every way except financially – he seems to have taken a lot of money out of Australia – wanting to spend his last days with his only living relatives, his nephews Wallace and Ira.

'That was all right with them. "Only living relatives" meant "only heirs" in their language. But by-and-by the nephews began to think it was better to be an heir than to be one of a couple of heirs – twice as good, in fact – and started fiddling for the inside track with the old man. At least, that's what Ira told me about Wallace, and I wouldn't be surprised if Wallace would say the same thing about Ira, though Wallace seems to be the harder up of the two. Anyhow, the nephews fell out, and then Uncle Tim, who had been staying at Ira's, came over here. That was a couple of months ago, and Ira hasn't seen Uncle Tim since, and hasn't been able to get in touch with him by phone or mail.

'That's what he wanted a private detective about. He didn't think Uncle Tim would come to any harm here – oh, no, he went to a lot of trouble to make that clear – but he thought maybe undue pressure was being brought to bear on the old boy, or he was being hornswoggled somehow, and at least being told lies about his loving nephew Ira. He wanted to know what was what. I waited until today, when a boat from Australia docked, and came up here as a Mr Ames with some important information for Uncle Tim about his properties down there. All I wanted was fifteen minutes alone with him.' Spade frowned thoughtfully. 'Well, I didn't get them. Wallace told me the old man refused to see me. I don't know.'

Suspicion had deepened in Dundy's cold blue eyes. 'And where is this Ira Binnett now?' he asked.

Spade's yellow-grey eyes were as guileless as his voice.

'I wish I knew. I phoned his house and office and left word for him to come right over, but I'm afraid—'

Knuckles knocked sharply twice on the other side of the room's one door. The three men in the room turned to face the door.

Dundy called, 'Come in.'

The door was opened by a sunburned blond policeman whose left hand held the right wrist of a plump man of forty or forty-five in well-fitting grey clothes. The policeman pushed the plump man into the room. 'Found him monkeying with the kitchen door,' he said.

Spade looked up and said, 'Ah!' His tone expressed satisfaction. 'Mr Ira Binnett, Lieutenant Dundy, Sergeant Polhaus.'

Ira Binnett said rapidly, 'Mr Spade, will you tell this man that—'

Dundy addressed the policeman: 'All right. Good work. You can leave him.'

The policeman moved a hand vaguely towards his cap and went away.

Dundy glowered at Ira Binnett and demanded, 'Well?'

Binnett looked from Dundy to Spade. 'Has something—'

Spade said, 'Better tell him why you were at the back door instead of the front.'

Ira Binnett suddenly blushed. He cleared his throat in embarrassment. He said, 'I – uh – I should explain. It wasn't my fault, of course, but when Jarboe – he's the butler – phoned me that Uncle Tim wanted to see me he told me he'd leave the kitchen door unlocked, so Wallace wouldn't have to know I'd—'

'What'd he want to see you about?' Dundy asked.

'I don't know. He didn't say. He said it was very important.'

'Didn't you get my message?' Spade asked.

Ira Binnett's eyes widened. 'No. What was it? Has anything happened? What is – .'

Spade was moving towards the door. 'Go ahead,' he said to Dundy. 'I'll be right back.'

He shut the door carefully behind him and went up to the third floor.

The butler Jarboe was on his knees at Timothy Binnett's door with an eye to the keyhole. On the floor beside him was a tray holding an egg in an eggcup, toast, a pot of coffee, china, silver, and a napkin.

Spade said, 'Your toast's going to get cold.'

Jarboe, scrambling to his feet, almost upsetting the coffee pot in his haste, his face red and sheepish, stammered, 'I – er – beg your pardon, sir. I wanted to make sure Mr Timothy was awake before I took this in.' He picked up the tray. 'I didn't want to disturb his rest if – '

Spade, who had reached the door, said, 'Sure, sure,' and bent over to put his eye to the keyhole. When he straightened up he said in a mildly complaining tone, 'You can't see the bed – only a chair and part of the window.'

The butler replied quickly. 'Yes, sir, I found that out.'

Spade laughed.

The butler coughed, seemed about to say something, but did not. He hesitated, then knocked lightly on the door.

A tired voice said, 'Come in.'

Spade asked quickly in a low voice, 'Where's Miss Court?'

'In her room, I think, sir, the second door on the left,' the butler said.

The tired voice inside the room said petulantly, 'Well, come on in.'

The butler opened the door and went in. Through the

door, before the butler shut it, Spade caught a glimpse of Timothy Binnett propped up on pillows in his bed.

Spade went to the second door on the left and knocked. The door was opened almost immediately by Joyce Court. She stood in the doorway, not smiling, not speaking.

He said, 'Miss Court, when you came into the room where I was with your brother-in-law you said "Wally, that old fool has—" Meaning Timothy?'

She stared at Spade for a moment. Then, 'Yes.'

'Mind telling me what the rest of the sentence would have been?'

She said slowly, 'I don't know who you really are or why you ask, but I don't mind telling you. It would have been sent for Ira. Jarboe had just told me.'

'Thanks.'

She shut the door before he had turned away.

He returned to Timothy Binnett's door and knocked on it.

'Who is it now?' the old man's voice demanded.

Spade opened the door. The old man was sitting up in bed.

Spade said, 'This Jarboe was peeping through your keyhole a few minutes ago,' and returned to the library.

Ira Binnett, seated in the chair Spade had occupied, was saying to Dundy and Polhaus, 'And Wallace got caught in the crash, like most of us, but he seems to have juggled accounts trying to save himself. He was expelled from the Stock Exchange.'

Dundy waved a hand to indicate the room and its furnishings. 'Pretty classy lay-out for a man that's busted.'

'His wife has some money,' Ira Binnett said, 'and he always lived beyond his means.'

Dundy scowled at Binnett. 'And you really think he and his missus weren't on good terms?'

'I don't think it,' Binnett replied evenly. 'I know it.'

Dundy nodded. 'And you know he's got a yen for the sister-in-law, this Court?'

'I don't know that. But I've heard plenty of gossip to the same effect.'

Dundy made a growling noise in his throat, then asked sharply, 'How does the old man's will read?'

'I don't know. I don't know whether he's made one.' He addressed Spade now, earnestly: 'I've told everything I know, every single thing.'

Dundy said, 'It's not enough.' He jerked a thumb at the door. 'Show him where to wait, Tom, and let's have the widower in again.'

Big Polhaus said, 'Right,' went out with Ira Binnett, and returned with Wallace Binnett, whose face was hard and pale.

Dundy asked, 'Has your uncle made a will?'

'I don't know,' Binnett replied.

Spade put the next question softly: 'Did your wife?'

Binnett's mouth tightened in a mirthless smile. He spoke deliberately: 'I'm going to say some things I'd rather not have to say. My wife, properly, had no money. When I got into financial trouble some time ago I made some property over to her to save it. She turned it into money without my knowing about it till afterwards. She paid our bills – our living expenses – out of it, but she refused to return it to me, and she assured me that in no event – whether she lived or died or we stayed together or were divorced – would I ever be able to get hold of a penny of it. I believed her, and still do.'

'You wanted a divorce?' Dundy asked.

'Yes.'

'Why?'

'It wasn't a happy marriage.'

'Joyce Court?'

Binnett's face flushed. He said stiffly, 'I admire Joyce

Court tremendously, but I'd have wanted a divorce anyway.'

Spade said, 'And you're sure – still absolutely sure – you don't know anybody who fits your uncle's description of the man who choked him?'

'Absolutely sure.'

The sound of the doorbell ringing came faintly into the room.

Dundy said sharply, 'That'll do.'

Binnett went out.

Polhaus said, 'That guy's as wrong as they make them. And—'

From below came the heavy report of a pistol fired indoors.

The lights went out.

In darkness the three detectives collided with one another going through the doorway into the dark hall. Spade reached the stairs first. There was a clatter of footsteps below him, but nothing could be seen until he reached a bend in the stairs. Then enough light came from the street through the open front door to show the dark figure of a man standing with his back to the open door.

A flashlight clicked in Dundy's hand – he was at Spade's heel – and threw a glaring white beam of light on the man's face. He was Ira Binnett. He blinked in the light and pointed at something on the floor in front of him.

Dundy turned the beam of his light down on the floor. Jarboe lay there on his face, bleeding from a bullet hole in the back of his head.

Spade grunted softly.

Tom Polhaus came blundering down the stairs, Wallace Binnett close behind him. Joyce Court's frightened voice came from farther up: 'Oh, what's happened? Wally, what's happened?'

'Where's the light switch?' Dundy asked.

'Inside the cellar door, under these stairs,' Wallace Binnett said. 'What is it?'

Polhaus pushed past Binnett towards the cellar door.

Spade made an inarticulate sound in his throat, and, pushing Wallace Binnett aside, sprang up the stairs. He brushed past Joyce Court and went on, heedless of her startled scream. He was halfway up the stairs to the third floor when the pistol went off up there.

He ran to Timothy Binnett's door. The door was open. He went on.

Something hard and angular struck him above his ear, knocking him across the room, bringing him down on one knee. Something thumped and clattered on the floor just outside the door.

The lights came on.

On the floor, in the centre of the room, Timothy Binnett lay bleeding from a bullet wound in his left forearm. His pyjama jacket was torn. His eyes were shut.

Spade stood up and put a hand to his head. He scowled at the old man on the floor, at the room, at the black automatic pistol lying on the hallway floor. He said, 'Come on, you old cut-throat. Get up and sit on a chair and I'll see if I can stop that bleeding till the doctor gets here.'

The man on the floor did not move.

There were footsteps in the hallway and Dundy came in, followed by the two younger Binnetts. Dundy's face was dark, and furious. 'Kitchen door wide open,' he said in a choked voice. 'They run in and out like—'

'Forget it,' Spade said. 'Uncle Tim is our meat.' He paid no attention to Wallace Binnett's gasp, to the incredulous looks on Dundy's and Ira Binnett's faces. 'Come on, get up,' he said to the old man on the floor, 'and tell us what it was the butler saw when he peeped through the keyhole.'

The old man did not stir.

'He killed the butler because I told him the butler had peeped,' Spade explained to Dundy. 'I peeped, too, but didn't see anything except that chair and the window, though we'd made enough racket by then to scare him back to bed. Suppose you take the chair apart while I go over the window.' He went to the window and began to examine it carefully. He shook his head, put a hand out behind him, and said, 'Give me the flashlight.'

Dundy put the flashlight in his hand.

Spade raised the window and leaned out, turning the light on the outside of the building. Presently he grunted and put his other hand out, tugging at a brick a little below the sill. Presently the brick came loose. He put it on the windowsill and stuck his hand into the hole its removal had made. Out of the opening, one at a time, he brought an empty black pistol holster, a partly filled box of cartridges, and an unsealed manila envelope.

Holding these things in his hands, he turned to face the others. Joyce Court came in with a basin of water and a roll of gauze and knelt beside Timothy Binnett. Spade put the holster and cartridges on a table and opened the manila envelope. Inside were two sheets of paper, covered on both sides with boldly pencilled writing. Spade read a paragraph to himself, suddenly laughed, and began at the beginning again, reading aloud:

' "I, Timothy Kieran Binnett, being sound of mind and body, do declare this to be my last will and testament. To my dear nephews, Ira Binnett and Wallace Bourke Binnett, in recognition of the loving kindness with which they have received me into their homes and attended my declining years, I give and bequeath, share and share alike all my worldly possessions of whatever kind, to wit, my carcase and the clothes I stand in.

' "I bequeath them, furthermore, the expense of my funeral and these memories: first, the memory of their credulity in believing that the fifteen years I spent in Sing Sing were spent in Australia; second, the memory of their optimism in supposing that those fifteen years had brought me great wealth, and that if I lived on them, borrowed from them, and never spent any of my own money, it was because I was a miser whose hoard they would inherit; and not because I had no money except what I shook them down for; third, for their hopefulness in thinking that I would leave either of them anything if I had it: and lastly, because their painful lack of any decent sense of humour will keep them from even seeing how funny this has all been. Signed and sealed this—" '

Spade looked up to say, 'There is no date, but it's signed Timothy Kieran Binnett with flourishes.'

Ira Binnett was purple with anger. Wallace's face was ghastly in its pallor, and his whole body was trembling. Joyce Court had stopped working on Timothy Binnett's arm.

The old man sat up and opened his eyes. He looked at his nephews and began to laugh. There was in his laughter neither hysteria nor madness; it was sane, hearty laughter, and subsided slowly.

Spade said, 'All right, now you've had your fun. Let's talk about the killings.'

'I know nothing more about the first one than I've told you,' the old man said, 'and this one's not a killing, since I'm only – '

Wallace Binnett, still trembling violently, said painfully through his teeth, 'That's a lie. You killed Molly. Joyce and I came out of her room when we heard Molly scream, and heard the shot and saw her fall out of your room, and nobody came out afterwards.'

The old man said calmly, 'Well, I'll tell you: it was an accident. They told me there was a fellow from Australia here to see me about some of my properties there. I knew there was something funny about that somewhere' – he grinned – 'not ever having been there. I didn't know whether one of my dear nephews was getting suspicious and putting up a game on me or what, but I knew that if Wally wasn't in on it he'd certainly try to pump the gentleman from Australia about me and maybe I'd lose one of my free boarding-houses.' He chuckled.

'So I figured I'd get in touch with Ira so I could go back to his house if things work out bad here, and I'd try to get rid of this Australian. Wally's always thought I'm half cracked' – he leered at his nephew – 'and is afraid they'll lug me off to a madhouse before I could make a will in his favour, or they'll break it if I do. You see, he's got a pretty bad reputation, what with that Stock Exchange trouble and all, and he knows no court would appoint him to handle my affairs if I went screwy – not as long as I've got another nephew' – he turned his leer on Ira – 'who's a respectable lawyer. So now I know that rather than have me kick up a row that might wind me up in the madhouse, he'll chase this visitor, and I put on a show for Molly, who happened to be the nearest one to hand. She took it too seriously, though.

'I had a gun, and I did a lot of raving about being spied on by my enemies in Australia and that I was going down to shoot this fellow. But she got too excited and tried to take the gun away from me, and the first thing I knew it had gone off, and I had to make these marks on my neck and think up that story about the big dark man.' He looked contemptuously at Wallace. 'I didn't know he was covering me up. Little as I thought of him, I never thought he'd be low enough to cover up his wife's murder – even if he didn't like her – just for the sake of the money.'

Spade said, 'Never mind that. Now about the butler?'

'I don't know anything about the butler,' the old man replied, looking at Spade with steady eyes.

Spade said, 'You had to kill him quick, before he had

time to do or say anything. So you slip down the back stairs, open the kitchen door to fool people, go to the front door, ring the bell, shut the door, and hide in the shadow of the cellar door under the front steps. When Jarboe answered the doorbell you shot him – the hole was in the back of his head – pulled the light switch just inside the cellar door, and ducked up the back stairs in the dark and shot yourself carefully in the arm. I got up there too soon for you, so you smacked me with the gun, chucked it through the door, and spread yourself on the floor while I was shaking pinwheels out of my noodle.'

The old man sniffed again. 'You're just—'

'Stop it,' Spade said patiently. 'Don't let's argue. The first killing was an accident – all right. The second couldn't be. And it ought to be easy to show that both bullets, and the one in your arm, were fired from the same gun. What difference does it make which killing we can prove first-degree murder on? They can only hang you once.' He smiled pleasantly. 'And they will.'

Black Out

PETER CHEYNEY

INVESTIGATOR FILE

NAME: Slim Callaghan, Private Detective

PLACE: London

TIME: 1941

CASES: *The Urgent Hangman* (1938), *The Unscrupulous Mr Callaghan* (1943), *They Never Say When* (1944), *Calling Mr Callaghan* (1953) etc.

DOSSIER: Slim Callaghan is a tough, cynical and hard-drinking private investigator with an office in Berkeley Square, London, and an intimate knowledge of the West End nightclubs and gambling casinos which provide many of his cases. In his early forties, Slim is suave when it suits him and handy with either his fists or a gun when in trouble. Several English critics have referred to him as 'fiction's most ruthless detective', a status he certainly lived up to during the heyday of his career in the late 'thirties and 'forties. Callaghan employs an attractive young secretary, Effie Thompson, and a pair of assistants, 'Windy' Nikolls, a fat, wise-cracking Canadian, and the more pragmatic Englishman, MacOliver. All three are tolerant of Callaghan's occasional binges and cover for him with clients when he is nursing a hangover because they admire his quick mind and ability to get to the bottom of often complex cases of theft, fraud and murder. Although Slim is happiest investigating crime in the city, he will occasionally leave town for the country, although his manner is not always welcomed by the local police. He is, in every sense, a man who could rub shoulders with the toughest American private eyes – and is widely regarded as the first and best of the English tough detectives.

CREATOR: Like Dashiell Hammett, whose books provided the inspiration for Slim Callaghan, Peter Cheyney (1896–1951) had also been a detective – the proprietor and leading agent of Cheyney Research Investigations in London – before making his fortune writing crime stories. His interest in American crime fiction actually led to the creation of two quite different investigators: Lemmy Caution, a New York G-Man who narrates his own adventures in the first person, and Slim Callaghan. Unfortunately, the Caution novels were flawed by Cheyney's lack of first-hand knowledge of the American underworld, but he was on much safer ground with Callaghan, who operates in a milieu that he knew from his own detective work, and in which he had been a regular figure even before the success of his books. Both series were, however, attacked by critics for their violence, but nevertheless pioneered a new tough school of British crime writing which was later exploited by other writers including James Hadley Chase, Hartley Howard, Peter Chambers and Hank Janson. 'Black Out' is unusual among Callaghan's cases in that it is set during the Second World War when, as is evident, the criminal underworld was still flourishing. Not that this makes any difference to Slim when the cry goes out again (in his creator's words), 'Call for Callaghan!'

***

The nurse left and Ferdie Phelps turned slowly over on to his back. His eyes, half dimmed with morphia, regained, for a moment, a suggestion of their old twinkle.

'Nice of you to come an' see me, Mr Callaghan,' he said softly. 'I'm glad you come here. I wanted to say "thank you". They tell me that you been lookin' after my missus since I 'ad this smash-up. My number's up an' I know it.'

Callaghan looked down the empty hospital ward, dimly lit, the windows carefully shaded for the black-out.

He said, 'You'll be all right, Ferdie. Just keep your chin up. You'll pull through.'

'Pull through nothin',' said Ferdie weakly. 'This is the end of me. An' I must say I never expected to get myself knocked over in a London street by a blinkin' motorcar. Cuss the bloomin' black-out.'

He coughed weakly. Then he went on, 'Get it orf your chest, Mr Callaghan. I bet you didn't come around 'ere to ask after my 'ealth.' He grinned again. 'Wot are you after? A deathbed confession? Maybe you thought I'd be feelin' like talkin' about somethin', eh?'

Callaghan said, 'Ferdie, I thought you might know something about that Amalgamated Jewellers steal. I always had a sneaking idea that Willie the Mug never pulled that job.'

Ferdie shifted a little. He was still grinning. 'You don't say,' he said. 'Look, Mr Callaghan, you ain't tryin' to tell me that you're interested in who pulled it or who didn't, are you? *I* know wot you're interested in. You're interested in where the stuff is. I reckon that insurance company you work for would give something to know where it is. Ain't that it?'

'That's it,' Callaghan agreed.

He lit a cigarette slowly.

There was a pause. Then Phelps said, ' 'Ooever it was christened 'im Willie the Mug knew wot they was talkin' about. 'E was a mug all right, an' 'e's doin' seven years for somethin' 'e didn't do – see? Willie never pinched that stuff. *I* know 'oo done it.'

Callaghan said, 'I always thought Willie didn't do it. He hasn't enough brains. But I think I know who was behind it. It was Narkat, wasn't it?'

Ferdie looked at the private detective for a moment. Then he said, 'I'll make a deal with you, Mr Callaghan. Maybe I'll feel better if I do a bit of talkin'. But you got to promise me somethin'. You got to promise me that as well as getting that jewellery back you'll do your best for Willie. You got to get Willie out of quod.'

Callaghan nodded. 'I give you my word, Ferdie, I'll do my best.'

Phelps nodded weakly. Then he muttered, 'Narkat was be'ind the whole thing. Willie the Mug only comes into it becos of that girl of 'is. She was a proper wrong 'un. She was two-timin' 'im with Narkat all the time an' the poor mug never knew it.

'Narkat 'ad fixed to get rid of the stuff after it was pinched an 'e'd arranged for Blooey Stevens to crack the safe. Orl right – well the lay was that Blooey was to get the stuff an' pass it to Miranda – Willie's girl – 'oo was to be waitin' for 'im on the corner of the street.

'She was goin' to take the attaché case along to Narkat an' Narkat was goin' to get rid of the stuff abroad.

'Stevens got into the Amalgamated Jewellers' place at twelve. 'E 'ad the job finished at a quarter to one. He passed the attaché case to Miranda on the corner of Green Street an' she started to walk towards Narkat's flat.

'All right. Well, she was nearly there when she sees Viners, a CID man, 'angin' about outside. She got the wind up proper, I can tell you. She turned about an' streaked through the alley into Long Acre. Viners went after 'er. 'E didn't know a thing, but 'e knew '*er* an' 'e thought she was actin' suspicious.

'She went to Willie the Mug's place off Long Acre. Willie come down an' opened the door. She 'anded 'im the attaché case, which was locked, an' told 'im some phoney story about it. She asked 'im to keep it for 'er until next day. Willie said OK an' off she went. She didn't know Viner's 'ad been watchin' 'er.

'Directly she'd gone, Viners went over an' rang the bell. 'E was goin' to ask Willie wot was in that attaché case. Willie 'ad a look out of the window an' saw it was Viners. 'E smelt a rat. 'E broke open the case and saw the jewellery inside, an' the only thing the poor mug thought of was lookin' after Miranda.

'So 'e rushed out to the back an' stuck the case out in the yard underneath a loose pavin' stone. Then 'e went an' opened the door for Viners.'

Ferdie grinned. 'I reckon you know the rest of the story, Mr Callaghan,' he said. Callaghan nodded.

'Go on, Ferdie,' he said quietly.

'Well, next day,' said Ferdie, 'they find out about the jewel robbery. Viners remembers seein' Miranda with the case. They pull 'er in an' they pull Willie in. An' all Willie is thinkin' of is lookin' after the skirt 'oo 'e thinks is struck on 'im – Miranda.

'Just so's to keep 'er in the clear 'e says 'e pinched the jewellery, an' that the case that Viners saw Miranda carryin' was just some laundry she was bringin' round to 'is place.

'When they ask him where the jewellery is 'e won't say. 'E's afraid to. Becos if he tells 'em an' they find the case under the pavin' stone in the back yard 'e knows that Viners will remember it an' they'll pinch Miranda as an accessory.

'OK. Well, they tell 'im that if 'e says where the jewellery is, 'e'll get off with a short sentence an' if 'e don't he'll get a seven-year stretch. But 'e prefers to be a little 'ero an' keep 'is mouth shut, so he gets seven years for somethin' 'e didn't do, an' Narkat, Miranda an' Blooey are laughin' their 'eads off.'

Ferdie coughed again.

'There's only one thing that's worryin' 'em,' he continued. 'An' that is they don't know where the jewellery is. It's still there, in the attaché case under the pavin' stone at the back of Willie's place in Sellers Alley.'

Callaghan said, 'Thanks, Ferdie. When that jewellery goes back, there'll be a reward. I'll see your missus gets it.'

The dying man smiled. 'That's OK,' he said weakly. 'But wot about Willie?'

Callaghan got up. He pressed Ferdie's hand.

'Don't worry, Ferdie,' he said. 'I'll look after him. I'll be seein' you.'

'No, you won't,' said Ferdie. 'I got my ticket this time. I got to hand in my dinner pail. I know. I got second sight.'

He grinned feebly at his own joke.

Callaghan went out as the ward sister came in.

Callaghan switched off the office lights, pulled aside the curtains before the window and stood looking out into the black void beneath him. Streets which usually twinkled with light were absolutely black.

He began to think about Willie the Mug, Narkat, the big boy – the man who ran the gang and never took any risks himself – and Miranda. Callaghan thought he didn't like Miranda very much.

He stood there looking out into the darkness, thinking. Then he began to smile. He pulled back the curtains, switched on the light, went to his desk and took up the telephone. He rang his assistant's flat.

'Listen, MacOliver,' he said. 'I'm getting a line on that

Amalgamated Jewellers steal. You remember that feller, Jelks, who used to work for us? Go round to his place and knock him up. Tell him I want him to do a little job for me.

'Tell him to wait for me at the works. Then get around and find out where Blooey Stevens is. He'll be somewhere round the West End. Meet me at Jelks's place at eleven. You can tell me about Stevens then.'

Blooey Stevens, thickset, overdressed, red faced, was sitting in the corner of the Blue Horse Club drinking whisky when Callaghan came in. The Blue Horse Club was an underground dive in the region of Shaftesbury Avenue. Tonight it was crowded.

Most of the members who, but for the black-out, would have been engaged in their different questionable occupations, were preparing to stay under cover and do a little quiet drinking. They had heard that the police had made very adequate war arrangements about crooks.

It was eleven-thirty. Callaghan threaded his way between the closely set tables. He sat down opposite Stevens and lit a cigarette.

'Good evening, Blooey,' he said. 'How are things?'

Stevens looked at Callaghan. His eyes were hard.

'None the better for seeing you,' he said. 'And I'll be glad if you'll go somewhere else. I don't like private detectives.'

Callaghan smiled. 'Don't you, Blooey?' he said. 'Well, I'd forget that if I were you. I think you're rather a tough jam.'

'Oh yes!' said Stevens.

His voice was insolent. He blew a cloud of cigarette smoke across the table in Callaghan's face.

'You can't bluff me, Callaghan,' he said aggressively. 'You've got nothing on me.'

Callaghan smiled amiably.

'Maybe not,' he said. 'But I've got an idea the police soon will have. Did you read the paper tonight?'

Stevens said, 'No, I didn't, and what's it got to do with you?'

Callaghan put his hand in his overcoat pocket and produced a copy of the evening paper.

He said, 'You know I've been trying to get a line on that stuff that was stolen from the Amalgamated Jewellers. Tonight I got the story from Ferdie Phelps. He was knocked down the other day. He's dying. Well – that was that – but the funny thing was that when I got back to the office I read this.'

He handed the paper, folded at the stop-press news, across the table.

Stevens read, 'Early this afternoon, taking advantage of the special black-out arrangements in Maidstone Prison, William James Farrell, commonly known as Willie the Mug, made his escape from the prison hospital. The authorities believe he will make for London. Farrell is suffering from chronic bronchitis and will probably be arrested within the next few hours.'

Stevens's face was ashy pale. He ran a finger between his collar and his neck.

'I don't think it's going to be so good for you, Blooey,' said Callaghan amiably. 'Willie the Mug's wise to things – how you and Miranda and Narkat let him in for that Amalgamated Jewellery steal. He knows you did it.

'I should think he'd be in London fairly soon. And I hear he's got a gun. I wouldn't like to be any one of you three tonight if Willie finds you,' he finished.

Stevens said, 'I don't know what the hell you're talking about.'

'No,' said Callaghan. 'I suppose you'll tell me in a minute that you didn't crack that safe, that you weren't the feller who handed the attaché case to Miranda, who planted it on poor old Willie, who took the rap for that cheap skirt.'

He got up, 'Well, Blooey,' he said, 'I expect you'll get what's coming to you. Good night.'

He turned on his heel and walked out of the club. Outside in the darkness, pressed close against the wall, was MacOliver.

Callaghan said, 'He'll be coming out in a minute. It'll be easy for you to tail him. He'll go straight round to Narkat to warn him and Miranda. Don't lose him. Directly he gets there, give me a ring on the telephone. I'll be at the office.'

Callaghan disappeared in the darkness.

At twelve o'clock Blooey Stevens, gasping a little, walked up the stairs to Narkat's flat in Charing Cross. He put his finger on the doorbell and kept it there. Two minutes afterwards the door opened. Narkat stood in the door-way. He was tall, slim, overdressed. He raised his eyebrows in surprise when he saw Stevens.

'Well, if it isn't Blooey,' he said. 'Fancy you out on a night like this. What's the trouble?'

'There's plenty of trouble,' said Stevens. 'Willie the Mug's wise to that Amalgamated frame-up. He's broken out of Maidstone this afternoon.'

They stood looking at each other. After a minute Narkat produced an uneasy grin.

'Come in,' he said. 'Miranda's inside. We'd better talk this over.'

It was one o'clock. Blooey Stevens, fortified with several large whiskies and sodas, was feeling distinctly better. Narkat, his nerve recovered, stood in front of the fireplace. On the other side of the fire, in an armchair, sat Miranda.

'Look,' said Narkat. 'I don't see what we've got to worry about. If Willie's found out what we've pulled on him, he's not going to be feeling good. But I don't think he's going as far as murder. I don't think he'd take a chance on that. After all, seven years is better than a rope. I've got another idea. If he shows up I'll try it on.'

'What's the idea, boss?' said Blooey.

'I'll buy that stuff off him,' said Narkat with a grin.

'Work it out for yourself. He's got out of prison and he's broke. With all this war trouble on, if he's got some money, there's a good chance of him getting away. He knows he's got that jewellery hidden somewhere and he knows we don't know where it is. I'll do a deal with him.

'If he likes to hand it over, I'll give him a thousand. With that money and a bit of luck he might make a getaway.'

Stevens said uneasily, 'Do you think he'll want to do a deal?'

Narkat shrugged his shoulders.

'Well, what else can we do?' he asked. 'We can't go round to the police and ask for protection, not unless we tell 'em the whole story. Anyway, he hasn't appeared yet.'

The words were hardly out of his mouth before the telephone rang. Narkat crossed to the instrument. He stiffened as a hoarse voice came over the wire.

'Good evening, Narkat,' said the voice. 'How d'you do? This is Willie the Mug. I'd recognise that voice of yours anywhere. Well, what have you got to say?'

Narkat said nothing. He looked at Miranda and Blooey.

'Now you listen to me,' the voice went on. 'I've got out of stir, and I'm going to stay out, see? And you're going to do what I tell you, Narkat, or I'm going to get the lot of you.'

'Look, Willie,' said Narkat, 'I'm not unreasonable. Why not let bygones be bygones? If I can do anything for you, you know I'll do it.'

'Like hell you will,' said Willie the Mug. 'Well, I'll tell you what you're going to do now. I'm speaking from the callbox just opposite your flat. I've got a gun in my pocket. If you don't do what I tell you, I'm coming over there to use it. Have you got any money?'

Narkat winked at Blooey.

'Yes, Willie,' he said. 'I've got a thousand. I'll tell you what I'll do with you. If you like to let me know where that jewellery is, I'll hand over the thousand and I'll fix a hide-out for you.'

'All right,' said Willie the Mug. 'You get that thousand an' you come downstairs an' walk round to my place in Sellers Alley. The door'll be open. An' remember I'll be just be'ind you. If you try any funny business I'll let you 'ave it.'

He wheezed hoarsely.

'OK, Willie,' said Narkat. 'I'll be there.'

He hung up.

'It's all right,' he said to the others. 'He'll do a deal. We'll get that stuff and there'll be a sweet profit.'

Narkat stumbled along Sellers Alley in the darkness. He found the door of Willie the Mug's place open. He went in and stood in the hallway. The door shut behind him. He could hear Willie the Mug wheezing. Narkat thought he sounded pretty bad.

He felt himself pushed into the room on the right of the hallway. He stood there leaning with his back against the wall.

'I've got the dough, Willie,' he said. 'Where's the stuff?'

'It's under a pavin' stone at the back,' wheezed the other. 'I'll get it. But I want to talk to you first. You tell Miranda that one of these fine days I'm going' to fix 'er. You can tell 'er that!'

Narkat said, 'It was tough on you, Willie, but what could she do? When Blooey did the job he handed the stuff to her to bring to me. She saw that flycop Viners, an' got the wind up. So she planted it on you. She never thought that you'd get pinched for it – or that when you did you wouldn't find a way out of it.'

Willie said, 'Shut up an' hand over the money.'

Narkat put his hand out in the darkness with the notes in it. Suddenly a light went on. Narkat found himself looking at Callaghan. On the other side of the room, standing by the windows which were shielded by blankets, stood two more men – they were Flying Squad men.

Callaghan said, 'So you fell for it, Narkat. We've got all we want on you now.'

Narkat muttered a curse.

'So you got at Stevens,' he said. 'I'll fix him for this – one day.'

'No, we didn't,' said Callaghan with a grin. 'I got the story from Ferdie Phelps tonight. Then I got in touch with a printer who does odd jobs for me. We got him to print a fake press report in the stop-press column of the evening paper.

'Blooey fell for it. I knew he'd come running round to you with the story. Then all I had to do was to telephone through to you and say I was Willie. You fell for that too.'

One of the Flying Squad men produced a pair of handcuffs.

'We've got the jewellery,' Callaghan went on. 'But I promised old Ferdie Phelps that I'd get Willie out. This was the way we did it. By this time they've picked up Miranda and Blooey.'

He grinned.

'You three are going to have a nice war,' he said. 'Inside!'

The Sleeping Dog

ROSS MACDONALD

INVESTIGATOR FILE

NAME: Lew Archer, Private Eye

PLACE: Malibu, California

TIME: 1965

CASES: *The Moving Target* (1949), *The Barbarous Coast* (1956), *Black Money* (1966), *Sleeping Beauty* (1973) etc.

DOSSIER: Lew Archer, policeman turned private eye, has been called 'the model slob sleuth' because unlike his predecessors he is not bothered about his appearance and more concerned with solving crimes than in creating an impression. He is also known as the most famous fictional detective of the 'sixties and 'seventies. Born in 1913, Archer was a policeman in Long Beach, California until his conscience would no longer allow him to work for what he knew was a corrupt police administration. Instead, he set himself up as a private investigator, and now often sleeps in his office since his wife, Sue, divorced him ('She didn't like the company I kept,' he once explained). He reuses yesterday's coffee grounds, dresses in dishevelled chinos and sports jacket, and drives the southern California freeways in a shabby car still scarred by half-finished repairs. Archer is cool, sardonic and driven by a strong moral sense, though he is more of a questioner than a doer. He can, though, be a catalyst for trouble whenever he begins to probe into the lives of the people involved in his cases. Lew is unusual in being a campaigner for the environment – a cause in which he was interested long before it became fashionable – and is always sympathetic to the problems of the young. Unlike his other contemporaries, he does not have a promiscuous sex life and prefers to read or study art – the paintings of the Japanese artist Kuniyoshi are among his favourites – and often surprises the wealthy Californians who form the majority of his clients and suspects with his knowledge and erudition.

CREATOR: Ross Macdonald (1915–83) was the pen name of Kenneth Miller, an erudite man himself, whom the *New York Times* described as 'one of the few mystery writers also regarded as a major American novelist'. Encouraged by his wife, Margaret, who was already established in the mystery field, Ross created Lew Archer in 1949 – his character's name having been lifted from Sam Spade's erstwhile partner, Miles Archer, according to some sources; but from his sign of the zodiac, Sagittarius, according to the author himself. Notwithstanding this, Archer immediately appealed to readers because he was essentially different from his hardboiled predecessors. 'He had enough feelings to be hurt and enough complexity to do wrong,' was how critic Anthony Boucher defined his magnetism. When *Moving Target* was adapted for the screen in 1966 it helped to make a superstar of its leading man, Paul Newman – although both Archer himself and the film were mysteriously renamed Harper. 'The Sleeping Dog' is a high point among the Archer short stories, which begins with the detective searching for a missing dog and quickly realising he is into something considerably stranger . . .

***

The Sleeping Dog

The day after her dog disappeared, Fay Hooper called me early. Her normal voice was like waltzing violins, but this morning the violins were out of tune. She sounded as though she'd been crying.

'Otto's gone.'

Otto was her one-year-old German shepherd.

'He jumped the fence yesterday afternoon and ran away. Or else he was kidnapped – dognapped, I suppose is the right word to use.'

'What makes you think that?'

'You know, Otto, Mr Archer – how loyal he was. He wouldn't deliberately stay away from me overnight, not under his own power. There must be thieves involved.'

She caught her breath. 'I realise searching for stolen dogs isn't your métier. But you *are* a detective, and I thought, since we knew one another . . .'

She allowed her voice to suggest, ever so chastely, that we might get to know one another better.

I liked the woman. I liked the dog, I liked the breed. I was taking my own German shepherd pup to obedience school, which is where I met Fay Hooper. Otto and she were the handsomest and most expensive members of the class.

'How do I get to your place?'

She lived in the hills north of Malibu she said, on the far side of the county line. If she wasn't home when I got there, her husband would be.

On my way out I stopped at the dog school in Pacific Palisades to talk to the man who ran it, Fernando Rambeau. The kennels behind the house burst into clamour when I knocked on the front door. Rambeau boarded dogs as well as trained them.

A dark-haired girl looked out and informed me that her husband was feeding the animals. 'Maybe I can help,' she added doubtfully, and then she let me into a small living-room.

I told her about the missing dog. 'It would help if you called the vets and animal shelters and gave them a description,' I said.

'We've already been doing that. Mrs Hooper was on the phone to Fernando last night.' She sounded vaguely resentful. 'I'll get him.'

Setting her face against the continuing noise, she went out the back door. Rambeau came in with her, wiping his hands on a rag. He was a square-shouldered Canadian with a curly black beard that failed to conceal his youth. Over the beard, his intense dark eyes peered at me warily, like an animal's sensing trouble.

Rambeau handled dogs as if he loved them. He wasn't quite so patient with human beings. His current class was only in its third week, but he was already having drop-outs. The man was loaded with explosive feeling, and it was close to the surface now.

'I'm sorry about Mrs Hooper and her dog. They were my best pupils. He was, anyway. But I can't drop everything and spend the next week looking for him.'

'Nobody expects that. I take it you've had no luck with your contacts.'

'I don't have such good contacts. Marie and I, we just moved down here last year, from British Columbia.'

'That was a mistake,' his wife said from the doorway.

Rambeau pretended not to hear her. 'Anyway, I know nothing about dog thieves.' With both hands he pushed the possibility away from him. 'If I hear any word of the dog I'll let you know, naturally. I've got nothing against Mrs Hooper.'

His wife gave him a quick look. It was one of those revealing looks which said, among other things, that she loved him but didn't know if he loved her, and she was worried about him. She caught me watching her and lowered her eyes. Then she burst out, 'Do you think somebody killed the dog?'

'I have no reason to think so.'

'Some people shoot dogs, don't they?'

'Not around here,' Rambeau said. 'Maybe back in the bush someplace.' He turned to me with a sweeping explanatory gesture. 'These things make her nervous and she gets wild ideas. You know Marie is a country girl – '

'I am not. I was born in Chilliwack.' Flinging a bitter look at him, she left the room.

'Was Otto shot?' I asked Rambeau.

'Not that I know of. Listen, Mr Archer, you're a good customer, but I can't stand here talking all day. I've got twenty dogs to feed.'

They were still barking when I drove up the coast highway out of hearing. It was nearly forty miles to the Hoopers' mailbox, and another mile up a black-top lane which climbed the side of a canyon to the gate. On both sides of the heavy wire gate, which had a new combination padlock on it, a hurricane fence, eight feet high and topped with barbed wire, extended out of sight. Otto would have to be quite a jumper to clear it. So would I.

The house beyond the gate was low and massive, made of fieldstone and steel and glass. I honked at it and waited. A man in blue bathing trunks came out of the house with a shotgun. The sun glinted on its twin barrels and on the man's bald head and round, brown, burnished belly. He walked quite slowly, a short heavy man in his sixties, scuffling along in huaraches. The flabby brown shell of fat on him jiggled lugubriously.

When he approached the gate, I could see the stiff grey pallor under his tan, like stone under varnish. He was sick, or afraid, or both. His mouth was profoundly discouraged.

'What do you want?' he said over his shotgun.

'Mrs Hooper asked me to help find her dog. My name is Lew Archer.'

He was not impressed. 'My wife isn't here, and I'm

busy. I happen to be following soy-bean futures rather closely.'

'Look here, I've come quite a distance to lend a hand. I met Mrs Hooper at dog school and—'

Hooper uttered a short savage laugh. 'That hardly constitutes an introduction to either of us. You'd better be on your way right now.'

'I think I'll wait for your wife.'

'I think you won't.' He raised the shotgun and let me look into its close-set, hollow, round eyes. 'This is my property all the way down to the road, and you're trespassing. That means I can shoot you if I have to.'

'What sense would that make? I came out here to help you.'

'You can't help me.' He looked at me through the wire gate with a kind of pathetic arrogance, like a lion that had grown old in captivity. 'Go away.'

I drove back down to the road and waited for Fay Hooper. The sun slid up the sky. The inside of my car turned oven-hot. I went for a walk down the canyon. The brown September grass crunched under my feet. Away up on the far side of the canyon an earth mover that looked like a crazy red insect was cutting the ridge to pieces.

A very fast black car came up the canyon and stopped abruptly beside me. A gaunt man in a wrinkled brown suit climbed out, with his hand on his holster, told me that he was Sheriff Carlson, and asked me what I was doing there. I told him.

He pushed back his wide cream-coloured hat and scratched at his hairline. The pale eyes in his sun-fired face were like clouded glass inserts in a brick wall.

'I'm surprised Mr Hooper takes that attitude. Mrs Hooper just came to see me in the courthouse. But I can't take you up there with me if Mr Hooper says no.'

'Why not?'

'He owns most of the county and holds the mortgage

on the rest of it. Besides,' he added with careful logic, 'Mr
Hooper is a friend of mine.'

'Then you better get him a keeper.'

The sheriff glanced around uneasily, as if the Hoopers'
mailbox might be bugged. 'I'm surprised he has a gun, let
alone threatening you with it. He must be upset about the
dog.'

'He didn't seem to care about the dog.'

'He does, though. *She* cares, so *he* cares,' Carlson said.

'What did she have to tell you?'

'She can talk to you herself. She should be along any
minute. She told me that she was going to follow me out
of town.'

He drove his black car up the lane. A few minutes later
Fay Hooper stopped her Mercedes at the mailbox. She
must have seen the impatience on my face. She got out
and came towards me in a little run, making noises of
dismayed regret.

Fay was in her late thirties and fading slightly, as if a
light frost had touched her pale gold head, but she was
still a beautiful woman. She turned the gentle force of her
charm on me.

'I'm dreadfully sorry,' she said. 'Have I kept you
waiting long?'

'Your husband did. He ran me off with a shotgun.'

Her gloved hand lighted on my arm, and stayed. She
had an electric touch, even through layers of cloth.

'That's terrible. I had no idea that Allan still had a
gun.'

Her mouth was blue behind her lipstick, as if the
information had chilled her to the marrow. She took me
up the hill in the Mercedes. The gate was standing open,
but she didn't drive in right away.

'I might as well be perfectly frank,' she said without
looking at me. 'Ever since Otto disappeared yesterday,
there's been a nagging question in my mind. What you've

just told me raises the question again. I was in town all day yesterday so that Otto was alone here with Allan when – when it happened.'

The values her voice gave to the two names made it sound as if Allan were the dog and Otto the husband.

'When what happened, Mrs Hooper?' I wanted to know.

Her voice sank lower. 'I can't help suspecting that Allan shot him. He's never liked any of the dogs. The only dogs he appreciates are hunting dogs – and he was particularly jealous of Otto. Besides, when I got back from town, Allan was getting the ground ready to plant some roses. He's never enjoyed gardening, particularly in the heat. We have professionals to do our work. And this really isn't the time of year to put in a bed of roses.'

'You think your husband was planting a dog?' I asked.

'If he was, I have to know.' She turned towards me, and the leather seat squeaked softly under her movement. 'Find out for me, Mr Archer. If Allan killed my beautiful big old dog, I couldn't stay with him.'

'Something you said implied that Allan used to have a gun or guns, but gave them up. Is that right?'

'He had a small arsenal when I married him. He was an infantry officer in the war and a big-game hunter in peacetime. But he swore off hunting years ago.'

'Why?'

'I don't really know. We came home from a hunting trip one fall and Allan sold all his guns. He never said a word about it to me but it was the fall after the war ended, and I always thought that it must have had something to do with the war.'

'Have you been married so long?'

'Thank you for that question.' She produced a rueful smile. 'I met Allan during the war, the year I came out, and I knew I'd met my fate. He was a very powerful person.'

'And a very wealthy one.'

She gave me a flashing, haughty look and stepped so hard on the accelerator that she almost ran into the sheriff's car parked in front of the house. We walked around to the back, past a freeform swimming pool that looked inviting, into a walled garden. A few Greek statues stood around in elegant disrepair. Bees murmured like distant bombers among the flowers.

The bed where Allan Hooper had been digging was about five feet long and three feet wide, and it reminded me of graves.

'Get me a spade,' I said.

'Are you going to dig him up?'

'You're pretty sure he's in there, aren't you, Mrs Hooper?'

'I guess I am.'

From a lath house at the end of the garden she fetched a square-edged spade. I asked her to stick around.

I took off my jacket and hung it on a marble torso where it didn't look too bad. It was easy digging in the newly worked soil. In a few minutes I was two feet below the surface, and the ground was still soft and penetrable.

The edge of my spade struck something soft but not so penetrable. Fay Hooper heard the peculiar dull sound it made. She made a dull sound of her own. I scooped away more earth. Dog fur sprouted like stiff black grass at the bottom of the grave.

Fay got down on her knees and began to dig with her lacquered fingernails. Once she cried out in a loud harsh voice, 'Dirty murderer!'

Her husband must have heard her. He came out of the house and looked over the stone wall. His head seemed poised on top of the wall, hairless and bodyless, like Humpty-Dumpty. He had that look on his face, of not being able to be put together again.

'I didn't kill your dog, Fay. Honest to God, I didn't.'

She didn't hear him. She was talking to Otto. 'Poor boy, poor boy,' she said. 'Poor beautiful boy.'

Sheriff Carlson came into the garden. He reached down into the grave and freed the dog's head from the earth. His large hands moved gently on the great wedge of the skull.

Fay knelt beside him in torn and dirty stockings. 'What are you doing?'

Carlson held up a red-tipped finger. 'Your dog was shot through the head, Mrs Hooper, but it's no shotgun wound. Looks to me more like a deer rifle.'

'I don't even own a rifle,' Hooper said over the wall. 'I haven't owned one for nearly twenty years. Anyway, I wouldn't shoot your dog.'

Fay scrambled to her feet. She looked ready to climb the wall. 'Then why did you bury him?'

His mouth opened and closed.

'Why did you buy a shotgun without telling me?'

'For protection.'

'Against my dog?'

Hooper shook his head. He edged along the wall and came in tentatively through the gate. He had on slacks and a short-sleeved yellow jersey which somehow emphasised his shortness and his fatness and his age.

'Mr Hooper had some threatening calls,' the sheriff said. 'Somebody got hold of his unlisted number. He was just telling me about it now.'

'Why didn't you tell me, Allan?'

'I didn't want to alarm you. You weren't the one they were after, anyway. I bought a shotgun and kept it in my study.'

'Do you know who they are?'

'No. I make enemies in the course of business, especially the farming operations. Some crackpot shot your dog, gunning for me. I heard a shot and found him dead in the driveway.'

'But how could you bury him without telling me?'

Hooper spread his hands in front of him. 'I wasn't thinking too well. I felt guilty, I suppose, because whoever got him was after me. And I didn't want you to see him dead. I guess I wanted to break it to you gently.'

'This is gently?'

'It's not the way I planned it. I thought if I had a chance to get you another pup—'

'No one will ever take Otto's place.'

Allan Hooper stood and looked at her wistfully across the open grave, as if he would have liked to take Otto's place. After a while the two of them went into the house.

Carlson and I finished digging Otto up and carried him out to the sheriff's car. His inert blackness filled the trunk from side to side.

'What are you going to do with him, Sheriff?' I asked.

'Get a vet I know to recover the slug in him. Then if we nab the sniper we can use ballistics to convict him.'

'You're taking this just as seriously as a real murder, aren't you?' I observed.

'They want me to,' he said with a respectful look toward the house.

Mrs Hooper came out carrying a white leather suitcase which she deposited in the back seat of her Mercedes.

'Are you going someplace?' I asked her.

'Yes, I am.' She didn't say where.

Her husband, who was watching her from the doorway, didn't speak. The Mercedes went away. He closed the door. Both of them had looked sick.

'She doesn't seem to believe he didn't do it. Do you, Sheriff?'

Carlson jabbed me with his forefinger. 'Mr Hooper is no liar. If you want to get along with me, get that through your head. I've known Mr Hooper for over twenty years – served under him in the war – and I never heard him twist the truth.'

'I'll have to take your word for it. What about those threatening phone calls? Did he report them to you before today?'

'No.'

'What was said on the phone?'

'He didn't tell me.'

'Does Hooper have any idea who shot the dog?'

'Well, he did say he saw a man slinking around outside the fence. He didn't get close enough to the guy to give me a good description, but he did make out that he had a black beard.'

'There's a dog trainer in Pacific Palisades named Rambeau who fits the description. Mrs Hooper has been taking Otto to his school.'

'Rambeau?' Carlson said with interest.

'Fernando Rambeau. He seemed pretty upset when I talked to him this morning.'

'What did he say?'

'A good deal less than he knows, I think. I'll talk to him again.'

Rambeau was not at home. My repeated knocking was answered only by the barking of the dogs. I retreated up the highway to a drive-in where I ate a torpedo sandwich. When I was on my second cup of coffee, Marie Rambeau drove by in a pick-up truck. I followed her home.

'Where's Fernando?' I asked.

'I don't know. I've been looking for him.'

'Is he in a bad way?'

'I don't know how you mean.'

'Emotionally upset.'

'He has been ever since that woman came into the class.'

'Mrs Hooper?'

Her head bobbed slightly.

'Are they having an affair?'

'They better not be.' Her small red mouth looked quite

implacable. 'He was out with her night before last. I heard him make the date. He was gone all night, and when he came home he was on one of his black drunks and he wouldn't go to bed. He sat in the kitchen and drank himself glassy-eyed.' She got out of the pick-up facing me. 'Is shooting a dog a serious crime?'

'It is to me, but not to the law. It's not like shooting a human being.'

'It would be to Fernando. He loves dogs the way other people love human beings. That included Otto.'

'But he shot him.'

Her head drooped. I could see the straight white part dividing her black hair. 'I'm afraid he did. He's got a crazy streak and it comes out in him when he drinks. You should have heard him in the kitchen yesterday morning. He was moaning and groaning about his brother.'

'His brother?'

'Fernando had an older brother, George, who died back in Canada after the war. Fernando was just a kid when it happened and it was a big loss to him. His parents were dead, too, and they put him in a foster home in Chiliwack. He still has nightmares about it.'

'What did his brother die of?'

'He never told me exactly, but I think he was shot in some kind of hunting accident. George was a guide and packer in the Fraser River valley below Mount Robson. That's where Fernando comes from, the Mount Robson country. He won't go back, on account of what happened to his brother.'

'What did he say about his brother yesterday?' I asked.

'That he was going to get his revenge for George. I got so scared I couldn't listen to him. I went out and fed the dogs. When I came back in, Fernando was loading his deer rifle. I asked him what he was planning to do, but he walked right out and drove away.'

'May I see the rifle?'

'It isn't in the house. I looked for it after he left today. He must have taken it with him again. I'm so afraid that he'll kill somebody.'

'What's he driving?'

'Our car. It's an old blue Meteor sedan.'

Keeping an eye out for it, I drove up the highway to the Hoopers' canyon. Everything there was very peaceful. Too peaceful. Just inside the locked gate, Allan Hooper was lying face down on his shotgun. I could see small ants in single file trekking across the crown of his bald head.

I got a hammer out of the trunk on my car and used it to break the padlock. I lifted his head. His skin was hot in the sun, as if death had fallen on him like a fever. But he had been shot neatly between the eyes. There was no exit wound; the bullet was still in his head. Now the ants were crawling on my hands.

I found my way into the Hoopers' study, turned off the stuttering teletype, and sat down under an elk head to telephone the courthouse. Carlson was in his office.

'I have bad news, Sheriff. Allan Hooper's been shot.'

I heard him draw in his breath quickly. 'Is he dead?'

'Extremely dead. You better put out a general alarm for Rambeau.'

Carlson said with gloomy satisfaction, 'I already have him.'

'You have him?'

'That's correct. I picked him up in Hoopers' canyon and brought him in just a few minutes ago.' Carlson's voice sank to a mournful mumble. 'I picked him up a little too late, I guess.'

'Did Rambeau do any talking?'

'He hasn't had a chance to yet. When I stopped his car, he piled out and threatened me with a rifle. I clobbered him one good.'

I went outside to wait for Carlson and his men. A very

pale afternoon moon hung like a ghost in the sky. For some reason it made me think of Fay. She ought to be here. It occurred to me that possibly she had been.

I went and looked at Hooper's body again. He had nothing to tell me. He lay as if he had fallen from a height, perhaps all the way from the moon.

They came in a black county wagon and took him away. I followed them inland to the county seat, which rose like a dusty island in a dark green lake of orange groves. We parked in the courthouse parking lot, and the sheriff and I went inside.

Rambeau was under guard in a second-floor room with barred windows. Carlson said it was used for interrogation. There was nothing in the room but an old deal table and some wooden chairs. Rambeau sat hunched forward in one of them, his hands hanging limp between his knees. Part of his head had been shaved and plastered with bandages.

'I had to cool him with my gun butt,' Carlson said. 'You're lucky I didn't shoot you – you know that, Fernando?'

Rambeau made no response. His black eyes were set and dull.

'Had his rifle been fired?'

'Yeah. Chet Scott is working on it now. Chet's my identification lieutenant and he's a bear on ballistics.' The sheriff turned back to Rambeau. 'You might as well give us a full confession, boy. If you shot Mr Hooper and his dog, we can link the bullets to your gun. You know that.'

Rambeau didn't speak or move.

'What did you have against Mr Hooper?' Carlson said.

No answer. Rambeau's mouth was set like a trap in the thicket of his beard.

'Your older brother,' I said to him, 'was killed in a hunting accident in British Columbia. Was Hooper at the other end of the gun that killed George?'

Rambeau didn't answer me, but Carlson's head came up. 'Where did you get that, Archer?'

'From a couple of things I was told. According to Rambeau's wife, he was talking yesterday about revenge for his brother's death. According to Fay Hooper, her husband swore off guns when he came back from a hunting trip after the war. Would you know if that trip was to British Columbia?'

'Yeah. Mr Hooper took me and the wife with him.'

'Whose wife?'

'Both our wives.'

'To the Mount Robson area?'

'That's correct. We went up after elk.'

'And did he shoot somebody accidentally?'

'Not that I know of. I wasn't with him all the time, understand. He often went out alone, or with Mrs Hooper,' Carlson replied.

'Did he use a packer named George Rambeau?'

'I wouldn't know. Ask Fernando here.'

I asked Fernando. He didn't speak or move. Only his eyes had changed. They were wet and glistening-black, visible parts of a grief that filled his head like a dark underground river.

The questioning went on and produced nothing. It was night when I went outside. The moon was slipping down behind the dark hills. I took a room in a hotel and checked in with my answering service in Hollywood.

About an hour before, Fay Hooper had called me from a Las Vegas hotel. When I tried to return the call, she wasn't in her room and didn't respond to paging. I left a message for her to come home, that her husband was dead.

Next, I called RCMP headquarters in Vancouver to ask some questions about George Rambeau. The answers came over the line in clipped Canadian tones. George and his dog had disappeared from his cabin below Red Pass in the fall of 1945. Their bodies hadn't been recovered until the following May, and by that time they consisted of parts of the two skeletons. These included George Rambeau's skull, which had been pierced in the right front and left rear quadrants by a heavy-calibre bullet. The bullet had not been recovered. Who fired it, or when, or why, had never been determined. The dog, a husky, had also been shot through the head.

I walked over to the courthouse to pass the word to Carlson. He was in the basement shooting gallery with Lieutenant Scott, who was firing test rounds from Fernando Rambeau's .30/30 repeater.

I gave them the official account of the accident. 'But since George Rambeau's dog was shot, too, it probably wasn't an accident,' I said.

'I see what you mean,' Carlson said. 'It's going to be rough, spreading all this stuff out in court about Mr Hooper. We have to nail it down, though.'

I went back to my hotel and to bed, but the process of nailing down the case against Rambeau continued through the night. By morning Lieutenant Scott had detailed comparisons set up between the test-fired slugs and the ones dug out of Hooper and the dog.

I looked at his evidence through a comparison microscope. It left no doubt in my mind that the slugs that killed Allan Hooper and the dog, Otto, had come from Rambeau's gun.

But Rambeau still wouldn't talk, even to phone his wife or ask for a lawyer.

'We'll take you out to the scene of the crime,' Carlson said. 'I've cracked tougher nuts than you, boy.'

We rode in the back seat of his car with Fernando handcuffed between us. Lieutenant Scott did the driving. Rambeau groaned and pulled against his handcuffs. He was very close to the breaking point, I thought.

It came a few minutes later when the car turned up the

lane past the Hooper's mailbox. He burst into sudden fierce tears as if a pressure gauge in his head had broken. It was strange to see a bearded man crying like a boy. 'I don't want to go up there.'

'Because you shot him?' Carlson said.

'I shot the dog. I confess I shot the dog,' Rambeau said.

'And the man?'

'No!' he cried. 'I never killed a man. Mr Hooper was the one who did. He followed my brother out in the woods and shot him.'

'If you knew that,' I said, 'why didn't you tell the Mounties years ago?'

'I didn't know it then. I was seven years old. How would I understand? When Mrs Hooper came to our cabin to be with my brother, how would I know it was a serious thing? Or when Mr Hooper asked me if she had been there? I didn't know he was her husband. I thought he was her father checking up. I knew I shouldn't have told him – I could see it in his face the minute after – but I didn't understand the situation till the other night, when I talked to Mrs Hooper.'

'Did she know that her husband had shot George?'

'She didn't even know George had been killed. They never went back to the Fraser River after nineteen forty-five. But when we put our facts together, we agreed he must have done it. I came out here next morning to get even. The dog came out to the gate. It wasn't real to me – I'd been drinking most of the night – it wasn't real to me until the dog went down. I shot him. Mr Hooper shot *my* dog. But when he came out of the house himself, I couldn't pull the trigger. I yelled at him and ran away.'

'What did you yell?' I said.

'The same thing I told him on the telephone: "Remember Mount Robson." '

A yellow cab, which looked out of place in the canyon, came over the ridge above us. Lieutenant Scott waved it to a stop. The driver said he'd just brought Mrs Hooper home from the airport and wanted to know if that constituted a felony. Scott waved him on.

'I wonder what she was doing at the airport,' Carlson said.

'Coming home from Vegas. She tried to call me from there last night. I forgot to tell you.'

'You don't forget important things like that,' Carlson said.

'I suppose I wanted her to come home under her own power.'

'In case she shot her husband?'

'More or less.'

'She didn't. Fernando shot him, didn't you, boy?'

'I shot the dog. I am innocent of the man.' He turned to me. 'Tell her that. Tell her I am sorry about the dog. I came out here to surrender the gun and tell her yesterday. I don't trust myself with guns.'

'With darn good reason,' Carlson said. 'We know you shot Mr Hooper. Ballistic evidence doesn't lie.'

Rambeau screeched in his ear, 'You're a liar! You're all liars!'

Carlson swung his open hand against the side of Rambeau's face. 'Don't call me names, little man.'

Lieutenant Scott spoke without taking his eyes from the road. 'I wouldn't hit him, Chief. You wouldn't want to damage our case.'

Carlson subsided, and we drove on up to the house. Carlson went in without knocking. The guard at the door discouraged me from following him.

I couldn't hear Fay's voice on the other side of the door, too low to be understood. Carlson said something to her.

'Get out! Get out of my house, you killer!' Fay cried out sharply.

Carlson didn't come out. I went in instead. One of his

arms was wrapped around her body, the other hand was covering her mouth. I got his Adam's apple in the crook of my left arm, pulled him away from her, and threw him over my left hip. He went down clanking and got up holding his revolver.

He should have shot me right away. But he gave Fay Hooper time to save my life.

She stepped in front of me. 'Shoot me, Mr Carlson. You might as well. You shot the one man I ever cared for.'

'Your husband shot George Rambeau, if that's who you mean. I ought to know. I was there.' Carlson scowled down at his gun and replaced it in his holster.

Lieutenant Scott was watching him from the doorway.

'You were there?' I said to Carlson. 'Yesterday you told me Hooper was alone when he shot Rambeau.'

'He was. When I said I was there, I meant in the general neighbourhood.'

'Don't believe him,' Fay said. 'He fired the gun that killed George, and it was no accident. The two of them hunted George down in the woods. My husband planned to shoot him himself, but George's dog came at him and he had to dispose of it. By that time George had drawn a bead on Allan. Mr Carlson shot him. It was hardly a coincidence that the next spring Allan financed his campaign for sheriff.'

'She's making it up,' Carlson said. 'She wasn't within ten miles of the place.'

'But you were, Mr Carlson, and so was Allan. He told me the whole story yesterday, after we found Otto. Once that happened, he knew that everything was bound to come out. I already suspected him, of course, after I talked to Fernando. Allan filled in the details himself. He thought, since he hadn't killed George personally, I would be able to forgive him. But I couldn't. I left him and flew to Nevada, intending to divorce him. I've been intending to for twenty years.'

Carlson said, 'Are you sure you didn't shoot him before you left?'

'How could she have?' I said. 'Ballistics don't lie, and the ballistic evidence says he was shot with Fernando's rifle. Nobody had access to it but Fernando – and you. You stopped him on the road and knocked him out, took his rifle, and used it to kill Hooper. You killed him for the same reason that Hooper buried the dog – to keep the past buried. You thought Hooper was the only witness to the murder of George Rambeau. But by that time Mrs Hooper knew about it, too.'

'It wasn't murder. It was self-defence, just like the war. Anyway, you'll never hang it on me.'

'We don't have to. We'll hang Hooper on you. How about it, Lieutenant?'

Scott nodded grimly, not looking at his chief. I relieved Carlson of his gun. He winced, as if I were amputating part of his body. He offered no resistance when Scott took him to the car.

I stayed behind for a final word with Fay. 'Fernando asked me to tell you he's sorry for shooting your dog.'

'We're both sorry.' She stood with her eyes down, as if the past was swirling visibly around her feet. 'I'll talk to Fernando later. Much later.'

'There's one coincidence that bothers me. How did you happen to take your dog to his school?'

'I happened to see his sign, and Fernando Rambeau isn't a common name. I couldn't resist going there. I had to know what had happened to George. I think perhaps Fernando came to California for the same reason.'

'Now you both know,' I said.

Caribbean Clues

PATRICIA MCGERR

INVESTIGATOR FILE

NAME: Selena Mead, Government Agent

PLACE: The Caribbean

TIME: 1983

CASES: *The King Will Die Tonight* (1963), *Is There a Traitor in the House?* (1964), *Legacy of Danger* (1970), *The Writing on the Wall* (1978) etc.

DOSSIER: Selena Mead is a resourceful government agent *extraordinaire* who has been described as 'one of the first women protagonists without womanly frills'. Although born to wealth and social status – her mother is a descendant of Robert E. Lee and her father a leading industrialist and occasional ambassador – Selena has proved herself equally at home investigating subversive activities in the farflung corners of the world or dancing with visiting statesmen at the White House. Attractive and engaging, she prefers to avoid the use of violence in favour of wit and guile despite the trauma which brought her into her present role. Profoundly happy in her marriage, Selena had her world shattered when her husband, Simon Mead, an agent for a secretive branch of the US National Security, known as Section Q, was knifed by an enemy agent in a Washington back-street in 1963. Distraught but resolute, she tracked down the killer, cleared a US senator of suspicion of treason, and found herself drawn into her late husband's network. Since then she has foiled a plot against the First Family, rescued a king, and tracked down criminal masterminds in places as far apart as Eastern Europe and South America. Although once dubbed by the *Wall Street Journal* as 'the female James Bond' – an epithet she denies and intensely dislikes – Selena avoids the use of guns and has the highest moral standards. She is now remarried to Hugh Pierce, her immediate superior in Section Q, and also works as a journalist covering stories for a Washington magazine – facts which enable the couple to work together often on investigations.

CREATOR: Patricia McGerr (b. 1917) was educated in Washington and worked as a public relations officer and journalist before becoming a fulltime writer in the 'fifties. Attracted to the crime genre by the announcement of a mystery story contest – which she did not win – she has since produced a string of exceptional novels and short stories which have earned her the accolade of having created a new development in the genre: the 'whodunnin?' in which the victim of the crime, rather than the culprit, is unknown. But it is for her memorable series character, Selena Mead, that she is best known, and the stories about the agent, with their elements of intrigue, suspense and humour, have not only won Patricia McGerr awards in the US but made her one of the few Americans to be honoured with the Grand Prix de Littérature Policière of France. 'Caribbean Clues' is one of Selena's more recent cases, in which the author again uses her strategy of starting with a solution and working backwards to create the mystery which unravels against the background of a luxury cruise . . .

***

Selena was at her desk paying bills when Hugh came in and dropped an illustrated folder on top of her cheque-book.

'Look that over,' he said. 'It's time we had a vacation.'

'Vacation?'

She glanced at the red-letter headline – 'Six Sun-filled Fun-filled Days in the Caribbean' – then raised her eyes to regard her husband with scepticism. 'While I bask in the sun, what will you be doing for Section Q?'

'Nothing consequential. A little courier duty.'

'Really? I know budgets are being cut all over Washington but I didn't think it had reached the point where agency heads have to run their own errands.'

'What's the good of being chief,' he countered, 'if I can't give myself a plum assignment? Read the brochure. Look at the pictures. It's a great trip. A quarter of an hour for business and the rest of the week to enjoy ourselves. Aren't you tempted?'

'I might be.' The cover picture was of scantily clad couples holding tall glasses and reclining in deckchairs around a sun-drenched pool. It was in sharp contrast to the snow and ice and blistering winds outside their door. 'But only if you tell me the real reason for the trip.'

'I have a piece of paper to deliver, that's all.'

'That's not all.' She swivelled her chair to look at him directly. 'This is a secret operation and it's important enough, or risky enough, for you to go yourself. If I'm to be involved, even if only as part of your cover as a cruising couple, I've a right to know what I'm walking – or sailing – into.'

'In intelligence work,' he reminded her, 'nobody has rights. Information is given on a need-to-know basis and for this trip you only need to know what to pack.'

'I can refuse to go.'

'And send me off alone?' He grinned at her. 'They say

these cruise ships are filled with seductive females lying in wait for unattached men.'

'In that case you might like to withdraw your invitation.'

'What do you say we compromise?' Hugh said. 'I'll give you a rough outline of the mission and you do without names or specific details.'

'Very well,' she agreed. 'Just tell me what's on the paper and to whom you're going to deliver it.'

'OK, here's the plan.' He sat down, pulling the chair closer to her desk. 'Next Friday we'll fly to Miami and sail from there. The ship stops in four ports. During the second stop, a leader of the resistance forces of one of the Latin American countries will come aboard. There's a heavy price on his head, so his movements must be kept top secret. Going myself keeps the people who know about the meeting to a minimum.'

'And when you meet, what then?'

'I have a list of names to give him and a map. People who are sympathetic to the cause, and dates and places where they will make contact. Once delivery is made, he'll get off the ship and my job is ended. You see, it's a very simple operation.'

'You make it sound that way,' she conceded, then let enthusiasm override her misgivings. 'All right, Hugh, I'd love to cruise the Caribbean with you.'

The first two days lived up to the brochure's promise. It was an unaccustomed luxury to wake in the morning with no plans, no appointments, no deadlines. They were free to concentrate on such important decisions as whether to take a brisk walk around the deck, play shuffleboard, or lie immobile and watch the smooth sea blend with an almost cloudless sky. In the evening they danced to the accompaniment of a five-piece band whose repertoire bridged the generations from the waltz through ragtime to the latest hard rock. It was an idyllic time, the first extended period since their marriage that they could count on uninterrupted time together, their tranquillity unbroken by newspapers or telephones. The single distraction was the list that Hugh was carrying with him. Soon, Selena told herself, he'll pass that on. Then we'll have the rest of the cruise to rest, relax, and enjoy each other.

Early in the morning of the third day the ship sailed into its first port. Many of the passengers boarded buses for a guided tour of the small island republic. Hugh and Selena chose to explore on their own, shop for souvenirs, and lunch at a restaurant recommended by friends. They were walking up the broad tree-lined avenue when a young boy, running fast, brushed Hugh's right hip and sped on to disappear up a side-street.

'Your wallet!' Selena exclaimed. 'Did he—'

'No, that's inside my coat. But I think – ' he reached into his back pocket and pulled out a screwed-up paper '– yes, he left a message.' Unfolding it he read the words, 'Call your office.'

'Trouble,' Selena said. 'I knew things were going too well.'

'Not necessarily,' he returned. 'It may be a minor change of plans. I've been out of touch for two days.'

They reversed their steps and went to the American consulate, where Hugh's credentials procured a private room with a secure phone. Selena drank coffee with the consul's wife while he made his call. Soon he joined them, looking grim.

'Bad news?' she asked when, having declined an invitation to lunch, they were outside the consulate.

'The worst.' He said no more until they were seated on a bench in the centre of a small park where they could talk without fear of eavesdroppers.

'Raul,' he told her then, 'has been taken.'

'Raul? Is that the man you're supposed to meet?'

'Yes. Word reached headquarters yesterday that he was caught in an ambush and delivered to the security police.'

'Then your meeting is cancelled.'

'Not exactly. According to our source – an informer with links to the security forces – his capture has been kept secret. He was compelled, probably under torture, to give them full details of tomorrow's rendezvous. They're sending one of their own people in his place.'

'Then you can at least be thankful that you found out in time. I gather it would be unfortunate if the data you're carrying went to the other side.'

'A disaster,' he confirmed. 'In the wrong hands, my list would endanger some very good men.'

'Will you meet the impostor or just let him dangle?'

'Oh, I'll keep the appointment. But I'll draw up a new list of names. Men who are solidly behind the government, some with important jobs. If we can start them distrusting each other, that will salvage something from Raul's loss. Come on.' He rose from the bench, cheered by the thought of counterattack. 'We'll have to have a quick lunch or we'll miss the sailing.'

After returning to the ship, Hugh went at once to their stateroom to prepare a counterfeit message for the counterfeit Raul. Selena stayed on deck to watch the liner manoeuvre through the harbour's narrow passage while young islanders dived for coins tossed by the passengers.

Hugh had finished his work by the time she went down to dress for dinner, but with habitual caution they did not speak of it while in their cabin or later in the dining salon.

They were finishing dinner when the room's lights dimmed and the pastry chef emerged from the galley bearing aloft a cake lighted by candles.

'Somebody's birthday,' Selena guessed as, with everyone's eyes upon him, he carried his sparkling burden toward the corner where they sat. A waiter followed with a bottle of champagne and, from the opposite direction, one of the ship's musicians, guitar in hand, came to meet them. Stopping at Selena and Hugh's table, the chef, with a flourish, placed the cake before them, the waiter uncorked the champagne, and the guitarist began to play and sing the 'Anniversary Waltz'. Other voices, scattered around the room, joined him.

Our anniversary was last month, Selena thought. They've come to the wrong table. I hope they can correct the mistake without too much embarrassment. She looked at Hugh, expecting him to protest, but he responded with an almost imperceptible shake of his head, reminding her of an agency rule. When the inexplicable occurs, do nothing and wait for an explanation.

As the song ended, the cruise director stepped forward to hand Hugh a white envelope.

'Happy anniversary, Mr and Mrs Pierce,' she said. 'This message came through shortly before dinner and the radio operator tipped us off. I hope you don't mind our holding it back in order to arrange the surprise.'

'It was indeed a surprise.' Hugh's glance circled the foursome – chef, waiter, guitarist, and cruise director. 'My wife and I are very grateful. Will you blow out the candles, darling?'

'It was most kind of you.' Selena smiled at them, took a deep breath, and bent toward the cake. The candles flickered and went out and the other diners applauded. The waiter poured the champagne, Selena cut the cake, and the staff members, satisfied with the celebration's success, left them alone.

Hugh tore open the envelope and, with unchanging expression, read the message silently and passed it to Selena. It was brief. 'Happy Anniversary. Love from Sophie, Craig, and Doris.' The greeting, she assumed, was camouflage. The coded message was in the signatures.

'Sophie, Craig, and Doris,' she repeated.

'Yes, aren't they the thoughtful ones.' Leaning close, his mouth at her ear, Hugh translated. 'Source credibility doubtful.'

'Oh.' For the benefit of anyone still watching, she smiled demurely and lowered her eyes.

While they ate the cake and sipped the wine, she thought about the message. The source referred to must be the informer who had reported Raul's capture and replacement. That he should be of dubious credibility was not surprising. Informers are often turned into double agents. If they discovered he was sending reports to Section Q, they might well use him to feed us misinformation. But what would be the point of saying Raul was in custody if it wasn't true?

'Congratulations, you two.' Passing their table with his wife in tow, a fellow passenger interrupted her thoughts. 'How long since you tied the knot?'

'Fifteen years,' Hugh answered.

'Let's hope you have fifteen more,' he said heartily and moved on.

He was the first of a stream of wellwishers who followed them from the dining-room, eager to help them celebrate the fictitious anniversary. They bought them drinks, offered toasts, shook Hugh's hand, kissed Selena.

'Next time,' she suggested when they had a moment's privacy, 'tell your colleagues to send condolences.'

'I think,' he returned, 'it's time for the happy couple to take a walk in the moonlight.'

They escaped from the lounge, climbed to the next deck, and walked back to the dark deserted swimming pool. There Selena was at last able to ask her question.

'If they somehow found out about Raul's mission,' he explained, 'but weren't able to stop him, they could plant the impostor story to block his getting the information we have for him.'

'And if you give the real Raul the wrong list of names and the resistance goes to them expecting to find friends – '

'Exactly.' He finished her sentence. 'That would turn into a trap for him and his fellow freedom fighters.'

'Then it's lucky you learned about the trick before your meeting.'

'If it is a trick,' he said sombrely. 'The message doesn't say that our source has been proved a liar, only that his credibility is doubtful. The conclusion is that the information he sent us may or may not be accurate.'

'So the man coming tomorrow may or may not be Raul. Then the only safe course is to give him nothing.'

'That's how it appears.' He frowned, shook his head. 'But if it *is* Raul, he will have taken great risks to come here. If I send him away empty handed, all his efforts, the dangers he's faced, will be for nothing.'

'There must be some way to check his identity. Aren't there pictures of him?'

'Yes, I've seen his picture. I've also seen Diego, the man they say is coming in his place. They're cousins and they look very much alike. That's one of the tragedies of civil war. It splits families. And that lets them send in a ringer who can easily pass for the man we're expecting. You can be sure he'll have all the right IDs and be fully briefed on what to say and do.'

'You say you've seen pictures of both of them?'

'Pictures of Raul,' he corrected. 'Diego I've seen in person. So have you.'

'I've seen Diego? When? Where?'

'About three years ago. Remember we went a few times to a nightclub on M street near Wisconsin?'

'Jazz-o-mania?'

'That's the one,' he said. 'It's out of business now. You know how those spots come and go. But the music was good. Diego was on the drums.'

'So he's lived in Washington.'

'Not for long. After the club failed, he had a couple of other jobs but finally gave up and went home. They tell me he has his own band now and plays for all the official functions.'

'But he's not part of the government?'

'No, his interest is music not politics. The only reason for using him as messenger is the family resemblance.'

'And they'd have the same reason for giving his name as substitute if the report is a hoax. There must be some way to distinguish between them.'

'I'm sure there is,' Hugh agreed. 'Given enough time, we could uncover the difference. But H-hour is noon tomorrow. By then I have to decide whether to give him the right list, the wrong list, or no list at all.'

The ship docked at its second port at ten o'clock the next morning. Since most of the passengers would spend the day ashore, the company had sold vouchers to island residents and tourists that entitled them to a tour of the ship and buffet lunch. The arrangement supplied protective cover for the Section Q-arranged rendezvous. The scenario called for Raul to come aboard with the touring party and, shortly before noon, to go to the Carib Bar and order a drink. To assure recognition, he was to wear a bright-orange shirt decorated with brown ponies. Hugh would take the stool next to his and identify himself by ordering a quinine and gin. While sipping their drinks, they would exchange comments on the weather or other small talk appropriate to strangers at a bar. And Hugh would inconspicuously pass on the list of names.

'That means I'll have approximately ten minutes to judge whether I'm talking to Raul or Diego,' Hugh told Selena as they stood at the rail on the top deck watching the visitors come aboard. He shook his head.

'There ought to be something you could ask him,' Selena

said. 'A question to which only Raul would know the answer.'

'Too bad it's not the other way around,' he returned. 'If Raul were trying to pass as Diego, I might stump him with a musical question. But as things stand, there's no way—'

'Maybe there is,' she interrupted. 'There just may be.'

'You've an idea?'

'I'm not sure but – yes, it might work. Anyway, it's worth a try.' She turned from the rail and started away.

'Where are you going? What's your plan?'

'There's no time to explain. But I'll see you in a few minutes. Outside the Carib Bar.'

Her first stop was the purser's office to ask where to find the guitarist.

'He may have gone ashore,' he told her, 'but I doubt it. He's probably resting in his cabin. Number 721 on B deck. Or there may be a card game going in the crew lounge.'

She hurried to the cabin, knocked, and waited tensely until the shirt-sleeved young man opened the door.

'Mrs Pierce.' His tone showed surprise.

'I don't believe I thanked you properly for serenading us last night.'

'Your husband did. He was very generous.'

'I'm glad to hear it. Because I've come to ask another favour.' She improvised quickly. 'Actually, the celebration was a day early. This is our real anniversary. And there's a tune that has special meaning for us. "Rhapsody in Blue". Can you play it?'

'Yes of course.'

'Then can you come right away to the Carib Bar? My husband's on his way there and I – oh, I know I must sound terribly sentimental –'

'Not at all. I'm happy to be involved in a romantic plot. Just let me get my jacket.'

'I'll go ahead,' she said, 'and meet you there.'

She took the elevator to the Promenade Deck and looked in the small bar. There were two customers, seated at opposite ends of the counter. One was an elderly passenger, the other a dark man in an orange shirt speckled with small brown horses. She waited in the doorway for the guitarist.

'Will you sit in that alcove, please?' She indicated a spot on the other side of the room. Crossing with him, she spoke again as they passed behind the orange shirt. 'I'd love to hear you play Gershwin's "Rhapsody in Blue".'

' "Rhapsody in Blue",' he repeated. 'You've got it.'

He sat down, strummed a few introductory notes, then began the familiar melody. Selena glanced at her watch. Two minutes to twelve.

She slipped out the other door to meet Hugh on deck.

'You have the lists?'

'Both of them. The right one here.' He patted his shirt pocket. 'And the other one here.' He touched his belt.

'I'll stand where you can see my signal. Ask him to name that tune.'

'You think he'll give himself away? He's not that stupid. I don't—'

'Trust me.'

'It appears,' he said, 'I have no choice.'

She waited on deck until Hugh was seated on the bar stool, then followed him inside. Passing the guitar player, she gave him an encouraging smile, then stationed herself close enough to the bar to hear the conversation. She was behind the orange-shirted man, out of his sight, but in Hugh's line of vision.

'This is the best drink in hot weather,' Hugh opened the conversation when the barman put down his quinine and gin.

'I prefer rum,' the other returned, 'in any weather.'

'That's good, too,' Hugh agreed. He picked up his glass, took a long sip, and seemed for the first time to become aware of the music. 'I've heard that tune before, but I can't put a name to it. Do you recognise it?'

'Sorry. I don't know anything about American music.'

Hugh glanced toward Selena. She put out her hand, thumb turned downward. He frowned, looking dubious. She repeated the gesture and he shrugged, accepting her judgment. He picked up a cocktail napkin and pressed it to his belt as if wiping off dripped liquid, then returned the crumpled napkin to the bar, near his companion's glass. A few seconds later the other man picked up both glass and napkin. He drained the glass and wiped his lips with the napkin while palming the paper Hugh had placed inside it.

'I hope you enjoy the rest of your cruise,' he said politely as he got off the stool.

'Thanks,' Hugh said. 'Nice talking to you.'

Selena watched him leave the bar, then took his place beside Hugh.

'I hope you understand what just happened,' he told her. 'Because I don't.'

'That was Diego,' she answered positively, 'and you gave him the false list.'

'I grant you that Diego would be suspicious of a musical clue and try to protect himself by pretending ignorance. But Raul would be genuinely ignorant. So how did that tell us which one it was?'

'Because I made sure he heard the title before our friend began to play. He knew it was "Rhapsody in Blue" and Raul would have told you so. Only Diego, needing to hide his identity, would deny his knowledge. And now your work is done, so let's thank the musician for playing our song.'

Virgil Tibbs and the Fallen Body

JOHN BALL

INVESTIGATOR FILE

NAME: Virgil Tibbs, Detective

PLACE: Pasadena, California

TIME: 1978

CASES: *In the Heat of the Night* (1965), *The Cool Cottontail* (1966), *The Eyes of the Buddha* (1976), *One For Virgil Tibbs* (1976) etc.

DOSSIER: Virgil Tibbs, the expert homicide investigator based in Pasadena, was the first black detective in fiction and became the archetypal black hero of the late 'sixties and 'seventies – strong, intelligent and defiant. Born in the Deep South where his mother still lives, Tibbs took menial jobs in a restaurant to pay his way through university before joining the police force. By the time he was in his early thirties he had earned an enviable reputation for interpreting clues in difficult cases and being able to look after himself in any physical confrontation. He is, in fact, a master of karate (having reached the grade of black belt) and has studied the even more advanced art of aikido. To help his career, he has also read law and science, while at the same time coming to terms with the humiliations of racial intolerance which he frequently meets on investigations. This was particularly evident in his first case, *In the Heat of the Night*, when he visited his mother and had to overcome being suspected of murder purely because of his colour and the prejudice of the local white police chief with whom he had to work to solve the brutal crime and preserve his own reputation. His dignified reaction to one hate-filled remark by another police officer is now part of detective fiction lore: 'They call me *Mr* Tibbs.' Today ranked as one of the great detectives of the genre, Tibbs uses his colour both as a badge of pride and a form of disguise when confronting prejudice – although despite his frequent encounters with intolerance he is not obsessed by the problem. A shrewd and proud man, he has come to understand both the black and white cultures and this gives him a unique freedom of movement and effectiveness denied to other conventional investigators.

CREATOR: John Ball (b. 1911), a former Air Force and commercial pilot, radio commentator and science journalist, is credited with having initiated the new breed of cross-cultural detectives who appeared during the development of ethnic consciousness in the 'sixties and 'seventies. A writer who researches his facts with painstaking care, Ball became a bestseller overnight with the publication of the first Virgil Tibbs case, which was faithfully adapted for the screen in 1967, with Sydney Poitier making the first of three landmark appearances in the leading role. The book was awarded an Edgar for the Best First Novel by the Mystery Writers of America while the movie garnered five Oscars. Ball has only written a handful of short stories about his prototype black investigator, of which 'Virgil Tibbs and the Fallen Body' is a good example. And when originally published in *Ellery Queen's Mystery Magazine* in September 1978, the editor confided proudly to his readers, 'It is unlikely that this story could have been written twenty years ago . . .'

The first thing Officer Frank Mitchell heard was a violent thud directly behind him; it was so powerful it seemed for a second that the very ground had shaken under his feet. He turned quickly, saw the body scarcely thirty feet away, and had a sudden, compelling desire to be sick. Only seven months out of the academy, he was still not used to the sight of sudden and violent death.

The body of the suicide, if that's what it was, had landed so hard the skull had split and what was revealed took all of Officer Mitchell's courage to face. Partly by reflex action he looked up, far up the side of the towering building in front of which he was standing. He saw an immensity of structure and glass that was totally unmoved by what had just happened. On Mitchell's first inspection the building gave no clue to the point from which the now smashed body had been launched into the air.

When he had seen and noted that, Officer Mitchell turned to do his unwelcome but necessary duty. There were a few others who had witnessed the terrible death; they hung back in a kind of hypnotised horror, unwilling either to come closer or to go away. Then through the small ring of spectators a slender but well-built black man came running forward, peeling off his coat at the same time. Because the man was headed straight toward the body on the sidewalk, Officer Mitchell held up his hands to stop him.

He could have saved himself the trouble; he was ignored. Instead, the intruder dropped to one knee and threw his coat over the head and shoulders of the fallen man. Then he looked up at Mitchell. 'Tibbs,' the man said. 'Pasadena Police. Get some back-up and an ambulance.'

Mitchell came out of his near shock and responded by taking his small portable police radio out of its belt carrier. He raised it to his face and put out an urgent call.

His immediate duty done, he walked the few steps to where the now covered body lay grimly still on the concrete. 'Thank you,' he said. 'It got to me for a moment.'

'Of course.' The Pasadena policeman got to his feet and had his own look at the sheer face of the massive building. 'He probably came from halfway up, or more. Did you note the condition of the skull?'

Mitchell swallowed and nodded. 'Frank Mitchell,' he introduced himself.

'Virgil Tibbs.'

'What do you work?'

'Robbery homicide.'

'Look, if you'd care to stick around until my back-up—'

'Of course. This isn't my jurisdiction, but I'll do what I can.' He took out his Pasadena ID and clipped it to his shirt pocket.

Mercifully, the gathering crowd showed no signs of wanting to come closer. A single young man armed with a small pocket camera started to move in, but retreated when Mitchell waved him away. After that the scene was static until a black and white patrol car coming Code Two pulled up with its roof lights still on. A sergeant got out; he was closing the car door when a second unit rolled in.

The sergeant took in the situation with a single careful look, then he too scanned the vast side of the huge building. He raised a hand to wave Virgil Tibbs away, then he saw the plastic identification clipped to his pocket. He came close enough to read it before he spoke. 'You covered the body.' It was a statement.

'Yes.'

'Thank you. The ambulance will be here right away.'

As he spoke, a red paramedic unit from the fire department rolled up. The two-man crew had already been notified what to expect; one man riding on the passenger side had a blanket ready on his lap. He jumped out, walked quickly to the body, took off Tibbs's coat, and satisfied himself that life was extinct. Then he snapped the blanket open and dropped it over the corpse. After that he picked up the coat once more and returned it to its owner. 'It may be stained,' he warned.

Tibbs checked it carefully, then put it back on. 'It's all right,' he said. 'I'll have it cleaned.'

Mitchell was talking to his sergeant, reporting on what he had seen. It took him only a few moments, then he introduced Tibbs.

The Los Angeles sergeant was obviously experienced, but unpretentious. 'I'm glad you were here to give us a hand,' he said. 'Bob Opper.'

'Anything else I can do?'

'If you've got the time, I'd like to get your account of this.'

'Whatever you want.'

'You work homicide?'

'Yes.'

'It looks like a jumper, of course, but I want to check it out. You're welcome if you want to come along.'

That didn't call for an answer, as the sergeant turned toward the entrance of the very high building. Tibbs fell in beside him. 'Did you get a look at the body before it was covered with the blanket?' Virgil asked.

'Partially. Why, did you catch something?'

'Perhaps,' Tibbs replied.

They walked together into the huge lobby. By that time there were blue uniforms everywhere; the LAPD was definitely efficient. Behind them a coroner's unit arrived and two men got out. It was hardly ten minutes since the body had hit the sidewalk, but the official machinery to clean up was already functioning smoothly.

There was a uniformed guard in the lobby; at the sergeant's instruction he rang for the building manager.

That done, Opper turned to his black colleague from Pasadena. 'You said you caught something.'

'The deceased had on a brand new pair of shoes. The soles were hardly scratched.'

'And you figure that a man wouldn't go buy himself a new pair of shoes just before he killed himself.'

'That's right. Buying a pair of shoes takes selection and fitting: if he was planning to take his life within the next hour, that wouldn't be a logical thing for him to do. From the condition of the soles he couldn't have walked more than two or three blocks at the most.'

'He could have put on a new pair of shoes and then driven here.'

'Agreed, but the percentages are against it; again, it wouldn't be logical unless his decision to kill himself was very sudden.'

A patrolman came in with a wallet in his hands. 'Here's the ID of the deceased,' he said. 'Robert T. Williamson, DOB 13 June, 1932. His home address is in Orange Country.'

'Run him – see if he was in any trouble or had a rap sheet.'

'Yes, sir.' The patrolman reached for his radio.

A man was hurrying up to them. He was middle-aged and well dressed in an expensive business suit. His shoes were shined and his tie was a model of good taste. He turned his attention at once to the sergeant. 'Excuse me, I've been on the phone,' he said. 'My name is Phillips, I'm the general manager of this building. Tell me how I can help you.'

'You know what happened?' Opper asked.

'Yes, unfortunately. I presume it had to come at some time, but this is the first such – tragedy – we've ever had.'

As the two men were talking, Virgil Tibbs stepped over

to the building directory and looked over the posted entries. When he came back, he had a question of his own. 'Mr Phillips, I notice that only the first thirty-two floors of the building appear to be occupied. Can you tell us about that?'

Phillips noted the police ID now clipped on the outside of Tibbs's coat, then responded. 'Yes, that's true, although we don't advertise that fact. You see, the higher floors, while very desirable from a tenant's point of view, haven't been finished yet. Frankly, we found that rentals were way below our expectations while the building was going up, so the builders decided to hold off on the expense of completing the upper floors until there was a demand for the space. In that way, they could be finished to suit the wishes of the tenants who lease them.'

'The whole building is air-conditioned,' Tibbs said.

'Yes, of course. There's a great deal of glass, you see.'

'My point is, Mr Phillips, do the windows open or are they all sealed shut?'

Opper looked at Tibbs and clearly approved the question.

'Most of the windows are sealed shut. A few do open, because the tenants wanted them that way.'

'On a building this high, isn't that dangerous?' the sergeant asked.

'Yes, so we designed them as casement types and set the handles so that they will only open a little way.'

'Could a determined man squeeze his body out of the opening?' the sergeant continued.

Phillips hesitated. 'That would depend, of course, on the man. Offhand, I would say that it would be very difficult.'

'Do you have a list of the personnel who work in this building?'

'No, you'd have to get that from the individual tenants.'

'Do you know a Robert Williamson? About forty-five, medium build?'

'No, not as far as I know.'

Virgil took over. 'Mr Phillips, suppose someone wanted to get onto one of the higher floors, even though they're unfinished. Could he do that easily?'

Phillips was prompt and emphatic with his answer. 'I don't think he could do it at all. Since there are no tenants, the stairwells are blocked off above the thirty-second floor. The elevators are all in, but only one of them will go above the thirty-second floor, and it takes a key to operate it.'

'You have the key, of course.'

'Yes. Do you want to go up there?'

'First, can you tell us offhand whether or not any of the windows on the north face of the building above the occupied floors can be opened?'

'I'm almost certain they are all sealed. I can have it checked.'

'How about the roof?'

'The maintenance people go up there regularly, and our resident building inspector. He works for us; his job is to keep a continual check on the building structure and all its systems. A building of this size—'

'I understand,' Tibbs cut him off. 'Now sir, if you please, we'd like to see the roof.'

At that point the patrolman who had been checking on the dead man reappeared; Sergeant Opper stepped aside to hear his report. As he did so, he motioned Tibbs to join him.

'No wants or warrants,' the patrolman said. 'Several traffic violations – nothing heavy. I also checked with Orange County sheriffs and they gave me a little more.'

'Good work,' Opper said.

'Williamson was apparently wealthy, but the source of his funds isn't known. He was hospitalised about a year ago; he fell down and cracked some ribs. In the course of treating him, they found some evidence of illegal narcotics use.'

'How did they get hold of information like that?' Tibbs asked. 'That's privileged.'

'I know, sir, but they still knew about it, don't ask me how. Apparently he wasn't hooked or anything like that, but he had some kind of medical history of narcotics. No action was taken at the time.'

'Probably the patient gave permission to have his chart seen,' Opper said, 'without realising that the narcotics data was on there. Anyhow, it explains a lot. He could have dropped acid some time back when it was still popular. Then, without warning, he went off on another trip – you know it works that way. Somehow he got to the roof and, like a lot of others, thought he could fly.'

'Let's go up to the roof,' Tibbs suggested.

On top of the building the height was terrifying anywhere near to the edge. The rooftop itself had many pieces of equipment installed – huge air ducts, antennae, and housings for elevator machinery. A sharp wind reminded all three men how high they were.

When Tibbs looked up, the movement of the clouds overhead gave him the illusion that the building was leaning. After he recovered himself, he walked carefully across the cement to the comparatively low parapet, judged the wind once again, and then began a meticulous examination of a section of the protective wall. He spent so much time doing it that his LAPD colleague began to show impatience. 'Find anything?' he asked.

Tibbs looked back at him. 'No,' he answered, 'and I'm strongly reminded of the dog in the night time.'

'The dog did nothing in the night time,' the sergeant responded promptly.

'You have just increased my admiration of the LAPD,' Tibbs said. 'You know your Sherlock Holmes. If you're through, let's go back down. This place is a little awesome.'

When they were back on the ground floor, Tibbs noticed a coffee shop set in one corner. After thanking Phillips for the trip to the roof, and the rest of his co-operation, Tibbs suggested that the LAPD sergeant join him for a cup of coffee. Sergeant Opper, who understood completely, accepted and saw to it that they were seated in a secluded booth.

'Now, what have you got?' he asked after their order had been taken.

'You've got one of two things – accident or homicide. At the moment I like homicide better.'

Opper was careful. 'From the condition of the body, the victim came off the roof, because he wouldn't have landed that hard from a lower floor. At least I don't think so; I'm no expert on jumpers.'

'He didn't jump,' Tibbs said. 'The PM may show a percentage of drugs in his body, and a careful check should be made for past acid use – that's the most likely thing if it was an accident. But this may help you a little – he definitely *didn't* come off the roof.'

Opper was thoughtful. 'If Phillips is right, none of the windows on the unoccupied floors open. We haven't checked yet for a broken pane.'

'In a way we have. If Williamson had broken a window in order to jump, there'd be some glass on the sidewalk. Your man out there might have been hurt, or some innocent pedestrians. No, I'm sure he didn't break a window.'

'How certain are you that he didn't come off the roof?'

'You felt the wind up there. Despite it there was some dust on the roof. It wasn't disturbed where he would have had to have gone over. And the parapet was unmarked.'

'Plus which, of course, just anybody couldn't get up on

to the roof without a key to the special elevator. And Phillips, the building manager, had never heard of the dead man.'

'Which leaves only one possibility,' Tibbs said. He stopped then and waited while the coffee was served.

'He couldn't have fallen out of the sky,' Opper mused. 'You can't get out of modern aircraft the way that – what was his name? – did. Over the English Channel, wasn't it?'

'Helicopter,' Tibbs said, and stirred his coffee.

'Someone would have seen it.'

'Twenty years ago, yes, but not now. Police and media helicopters fly over the city at low altitude all the time and they're commonplace. The fire department has some too. The point is, no one notices them or hears them any more, except under unusual circumstances. They don't look up just to see them fly by.'

Sergeant Opper drank some coffee while he thought. 'All right, he could have come out of a helicopter, and come to think of it, some of them don't even have doors, or the doors are very easily opened.'

'True.'

'But the pilot would have reported it.'

Tibbs smiled, not very much, and it was a little grim. 'All the helicopters operating in the greater Los Angeles area have a special frequency for talking to each other, it's one two two point nine five. If it had been an accident, then the pilot would have gone on the air immediately, knowing that all the law-enforcement helicopters airborne in the area would hear him. But he didn't. That's why I think it was a homicide.'

'Anything else?'

'Yes. Helicopters can fly at almost any speed they like, up to their maximum. They can turn on a dime, hover, and do lots of other things.'

'Therefore?'

'Therefore I think that Williamson was dumped out of a helicopter just at the point where it would appear he had jumped from the building. Remember, a good helicopter pilot can manoeuvre his machine with great precision, even in a wind.'

'One objection, Tibbs, and it's a strong one. Williamson would have struggled. He would have grabbed on to something. He was a well-set-up man and the pilot had to keep flying. Unless there were other people in the chopper. Even then, throwing a man out against his will would take a lot of doing. I wouldn't care to try it.'

Tibbs nodded. 'Let me put together a theory – you can check it easily enough. The man had traces of narcotics use, but he wasn't hooked. That suggests someone who handled the stuff, but who was too smart to use it himself. That's supported by his evident wealth with no obvious source for the money – you can check that too. If I'm right so far, then we're talking about some very ruthless people who are engaged in one of the most profitable forms of crime known.'

Opper took out his inevitable notebook. 'I'll check with our narcotics people. If they knew Williamson, or of him, you've got something.'

'Do you want the rest?'

'By all means.'

'I don't think the fall killed him. Or if it did, he was unconscious when he was tossed from the chopper. Suppose he was given a shot and taken out. Then he was dumped from the chopper so that he would appear to have jumped from the building. No one saw the helicopter for the reasons already given.'

'Father Brown's postman.'

'Exactly. Getting rid of an unconscious man, or a dead one, could be done without too much trouble. The cause of death would be so obvious that extensive tests probably wouldn't be run.'

'Not everybody has a helicopter,' Opper said.

'And that's the point where your investigation should begin. If you'll allow me.'

Opper got up. 'I'll call you tomorrow,' he promised.

MR TIBBS:

WHILE YOU WERE OUT SGT OPPER OF LAPD CALLED YOU. HE SAID CORONER DETERMINED CAUSE OF DEATH OD HEROIN, NOT FALL (???) CHECK WITH SHERIFF'S ARGUS PATROL AND FIRE DEPARTMENT CONFIRMS NO MESSAGE RECEIVED ON 122.95 AT TIME OF INCIDENT. HE SAYS ONLY A MATTER OF TIME UNTIL CHOPPER ID'ED. CASE DEFINITELY HOMICIDE, MANY THANKS YOUR CO-OPERATION, LETTER COMING TO CHIEF MCGOWAN RE YOUR HELP. HE ALSO SAID NARCO HAD FOLDER ON WILLIAMSON.

MARGE

Hey, Virg, what the hell happened, anyway?
M.

Full Moon

GEORGE BAXT

INVESTIGATOR FILE

NAME: Pharaoh Love, Homicide Detective

PLACE: New York

TIME: 1994

CASES: *A Queer Kind of Death* (1966), *Swing Low, Sweet Harriet* (1967), *Topsy and Evil* (1968), *A Queer Kind of Love* (1994) etc.

DOSSIER: Pharoah Love, the New York City investigator, has been described flippantly in the kind of language he enjoys as 'gay, black and as fast with a pun as he is with his gun'. In fact, he enjoys a much higher rating in the pantheon of great fictional detectives as the first homosexual sleuth. A muscular Afro-American, Love rejects the conventional dress style of officers of the law and favours a T-shirt – normally complete with an obscene motif – and wears a ponytail. He is a confirmed pacifist who recoils from violence, but is still a streetwise detective with a particular ability to spot hidden clues. Famous among his superiors for breaking just about every rule in the book, his lack of modesty is equally legendary. When not working, Pharaoh is struggling to become a writer and has already had several short stories published. He is attractive to other gays, and despite his offhand remarks is very careful about his liaisons in these days of Aids, which he refers to as 'the plague'. Pharaoh first appeared to solve a murder in *A Queer Kind of Death* which critic Jeff Banks has described as unique because of 'its verisimilitude-laden portrayal of the homosexual underground of New York to which victim, murderer and detective *all* belong'. Several cases later, he is firmly established as a major figure in contemporary crime fiction.

CREATOR: George Baxt (b. 1923), who was born and raised in Brooklyn, 'exploded across the skies of mystery fiction like a meteor in 1966', according to *Ellery Queen's Mystery Magazine*, which joined all the other newspaper and magazine critics in praising his debut novel about Pharaoh Love. At a stroke, Baxt showed himself to be at the forefront of writers in the late 'sixties who were putting the emphasis in their work on black humour. He was also a pioneer through his introduction of faithfully portrayed homosexuality into the mystery story. Despite the fact that some critics have found his later books 'grotesque and nasty', he has built up a huge circle of admirers, won several awards, including an Edgar from the Mystery Writers of America, and become a busy film and television scriptwriter. 'Full Moon' is the most recent exploit about Pharaoh Love, and a curious link with the earlier story about the Saint finds him in the world of publishing, too – though this time the criminal is a killer . . .

* * *

Poor Richard's Almanac was the talk of New York City within hours after the first issue went on sale. There were many who wished this offspring of the eccentric millionaire Lucian Wallace had been stillborn. It was nasty, mean spirited, frequently hilarious, carefully walking the tightrope of slander, dishing the dirt about anyone and everyone, slinging the mud with the uncanny eye of a major league baseball pitcher, and wallowing in its rarefied notoriety like a pig in a trough of slop.

Pharaoh Love, who referred to himself happily as detective no class, loved the rag. Lucian Wallace was a special friend of his, having once helped Pharaoh solve a particularly knotty problem by hiring two goons to beat up and torture Pharaoh's number one suspect. The killer's confession brought Pharaoh accolades from his immediate superior, chief of detectives Walt McIntyre, who Pharaoh suspected couldn't spell accolade.

Pharaoh recalled the chief asking him suspiciously, 'You're *sure* you didn't lay a hand on him?'

'Not a finger.'

'Would you swear on a stack of Bibles?'

'You got a stack of Bibles?' Pharaoh smiled. 'You know I'm a pacifist. I never strike the first blow or throw the first stone. What's your beef, Walt? He confessed to cutting the victim's throat.'

'But he was so eager when he confessed. In a room full of cops he kept looking over his shoulder, even with his right eye almost hanging out of the socket.'

'He never tried to recant. Even safe behind bars he didn't yell frame-up. He didn't even try for a plea bargain.'

McIntyre stated flatly, 'You know who did the number on him.'

'Even if I did, I wouldn't tell you. You're such a blabbermouth. Your wife says you talk in your sleep.' He added slyly, 'And that nothing's sacred.'

McIntyre bristled. 'When did you talk to my wife?'

'When I needed a suggestion as to what to get you for your birthday. She suggested a high colonic.'

Pharaoh swiftly dodged the ashtray that went sailing past his ear to crash against the wall behind him.

Pharaoh wigwagged a finger and admonished, 'Temper, temper.'

That was forgotten months ago. A lot of murder cases under the bridge. Walt McIntyre was almost abnormally fond of Pharaoh Love. The young Afro-American broke every rule in the book, and was eagerly awaiting some fresh ones to turn topsy-turvy. He sported a ponytail despite ponytails being frowned upon and considered much too frivolous for an officer of the law. He wore shirts that were frequently paradigms of obscenity. He claimed they made a collar easier while the perp was temporarily paralysed with shock. Take for example his Madonna T-shirt which he had flashed at her in a restaurant. He insisted it took minutes before she could raise her jaw. The rest of his attire was distinctively colourful and showed to advantage his muscular, well-proportioned body, while camouflaging his holster.

Now Pharaoh sat in McIntyre's office, his feet up on the desk and chuckling while reading today's issue of *Poor Richard's Almanac*.

'What's so funny?' asked McIntyre, who would never admit to sneaking a peak at the rag when no one was looking.

'This obituary of Norman Taylor.'

'Wall Street Norman Taylor? When did he die?'

'Not a moment too soon. The Feds were catching up with him. A stock swindle of some kind.' Pharaoh looked at his chief.

'I never understand these guys who have to pull a swindle when they've got more money than they can ever spend in their lifetime,' said McIntyre.

'It's August. There's always a lot of everything in August. Tonight's a full moon. Second one this month. It's called the Blue Moon. Two full moons in one month is very rare. But it's August.' Pharaoh winked at McIntyre. 'August is the bad luck month.'

'Where'd you hear that?'

'I read it someplace.'

'Probably in that rag you're reading.'

Pharaoh said, 'August is also the crazy month. That's when most psychiatrists take their vacations and go offshore to check up on their hidden bank accounts. There's more hidden bank accounts then hidden ids.'

McIntyre did not pretend to hide his astonishment. 'Where do you find out things like this?'

'Mostly from Lucian Wallace.'

McIntyre gestured lavishly. 'How the hell does a nothing like you come to meet a Lucian Wallace?'

'In the men's room of the Metropolitan Opera during a very bad performance of *Manon*. I remember the *Times*, headline, "*Manon* Overboard".'

'He cruised you?'

'Don't be crude, it's unbecoming in nothings like us.' Pharaoh bore down on the last three words. He didn't look to see if the chief got his point. 'We got to talking washing our hands and yes, I could hear him with the water running. When I told him I was a detective he invited me for a drink. We never did get to see the rest of Act One. I fascinated him.'

'Modesty was never your strong point,' said McIntyre wryly.

'When you've got it, flaunt it. Nobody'll do it for you.' He set the newspaper aside. 'Lucian is a very fascinating guy. It's three, maybe four years I know him now. He's been a good friend, a very good friend. He's done me a lot of favours.'

'Such as hire some thugs to beat up a murder suspect so your hands can stay clean.'

'Lucian admires my clean hands. He thinks they should be sculpted. He encouraged me to write those early short stories of mine.'

'Oh yeah. Them. I forgot you've got two careers now. How many you've published?'

'Four.' Pharaoh preened at the wall mirror while reciting the names of the magazines in which he had been published.

'Doesn't Lucian Wallace publish those?'

'That's right.'

McIntyre was lighting a cigar and squinting as the smoke attacked his eyes. 'You having an affair with him?'

Pharaoh smiled at the expected question. 'I don't have affairs, they're too expensive. And much as I loathe it, I have a great deal of respect for the plague. I respect anything I can't beat.'

McIntyre was flipping pages in the *New York Times*. He found the page he was looking for and grunted. 'There's no obituary of Norman Taylor in the *Times*.'

'Maybe they didn't like him. He once cornered the market in newsprint and monopolised it for years, sending the price skyrocketing and breaking the hump of a lot of newspapers and magazines across the country.'

'Lucian Wallace tell you that?'

'That's right.'

'Do you suppose he could find out what the winning numbers will be in today's lottery?'

Pharaoh moved away from the mirror while brushing nonexistent lint from his lapels. 'Shame on you, Walt McIntyre, for even suggesting the lottery might be rigged.' He looked at his wristwatch. 'My goodness. It's time for tea.'

'What's new with the homeless murders?' It was feared a serial killer was stalking the homeless population. There had been four killings in the past two weeks and McIntyre fretted it might reach epidemic proportions.

'It's not an easy one, chief, it's just not an easy one.'

McIntyre said with sincere confidence, 'My money's on

you, Pharaoh.' And then he added unkindly, 'The only good thing about it, there's four less homeless in the city.'

'Now *that* is unbecoming.' As he left McIntyre's office without waiting for a response, he wondered if the killer was someone fed up with being badgered on the streets for contributions to a battered, used cardboard coffee container. He walked slowly down the hallway to his office. He passed the office of his friend and colleague, Albert West, whom he could see through the open doorway sitting at his desk and seemingly staring into space. West, as always, was immaculately attired, as though expecting an invitation momentarily to an executive dinner.

Pharaoh said, 'Albert, you look embalmed.'

West sat back in his chair and invited Pharaoh to join him. 'Cute T-shirt.' It said, I owe, I owe, so off to work I go.

'One of your least offensive.'

'I must do something about that.' He saw a copy of *Poor Richard's Almanac* on his confrère's desk. 'I thought you disapproved of such literature.'

'How dare you dignify this crap by calling it literature.'

'I like it. It's funny.'

'It's outrageous.'

'It's outrageously funny.'

'How can Lucian Wallace publish this garbage and crow about it?' He rearranged himself. 'I saw him on *Geraldo* and he was positively offensive.'

'I missed the show. You sure it was offensive as opposed to defensive?'

'I have to admit, he gave as good as he got. He left Geraldo staggering against the ropes a couple of times.'

'I must ask Lucian about that.'

'He still a friend of yours?'

'No reason for him not to be.'

'Then how's about helping a friend who's on the horns of a dilemma?'

'What's the problem?'

'I know you read that rag of his religiously, so you've probably read Norman Taylor's obituary.'

'It was a scream.'

'His family doesn't find it particularly funny.'

'Who told you?'

'His son, Shea. We were at Yale together.'

Pharaoh's eyes widened. 'Yale? You went to Yale? How come you never brag about it?'

'What's to brag? I was there less than a year before they caught wise and gave me directions to the nearest exit. I saw Shea today. He asked me to his office. He thinks there's something suspicious about his father's death.'

'Meaning murder?' Albert nodded. 'Then ask the family to release the body for an autopsy,' suggested Pharaoh.

'I have and they did. Over the past six months there have been three other deaths of financiers under circumstances similar to Norman Taylor's. Those three were also in danger of investigation and having the boom lowered on them.'

'Coincidence?'

'I don't think so. They were all involved in a stock scheme called "Valley Forge". Maybe you've read about it.'

'I did but I have no head for finances. You know that. I'm always in trouble when we're splitting a cheque.'

'Shea told me it was a kind of pyramid thing, perfectly legal on the surface.'

'But the surface is being penetrated.'

'It doesn't worry Shea if that's what you're thinking. Though he's on Wall Street, his operation is in no way connected with his father's company or anything else.

He's just a plain old legitimate stockbroker. Too square to manipulate. He's strictly white bread and mayonnaise. But he knows his father was involved in this scheme and he suspected it was in some way fraudulent and that they'd sooner or later get caught and exposed. He convinced his father to get out just as the other three were trying to uninvolve themselves, but dying suddenly.' Albert added matter of factly, 'They weren't elderly men, Pharaoh. They were middle aged.'

'In other words, too soon to die.'

'That's right.'

'How can I help? I'm up to my hips in a serial killer.'

Albert was on his feet pacing. 'Pharaoh, in all four deaths, the *Almanac* ran the obituary before it appeared in any other daily.'

'The *Almanac* is on its toes. You know that. They blew the lid of the Michael Jackson story before anyone else had it.'

'Since when is a paper anxious to scoop an obituary? Who runs their obituaries?'

'How the hell would I know?' He thought for a moment. 'Why don't you phone them and ask?'

'I did. They said lots of writers contributed.'

'But they didn't say who was in charge.'

'No. They didn't.'

'What does it matter, anyway?'

'Four deaths. Similar circumstances. The four of them involved in a dicey operation.' He paused. 'Couldn't Lucian Wallace help?'

'Probably. I'm having a drink with him up at his place. I'll ask him. Were the other three corpses autopsied?'

'If the results of Norman Taylor's are suspicious, I'll request permission for their autopsies.'

Pharaoh made a fist and dramatically pressed it against his forehead. 'Oh God! Is there no rest for the wicked?'

Lucian Wallace's twenty-room apartment on upper Fifth Avenue contained so many bathrooms, Pharaoh commented in his first visit, it could easily accommodate an epidemic of diarrhoea. It was one of many outrageous comments that endeared him to Lucian Wallace, whose own sense of humour was as perverted and off the wall. As a former friend of Lucian's observed, 'Lucian's idea of a good time is driving someone to suicide.'

In his suitably decorated and furnished study, Lucian Wallace sat at his oversized desk staring at a family heirloom, a Smith-Corona portable typewriter which he was leaving to the Smithsonian Institute. He typed a few words and then sat back with a sigh while directing his eyes to a framed portrait of his immediate family. He stared at his wife, a lovely woman with perfectly coiffured hair in a perfectly designed Balenciaga which was the height of fashion a decade ago. Rebecca sat in a throne chair guarded on the left by her oldest son, Myron, and on her right by his younger brother, Avery. The expressions on their faces were pained. They hated having their pictures taken. Myron was now almost two years deceased, having perished on an Alpine ski slope when he lost a race with a thundering avalanche. His body was never recovered. Lucian never stopped hoping that some day, like H. Rider Haggard's Leo who was forever entombed in ice in the novel *She*, some future expedition might uncover Myron's perfectly preserved body. If they did, he hoped they'd give it a proper Christian burial. Rebecca was also dead, having succumbed to the ravages of a cancer she had bravely battled for several years. On her deathbed she held on to Lucian's hand so tightly he began to suspect she was planning to take him with her. Panicking, he slapped her hand away. With an enigmatic smile, she closed her eyes and set off on the big adventure.

And Avery. His favourite. Shea Taylor's tennis partner

at the club. Shea had suspicions about his father's sudden death and shared them with Avery. This made Avery unhappy and when Avery was unhappy, he always sought solace from the father he loved and respected. He'd been with Lucian an hour ago, but Lucian, for the first time in Avery's experience, had no words with which to comfort him. Avery left dissatisfied.

Pharaoh drove an unmarked police car to his appointment with Lucian Wallace. August. The crazy month. Full moon. Blue moon. He was uneasy for the first time in days. The serial killer case was a backbreaker, they always were. There were too many of them. Why doesn't somebody think of something new in the way of murder cases? Maybe bring back the iron maiden (she was a load of laughs) or the garrotte. Pharaoh made his way up Madison Avenue, hung a left at Eighth and then another left into Fifth and parked in front of the building which contained Lucian Wallace's apartment. The doorman came forth to do battle but Pharaoh held up his police sign and placed it against the windshield. The doorman backed off somewhat obsequiously once he recognised Pharaoh from previous visits. He hurried to the house phone to announce him.

In the library, Lucian told the butler to bring Pharaoh straight in. He typed one last sentence and then pulled the sheet of paper out of the typewriter, folded it neatly and placed it in an envelope which he then sealed. Pharaoh came sailing into the room with a false jauntiness to mask his unease and they greeted each other warmly. Pharaoh indicated the typewriter and asked, 'Writing your memoirs?'

'Who'd want to read those?' asked Lucian as he poured two vodkas on the rocks.

'I certainly would,' said Pharaoh. 'That was a real funny obit in today's *Almanac*.'

'Oh? Which one?'

'Norman Taylor. I liked that bit about him leaving a wife, a son, two grandchildren, a mistress and a pile of debts. You write this one yourself? It smacks of your own bitchy style.'

'It does, come to think of it, doesn't it? We were occasional business associates.'

'Yeah. Albert West told me. You remember Albert, the detective with the rigid spine, as you described him.'

'Of course I remember him. He's quite memorable.'

'He went to Yale with Shea Taylor. Briefly. Shea thinks there's something fishy about his father's death. A little too sudden.'

'Heart attacks are always a little too sudden,' said Lucian.

'How do you know it was a heart attack?'

'I'm just surmising as much. Heart attacks. Strokes. Cerebral haemorrhages. They're endemic to financial circles.' Lucian shifted in his seat.

'Well, we'll know for sure within the next couple of days. Albert's asked for an autopsy.'

'Albert sounds terribly competent.'

'Three other associates of Taylor's died recently under similar circumstances.'

'I'm aware of that.' Lucian sank into silence. Then, 'Is your drink OK?'

'Real cool.'

Lucian briefly wondered if there was too much ice.

Then Pharaoh asked, 'What's Avery up to these days besides making money?'

'I saw him today. He didn't seem too happy. Avery and Shea, Taylor's son, are friends. Shea has also shared his suspicion of his father's death with Avery. Avery thought I might have some suspicions of my own.'

'Do you?' asked the detective.

'Pharaoh, I've written you a letter.' He crossed to the desk, picked up the envelope and brought it to Pharaoh.

Pharaoh started to open it. 'Not now,' said Lucian sharply. 'I meant for you to read it later.' Pharaoh stared into the man's eyes. There was no twinkle where there was usually a twinkle. 'It's only for you. A scoop. I'm sure you know what a scoop is, in the newspaper world at any rate.'

'Getting it first. Like some of your obituaries.'

'Yes, I did have a few scoops there. I love the *Almanac*. It's outrageous. It's nasty. It's every awful thing everyone says it is, but no one has ever accused it of being dishonest. It told the truth because all my life I have always insisted on the truth. I was brought up that way. The *Almanac* doesn't make up gossip. It tells it like it is. There's no excuse for its outlandishness, for its pandering to the prurient and the morbid, and it has found a large readership. Here's a scoop for you. Today was the last edition.' Pharaoh reacted but said nothing. 'It's all in the letter.'

Pharaoh put the letter in his inside jacket pocket. 'We having dinner?'

'Forgive me, but I'm begging off. I'm having a really bad day.'

'Full moon.'

'Oh, is there one tonight? Well, that explains it. Well, old buddy, forgive me if I don't see you out.'

'Lucian, I don't like the way you look.'

'It's my medication. I took some before you arrived. Norman Taylor and the others took the same medication. We have the same doctor. I pay him handsomely. Pharaoh, give me a hug.'

Pharaoh hugged him and hurried out.

Lucian shut the study door. He returned to the desk, sat, closed his eyes, and waited.

Pharaoh, back at the precinct, shared the letter with Albert West and Walt McIntyre. It was succinct and to the point. It told of a carefully planned stock swindle that backfired and was to be Lucian's ruination. He eliminated Taylor and the other three in the hope of rescuing himself. He couldn't resist writing their obituaries.

Pharaoh laughed. 'You got to hand it to Lucian. He was one of the wickedest bastards on earth. But mind you, he set a good table.'

'Why that weird look on your face, Pharaoh?' asked McIntyre.

'I was thinking, what a lousy shame no *Almanac* tomorrow. It could have been Lucian's greatest scoop.' He waved the letter at them. 'His own obituary. The son of a bitch, I loved him so, I have to forgive him. Anyone for a pizza?'

Willing to Kill

DON PENDLETON

INVESTIGATOR FILE

NAME: Mack Bolan, aka the Executioner

PLACE: Dallas, Texas

TIME: 1978

CASES: *War Against the Mafia* (1969), *Nightmare in New York* (1971), *Hawaiian Hellground* (1975), *Friday's Feast* (1979) etc.

DOSSIER: Mack Bolan, the Vietnam veteran known as the Executioner, introduced another new figure into the crime genre: the Aggressor, a one-man army who takes on the enemies of society and destroys them without mercy or a moment's reflection. He has been called the 'Everyman of the 'seventies', a mixture of professional killer, idealist and avenger who sums up his philosophy in one terse sentence: 'Live large and stay hard.' Bolan unwittingly adopted his fearsome new identity after serving with distinction as a sergeant in Vietnam where he carried out almost one hundred killings in the line of duty, which earned him the nickname of 'the Executioner' among his fellow soldiers. On his return home to Pittsfield, Massachusetts, he found that his family – father, mother and sister – had been killed in his absence by the local Mafia. Not content to let the law take its own course, Mack became a lone crusader, and armed only with a game rifle proceeded to wipe out the Mafiosi in a spectacular explosion of bloodshed. In those moments he discovered his mission in life and now uses many of the techniques that he learned in the army – observation, pursuit, psychological warfare and, especially, killing – to exterminate criminals wherever he finds them. Bolan is, of necessity, a loner, trusting in his own skills as a former combat soldier to survive in the urban jungles where so many of his enemies operate. Although a believer in the sanctity of life, he never shies from wholesale slaughter against those who corrupt and exploit their fellow men. He is an anarchist by nature and undoubtedly most strongly motivated by cases of vengeance. Though the Executioner has yet to be portrayed in the movies, his like has been seen over and again in the roles played by such Hollywood stars as Sylvester Stallone (*Rambo*) and Arnold Schwarzenegger (*The Terminator*).

CREATOR: Donald Pendleton (b. 1927) served in the US Navy during the Second World War, winning a Navy Commendation Medal at Iwo Jima in 1945, and thereafter worked in the engineering industry and as a columnist on *Orion* magazine. In the late 'sixties he wrote a large number of westerns and science fiction paperbacks before, as he puts it, 'striking it lucky' with the Executioner in 1969, and thereafter being able to devote all his time to the series. Pendleton's achievement in creating a new sub-genre in the crime field has earned him huge international sales and ultimately allowed him to hand the series over to other writers. 'Willing to Kill' is the only short story about Mack Bolan that he wrote and it has been out of print now for almost twenty years.

***

At the beginning of his impossible war, Mack Bolan had not envisioned himself as the arch foe of the Mafia world. He had simply reacted to a terribly disheartening situation – in the same way in which any man of like talents and ideals would have done – with no thought that soon he would become the most feared and hated enemy of the crime kingdoms.

He had been a death master in 'Nam, sure, but he was, after all, just a man – a soldier, not a cop – an individual, not an army. There were limitations to what one man could do. Weren't there? Perhaps – but the resourceful and daring young soldier's 'last mile' on earth had stretched to encompass the entire Western world as he carried his personal brand of stunning warfare to this new enemy.

And Bolan had not expected to come so far. He was living 'on the heartbeat' – with no thought beyond the next battle-line – or beyond the next police trap. The men behind the badges were, in Bolan's understanding, 'soldiers of the same side' and he would not engage them in hostilities. But the official police reaction to Mack Bolan's war was, naturally, unsympathetic. The law was blind so could not distinguish between constructive and destructive violations. In the official book, then, Mack Bolan was the largest criminal of all. And he accepted that. He would, in fact, have it no other way.

Though several quiet offers of official sponsorship had been extended from the highest level of government, the one-man army had declined them all, preferring to wage his own war his own way. Bolan had never turned away a hand of personal friendship from those in the police community, however, and he often worked in quiet collaboration with individual law officers. His best friend in all the world was one Leo Turrin, undercover fed extraordinary and underboss of an eastern US crime family.

Another powerful on-and-off ally was none other than Harold Brognola, the country's top cop in the official war on organised crime. So Bolan was not entirely without friends. It was just that he had learned early in his war that he was stronger when standing alone – and, indeed, this was how he preferred to operate.

He was not 'operating' at all, though, that fated morning in Dallas when he stumbled on to the hit team from Los Angeles. He was simply passing through the area and he'd gone to the regional airport to claim an air-express package containing routine intelligence from Leo Turrin. After picking up the package – a rundown on the mob invasion of Wall Street – he followed one of those subliminal quivers of psyche which led him towards a quick-pass through the passenger terminal. And suddenly he was eye to eye with Jersey Jake Natti, a grizzled survivor of the old Murder Incorporated group.

Natti was on the downslope of life, now, and that fact alone was enough to support his reputation as the wiliest and most effective death contractor in the business. Longevity, in his business, was the stamp of success.

For Bolan it had been instant recognition – a bright spotlight illuminating the mental mugfile. Not so for Natti. He saw only a young Texan wearing Levi's, T-shirt, dungaree jacket, dusty boots, corduroy range hat – softly drawling an apology for getting in the way. The lack of recognition was understandable. Few living Mafiosi had ever stood eye to eye with Mack Bolan; even those few had carried away from the experience only a confused and faulty impression of what the guy actually looked like. The many composite sketches provided by police artists and mob headhunters alike agreed in but one detail, the eyes – and, indeed, though they captured one essence of the subject, these were without exception the coldly purposeful eyes of the combatman, which seemed to be the one detail which never escaped the living memory of a Bolan encounter. The Bolan gaze was actually composed of many diverse qualities and could flick from cold death to warm compassion in a single leap – or could contain both together at the one moment.

So it was no shame to the reputation of Jersey Jake Natti that he saw only what Mack Bolan permitted him to see. It was, though, perhaps a fatal failure.

Bolan stepped around the death specialist and moved casually on, but he had the guy in his peripheral vision and he kept him there. Natti was not alone. Another guy was at his left elbow and a third cold-eye kept pace two strides to the rear.

They would not be packing hardware, of course – not here, not yet. They had obviously just arrived on an incoming flight and were making their way to the baggage-claim area. None had given Bolan a second glance. He tagged along far to the rear, keeping plenty of bodies between, curiosity more than anything directing his movements.

The head party pulled up at a baggage carousel and stood in casual non-communication, awaiting the baggage offload from their flight. Quite a crowd was gathering there.

Bolan moved alongside an elderly man at the edge of the crowd and asked him, 'Is this the Denver flight?'

The man chuckled as he replied, 'I hope not. They told me the LA baggage would be here.'

Bolan thanked the man for that interesting information and moved on, taking position in the background from where a soft surveillance could be maintained.

There had been no Mafia rumbles out of Texas since Bolan's own firestorm through that state some months earlier. An embarrassed police establishment had quickly closed ranks in the wake of that sweep, determined to keep the lid on any reawakening mob activities in the area. So far as the intelligence could ascertain, there had been none.

So, yes, Jersey Jake's presence in Dallas could be a matter of considerable interest to Mack Bolan.

The two guys accompanying Natti were youngbloods. The faces had no place in Bolan's mental file. But those eyes had seen death, many times – no mistake about that. The tagman could hardly be more than twenty-two or twenty-three years old; a lanky kid with a nervous thumb. The guy at Natti's elbow could be anywhere less than thirty. He was short, stocky, hard – the lips set in a perpetual smile of which the eyes never became aware.

It was a death team, for sure. Guys like these did not travel in sets without very good reason.

Natti had a contract in the pocket, for sure.

Bolan moved closer and mixed with the crowd at the carousel as the baggage flow began. The first bag on the wheel was Natti's. No coincidence there, either. It was a large, square case with rigid sides – more of a box than a bag – and the baggage check was not the standard type; evidently it had received very special handling, to the enrichment of some lucky handler. Uh huh. Weapons.

The hit team claimed one other bag and went on towards the car-rental desks. The other guys awaited them there, familiar yellow rental envelopes in hand. Obviously those two had gone ahead to handle the transportation requirements while Natti claimed the baggage. But why two cars?

For that matter, why *five* hitmen? Who in Texas rated that kind of firepower? But that was not the end of wonderment. Another *five* cold-eyes loitered just outside the exit to the rental parking lot.

Hell, it was a war party.

Something large was going down.

Bolan peeled off and went quickly to his own vehicle.

He intended to be in tracking position when those headhunters got their show on the road.

The Executioner had invited himself to the war.

They had circled the northern rim of Dallas on the bypass and were now running east along Interstate 30. Bolan was tracking in the Warwagon, a twenty-six-foot GMC motorhome which served him admirably as base camp, scout ship, battle-cruiser, home. Dubbed 'the terran module' by the aerospace geniuses in New Orleans who installed the special systems, the big vehicle had provided fantastic dimensions to Bolan's one-man war against the Mafia. An onboard computer served as the heart of the space-age technology group which included electronic intelligence-gathering and processing capabilities, communications and navigation systems, unerring and massive firepower. But the big ship had her drawbacks, as well, in certain situations. For one, she stood out like a sore thumb. And though the big Toronado power plant moved her along at acceptable speeds in an open run, she was not as quick and nimble as Bolan would have preferred in heavy-traffic situations. Twice he had taken her back to the experts for modifications to partially offset the drawbacks. The tracking systems could now 'read' a target vehicle which could not be seen by the unaided eye, locking the navigation system on to the target for a sure track through the most disheartening traffic conditions. Also, a chameleon-like effect had been engineered into the outer skin of the vehicle, using an electronic system to colour-programme 'scale panels' and provide an almost infinite variety of colour schemes via the onboard computer.

That latter touch had been intended primarily to serve a confusion effect; however, it also provided excellent camouflage designs for off-road concealment, when needed.

Bolan was presently concerned about on-road conceal-ment. He was relying upon the distant-track capability to achieve that, dropping back to a healthy separation when it became evident that the killer force was definitely heading away from Dallas. Traffic on the interstate was moderately heavy and the quarry was travelling at a sedate sixty mph, pacing the flow.

As the final suburban exit flashed past, Bolan activated the mobile phone and worked the contact combination to his inside friend back east, Leo Turrin.

'I'm on the floater so watch it,' he told the double-lifer. 'I got your package – thanks.'

'Good,' was the relaxed response. 'How're things in God's country?'

'Ungodly, I guess,' Bolan replied casually. 'I just ran into a guy who's a dead ringer for Jersey Jake.'

'Oh, yeah?'

'Uh huh. Travelling heavy. With a big team. What do you hear from Jake?'

'I hear nothing,' Turrin said, that good voice still light and easy. 'Should I start listening?'

'Uh huh. Can you get back to me soon?'

'Right. Soon as possible. A whole team, eh?'

'In spades, yeah. And it looks like they came to play.'

'OK. I'll try to find a scorecard. Keep the floater open.'

Bolan said, 'Always,' and killed the loop.

He settled into the track and tried to allow the questions to rest awhile. They would not do so. Not that there was a lack of confidence in Leo Turrin's abilities. The little undercover fed had an incredible talent for pulling together bits and pieces of a distant picture. But there was no comfort in waiting while those same bits and pieces were hurtling together at a closure rate of a mile a minute – especially when each mile could be the final one. Well and good enough, sure, if this war party was moving against another Mafia faction; Bolan felt no need to interfere when the enemy engaged itself. They were welcome to kill off one another to their little hearts' content, and certainly there was no desire to take on a bunch like this if there was no need to do so. Bolan was hoping there would be no such need. He did not like extemporaneous engagements. There was too much to be lost and usually not enough gained. This methodical warrior spent his combat energies with the best strategic efficiency possible, not in wild-assed games.

At the moment, he was not all that prepared for an encounter with a superior force. He was low on personal energy and his armaments greatly depleted. He had, indeed, come to Texas to restock the armoury and to pick up a bit of R&R on the coast. There was but one firebird left for the warwagon's big punch. As for personal munitions – there were hardly enough in the boodle to supply a brief firefight.

But that killer force ahead continued streaking eastwards, the hounds of hell running towards God-knew-whose blood. What were ten guns looking for in east Texas? What the hell was *here*? What was at stake?

A quick little chill tickled the Bolan spine, emanating from some subliminal tremor of the combat instinct.

And Mack Bolan knew, without knowing why, that he would be there . . . at the kill.

They were lunching at a truck stop outside Texarkana, on the Texas–Arkansas border. It had been a three-and-one-half-hour run, without let-up, and Bolan had begun to worry about his fuel supply. The headhunters were already seated in the restaurant when he pulled into the service area. He gassed up, then changed clothes quickly and went inside. The group occupied three separate tables. They all seemed a bit uptight, restrained – perhaps intent only upon blending in, non-notable. Bolan gave them only a quick and apparently disinterested glance as he moved on through the lobby and into the truckers' lounge – but he had their measure. They were all packing hardware, now. And they were as notable as the death look they wore.

He went to a phone booth and began the complicated calling code which would route him into Leo Turrin's 'clean phone'. The little guy had dropped a quickie on the floater an hour earlier: 'Call me clean as quick as possible.'

That usually meant something too hot to relate via open circuits.

But that good voice was droll and relaxed as it swelled into the clean connection. 'Natti is the only Jersey Jake I know of, Sarge.'

'That's the one,' Bolan assured him.

'OK. He operates out of an office in Santa Monica. Calls himself a business consultant. But all the wiseguys know what his business is.'

'What's he doing in Texas with a war party, Leo?'

'I got no wires on that. Couldn't get any. I did call his office in Santa Monica. Got an answering service. Said he would be unavailable for the next twenty-four hours. So.'

'Yeah,' Bolan said. 'So.'

'Where are you now?'

'Texarkana. For lunch.'

'That's just about in Arkansas, isn't it?'

'Half and half, yeah. What's the hot, Leo?'

The double-lifer laughed nervously. 'Maybe it's nothing. I just had the hunch. And now you say Texarkana. I, uh, picked up something from the other side of the street.'

Which explained the 'hot'. Turrin never felt comfortable divulging, even to Mack Bolan, important secrets from the official side of his life.

Bolan said, 'Suit yourself, buddy. But I'm getting spinal shivers, myelf. So . . .'

'Yeah. Me, too. Well. It's a long shot, but . . .'

'Your shivers are good enough for me, Leo. Let's play it.'

'OK. There's a place down in the western region of Arkansas. Long ways from Dallas – long ways from Texarkana, for that matter, but it's in the ballpark, at least. And you don't want to discount the fancy footwork getting there.'

'What sort of place?'

'They got an FBI safe house there.'

A new chill chased itself along the military spine. 'Who's in it?'

'I couldn't get that. I only know that it's suddenly very hot. I tried to get Brognola a while ago, after I talked to you. He's totally out of reach. En route to Arkansas, I get it. I left a page for him at the Little Rock airport. I figure he'll be taking a chopper from there. Some VIP they've got stashed in this safe house is ready to start talking about a whole new subject. The gossip off of Capitol Hill has it connected somehow with three presidential admin- istrations, the CIA, the Bay of Pigs, and the death of a president plus the undoing of another. I don't know, it's very garbled and all I get is echoes. But it's very hot. And I'm guessing that Brognola is headed down there to begin the formalities.'

Bolan mused, 'This, uh, VIP had some high visibility?'

'Oh, it's all in the family, for sure. He wouldn't be VIP otherwise, Sarge. They don't set up button men in mountain retreats.'

'Where's the stash, Leo?'

'Has something to do with a place called Petit Jean.'

'Is that in the Hot Springs area?'

'Not really, no. I know what you're thinking of – but that's downstate a bit. This joint is up near the Rockefel- ler ranch, up in the mountain boonies.'

'That's all you know, eh?'

'Sorry, that's it.'

'Maybe it's enough. How would these guys get on to a safe house, Leo?'

'Well, you know, Congress has been looking into this stuff. And certain people have been getting very nervous about the direction the inquiries are taking. Already in the last few weeks we've had – what? – three big hits? Yeah, it's damn hot. And once it gets on to Capitol Hill, man – well, anybody who wants to know *can* know.'

Yeah. Capitol Hill, and the things that went on there, were simply the price a people paid for their democracy. And sometimes they paid in blood.

The conversation concluded with an exchange of quiet pleasantries. Bolan returned to the dining-room and took a stool at the counter. He had a ham and cheese sandwich while the wolf pack devoured giant Texas steaks, and he managed to get back outside ahead of them.

It was a fortunate circumstance that he did so. The two rented cars from Dallas Fort Worth airport had reached their intended destination. Three fresh vehicles had evidently been waiting at the Texarkana truck stop. When the killer force from Santa Monica invaded the state of Arkansas, it was separated into three fire teams and the headcount had swollen to fifteen.

Something was damned 'hot', for sure.

And yeah, Leo, the footwork was becoming dazzling.

The new cars bore Arkansas plates and they were radio-equipped. Fifteen minutes of patient scanning by the war-wagon's monitors finally caught them in an exchange on the UHF range. The voices meant nothing in particular to Bolan except that they were obviously foreign in this region of the country – and the words themselves fit the occasion.

'Do we take Highway Seven?'

'Right. It's nearly an hour ahead. So relax.'

'That's pretty country up there, I hear.'

'Depends on what we find, I guess. Let's stay off the radio as much as possible.'

'Right.'

No mistake, it was them. Bolan locked his primary transceiver to the frequency but kept the scanners working, just in case. He punched in an area map for display on the command console and programmed his present position, then gave it over to the navigation computer. This would keep him 'related' not only to the chase track but also to surrounding terrain as well. His own position in the display appeared as a tiny pulse moving steadily along Interstate 30. If the force intended to diverge from that track at State Highway 7 – then, yeah – it was paydirt, OK.

Highway 7 headed off due north from the interstate route to pass through Hot Springs as it continued on through the mountainous western section of the state. He punched in a finder code for 'Petit Jean' and was immediately rewarded with a red flare at the top of the display, indicating that the 'find' was beyond the hundred-mile display zone. He broadened the zone until the flare locked on to Petit Jean. It was a state park, according to the map, in the west-central region. The immediate region was served by no major highways. Though not too distant, really, from the capital city of Little Rock, the entire region surrounding Petit Jean seemed rather remote.

Good place for a 'safe house', sure. Until lips began to flap. Good place, then, for a hunt and kill exercise. Bad place for cat and mousing, though. Once they hit those hills, the tracking would become more difficult. He would have to hang closer. Even radio waves behaved unreliably in such areas. And the major problem, of course, was that Bolan did not know the exact destination. He was depending on the prey to lead him to the war.

The smart thing – strictly from the military standpoint – would be to take on the hellhounds right out here in open country, long before they could pose any sort of threat in the safe zone. But he could not risk open hostilities in these surroundings. Forget the inevitable police involvement. It was a major interstate route, heavily travelled and getting heavier as the afternoon wore on. A lot of innocent people could get hurt by a firestorm anywhere along here . . . and that was not the name of Mack Bolan's game.

So he settled into the patient track, dividing his consciousness for a thorough study of the terrain features in the Petit Jean area. The time was three o'clock when the optics monitor signalled a change of track. The killer force had turned north on to Arkansas 7.

Bolan immediately activated the floater and made mobile contact with Leo Turrin. 'Have you heard anything from Alice?' he inquired, referring to Hal Brognola, the head fed from Washington Wonderland.

'Not a breath,' was the nervous response. 'I was hoping for a call from Rock City. Maybe it didn't go that way.'

'Keep trying. Use every avenue. The doomsday machine is rolling, for sure. Looks like a scorched earth approach. I'd call the ETA at shortly after nightfall. If you should reach Alice in time, I recommend instant withdrawal and distant relocation under full seal.'

'I get that, right – but I'm afraid Alice has become untouchable. She could already be there. And she is the only avenue into that joint. The whole game may be up to you, buddy.'

'Don't rest it on me. I'm not that sure I can turn it.'

'Are you hurting?'

'A little, yeah. I'm undermanned.'

'Do what you can. And I'll try to find a panic button if you're sure it's all that urgent.'

'You can bet Alice's life on that, buddy?'

'See what you mean. OK. Keep the ears floating. I'll try to keep you updated.'

'Do that,' Bolan said quietly, terminating the contact.

A bit of chatter was commanding his attention to the UHF monitor.

'We need a piss call.'

'Cross your legs.'

'It's a long time to cross the legs, Jake.'

'Hang it out a window, then. We don't stop till the Springs.'

Looking back on that moment – a half-hour or so later – Bolan would regret that he had not analysed the brief exchange a bit closer. Yeah. He would really regret that.

Hot Springs is a charming and picturesque little resort city built around a health spa. The bath-houses, and their therapeutic waters, had attracted visitors from far and wide for more than half a century – and a national park had been established there. But 'the Springs' had its share of notoriety as well, for several decades supporting a flourishing traffic in gambling, prostitution, bootlegging, and what-have-you. Winthrop Rockefeller had officially closed the 'open city' of Hot Springs during his tenure as governor, though – at least on the surface of things – and the recent history of the area had been relatively clean. At least there were now no booming casinos operating along bath-house row in open contempt of the law. But old affections die hard and Bolan was aware that various older mobsters continued to visit and 'relax' in the area. So he was alert to a possibility of further intrigue at this stage of the chase and he had no alibis for himself to account for the dismal turn of affairs there.

He simply lost the track at Hot Springs.

The city is built along the side of a hill, highways feeding into it like spokes into a hub, the streets winding and plunging this way and that. Peak-season traffic through the city was horrendous and confused, the sidewalks jammed with tourists, parking lots overflowing, harried cops everywhere trying to control the situation.

It was impossible to keep the killer force in constant view. Their radios remained silent. He lost them completely at midtown – and when he again caught sight of the vehicles, several blocks farther along, they were turning onto US Highway 70, the main route to Little Rock. By the time he overtook the caravan, at the eastern edge of the city, he knew that he'd been had by another instance of 'fancy footwork'. Each of the cars contained a driver only – and not even the same drivers they'd had from Texarkana.

So. He'd lost the hellhounds. And he was realist enough to know that there would be no recovery possible – not in the confusion which was Hot Springs at high season.

With them, of course, he'd lost his only handle to the Petit Jean affair.

So . . . dammit, he'd just have to build another handle.

More was at stake than the health of a defecting Mafia VIP with important secrets to tell. At stake, also, were the lives of the entire 'safe house' staff – as well as that of a close and good friend, Hal Brognola.

Jake Natti and his West Coast killer force would show no compunction whatever about taking on a federal security staff. The mere fact that they had been 'sent' provided full assurances on that count. Had it been regarded as an easy hit, not so many would have been sent. Bolan had not been kidding Leo Turrin about 'scorched earth'. Those guys were not planning to leave a mouth behind to tell the tale – and they were going to fantastic lengths to cover their own trail behind them.

Yeah, Leo, it was plenty damned hot.

And Mack Bolan was not willing to bet Hal Brognola's life on the outcome.

He turned the warwagon about for a return to Highway 7. Somewhere, somehow, he simply had to find another handle.

The sun was grazing the peaks of the higher hills. It had been a damn long day already, and Bolan knew that *his* day was just beginning. Even allowing the possibility that Natti had beaten him out of Hot Springs and arrived in the target zone first, it did not seem likely that the guy would attack in daylight. If he was already on the scene, somewhere, then he was quite probably scouting the set-up and awaiting the cover of darkness.

But, hell, what a scene.

The warwagon's sector display was centred on Petit Jean Mountain. Highway 7 formed the western boundary, Highway 9 the eastern. At the bottom, running east–west, was State Highway 10 out of Little Rock. The Arkansas River formed the northern boundary. That was the fire zone. Somewhere in that sector Hal Brognola was preparing a Mafia defector for some rather large and spooky revelations. And, somewhere in there, a killer force intended to neutralise the whole hush-hush affair and save the Mafia nation a lot of harassment at the hands of the US Department of Justice. And Bolan could not even find the hot spot.

It was damned rugged country. Isolated, right. Hills and valleys, winding country roads, soaring bluffs, large cattle spreads, here and there a farmhouse or a cross-roads village – damn little else.

There was something else, though – and Bolan was staring at the marker through the windshield. *Winrock*

Farms. Santa Gertruda cattle, experimental livestock pastures. Winrock: Winthrop Rockefeller. Leo had said 'up near the Rockefeller ranch'.

Tickling the Bolan memory was something else concerning Win Rockefeller and his ambitions for a greater Arkansas, his adopted state. Long before his death – for years, even, before he became governor – the famed millionaire had sought to attract industry to the state . . . had flown in industrialists and investors, entertaining them at his . . . where? . . . Winrock Farms? The Rockefeller ranch? The place up near Petit Jean?

What a perfect set-up for a safe house!

It had to have an airstrip and the whole nine yards. Which may explain why Brognola had not responded to an airport page at Little Rock. He had not even gone through Little Rock. He could have flown directly to the safe house.

Bolan activated his optic and audio broad-surveillance systems and sent the warwagon cruising along the access road to Winrock. A fork at the top of the hill provided alternate routes, one marked Private Drive and the other Convention Centre. He opted for the private drive and wound on around toward the residence compound. In the distance could be seen the lush Arkansas River valley and the patchwork effect of pasturelands proliferating in varied designs. Clinging to the edge of an outcropping bluff in the foreground of that vista was an impressive structure of stone and glass – a millionaire's mansion in the modern vein, right – its curving walls designed to utilise fully the contours of the land upon which it perched and providing a spectacular overlook.

Barring passage to there, though, from about a quarter-mile out, stood a steel gate and a uniformed guard.

The guard pleasantly advised the Executioner, 'You missed it a couple miles back, sir.'

'Missed what?' Bolan asked, just as pleasantly.

'The state park. You're on private property. There's no camping here.'

'I'm not camping,' Bolan told him. 'I'm meeting Brognola here.'

The guy seemed genuinely confused by that. 'Who?'

'He said Winrock. Isn't this Winrock?'

'There's nobody here, sir. You must be looking for the convention centre.'

Bolan produced his stock ID wallet and flashed it at the guy. 'Are they here or aren't they?' he asked, growling just a bit.

It didn't shake the guy any. He knew where he was at. 'There's nobody here, sir,' he replied firmly. 'Try the convention centre.'

So Bolan sighed and tried the convention centre.

And he struck immediate paydirt there, just inside the parking area.

A couple of guys in standard FBI profile came loping out to intercept the intruding 'camper'.

Bolan did not try fake credentials with those guys. He cracked his window and told them. 'It's a red alert.' He handed down a small, sealed envelope. Inside was a card with a single word scrawled upon it: *Striker*. 'Get this to Brognola on the double damn quick. I'll wait here for him.'

The agents consulted each other with eyes only, then one trotted away with the envelope while the other stood in silent and wary regard of the visitor. Bolan was wearing smoked glasses and a hunter's cap set low over the brows but still he was uncomfortable with the scrutiny. It was no time for identity games with the cops. He told the guy, 'Relax – I'm not here to smoke your VIP. But it's not far away. So save your nerves. You're going to need them.'

The guy said nothing in reply but the eyes were massaging the message. Bolan lit a cigarette and took a moment to check the optic monitors. The whole area seemed clean – no movements anywhere within the optic range, nary a whisper from the radio monitors.

The 'convention centre' was a largish structure of simple architecture set into the hillside behind a respectable parking lot. It did not look like much from this approach, but Bolan suspected that the back side of the building would be mostly glass for scenic overlook effect – and it was quite large enough to handle a number of guests. A small motel, really. Also, stone walkways wandered off here and there, suggesting the presence somewhere of other nearby facilities – guest cottages, perhaps.

The grey of twilight was settling on to these hills, though, and a guy could not see all he would like to see.

Wherever the safe house may have been on those grounds, it took Brognola less than two minutes to respond to the summons. Bolan spotted him hurrying along one of the flagstoned walks, and the sudden appearance of the familiar figure only served warmly to remind the warrior of the urgency of the moment.

The head fed stepped aboard with a snort and a growl. 'F'God's sake, Striker! How the hell did you – what're you doing here! Are you out of – ?!'

'Save it,' Bolan growled back, cutting short the disturbed greeting. 'Fifteen hot guns are right now camped at your front door and they're not here for the scenic view. How many people do you have?'

Not a beat was lost in the uptake. 'I have four staff agents and two marshals. Who's gunning?'

'Jake Natti. I picked him up at the Dallas airport. He was ten strong, out of Dallas. Another five joined him at Texarkana. I lost the pack in Hot Springs – so he could be more than fifteen, by now. I figure they'll wait for nightfall. Which gives you very little time. I suggest you cut and run. Pack it out, as quick as you can.'

'I dislike the suggestion,' Brognola replied worriedly. 'I don't want to be running around in the dark with God knows how many guns on our ass.'

'How did you get here, Hal?'

'By chopper from Little Rock Air Force Base. I sent it home.'

'Call it back, then. How long could it take? You're not more than—'

'You can't just snap your fingers and get the goddamn things! I don't know how long it would – besides, you're talking about evacuating a dozen people. I've got—'

'Who are you safing, Hal?'

'Come on.'

'You come on. Who is it?'

The guy turned absolutely purple, but he came on. 'It's your old buddy from the Bronx. Chianti.'

Bolan's mind whistled at that. 'Sam the Bomber?'

'Yeah. Plus his wife and kids.'

Plus the wife and kids, sure – calm Theresa, the good lady whom Mack Bolan would not make a widow for all the nightmares in New York. Chianti had been an underboss for Freddie Gambella, and he'd been as large a savage as any. But somewhere in that kingdom of evil Sam the Bomber had found the good Theresa – and some of her had evidently rubbed into the monster of the Bronx. And even though Bolan had been an inch away from pinning a death medal on the guy, Theresa had apparently rubbed something on to the Man from Blood, as well.

'For *her*, Sam,' he'd told Chianti on that fated night as he let the guy off. 'Not for you. For *her*, one time only.'

So apparently the hunch had been right – and 'one time only' was the only time needed. Chianti had assured the Executioner that he would defect and seek federal protection. And so he had.

God, that seemed so long ago.

'So the wife and kids are here, too,' Bolan muttered to his friend from Wonderland.

'Sure they're here,' Brognola growled. 'Chianti isn't under any indictments. He's co-operating. We're giving him a blanket. And this guy has some stunning stuff, Striker. We simply can't let it go.'

'No way,' Bolan muttered in reply.

No, indeed, no way whatever. Quite aside from the human angle, and forgetting even the justice angle, there was no way they could allow the mob to pull off something like this. Those guys already thought they were gods – and they had a fair portion of the world convinced of that myth, also.

'Send for your chopper, Hal,' Bolan told Alice in Wonderland. 'Work out a foolproof recognition signal. Get those people out of here as quick as you can. Leave the rest to me.'

'Leave it to you, eh?' said the nation's top cop. But there was no sarcasm there. The tone was, if anything, resignation . . . to a reality.

And Mack Bolan had to be the most comfortable reality of Harold Brognola's present moment.

'Yeah,' quietly said the warrior. 'Leave the rest to me.'

They came with first dark, five heavy vehicles moving slowly up the mountain without lights – nothing cute – just a straight-on frontal assault like any cocky, élite force with massive power and supreme confidence. Five, now, yeah – count 'em – with a minimum of five guns per vehicle. Not a pistol force, either – bet on that – they would be toting automatics and big boomers, for sure.

Bolan's first quivery feeling about that bunch was borne out to the final sigh. They had come to scorch the earth around Petit Jean – to brazenly serve open notice on all potential defectors that there was no possible protection behind the law.

Bolan was as ready as he was likely to get. He had completely swept clean the personal arsenal. He was wearing the skintight combat blacks and soft black shoes. All exposed flesh was cosmetically darkened. The big .44 AutoMag was strapped to the right hip. An M-16 with extended clip dangled from a neck strap; riding its underside was the M-203 personal howitzer, forty flaming millimetres of firepower backing up the withering assault rifle. Belt-strung reloads circled the torso from each shoulder and various other items of military ordnance dangled from the belts.

It was not exactly a misnomer to call this guy a one-man army. He was – even in a depleted condition. And the warwagon, of course, even with just one bird aboard, added the final dimension. The big cruiser was poised at the overlook, roof-mounted rocket pod raised and locked in the firing ready. Laser-supplemented infra-red optics bathed the mountainside with invisible light, bringing an eerie red glow and negative-like images to the command console.

Bolan refined the optic focus and zoomed in on the point vehicle, then turned the system over to Target Acquisition. Rangemarks superimposed themselves upon the target image. He made a final fine adjustment and punched in Target Lock, then got the hell out of there on the combat double, pulling night goggles into place over the eyes as he went EVA.

He'd picked the spot with all the care that time allowed, with full knowledge in his soldier's heart that he had to get it all his first time out. There would be no second chance at this bunch.

He dropped down over the hill in a sliding plunge toward the final hairpin turn into the straightaway, taking position on the upslope about fifty feet above the roadway. There was no seeing them, now, but he could hear those powerful engines of the doomsday machine and he knew that they were no more than a few inches out of the firetrack.

Then, suddenly, there they were, yeah – creeping around that final curve and lining into the run to doomsday – picking up speed already – hungry for the kill – glowing feebly in the night goggles and for all the world a pack of hounds straight out of hell.

He gave them a five-count, then punched the EVA-Remote at his belly, summoning forth the fire. The fire responded instantly, leaping off the overlook with a rustling sigh – seeming to hesitate for a brief instant of initial flight to sniff the air and find a track – dipping, then, hot on the scent and sizzling along on a tail of flame and smoke.

They saw it, too, perhaps one lurching heartbeat before the intercept. An electrified foot stabbed at a brake pedal; the point vehicle staggered and nosed-down in a final, futile manoeuvre as the mighty little rocket slammed in.

Bolan glimpsed dismayed faces in there as that car lifted on a fireball and flung parts of itself back down the road upon the following vehicles. The fuel tank lent itself to an immediate secondary effect, blowing straight up and scattering flaming debris and smoking flesh all over that tortured hellground.

And there was little comfort in those closely following vehicles. The one-man army was striding along their flank with the M-203 at full bellow, roaring out angry little chunks of high explosives in forty-millimetre packages, bringing daylight to the night and final darkness to those who tarried too long in the midst of the firestorm.

It was twenty numbers into the hit and four of the cars were flaming wrecks – the fifth stalled broadside across the roadway – when the sporadic answering fire began. But those who still had the means and the will were finding very little to shoot at. Bolan was prowling the dark zone – the master in his own element – night goggles now abandoned as the leaping flames of combat illuminated the target zone with the dancing hues of hellfire. And the M-16 was raking that entire zone with quick bursts of lightning that never needed to strike twice in the same spot.

One silly guy came running out of the inferno with both hands on the head – and Bolan sent that silly guy sliding back with no head whatever.

No conventions governed this war; no meaningless gallantries extended to those savages who spat on civilised ideals. It was a war to the death. Mack Bolan intended to take as many as possible to hell with him. Let them make their peace with the devil; they would never find any from Mack Bolan.

Sam the Bomber had, of course. Plus a few others, here and there, when the right man and the right moment had coincided at the right place. But there had been not many of those.

'There are times,' Bolan had declared, early in his war, 'when a man will make his stand for what is right. It isn't enough to simply believe in something. To be truly alive, you have to be ready to *die* for something. Harder still, there are times when you have to be willing to *kill* for something. I am both ready to die and willing to kill.'

The deathmaster from Vietnam had made his stand on the home grounds. Over, and over, and over again. And he did so, again, that blighted night on Petit Jean Mountain.

Perversely enough, Jersey Jake Natti was the last to die in that stand. The veteran hitman was pinned by the legs beneath a burning vehicle and screaming for help when Bolan quit the darkness and moved in closer for the mop-up.

And the contractor knew his enemy when he saw him, this time. He knew what had come for him – and he was prepared to die as he had lived: with an utter contempt for life. 'Finish me off, huh?' he requested, as coolly as possible under the circumstances.

'It's why I'm here, Jake,' Bolan assured him as he shot the dying man once between the eyes with the thundering .44.

He dropped a marksman's medal into the mess and told Jake Natti's remains, 'My contempt is for *death*, guy.'

The air force chopper had arrived at the height of the festivities and was chugging away into the dark skies when Mack Bolan paid his final respects to Jersey Jake.

So much for that, then.

One more time, Theresa.

He devoted another minute or two to the clean-up, then went wearily up the hill to reclaim his cruiser and put those hellgrounds behind him. Isolated area, sure, but no more peace here for Bolan than anywhere else, following a firefight. No place in God's world was that secure.

But he was jarred a bit to find Brognola and his two marshals awaiting him at the overlook. Bolan could not afford to be *that* sure of *any* cop – not ever.

'You missed your plane,' he said quietly, speaking only to Brognola.

The top cop seemed a bit uncomfortable. 'Couldn't run off and leave you to face it alone, buddy. You just didn't give us any room for response.'

One of the marshals was grinning openly at the most-wanted 'criminal' in the country. 'That was the damnedest hit I ever saw,' he commented.

'Not me,' grunted the other. 'I was in New Orleans when—'

Brognola moved quickly and firmly to shut that off. He never referred to Mack Bolan by any name other than 'Striker' and obviously he wanted no open association whatever. But the embarrassment was still in the voice as he declared, 'I can't introduce you guys because I don't know the man's name – but if you boys want to shake his hand, you get in line behind me.'

Bolan grinned, shook hands all around, and returned to the only 'home' he would ever know.

He wiped off the cosmetic goop and pulled on Levi's over the bloodstained skinsuit, then sent the cruiser down the hill. He had to pick his way carefully through the debris of combat, but soon he was off and running free, the whole wide world lying before him in an entirely uncertain future.

Maybe he could catch some R&R now – some of that good Arkansas fishing, perhaps.

Then again, maybe he would find only another battle-field. Not that he thought of himself as the arch foe of the Mafia tribes. He was just a soldier, after all.

And there were certain limits to what one lone man could do.

Weren't there?

The Bottle Dungeon

ANTONIA FRASER

INVESTIGATOR FILE

NAME: Jemima Shore, TV Investigative Journalist

PLACE: Castle Crask, Scotland

TIME: 1992

CASES: *Quiet as a Nun* (1977), *Splash of Red* (1981), *Oxford Blood* (1985), *The Cavalier Case* (1990), *Jemima Shore at the Sunny Grave* (1993) etc.

DOSSIER: Jemima Shore, the glamorous, intelligent, self-assured television journalist, was the first female detective who was also a star. Described when she made her entrance as a mixture of Barbara Walters and Joan Bakewell, the elegant and stylish Jemima has also had to bear the epithet of 'the thinking man's crumpet', not to mention her fair share of male chauvinism in the circles in which she operates. Famed for her sweet smile and gentle manners, she can, none the less, disarm the most unco-operative interviewee and is always hard hitting in her presentations. Born in Bangalore and educated at various Catholic schools in England, she obtained a first-class Honours degree at Cambridge, and after a brief period in publishing is now the writer and presenter of her own TV series, *Jemima Shore Investigates*, which has probed a number of controversial issues from women's rights to racial conflict, housing shortages to juvenile crime – along the way winning a number of awards and making her a major television personality. Jemima has also proved herself a formidable detective to whom members of the public bring problems as diverse as theft and first-degree murder. The demands of her job mean that being single is a definite advantage, though she is never without a man in her life. Above all, Jemima is intensely feminine, which caused one fellow journalist to describe her as 'the woman most women would like to be – cool, self-reliant, physically brave and attractive'. Jemima lives in Holland Park, London, and describes her hobbies as 'listening to music and talking to cats', omitting to mention that she also has a taste for good champagne, driving her sports car fast, and lying in hot baths where, she says, 'I do my thinking' – until the phone rings and she is called away on another case . . .

CREATOR: Antonia Fraser (b. 1932), who made her name as an historian and biographer, created Jemima Shore because she was struck by the number of glamorous and intelligent women who have chosen their own profession and consequently gained fame as well as independence. She based Jemima's physical characteristics on one of her biographical subjects, Elizabeth I – the golden-red hair, white skin and virginal air – while her name is intended to be a combination of the repressed and the liberated: Jemima being a typical Puritan name, and Shore from Jane Shore, the beautiful and dissolute mistress of Edward IV. The success of the books made them a natural for television and to date Jemima has featured in two series: in the first played by Maria Aitken, and subsequently, Patricia Hodge. 'The Bottle Dungeon' is one of her most recent investigations and finds her far away from the bright lights and comforts of the London studios in a gloomy old Scottish castle celebrating the New Year, when the party spirit is suddenly turned chilly by a murder . .

'Quite rare nowadays, I believe,' said Joss Benmuir, looking down beyond his feet at the black hole.

'It may be quite rare but it's absolutely horrible! Really, Joss, I fail to see how you can – ' Lady Martin paused, then went on with fervour, ' – *tolerate* something so totally *foul*.'

'It's not a human rights issue, Aunt May, at least not now.' The intention of Robbie Benmuir was evidently to tease. May Martin was an extremely wealthy widow: since her husband's death she had occupied herself as an indefatigable campaigner for every conceivable liberal issue. Her figure was a familiar one, holding up a sandwich board of protest, spread across some newspaper.

Jemima Shore shivered as she too looked down. The Bottle Dungeon was carved – literally – out of rock. It consisted of a long narrow 'neck' which bellied out into a circular 'bottle', the shape of which could not be discerned from above until Joss Benmuir swung his flashlight into its depths. There were no steps cut in the 'neck'. The only method of getting down (or up) consisted of using a thick rope, currently coiled beside them, and fastened to an enormous iron ring in the stone.

Privately Jemima agreed with Lady Martin there was something foul about the gaping hole. She also fancied that there was a fetid smell. No light, not much air, and absolutely no sanitation beyond a tiny aperture in the rock at the bottom of the bottle which dropped to the sea – no wonder there was something dank and rotten in the atmosphere of the stone cell which contained the entrances to the dungeon. But since Jemima was an outsider at this house party, she decided to stay silent. She had been working with May Martin in recent months on a project for a television series tentatively entitled *A Woman's Right to Say Anything: The Female Political Voice in Various Totalitarian Countries*. She had become fond of the old lady, faintly ridiculous in her untidy appearance, certainly often ridiculed in the press for her views; yet ever gallant in her defence of those unable to speak for themselves. When her own New Year plans fell through, she had accepted Lady Martin's invitation to be her companion on the Scottish trip.

'Not really a party,' Lady Martin had pronounced. 'In spite of its being Hogmanay. There aren't any neighbours for miles. Plenty of time to work together.' She hesitated. 'Thank heaven you're not married; you'll take Joss's mind off that dreadful Clio Brown; then of course there's Robbie.'

A slightly uncomfortable silence followed Robbie Benmuir's little sally about human rights. To May Martin at least such things were not a laughing matter. It was broken by Joss, who continued to gaze down into the dungeon as he spoke. 'It's a tourist attraction, Aunt May. That's what it is. And a very fine one too. After all, who else would come to this desolate spot otherwise? So many finer castles, aren't there? And you know how I need the money.' His tone was perfectly equable; nevertheless, the words only increased the general embarrassment. Joss was being deliberately provocative, as Jemima Shore already knew enough about the Benmuir family set-up to appreciate.

May Martin was probably rich enough to restore the crumbling castle (what remained of it) single-handed, but preferred to spend her money on good causes – which did not include Castle Crask. And there was nothing to stop her doing so. Although Joss and Robbie, the children of her late brother, were her only blood relations, May Martin's money came entirely from the man she had married comparatively late in her life and very late in his, Sir Ludwig Martin, founder of LudMart. She had confided to Jemima on the way up: 'Joss wants me to "invest" in Crask – his phrase. He should know by now that I only make strictly philanthropic investments, which does not include ancient masonry even if it is owned by my family.'

As if there weren't enough tensions within the party already, thought Jemima, what with Clio Brown being once upon a time a girlfriend of Robbie. Clio Brown and her overweight and overanxious husband, Gerald (why on earth had she married him? The answer was, presumably, money), and now apparently – all too apparently this afternoon – Clio Brown and Joss. Jemima Shore had taken a strong dislike to Clio Brown. She hoped it was not jealousy on her part. Clio with her cat's face and fashionably cropped dark hair, so tall, so slim, and at the same time so curved, was certainly amazingly good looking. But there was something intensely disagreeable about her. Gerald bore the brunt of her bad moods: the sight of his red, perspiring face – even in the un-centrally heated castle he seemed perpetually hot – would remind Clio that she needed a handkerchief fetching from her bedroom. She seemed to take a malevolent pleasure in watching Gerald trying to fit his bulk up a curved stone staircase.

Joss Benmuir was right: Crask was indeed a desolate spot situated on a headland which ran out into the North Sea where even the harsh cries of the sea birds seemed to have something lonely and despairing about them. It had not always been so. Crask's moat was now dry, but its depth indicated that the castle had once acted as an important fortress, ready to repel foreign raiders and hand off domestic assailants with equal ferocity. Its strategic position meant that some kind of defensive structure must always have existed on the site – there were even traces of a prehistoric *dun* – but the present castle had been predominantly built in the fourteenth century. It had however been badly battered during the

Cromwellian invasion of Scotland and suffered again in the period of the Jacobite risings.

As Colonel Benmuir, father of Joss and Robbie, had been wont to lament: 'It's centuries since we Benmuirs managed to find ourselves on the winning side.' He sometimes added, 'Perhaps that's where poor May gets her taste for losers from – the spirit of her ancestors.'

Two substantial towers did however remain of the fourteenth-century castle: but they were no longer joined by a great hall or other buildings. The space in between was occupied by grass and stones, some of which were big enough to cause unwary guests to stumble as they moved between the two separate structures which together made up the living quarters of the modern Benmuir family. There was no protection on the head-land – mountains existed only in the distance – and the gusts of wind carried the seaspray inland and had been known to whirl umbrellas away. That had happened to Jemima Shore on the previous evening, so that her beautiful crushed velvet skirt had become sodden. Now, as they stood outside, a girl called Ellie MacSomething – attached to Robbie it seemed – who had suffered similarly with her tartan wool skirt, was bold enough to ask Joss why there was no covered way.

'It would blow away like your umbrella,' Joss remarked blandly. 'Wouldn't it, Robbie? At least you didn't stumble over a sheep: my father used to keep sheep here to deal with the grass. I got rid of them. Besides, we chaps like leading our own lives. Robbie has always got a home here. Until I marry, that is.'

'And will you and your wife have separate towers when you marry?' There was something provocative about the way Ellie MacSomething was pursuing the matter and it occurred to Jemima that she might be thinking of transferring her affections from Robbie to his elder brother. Joss, with his pale face, the black hair falling romantically over the eyes with their heavy lids, had more the air of a Spanish grandee – an El Greco – than a Scot. Robbie, on the other hand, with his rosy, almost ruddy cheeks, his freckles, his brownish curly hair already slipping back on his forehead, and stocky figure was the same physical type as his Aunt May. Although Jemima had the impression of intelligence beneath Robbie's jokey manner, there was no doubt which brother was the better looking, and Joss was after all the owner of Crask (whatever that might mean).

'Separate towers for married couples! What a good idea!' said Clio Brown suddenly. 'Gerald, I think we should get on much better like that. Towers with thick walls. Too thick for even your snores to penetrate.' She smiled in her peculiar cat-like manner, the corners of her small, perfectly bowed mouth turning up as though she were contemplating a small mouse before her. The mouse however was her large husband. One could not say that Gerald Brown flushed, since his face was red enough already, nevertheless it was clear that the remark had wounded him – but then that was presumably the intention.

By unspoken agreement, the other guests turned back to their contemplation of the Bottle Dungeon. They had all been taken on a visit to Crask's famous attraction – if a dungeon could really be so described – as a post-lunch treat by their host. The light faded early on a midwinter Scottish afternoon and as Joss Benmuir jocularly observed: 'We don't want to lose one of you down the neck, not on the eve of Hogmanay anyway, it might ruin our modest celebrations.'

He touched the aperture with his toe. 'There's one at St Andrew's Castle but ours is a whole foot deeper. Twenty-six foot deep.' Jemima shivered again. She still could not easily bear to contemplate the idea of a prisoner lowered into the depths and left – left without light, heat, food beyond what the captors condescended to lower, left in the filth, the prey to rats ... for there were apparently rats there in the past, probably introduced down the neck by the jailers, since the drainage hole at the bottom was minute, too small for a mouse let alone a rat to enter ...

In desperation Jemima found herself asking, 'Did anyone ever escape?' It was the best she could do to strike a more cheerful note. Before Joss could answer, May Martin said, very fiercely indeed, 'The terrible thing is that people *lived*, not that they died. Death was *merciful* compared to what people endured down there. Sometimes for years. An amazing aspect of the human spirit: some people are survivors. Joss, I really think you should seal it off, not exhibit it, show some respect for the sufferings of human beings ...' Fortunately for Joss, he was able to ignore his aunt in favour of answering Jemima. 'No one escaped.' He pointed to some lettering cut in the side of the stone cell. '*Initus non abeat*. Medieval Latin. It means: Once in, you can't get out. Carved shortly after the castle was built, they think.' Joss paused. 'No one escaped without help, that is. Some prisoner, put down there for supporting John Knox, at the time of the Reformation, that sort of thing, did get out. But it turned out that the jailer's daughter had helped him out with a rope. Otherwise: *Initus non abeat*. That's a bottle dungeon for you.'

'Just like marriage,' said Clio Brown suddenly. 'Once in, there's no way out. Unless you get help.' At first the company assumed that this was merely one of Clio's unpleasant interjections intended primarily to bait her husband. But it turned out that she had more to say. 'I want to go down, Joss. I want to see what it's like. It could be quite an experience. I want to spend the night down there. It should be – ' she lifted her lips in her little cat's smile again ' – gloriously private. Look how narrow that neck is. Gerald, I don't believe you could fit down there, even if the rope would hold you.'

There was polite laughter from those like Ellie and Jemima who decided to pretend that Clio was joking. Gerald merely spluttered: but this time there was no doubt at all in Jemima's mind that he was seriously angry, and Clio might find she had gone for once a little too far. She did not however act as if she was aware of her husband's rage. On the contrary, she persisted in talking about her descent, cajoled Joss into revealing that there was a rope ladder for emergencies, narrow but serviceable, in a locked cupboard in the corner of the cell, and finally provoked Gerald into shouting at her.

'If that's how you want to see the New Year in, goddammit, don't count on finding me in a very good mood tomorrow morning.'

'I don't count on finding you at all tomorrow morning, Gerald, if you go on shouting like this,' replied Clio smoothly. 'You're straining yourself dreadfully with all that shouting, and you know what the doctor said. Rage is not healthful.' Clio sounded so primly reproachful that you might almost have thought that the previous scene in which she deliberately provoked her husband's anger had not taken place.

'And wouldn't you be pleased?' snarled Gerald. 'A rich widow. Well, don't count on that either.' The embarrassment continued.

Afterwards it became important as to who had first suggested the bet. Was it Joss, his eyes black as he challenged Clio in a way that seemed positively sexual even at the comparatively asexual hour of three o'clock in the afternoon? Or perhaps frivolous, giggly Ellie, seeking to stir up further trouble? Or the much calmer and more self-possessed Robbie, with exactly the opposite aim of defusing the situation? Jemima had certainly not done so – she continued to regard the Bottle Dungeon with revulsion – while Lady Martin made her indignation quite obvious.

'Sensation-monger!' she said to Jemima in an aside which was clearly intended to be heard. 'The sort of person who collects Nazi mementoes for kicks.'

Gerald had been the first one actually to use the word 'bet'.

'I bet you won't stay down there for one hour, Clio, let alone for one night.' Then he stumped away from the party, with the words: 'Do what you damn well please! You always do.' But it was after that the real bet somehow evolved: the bet that Clio would be lowered down by the little ladder, as warmly clad as possible, with sleeping bag and flashlight, and a pocket heater, generally used out shooting, to warm her hands. This lowering would take place at eleven o'clock that night. She would be formally let out – let up – one hour later, with the New Year.

'And what does she get if she wins the bet?' asked Ellie, who had gone back to twining herself round Robbie again.

'I get to choose how I spend the rest of the night.' Jemima swore that Clio actually licked her lips when she said that; certainly there was a flicker of her little red tongue as she smiled. 'Which means,' she went on, looking at each of the three men in turn, ending with her husband, now some distance away, 'I get to spend it alone.'

It was not until dinnertime, when all had changed, including Clio, who wore a black Lycra cat suit, that Robbie made the obvious point.

'I've just realised she's bound to win the bet, isn't she? Unless she dies of fright or something awful like that. You see if Clio does want to come up – come up early and lose the bet – she has no way of letting us know, has

she? She just has to sit it out down there – yuk – until we
come and get her. Next year.'

So it was agreed that Clio should be installed with a
large noisy bell, which Robbie found, once used to
summon labourers for lunch. If the bell was heard to
ring, it would be regarded as a sign that Clio needed help
and the bet was off.

'Send not to know for whom the bell tolls' – Robbie
being jokey again – 'because it will definitely be Clio.
After all, once in you can't get out. Without help. Good
family motto that, Joss, we should use it. After all, we
Benmuirs are always getting into things we can't get out
of, aren't we – relationships, debt, that sort of thing.'
Lady Martin and Joss both frowned.

The presence of the bell meant that the door to the
stone cell had to be left open: Robbie was not sure the
clang from the depths would otherwise be heard. But no
one felt that to be a problem. The door was clearly visible
across the rough grass from the Big Tower where the
party was congregated in the big sitting-room on the first
floor, also used as a dining-room on festive occasions,
with its high windows and seats in the embrasures.
Nobody could rescue Clio early – supposing anyone was
minded to do so – without being observed.

'Not even to drop down the teeniest reviving malt
whisky' – Robbie, determinedly lighthearted again. But
none of the badinage was really very lighthearted.
Something – what exactly and when? – had gone too far.
A troublemaking young woman, a stupid bet, what a
recipe for New Year's Eve! (Jemima Shore wished she
were at home, celebrating with her cat, appropriately
named Midnight.) About ten-thirty both Gerald Brown
and Lady Martin decided to opt out of proceedings –
including the seeing-in of the New Year – and went to
their respective beds. The Browns were sleeping in the
Little Tower, or Robbie's Tower, together with Ellie and

Robbie himself; Lady Martin and Jemima were housed still higher up in the Big Tower. Joss, as host, now politely insisted on escorting Lady Martin upstairs, despite her protests about knowing the way perfectly well.

'But Joss, I grew up here!' she exclaimed. Perhaps he intended to make his touch at this point, thought Jemima, although it was scarcely a tactful moment with her disapproval so manifest. Gerald's bulky figure could be seen crossing the grass, bending slightly as he fronted the wind. The moon, almost full, had now risen, and with its eerie glow on the stones, did something to supplement the inadequate lighting of the passage between the two towers.

After a short while Clio said crossly: 'I hope he hasn't gone to sleep already. I've got to put a great many things over this.' She stretched out in her skintight black suit; she really did have the most beautiful lissom figure, small high breasts clearly visible under the Lycra, and the narrow thighs and long, long legs of a model; she actually could wear her cat suit and get away with it. 'I'll be back,' said Clio. 'May he not be *snoring*, that's all I ask.'

A few moments later they watched Clio in her turn cross the grass, a cumbersome parka over her cat suit, as the winds tossed her short hair. Whatever passed between the Browns on the first floor of the Little Tower must however have been vaguely conciliatory because they saw Gerald at the window, raising his hand and waving. His mood must have improved since he left. Clio reappeared shortly afterwards.

'Of course he's in a better temper!' she exclaimed. 'He just thinks I'll lose, that's why. He's really a cunning old sod, that one. Convinced I'll panic and ring the bell. Such a downer. I really can't think why I married him.' Jemima, looking at her, now more of a Michelin woman in her jerseys, thought: why did he marry you? Do some men just like to be humiliated? Answer, I suppose: yes.

In the event, the actual descent of Clio on the rope ladder was a slight anticlimax. Her sleek head had disappeared from view into the Bottle Dungeon without anything more dramatic happening than her own voice echoing upwards: 'It's great down here, the new holiday spot, can't think why those prisoners complained.'

'Any rats?' called Robbie.

'They're all upstairs,' Clio shouted back. 'Or asleep.' She was in her usual form. The flashlight was seen to cast its sepulchral glow upwards, the bell was tested (it sounded very loud), and then there was nothing to do but brave the wind and go back to the Big Tower again and wait.

There nobody could quite think how to fill the time. The general clear view of the open door of the cell meant that it was impossible to forget Clio. Joss, their host, had fallen moodily silent, his thoughts no doubt with her. The hour looked like passing slowly until Robbie decided to organise them.

'Here we are, four people in search of an occupation. Is it to be a foursome reel or bridge?'

Although Ellie clapped her hands and voted for a reel, Jemima hastily pointed out she did not know how to dance a reel. So they all four settled for bridge. After that the time did pass a little quicker, although the fact that the bridge table was placed in the embrasure containing the big window meant that the Bottle Dungeon – and Clio – remained somewhere in Jemima's thoughts at least. Nor did the bridge prove quite the engrossing occupation for herself and Ellie they might have antici- pated. The Benmuir brothers, Joss playing with Jemima, and Robbie with Ellie, played virtually every hand themselves, bidding, it seemed, with the aim of so doing. The one hand Jemima did play, Joss peered over her shoulder silently, but somehow, she felt, critically. Ellie never got to play a single hand.

It was actually Robbie who was busy making six spades – his luck was in – when they heard the bell ring. It rang loudly, the sound melted away into the wind, then it rang again. Instinctively Jemima looked at her watch: it was ten minutes to twelve. The others simply jumped up: then all of them started to run down the twisting stair, Joss pushing open the door, and out across the moonlit grass. Ellie stumbled twice but Robbie did not stop to help her. The brothers reached the cell together, leading Jemima herself by at least fifteen yards. By the time she arrived, the rope ladder was already being lowered and Joss was speaking soothing words to Clio – soothing and openly tender. But then Gerald was not present.

'Now then, darling, it's going to be all right. Trust Joss. Easy goes. Come on, my beautiful darling.'

And after a few moments, Clio's head emerged once again but it was a very different Clio, tear stained, dirty – filthy dirty and more or less incoherent. Jemima felt no particular pleasure at the sight; as a matter of fact, she found she preferred the confident if disagreeable Clio to this pathetic victim. Finally, how little Clio had known herself. She had been so sure of her own nerves, and so absolutely wrong when it came to the crunch. 'The shadows, the ghosts of the prisoners trying to kill me,' were some of the things Clio babbled about. At least Lady Martin might have been pleased at this last-minute sensitivity to the sufferings of people in the past. Still hysterical, Clio was led away in the direction of the Little Tower; it was now Robbie, not Joss, who took her arm, as though in tacit agreement that the Little Tower was 'Robbie's'. Joss, Ellie, and Jemima trailed after them.

'Nobody ever asked what would happen if she lost the bet!' cried Ellie suddenly: Jemima guessed she was annoyed at Robbie's attention to Clio.

'She gets to spend the night with Gerald,' snapped Joss, evidently made equally tense by the sight of Robbie's arm round Clio. Ellie continued to gaze after them.

'My room is on the ground floor, overlooking the sea,' she said. 'I suppose I'd better go to it. It must be midnight by now. Happy New Year.' Ellie did not even try to sound sincere. The door above their heads opened and shut; immediately Robbie came clattering back down the stairs: Clio had been tactfully left to face Gerald – if awake – by herself.

Ellie was therefore looking slightly happier when Clio started to scream for the second time that night. This time there were no sobs, just sheer horror. What Clio was screaming over and over again, as she half ran, half fell down the stairway till she reached Robbie (and Joss), was this: 'He's dead, he's dead.' Then: 'Gerald, Gerald.' Then more screams.

It was Robbie who slapped Clio's face but it was Joss who shouted at her – almost as loudly as her own screams: 'What do you mean, girl? How can he be dead?'

'He's dead,' wailed Clio in a quieter tone. 'I got into the bed, I touched something. It was a scarf. A long woollen scarf! A horrible thing. Red and purple squares.' She gulped. 'I pulled it. It didn't move. I put on the light. It was round his neck. He's dead. Gerald's dead.'

'My scarf!' screamed Ellie in her turn. 'That's my scarf!'

What followed was one of the most dreadful New Year's Days that Jemima had ever spent. The Crask headland and its castle was like something under an evil spell. Dawn came late and brought with it lurid red streaks over the North Sea: diabolic colours, thought Jemima.

The police in the person of one solitary officer took a long time to reach them: the nearest police station was after all over twenty-five miles away, and the Force in general was occupied by drivers in distress, drunken drivers, and drunks pure and simple. The police doctor, summoned by him, took even longer to arrive; arrangements to take away the corpse – yes, Gerald had been strangled and with Ellie's woollen scarf – would take a while to make. In the meantime the corpse was locked inside the Browns' room, while Robbie, Ellie, and of course Clio took refuge in the Big Tower.

No one could leave the castle, statements would have to be made, evidence taken. The remaining occupants of Crask sat around in the big sitting-room, as though in a daze.

At one point Ellie, who seemed personally angry with the situation so clearly devoid of any element of enjoyment, burst out: 'It must have been some tramp. He could have got in by the back door, through the kitchenette. Some maniac. He could still be lurking. And he took my scarf!' Nobody answered her. After a while Robbie patted her hand. But nobody for the time being chose to go and sleep. When Lady Martin was wakened – by Joss – and told of the tragedy, she too joined them: with her curly grey hair, in her tartan dressing gown, she had the air of some cosy family nanny.

What Lady Martin said to Jemima later that morning was however the reverse of cosy. Joss was talking to the police; Clio was lying down in his room (which he made over to her); Robbie and Ellie were in the kitchen trying to organise some kind of meal in the absence of any local help at Hogmanay.

'She did it! Of course that wicked Clio Brown did it.' Lady Martin's voice shook slightly in the passion of her conviction; she might have been lobbying a recalcitrant politician for the rights of the forgotten. 'I recognise evil when I see it. People think I'm blind to the bad side of life – but what do they know about me? On the contrary, I've seen so much of it that I recognise it instantly. Clio

Brown has no moral sense. She never had when she flirted with Robbie in the first place, then abandoned him for Gerald, all for the sake of the Brown money. Then she wasn't even grateful to Gerald for that – '

Jemima realised that May Martin, another woman who had married a rich man, was subconsciously contrasting Clio's behaviour with her own: she gathered May had been extremely attentive to Sir Ludwig during their brief and harmonious marriage.

'Now she's done away with him in order to marry Joss and queen it here at Benmuir.' Lady Martin paused in her harangue. 'Yes, Jemima, I'm afraid my nephew Joss is not exactly a moral person either. Clio and Joss: they're alike in that way. Oh ye gods! Money, and what people will do for it.' An unbidden thought came to Jemima that Lady Martin could perhaps have prevented all this, whatever it was that had happened, by helping her nephew with Benmuir. She dismissed the thought. Who was she, Jemima, to say that family feeling should be put before human rights? She herself had no family.

'Listen, my friend,' said Jemima in her most soothing interviewer's manner, patting the tartan-clad knee. 'It's out of the question. Clio couldn't have done it. Gerald was alive when she went into the Bottle Dungeon, we know he was, and dead when she came out of it. So she couldn't have done it. No one gets out of the Bottle Dungeon without help. That motto carved in the stone – how does it go?'

All the time, however, Jemima was thinking fiercely beneath her tranquil front: I'm right, aren't I? She couldn't have done it, could she? She went over to the Little Tower, we saw her go. Gerald waved her goodbye, we saw him. A few minutes later she was back with us. Then she went down into the dungeon, we watched her, the ladder was pulled up and put aside, we could all see the stone cell from the Big Tower window. She couldn't have got out without being seen. The boys, above all *Joss*: no, he was here, we were all here. Even when Joss was dummy, he kept looking over my shoulder. Robbie never left the bridge table. If anyone went to the loo – maybe Ellie did when she was dummy – she would simply have gone to that little turret cloakroom on the same floor, one instant away; you'd have noticed a longer absence.

Jemima pursued her thoughts. And yet Gerald was dead when Clio was released. He must have been. Robbie took her up to her bedroom door and came straight down, we heard him. Besides, Gerald's body was beginning to grow cold. Jemima shuddered as she thought: I touched him.

To distract herself, she repeated: 'How does the motto go?'

'Like this. *Initus* – once you're in – *non abeat* – you can't get out. The only Latin I know.' Lady Martin sounded weary. 'Girls in our family weren't taught Latin. Not that it would have been much use to me, as things turned out. I did learn first aid and nursing, much more useful, handling people the right way.' Her voice trailed away.

Afterwards Jemima would look back on this conversation as crucial, and Lady Martin as the person who in all fairness was really responsible for solving the case. At the time she merely felt some stirring of comprehension, as though recent events, if looked at from the opposite angle, might be understood altogether differently – and correctly.

Jemima jumped up. 'Will you be all right, May? I need – fresh air.' On her way out of the Big Tower, Jemima stopped by the open door to the sitting-room. Joss was standing there, looking out of the window. When she reached the ground floor, she could hear Robbie and Ellie in the kitchen. Jemima caught the words. 'My scarf.' Ellie was still complaining. She grabbed her own coat from the pile in the hall and passed rapidly out of doors. She walked across the grass, towards the stone cell, bending slightly in the wind. Jemima was conscious that Joss must be watching her from the window, as they had watched first Gerald, then Clio, the evening before. The door of the cell was still open; no one had thought to close it.

Jemima entered. The fetid reek from the open mouth of the Bottle Dungeon seemed to her stronger than ever: a reek of death. After all, if some prisoners had lived, in torment, others had died here. She remembered Clio's provocative comparison of the dungeon to marriage, a state from which she could not emerge without help. Gerald, of course, like some of the past prisoners, had emerged from it through death. The stone words were just visible above her head in the dim light. She traced them with her finger.

Initus ... Suddenly she understood.

At that moment there was a noise behind her. Jemima turned cautiously round; she did not want to lose her footing. 'Joss! You gave me a fright. I might have hurtled down into the depths.'

'I wouldn't have let that happen. No more tragedies.' Joss was blocking the light so that Jemima could not see his expression.

'How's Clio?'

'As well as can be expected.' It was impossible to tell whether the cliché was intended sarcastically without seeing Joss's face. The effect was to make Jemima eager to get out of the cell, away from the pervasive stink which came from the dungeon, into the sea wind. She moved towards the door but Joss continued to block it.

'Any theories?' he asked. 'Any theories, Jemima Shore Investigator?' He used the title of her television series by which the public generally identified her, but he made the words seem threatening. 'Do you buy Ellie's tramp or Ellie's maniac?'

'*Are* there tramps in this remote spot? You tell me. But as for maniacs, I suppose you find them anywhere.'

'Like criminals.'

'Exactly.' Jemima knew her voice was beginning to sound stifled. 'The air, Joss,' she began, 'the air in here – ' Then she realised what she must say. 'One thing I do know: nobody in the party could have done it.' May God forgive her for the lie: but like any prisoner she needed to get out.

'Is that so?'

'How could they? We were all together all the time, weren't we? Except for Clio, that is.'

'And she was – here.' Joss stepped forward as though to peer into the hole.

'Quite rare and absolutely horrible.' Jemima was pleased to find her voice was under control. 'No wonder Clio panicked and sounded the bell.'

Joss moved aside. Jemima stepped out. She was now in the full view of the first floor of the Big Tower, where she could make out Robbie and Ellie standing together. They must be able to see her. She was safe. Nevertheless, Jemima chose to walk a number of yards away from the stone cell in the direction of the Big Tower. Then she saw Clio coming out of the great door. Her short black hair became rapidly windblown; she was wearing a parka over the black suit she had worn the night before. Clio came and leant against Joss. He gave the impression of being quite indifferent to what anyone might think of this. Jemima had a fierce impulse to disturb that feline composure. She took a deep breath.

'Yes, you are alike,' she said sharply to Joss. 'Your aunt was right. Not only in your natures but physically alike. Both of you tall with short black hair. How could we tell the difference from the Big Tower? A parka over the trousers. We thought it was Clio. It was you, Joss. After you took May to her room. You killed him, didn't you?' Jemima still addressed Joss. 'You took Ellie's scarf from her room to kill him. Then you made him wave out of the window, took up his arm and manipulated him, handled him. So that we were certain he was alive. Minutes later Clio came back into the sitting-room, as if she'd just crossed the grass in the dark. But she'd been downstairs all along. And together you set up the bet. Another piece of handling.'

'What's she saying, darling? Why is she saying these horrible things?' Clio sounded merely plaintive; she still looked perfectly, composedly beautiful.

Joss said nothing. He continued to gaze impassively at Jemima. She was glad to be under the protective gaze of Robbie and Ellie.

'*Initus non abeat*. Once in, you can't get out. The motto,' cried Jemima. 'But Clio wasn't actually *in* the dungeon when Gerald died. That was all a plot, a distraction to get our attention. She was lurking downstairs among all the coats, finding jerseys there, letting *you* do it, Joss. Afterwards, Clio's panic in the dungeon may well have been genuine, ringing that bell that Robbie found. She was alone, she had connived at the murder of her husband: and of course the bell made for another distraction.'

'Prove it,' said Joss coldly to Jemima. To Clio he said: 'Pay no attention, she's mad. Media people! We should never have let Aunt May bring her. Unhinged!'

'I can't prove it. That's for the police.' As though on cue, Jemima was aware of the distinctive Scottish police car driving towards the gates of the castle to her right. 'All I know is: you were in it together. And you're still in it together: this is one Bottle Dungeon with two prisoners inside it. A desperate kind of marriage: your word, Clio. Until one of you turns on the other, that is.'

As the police car drove nearer, Jemima saw Clio's slanting cat's eyes slide away from Joss. Clio was in deep, as deep as she had been down in those fetid depths. But Clio was going to try to get out. She'll betray him, thought Jemima, and after all he did the killing. What was it May Martin said that afternoon by the dungeon? Some people are survivors.

The Takamoku Joseki

SARA PARETSKY

INVESTIGATOR FILE

NAME: V. I. Warshawski, Private Investigator

PLACE: Chicago

TIME: 1982

CASES: *Indemnity Only* (1982), *Bitter Medicine* (1987), *Burn Marks* (1990), *Tunnel Vision* (1994).

DOSSIER: The feisty, quirky and dedicated V. I. Warshawski – 'my first name is Victoria, my friends call me Vic, never Vicki' – is the second of the three female private eyes who have pioneered the latest development in detective fiction. Described admiringly by *Entertainment Weekly* as 'America's most convincing and engaging professional female private eye', she has also attracted the more caustic assessment by critic Allen J. Hubin of being 'a left-wing Mike Hammer in a bra'. She is, though, a lady far removed from such a generalisation. Working against the gritty background of Chicago, Vic is a woman now nearing forty, fiercely independent, professionally very competent and self-reliant. Although both her parents have been dead for some years, she still feels herself obliged to honour their old standards and obligations – though she does sometimes resent the occasional intrusions of family relations and their assumptions she should solve their problems. V. I. uses the same tough language as her predecessors and will put down clients and villains alike. She has regular run-ins with the police, is constantly fighting Chicago's bureaucratic machine and loathes the corruption she is forever encountering. Vic is, though, stoical when in pain and given to periods of brooding introspection and a swig or two of Johnny Walker Black Label whisky. She lives alone on the north side of the city and enjoys jogging around the lake and meals of pasta and fine Barolo wine. Though she is in some respects not unlike the male private eye of the 'thirties, V. I. has a defiant and private code of ethics that is uniquely her own and reflective of the 'nineties.

CREATOR: Attractive Sara Paretsky who also lives and works in Chicago, has admitted that the stories of Raymond Chandler were her biggest influence, and she has been particularly delighted by reviews that have drawn comparisons – *vide* the *Independent* which called her 'the only writer who is the natural inheritor of Damon Runyon's language plus Chandler's suspense'. She was, though, born in Kansas – both her parents were academic scientists – and it was not until she had obtained a Ph.D. in history that she moved to Chicago. There she worked as a secretary, sales promotions manager for an insurance company, and freelance writer before leaping to public attention with the V. I. War-shawski novels, which several reviewers have declared introduced new sensibilities and insights into the genre. In 1992, *Deadlock* was brought to the screen with Kathleen Turner as Vic, a role she has since repeated in two series on BBC Radio. 'The Takamoku *Joseki*' was the first V. I. short story published in *Alfred Hitchcock's Mystery Magazine* in November 1983 and for those who have not already met her provides an ideal introduction to this 'gumshoe for modern times' . . .

***

The *Takamoku* Joseki

Mr and Mrs Takamoku were a quiet, hardworking couple. Although they had lived in Chicago since the 1940s, when they were relocated from an Arizona detention camp, they spoke only halting English. Occasionally I ran into Mrs Takamoku in the foyer of the old three-flat we both lived in on Belmont, or at the corner grocery store. We would exchange a few stilted sentences. She knew I lived alone in my third-floor apartment, and she worried about it, although her manners were too perfect for her to come right out and tell me to get myself a husband.

As the time passed, I learned about her son, Akira, and her daughter, Yoshio, both professionals living on the West Coast. I always inquired after them, which pleased her.

With great difficulty I got her to understand that I was a private detective. This troubled her; she often wanted to know if I were doing something dangerous, and would shake her head and frown as she asked. I didn't see Mr Takamoku often. He worked for a printer and usually left long before me in the morning.

Unlike the De Paul students who formed an ever-changing collage on the second floor, the Takamokus did little entertaining, or at least little noisy entertaining. Every Sunday afternoon a procession of Asians came to their apartment, spent a quiet afternoon, and left. One or more Caucasians would join them, incongruous by their height and colour. After a while, I recognised the regulars: a tall, bearded white man, and six or seven Japanese and Koreans.

One Sunday evening in late November I was eating sushi and drinking sake in a storefront restaurant on Halsted. The Takamokus came in as I was finishing my first little pot of sake. I smiled and waved at them, and watched with idle amusement as they conferred earnestly, darting glances at me. While they argued, a waitress brought them bowls of noodles and a plate of sushi; they were clearly regular customers with regular tastes.

At last, Mr Takamoku came over to my table. I invited him and his wife to join me.

'Thank you, thank you,' he said in an agony of embarrassment. 'We only have question for you, not to disturb you.'

'You're not disturbing me. What do you want to know?'

'You are familiar with American customs.' That was a statement, not a question. I nodded, wondering what was coming.

'When a guest behaves badly in the house, what does an American do?'

I gave him my full attention. I had no idea what he was asking, but he would never have thought it up just to be frivolous.

'It depends,' I said carefully. 'Did they break up your sofa or spill tea?'

Mr Takamoku looked at me steadily, fishing for a cigarette. Then he shook his head slowly. 'Not as much as breaking furniture. Not as little as tea on sofa. In between.'

'I'd give him a second chance.'

A slight crease erased itself from Mr Takamoku's forehead. 'A second chance. A very good idea. A second chance.'

He went back to his wife and ate his noodles with the noisy appreciation that showed good Japanese manners. I had another pot of sake and finished about the same time as the Takamokus; we left the restaurant together. I topped them by a good five inches and perhaps twenty pounds, so I slowed my pace to a crawl to keep step with them.

Mrs Takamoku smiled. 'You are familiar with Go?' she asked, giggling nervously.

'I'm not sure,' I said cautiously, wondering if they wanted me to conjugate an intransitive irregular verb.

'It's a game. You have time to stop and see?'

'Sure,' I agreed, just as Mr Takamoku broke in with vigorous objections.

I couldn't tell whether he didn't want to inconvenience me or didn't want me intruding. However, Mrs Takamoku insisted, so I stopped at the first floor and went into the apartment with her.

The living-room was almost bare. The lack of furniture drew the eye to a beautiful Japanese doll on a stand in one corner, with a bowl of dried flowers in front of her. The only other furnishings were six little tables in a row. They were quite thick and stood low on carved wooden legs. Their tops, about eighteen inches square, were crisscrossed with black lines which formed dozens of little squares. Two covered wooden bowls stood on each table.

'Go-ban,' Mrs Takamoku said, pointing to one of the tables. I shook my head in incomprehension.

Mr Takamoku picked up a covered bowl. It was filled with smooth white discs, the size of nickels but much thicker. I held one up and saw beautiful shadows in it.

'Clamshell,' Mr Takamoku said. 'They cut, then polish.' He picked up a second bowl, filled with black discs. 'Shale.'

He knelt on a cushion in front of one of the tables and rapidly placed black and white discs on intersections of the lines. A pattern emerged.

'This is Go. Black play, then white, then black, then white. Each try to make territory, to make eyes.' He showed me an 'eye' – a clear space surrounded by black stones. 'White cannot play here. Black safe. Now white must play someplace else.'

'I see.' I didn't really, but I didn't think it mattered.

'This afternoon, someone knock stones from table, turn upside down, and scrape with knife.'

'This table?' I asked, tapping the one he was playing on.

'Yes.' He swept the stones off swiftly but carefully, and put them in their little pots. He turned the board over. In the middle was a hole, carved and sanded. The wood was very thick – I suppose the hole gave it resonance.

I knelt beside him and looked. I was probably thirty years younger, but I couldn't tuck my knees under me with his grace and ease; I sat cross-legged. A faint scratch marred the sanded bottom.

'Was he American?'

Mr and Mrs Takamoku exchanged a look. 'Japanese, but born in America,' she said. 'Like Akira and Yoshio.'

I shook my head. 'I don't understand. It's not an American custom.' I climbed awkwardly back to my feet. Mr Takamoku stood with one easy movement. He and Mrs Takamoku thanked me profusely. I assured them it was nothing and went to bed.

The next Sunday was a cold, grey day with a hint of snow. I sat in front of the television, in my living-room, drinking coffee, dividing my attention between November's income and watching the Bears. Both were equally feeble. I was trying to decide on something friendlier to do when a knock sounded on my door. The outside buzzer hadn't rung. I got up, stacking loose papers on one arm of the chair and balancing the coffee cup on the other.

Through the peephole I could see Mrs Takamoku. I opened the door. Her wrinkled ivory face was agitated, her eyes dilated. 'Oh, good, good, you here. You must come.' She tugged at my hand.

I pulled her gently into the apartment. 'What's wrong? Let me get you a drink.'

'No, no.' She wrung her hands in agitation, repeating that I must come, I must come.

I collected my keys and went down the worn, uncarpeted stairs with her. Her living-room was filled with cigarette smoke and a crowd of anxious men. Mr Takamoku detached himself from the group and hurried over to his wife and me. He clasped my hand and pumped it up and down.

'Good. Good you come. You are a detective, yes? You will see the police do not arrest Naoe and me.'

'What's wrong, Mr Takamoku?'

'He's dead. He's killed. Naoe and I were in camp during World War. They will arrest us.'

'Who's dead?'

He shrugged helplessly. 'I don't know name.'

I pushed through the group. A white man lay sprawled on the floor. His face had contorted in dreadful pain as he died, so it was hard to guess his age. His fair hair was thick and unmarked with grey; he must have been relatively young.

A small dribble of vomit trailed from his clenched teeth. I sniffed at it cautiously. Probably hydrocyanic acid. Not far from his body lay a teacup, a Japanese cup without handles. The contents sprayed out from it like a Rorschach. Without touching it, I sniffed again. The fumes were still discernible.

I got up. 'Has anyone left since this happened?'

The tall, bearded Caucasian I'd noticed on previous Sundays looked around and said 'No' in an authoritative voice.

'And have you called the police?'

Mrs Takamoku gave an agitated cry. 'No police. No. You are detective. You find the murderer yourself.'

I shook my head and took her gently by the hand. 'If we don't call the police, they will put us all in jail for concealing a murder. You must tell them.'

The bearded man said, 'I'll do that.'

'Who are you?'

'I'm Charles Welland. I'm a physicist at the University of Chicago, but on Sundays I'm a Go player.'

'I see . . . I'm V. I. Warshawski. I live upstairs. I'm a private investigator. The police look very dimly on all citizens who don't report murders, but especially on PIs.'

Welland went into the dining-room, where the Takamokus kept their phone. I told the Takamokus and their guests that no one could leave before the police gave them permission, then followed Welland to make sure he didn't call anyone besides the police, or take the opportunity to get rid of a vial of poison.

The Go players seemed resigned, albeit very nervous. All of them smoked ferociously; the thick air grew bluer. They split into small groups, five Japanese together, four Koreans in another clump. A lone Chinese fiddled with the stones on one of the Go-bans.

None of them spoke English well enough to give a clear account of how the young man died. When Welland came back, I asked him for a detailed report.

The physicist claimed not to know his name. The dead man had only been coming to the Go club the last month or two.

'Did someone bring him? Or did he just show up one day?'

Welland shrugged. 'He just showed up. Word gets around among Go players. I'm sure he told me his name – it just didn't stick. I think he worked for Hansen Electronic, the big computer firm.'

I asked if everyone there was a regular player. Welland knew all of them by sight, if not by name. They didn't all come every Sunday, but none of the others was a newcomer.

'I see. OK. What happened today?'

Welland scratched his beard. He had bushy, arched

eyebrows which jumped up to punctuate his stronger statements, kind of like Sean Connery. I found it pretty sexy. I pulled my mind back to what he was saying.

'I got here around one-thirty. I think three games were in progress. This guy' – he jerked his thumb towards the dead man – 'arrived a bit later. He and I played a game. Dr Han showed up, and he and I were playing when the whole thing happened. Mrs Takamoku sets out tea and snacks. We all wander around and help ourselves. About four, this guy took a swallow of tea, gave a terrible cry, and died.'

'Is there anything important about the game they were playing?'

Welland looked at the board. A handful of black-and-white stones stood on the corner points. He shook his head. 'They'd just started. It looks like our dead friend was trying one of the Takamoku *josekis*. That's a complicated one – I've never seen it used in actual play before.'

'What's that? Anything to do with Mr Takamoku?'

'The *joseki* are the beginning moves in the corners. Takamoku is this one' – he pointed at the far side – 'where black plays on the five-four point – the point where the fourth and fifth lines intersect. It wasn't named for our host. That's just coincidence.'

Sergeant McGonnigal didn't find out much more than I did. A thickset young detective, he had a lot of experience and treated his frightened audience gently. He was a little less kind to me, demanding roughly why I was there, what my connection with the dead man was, who my client was. It didn't cheer him up any to hear I was working for the Takamokus, but he let me stay with them while he questioned them. He sent for a young Korean officer to interrogate the Koreans in the group. Welland, who spoke fluent Japanese, translated the Japanese interviews. Dr Han, the lone Chinese, struggled along on his own.

McGonnigal learned that the dead man's name was Peter Folger. He learned that people were milling around all the time watching each other play. He also learned that no one paid attention to anything but the game they were playing, or watching.

'The Japanese say the Go player forgets his father's funeral,' Welland explained. 'It's a game of tremendous concentration.'

No one admitted knowing Folger outside the Go club. No one knew how he found out that the Takamokus hosted Go every Sunday.

My clients hovered tensely in the background, convinced that McGonnigal would arrest them at any minute. But they could add nothing to the story. Anyone who wanted to play was welcome at their apartment on Sunday afternoon. Why should he show a credential? If he knew how to play, that was the proof.

McGonnigal pounced on that. Was Folger a good player? Everyone looked around and nodded. Yes, not the best – that was clearly Dr Han or Mr Kim, one of the Koreans – but quite good enough. Perhaps first *kyu*, whatever that was.

After two hours of this, McGonnigal decided he was getting nowhere. Someone in the room must have had a connection with Folger, but we weren't going to find it by questioning the group. We'd have to dig into their backgrounds.

A uniformed man started collecting addresses while McGonnigal went to his car to radio for plainclothes reinforcements. He wanted everyone in the room tailed and wanted to call from a private phone. A useless precaution, I thought: the innocent wouldn't know they were being followed, and the guilty would expect it.

McGonnigal returned shortly, his face angry. He had a

bland-faced, square-jawed man in tow, Derek Hatfield of the FBI. He did computer fraud for them. Our paths had crossed a few times on white-collar crime. I'd found him smart and knowledgeable, but also humourless and overbearing.

'Hello, Derek,' I said, without getting up from the cushion I was sitting on. 'What brings you here?'

'He had the place under surveillance,' McGonnigal said, biting off the words. 'He won't tell me who he was looking for.'

Derek walked over to Folger's body, covered now with a sheet, which he pulled back. He looked at Folger's face and nodded. 'I'm going to have to phone my office for instructions.'

'Just a minute,' McGonnigal said. 'You know the guy, right? You tell me what you were watching him for.'

Derek raised his eyebrows haughtily. 'I'll have to make a call first.'

'Don't be an ass, Hatfield,' I said. 'You think you're impressing us with how mysterious the FBI is, but you're not, really. You know your boss will tell you to co-operate with the city if it's murder. And we might be able to clear this thing up right now, glory for everyone. We know Folger worked for Hansen Electronic. He wasn't one of your guys working undercover, was he?'

Hatfield glared at me. 'I can't answer that.'

'Look,' I said reasonably. 'Either he worked for you and was investigating problems at Hansen, or he worked for them and you suspected he was involved in some kind of fraud. I know there's a lot of talk about Hansen's new Series J computer – was he passing secrets?'

Hatfield put his hands in his pockets and scowled in thought. At last he said, to McGonnigal, 'Is there some place we can go and talk?'

I asked Mrs Takamoku if we could use her kitchen for a few minutes. Her lips moved nervously, but she took

Hatfield and me down the hall. Her apartment was laid out like mine and the kitchens were similar, at least in appliances. Hers was spotless; mine had that lived-in look.

McGonnigal told the uniformed man not to let anyone leave or make any phone calls, and followed us.

Hatfield leaned against the back door. I perched on a bar stool next to a high wooden table. McGonnigal stood in the doorway leading to the hall.

'You got someone here named Miyake?' Hatfield asked.

McGonnigal looked through the sheaf of notes in his hand and shook his head.

'Anyone here work for Kawamoto?'

Kawamoto is a big Japanese electronics firm, one of Mitsubishi's peers and a strong rival of Hansen in the megacomputer market.

'Hatfield, are you trying to tell us that Folger was passing Series J secrets to someone from Kawamoto over the Go boards here?'

Hatfield shifted uncomfortably. 'We only got in to it three weeks ago. Folger was just a go-between. We offered him immunity if he would finger the guy from Kawamoto. He couldn't describe him well enough for us to make a pick-up. He was going to shake hands with him or touch him in some way as they left the building.'

'The Judas trick,' I remarked.

'Huh?' Hatfield looked puzzled.

McGonnigal smiled for the first time that afternoon. 'That man I kiss is the one you want. You should've gone to Catholic school, Hatfield.'

'Yeah. Anyway, Folger must've told this guy Miyake we were closing in.' Hatfield shook his head disgustedly. 'Miyake must be part of that group, just using an assumed name. We got a tail put on all of them.' He straightened up and started back toward the hall.

'How was Folger passing the information?' I asked.

'It was on microdots.'

'Stay where you are. I might be able to tell you which one is Miyake without leaving the building.'

Of course, both Hatfield and McGonnigal started yelling at me at once. Why was I suppressing evidence, what did I know, they'd have me arrested.

'Calm down, boys,' I said. 'I don't have any evidence. But now that I know the crime, I think I know how it was done. I just need to talk to my clients.'

Mr and Mrs Takamoku looked at me anxiously when I came back to the living-room. I got them to follow me into the hall. 'They're not going to arrest you,' I assured them. 'But I need to know who turned over the Go board last week. Is he here today?'

They talked briefly in Japanese, then Mr Takamoku said, 'We should not betray a guest. But murder is much worse. Man in orange shirt, named Hamai.'

Hamai, or Miyake, as Hatfield called him, resisted valiantly. When the police started to put the handcuffs on him, he popped a gelatin capsule into his mouth. He was dead almost before they realised what he had done.

Hatfield, impersonal as always, searched his body for the microdot. Hamai had stuck it to his upper lip, where it looked like a mole against his dark skin.

'How did you know?' McGonnigal grumbled, after the bodies had been carried off and the Takamokus' efforts to turn their life savings over to me successfully averted.

'He turned over a Go board here last week. That troubled my clients enough that they asked me about it. Once I knew we were looking for the transfer of information, it was obvious that Folger had stuck the dot in the hole under the board. Hamai couldn't get at it, so he had to turn the whole board over. Today, Folger must have put it in a more accessible spot.'

Hatfield left to make his top-secret report. McGonnigal

followed his uniformed men out of the apartment. Welland held the door for me.

'Was his name Hamai or Miyake?'

'Oh, I think his real name was Hamai – that's what all his identification said. He must have used a false name with Folger. After all, he knew you guys never pay attention to each other's names – probably wouldn't even notice what Folger called him. If you could figure out who Folger was.'

Welland smiled; his busy eyebrows danced. 'How about a drink? I'd like to salute a lady clever enough to solve the Takamoku *joseki* unaided.'

I looked at my watch. Three hours ago I'd been trying to think of something friendlier to do than watch the Bears get pummelled. This sounded like a good bet. I slipped my hand through his arm and went outside with him.

She Didn't Come Home

SUE GRAFTON

INVESTIGATOR FILE

NAME: Kinsey Millhone, Private Investigator

PLACE: Santa Teresa, California

TIME: 1985

CASES: *A is for Alibi* (1982), *D is for Deadbeat* (1987), *G is for Gumshoe* (1990), *K is for Killer* (1994) etc.

DOSSIER: The euphoniously named Kinsey Millhone, who features in an 'alphabet' series of novels, is the third of the trio of landmark contemporary female private eyes, and has been compared to V. I. Warshawski as 'a sunnier-natured little sister who has the same attitude, the one-liners and the gumption, but manages to find adventure without the quota of death, destruction and dark moods of her northern compatriot,' according to a recent *Sunday Times* review. She is, though, undeniably one of the most convincing private investigators in business. Introduced as a thirty-two-year-old living in a converted garage in 'Santa Teresa' – which is quite obviously Santa Barbara – Kinsey is divorced, has no children, and is looking for fulfilment in her life. Although strong willed and feminine, she is not one for possessions, scorning cupboards full of dresses and preferring to eat out rather than cook. Flippantly described as a 'tough cookie heroine', she will certainly kill in a tight corner, but is also sensitive, compassionate and the deliverer of some of the best wise-cracks in the genre – 'Her impending nuptials had lowered her IQ several critical points,' being a typical example. Kinsey is not above the odd affair and does have a sort of ongoing relationship with Rosie, the cantankerous Hungarian-American owner of the bar where she often eats. Her cases have brought her into contact with all types of criminals, from a hired killer to a porn star, but her unquenchable spirit and innate strength of character have seen her through to the middle of the alphabet . . . so far.

CREATOR: Sue Grafton (b. 1940) was born in Louis-ville, Kentucky, the daughter of mystery writer C. W. Grafton, whose novels about a series character Gil Henry included *The Rat Began to Gnaw the Rope* (1943) and *The Rope Began to Hang the Butcher* (1944), and who proved a formative influence on her ambition to become a novelist. One of her early books, *The Lolly-Madonna War* (1969), was filmed in 1973 and this led to a career as a screenwriter until the acrimonious break-up of her marriage gave her the inspiration for the Kinsey Millhone series. As she explains, 'For months I lay awake and plotted how to kill my ex-husband . . . but I knew I'd bungle it and get caught, so I wrote it in a book instead.' Her private eye is, she says, a mixture of the hardboiled gumshoes of the 'thirties with the perceptions of a modern woman and quite a lot of Grafton herself. The worldwide success of the series has made her set her sights on Kinsey reaching the letter Z in middle age – though not a gentle or unexciting middle age. 'She Didn't Come Home', written for *Redbook* in 1985, is one of a small group of short stories about Millhone and, apart from revealing the acclaimed PI at the top of her form, demonstrates in its clever plotting and intriguing charac-ters just why the private investigator has played such a vital role in the development of crime fiction . . . and will surely continue to do so in the foreseeable future.

***

September in Santa Teresa. I've never known anyone yet who doesn't suffer a certain restlessness when autumn rolls around. It's the season of new school clothes, fresh notebooks, and finely sharpened pencils without any teeth marks in the wood. We're all eight years old again and anything is possible. The new year should never begin on 1 January. It begins in the fall and continues as long as our saddle oxfords remain unscuffed and our lunch boxes have no dents.

My name is Kinsey Millhone. I'm female, thirty-two, twice divorced, 'doing business' as Kinsey Millhone Investigations in a little town ninety-five miles north of Los Angeles. Mine isn't a walk-in trade like a beauty salon. Most of my clients find themselves in a bind and then seek my services, hoping I can offer a solution for a mere thirty bucks an hour, plus expenses. Robert Ackerman's message was waiting on my answering machine that Monday morning at nine when I got in.

'Hello. My name is Robert Ackerman and I wonder if you could give me a call. My wife is missing and I'm worried sick. I was hoping you could help me out.' In the background, I could hear whiney children, my favourite kind. He repeated his name and gave me a telephone number. I made a pot of coffee before I called him back.

A little person answered the phone. There was a murmured child-size hello and then I heard a lot of heavy breathing close to the mouthpiece.

'Hi,' I said, 'can I speak to your daddy?'

'Yes.' Long silence.

'Today?' I asked.

The receiver was clunked down on a tabletop and I

could hear the clatter of footsteps in a room that sounded as if it didn't have any carpeting. In due course, Robert Ackerman picked up the phone.

'Lucy?'

'It's Kinsey Millhone, Mr Ackerman. I just got your message on my answering machine. Can you tell me what's going on?'

'Oh wow, yeah . . .'

He was interrupted by a piercing shriek that sounded like one of those policeman's whistles you use to discourage obscene phone callers. I didn't jerk back quite in time. 'Shit, that hurt.'

I listened patiently while he dealt with the errant child.

'Sorry,' he said when he came back on the line. 'Look, is there any way you could come out to the house?' I've got my hands full and I just can't get away.'

I took his address and brief directions, then headed out to my car.

Robert and the missing Mrs Ackerman lived in a housing tract that looked like it was built in the 'forties before anyone ever dreamed up the notion of family rooms, country kitchens, and his 'n' hers solar spas. What we had here was a basic drywall box; cramped living-room with a dining L, a kitchen and one bathroom sandwiched between two nine-by-twelve-foot bedrooms. When Robert answered the door I could just about see the whole place at a glance. The only thing the builders had been lavish with was the hardwood floors, which, in this case, was unfortunate. Little children had banged and scraped these floors and had brought in some kind of foot grit that I sensed before I was even asked to step inside.

Robert, though harried, had a boyish appeal; a man in his early thirties perhaps, lean and handsome, with dark eyes and dark hair that came to a pixie point in the middle of his forehead. He was wearing chinos and a plain white T-shirt. He had a baby, maybe eight months old, propped on his hip like a grocery bag. Another child clung to his right leg, while a third rode his tricycle at various walls and doorways, making quite loud sounds with his mouth.

'Hi, come on in,' Robert said. 'We can talk out in the back yard while the kids play.' His smile was sweet.

I followed him through the tiny disorganised house and out to the back yard, where he set the baby down in a sandpile framed with two-by-fours. The second child held on to Robert's belt loops and stuck his thumb in its mouth, staring at me while the tricycle child tried to ride off the edge of the porch. I'm not fond of children. I'm really not. Especially the kind who wear hard brown shoes. Like dogs, these infants sensed my distaste and kept their distance, eyeing me with a mixture of rancour and disdain.

The back yard was scruffy, fenced in, and littered with the fifty-pound sacks the sand had come in. Robert gave the children homemade-style cookies out of a cardboard box and shooed them away. In fifteen minutes the sugar would probably turn them into lunatics. I gave my watch a quick glance, hoping to be gone by then.

'You want a lawn chair?'

'No, this is fine,' I said and settled on the grass. There wasn't a lawn chair in sight, but the offer was nice anyway.

He perched on the edge of the sandbox and ran a distracted hand across his head. 'God, I'm sorry everything is such a mess, but Lucy hasn't been here for two days. She didn't come home from work on Friday and I've been a wreck ever since.'

'I take it you notified the police.'

'Sure. Friday night. She never showed up at the babysitter's house to pick the kids up. I finally got a call here at seven asking where she was. I figured she'd just stopped off at the grocery store or something, so I went ahead and picked 'em up and brought 'em home. By ten o'clock when I hadn't heard from her, I knew something was wrong. I called her boss at home and he said as far as he knew she'd left work at five as usual, so that's when I called the police.'

'You filed a missing persons report?'

'I can do that today. With an adult, you have to wait seventy-two hours, and even then, there's not much they can do.'

'What else did they suggest?'

'The usual stuff, I guess. I mean, I called everyone we know. I talked to her mom in Bakersfield and this friend of hers at work. Nobody has any idea where she is. I'm scared something's happened to her.'

'You've checked with hospitals in the area, I take it.'

'Sure. That's the first thing I did.'

'Did she give you any indication that anything was wrong?'

'Not a word.'

'Was she depressed or behaving oddly?'

'Well, she was kind of restless the past couple of months. She always seemed to get excited around this time of year. She said it reminded her of her old elementary school days.' He shrugged. 'I hated mine.'

'But she's never disappeared like this before.'

'Oh, heck no. I just mentioned her mood because you asked. I don't think it amounted to anything.'

'Does she have any problems with alcohol or drugs?'

'Lucy isn't really like that,' he said. 'She's petite and kind of quiet. A homebody, I guess you'd say.'

'What about your relationship? Do the two of you get along OK?'

'As far as I'm concerned, we do. I mean, once in a while we get into it but never anything serious.'

'What are your disagreements about?'

He smiled ruefully. 'Money, mostly. With three kids, we never seem to have enough. I mean, I'm crazy about big families, but it's tough financially. I always wanted four or five, but she says three is plenty, especially with the oldest not in school yet. We fight about that some . . . having more kids.'

'You both work?'

'We have to. Just to make ends meet. She has a job in an escrow company downtown, and I work for the phone company.'

'Doing what?'

'Installer,' he said.

'Has there been any hint of someone else in her life?'

He sighed, plucking at the grass between his feet. 'In a way, I wish I could say yes. I'd like to think maybe she just got fed up or something and checked into a motel for the weekend. Something like that.'

'But you don't think she did.'

'Unh-uh and I'm going crazy with anxiety. Somebody's got to find out where she is.'

'Mr Ackerman . . .'

'You can call me Rob,' he said.

Clients always say that. I mean, unless their names are something else.

'Rob,' I said, 'the police are truly your best bet in a situation like this. I'm just one person. They've got a vast machinery they can put to work and it won't cost you a cent.'

'You charge a lot, huh?'

'Thirty bucks an hour plus expenses.'

He thought for a moment, then gave me a searching look. 'Could you maybe put in ten hours? I got three hundred bucks we were saving for a trip to the San Diego Zoo.'

I pretended to think about it, but the truth was, I knew I couldn't say no to that boyish face. Anyway, the kids were starting to whine and I wanted to get out of there. I waived the retainer and said I'd send him an itemised bill when the ten hours were up. I figured I could put a contract in the mail and reduce my contact with the short persons who were crowding around him now, begging for more sweets. I asked for a recent photograph of Lucy, but all he could come up with was a two-year-old snapshot of her with the two older kids. She looked beleaguered even then, and that was before the third baby came along. I thought about quiet little Lucy Ackerman whose three strapping sons had legs the size of my arms. If I were she, I knew where I'd be. Long gone.

Lucy Ackerman was employed as an escrow officer for a small company on State Street not far from my office. It was a modest establishment of white walls, rust and brown plaid furniture with burnt orange carpeting. There were Gauguin reproductions all around and a live plant on every desk. I introduced myself first to the office manager, a Mrs Merriman, who was in her sixties, had tall hair, and wore lace-up boots with stiletto heels. She looked like a woman who'd trade all her pension monies for a head-to-toe body tuck.

I said, 'Robert Ackerman has asked me to see if I can locate his wife.'

'Well, the poor man. I heard about that,' she said with her mouth. Her eyes said, 'Fat chance!'

'Do you have any idea where she might be?'

'I think you'd better talk to Mr Sotherland.' She had turned all prim and officious, but my guess was she knew something and was dying to be asked. I intended to accommodate her as soon as I'd talked to him. The protocol in small offices, I've found, is ironclad.

Gavin Sotherland got up from his swivel chair and stretched a big hand across the desk to shake mine. The other member of the office force, Barbara Hemdahl, the book-keeper, got up from her chair simultaneously and excused herself. Mr Sotherland watched her depart and then motioned me into the same seat. I sank into leather still hot from Barbara Hemdahl's backside, a curiously intimate effect. I made a mental note to find out what she knew, and then I looked, with interest, at the company vice president. I picked up all these names and job titles because his was cast in stand-up bronze letters on his desk, and the two women both had white plastic name tags affixed to their breasts, like nurses. As nearly as I could tell, there were only four of them in the office, including Lucy Ackerman, and I couldn't understand how they could fail to identify each other on sight. Maybe all the badges were for clients who couldn't be trusted to tell one from the other without the proper IDs.

Gavin Sotherland was large, an ex-jock to all appearances, maybe forty-five years old, with a heavy head of blond hair thinning slightly at the crown. He had a slight paunch, a slight stoop to his shoulders, and a grip that was damp with sweat. He had his coat off, and his once-starched white shirt was limp and wrinkled, his beige gabardine pants heavily creased across the lap. Altogether, he looked like a man who'd just crossed a continent by rail. Still, I was forced to credit him with good looks, even if he had let himself go to seed.

'Nice to meet you, Miss Millhone. I'm so glad you're here.' His voice was deep and rumbling, with confidence-inspiring undertones. On the other hand, I didn't like the look in his eyes. He could have been a conman, for all I knew. 'I understand Mrs Ackerman never got home Friday night,' he said.

'That's what I'm told,' I replied. 'Can you tell me anything about her day here?'

He studied me briefly. 'Well, now I'm going to have to be honest with you. Our book-keeper has come across some discrepancies in the accounts. It looks like Lucy

743

Ackerman has just walked off with half a million dollars entrusted to us.'

'How'd she manage that?'

I was picturing Lucy Ackerman, free of those truck-busting kids, lying on a beach in Rio, slurping some kind of rum drink out of a coconut.

Mr Sotherland looked pained. 'In the most straightforward manner imaginable,' he said. 'It looks like she opened a new bank account at a branch in Montebello and deposited ten cheques that should have gone into other accounts. Last Friday, she withdrew over five hundred thousand dollars in cash, claiming we were closing out a big real estate deal. We found the passbook in her bottom drawer.' He tossed the booklet across the desk to me and I picked it up. The word 'VOID' had been punched into the pages in a series of holes. A quick glance showed ten deposits at intervals dating back over the past three months and a zero balance as of last Friday's date.

'Didn't anybody else double-check this stuff?'

'We'd just undergone our annual audit in June. Everything was fine. We trusted this woman implicitly and had every reason to.'

'You discovered the loss this morning?'

'Yes, ma'am, but I'll admit I was suspicious Friday night when Robert Ackerman called me at home. It was completely unlike that woman to disappear without a word. She's worked here eight years, and she's been punctual and conscientious since the day she walked in.'

'Well, punctual at any rate,' I said. 'Have you notified the police?'

'I was just about to do that. I'll have to alert the Department of Corporations, too. God, I can't believe she did this to us. I'll be fired. They'll probably shut this entire office down.'

'Would you mind if I had a quick look around?'

'To what end?'

'There's always a chance we can figure out where she went. If we move fast enough, maybe we can catch her before she gets away with it.'

'Well, I doubt that,' he said. 'The last anybody saw her was Friday afternoon. That's two full days. She could be anywhere by now.'

'Mr Sotherland, her husband has already authorised three hundred dollars' worth of my time. Why not take advantage of it?'

He stared at me. 'Won't the police object?'

'Probably. But I don't intend to get in anybody's way, and whatever I find out, I'll turn over to them. They may not be able to get a fraud detective out here until late morning anyway. If I get a line on her, it'll make you look good to the company *and* to the cops.'

He gave a sigh of resignation and waved his hand. 'Hell, I don't care. Do what you want.'

When I left his office, he was putting the call through to the police department.

I sat briefly at Lucy's desk, which was neat and well organised. Her drawers contained the usual office supplies; no personal items at all. There was a calendar on her desktop, one of those loose-leaf affairs with a page for each day. I checked back through the past couple of months. The only personal notation was for an appointment at the Women's Health Centre, 2 August, and a second visit last Friday afternoon. It must have been a busy day for Lucy, what with a doctor's appointment and ripping off her company for half a million bucks. I made a note of the address she'd pencilled in at the time of her first visit. The other two women in the office were keeping an eye on me, I noticed, though both pretended to be occupied with paperwork.

When I finished my search, I got up and crossed the

room to Mrs Merriman's desk. 'Is there any way I can make a copy of the passbook for that account Mrs Ackerman opened?'

'Well, yes, if Mr Sotherland approves,' she said.

'I'm also wondering where she keeps her coat and purse during the day.'

'In the back. We each have a locker in the storage room.'

'I'd like to take a look at that, too.'

I waited patiently while she cleared both matters with her boss, and then I accompanied her to the rear. There was a door that opened on to the parking lot. To the left of it was a small rest room and, on the right, there was a storage room that housed four connecting upright metal lockers, the copy machine, and numerous shelves neatly stacked with office supplies. Each shoulder-high locker was marked with a name. Lucy Ackerman's was still securely padlocked. There was something about the blank look of that locker that seemed ominous somehow. I looked at the lock, fairly itching to have a crack at it with my little set of key picks, but I didn't want to push my luck with the cops on the way.

'I'd like for someone to let me know what's in that locker when it's finally opened,' I remarked while Mrs Merriman ran off the copy of the passbook pages for me.

'This, too,' I said, handing her a carbon of the withdrawal slip Lucy'd been required to sign in receipt of the cash. It had been folded and tucked into the back of the booklet. 'You have any theories about where she went?'

Mrs Merriman's mouth pursed piously, as though she were debating with herself about how much she might say.

'I wouldn't want to be accused of talking out of school,' she ventured.

'Mrs Merriman, it does look like a crime's been

committed,' I suggested. 'The police are going to ask you the same thing when they get here.'

'Oh. Well, in that case, I suppose it's all right. I mean, I don't have the faintest idea where she is, but I do think she's been acting oddly the past few months.'

'Like what?'

'She seemed secretive. Smug. Like she knew something the rest of us didn't know about.'

'That certainly turned out to be the case,' I said.

'Oh, I didn't mean it was related to that,' she said hesitantly. 'I think she was having an affair.'

That got my attention. 'An affair? With whom?'

She paused for a moment, touching at one of the hairpins that supported her ornate hairdo. She allowed her gaze to stray back towards Mr Sotherland's office. I turned and looked in that direction, too.

'Really?' I said. 'No wonder he was in a sweat,' I thought.

'I couldn't swear to it,' she murmured, 'but his marriage has been rocky for years, and I gather she hasn't been that happy herself. She has those beastly little boys, you know, and a husband who seems determined to spawn more. She and Mr Sotherland . . . Gavie, she calls him . . . have . . . well, I'm sure they've been together. Whether it's connected to this matter of the missing money, I wouldn't presume to guess.' Having said as much, she was suddenly uneasy. 'You won't repeat what I've said to the police, I hope.'

'Absolutely not,' I said. 'Unless they ask, of course.'

'Oh. Of course.'

'By the way, is there a company travel agent?'

'Right next door,' she replied.

I had a brief chat with the book-keeper, who added nothing to the general picture of Lucy Ackerman's last few days at work. I retrieved my VW from the parking lot and headed over to the health centre eight blocks away, wondering what Lucy had been up to. I was guessing birth control and probably the permanent sort. If she were having an affair (and determined not to get pregnant again in any event), it would seem logical, but I hadn't any idea how to verify the fact. Medical personnel are notoriously stingy with information like that.

I parked in front of the clinic and grabbed my clipboard from the back seat. I have a supply of all-purpose forms for occasions like this. They look like a cross between a job application and an insurance claim. I filled one out now in Lucy's name and forged her signature at the bottom where it said 'authorisation to release information'. As a model, I used the Xerox copy of the withdrawal slip she'd tucked in her passbook. I'll admit my methods would be considered unorthodox, nay illegal, in the eyes of law-enforcement officers every-where, but I reasoned that the information I was seeking would never actually be used in court, and therefore it couldn't matter *that* much how it was obtained.

I went into the clinic, noting gratefully the near-empty waiting room. I approached the counter and took out my wallet with my California Fidelity ID. I do occasional insurance investigations for CF in exchange for office space. They once made the mistake of issuing me a company identification card with my picture right on it that I've been flashing around quite shamelessly ever since.

I had a choice of three female clerks and, after a brief assessment, I made eye contact with the oldest of them. In places like this, the younger employees usually have no authority at all and are, thus, impossible to con. People without authority will often simply stand there, reciting the rules like mynah birds. Having no power, they also seem to take a vicious satisfaction in forcing others to comply.

The woman approached the counter on her side, looking at me expectantly. I showed her my CF ID and made the form on the clipboard conspicuous, as though I had nothing to hide.

'Hi. My name is Kinsey Millhone,' I said, 'I wonder if you can give me some help. Your name is what?'

She seemed wary of the request, as though her name had magical powers that might be taken from her by force. 'Lillian Vincent,' she said reluctantly. 'What sort of help did you need?'

'Lucy Ackerman has applied for some insurance benefits and we need verification of the claim. You'll want a copy of the release form for your files, of course.'

I passed the forged paper to her and then busied myself with my clipboard as though it was all perfectly matter-of-fact.

She was instantly alert. 'What is this?'

I gave her a look. 'Oh, sorry. She's applying for maternity leave and we need her due date.'

'Maternity leave?'

'Isn't she a patient here?'

Lillian Vincent looked at me. 'Just a moment,' she said, and moved away from the desk with the form in her hand. She went to a file cabinet and extracted a chart, returning to the counter. She pushed it over to me. 'The woman has had a tubal ligation,' she said, her manner crisp.

I blinked, smiling slightly as though she were making a joke. 'There must be some mistake.'

'Lucy Ackerman must have made it then if she thinks she can pull this off.' She opened the chart and tapped significantly at the 2 August date. 'She was just in here Friday for a final checkup and a medical release. She's sterile.'

I looked at the chart. Sure enough, that's what it said. I

raised my eyebrows and then shook my head slightly. 'God. Well. I guess I better have a copy of that.'

'I should think so,' the woman said and ran one off for me on the desktop dry copier. She placed it on the counter and watched as I tucked it on to my clipboard.

She said, 'I don't know how they think they can get away with it.'

'People love to cheat,' I replied.

It was nearly noon by the time I got back to the travel agency next door to the place where Lucy Ackerman had worked. It didn't take any time at all to unearth the reservations she'd made two weeks before. Buenos Aires, first class on Pan Am. For one. She'd picked up the ticket Friday afternoon just before the agency closed for the weekend.

The travel agent rested his elbows on the counter and looked at me with interest, hoping to hear all the gory details, I'm sure. 'I heard about that business next door,' he said. He was young, maybe twenty-four, with a pug nose, auburn hair and a gap between his teeth. He'd make the perfect co-star on a wholesome family TV show.

'How'd she pay for the tickets?'

'Cash,' he said. 'I mean, who'd have thunk?'

'Did she say anything in particular at the time?'

'Not really. She seemed jazzed and we joked some about Montezuma's revenge and stuff like that. I knew she was married, and I was asking her all about who was keeping the kids and what her old man was going to do while she was gone. God, I never in a million *years* guessed she was pulling off a scam like that, you know?'

'Did you ask why she was going to Argentina by herself?'

'Well, yeah, and she said it was a surprise.' He shrugged. 'It didn't really make sense, but she was laughing like a kid, and I thought I just didn't get the joke.'

I asked for a copy of the itinerary, such as it was. She had paid for a round-trip ticket, but there were no reservations coming back. Maybe she intended to cash in the return ticket once she got down there. I tucked the travel docs on to my clipboard along with the copy of her medical forms. Something about this whole deal had begun to chafe, but I couldn't figure out quite why.

'Thanks for your help,' I said, heading towards the door.

'No problem. I guess the other guy didn't get it either,' he remarked.

I paused, midstride, turning back. 'Get what?'

'The joke. I heard 'em next door and they were fighting like cats and dogs. He was pissed.'

'Really?' I asked. I stared at him. 'What time was this?'

'Five-fifteen. Something like that. They were closed and so were we, but Dad wanted me to stick around for a while until the cleaning crew got here. He owns this place, which is how I got in the business myself. These new guys were starting and he wanted me to make sure they understood what to do.'

'Are you going to be here for a while?'

'Sure.'

'Good. The police may want to hear about this.'

I went back into the escrow office with mental alarm bells clanging away like crazy. Both Barbara Hemdahl and Mrs Merriman had opted to eat lunch in. Or maybe the cops had ordered them to stay where they were. The book-keeper sat at her desk with a sandwich, apple, and a carton of milk neatly arranged in front of her, while Mrs Merriman picked at something in a plastic container she must have brought in from a fast-food place.

'How's it going?' I asked.

Barbara Hemdahl spoke up from her side of the room. 'The detectives went off for a search warrant so they can get in all the lockers back there, collecting evidence.'

'Only one of 'em is locked,' I pointed out.

She shrugged. 'I guess they can't even peek without the paperwork.'

Mrs Merriman spoke up then, her expression tinged with guilt. 'Actually, they asked the rest of us if we'd open our lockers voluntarily, so of course we did.'

Mrs Merriman and Barbara Hemdahl exchanged a look.

'And?'

Mrs Merriman coloured slightly. 'There was an overnight case in Mr Sotherland's locker, and I guess the things in it were hers.'

'Is it still back there?'

'Well, yes, but they left a uniformed officer on guard so nobody'd walk off with it. They've got everything spread out on the copy machine.'

I went through the rear of the office, peering into the storage room. I knew the guy on duty and he didn't object to my doing a visual survey of the items, as long as I didn't touch anything. The overnight case had been packed with all the personal belongings women like to keep on hand in case the rest of the luggage gets sent to Mexicali by mistake. I spotted a toothbrush and toothpaste, slippers, a filmy nightie, prescription drugs, hairbrush, extra eyeglasses in a case. Tucked under a change of underwear, I spotted a round plastic container, slightly convex, about the size of a compact.

Gavin Sotherland was still sitting at his desk when I stopped by his office. His skin tone was grey and his shirt was hanging out, big rings of sweat under each arm. He was smoking a cigarette with the air of a man who's quit the habit and has taken it up again under duress. A second uniformed officer was standing just inside the door to my right.

I leaned against the frame, but Gavin scarcely looked up.

I said, 'You knew what she was doing, but you thought she'd take you with her when she left.'

His smile was bitter. 'Life is full of surprises,' he said.

I was going to have to tell Robert Ackerman what I'd discovered, and I dreaded it. As a stalling manoeuvre, just to demonstrate what a good girl I was, I drove over to the police station first and dropped off the data I'd collected, filling them in on the theory I'd come up with. They didn't exactly pin a medal on me, but they weren't as pissed off as I thought they'd be, given the number of civil codes I'd violated in the process. They were even moderately courteous, which is unusual in their treatment of me. Unfortunately, none of it took that long and before I knew it, I was standing at the Ackermans' front door again.

I rang the bell and waited, bad jokes running through my head. Well, there's good news and bad news, Robert. The good news is we've wrapped it up with hours to spare so you won't have to pay me the full three hundred dollars we agreed to. The bad news is your wife's a thief, she's probably dead, and we're just getting out a warrant now, because we think we know where the body's stashed.

The door opened and Robert was standing there with a finger to his lips. 'The kids are down for their naps,' he whispered.

I nodded elaborately, pantomiming my understanding, as though the silence he'd imposed required this special behaviour on my part.

He motioned me in and together we tiptoed through the house and out to the back yard, where we continued to talk in low tones. I wasn't sure which bedroom the little rugrats slept in, and didn't want to be responsible for waking them.

Half a day of playing papa to the boys had left Robert looking dishevelled and sorely in need of relief.

'I didn't expect you back this soon,' he whispered.

I found myself whispering too, feeling anxious at the sense of secrecy. It reminded me of grade school somehow: the smell of autumn hanging in the air, the two of us perched on the edge of the sandbox like little kids, conspiring. I didn't want to break his heart, but what was I to do?

'I think we've got it wrapped up,' I said.

He looked at me for a moment, apparently guessing from my expression that the news wasn't good. 'Is she OK?'

'We don't think so,' I said. And then I told him what I'd learned, starting with the embezzlement and the relationship with Gavin, taking it right through to the quarrel the travel agent had heard. Robert was ahead of me.

'She's dead, isn't she?'

'We don't know it for a fact, but we suspect as much.'

He nodded, tears welling up. He wrapped his arms around his knees and propped his chin on his fists. He looked so young, I wanted to reach out and touch him. 'She was really having an affair?' he asked plaintively.

'You must have suspected as much,' I said. 'You said she was restless and excited for months. Didn't that give you a clue?'

He shrugged one shoulder, using the sleeve of his T-shirt to dash at the tears trickling down his cheeks. 'I don't know,' he said. 'I guess.'

'And then you stopped by the office Friday afternoon and found her getting ready to leave the country. That's when you killed her, isn't it?'

He froze, staring at me. At first, I thought he'd deny it,

but maybe he realised there wasn't any point. He nodded mutely.

'And then you hired me to make it look good, right?'

He made a kind of squeaking sound in the back of his throat and sobbed once, his voice reduced to a whisper again. 'She shouldn't have done it . . . betrayed us like that. We loved her so much . . .'

'Have you got the money here?'

He nodded, looking miserable. 'I wasn't going to pay your fee out of that,' he said incongruously. 'We really did have a little fund so we could go to San Diego one day.'

'I'm sorry things didn't work out,' I said.

'I didn't do so bad, though, did I? I mean, I could have gotten away with it, don't you think?'

I'd been talking about the trip to the zoo. He thought I was referring to his murdering his wife. Talk about poor communication. God.

'Well, you nearly pulled it off,' I said. Shit, I was sitting there trying to make the guy *feel* good.

He looked at me piteously, eyes red and flooded, his mouth trembling. 'But where did I slip up? What did I do wrong?'

'You put her diaphragm in the overnight case you packed. You thought you'd shift suspicion on to Gavin Sotherland, but you didn't realise she'd had her tubes tied.'

A momentary rage flashed through his eyes and then flickered out. I suspected that her voluntary sterilisation was more insulting to him than the affair with her boss.

'Jesus, I don't know what she saw in him,' he breathed. 'He was such a pig.'

'Well,' I said, 'if it's any comfort to you, she wasn't going to take *him* with her, either. She just wanted freedom, you know?'

He pulled out a handkerchief and blew his nose, trying

to compose himself. He mopped his eyes, shivering with tension. 'How can you prove it, though, without a body? Do you know where she is?'

'I think we do,' I said softly. 'The sandbox, Robert. Right under us.'

He seemed to shrink. 'Oh, God,' he whispered, 'Oh, God, don't turn me in. I'll give you the money, I don't give a damn. Just let me stay here with my kids. The little guys need me. I did it for them. I swear I did. You don't have to tell the cops, do you?'

I shook my head and opened my shirt collar, showing him the mike. 'I don't have to tell a soul. I'm wired for sound,' I said, and then I looked over toward the side yard.

For once, I was glad to see Lieutenant Dolan amble into view.

Acknowledgements

BOOK ONE

The editor is grateful to the following authors, agents and publishers for permission to include copyright stories in this collection: the author and A. M. Heath Literary Agency for 'Man With a Hobby' by Robert Bloch; Hughes Massie Ltd for 'Accident' by Agatha Christie; Random Publishing Group for 'Evidence in Camera' by Margery Allingham and Random House Inc for 'A Flash of White' by Andrew Vachss; H. N. Swanson Inc. for 'Round Trip' by W. R. Burnett; Robert Hale Ltd for 'Morning Visit' by James Hadley Chase; William Morris Agency for 'Murder Comes Easy' by Evan Hunter; Richard Curtis Associates Inc. for 'The Flaw in the System' by Jim Thompson; United Newspapers Magazine Corporation for 'Blurred View' by John D. MacDonald; Davis Publications Inc. for 'The Sweetest Man in the World' by Donald E. Westlake and 'Going Through The Motions' by Lawrence Block; Michael Joseph Publishers Ltd for 'Prediction' by Chester Himes; Vanessa Holt Ltd for 'The Corder Figure' by Peter Lovesey; Dell Publishing for 'Gravy Train' by James Ellroy; Observer Newspapers Ltd for 'Remain Nameless' by Lynda La Plante. While every effort has been made to contact the copyright holders of material used in this collection, in the case of any accidental infringement, concerned parties are asked to contact the editor in care of the publishers.

BOOK TWO

The editor is grateful to the following authors, agents and publishers for permission to include copyright stories in this collection: Lawrence Pollinger Literary Agency Ltd for 'A Case of Christmas Spirit' by Nicholas Rhea; the author and *Ellery Queen's Mystery Magazine* for 'The Second Skin' by Michael Gilbert; Davis Publications for 'Blood Brothers' by Christianna Brand, 'Sweating It Out With Dover' by Joyce Porter and 'Gideon and the Young Toughs' by John Creasey; Victor Gollancz Ltd for 'Duello' by Henry Wade and 'The Memorial Service' by Michael Innes; HarperCollins Publishers for 'The Suitcase' by Freeman Wills Crofts; Blake Friedmann Literary Agency for 'Confirmation' by John Harvey; Curtis Brown Literary Agency for 'Auld Lang Syne' by Ian Rankin; Peters, Fraser & Dunlop for 'Clutching at Straws' by Ruth Rendell; *Mail on Sunday* and the author for 'The Burglar' by Colin Dexter; A. P. Watt Ltd for 'Where The Snow Lay Dinted' by Reginald Hill; The Regent Trust Company Ltd for 'The Little Copplestone Mystery' by Ngaio Marsh; United Newspapers Ltd for 'Before Insulin' by J. J. Connington. While every effort has been made to contact the copyright holders of material used in this collection, in the case of any accidental infringement, concerned parties are asked to contact the editor in care of the publishers.

BOOK THREE

The editor is grateful to the following authors, agents and publishers for permission to include copyright stories in this collection: Berkeley Publishing Group for 'Somewhere in the City' by Marcia Muller; Hodder Headline Publishing Group for 'A Classic Forgery' by Roy Vickers; Mrs Leslie Charteris for 'The Smashing of Another Racket' by Leslie Charteris; Davis Publications for 'Raffles and the Dangerous Game' by Barry Perowne, 'The Sleeping Dog' by Ross Macdonald, 'Caribbean Clues' by Patricia McGerr and 'The Bottle Dungeon' by Antonia Fraser; Random Publishing Group for 'They

Acknowledgements

Can Only Hang You Once' by Dashiell Hammett; HarperCollins for 'Black Out' by Peter Cheyney; Brandt & Brandt for 'Virgil Tibbs and the Fallen Body' by John Ball; *Armchair Detective* for 'Full Moon' by George Baxt; Scott Meredith Literary Agency for 'Willing to Kill' by Don Pendleton; Hamish Hamilton Ltd for 'The Takamoku *Joseki*' by Sara Paretsky; Redbook and Ballantine Books for 'She Didn't Come Home' by Sue Grafton. While every effort has been made to contact the copyright holders of material used in this collection, in case of any accidental infringement, concerned parties are asked to contact the editor in care of the publishers.

All Orion/Phoenix titles are available at your local bookshop or from the following address:

Littlehampton Book Services
Cash Sales Department L
14 Eldon Way, Lineside Industrial Estate
Littlehampton
West Sussex BN17 7HE
telephone 01903 721596, *facsimile* 01903 730914

Payment can either be made by credit card (Visa and Mastercard accepted) or by sending a cheque or postal order made payable to *Littlehampton Book Services*.
DO NOT SEND CASH OR CURRENCY.

Please add the following to cover postage and packing

UK and BFPO:
£1.50 for the first book, and 50P for each additional book to a maximum of £3.50

Overseas and Eire:
£2.50 for the first book plus £1.00 for the second book and 50p for each additional book ordered

----

BLOCK CAPITALS PLEASE

name of cardholder ....   *delivery address*
....   *(if different from cardholder)*
address of cardholder ....
....
....
....
postcode ....   *postcode* ....

☐ I enclose my remittance for £...........................

☐ please debit my Mastercard/Visa (delete as appropriate)

card number ☐☐☐☐☐☐☐☐☐☐☐☐☐☐☐☐☐☐☐

expiry date ☐☐☐☐

signature ....

prices and availability are subject to change without notice